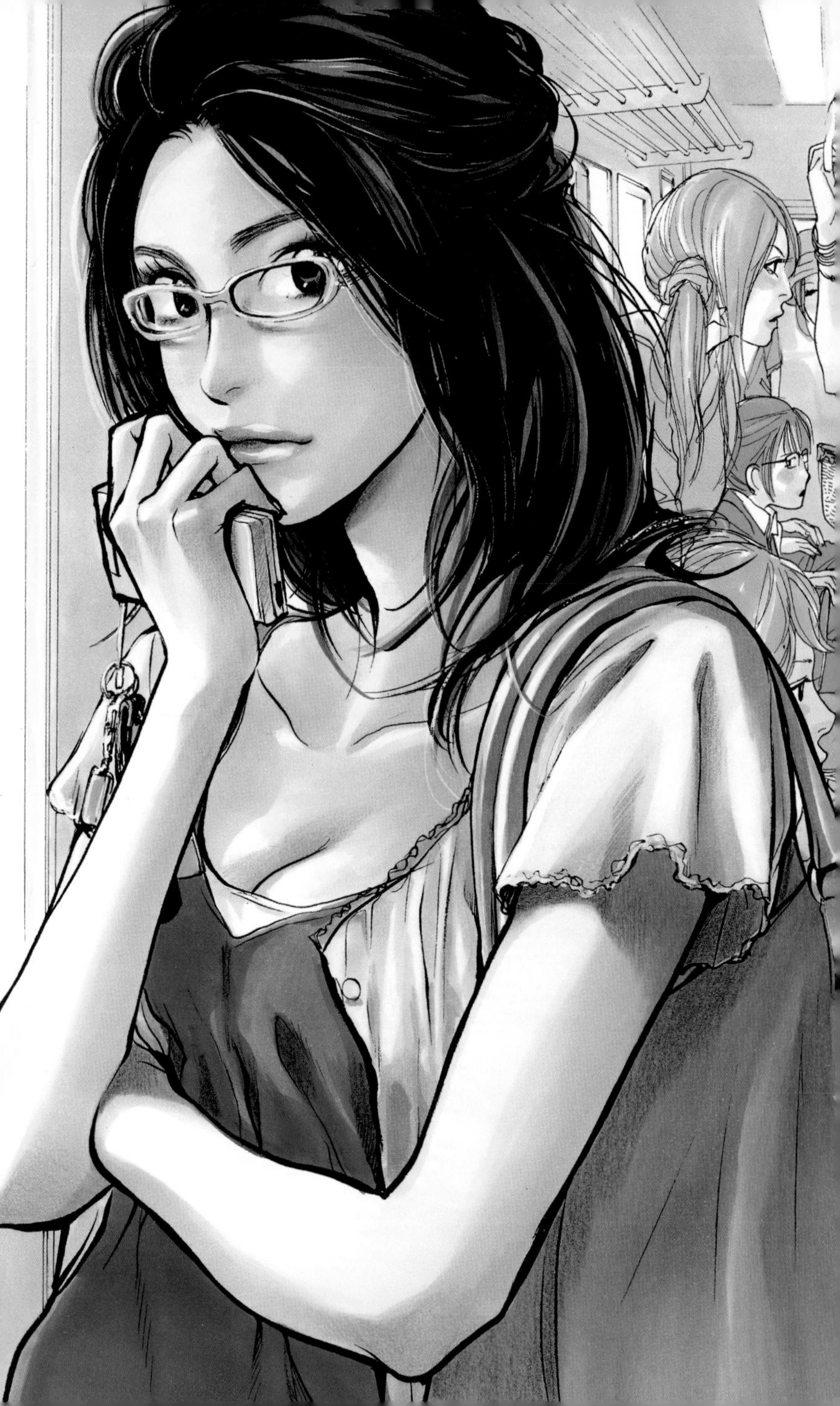

Moteki

Mitsurou Kubo

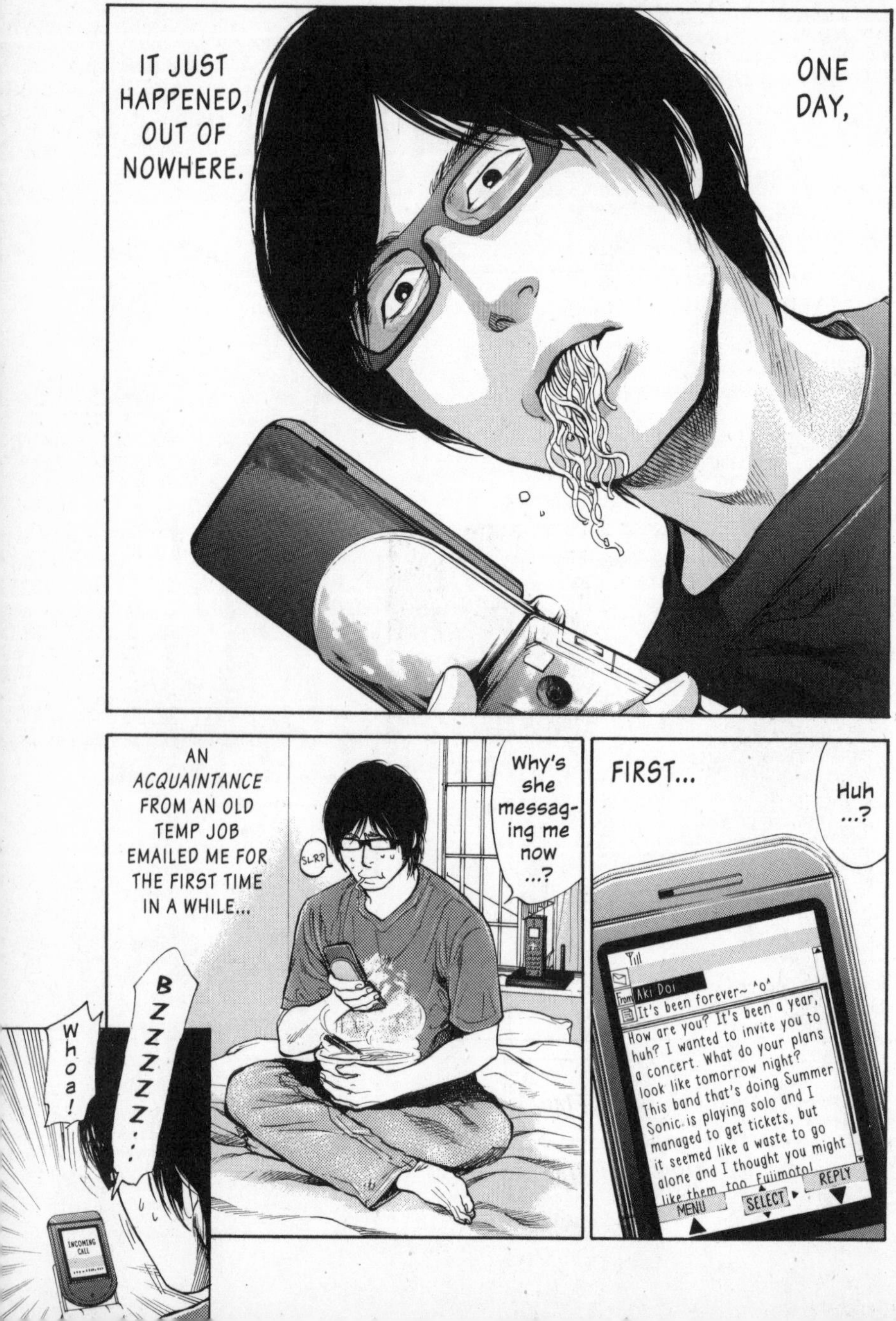
ONE DAY,
IT JUST HAPPENED, OUT OF NOWHERE.
FIRST...
Huh ...?
Aki Doi
It's been forever~ ^o^
How are you? It's been a year, huh? I wanted to invite you to a concert. What do your plans look like tomorrow night? This band that's doing Summer Sonic is playing solo and I managed to get tickets, but it seemed like a waste to go alone and I thought you might like them, too, Fujimoto!
MENU
SELECT
REPLY
Why's she messaging me now ...?
AN ACQUAINTANCE FROM AN OLD TEMP JOB EMAILED ME FOR THE FIRST TIME IN A WHILE...
SLRP
BZZZZZ...
Whoa!
INCOMING CALL

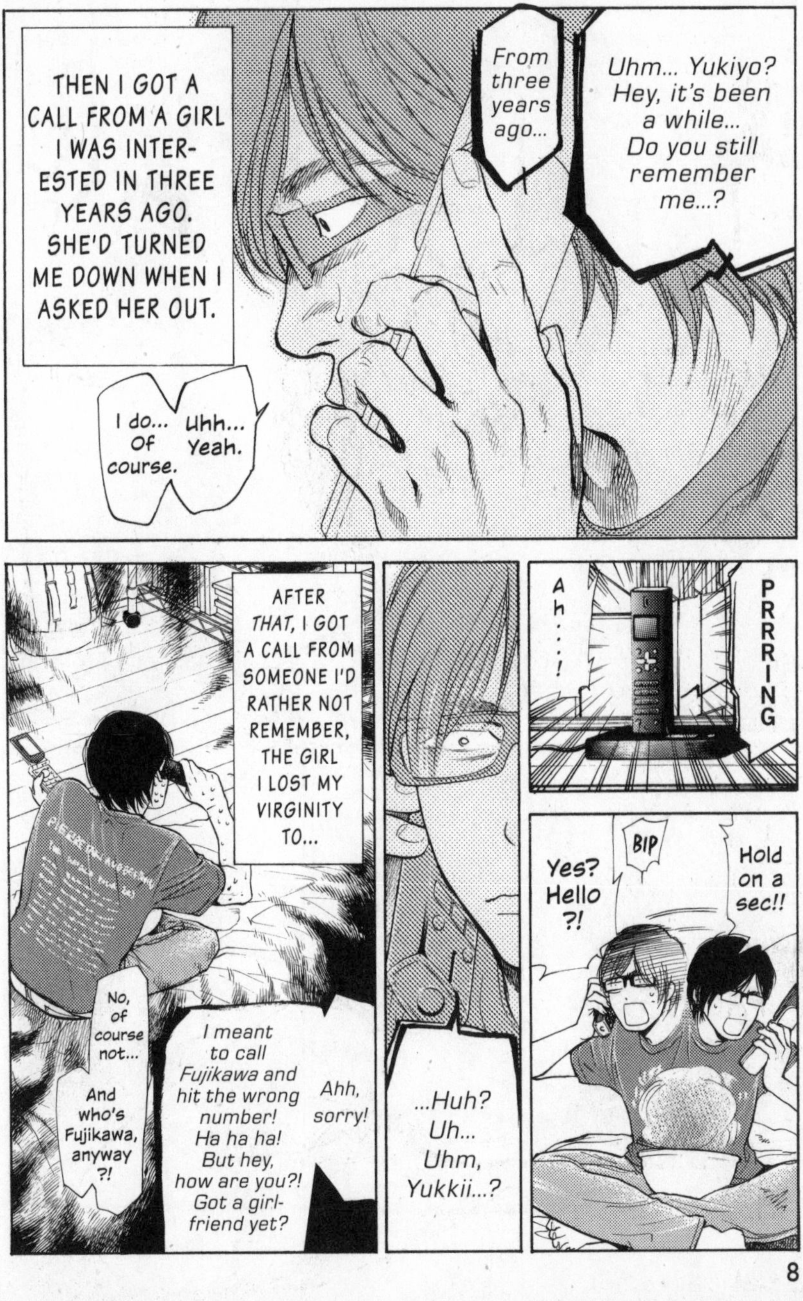
Uhm... Yukiyo? Hey, it's been a while... Do you still remember me...?
From three years ago...
THEN I GOT A CALL FROM A GIRL I WAS INTER-ESTED IN THREE YEARS AGO. SHE'D TURNED ME DOWN WHEN I ASKED HER OUT.
Uhh... Yeah.
I do... Of course.
PRRRING
Ah...!
Hold on a sec!!
BIP
Yes? Hello ?!
...Huh? Uh... Uhm, Yukkii...?
AFTER THAT, I GOT A CALL FROM SOMEONE I'D RATHER NOT REMEMBER, THE GIRL I LOST MY VIRGINITY TO...
Ahh, sorry!
I meant to call Fujikawa and hit the wrong number! Ha ha ha! But hey, how are you?! Got a girl-friend yet?
No, of course not...
And who's Fujikawa, anyway ?!

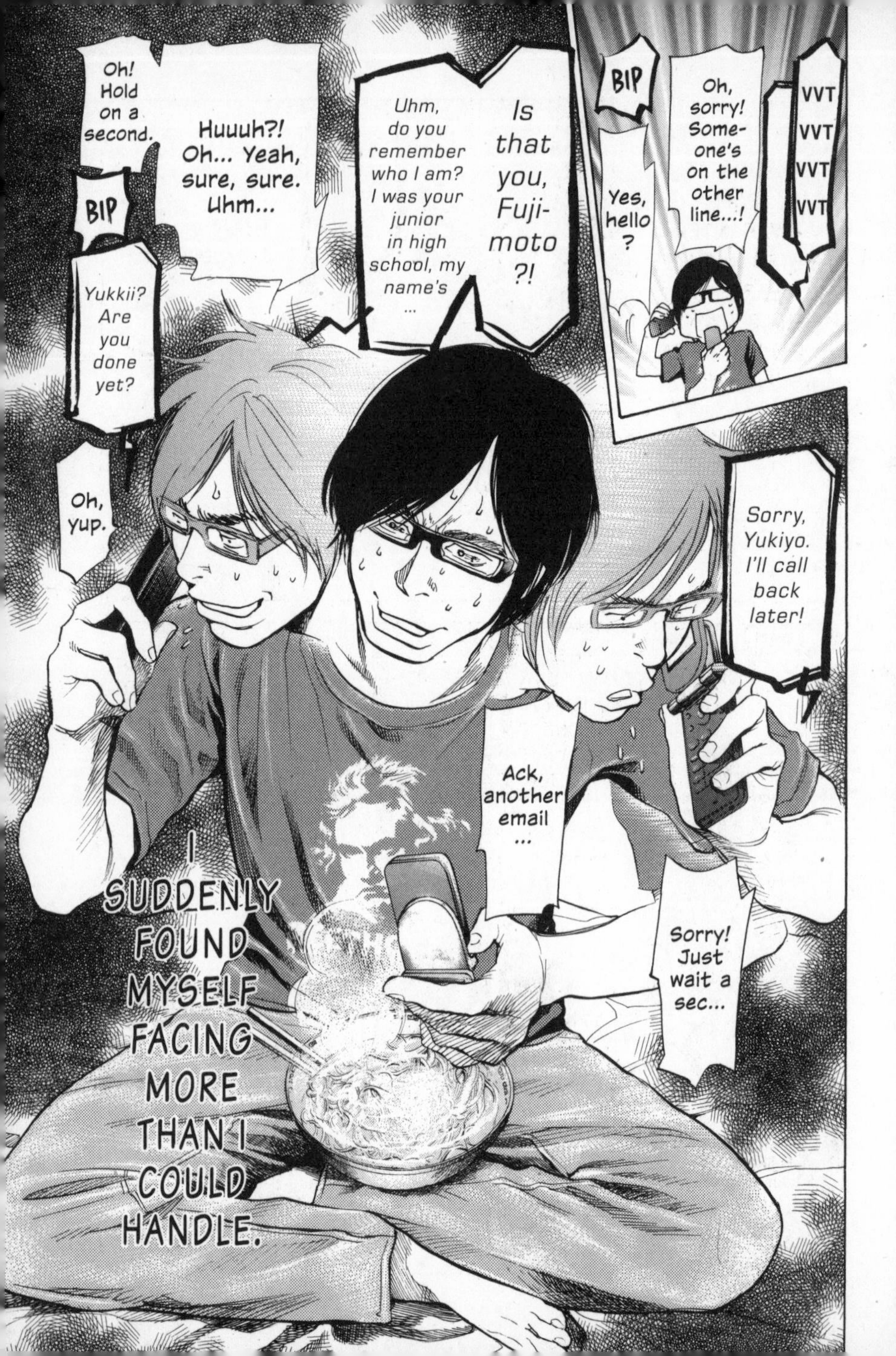
VVT VVT VVT VVT
Oh, sorry! Someone's on the other line...!
BIP
Yes, hello?
Is that you, Fujimoto?!
Uhm, do you remember who I am? I was your junior in high school, my name's ...
Huuuh?! Oh... Yeah, sure, sure. Uhm...
Oh! Hold on a second.
BIP
Yukkii? Are you done yet?
Oh, yup.
Sorry, Yukiyo. I'll call back later!
Ack, another email ...
Sorry! Just wait a sec...
I SUDDENLY FOUND MYSELF FACING MORE THAN I COULD HANDLE.

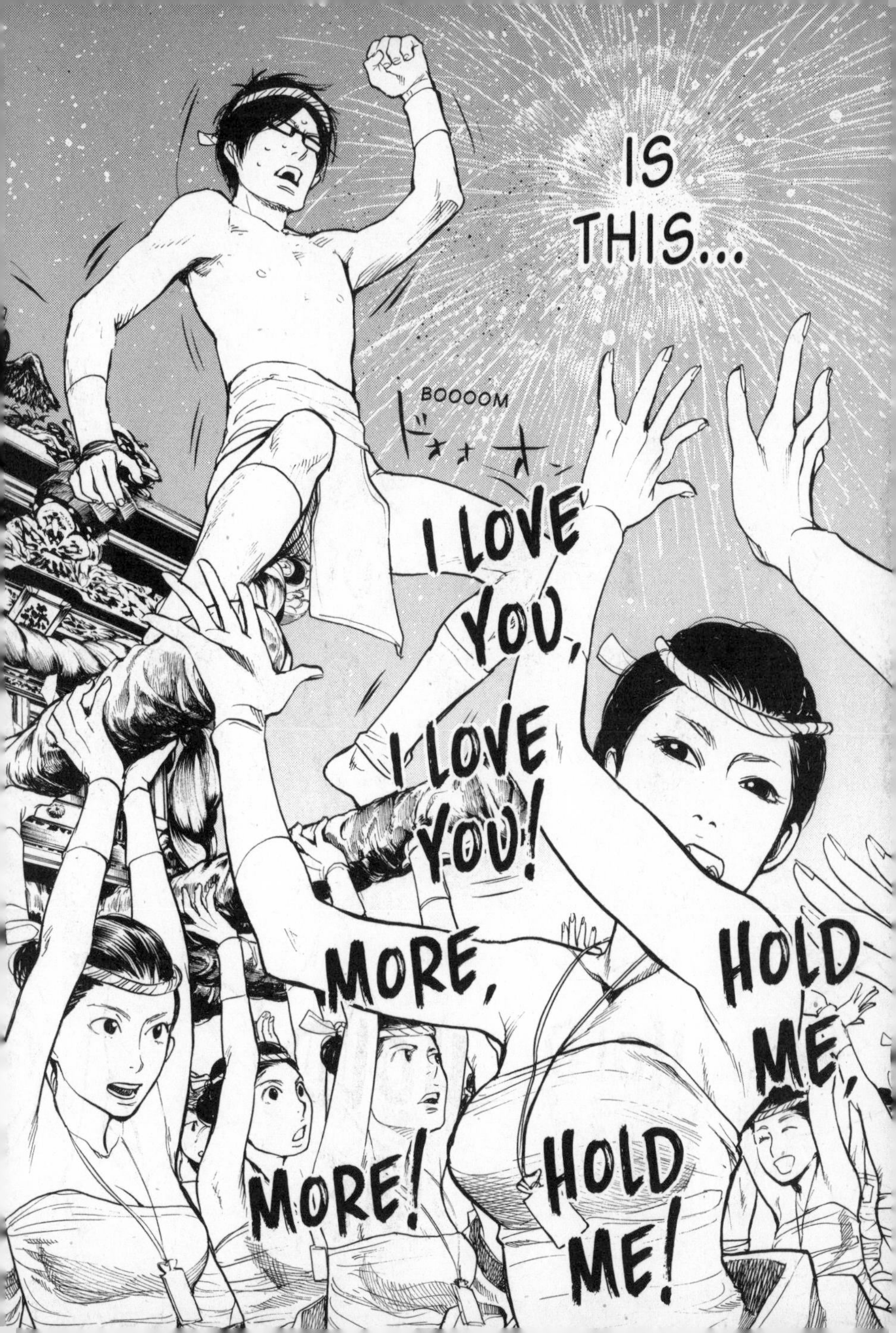
IS THIS...
BOOOOM
I LOVE YOU, I LOVE YOU!
HOLD ME, HOLD ME!
MORE, MORE!

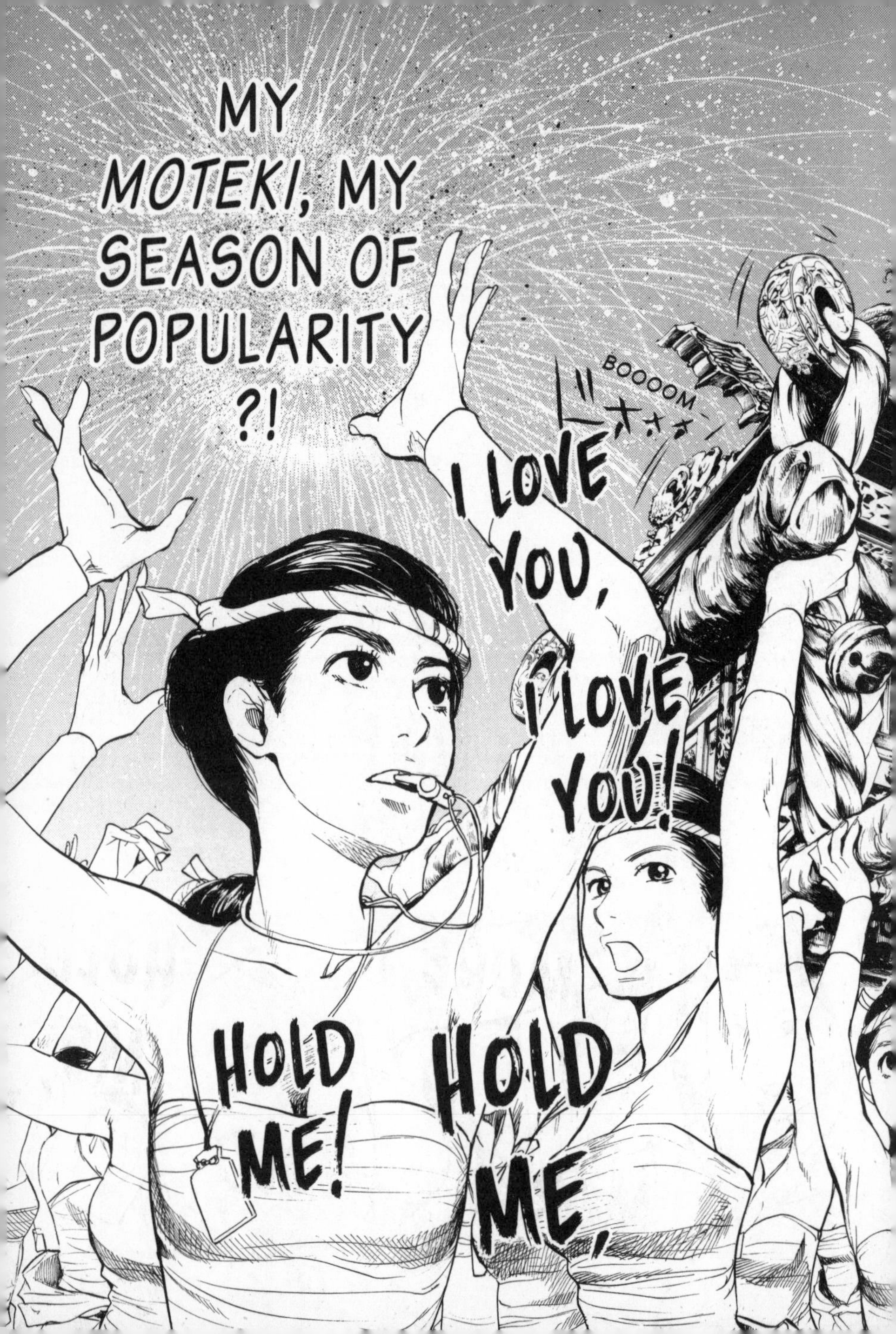
BOOOOM
I LOVE YOU, I LOVE YOU!
MY MOTEKI, MY SEASON OF POPULARITY ?!
HOLD ME,
HOLD ME!

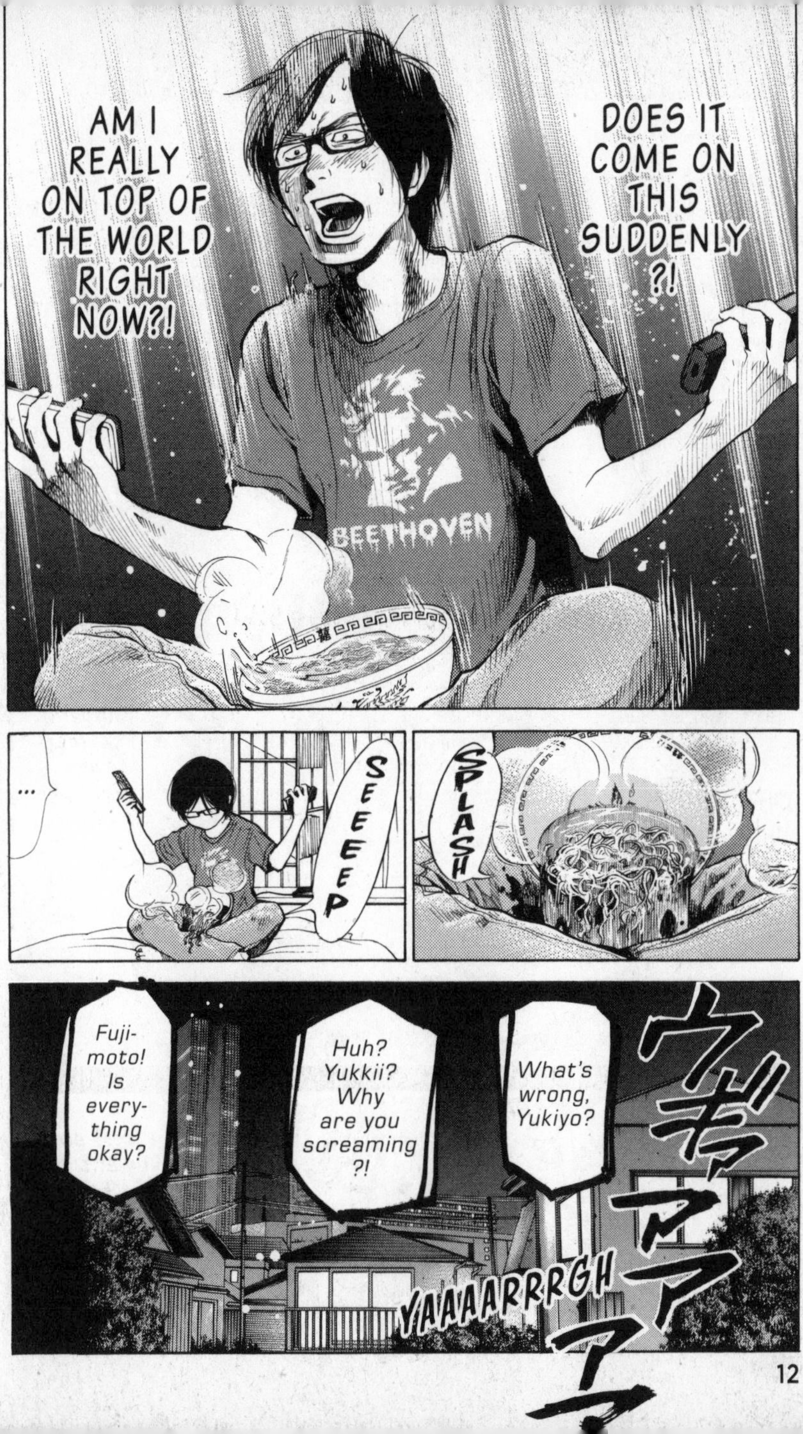
DOES IT COME ON THIS SUDDENLY?!
AM I REALLY ON TOP OF THE WORLD RIGHT NOW?!
BEETHOVEN
SPLASH
SEEEEEP
...
ウギャアアア
YAAAARRRGH
What's wrong, Yukiyo?
Huh? Yukkii? Why are you screaming?!
Fuji-moto! Is every-thing okay?

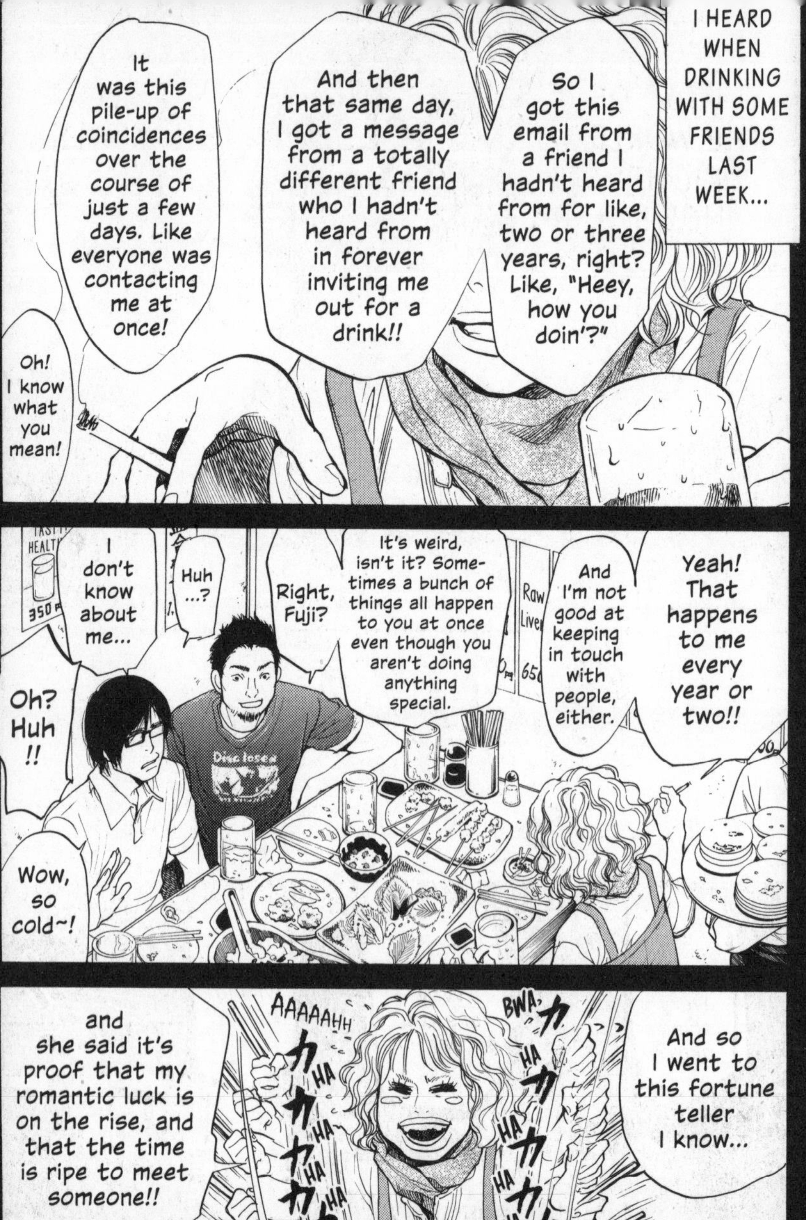
I HEARD WHEN DRINKING WITH SOME FRIENDS LAST WEEK...
So I got this email from a friend I hadn't heard from for like, two or three years, right? Like, "Heey, how you doin'?"
And then that same day, I got a message from a totally different friend who I hadn't heard from in forever inviting me out for a drink!!
It was this pile-up of coincidences over the course of just a few days. Like everyone was contacting me at once!
Oh! I know what you mean!
Yeah! That happens to me every year or two!!
And I'm not good at keeping in touch with people, either.
It's weird, isn't it? Sometimes a bunch of things all happen to you at once even though you aren't doing anything special.
Right, Fuji?
Huh ...?
I don't know about me...
Oh? Huh !!
Wow, so cold~!
And so I went to this fortune teller I know...
BWA HA HA HA HA HA HA HA
AAAAAHH
and she said it's proof that my romantic luck is on the rise, and that the time is ripe to meet someone!!

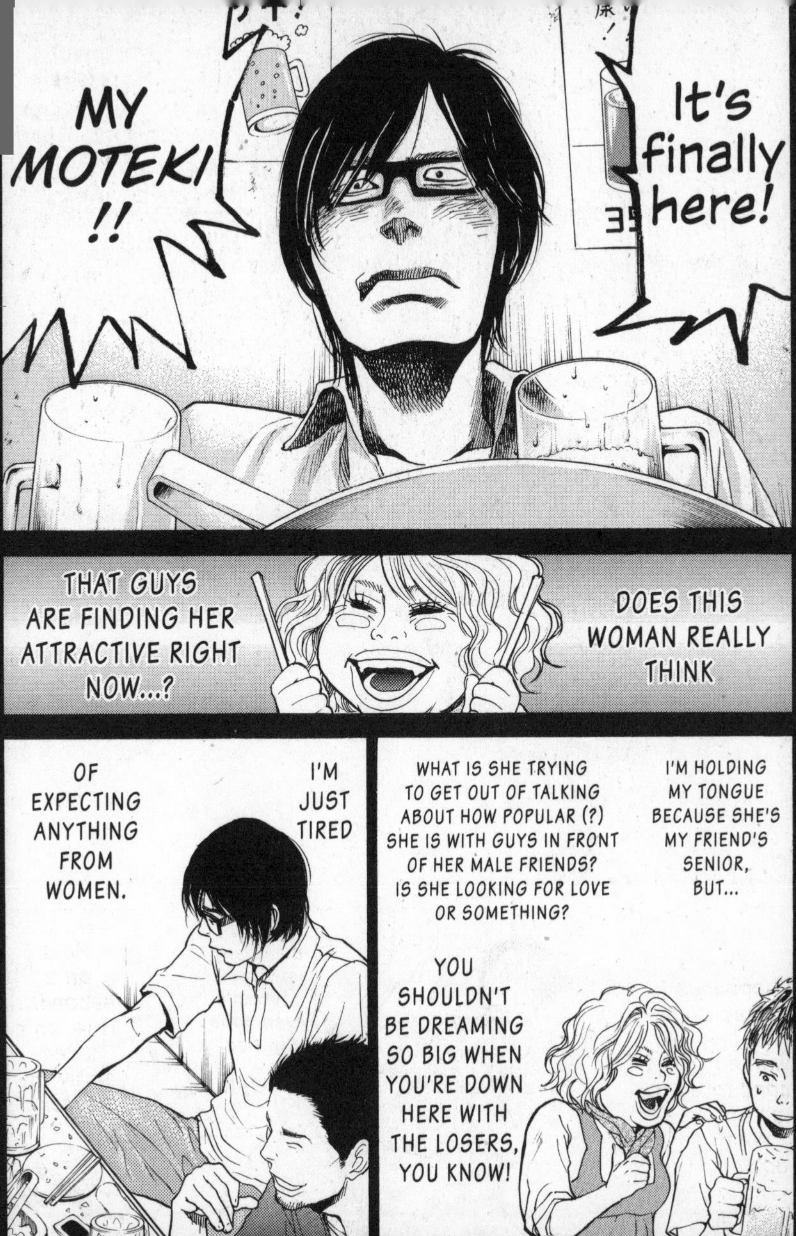
It's finally here!
MY MOTEKI!!
DOES THIS WOMAN REALLY THINK
THAT GUYS ARE FINDING HER ATTRACTIVE RIGHT NOW...?
I'M HOLDING MY TONGUE BECAUSE SHE'S MY FRIEND'S SENIOR, BUT...
WHAT IS SHE TRYING TO GET OUT OF TALKING ABOUT HOW POPULAR (?) SHE IS WITH GUYS IN FRONT OF HER MALE FRIENDS? IS SHE LOOKING FOR LOVE OR SOMETHING?
YOU SHOULDN'T BE DREAMING SO BIG WHEN YOU'RE DOWN HERE WITH THE LOSERS, YOU KNOW!
I'M JUST TIRED
OF EXPECTING ANYTHING FROM WOMEN.

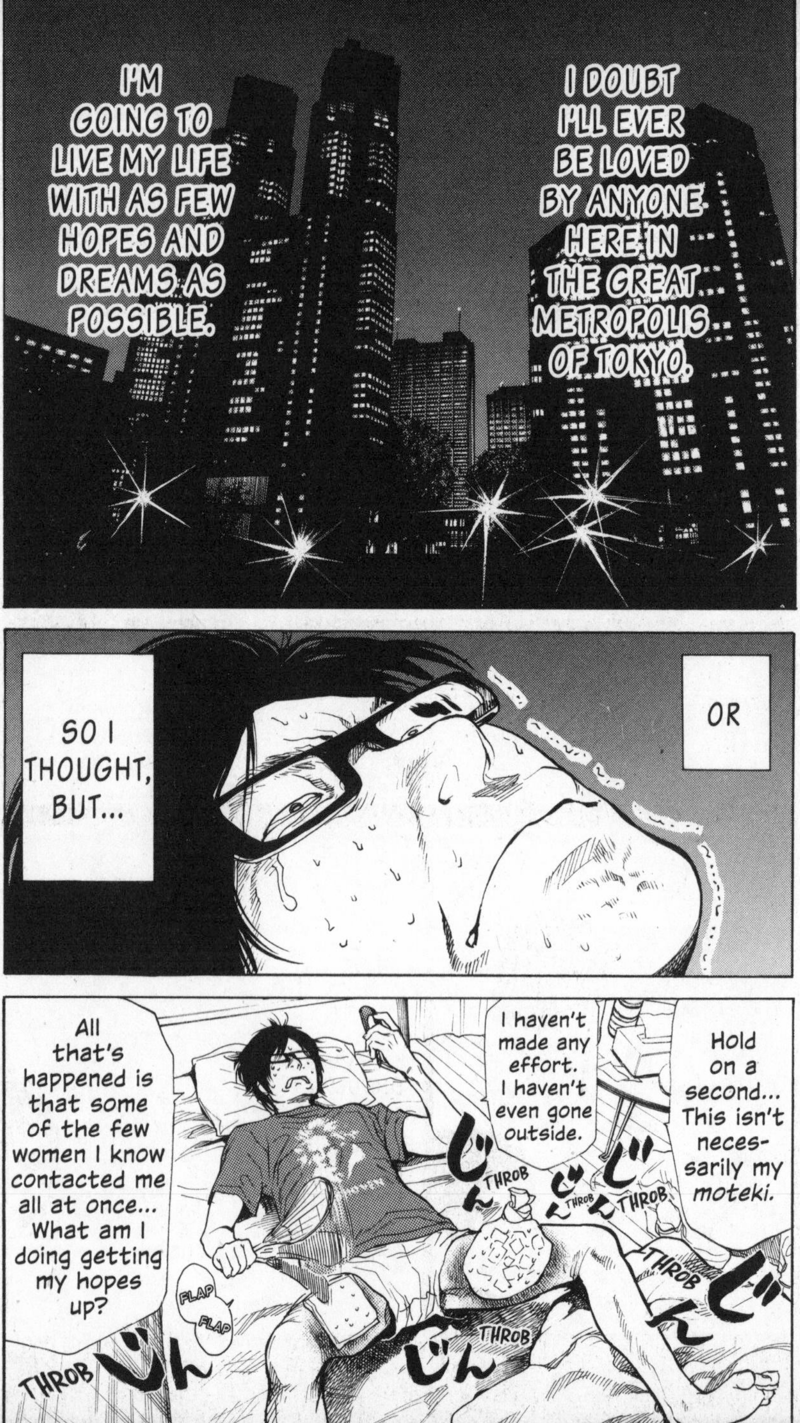
I DOUBT I'LL EVER BE LOVED BY ANYONE HERE IN THE GREAT METROPOLIS OF TOKYO.
I'M GOING TO LIVE MY LIFE WITH AS FEW HOPES AND DREAMS AS POSSIBLE.
OR
SO I THOUGHT, BUT...
Hold on a second... This isn't neces-sarily my *moteki.*
I haven't made any effort. I haven't even gone outside.
All that's happened is that some of the few women I know contacted me all at once... What am I doing getting my hopes up?
じん THROB
じん THROB
じん THROB
じん THROB
じん THROB
FLAP FLAP
じん THROB
じん THROB

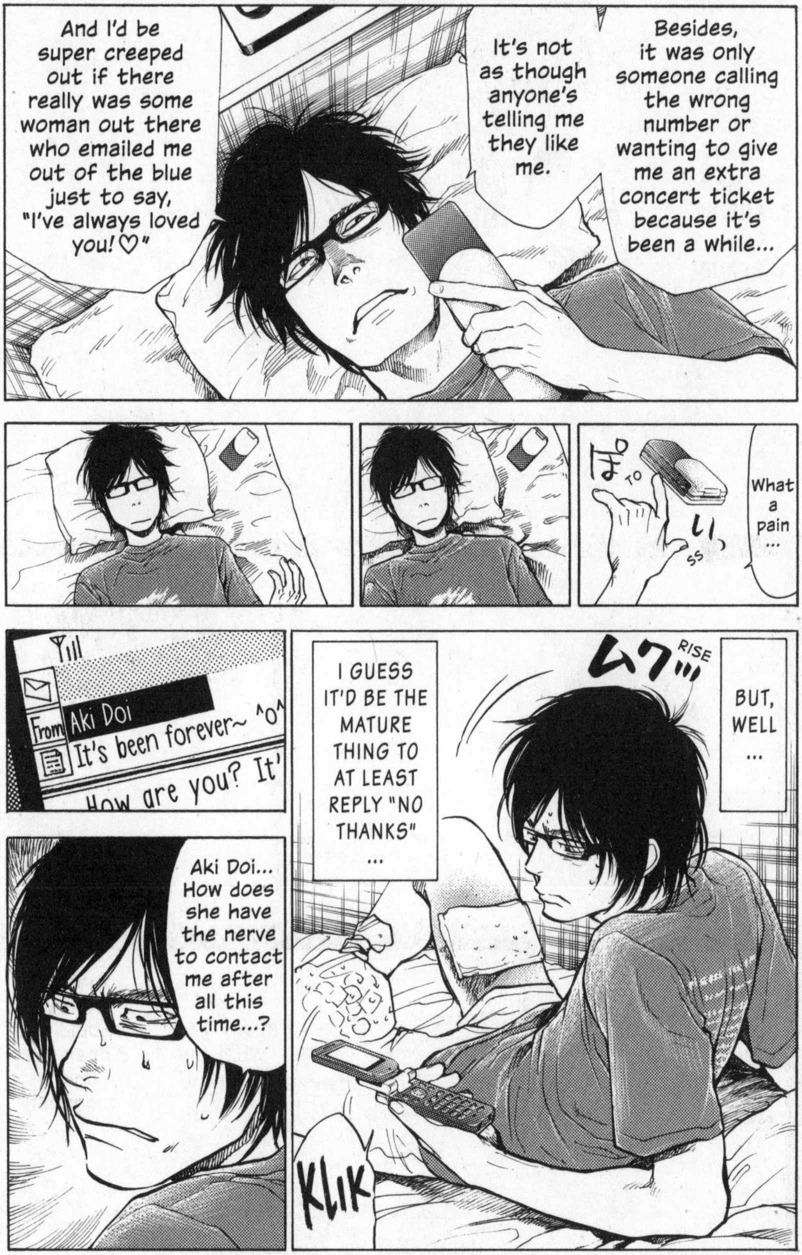
Besides, it was only someone calling the wrong number or wanting to give me an extra concert ticket because it's been a while...
It's not as though anyone's telling me they like me.
And I'd be super creeped out if there really was some woman out there who emailed me out of the blue just to say, "I've always loved you!♡"
What a pain...
ぽ TO
い SS
ムクッ RISE
BUT, WELL...
I GUESS IT'D BE THE MATURE THING TO AT LEAST REPLY "NO THANKS"...
KLIK
From Aki Doi
It's been forever~ ^o^
How are you? It'
Aki Doi... How does she have the nerve to contact me after all this time...?

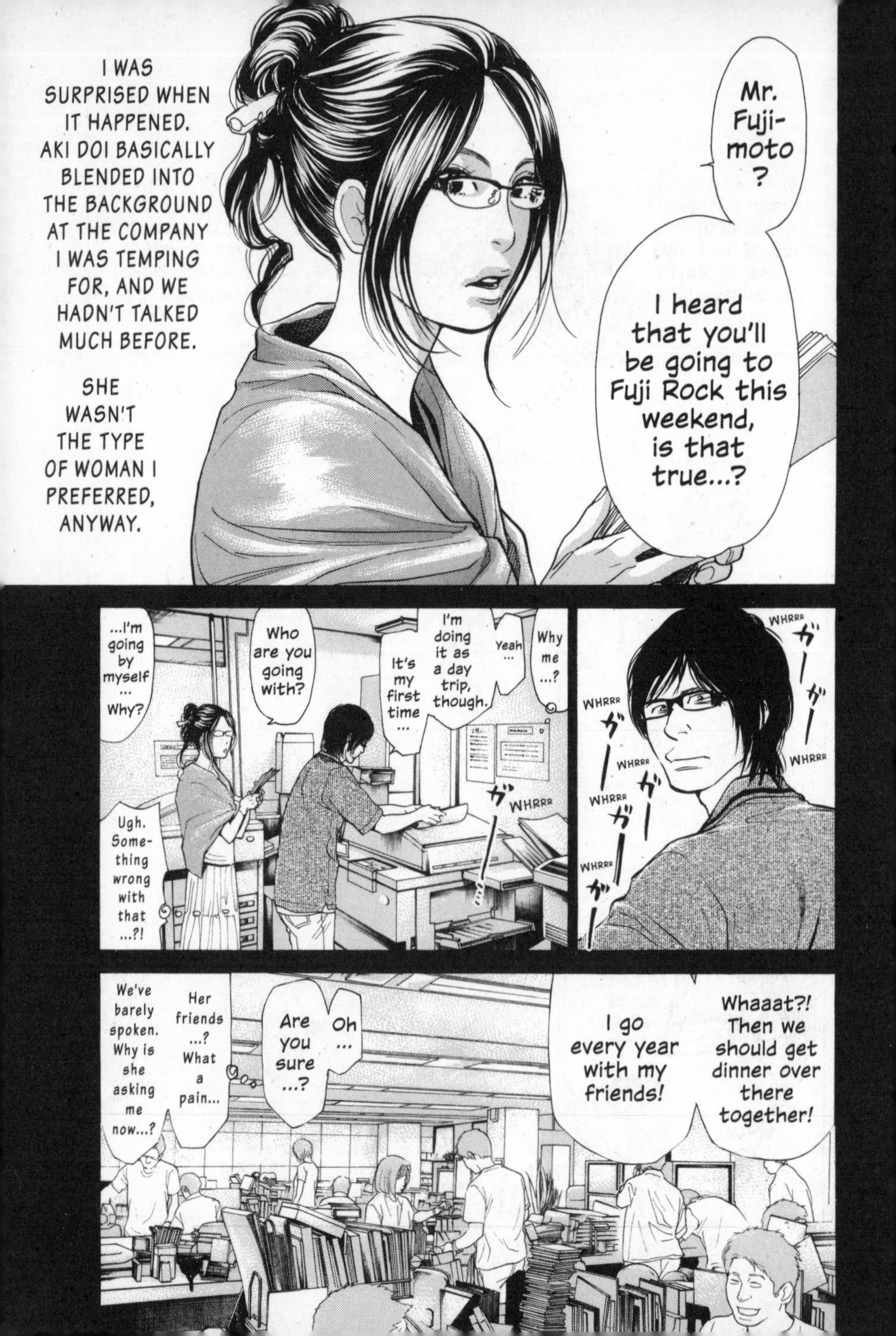
Mr. Fuji-moto?
I heard that you'll be going to Fuji Rock this weekend, is that true...?
I WAS SURPRISED WHEN IT HAPPENED. AKI DOI BASICALLY BLENDED INTO THE BACKGROUND AT THE COMPANY I WAS TEMPING FOR, AND WE HADN'T TALKED MUCH BEFORE.
SHE WASN'T THE TYPE OF WOMAN I PREFERRED, ANYWAY.
WHRRR
ガーガー
WHRRR
WHRRR
ガー
WHRRR
ガー
WHRRR
ガー
WHRRR
ガー
Why me...?
Yeah...
I'm doing it as a day trip, though.
It's my first time...
ガ
WHRRR
Who are you going with?
...I'm going by myself... Why?
Ugh. Something wrong with that...?!
Whaaat?! Then we should get dinner over there together!
I go every year with my friends!
Oh...
Are you sure...?
Her friends...? What a pain...
We've barely spoken. Why is she asking me now...?

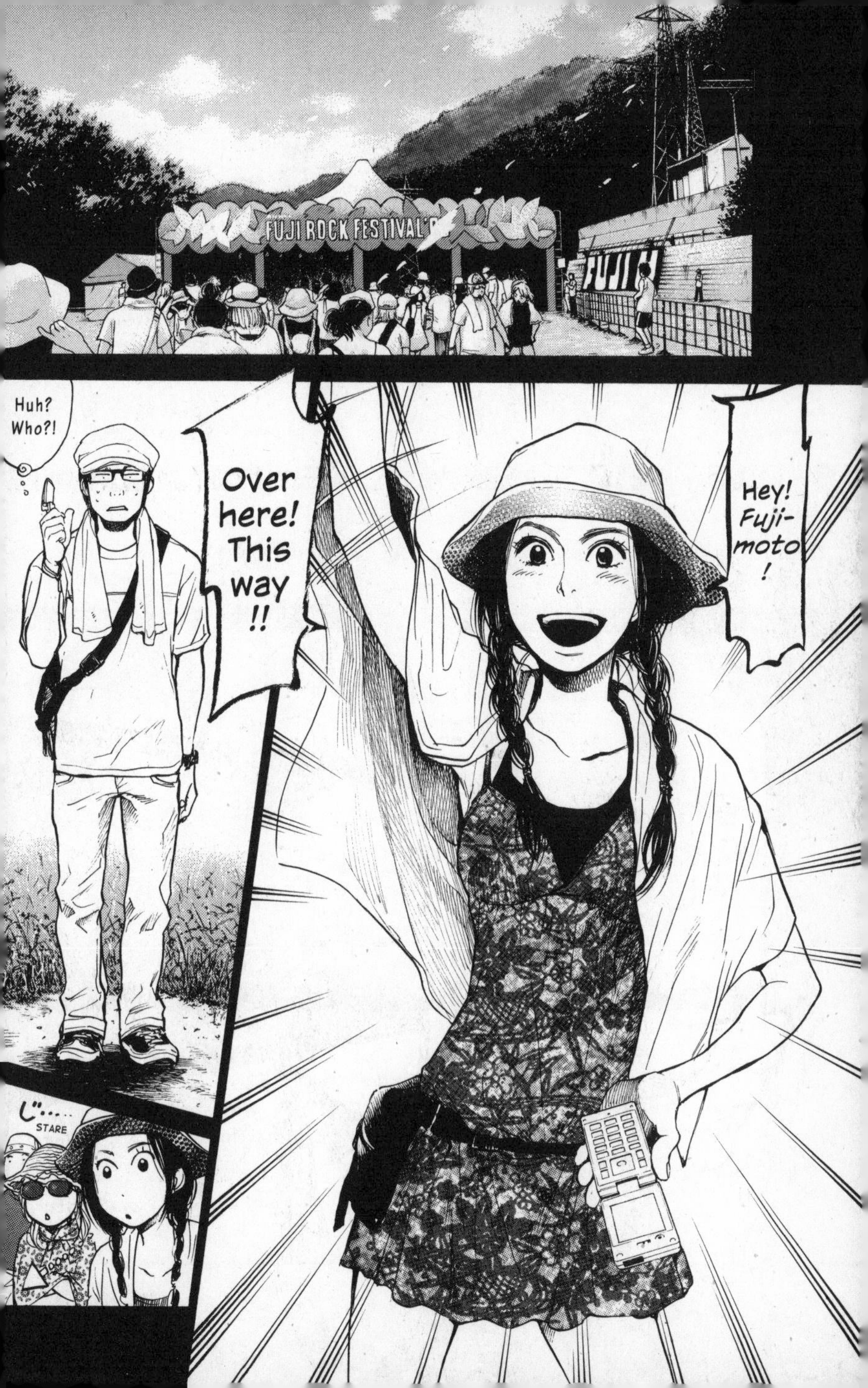
FUJI ROCK FESTIVAL'
Hey! Fuji-moto!
Over here! This way!!
Huh? Who?!
じ…… STARE

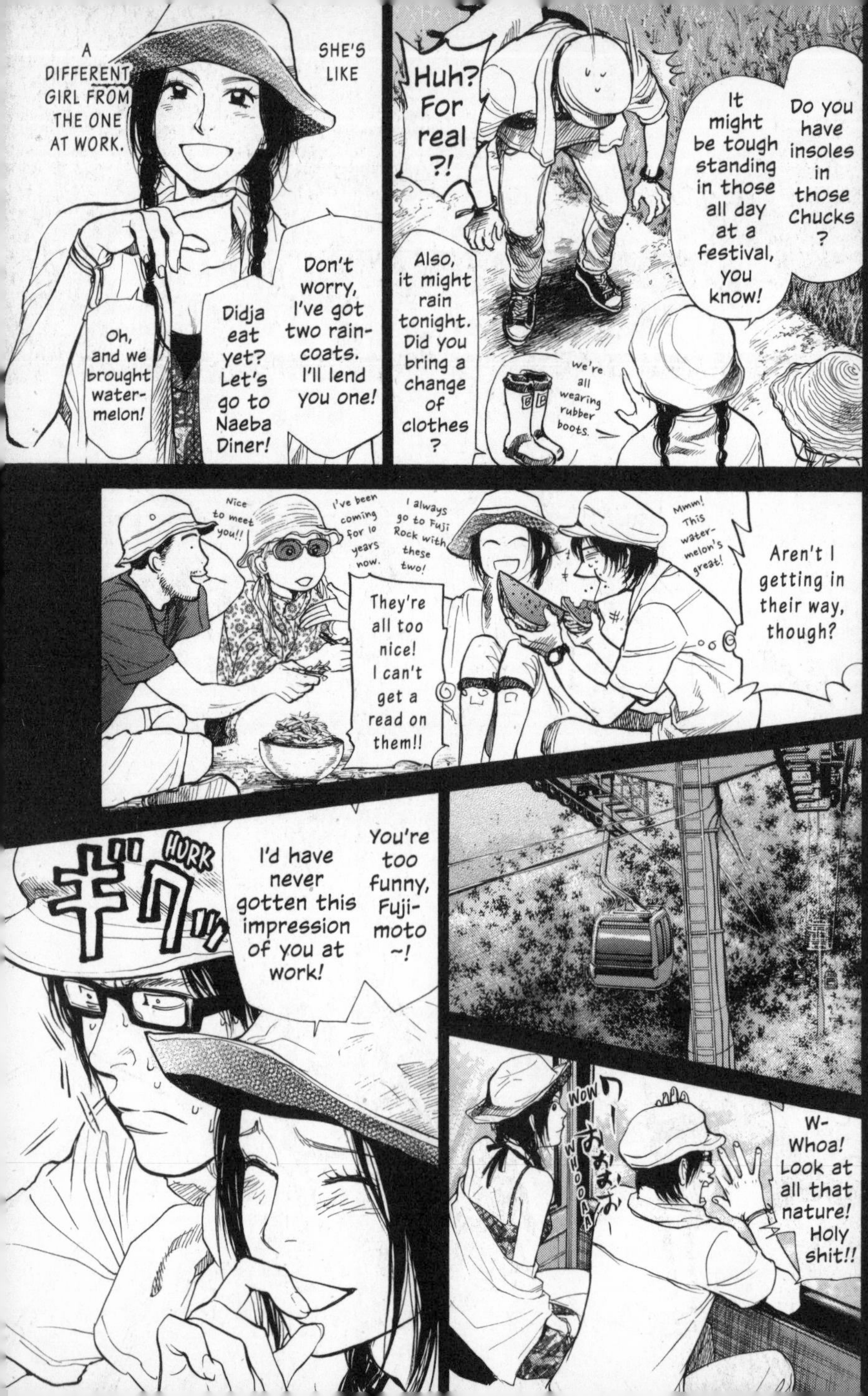
Do you have insoles in those Chucks?
It might be tough standing in those all day at a festival, you know!
Huh? For real?!
We're all wearing rubber boots.
Also, it might rain tonight. Did you bring a change of clothes?
SHE'S LIKE
A DIFFERENT GIRL FROM THE ONE AT WORK.
Don't worry, I've got two rain-coats. I'll lend you one!
Didja eat yet? Let's go to Naeba Diner!
Oh, and we brought water-melon!
Aren't I getting in their way, though?
Mmm! This water-melon's great!
I always go to Fuji Rock with these two!
I've been coming for 10 years now.
Nice to meet you!!
They're all too nice! I can't get a read on them!!
W-Whoa! Look at all that nature! Holy shit!!
WOW
WHOOAA
You're too funny, Fuji-moto~!
I'd have never gotten this impression of you at work!
HURK

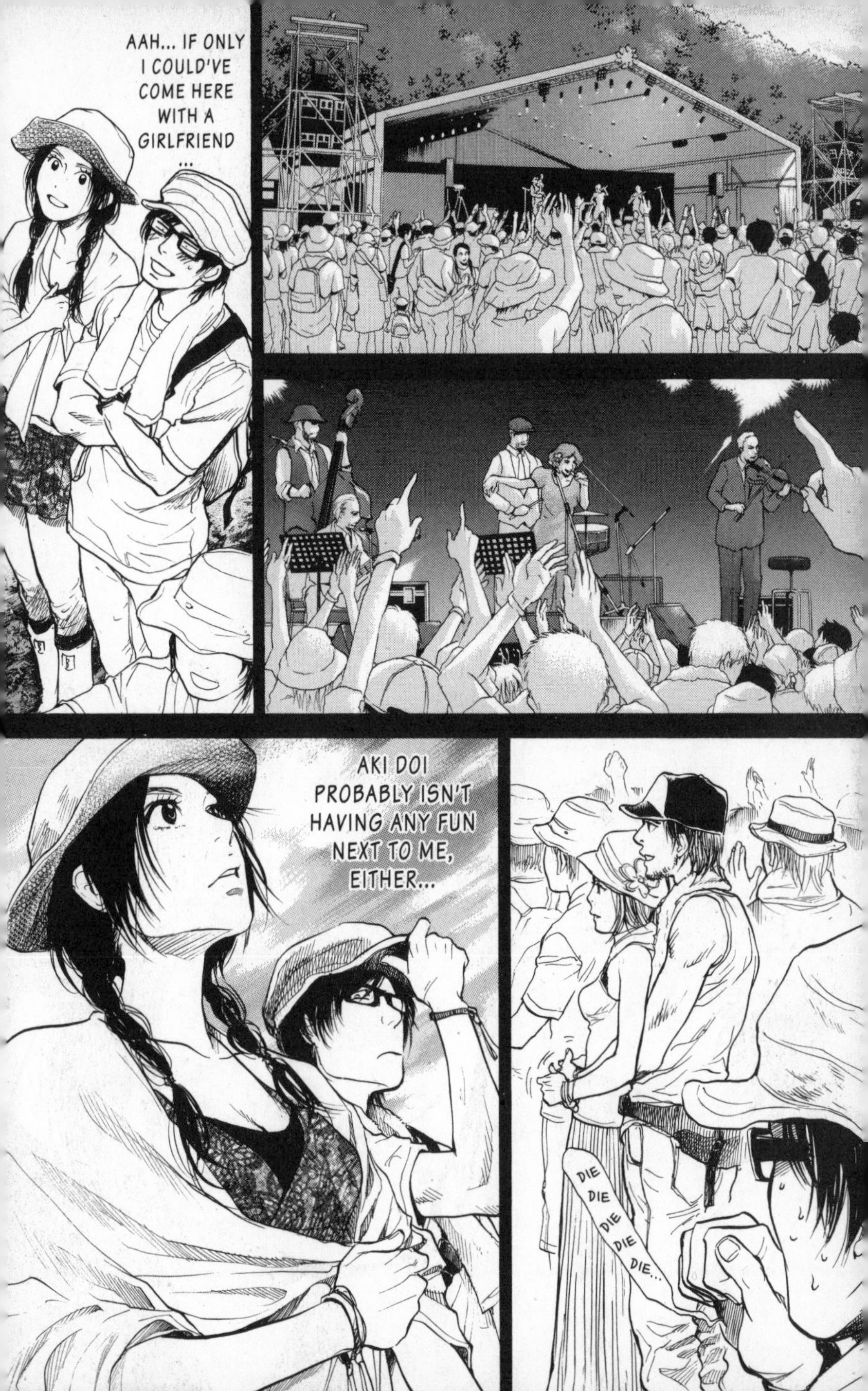
AAH... IF ONLY I COULD'VE COME HERE WITH A GIRLFRIEND ...
DIE DIE DIE DIE DIE...
AKI DOI PROBABLY ISN'T HAVING ANY FUN NEXT TO ME, EITHER...

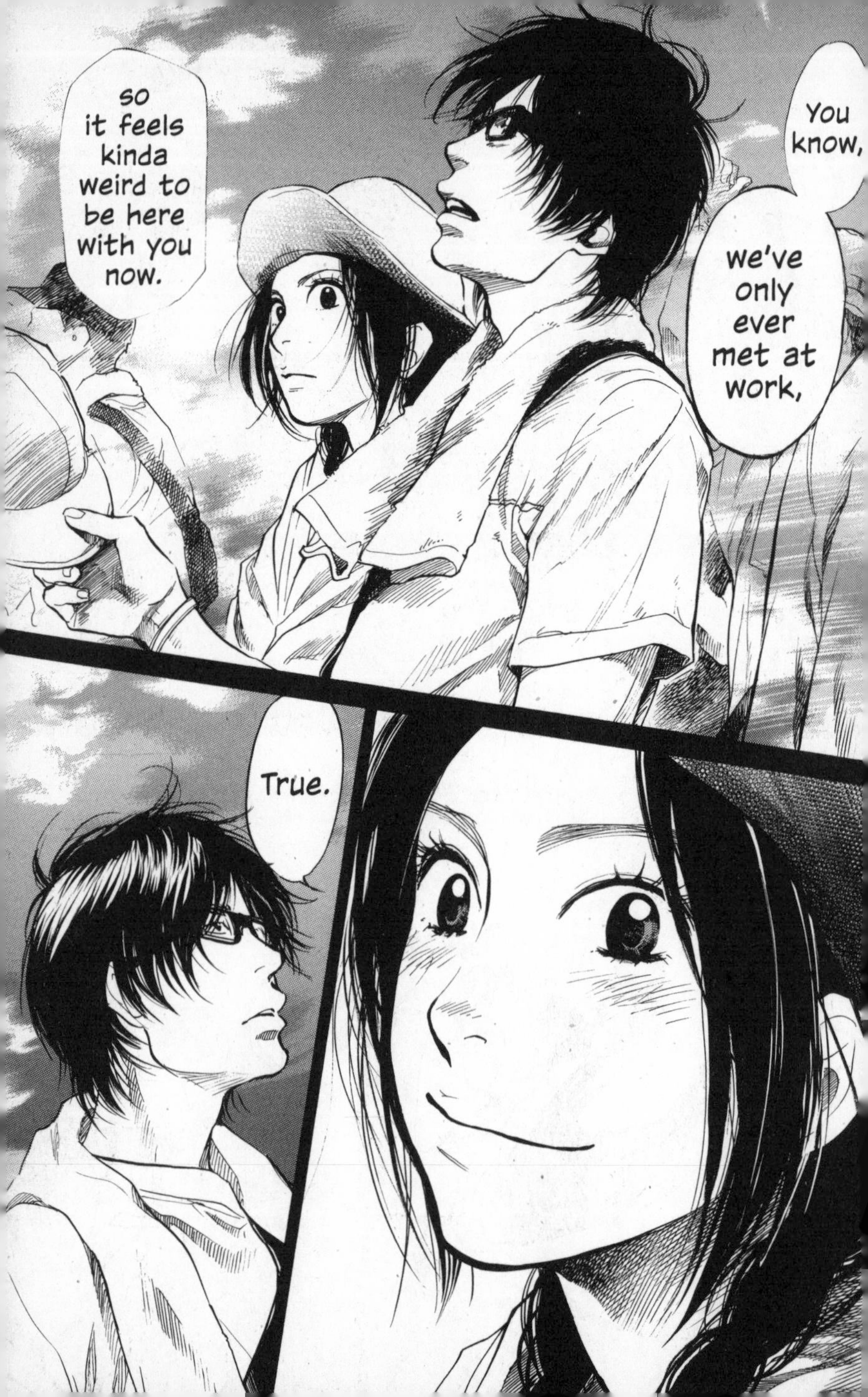
You know,
we've only ever met at work,
so it feels kinda weird to be here with you now.
True.

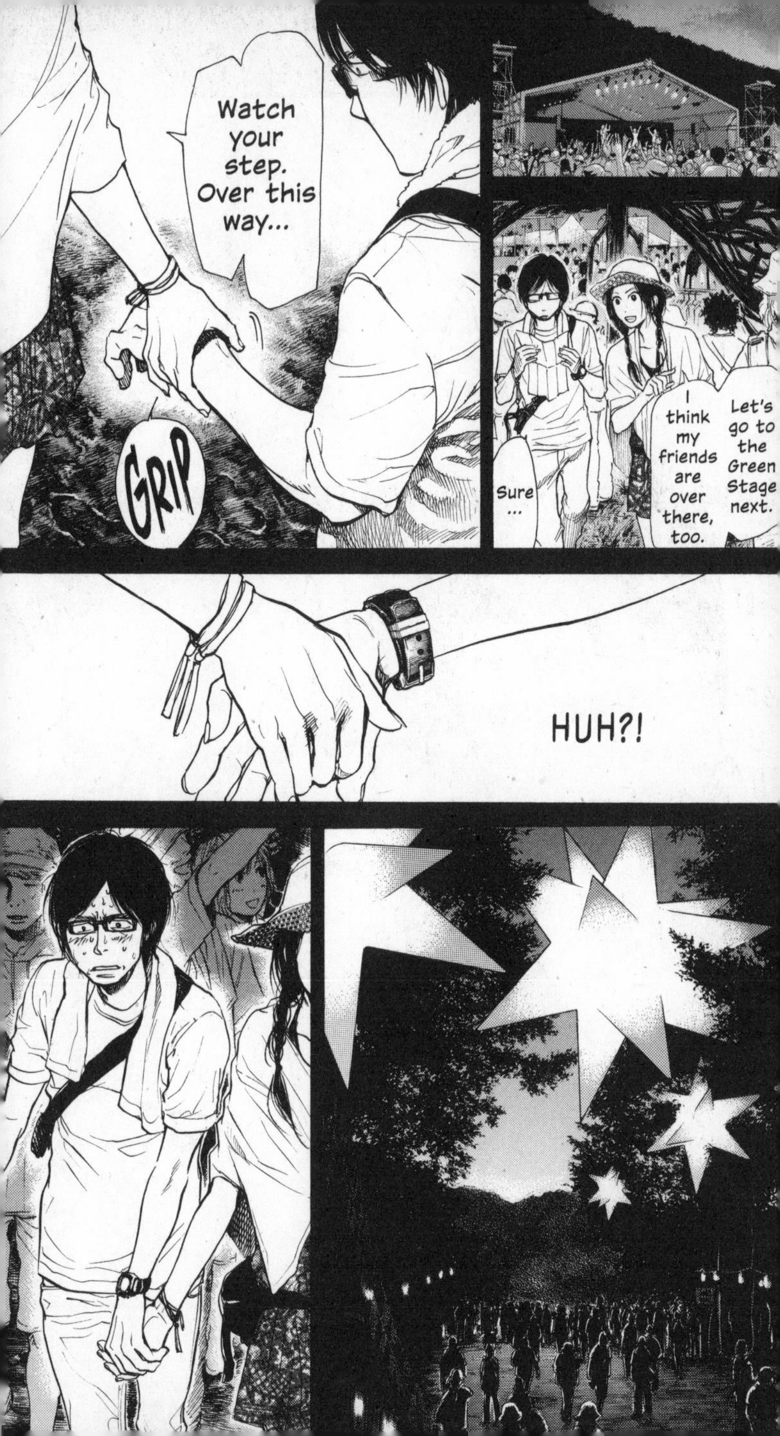
Let's go to the Green Stage next.
I think my friends are over there, too.
Sure...
Watch your step. Over this way...
GRIP
HUH?!

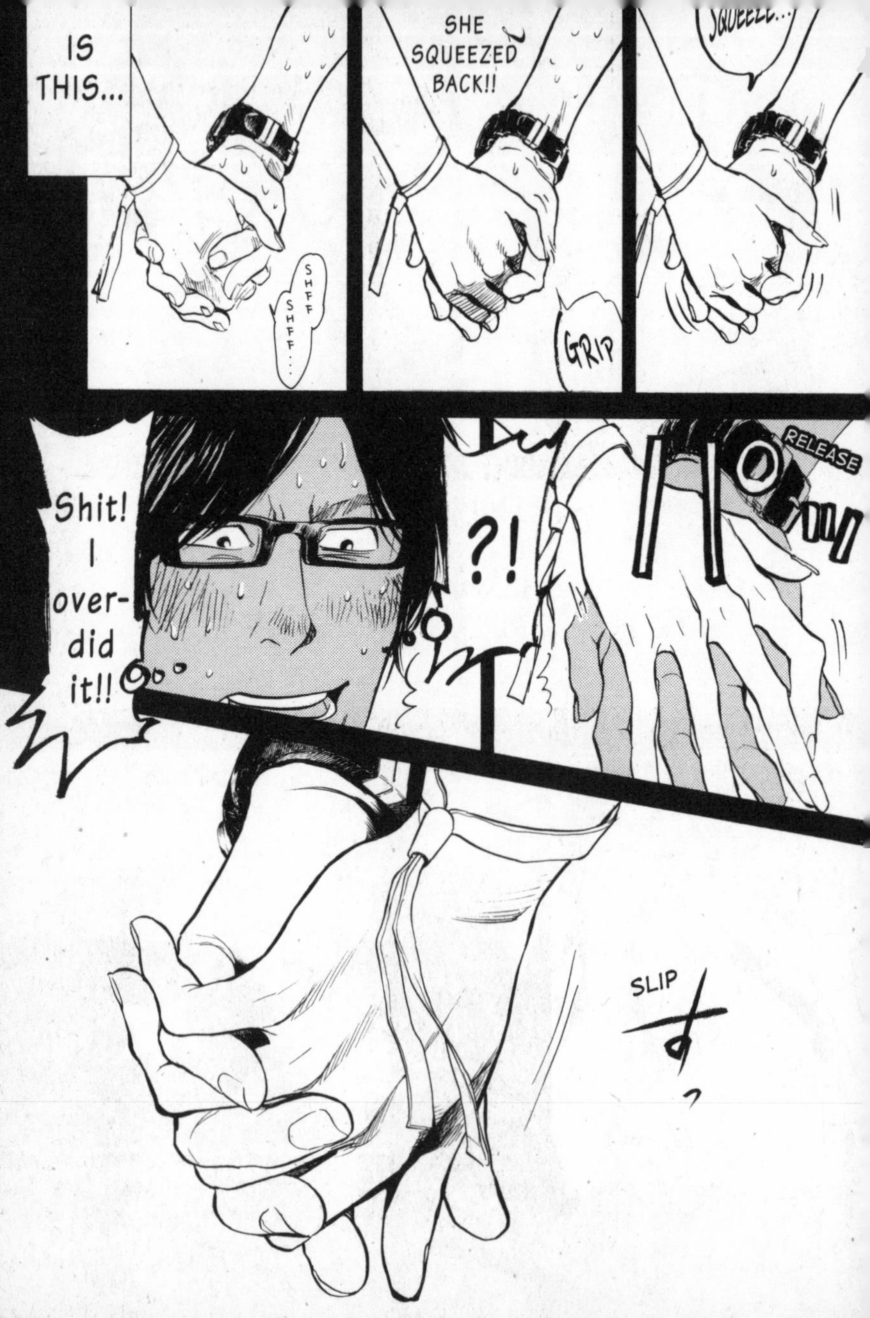
SQUEEZE...
SHE SQUEEZED BACK!!
GRIP
IS THIS...
SHFF SHFF...
RELEASE
?!
Shit! I over-did it!!
SLIP

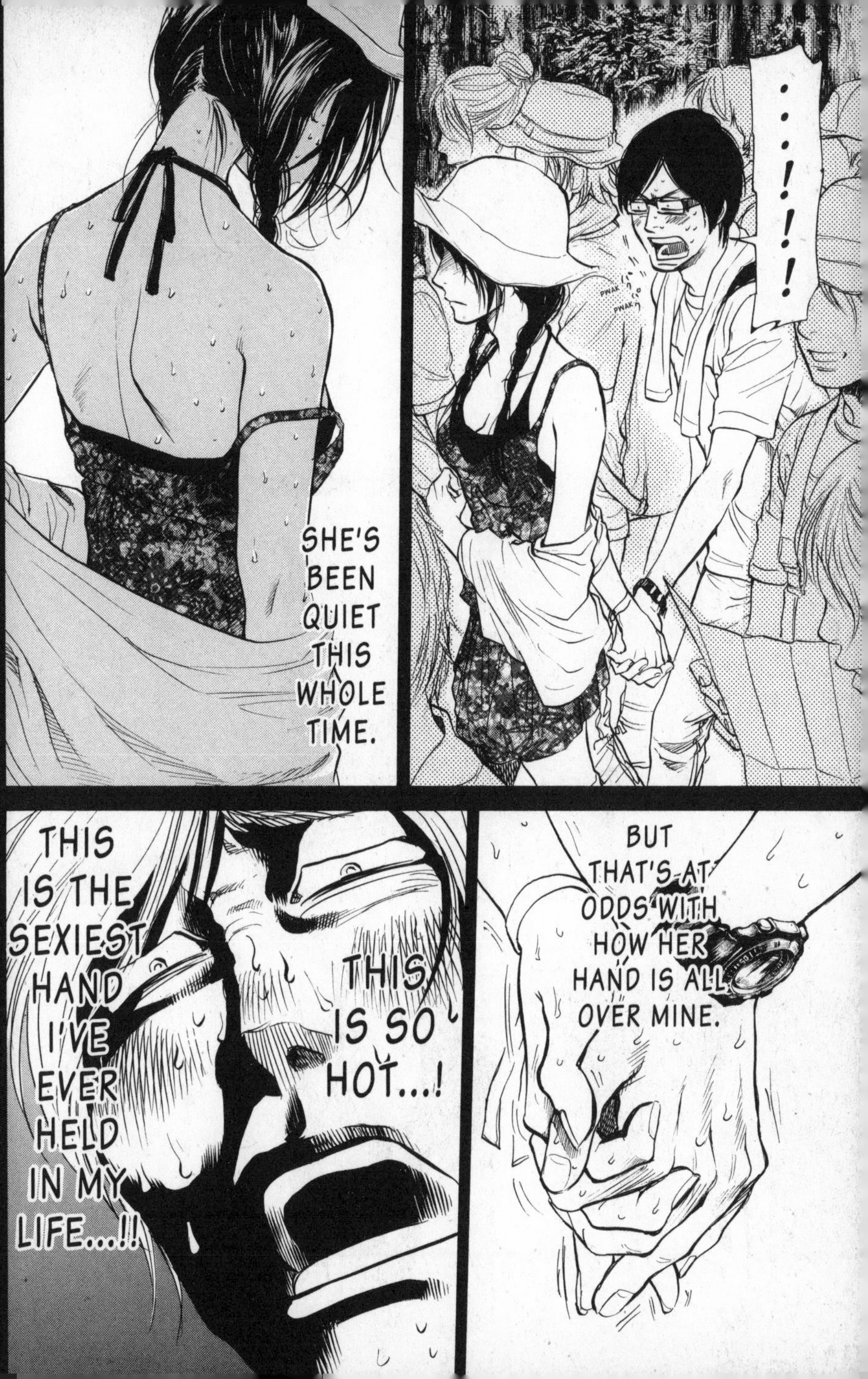
...!!!
PWAK PWAK
SHE'S BEEN QUIET THIS WHOLE TIME.
BUT THAT'S AT ODDS WITH HOW HER HAND IS ALL OVER MINE.
THIS IS SO HOT...!
THIS IS THE SEXIEST HAND I'VE EVER HELD IN MY LIFE...!!

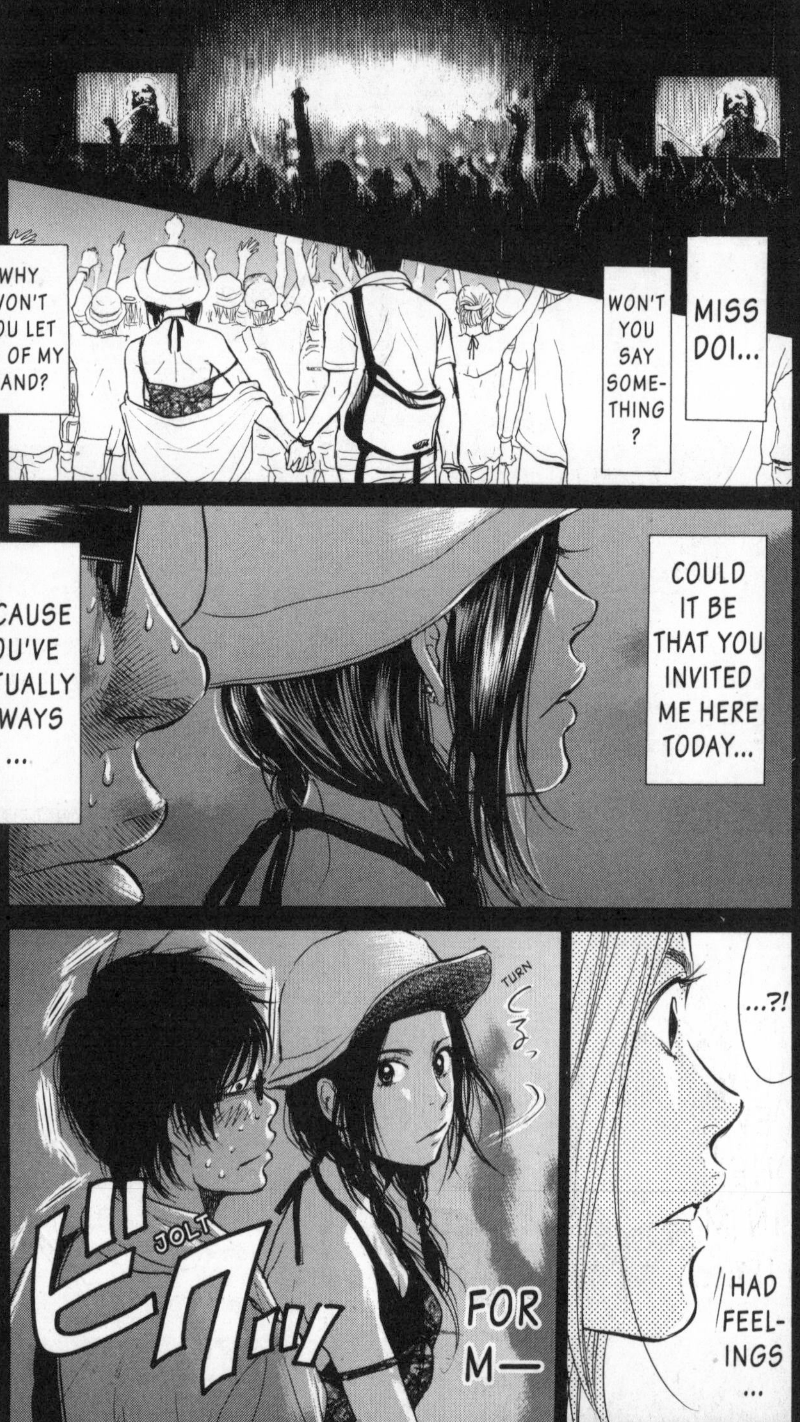
MISS DOI...
WON'T YOU SAY SOME-THING?
WHY WON'T YOU LET GO OF MY HAND?
COULD IT BE THAT YOU INVITED ME HERE TODAY...
BECAUSE YOU'VE ACTUALLY ALWAYS ...
...?!
HAD FEEL-INGS ...
TURN
FOR M—
JOLT

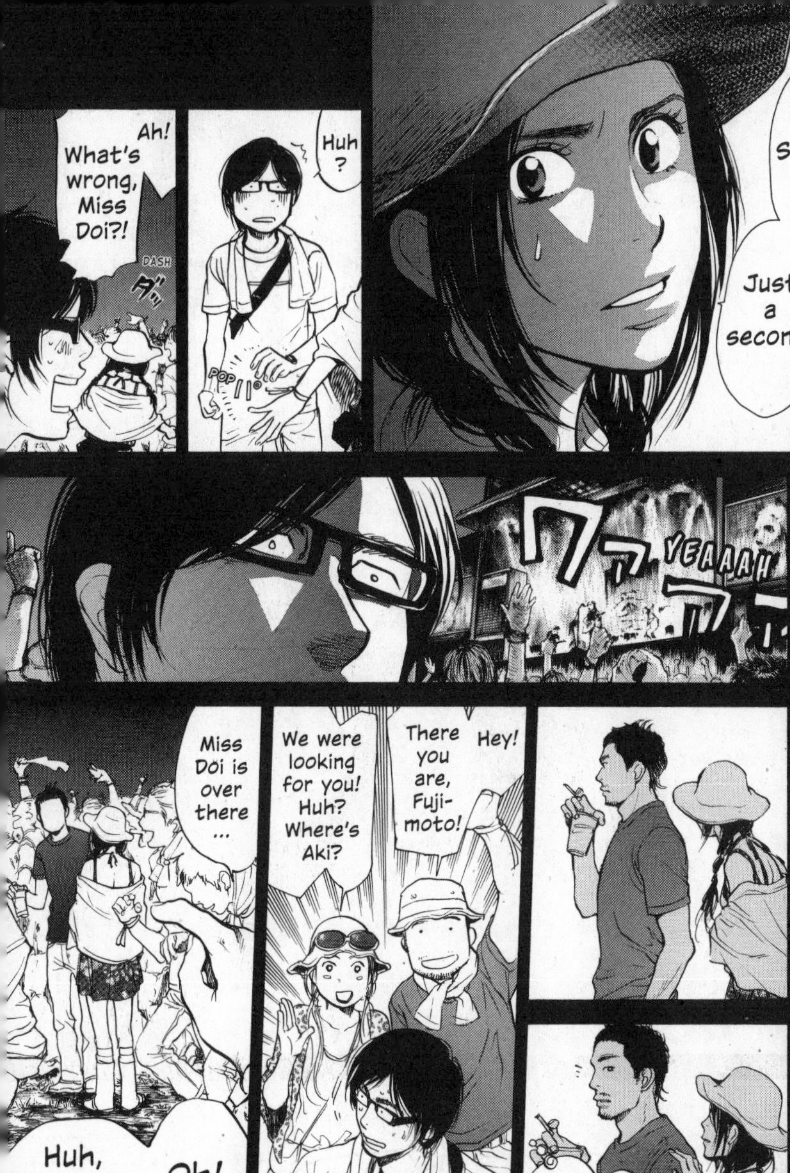

Sorry...
Just a second.
Huh?
Ah! What's wrong, Miss Doi?!
DASH
ダッ
POP
YEAAAH
Who's that...? Someone she knows?
Hey!
There you are, Fujimoto!
We were looking for you! Huh? Where's Aki?
Miss Doi is over there...
Oh! There she is!
Huh, look at that! She's with Masanori!

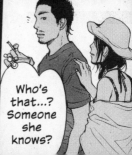

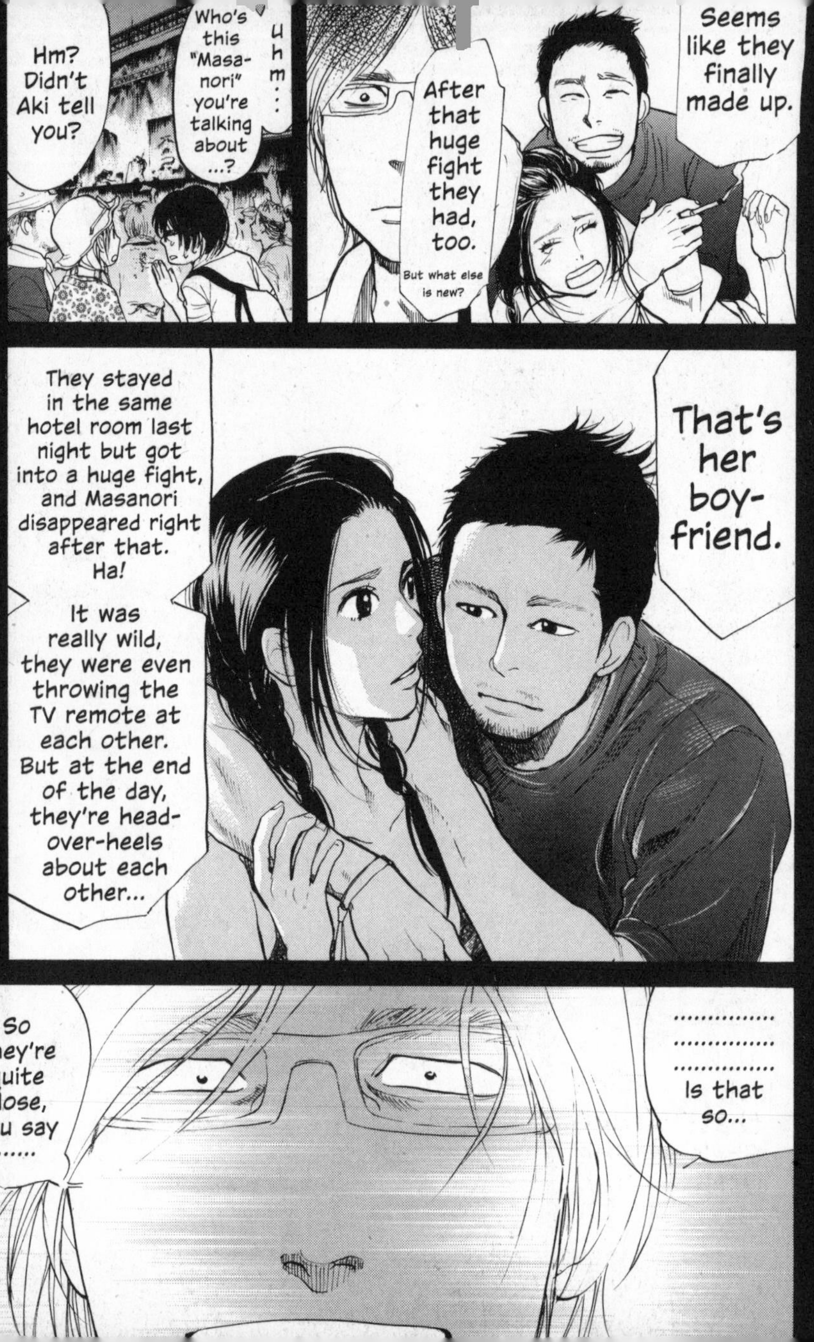
Seems like they finally made up.
After that huge fight they had, too.
But what else is new?
Uhm...
Who's this "Masanori" you're talking about ...?
Hm? Didn't Aki tell you?
That's her boyfriend.
They stayed in the same hotel room last night but got into a huge fight, and Masanori disappeared right after that. Ha!
It was really wild, they were even throwing the TV remote at each other. But at the end of the day, they're head-over-heels about each other...
.... Is that so...
So they're quite close, you say ......

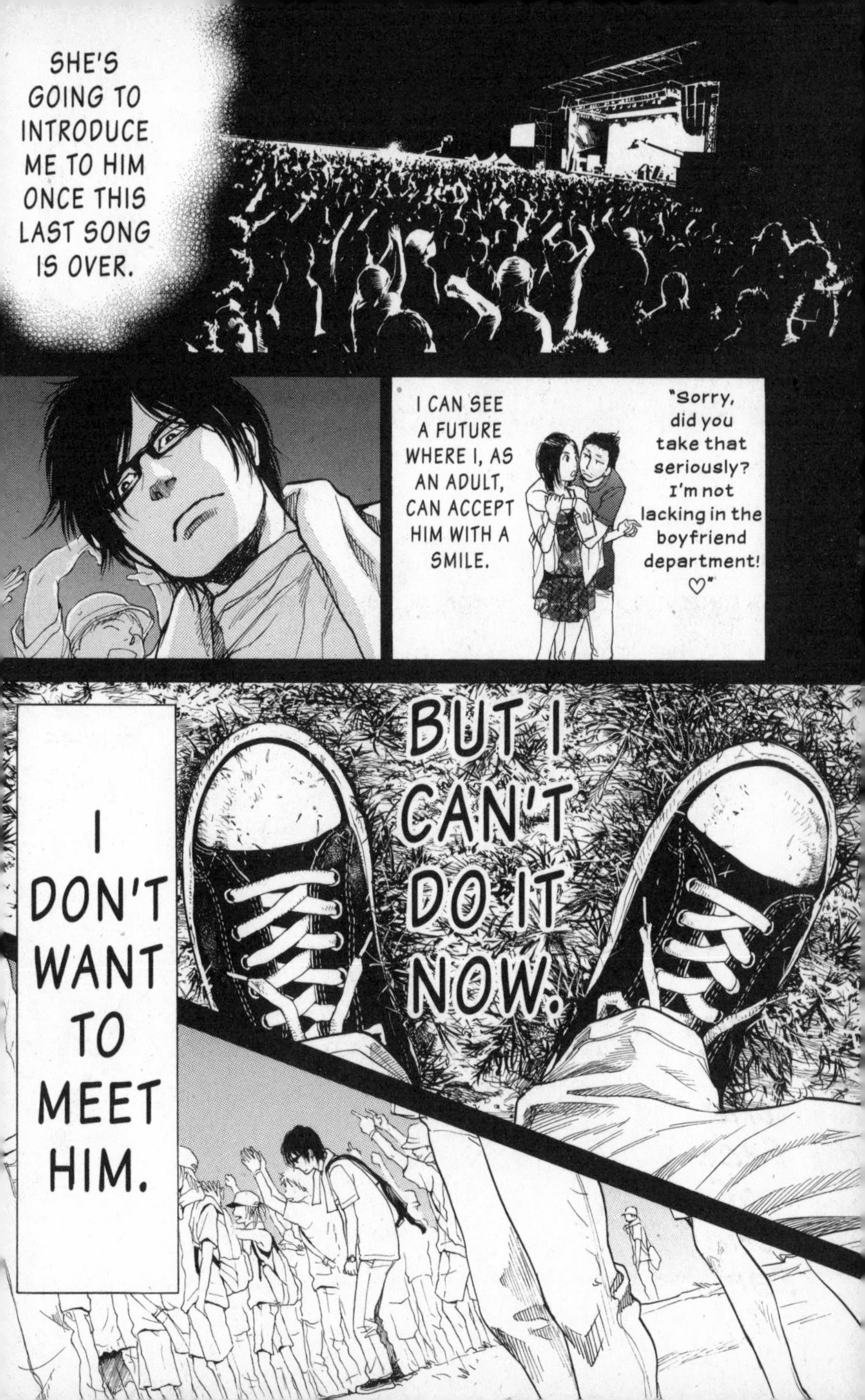
SHE'S GOING TO INTRODUCE ME TO HIM ONCE THIS LAST SONG IS OVER.
"Sorry, did you take that seriously? I'm not lacking in the boyfriend department! ♡"
I CAN SEE A FUTURE WHERE I, AS AN ADULT, CAN ACCEPT HIM WITH A SMILE.
BUT I CAN'T DO IT NOW.
I DON'T WANT TO MEET HIM.

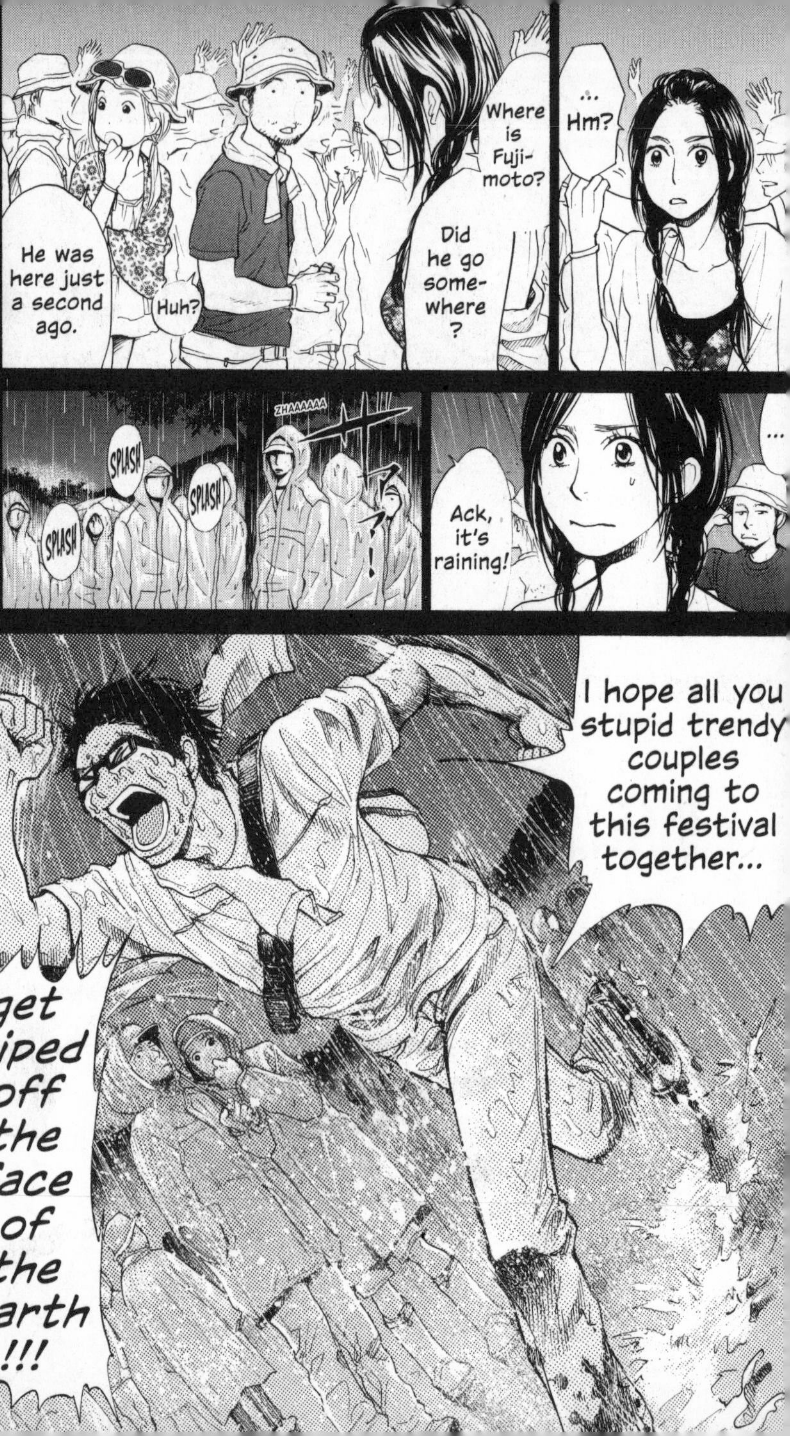
... Hm?
Where is Fuji-moto?
Did he go some-where?
Huh?
He was here just a second ago.
...
Ack, it's raining!
ZHAAAAAA
SPLASH
SPLASH
SPLASH
I hope all you stupid trendy couples coming to this festival together...
get wiped off the face of the Earth!!!

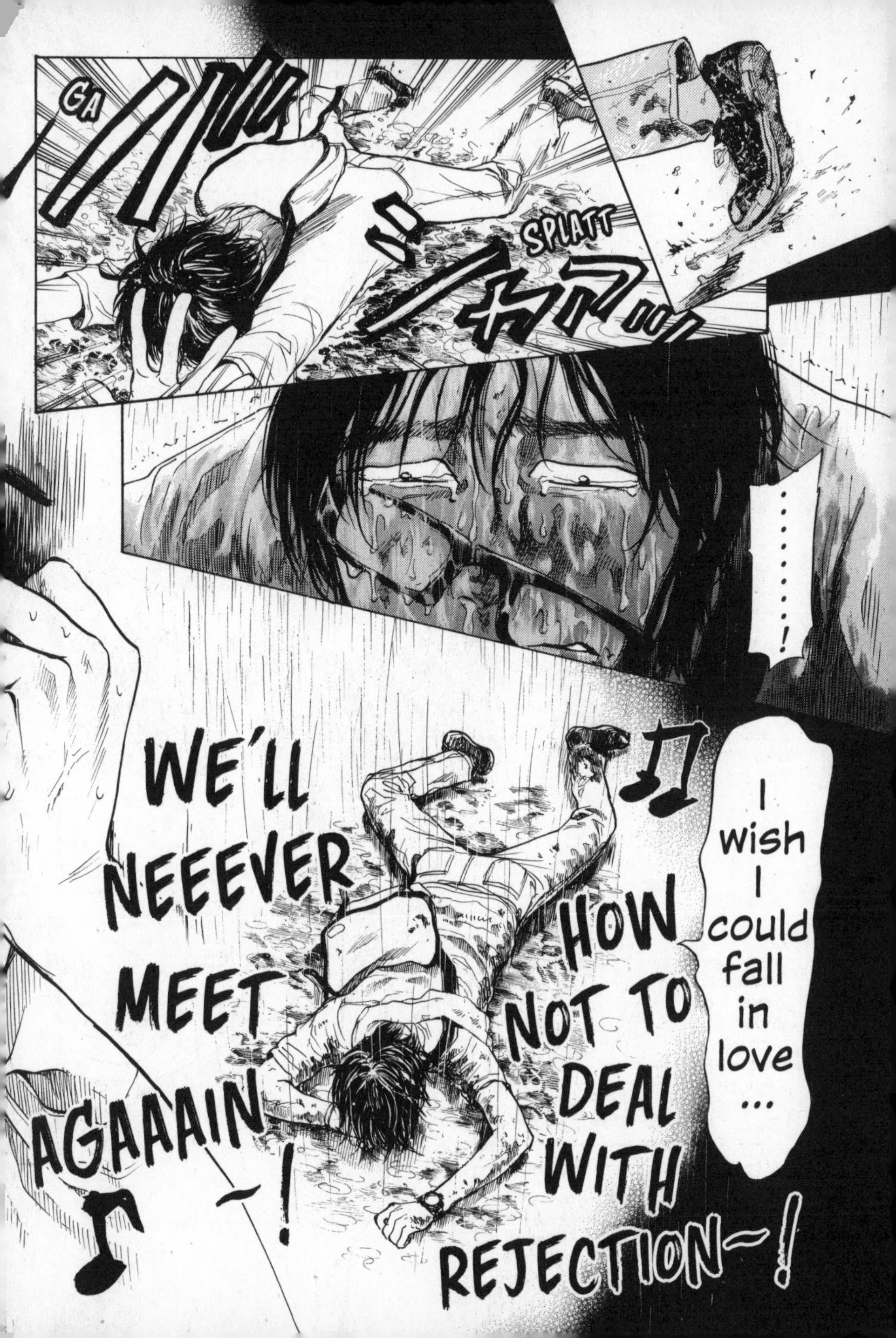
GA
SPLATT
......!
I wish I could fall in love...
HOW NOT TO DEAL WITH REJECTION~!
WE'LL NEEEVER MEET AGAAAIN~!

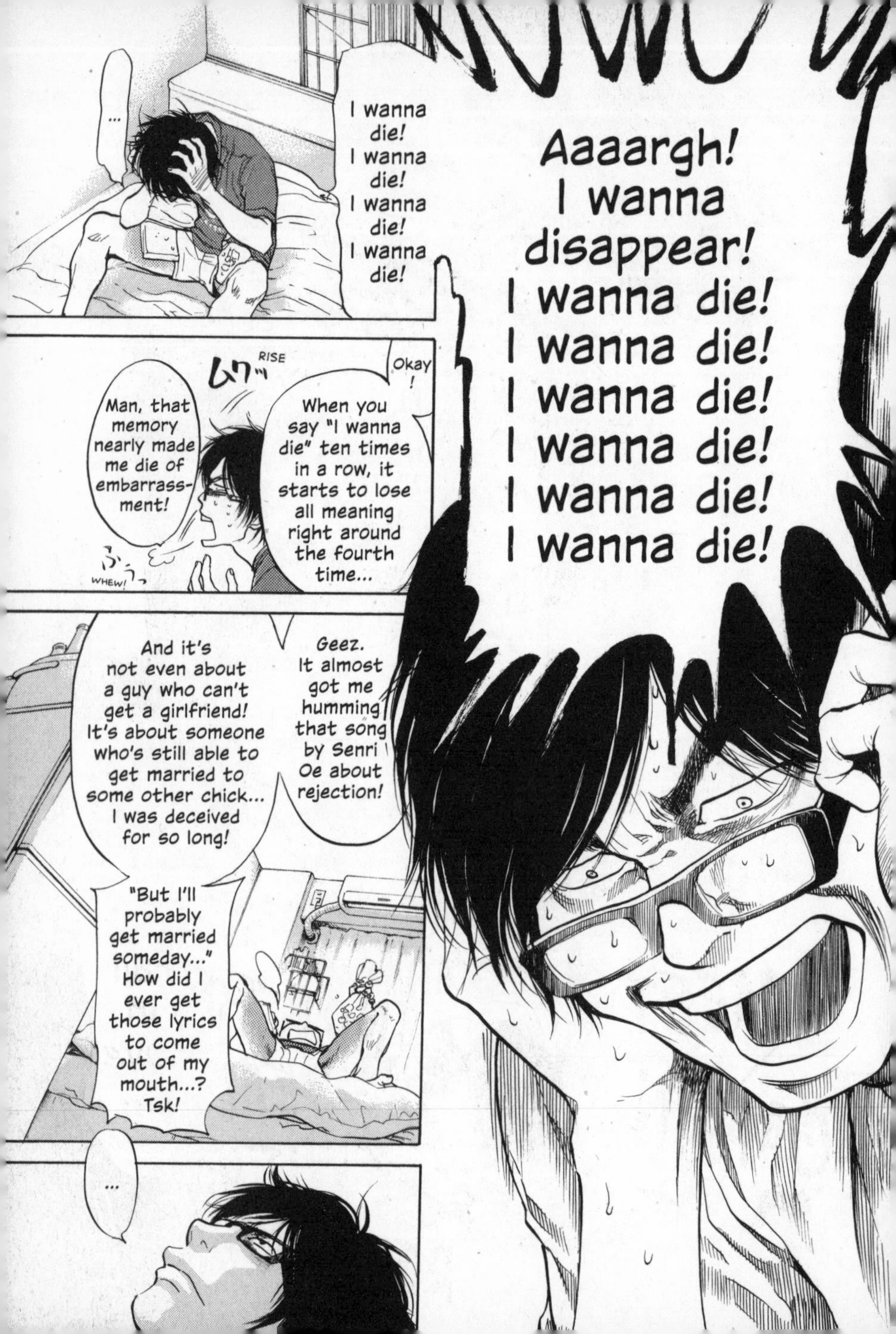

Aaaargh! I wanna disappear! I wanna die! I wanna die! I wanna die! I wanna die! I wanna die! I wanna die!
I wanna die! I wanna die! I wanna die! I wanna die!
...
Okay!
RISE
When you say "I wanna die" ten times in a row, it starts to lose all meaning right around the fourth time...
Man, that memory nearly made me die of embarrass-ment!
WHEW!
Geez. It almost got me humming that song by Senri Oe about rejection!
And it's not even about a guy who can't get a girlfriend! It's about someone who's still able to get married to some other chick... I was deceived for so long!
"But I'll probably get married someday..." How did I ever get those lyrics to come out of my mouth...? Tsk!
...

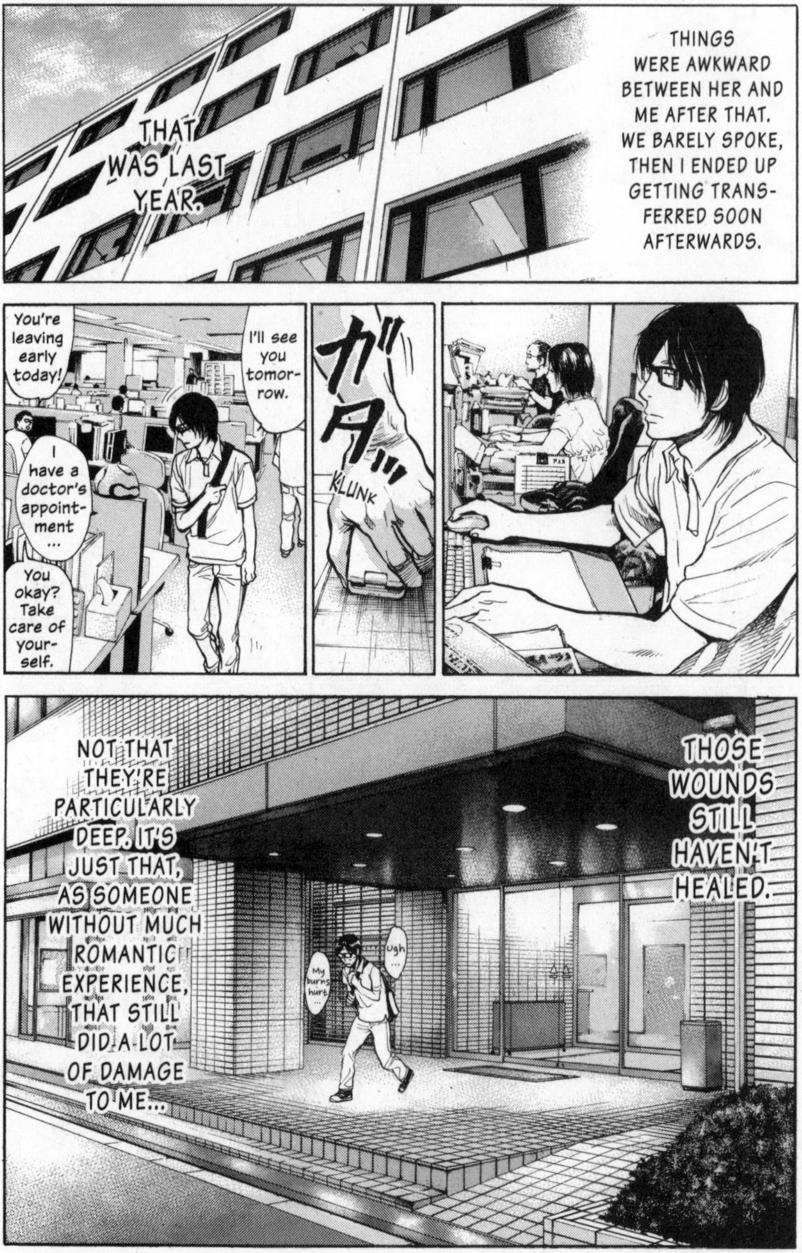
THINGS WERE AWKWARD BETWEEN HER AND ME AFTER THAT. WE BARELY SPOKE, THEN I ENDED UP GETTING TRANSFERRED SOON AFTERWARDS.
THAT WAS LAST YEAR.
ガタッ
KLUNK
You're leaving early today!
I have a doctor's appointment...
You okay? Take care of yourself.
I'll see you tomorrow.
THOSE WOUNDS STILL HAVEN'T HEALED.
NOT THAT THEY'RE PARTICULARLY DEEP. IT'S JUST THAT, AS SOMEONE WITHOUT MUCH ROMANTIC EXPERIENCE, THAT STILL DID A LOT OF DAMAGE TO ME...
ugh...
My burns hurt...

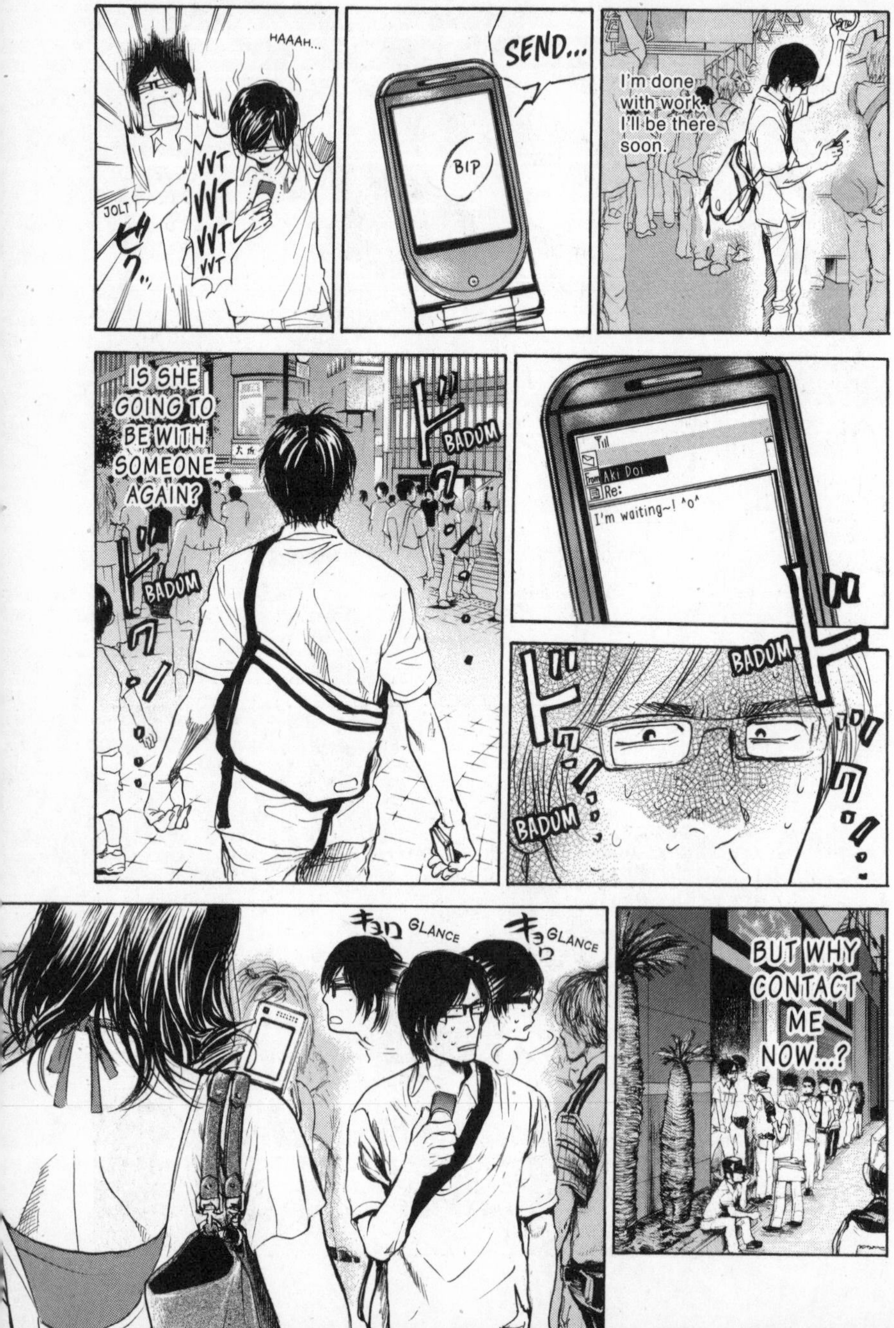
I'm done with work. I'll be there soon.
SEND...
BIP
HAAAH...
VVT VVT VVT VVT
JOLT
Aki Doi
Re:
I'm waiting~! ^o^
BADUM
BADUM
IS SHE GOING TO BE WITH SOMEONE AGAIN?
BADUM
BADUM
BUT WHY CONTACT ME NOW...?
GLANCE
GLANCE

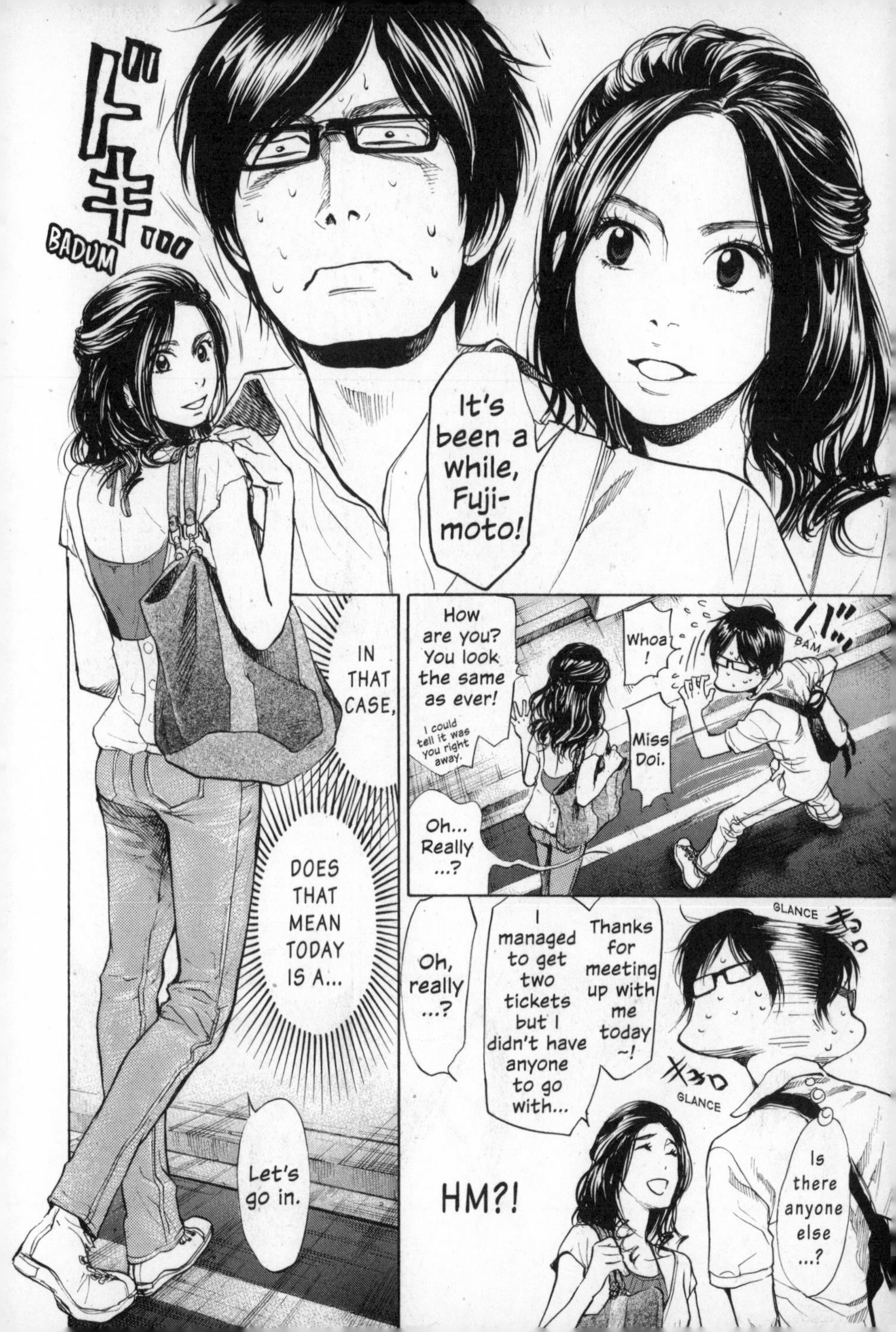
BADUM
It's been a while, Fuji-moto!
How are you? You look the same as ever!
I could tell it was you right away.
BAM
Whoa!
Miss Doi.
Oh... Really ...?
Thanks for meeting up with me today ~!
I managed to get two tickets but I didn't have anyone to go with...
Oh, really ...?
GLANCE
GLANCE
HM?!
Is there anyone else ...?
IN THAT CASE,
DOES THAT MEAN TODAY IS A...
Let's go in.

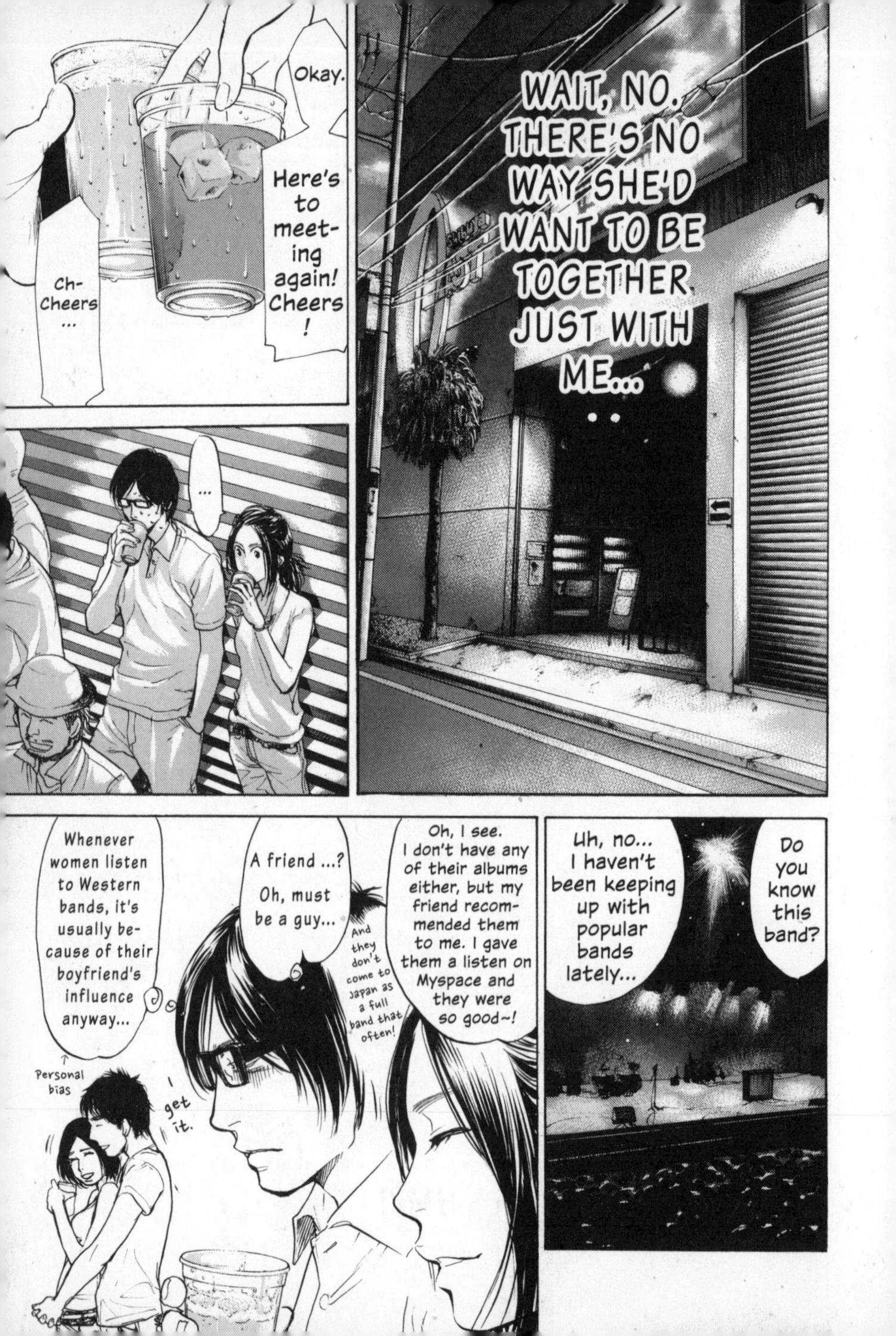
WAIT, NO. THERE'S NO WAY SHE'D WANT TO BE TOGETHER JUST WITH ME...
Okay.
Here's to meet-ing again! Cheers!
Ch-Cheers...
...
...
Do you know this band?
Uh, no... I haven't been keeping up with popular bands lately...
Oh, I see. I don't have any of their albums either, but my friend recom-mended them to me. I gave them a listen on Myspace and they were so good~!
And they don't come to Japan as a full band that often!
A friend ...?
Oh, must be a guy...
Whenever women listen to Western bands, it's usually be-cause of their boyfriend's influence anyway...
Personal bias
I get it.

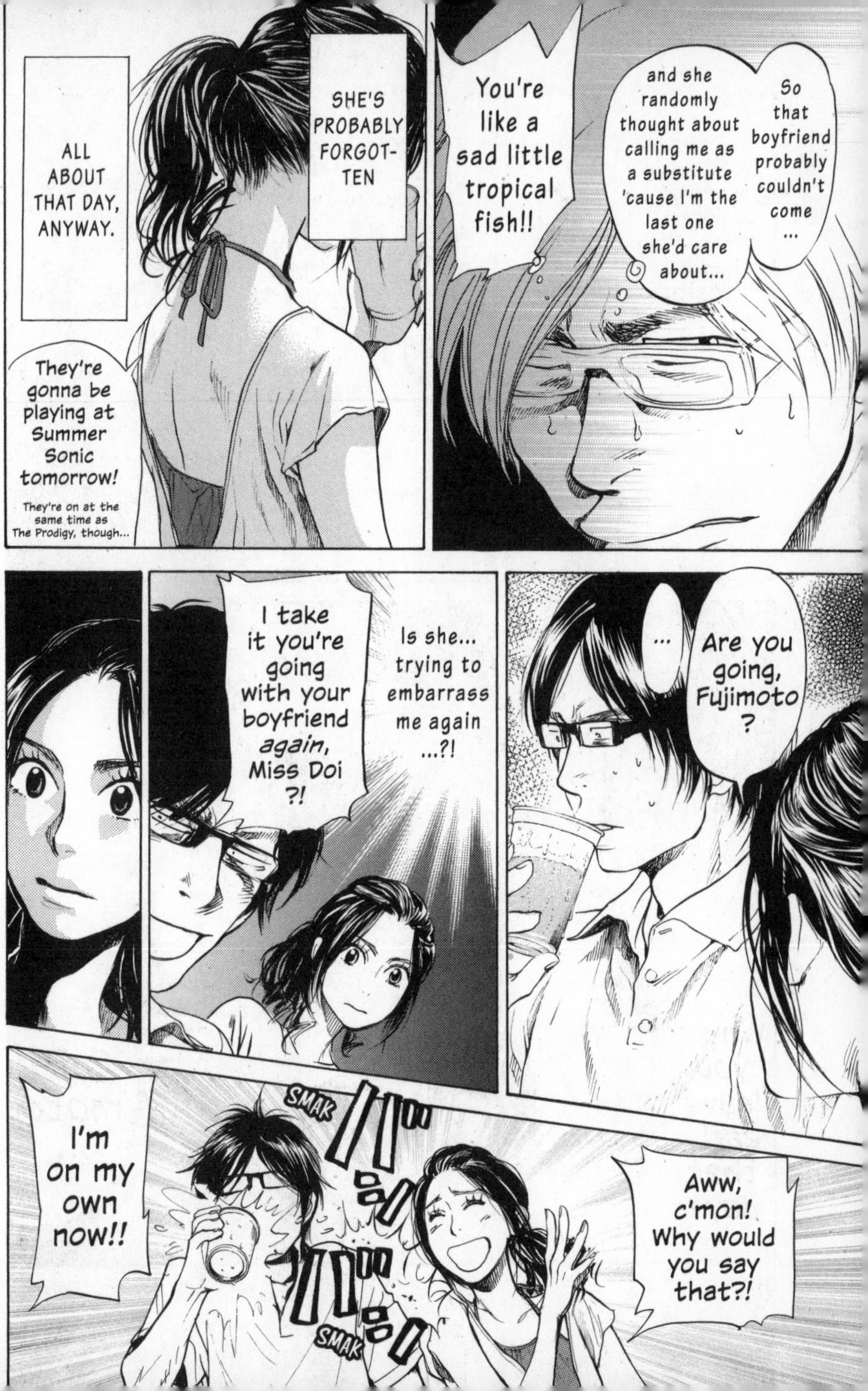

So that boyfriend probably couldn't come ...
and she randomly thought about calling me as a substitute 'cause I'm the last one she'd care about...
You're like a sad little tropical fish!!
SHE'S PROBABLY FORGOT-TEN
ALL ABOUT THAT DAY, ANYWAY.
They're gonna be playing at Summer Sonic tomorrow!
They're on at the same time as The Prodigy, though...
Are you going, Fujimoto ?
...
Is she... trying to embarrass me again ...?!
I take it you're going with your boyfriend *again*, Miss Doi ?!
Aww, c'mon! Why would you say that?!
SMAK
SMAK
I'm on my own now!!

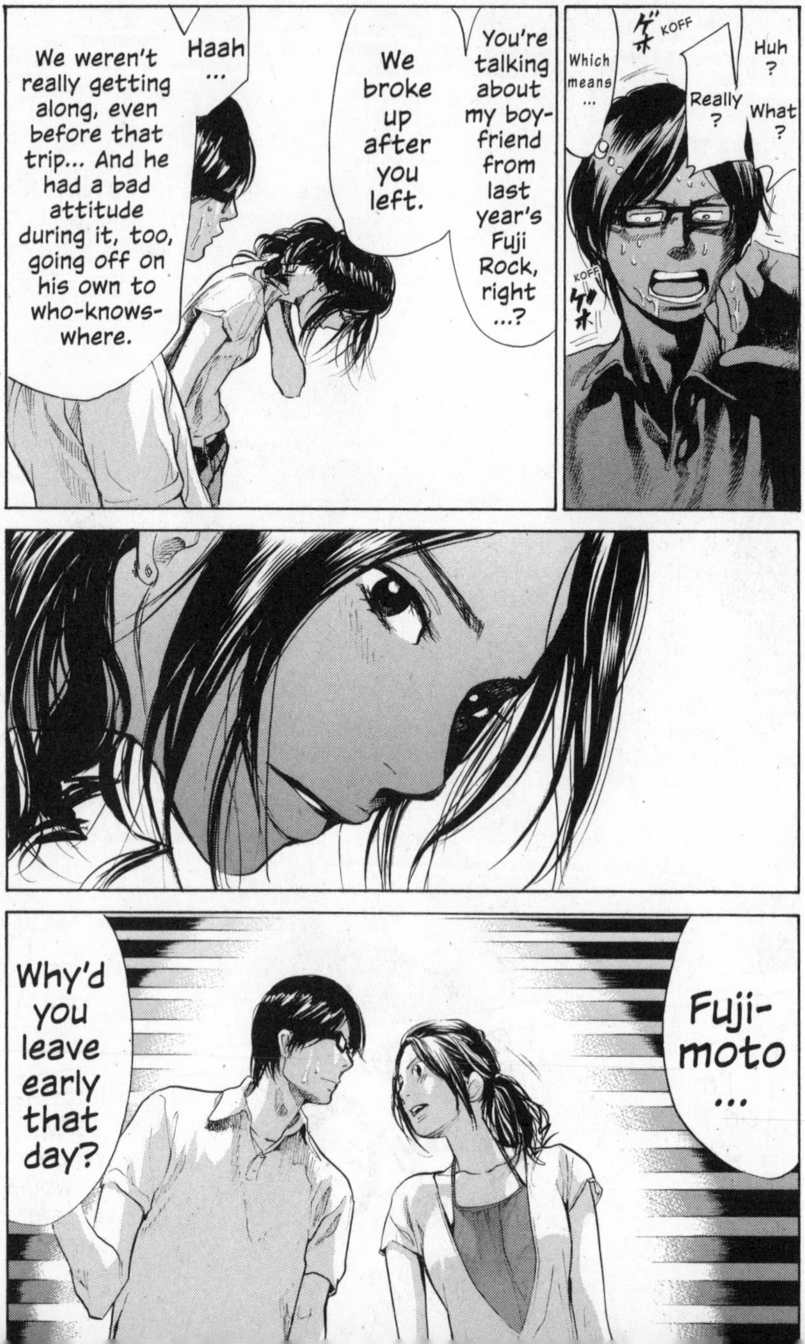
Huh?
What?
Really?
ゲホ KOFF
Which means...
ゲホ KOFF
You're talking about my boyfriend from last year's Fuji Rock, right...?
We broke up after you left.
Haah...
We weren't really getting along, even before that trip... And he had a bad attitude during it, too, going off on his own to who-knows-where.
Fuji-moto...
Why'd you leave early that day?

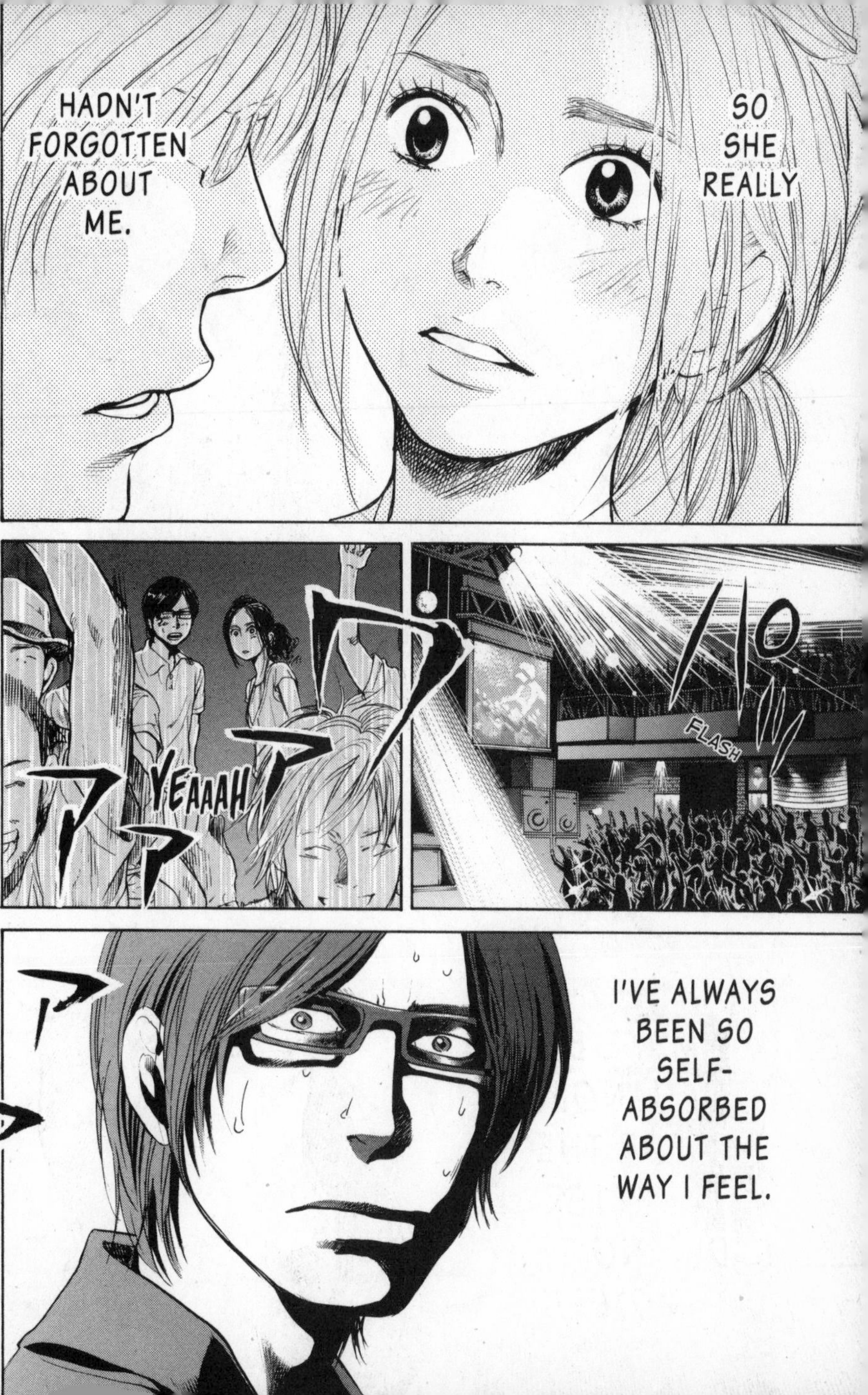
SO SHE REALLY
HADN'T FORGOTTEN ABOUT ME.
FLASH
YEAAAH
I'VE ALWAYS BEEN SO SELF-ABSORBED ABOUT THE WAY I FEEL.

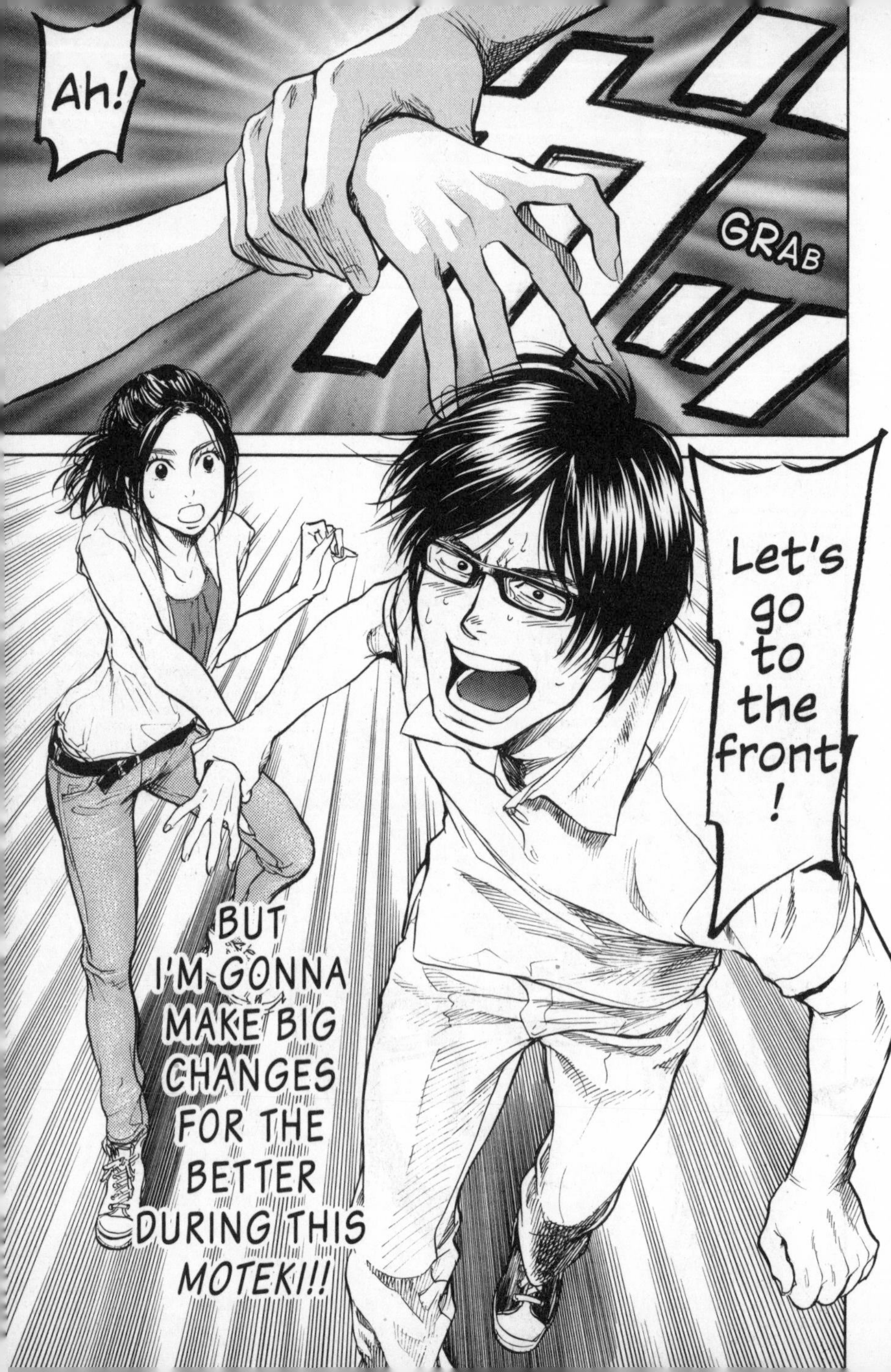
GRAB
Ah!
Let's go to the front!
BUT I'M GONNA MAKE BIG CHANGES FOR THE BETTER DURING THIS MOTEKI!!

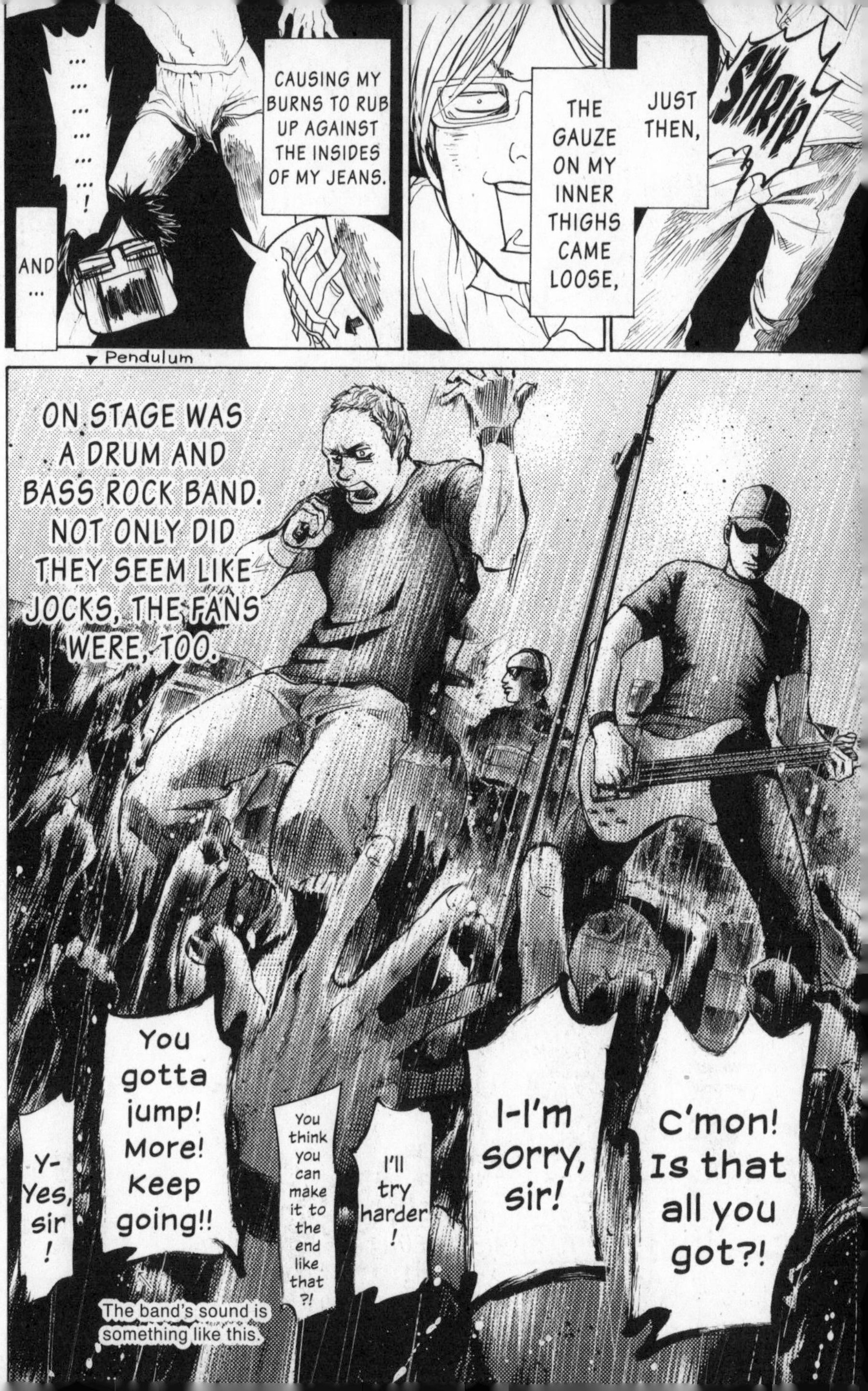
JUST THEN,
SHRIP
THE GAUZE ON MY INNER THIGHS CAME LOOSE,
CAUSING MY BURNS TO RUB UP AGAINST THE INSIDES OF MY JEANS.
... ... !
AND ...
Pendulum
ON STAGE WAS A DRUM AND BASS ROCK BAND. NOT ONLY DID THEY SEEM LIKE JOCKS, THE FANS WERE, TOO.
C'mon! Is that all you got?!
I-I'm sorry, sir!
You think you can make it to the end like that?!
I'll try harder!
You gotta jump! More! Keep going!!
Y-Yes, sir!
The band's sound is something like this.

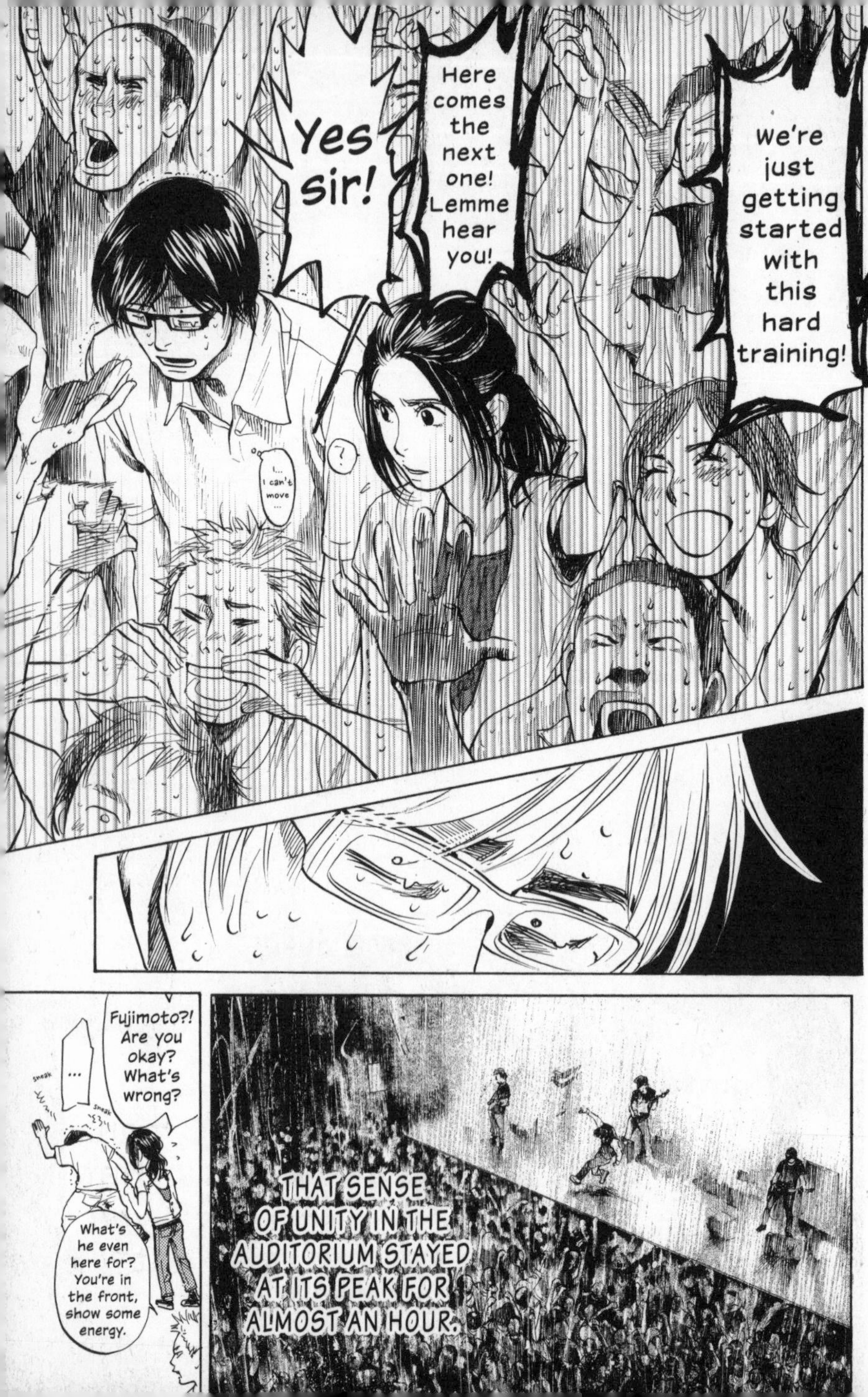
We're just getting started with this hard training!
Here comes the next one! Lemme hear you!
Yes sir!
?
I... I can't move ...
THAT SENSE OF UNITY IN THE AUDITORIUM STAYED AT ITS PEAK FOR ALMOST AN HOUR.
Fujimoto?! Are you okay? What's wrong?
...
sneak
sneak
What's he even here for? You're in the front, show some energy.

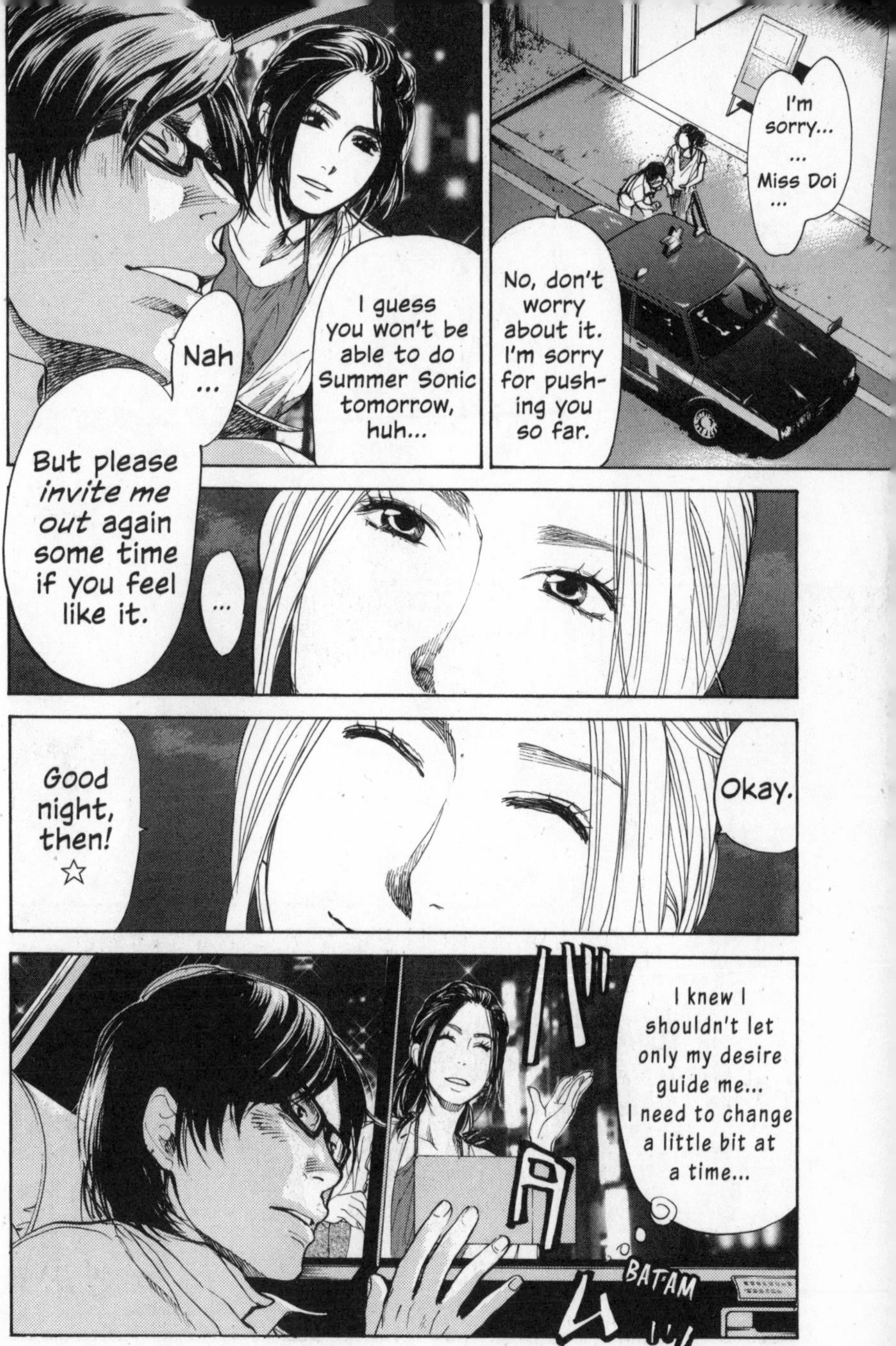
I'm sorry... ... Miss Doi ...
No, don't worry about it. I'm sorry for pushing you so far.
I guess you won't be able to do Summer Sonic tomorrow, huh...
Nah ...
But please *invite me out* again some time if you feel like it.
...
Okay.
Good night, then! ☆
I knew I shouldn't let only my desire guide me... I need to change a little bit at a time...
BATAM

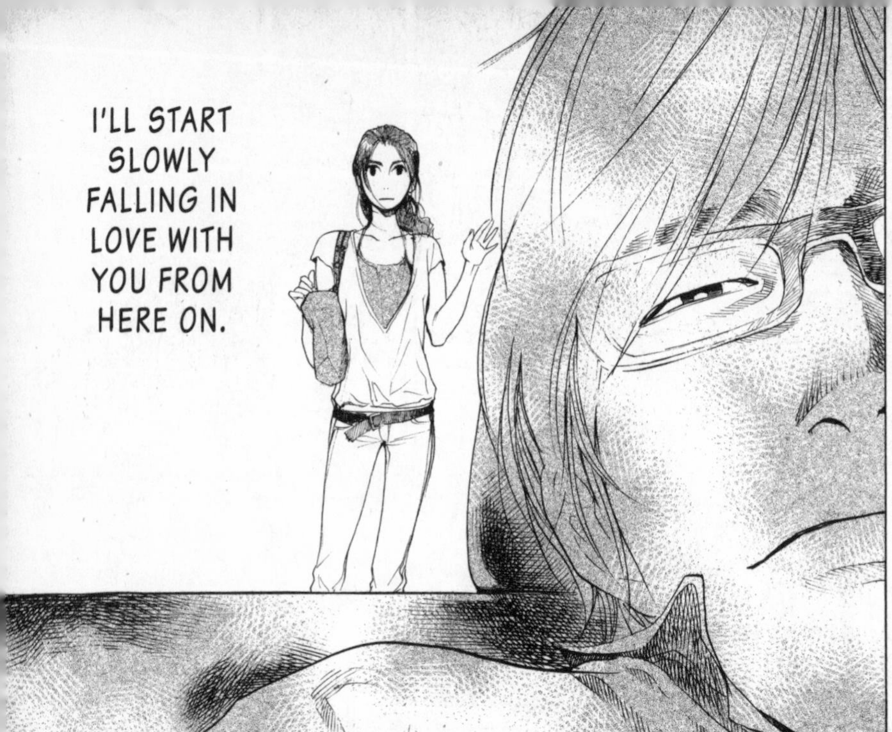
I'LL START SLOWLY FALLING IN LOVE WITH YOU FROM HERE ON.
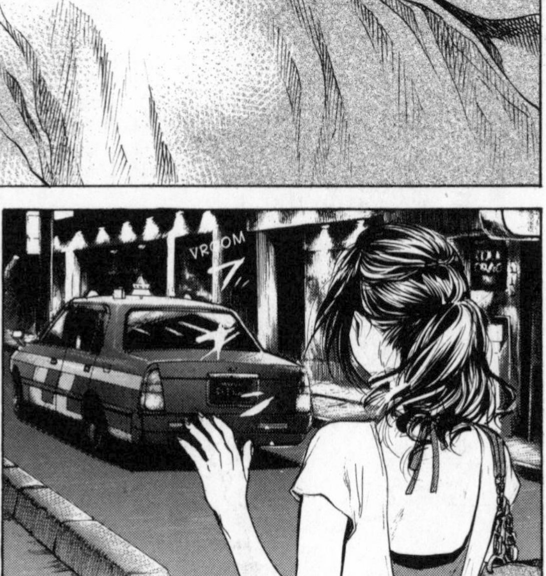
VROOM
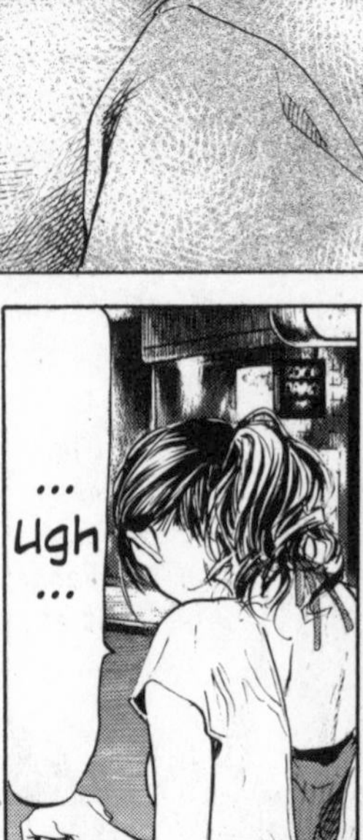
...ugh...

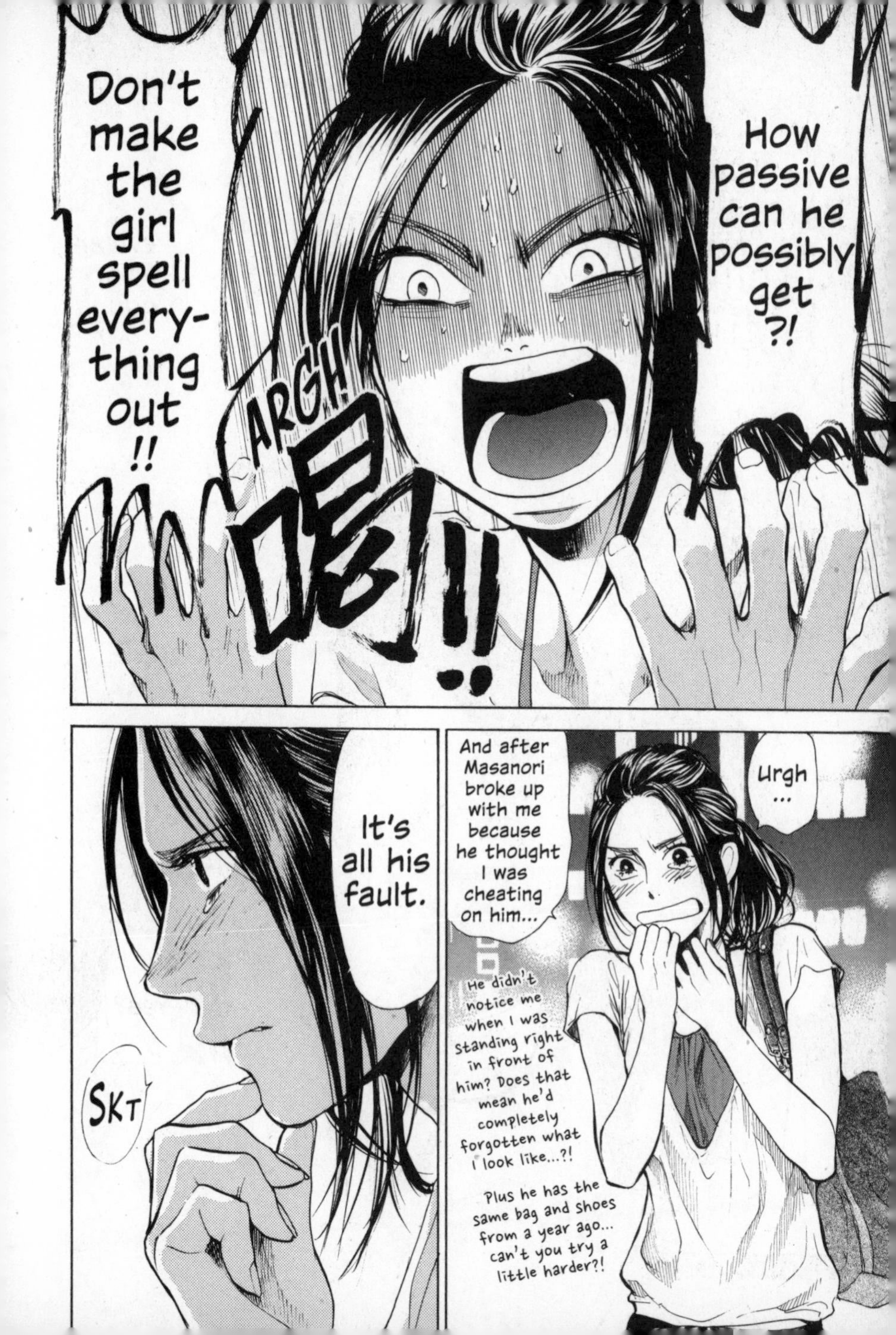
How passive can he possibly get?!
Don't make the girl spell every-thing out!!
ARGH
Urgh...
And after Masanori broke up with me because he thought I was cheating on him...
He didn't notice me when I was standing right in front of him? Does that mean he'd completely forgotten what I look like...?!
Plus he has the same bag and shoes from a year ago... can't you try a little harder?!
It's all his fault.
SKT

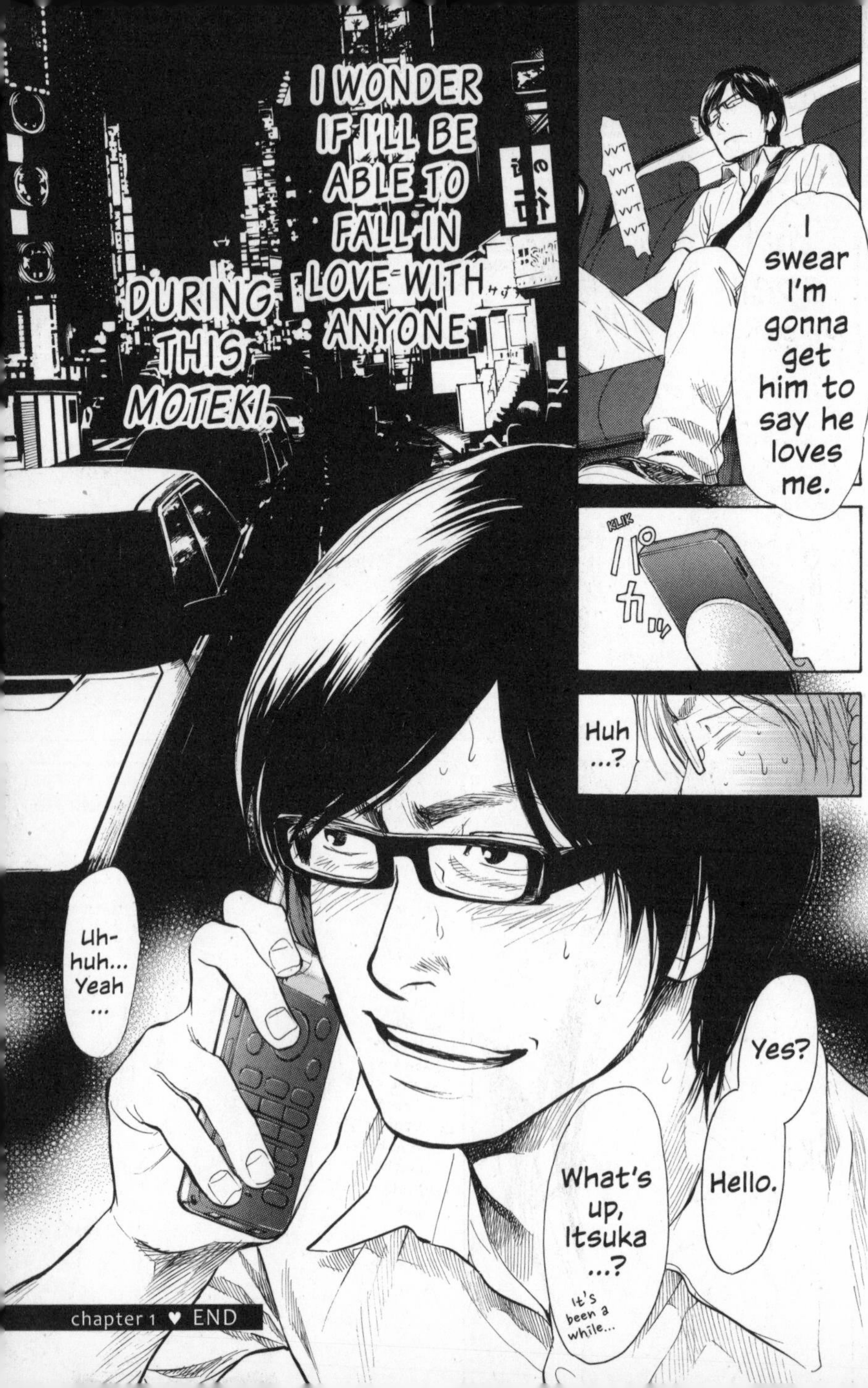
VVT VVT VVT VVT VVT
I swear I'm gonna get him to say he loves me.
KLIK
パカッ
Huh ...?
I WONDER IF I'LL BE ABLE TO FALL IN LOVE WITH ANYONE
DURING THIS MOTEKI.
Yes?
Hello.
What's up, Itsuka ...?
It's been a while...
Uh-huh... Yeah ...
chapter 1 ♥ END

M o t e k i

M i t s u r o u   K u b o

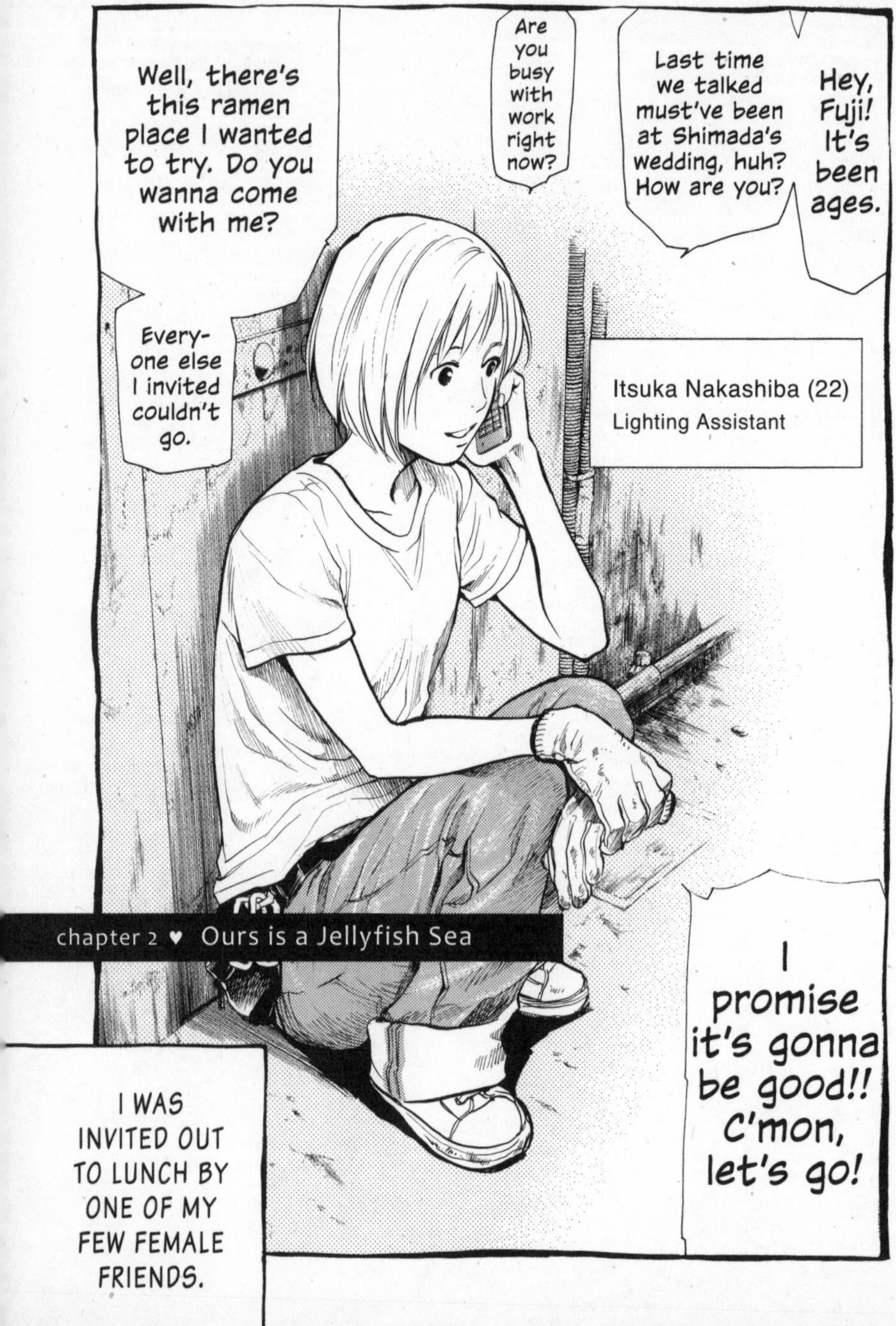
Hey, Fuji! It's been ages.
Last time we talked must've been at Shimada's wedding, huh? How are you?
Are you busy with work right now?
Well, there's this ramen place I wanted to try. Do you wanna come with me?
Itsuka Nakashiba (22)
Lighting Assistant
Every-one else I invited couldn't go.
chapter 2 ♥ Ours is a Jellyfish Sea
I promise it's gonna be good!! C'mon, let's go!
I WAS INVITED OUT TO LUNCH BY ONE OF MY FEW FEMALE FRIENDS.

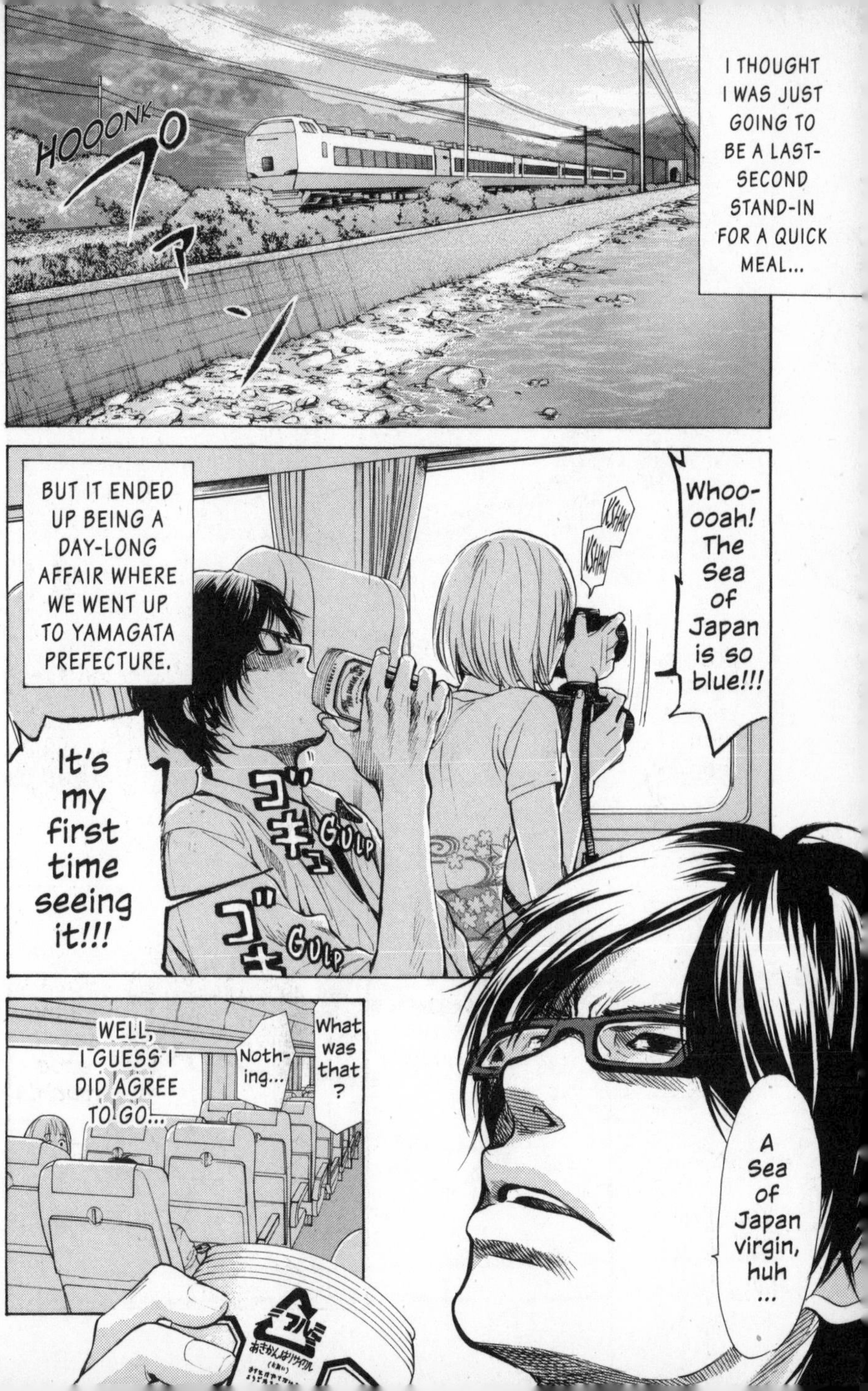
I THOUGHT I WAS JUST GOING TO BE A LAST-SECOND STAND-IN FOR A QUICK MEAL...
HOOONK
Whoo-ooah! The Sea of Japan is so blue!!!
KSHAK KSHAK
BUT IT ENDED UP BEING A DAY-LONG AFFAIR WHERE WE WENT UP TO YAMAGATA PREFECTURE.
It's my first time seeing it!!!
GULP
GULP
A Sea of Japan virgin, huh ...
What was that?
Noth-ing...
WELL, I GUESS I DID AGREE TO GO...

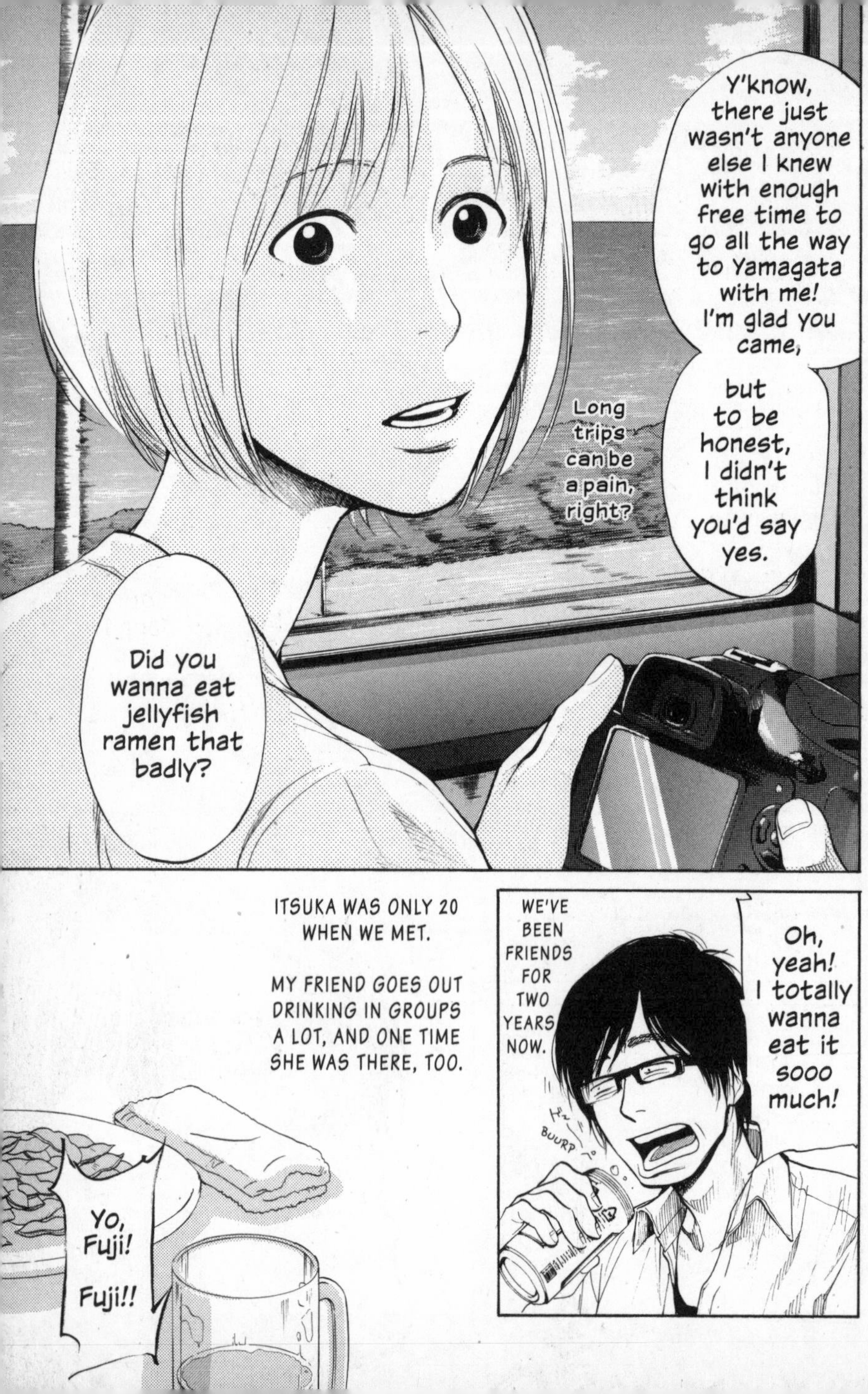
Y'know, there just wasn't anyone else I knew with enough free time to go all the way to Yamagata with me! I'm glad you came,
but to be honest, I didn't think you'd say yes.
Long trips can be a pain, right?
Did you wanna eat jellyfish ramen that badly?
Oh, yeah! I totally wanna eat it sooo much!
WE'VE BEEN FRIENDS FOR TWO YEARS NOW.
BUURP
ITSUKA WAS ONLY 20 WHEN WE MET.
MY FRIEND GOES OUT DRINKING IN GROUPS A LOT, AND ONE TIME SHE WAS THERE, TOO.
Yo, Fuji!
Fuji!!

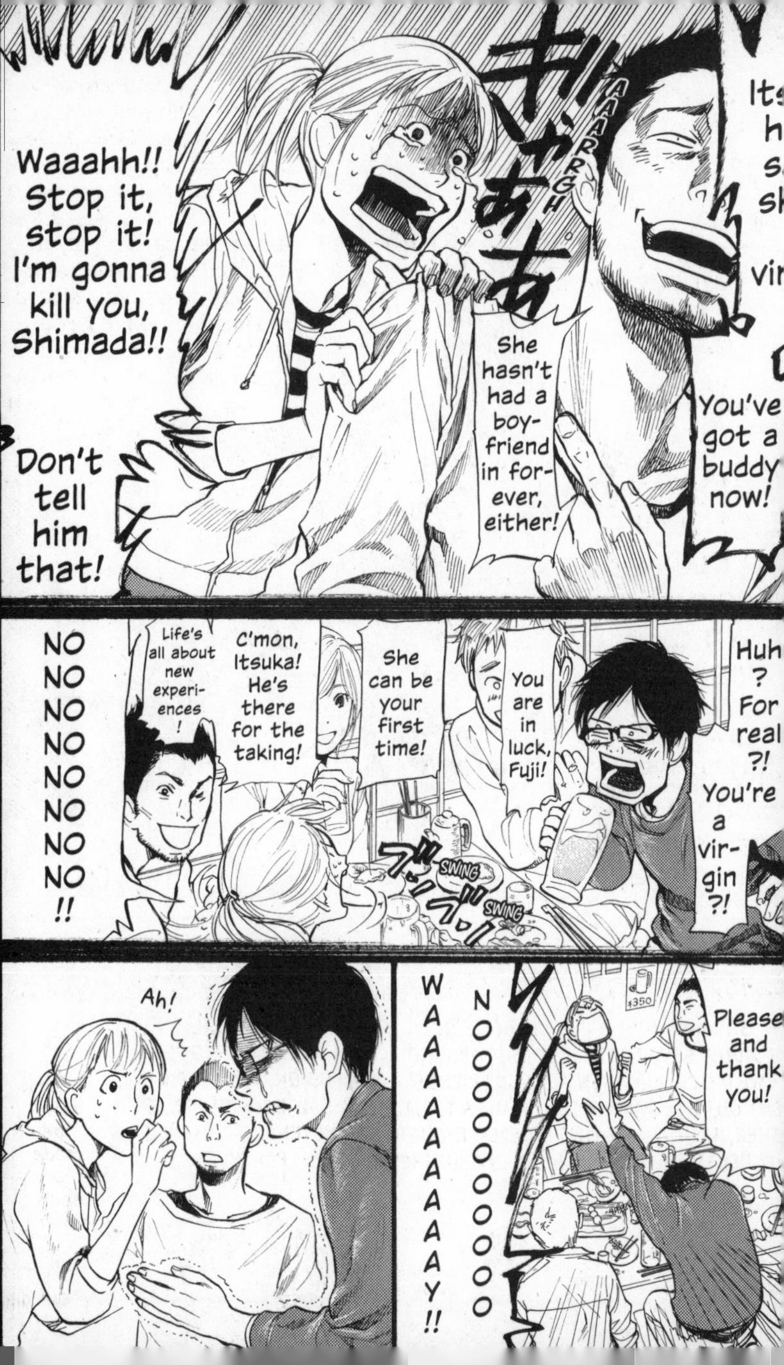
You've got a buddy now!
AAAARGH
She hasn't had a boyfriend in forever, either!
Waaahh!! Stop it, stop it! I'm gonna kill you, Shimada!!
Don't tell him that!
Huh? For real?! You're a virgin?!
You are in luck, Fuji!
She can be your first time!
C'mon, Itsuka! He's there for the taking!
Life's all about new experiences!
SWING
SWING
NO NO NO NO NO NO NO NO!!
Please and thank you!
NOOOOOOOOOOO
WAAAAAAAAAAY!!
Ah!

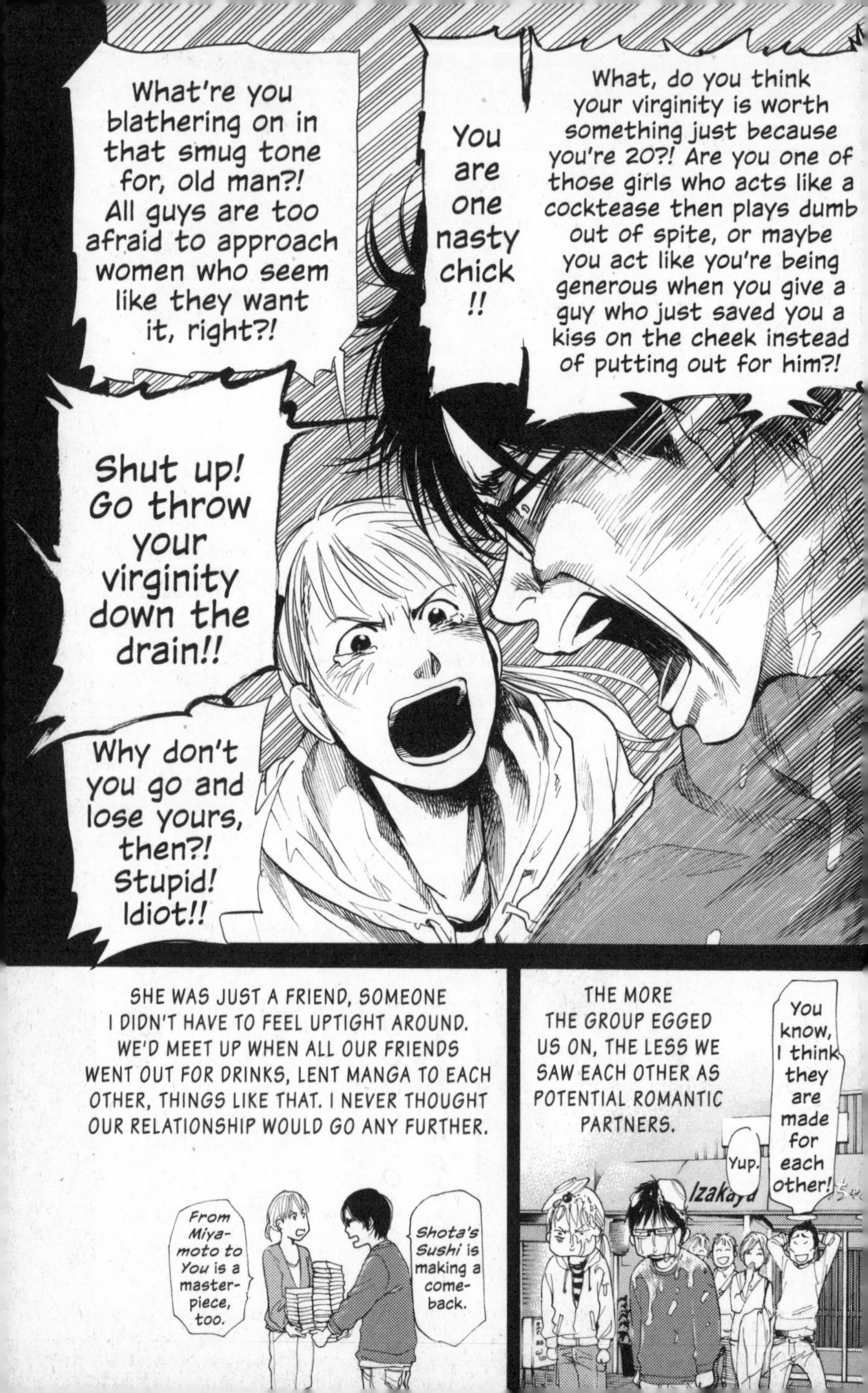
What, do you think your virginity is worth something just because you're 20?! Are you one of those girls who acts like a cocktease then plays dumb out of spite, or maybe you act like you're being generous when you give a guy who just saved you a kiss on the cheek instead of putting out for him?!
You are one nasty chick!!
What're you blathering on in that smug tone for, old man?! All guys are too afraid to approach women who seem like they want it, right?!
Shut up! Go throw your virginity down the drain!!
Why don't you go and lose yours, then?! Stupid! Idiot!!
THE MORE THE GROUP EGGED US ON, THE LESS WE SAW EACH OTHER AS POTENTIAL ROMANTIC PARTNERS.
You know, I think they are made for each other!
Yup.
Izakaya
SHE WAS JUST A FRIEND, SOMEONE I DIDN'T HAVE TO FEEL UPTIGHT AROUND. WE'D MEET UP WHEN ALL OUR FRIENDS WENT OUT FOR DRINKS, LENT MANGA TO EACH OTHER, THINGS LIKE THAT. I NEVER THOUGHT OUR RELATIONSHIP WOULD GO ANY FURTHER.
Shota's Sushi is making a comeback.
From Miyamoto to You is a masterpiece, too.

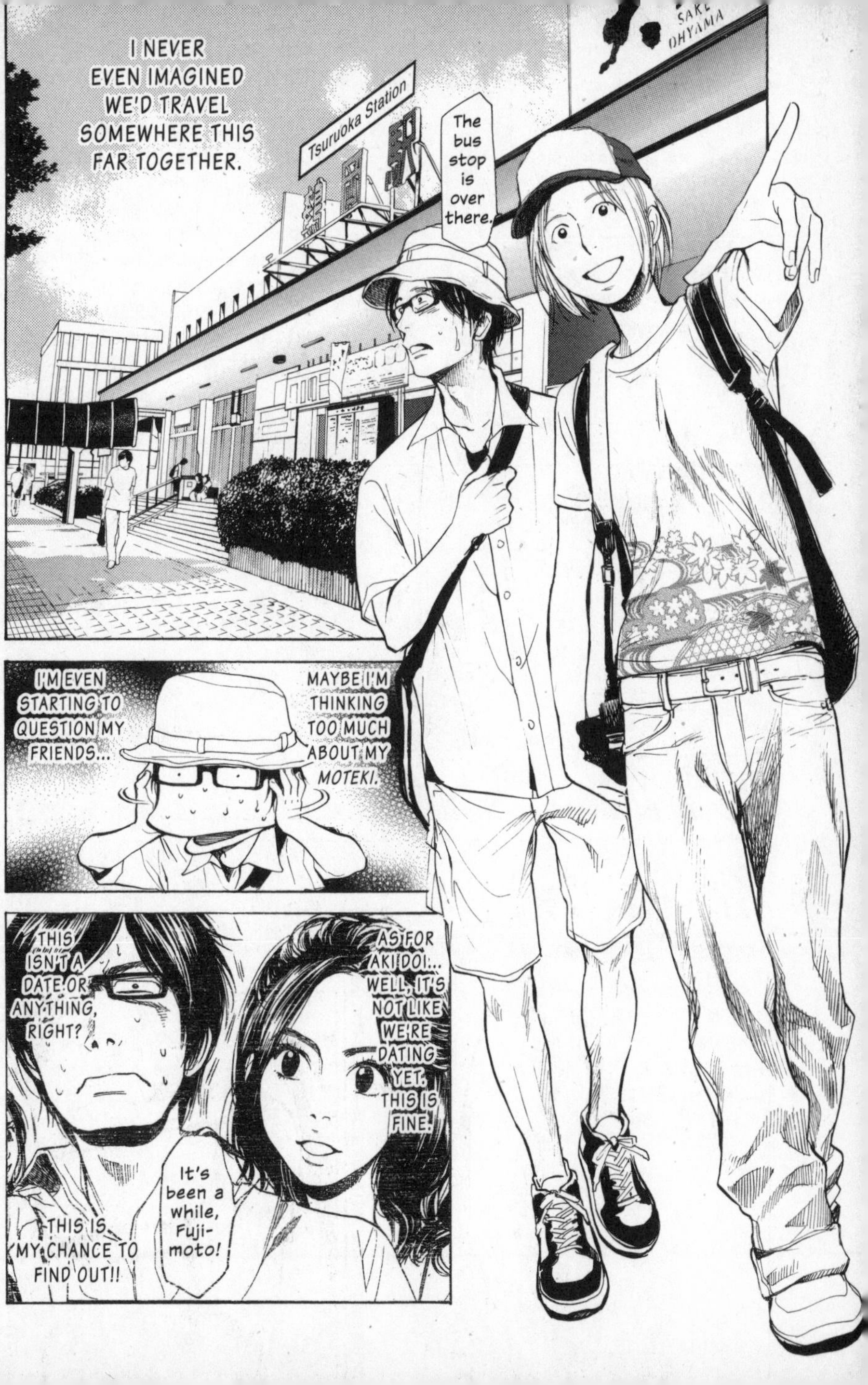
SAKE OHYAMA
The bus stop is over there.
Tsuruoka Station
I NEVER EVEN IMAGINED WE'D TRAVEL SOMEWHERE THIS FAR TOGETHER.
MAYBE I'M THINKING TOO MUCH ABOUT MY MOTEKI.
I'M EVEN STARTING TO QUESTION MY FRIENDS...
AS FOR AKI DOI... WELL, IT'S NOT LIKE WE'RE DATING YET. THIS IS FINE.
THIS ISN'T A DATE OR ANYTHING, RIGHT?
It's been a while, Fujimoto!
THIS IS MY CHANCE TO FIND OUT!!

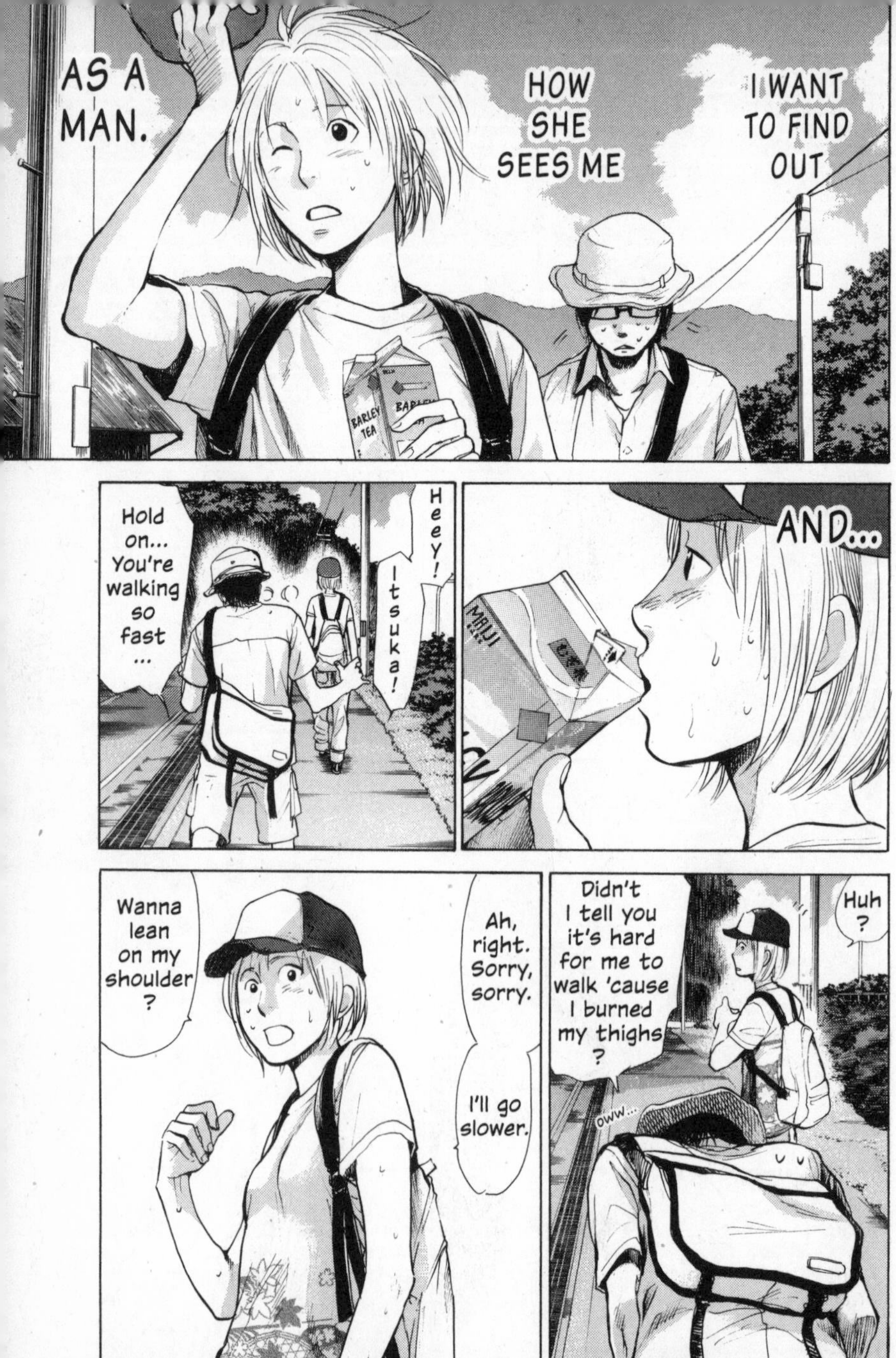
I WANT TO FIND OUT
HOW SHE SEES ME
AS A MAN.
BARLEY TEA
AND...
HeeY! Itsuka!
Hold on... You're walking so fast ...
Huh?
Didn't I tell you it's hard for me to walk 'cause I burned my thighs?
oww...
Ah, right. Sorry, sorry.
I'll go slower.
Wanna lean on my shoulder?

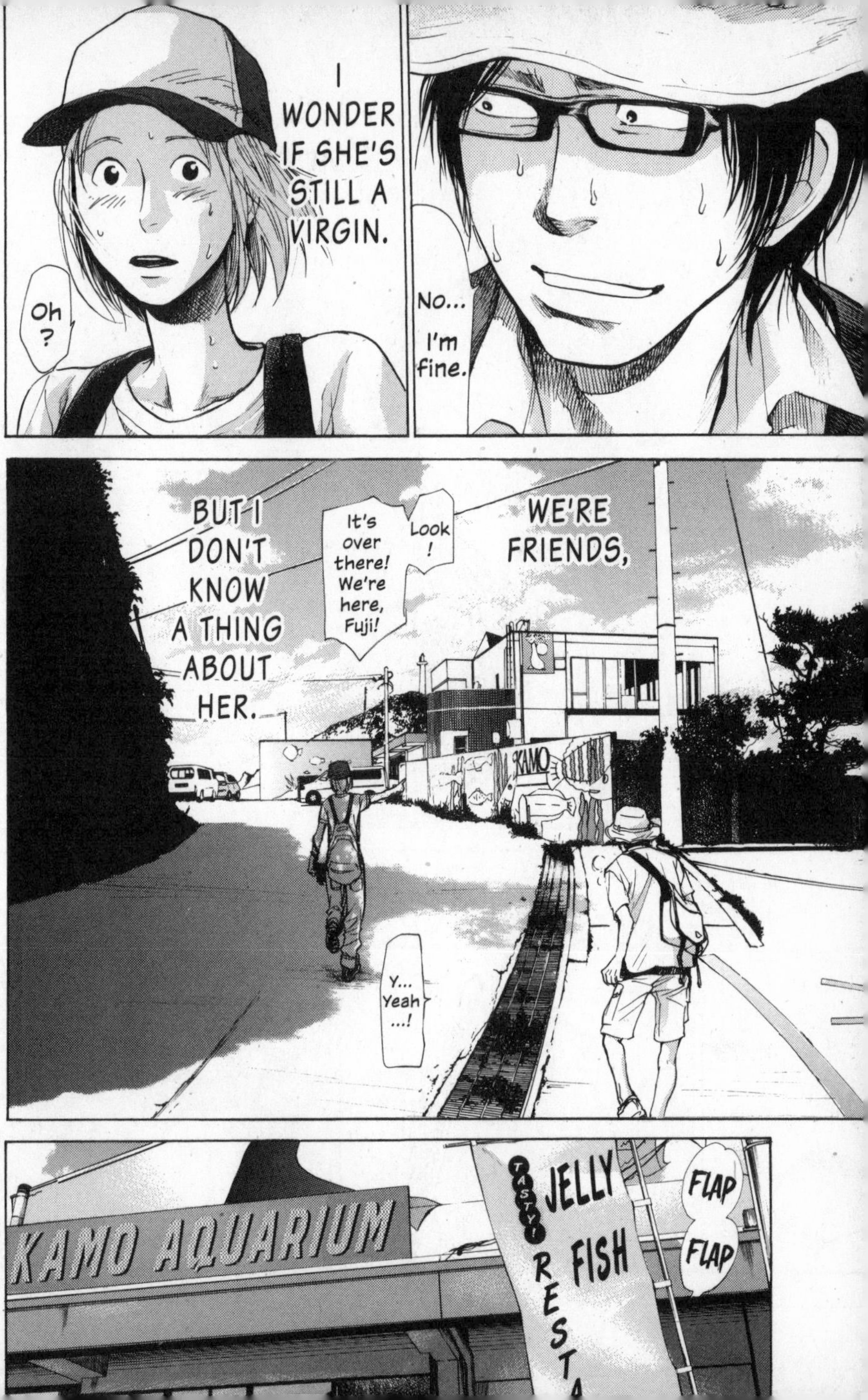
No...
I'm fine.
Oh?
I WONDER IF SHE'S STILL A VIRGIN.
WE'RE FRIENDS,
Look!
It's over there! We're here, Fuji!
BUT I DON'T KNOW A THING ABOUT HER.
KAMO
Y... Yeah...!
FLAP
FLAP
TASTY! JELLY FISH RESTA
KAMO AQUARIUM

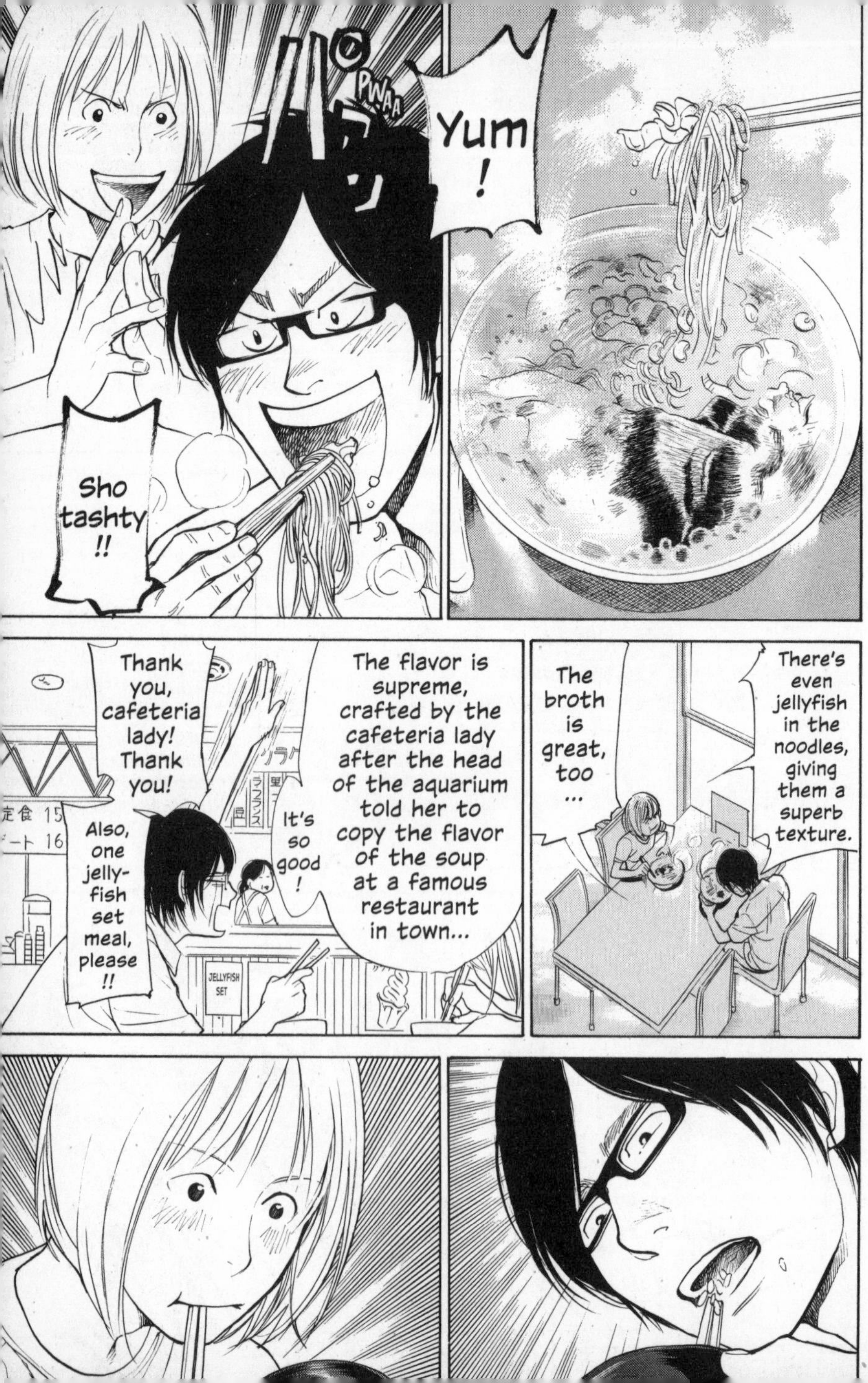
PWAA
Yum!
Sho tashty!!
There's even jellyfish in the noodles, giving them a superb texture.
The broth is great, too ...
The flavor is supreme, crafted by the cafeteria lady after the head of the aquarium told her to copy the flavor of the soup at a famous restaurant in town...
It's so good!
Thank you, cafeteria lady! Thank you!
Also, one jellyfish set meal, please!!
JELLYFISH SET

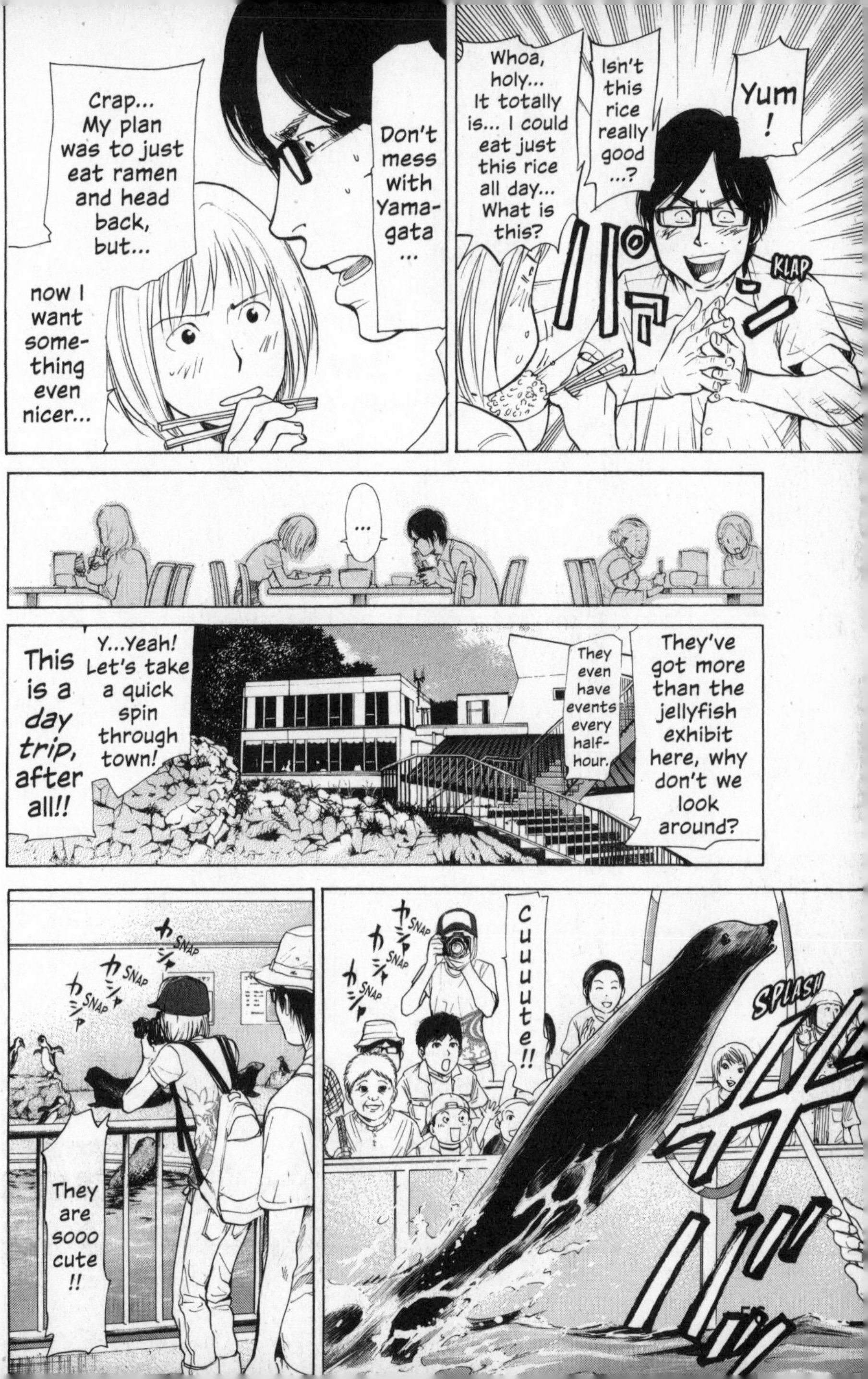
Yum!
Isn't this rice really good ...?
Whoa, holy... It totally is... I could eat just this rice all day... What is this?
KLAP
Don't mess with Yamagata ...
Crap... My plan was to just eat ramen and head back, but...
now I want something even nicer...
...
They've got more than the jellyfish exhibit here, why don't we look around?
They even have events every half-hour.
Y...Yeah! Let's take a quick spin through town!
This is a *day trip*, after all!!
SPLASH
Cuuuute!!
SNAP
SNAP
SNAP
SNAP
SNAP
SNAP
They are sooo cute!!

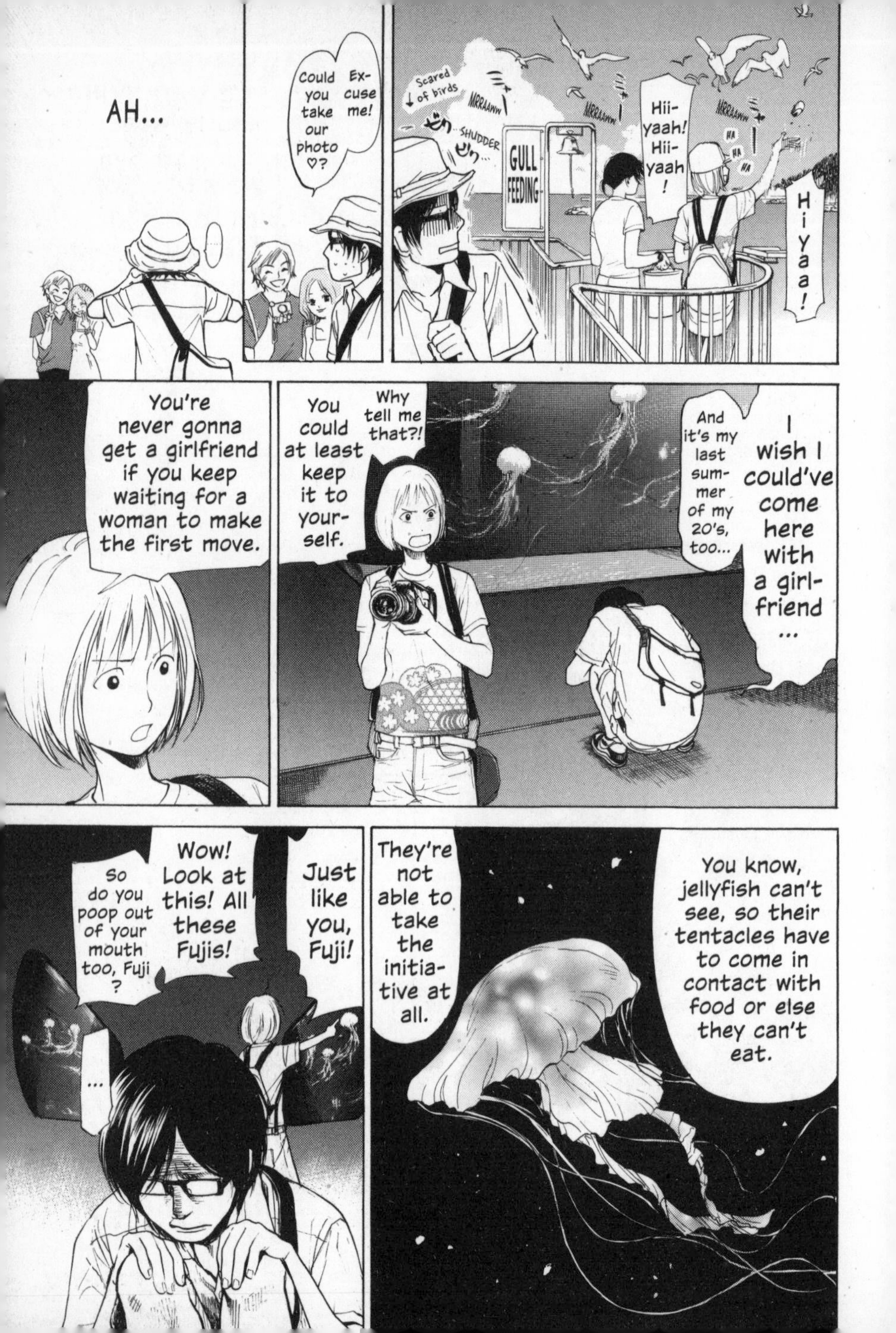

Hi Yaa!
Hii-yaah! Hii-yaah!
MRRAAWW
HA HA HA
MRRAAWW
MRRAAWW
GULL FEEDING
Scared of birds
SHUDDER
Ex-cuse me!
Could you take our photo ♡?
...
AH...
I wish I could've come here with a girlfriend...
And it's my last summer of my 20's, too...
Why tell me that?!
You could at least keep it to yourself.
You're never gonna get a girlfriend if you keep waiting for a woman to make the first move.
You know, jellyfish can't see, so their tentacles have to come in contact with food or else they can't eat.
They're not able to take the initiative at all.
Just like you, Fuji!
Wow! Look at this! All these Fujis!
So do you poop out of your mouth too, Fuji?
...

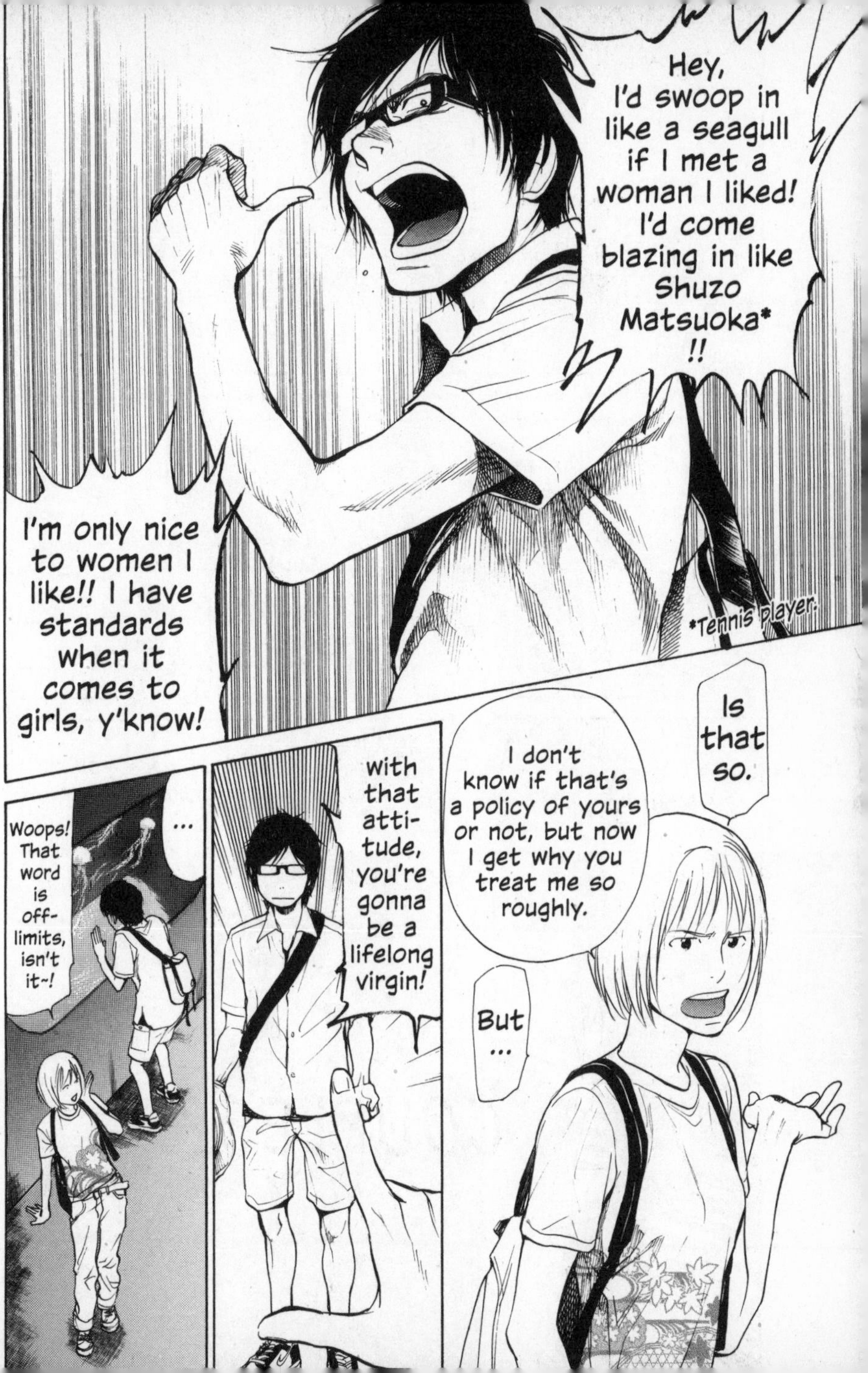
Hey, I'd swoop in like a seagull if I met a woman I liked! I'd come blazing in like Shuzo Matsuoka* !!
I'm only nice to women I like!! I have standards when it comes to girls, y'know!
*Tennis player.
Is that so.
I don't know if that's a policy of yours or not, but now I get why you treat me so roughly.
But ...
with that atti-tude, you're gonna be a lifelong virgin!
...
Woops! That word is off-limits, isn't it~!

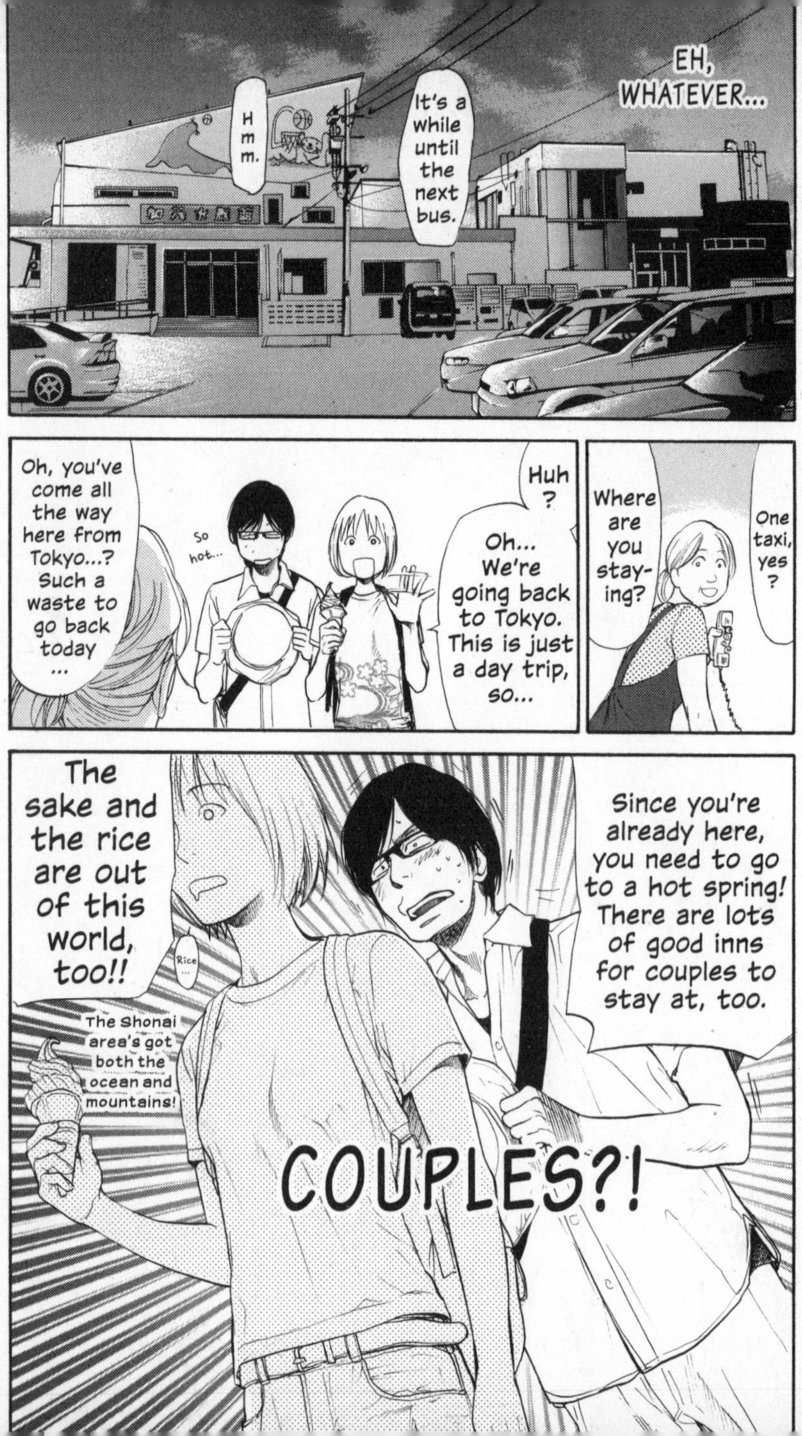
EH, WHATEVER...
It's a while until the next bus.
Hmm.
One taxi, yes?
Where are you staying?
Huh?
Oh... We're going back to Tokyo. This is just a day trip, so...
So hot...
Oh, you've come all the way here from Tokyo...? Such a waste to go back today...
Since you're already here, you need to go to a hot spring! There are lots of good inns for couples to stay at, too.
The sake and the rice are out of this world, too!!
Rice...
The Shonai area's got both the ocean and mountains!
COUPLES?!

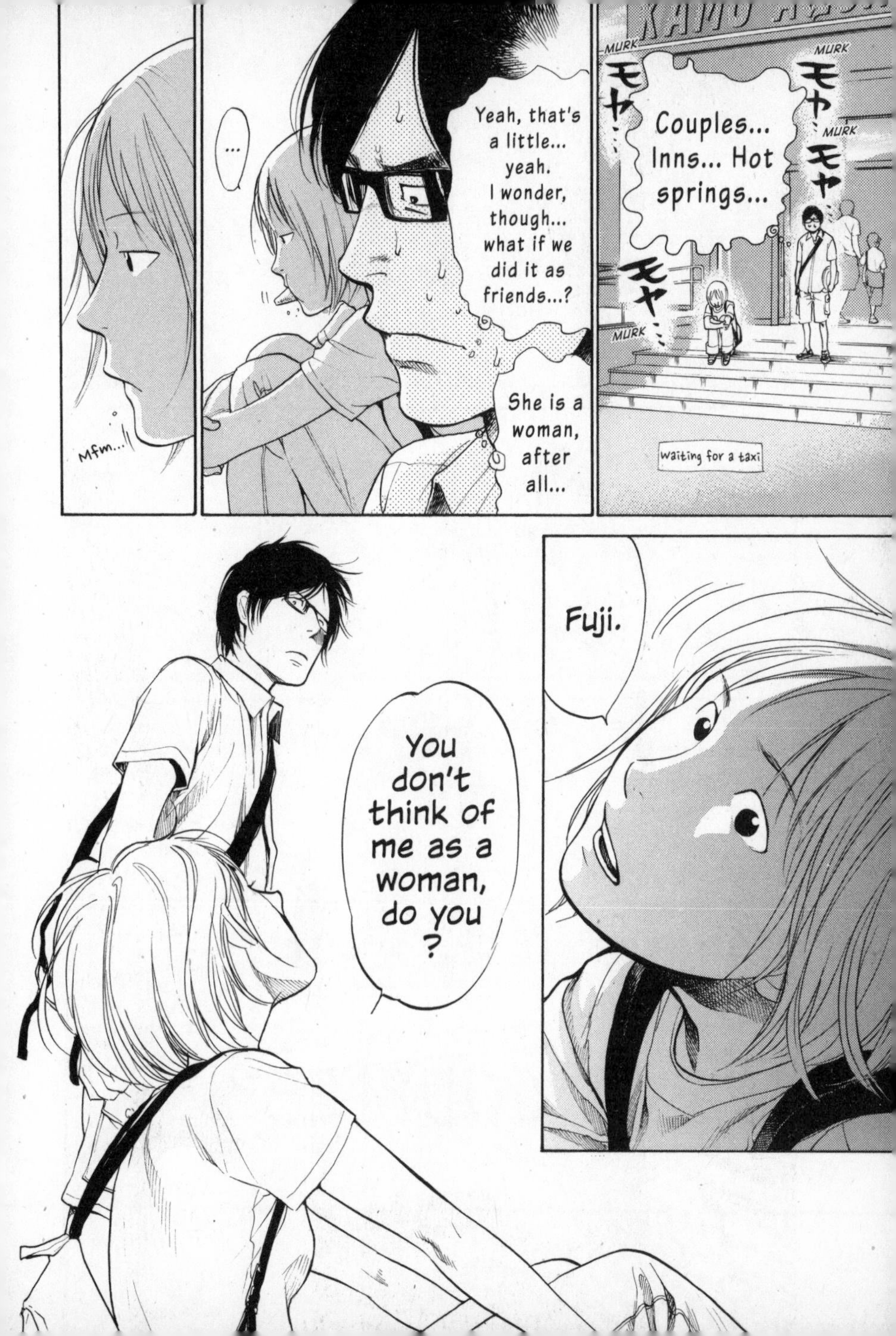
MURK
モヤ…
MURK
モヤ…
MURK
モヤ…
MURK
Couples... Inns... Hot springs...
Waiting for a taxi
Yeah, that's a little... yeah. I wonder, though... what if we did it as friends...?
She is a woman, after all...
...
Mfm...
Fuji.
You don't think of me as a woman, do you?

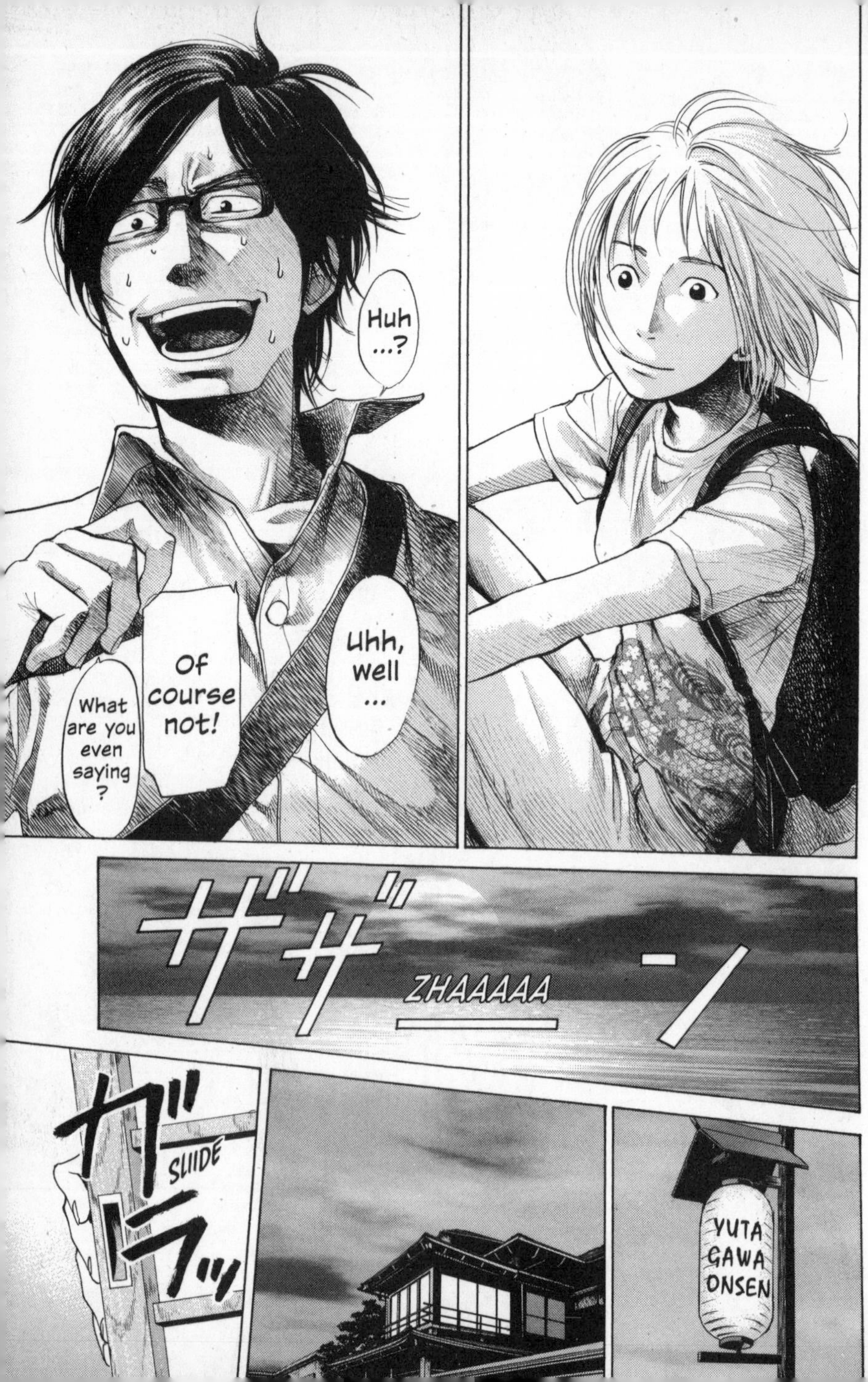
Huh ...?
Uhh, well ...
Of course not!
What are you even saying?
ザザーン
ZHAAAAA
YUTA GAWA ONSEN
ガラッ
SLIIDE

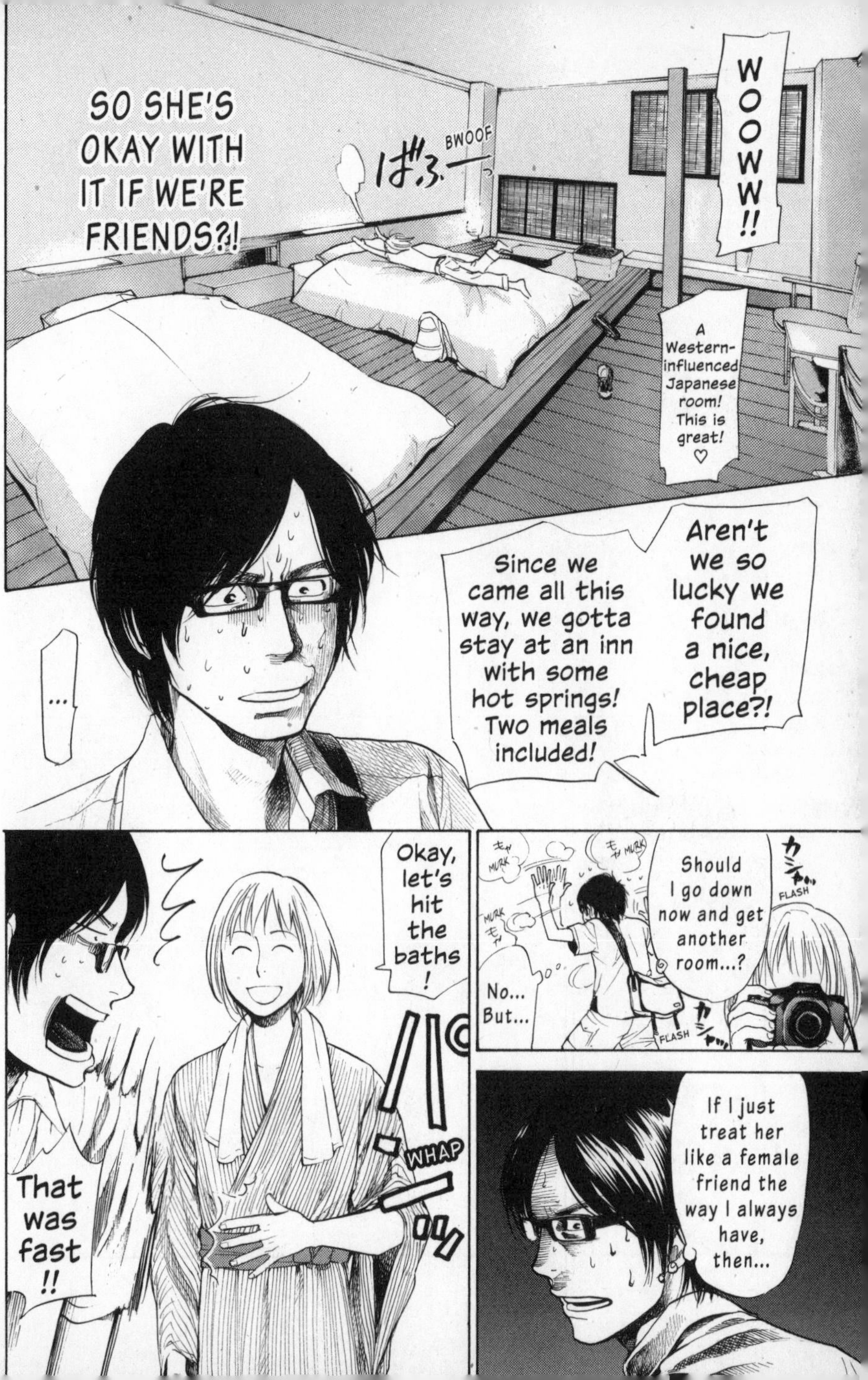
WOOOWW!!
A Western-influenced Japanese room! This is great! ♡
ばふ BWOOF
SO SHE'S OKAY WITH IT IF WE'RE FRIENDS?!
Aren't we so lucky we found a nice, cheap place?!
Since we came all this way, we gotta stay at an inn with some hot springs! Two meals included!
...
FLASH
Should I go down now and get another room...?
MURK
MURK
MURK
No... But...
FLASH
If I just treat her like a female friend the way I always have, then...
Okay, let's hit the baths!
WHAP
That was fast!!

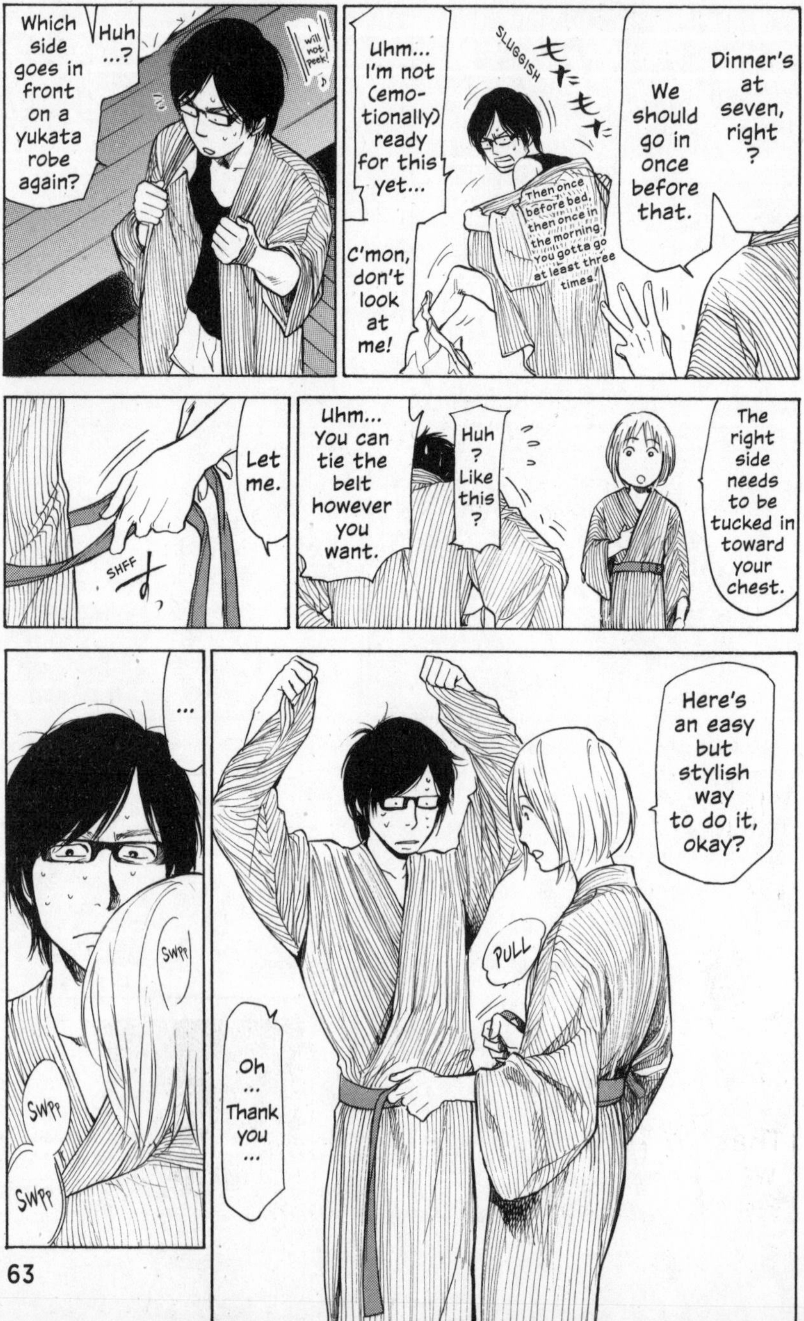
Dinner's at seven, right?
We should go in once before that.
Then once before bed, then once in the morning. You gotta go at least three times!
SLUGGISH
Uhm... I'm not (emotionally) ready for this yet...
C'mon, don't look at me!
I will not peek!
Huh ...?
Which side goes in front on a yukata robe again?
The right side needs to be tucked in toward your chest.
Huh? Like this?
Uhm... You can tie the belt however you want.
Let me.
SHFF
Here's an easy but stylish way to do it, okay?
PULL
Oh ... Thank you ...
...
SWPP
SWPP
SWPP

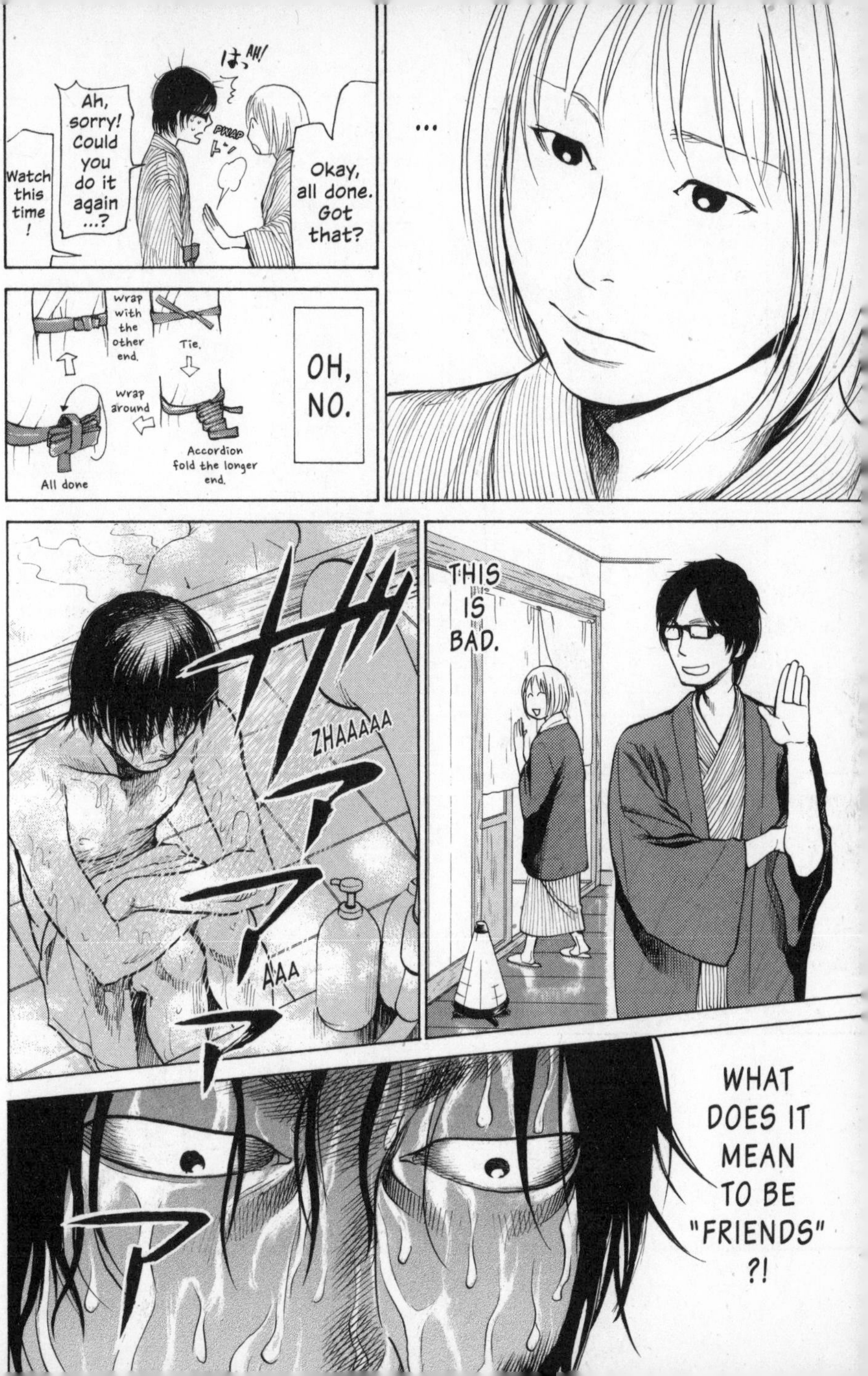
...
Okay, all done. Got that?
はっ AH!
PWAP
Ah, sorry! Could you do it again ...?
Watch this time!
OH, NO.
Wrap with the other end.
Tie.
Wrap around
Accordion fold the longer end.
All done
THIS IS BAD.
ZHAAAAA
AAA
WHAT DOES IT MEAN TO BE "FRIENDS" ?!

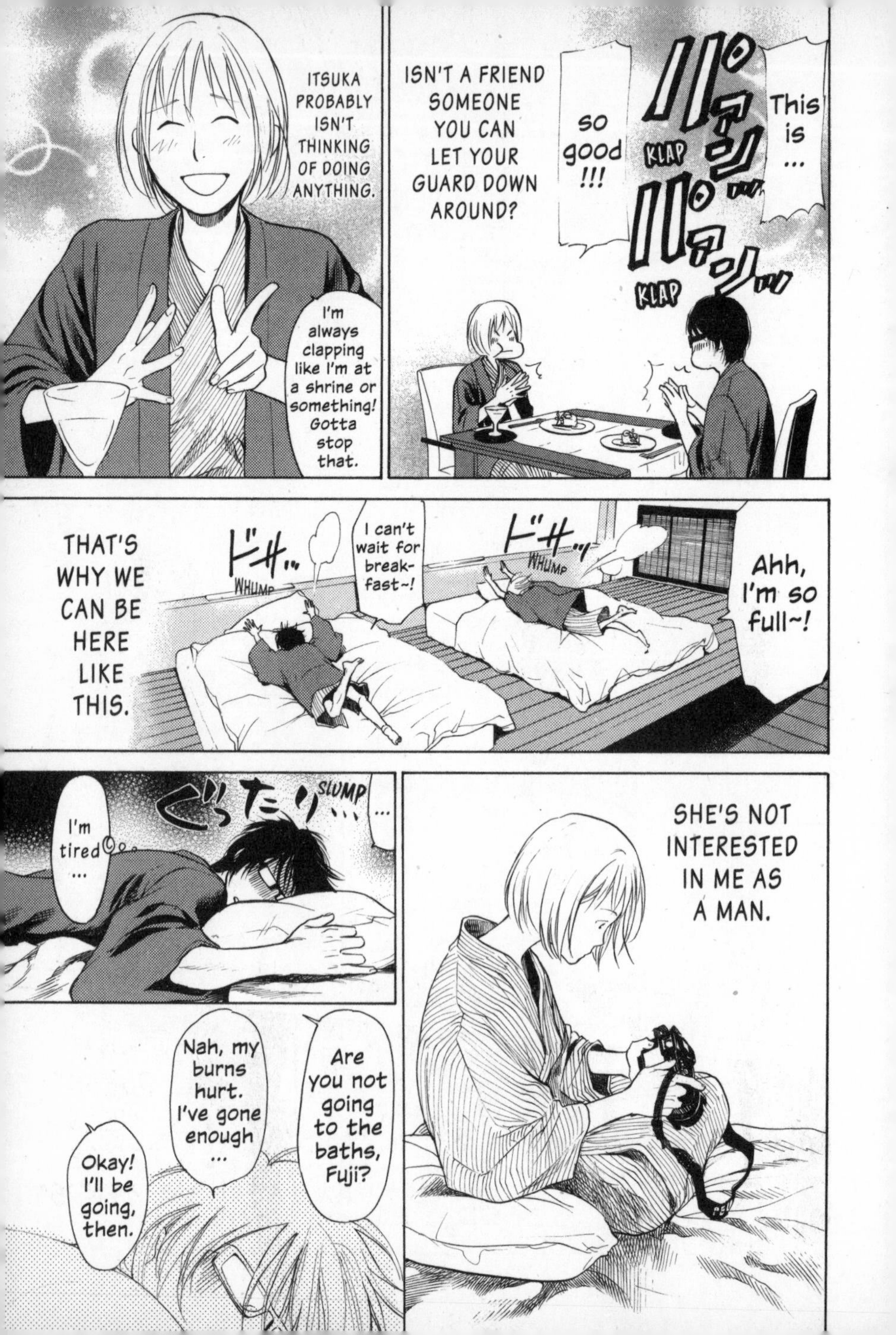
This is ...
so good !!!
パァン KLAP
パァン KLAP
ISN'T A FRIEND SOMEONE YOU CAN LET YOUR GUARD DOWN AROUND?
ITSUKA PROBABLY ISN'T THINKING OF DOING ANYTHING.
I'm always clapping like I'm at a shrine or something! Gotta stop that.
Ahh, I'm so full~!
ドサッ WHUMP
I can't wait for break-fast~!
ドサッ WHUMP
THAT'S WHY WE CAN BE HERE LIKE THIS.
SHE'S NOT INTERESTED IN ME AS A MAN.
ぐったり SLUMP
...
I'm tired ...
Are you not going to the baths, Fuji?
Nah, my burns hurt. I've gone enough ...
Okay! I'll be going, then.

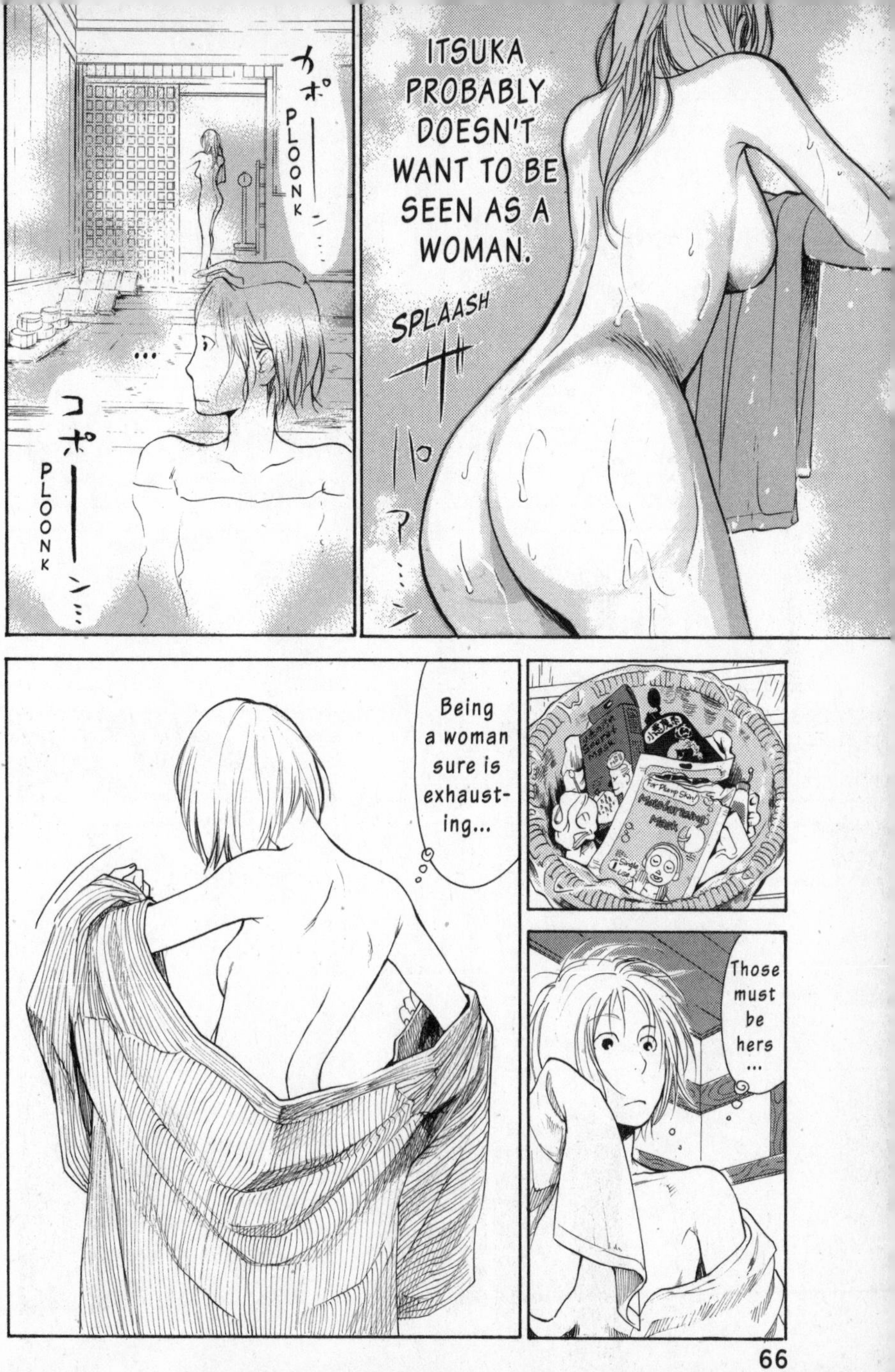
ITSUKA PROBABLY DOESN'T WANT TO BE SEEN AS A WOMAN.
SPLAASH
PLOONK
...
PLOONK
Those must be hers...
Being a woman sure is exhausting...

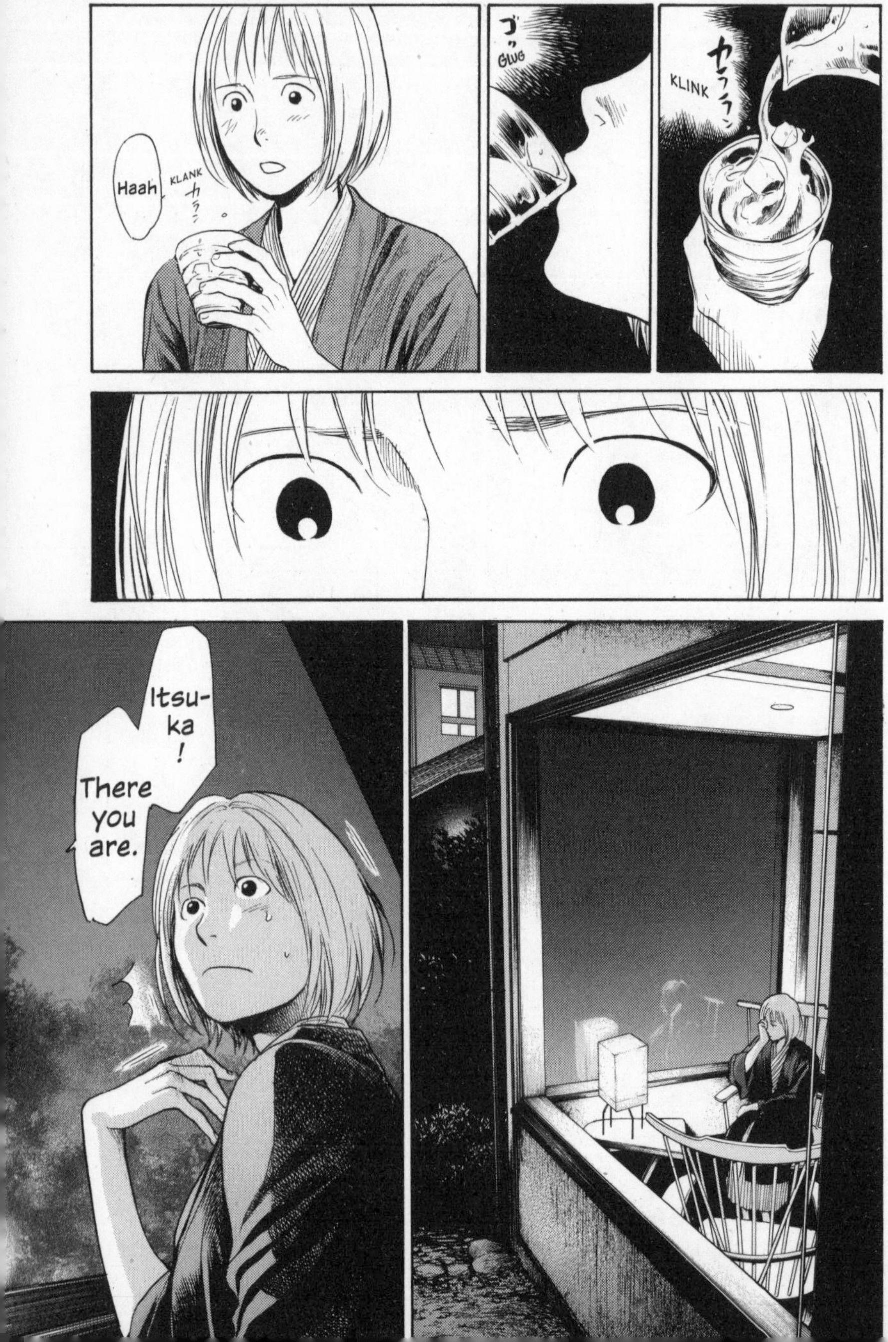
KLINK
カラン
ゴッ
GLUG
Haah
KLANK
カラン
Itsu-ka! There you are.

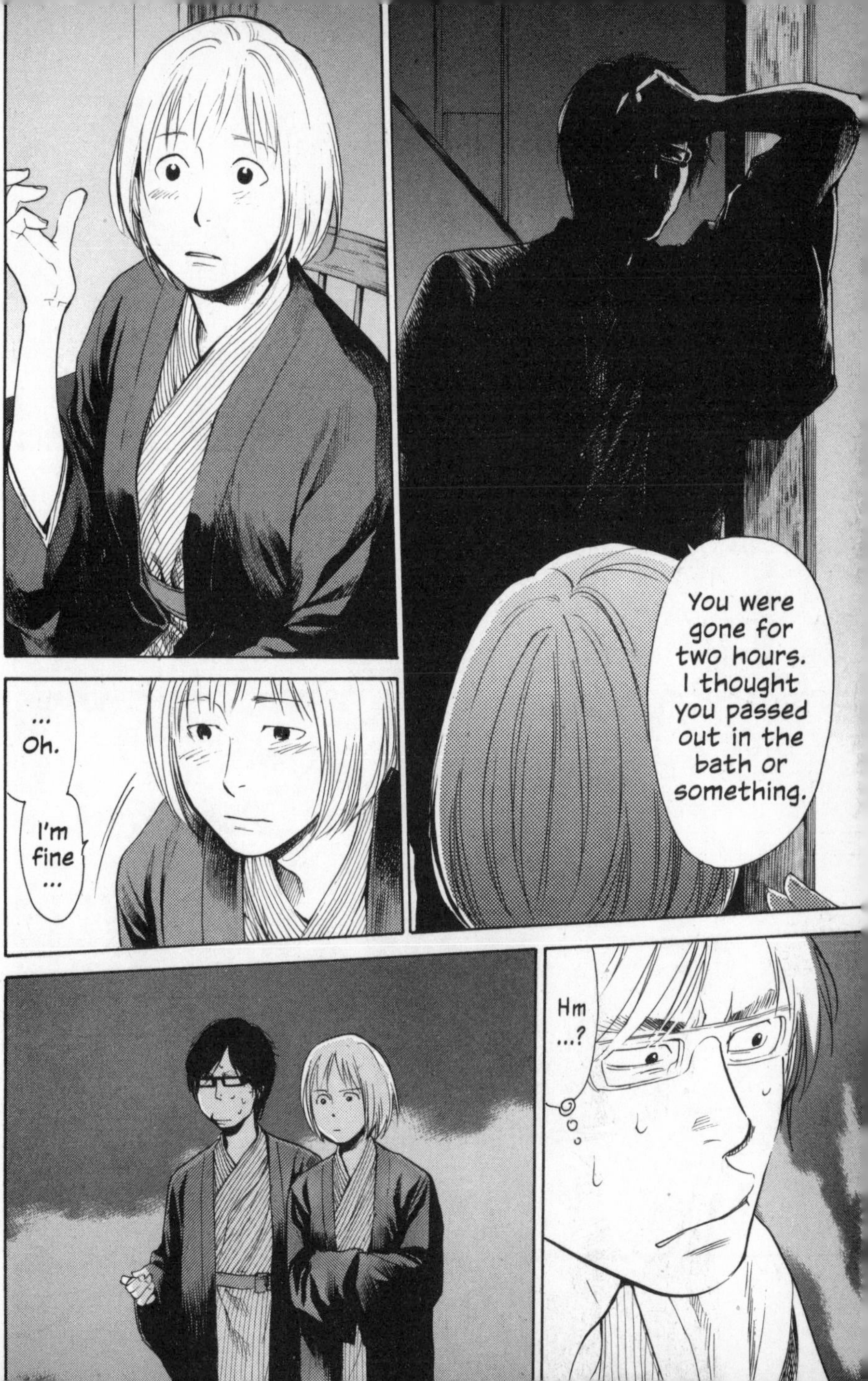
You were gone for two hours. I thought you passed out in the bath or something.
... Oh.
I'm fine ...
Hm ...?

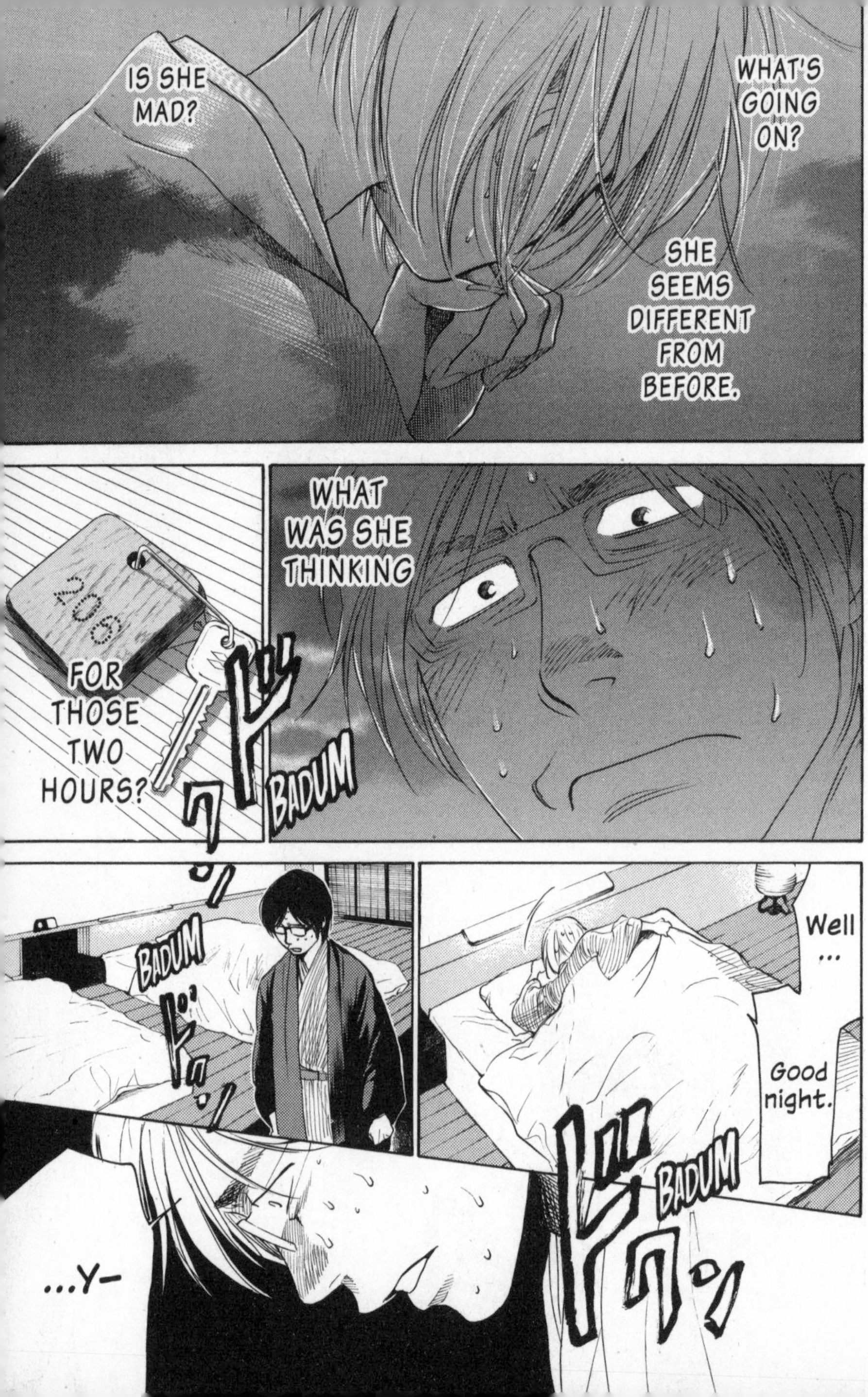
WHAT'S GOING ON?
IS SHE MAD?
SHE SEEMS DIFFERENT FROM BEFORE.
WHAT WAS SHE THINKING
BADUM
FOR THOSE TWO HOURS?
Well ...
Good night.
BADUM
BADUM
...Y-

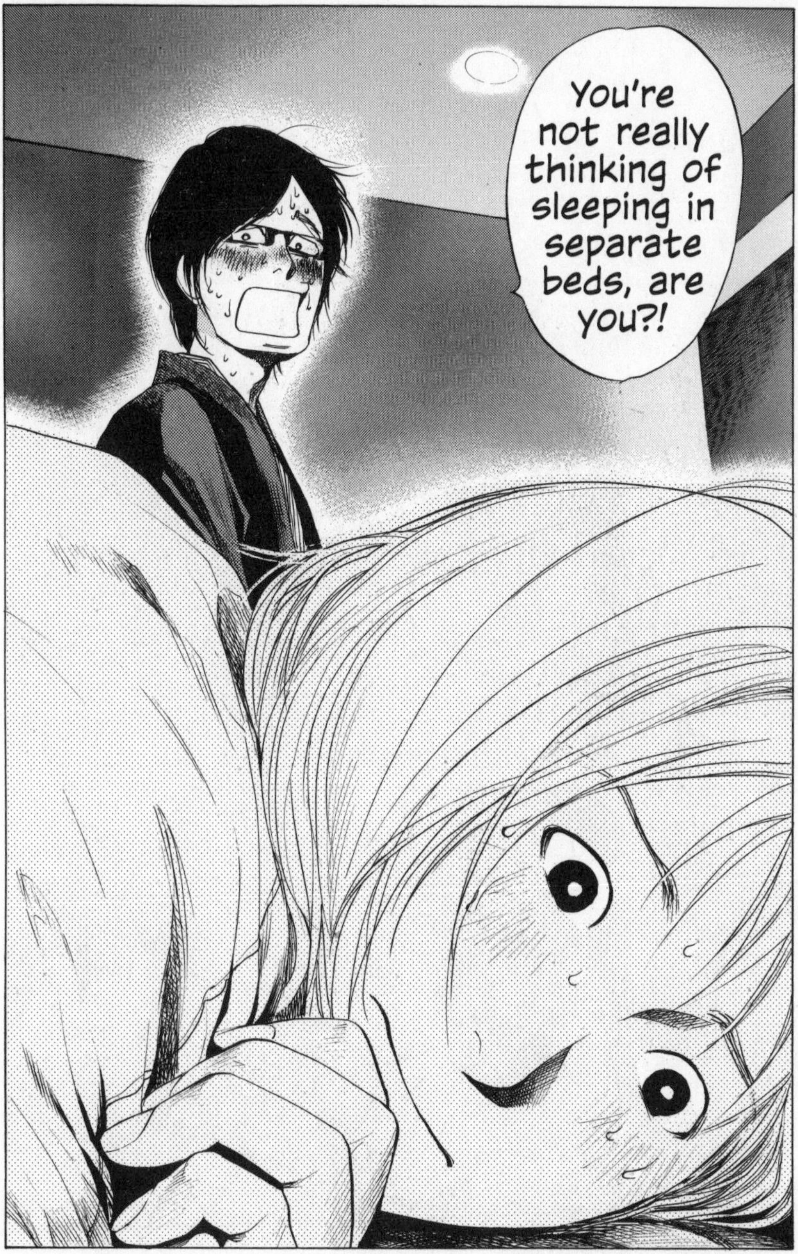
You're not really thinking of sleeping in separate beds, are you?!

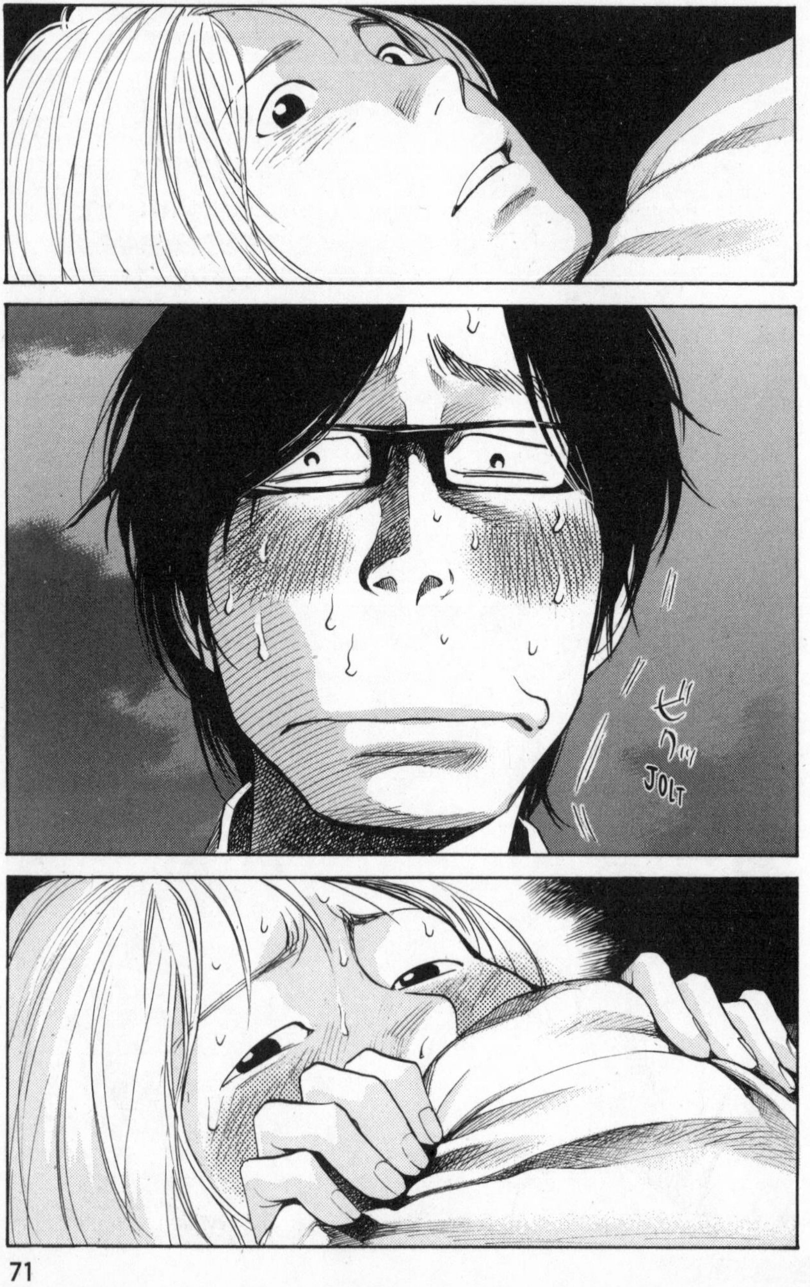
ビクッ
JOLT

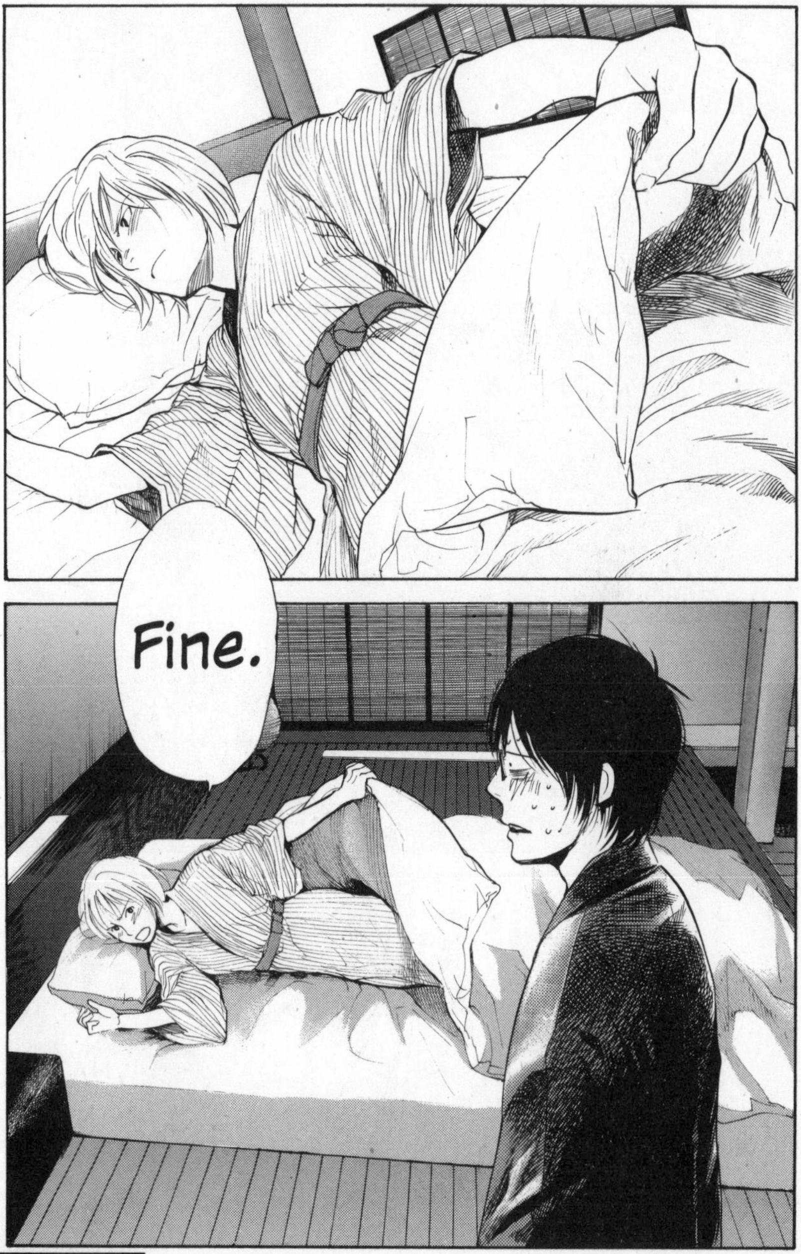
Fine.

chapter 2 ♥ END

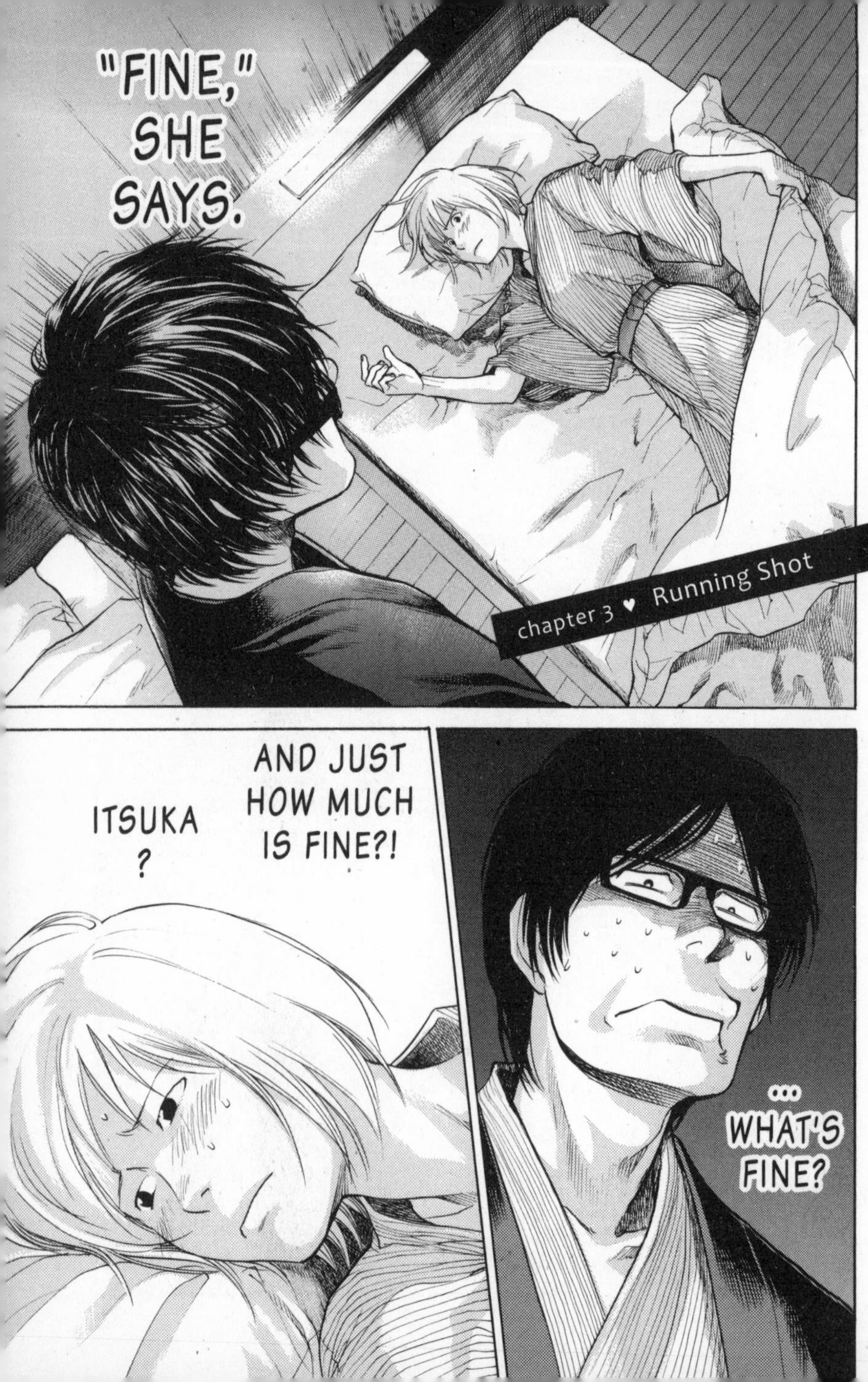
"FINE," SHE SAYS.
chapter 3 ♥ Running Shot
... WHAT'S FINE?
AND JUST HOW MUCH IS FINE?!
ITSUKA ?

I-
I'll turn off the lights!
Is it here?
Huh?
BAM
No?
Maybe it was over here?
Sorry, just a sec!!
KLIK
All right, they are off!!
OWW...!!!
GRAK
You okay, Fuji?
...!
THROB
THROB
GOD, I LOOK SO LAME ...
WHY DIDN'T I GET THIS KIND OF THING OUT OF THE WAY IN MY TEENS...? OR AT LEAST IN MY EARLY 20'S...
I'M ALMOST 30! CAN YOU BELIEVE IT? GROSS, RIGHT?

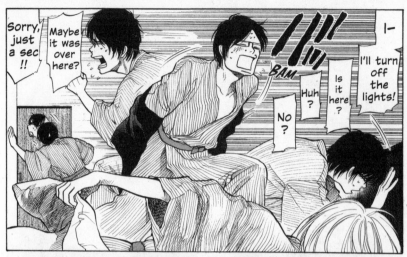

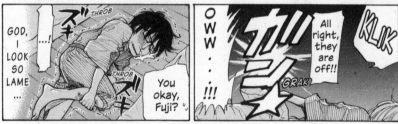

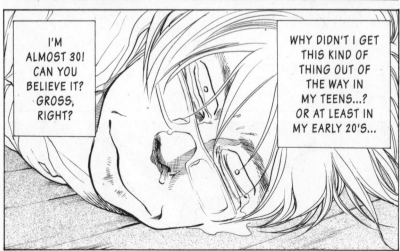

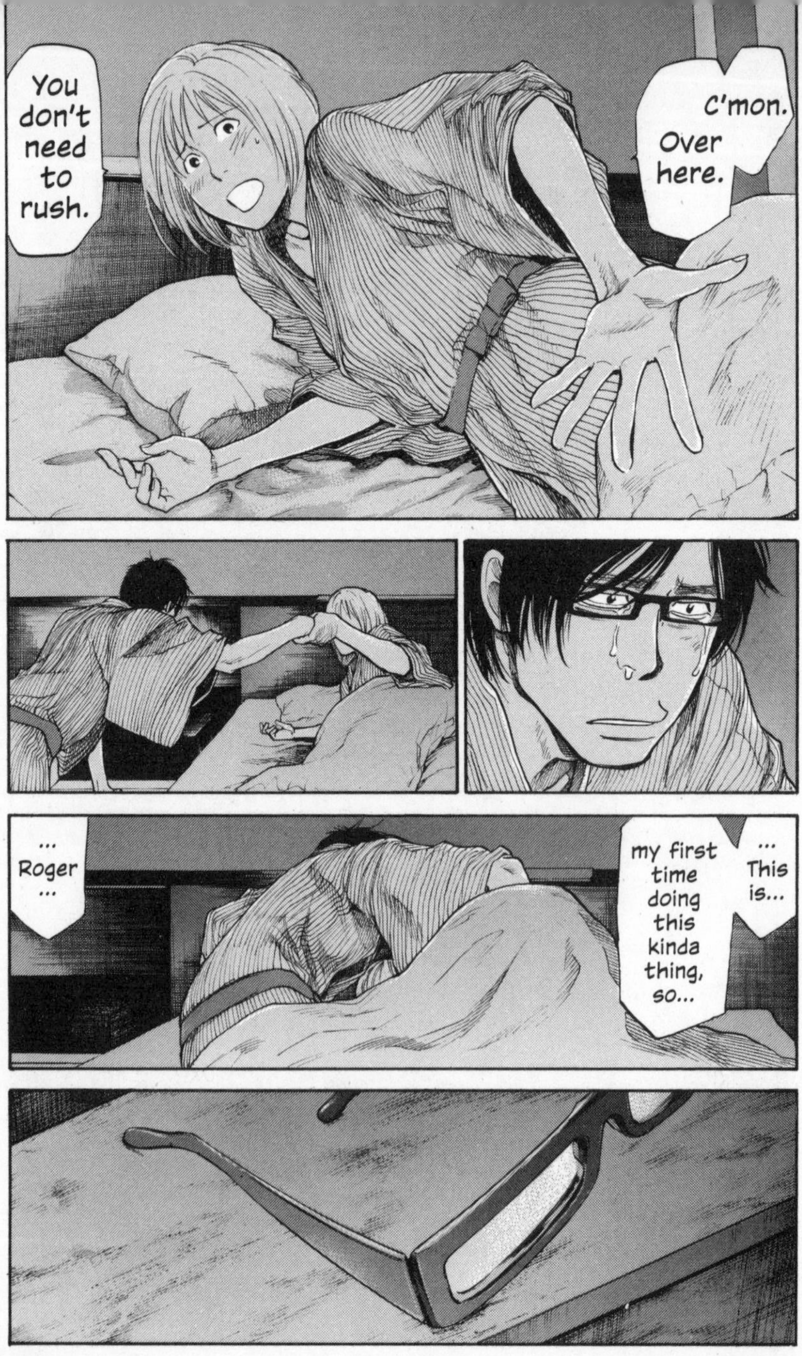
C'mon. Over here.
You don't need to rush.
... This is...
my first time doing this kinda thing, so...
... Roger ...

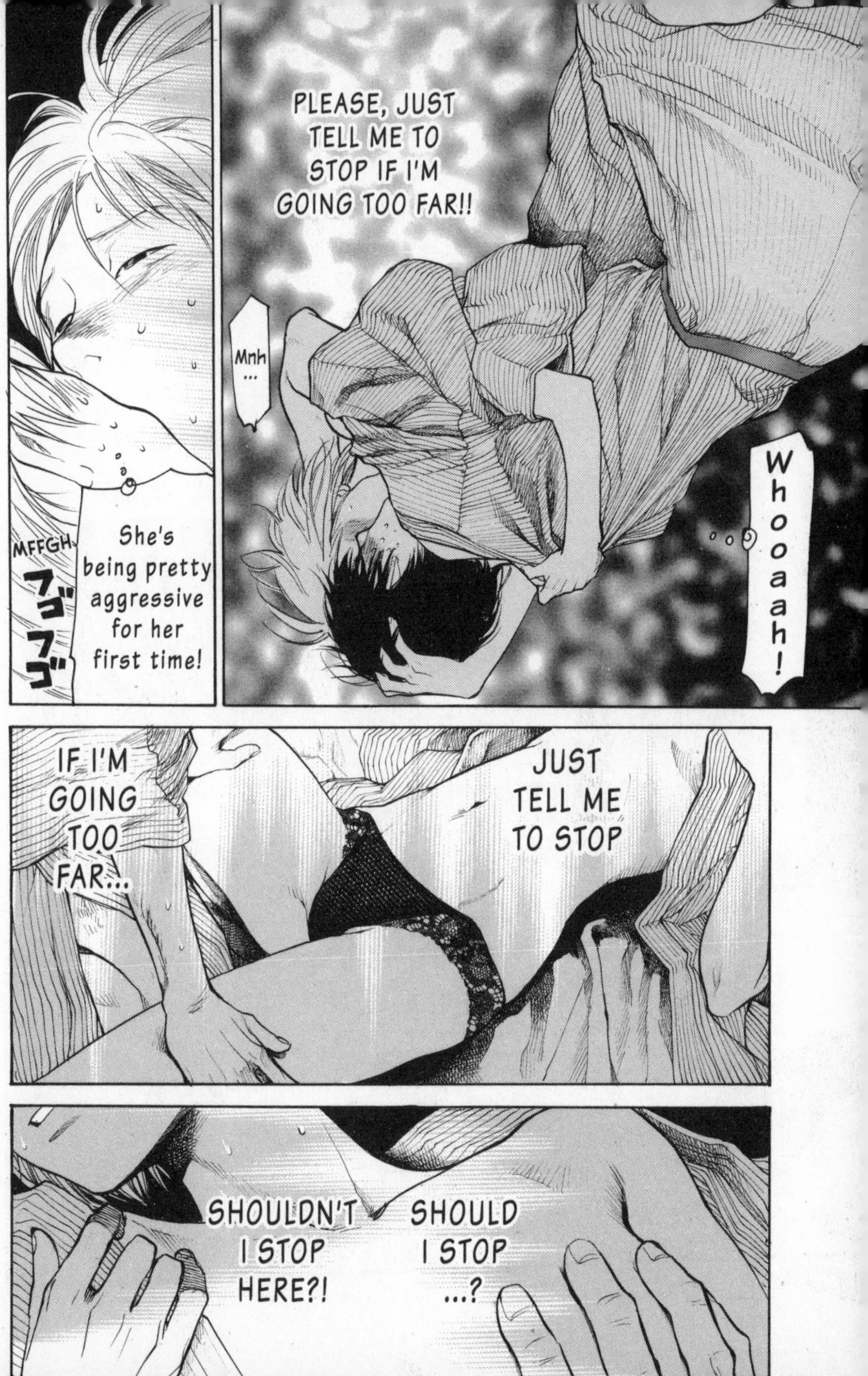
PLEASE, JUST TELL ME TO STOP IF I'M GOING TOO FAR!!
Whooaah!
Mnh...
She's being pretty aggressive for her first time!
MFFGH
フゴフゴ
JUST TELL ME TO STOP
IF I'M GOING TOO FAR...
SHOULD I STOP ...?
SHOULDN'T I STOP HERE?!

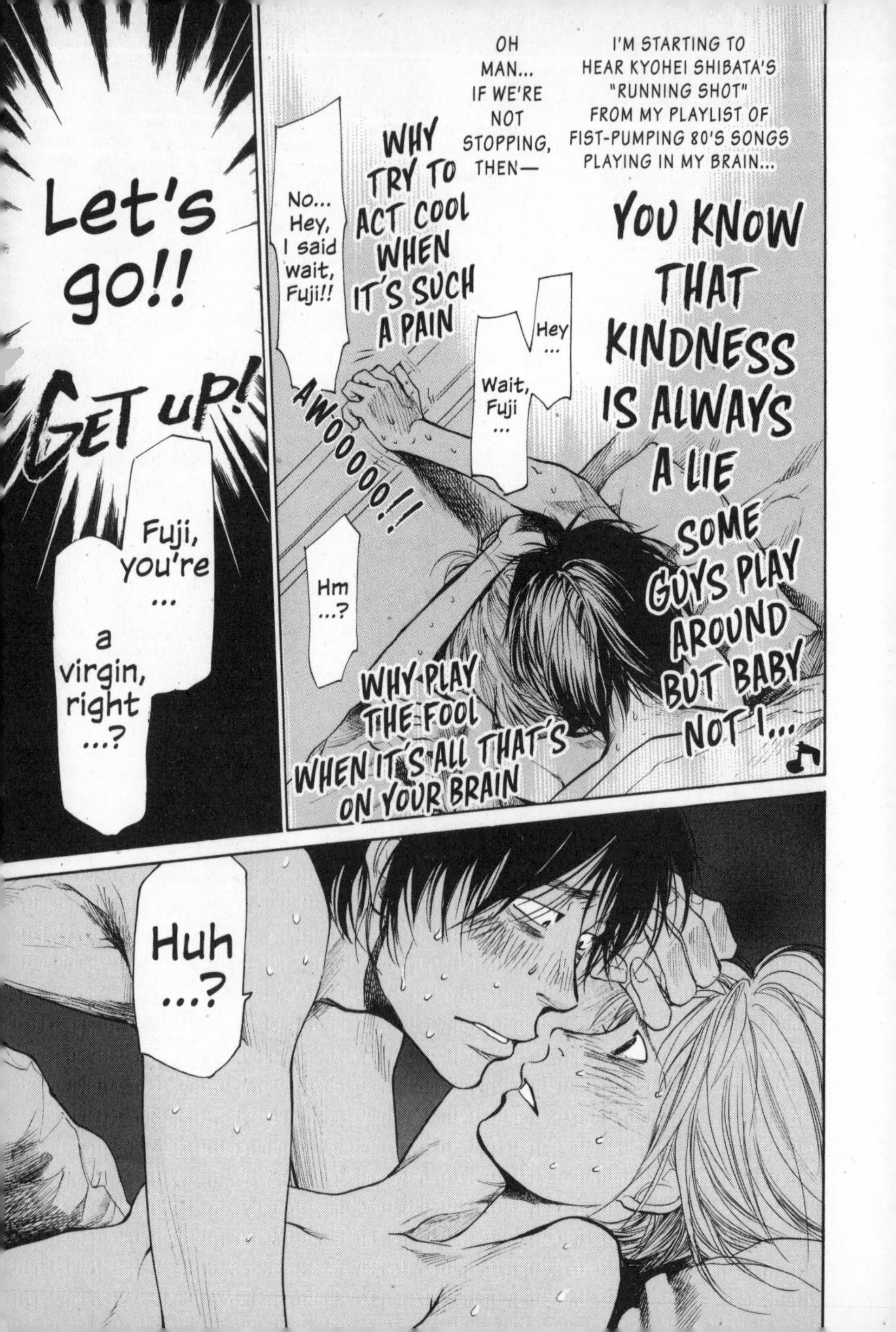
I'M STARTING TO HEAR KYOHEI SHIBATA'S "RUNNING SHOT" FROM MY PLAYLIST OF FIST-PUMPING 80'S SONGS PLAYING IN MY BRAIN...
OH MAN... IF WE'RE NOT STOPPING, THEN—
YOU KNOW THAT KINDNESS IS ALWAYS A LIE
WHY TRY TO ACT COOL WHEN IT'S SUCH A PAIN
No... Hey, I said wait, Fuji!!
Hey ...
Wait, Fuji ...
AWOOOOOO!!
SOME GUYS PLAY AROUND BUT BABY NOT I...
Hm ...?
WHY PLAY THE FOOL WHEN IT'S ALL THAT'S ON YOUR BRAIN
Let's go!!
GET UP!
Fuji, you're ... a virgin, right ...?
Huh ...?

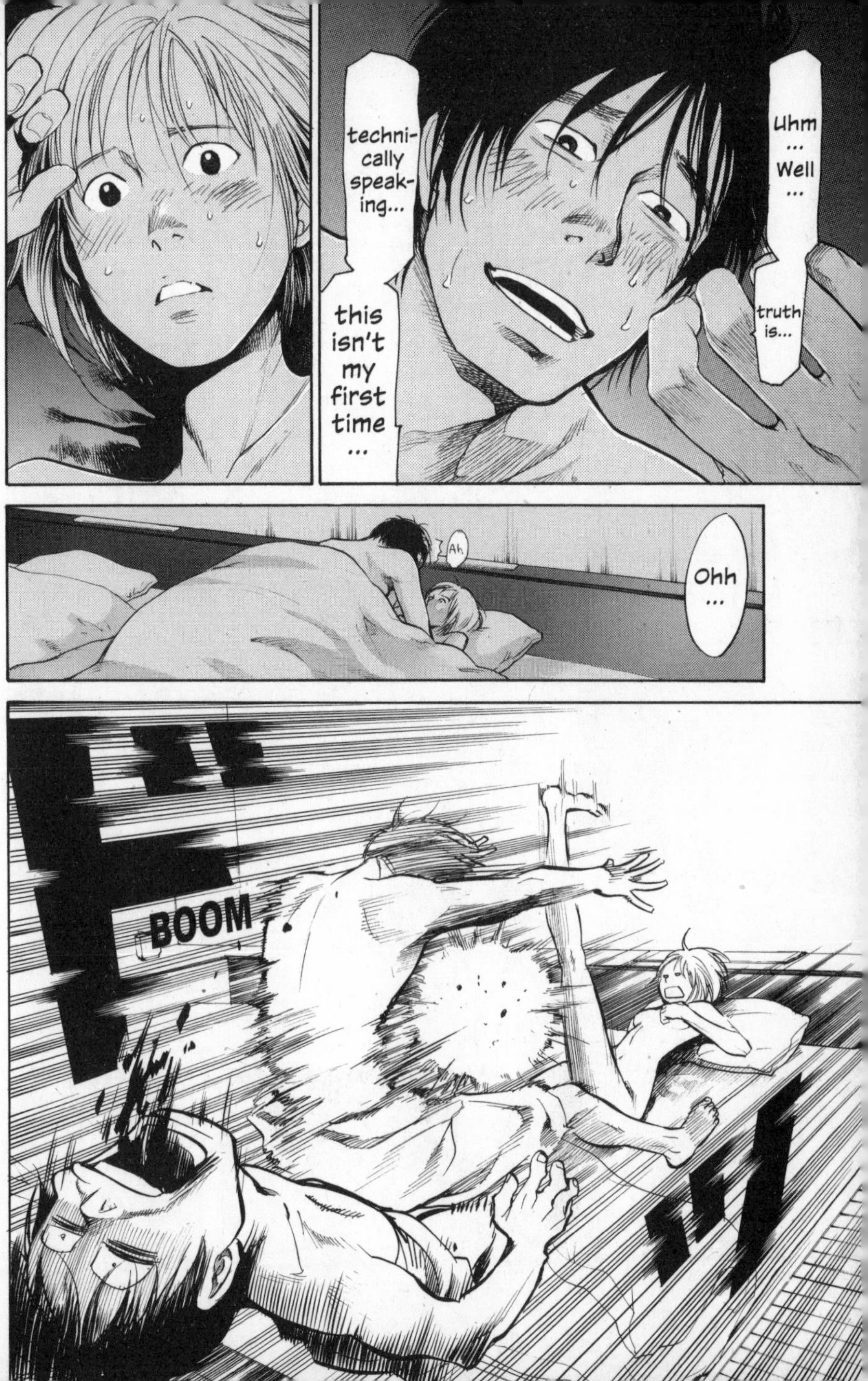
Uhm ... Well ...
truth is...
techni-cally speak-ing...
this isn't my first time ...
Ohh ...
Ah
BOOM

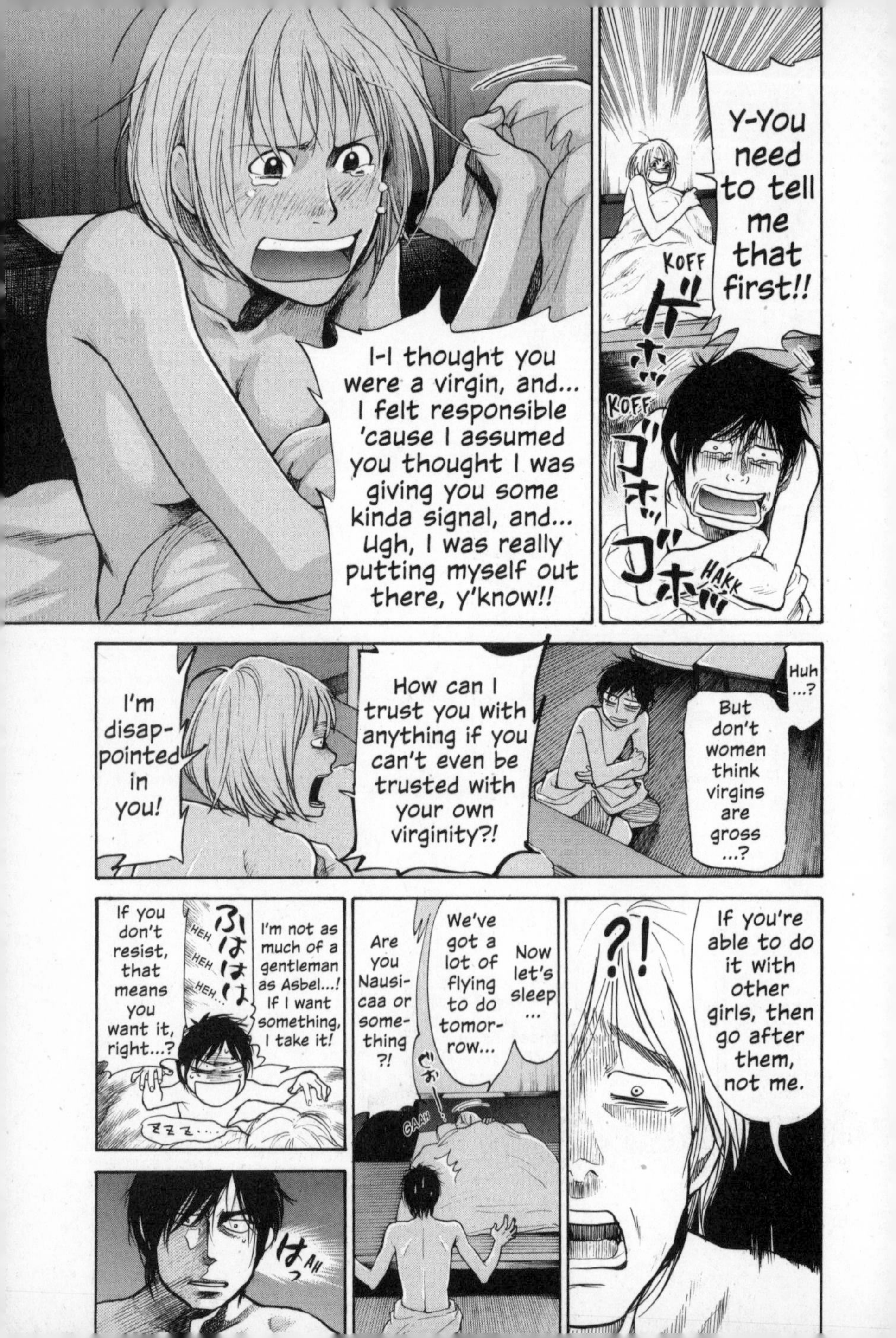

Y-You need to tell me that first!!
KOFF
ゲホッ
KOFF
ゴホッ
HAKK
ゴホッ
I-I thought you were a virgin, and... I felt responsible 'cause I assumed you thought I was giving you some kinda signal, and... Ugh, I was really putting myself out there, y'know!!
Huh ...?
But don't women think virgins are gross ...?
How can I trust you with anything if you can't even be trusted with your own virginity?!
I'm disap-pointed in you!
?!
If you're able to do it with other girls, then go after them, not me.
Now let's sleep ...
We've got a lot of flying to do tomor-row...
Are you Nausi-caa or some-thing ?!
GAAH
I'm not as much of a gentleman as Asbel...! If I want something, I take it!
ふははは
HEH HEH HEH...
If you don't resist, that means you want it, right...?
はっ
AH

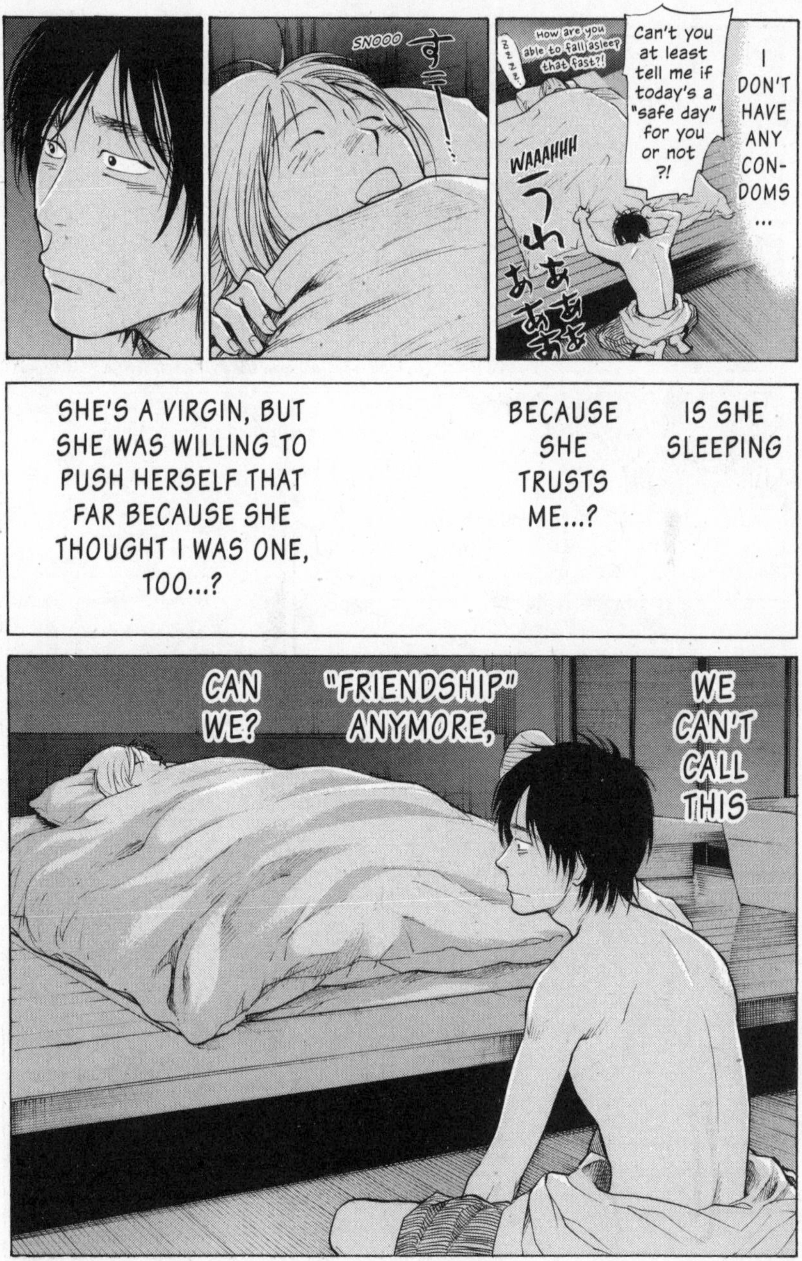
I DON'T HAVE ANY CON-DOMS ...
Can't you at least tell me if today's a "safe day" for you or not ?!
How are you able to fall asleep that fast?!
WAAAHHH
SNOOO
すー
IS SHE SLEEPING
BECAUSE SHE TRUSTS ME...?
SHE'S A VIRGIN, BUT SHE WAS WILLING TO PUSH HERSELF THAT FAR BECAUSE SHE THOUGHT I WAS ONE, TOO...?
WE CAN'T CALL THIS
"FRIENDSHIP" ANYMORE,
CAN WE?

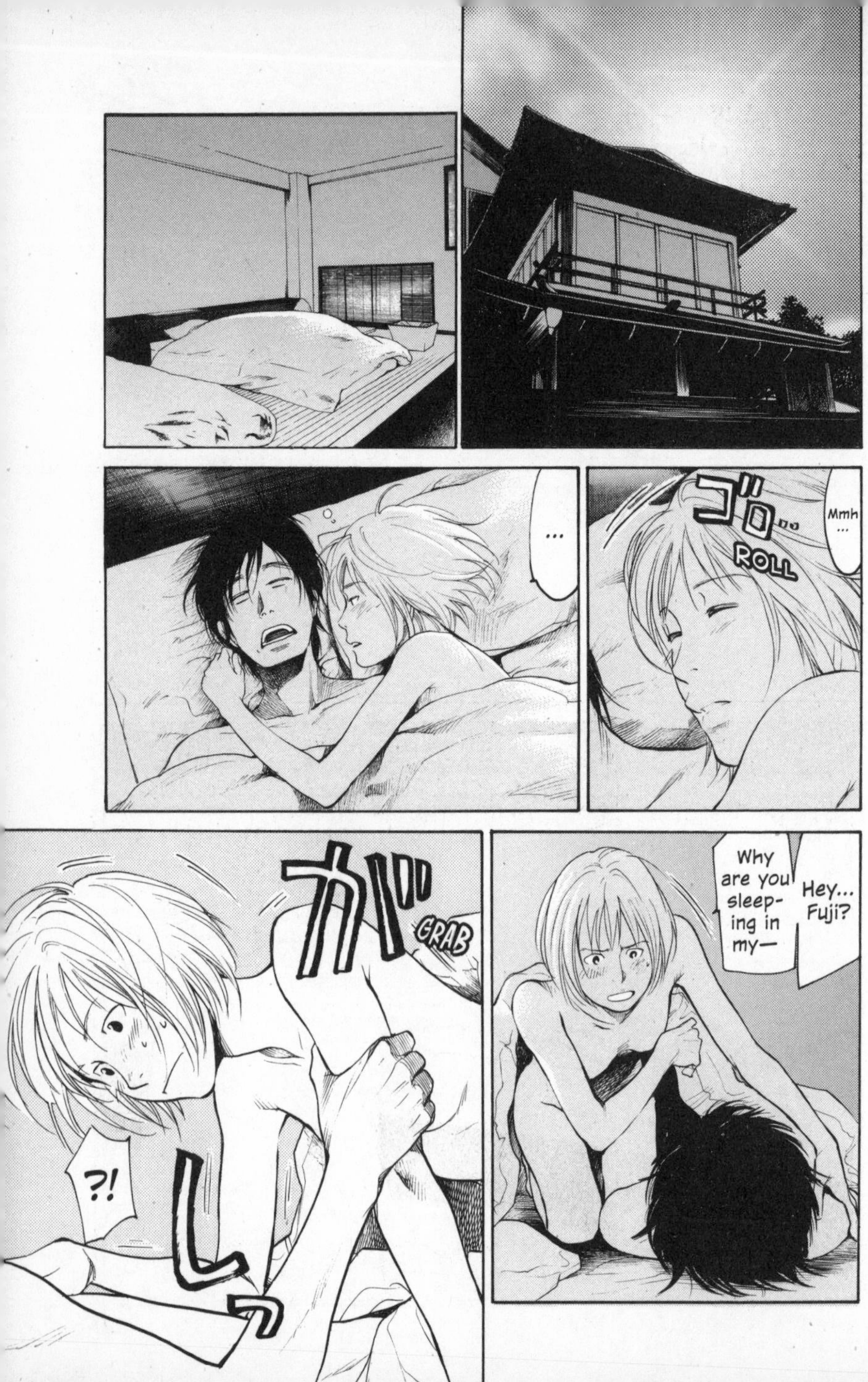
ゴロ..
ROLL
Mmh...
...
Hey... Fuji?
Why are you sleeping in my—
カバ
GRAB
?!
しっ

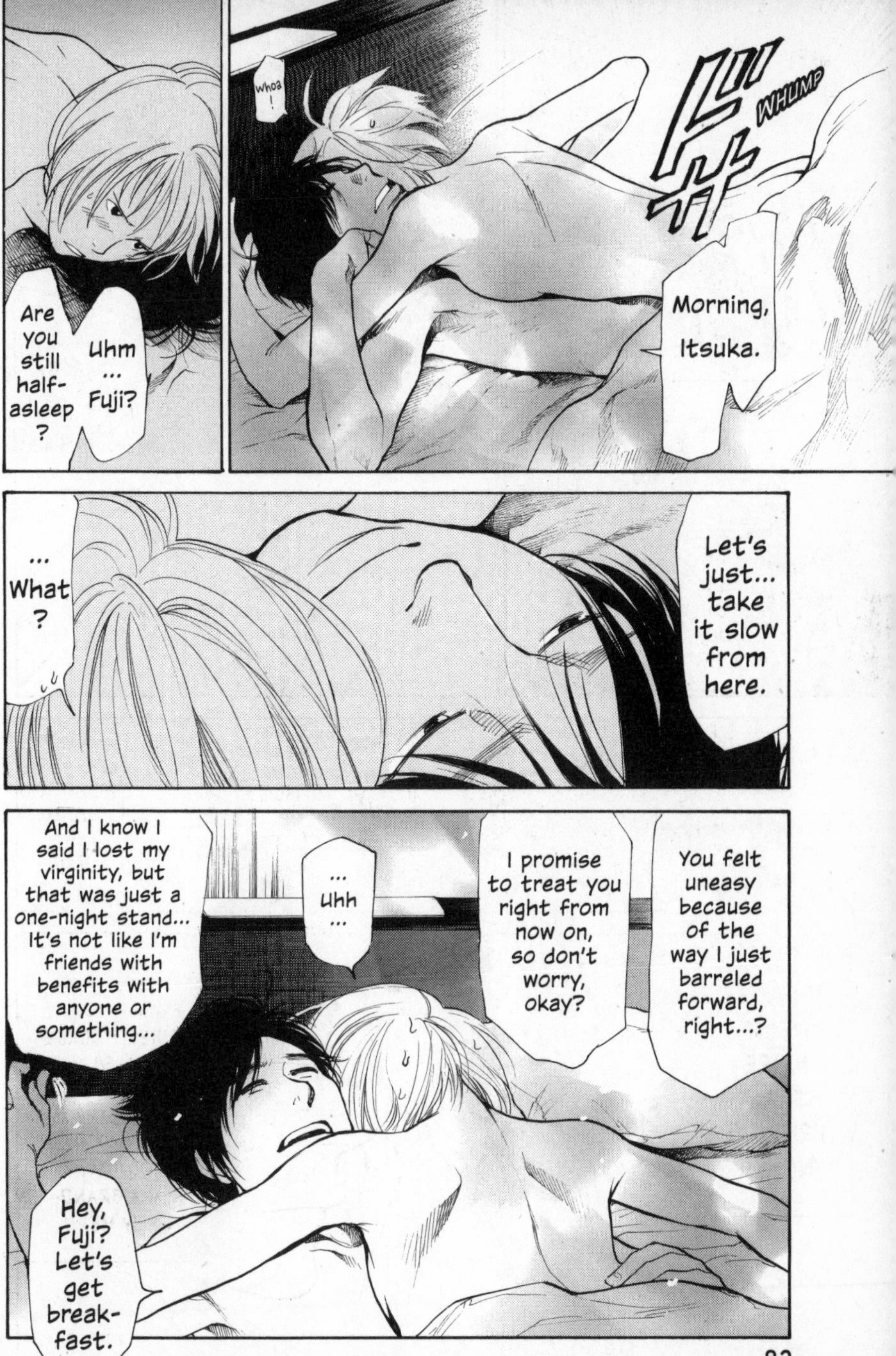
WHUMP
Whoa!
Morning, Itsuka.
Uhm ... Fuji?
Are you still half-asleep?
Let's just... take it slow from here.
... What?
You felt uneasy because of the way I just barreled forward, right...?
I promise to treat you right from now on, so don't worry, okay?
... Uhh ...
And I know I said I lost my virginity, but that was just a one-night stand... It's not like I'm friends with benefits with anyone or something...
Hey, Fuji? Let's get breakfast.

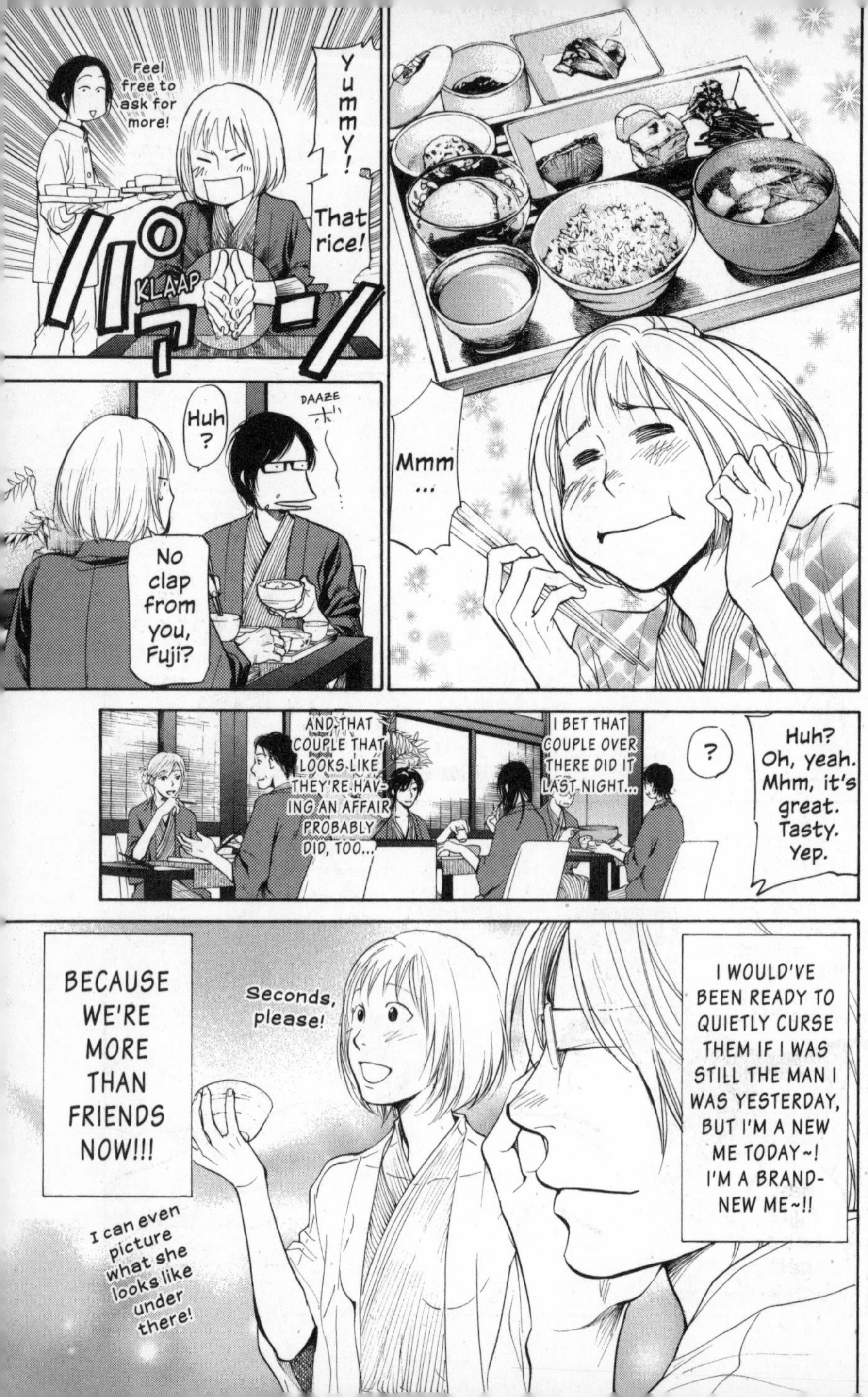

Mmm...
Yummy!
That rice!
Feel free to ask for more!
KLAAP
DAAZE
Huh?
No clap from you, Fuji?
Huh? Oh, yeah. Mhm, it's great. Tasty. Yep.
?
I BET THAT COUPLE OVER THERE DID IT LAST NIGHT...
AND THAT COUPLE THAT LOOKS LIKE THEY'RE HAVING AN AFFAIR PROBABLY DID, TOO...
I WOULD'VE BEEN READY TO QUIETLY CURSE THEM IF I WAS STILL THE MAN I WAS YESTERDAY, BUT I'M A NEW ME TODAY~! I'M A BRAND-NEW ME~!!
Seconds, please!
BECAUSE WE'RE MORE THAN FRIENDS NOW!!!
I can even picture what she looks like under there!

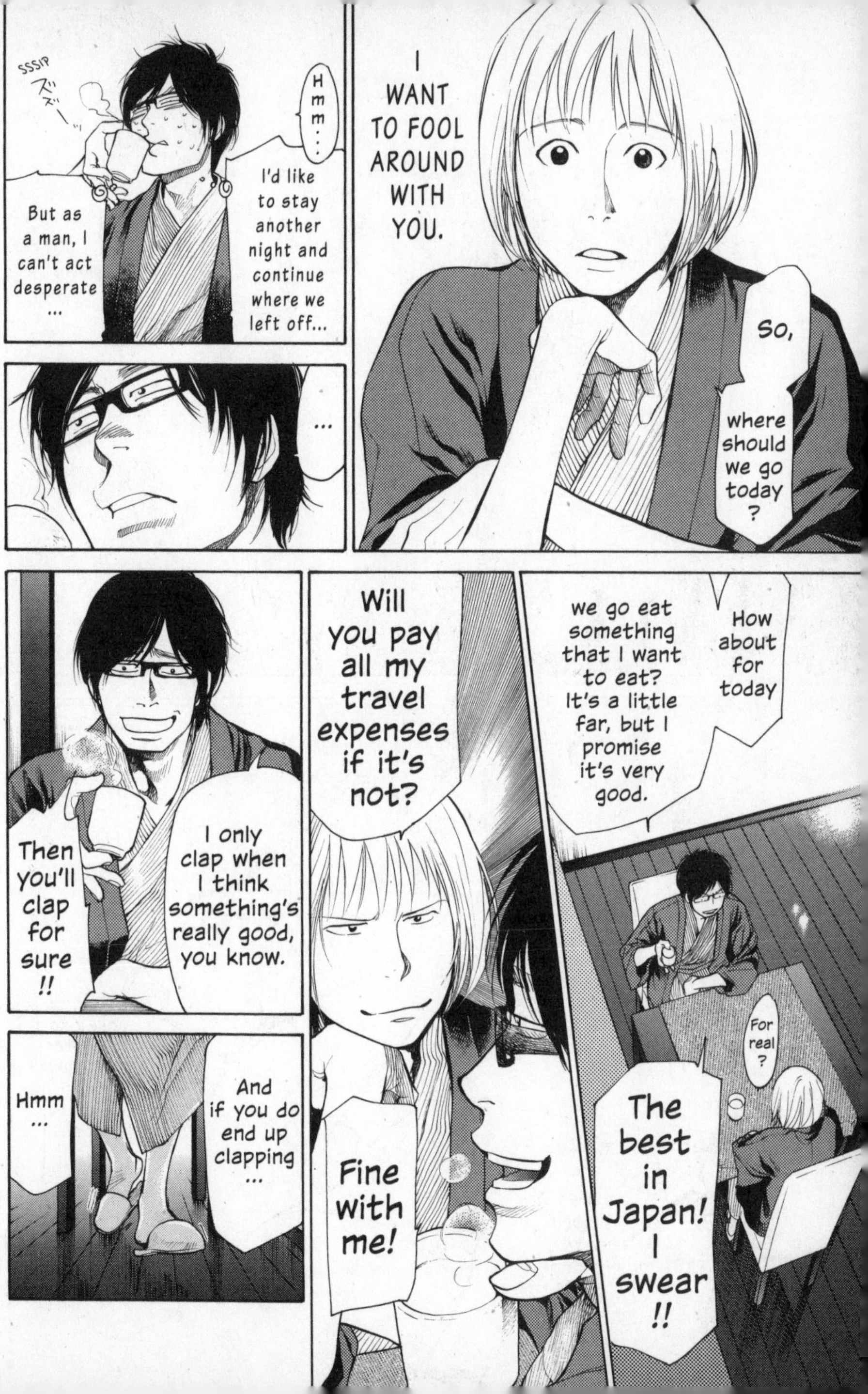
I WANT TO FOOL AROUND WITH YOU.
So, where should we go today?
Hmm...
SSSIP
I'd like to stay another night and continue where we left off...
But as a man, I can't act desperate...
...
How about for today
we go eat something that I want to eat? It's a little far, but I promise it's very good.
For real?
The best in Japan! I swear!!
Will you pay all my travel expenses if it's not?
Fine with me!
I only clap when I think something's really good, you know.
Then you'll clap for sure!!
And if you do end up clapping...
Hmm...

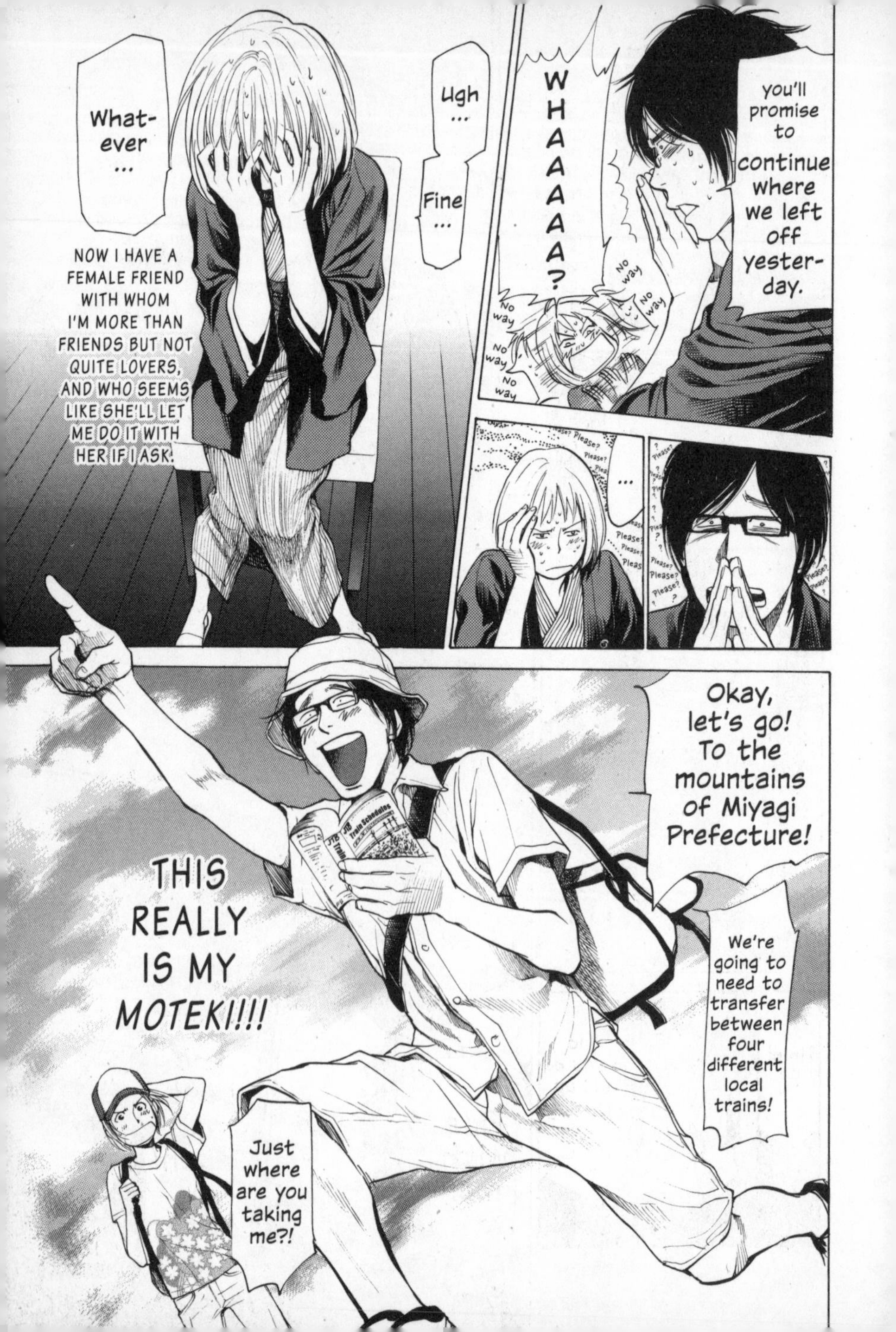
you'll promise to continue where we left off yester-day.
WHAAAAAA?
No way
No way
No way
No way
No way
Please? Please? Please?
...
Please? Please? Please?
Ugh... Fine...
What-ever...
NOW I HAVE A FEMALE FRIEND WITH WHOM I'M MORE THAN FRIENDS BUT NOT QUITE LOVERS, AND WHO SEEMS LIKE SHE'LL LET ME DO IT WITH HER IF I ASK.
Okay, let's go! To the mountains of Miyagi Prefecture!
Train Schedules
We're going to need to transfer between four different local trains!
THIS REALLY IS MY MOTEKI!!!
Just where are you taking me?!

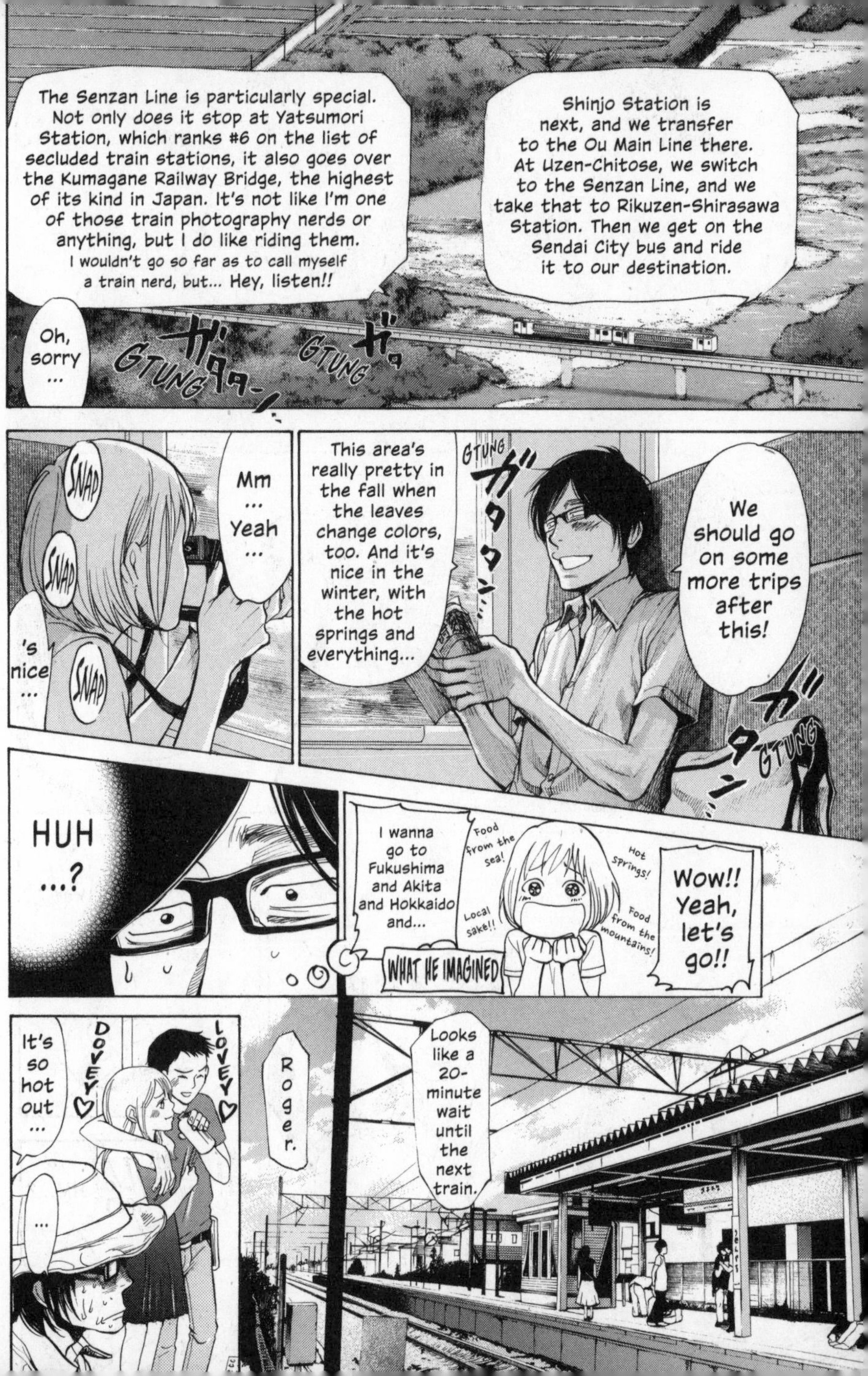
Shinjo Station is next, and we transfer to the Ou Main Line there. At Uzen-Chitose, we switch to the Senzan Line, and we take that to Rikuzen-Shirasawa Station. Then we get on the Sendai City bus and ride it to our destination.
The Senzan Line is particularly special. Not only does it stop at Yatsumori Station, which ranks #6 on the list of secluded train stations, it also goes over the Kumagane Railway Bridge, the highest of its kind in Japan. It's not like I'm one of those train photography nerds or anything, but I do like riding them.
I wouldn't go so far as to call myself a train nerd, but... Hey, listen!!
GTUNG
GTUNG
Oh, sorry ...
GTUNG
This area's really pretty in the fall when the leaves change colors, too. And it's nice in the winter, with the hot springs and everything...
We should go on some more trips after this!
GTUNG
Mm ... Yeah ...
SNAP
SNAP
SNAP
's nice ...
Wow!! Yeah, let's go!!
Hot Springs!
Food from the mountains!
Food from the Sea!
Local sake!!
I wanna go to Fukushima and Akita and Hokkaido and...
WHAT HE IMAGINED
HUH ...?
Looks like a 20-minute wait until the next train.
Roger.
LOVEY
DOVEY
It's so hot out ...
...

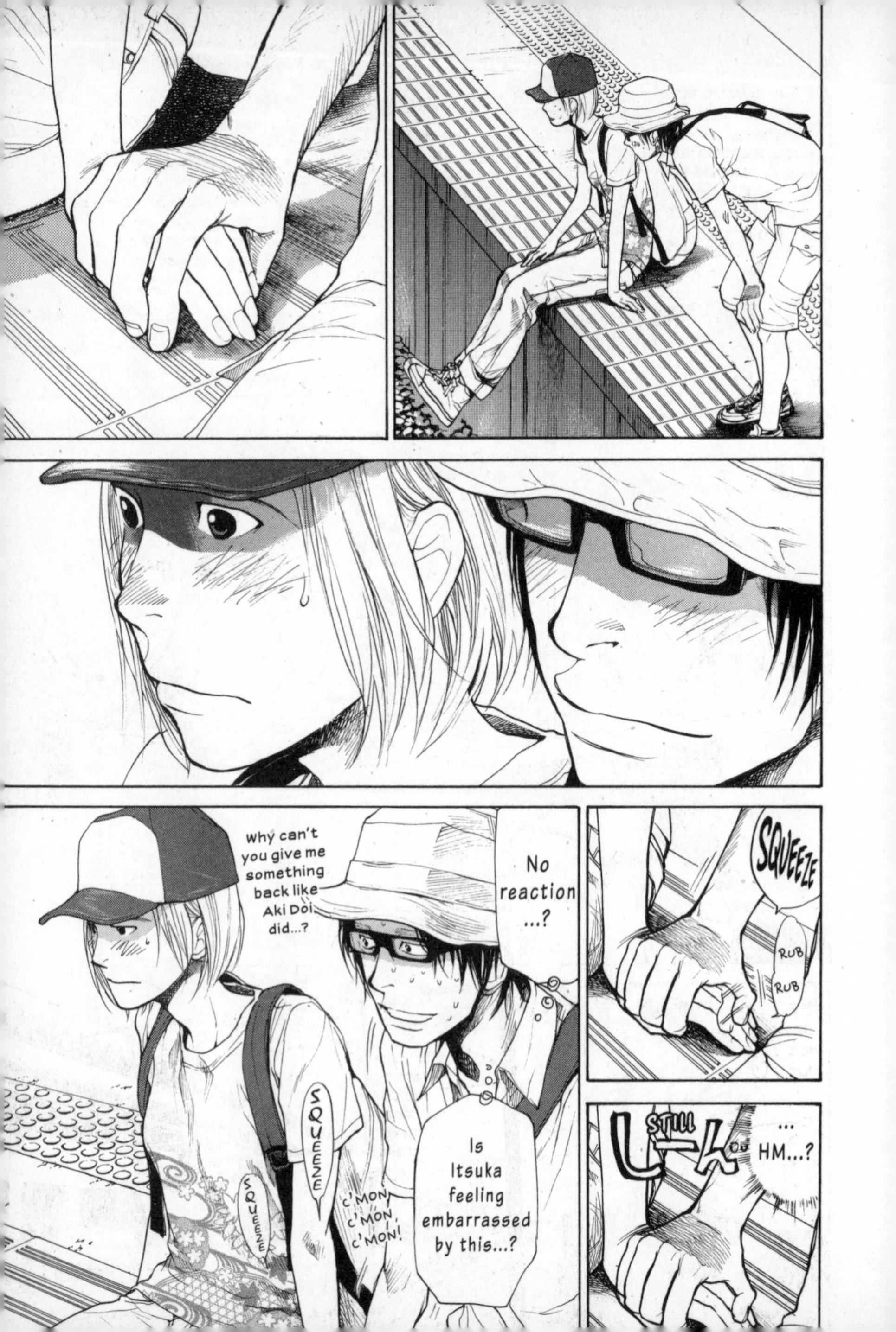
SQUEEZE
RUB RUB
STILL
... HM...?
No reaction ...?
Why can't you give me something back like Aki Doi did...?
Is Itsuka feeling embarrassed by this...?
C'MON C'MON C'MON!
SQUEEZE
SQUEEZE

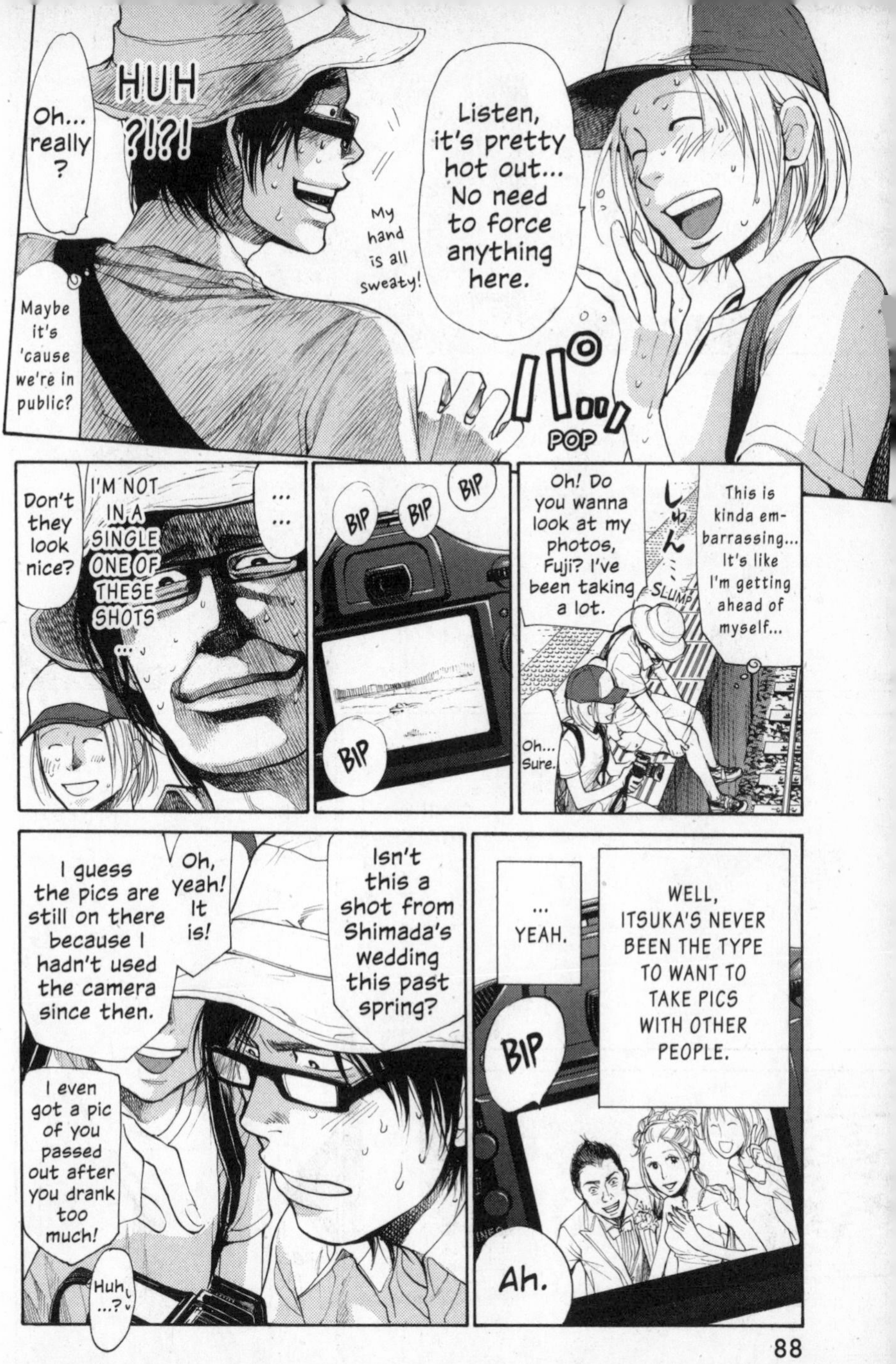
Listen, it's pretty hot out... No need to force anything here.
My hand is all sweaty!
HUH ?!?!
Oh... really ?
Maybe it's 'cause we're in public?
POP
This is kinda em-barrassing... It's like I'm getting ahead of myself...
Oh! Do you wanna look at my photos, Fuji? I've been taking a lot.
しゅん…
SLUMP
Oh... Sure.
BIP
BIP
BIP
BIP
... ...
I'M NOT IN A SINGLE ONE OF THESE SHOTS...
Don't they look nice?
WELL, ITSUKA'S NEVER BEEN THE TYPE TO WANT TO TAKE PICS WITH OTHER PEOPLE.
... YEAH.
BIP
Ah.
Isn't this a shot from Shimada's wedding this past spring?
Oh, yeah! It is!
I guess the pics are still on there because I hadn't used the camera since then.
I even got a pic of you passed out after you drank too much!
Huh ...?

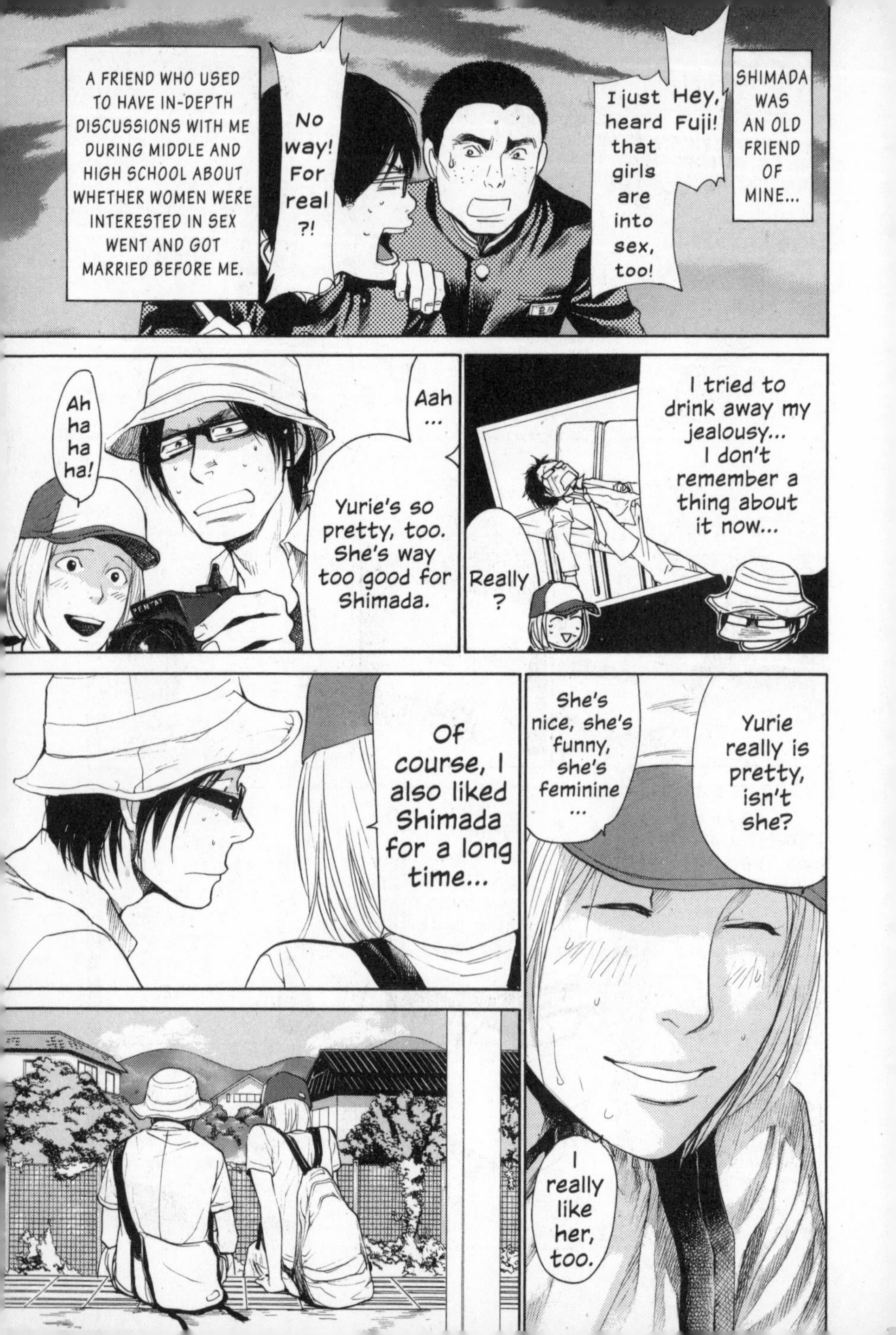
SHIMADA WAS AN OLD FRIEND OF MINE...
Hey, Fuji!
I just heard that girls are into sex, too!
No way! For real?!
A FRIEND WHO USED TO HAVE IN-DEPTH DISCUSSIONS WITH ME DURING MIDDLE AND HIGH SCHOOL ABOUT WHETHER WOMEN WERE INTERESTED IN SEX WENT AND GOT MARRIED BEFORE ME.
I tried to drink away my jealousy... I don't remember a thing about it now...
Really?
Aah...
Yurie's so pretty, too. She's way too good for Shimada.
Ah ha ha ha!
Yurie really is pretty, isn't she?
She's nice, she's funny, she's feminine...
I really like her, too.
Of course, I also liked Shimada for a long time...

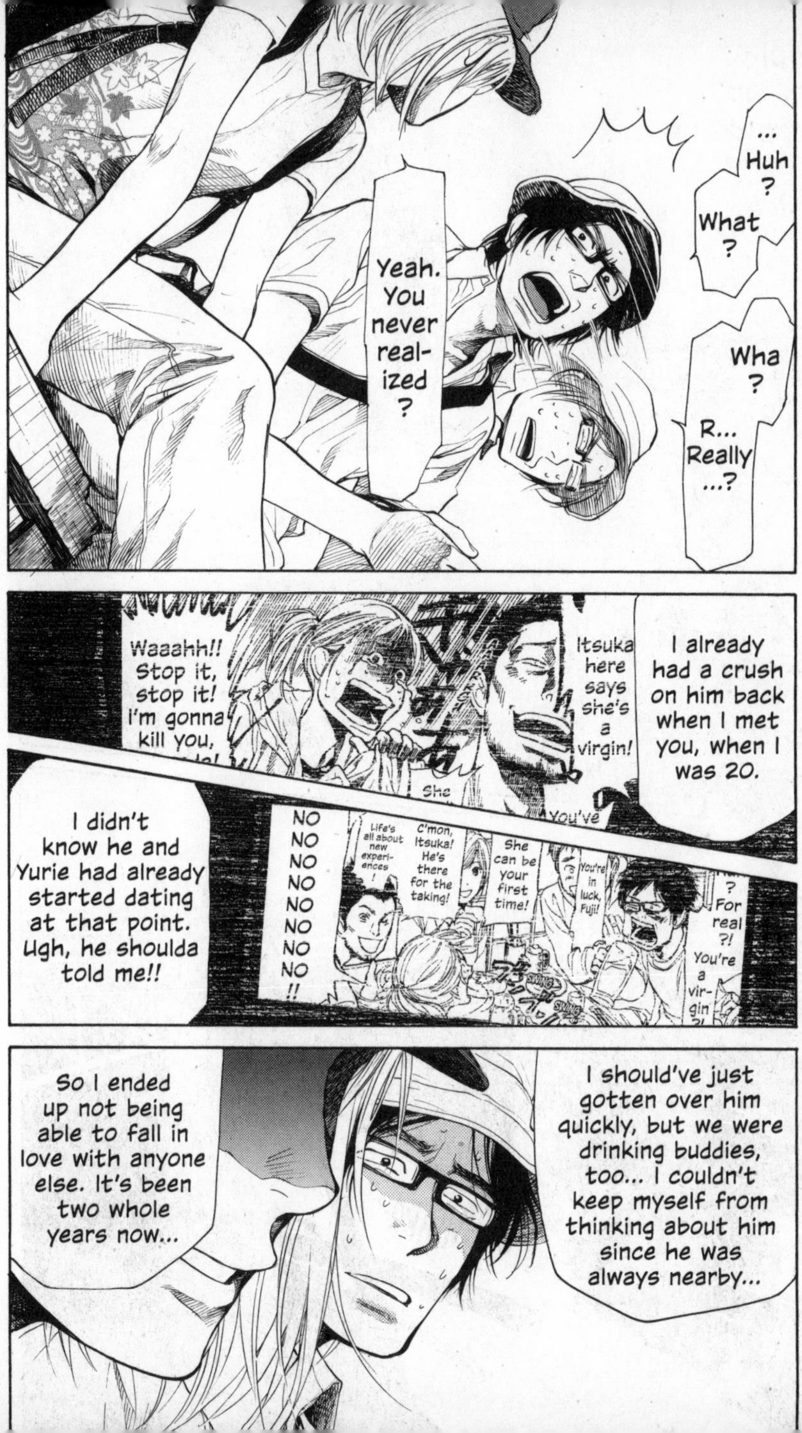
... Huh?
What?
Wha? R... Really...?
Yeah. You never realized?
I already had a crush on him back when I met you, when I was 20.
Itsuka here says she's a virgin!
Waaahh!! Stop it, stop it! I'm gonna kill you,
For real?! You're a virgin
You're in luck, Fuji!
She can be your first time!
C'mon, Itsuka! He's there for the taking!
Life's all about new experiences!
NO NO NO NO NO NO NO NO NO !!
SWING
SWING
I didn't know he and Yurie had already started dating at that point. Ugh, he shoulda told me!!
I should've just gotten over him quickly, but we were drinking buddies, too... I couldn't keep myself from thinking about him since he was always nearby...
So I ended up not being able to fall in love with anyone else. It's been two whole years now...

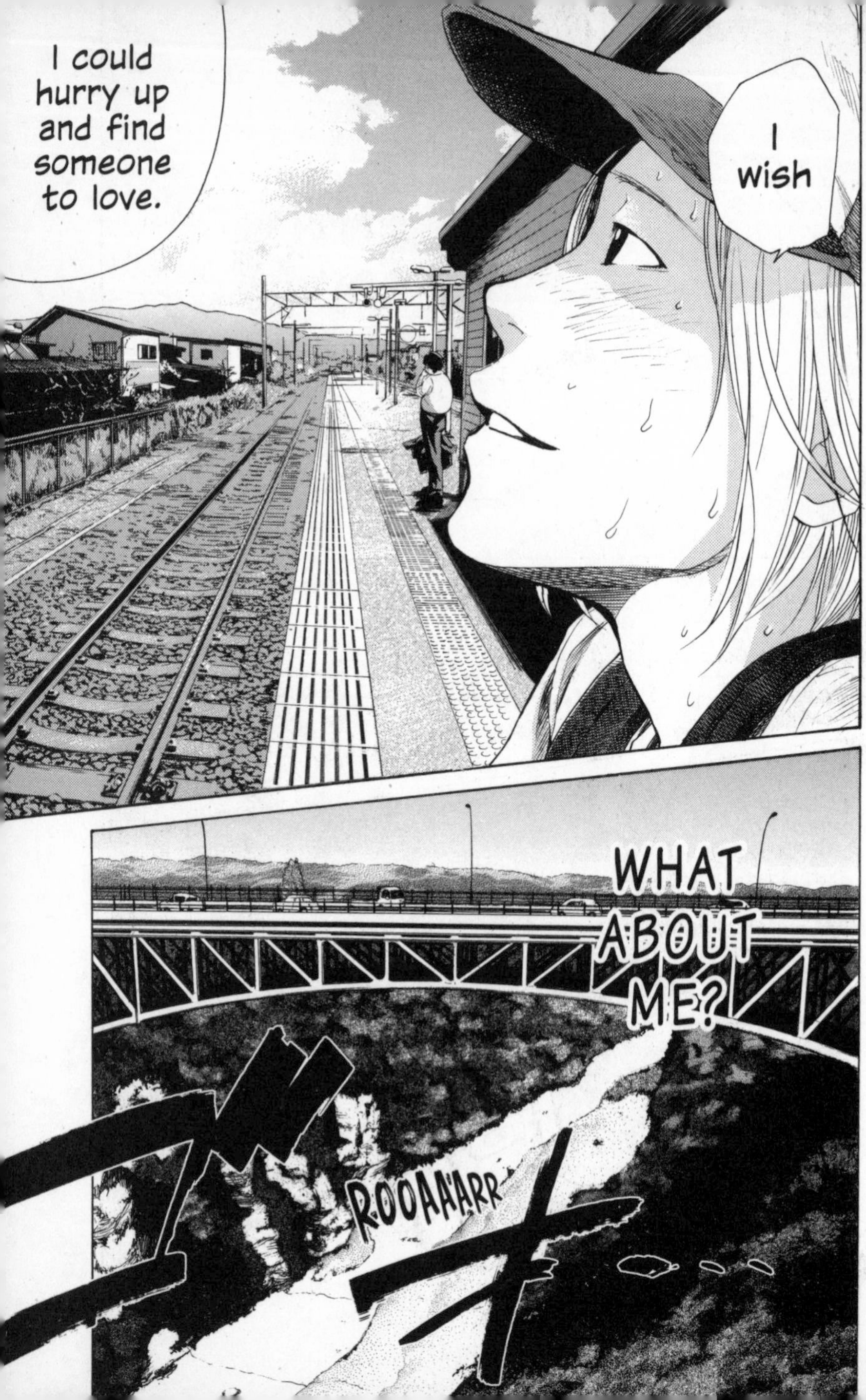
I wish
I could hurry up and find someone to love.
WHAT ABOUT ME?
ROOAAARR

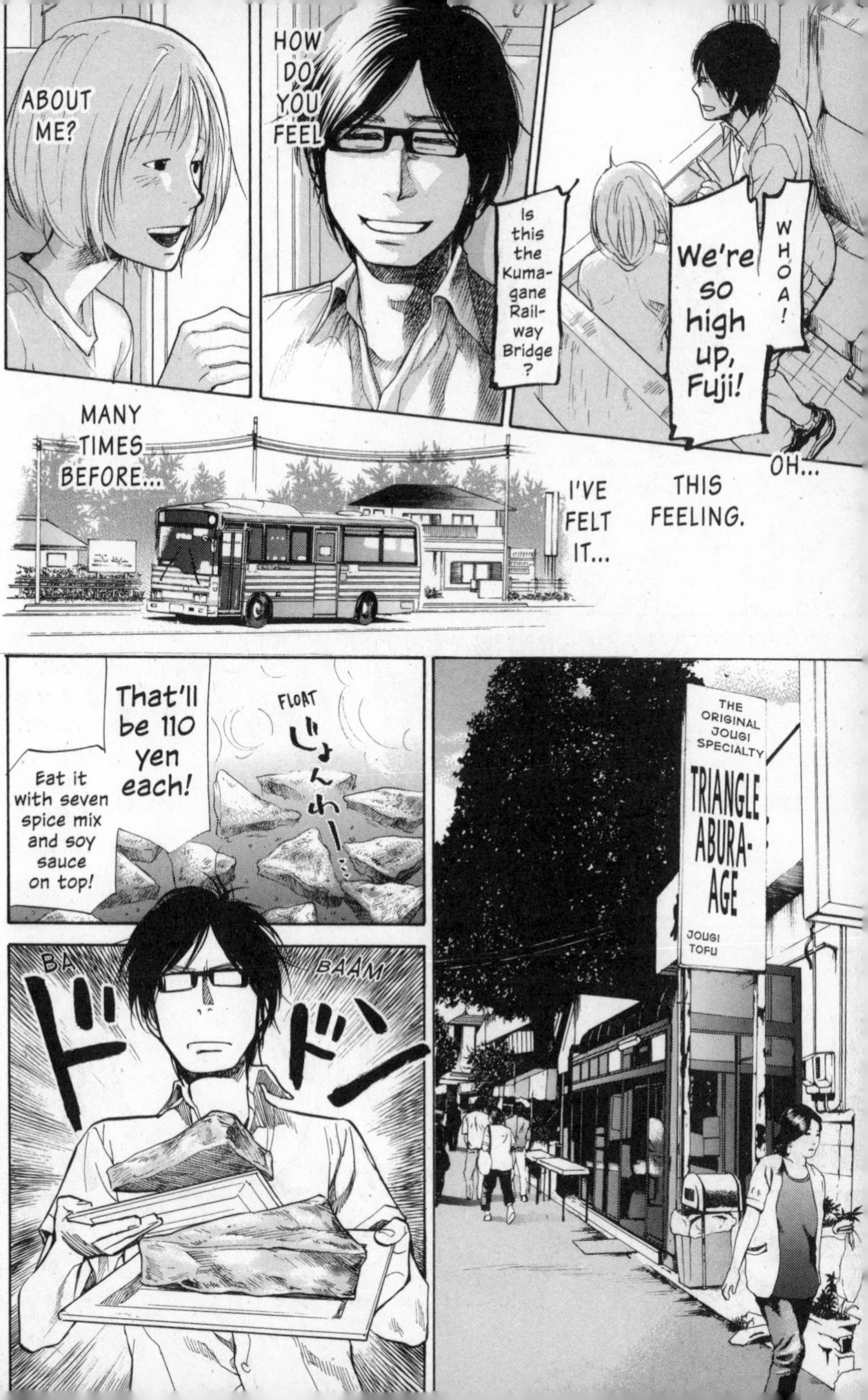
WHOA!
We're so high up, Fuji!
HOW DO YOU FEEL
Is this the Kumagane Railway Bridge?
ABOUT ME?
OH...
THIS FEELING.
I'VE FELT IT...
MANY TIMES BEFORE...
THE ORIGINAL JOUGI SPECIALTY
TRIANGLE ABURA-AGE
JOUGI TOFU
That'll be 110 yen each!
FLOAT
Eat it with seven spice mix and soy sauce on top!
BA
BAAM

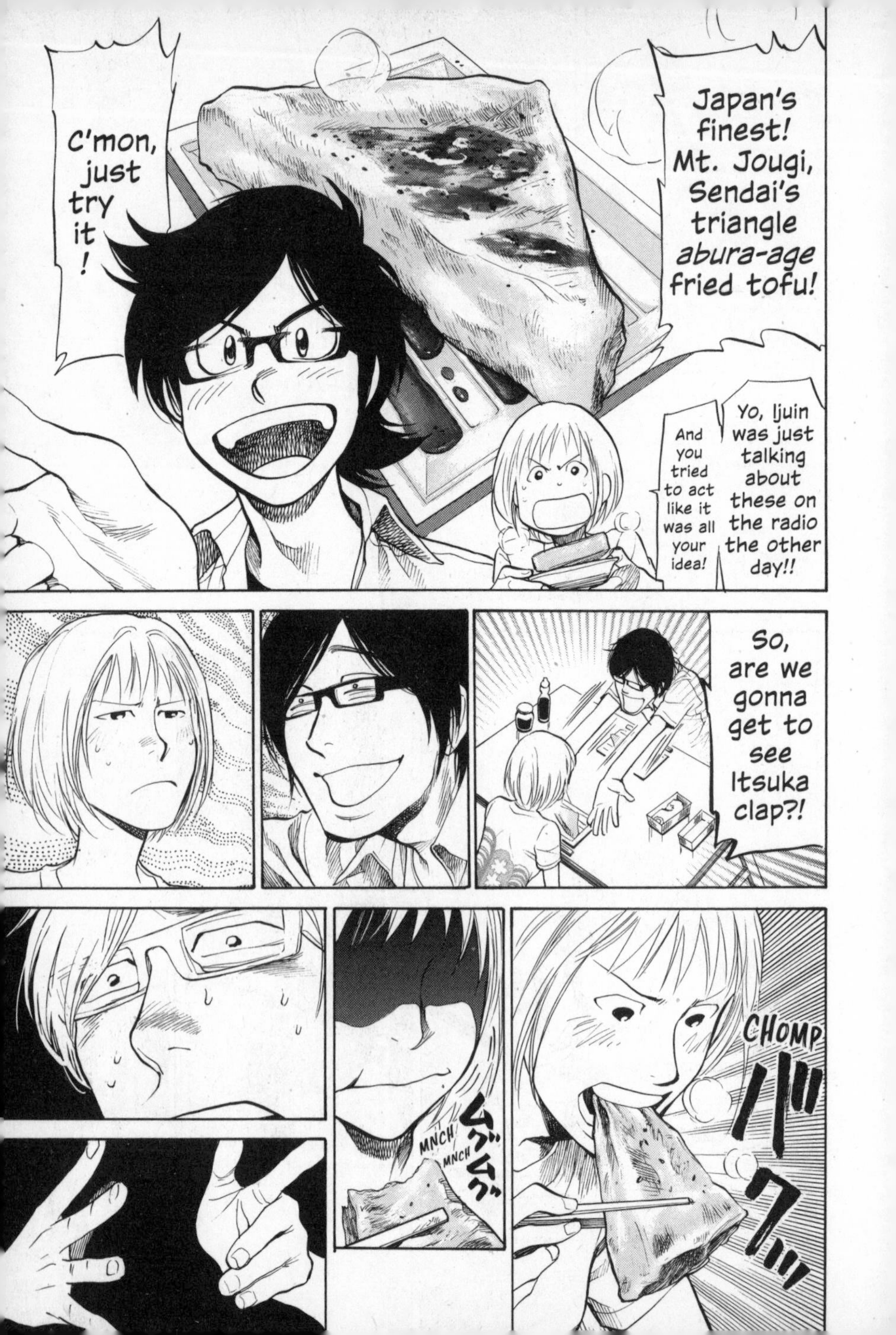
Japan's finest! Mt. Jougi, Sendai's triangle *abura-age* fried tofu!
C'mon, just try it!
Yo, Ijuin was just talking about these on the radio the other day!!
And you tried to act like it was all your idea!
So, are we gonna get to see Itsuka clap?!
CHOMP
MNCH MNCH

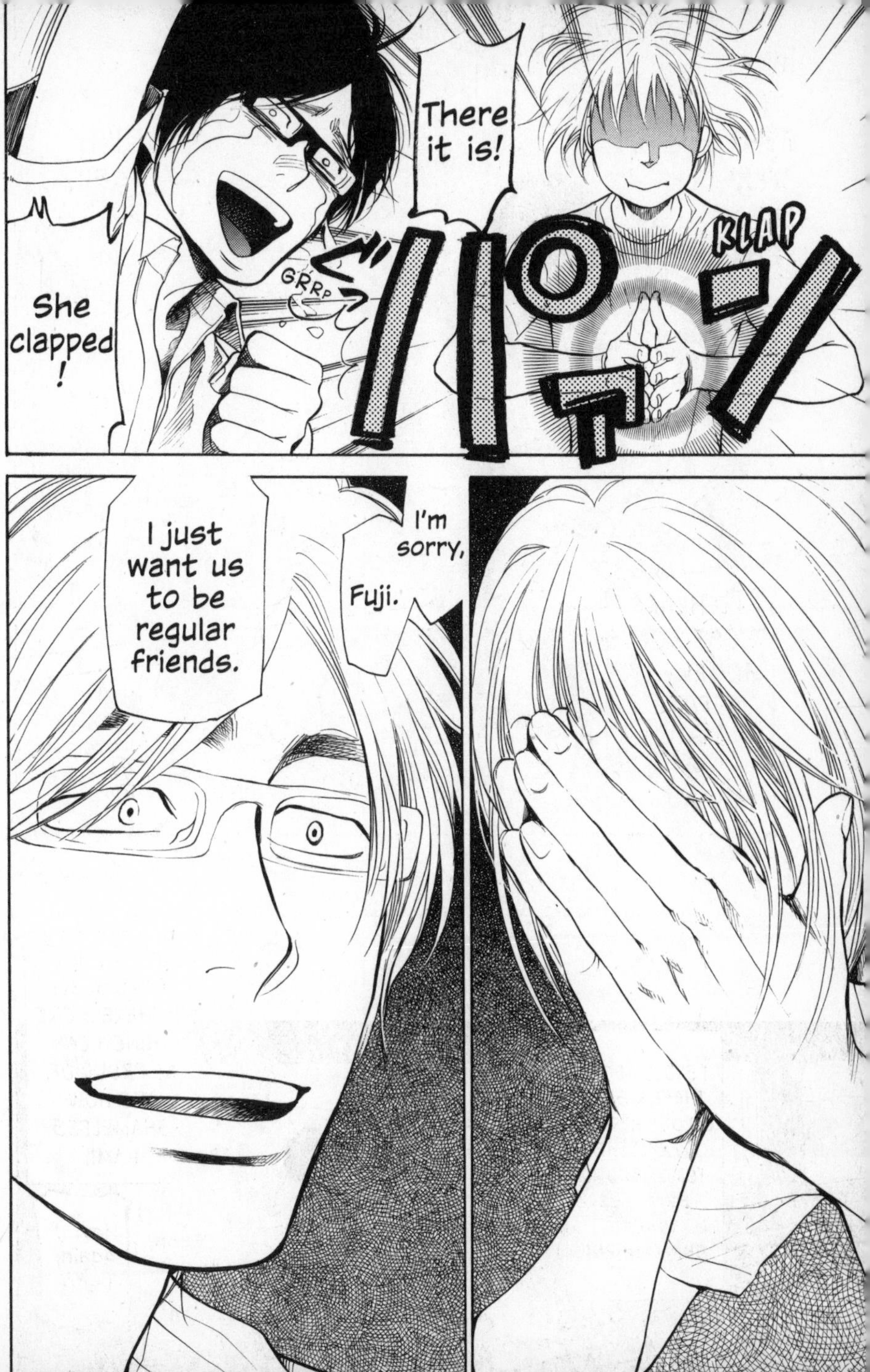
KLAP
There it is!
GRRP
She clapped!
I'm sorry, Fuji.
I just want us to be regular friends.

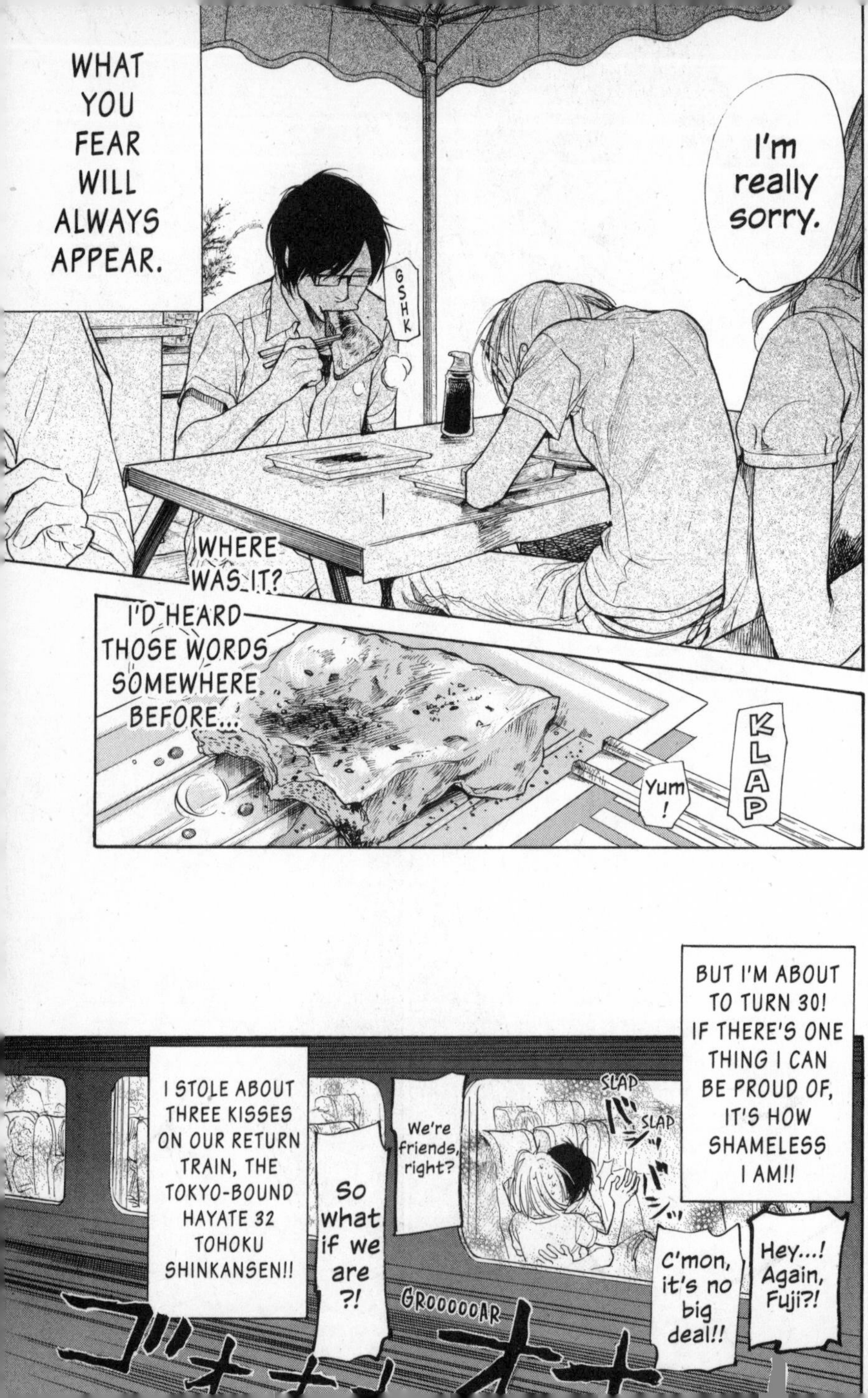
I'm really sorry.
GSHK
WHAT YOU FEAR WILL ALWAYS APPEAR.
WHERE WAS IT?
KLAP
Yum!
I'D HEARD THOSE WORDS SOMEWHERE BEFORE...
BUT I'M ABOUT TO TURN 30! IF THERE'S ONE THING I CAN BE PROUD OF, IT'S HOW SHAMELESS I AM!!
Hey...! Again, Fuji?!
C'mon, it's no big deal!!
SLAP
SLAP
We're friends, right?
So what if we are?!
I STOLE ABOUT THREE KISSES ON OUR RETURN TRAIN, THE TOKYO-BOUND HAYATE 32 TOHOKU SHINKANSEN!!
GROOOOOAR

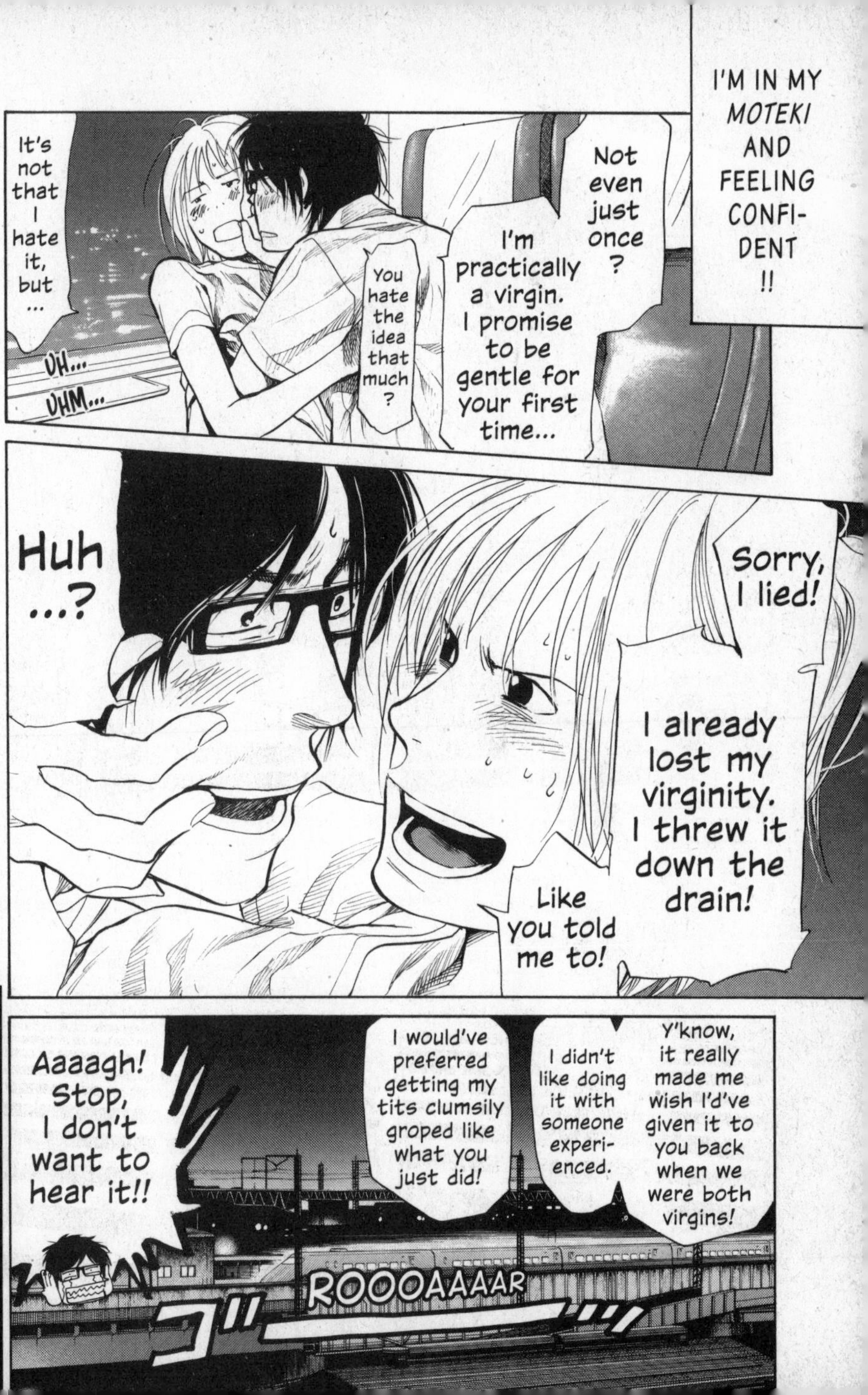
I'M IN MY MOTEKI AND FEELING CONFI-DENT !!
Not even just once ?
I'm practically a virgin. I promise to be gentle for your first time...
You hate the idea that much ?
It's not that I hate it, but ...
UH...
UHM...
Sorry, I lied!
I already lost my virginity. I threw it down the drain!
Like you told me to!
Huh ...?
Y'know, it really made me wish I'd've given it to you back when we were both virgins!
I didn't like doing it with someone experi-enced.
I would've preferred getting my tits clumsily groped like what you just did!
Aaaagh! Stop, I don't want to hear it!!
ROOOAAAAR
ゴー

chapter 3 ♥ END

chapter 4 ♥ Love is Like a Mirage

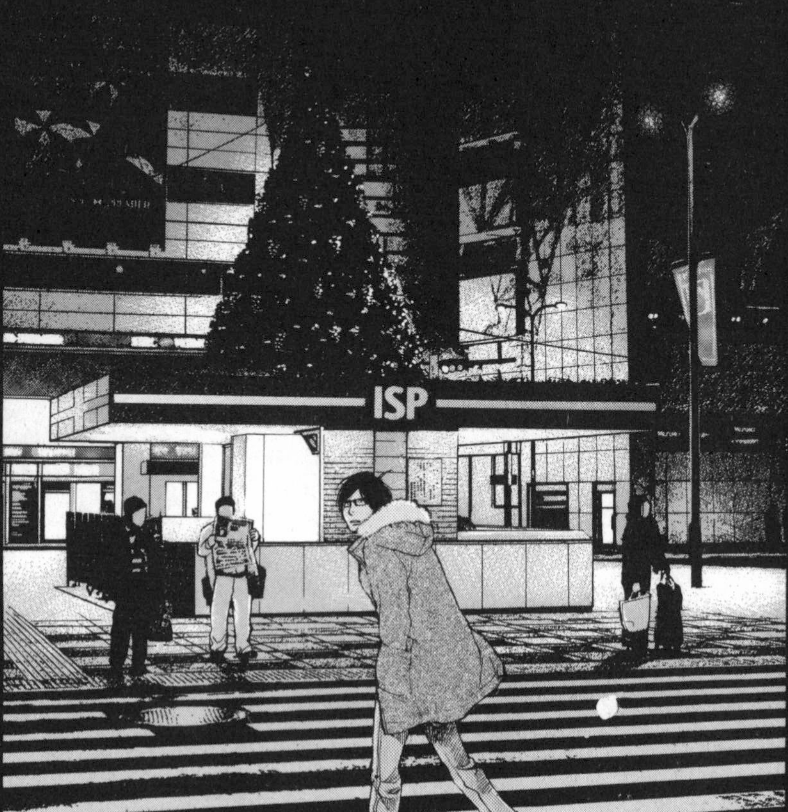
ISP

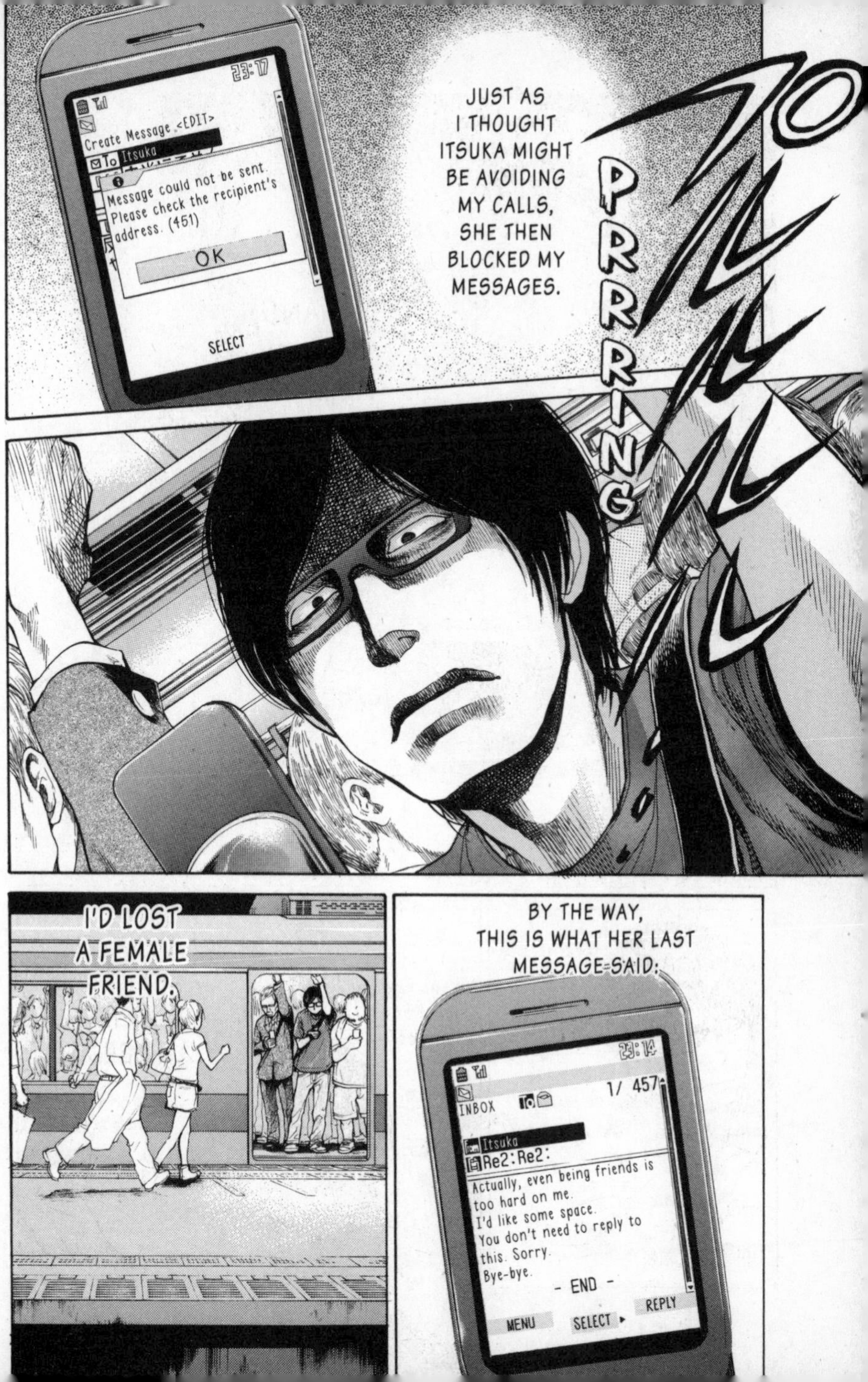
JUST AS I THOUGHT ITSUKA MIGHT BE AVOIDING MY CALLS, SHE THEN BLOCKED MY MESSAGES.
PRRRING
23:17
Create Message <EDIT>
To Itsuka
Message could not be sent. Please check the recipient's address. (451)
OK
SELECT
BY THE WAY, THIS IS WHAT HER LAST MESSAGE SAID:
23:14
1/ 457
INBOX
Itsuka
Re2:Re2:
Actually, even being friends is too hard on me.
I'd like some space.
You don't need to reply to this. Sorry.
Bye-bye.
- END -
REPLY
MENU
SELECT
I'D LOST A FEMALE FRIEND.

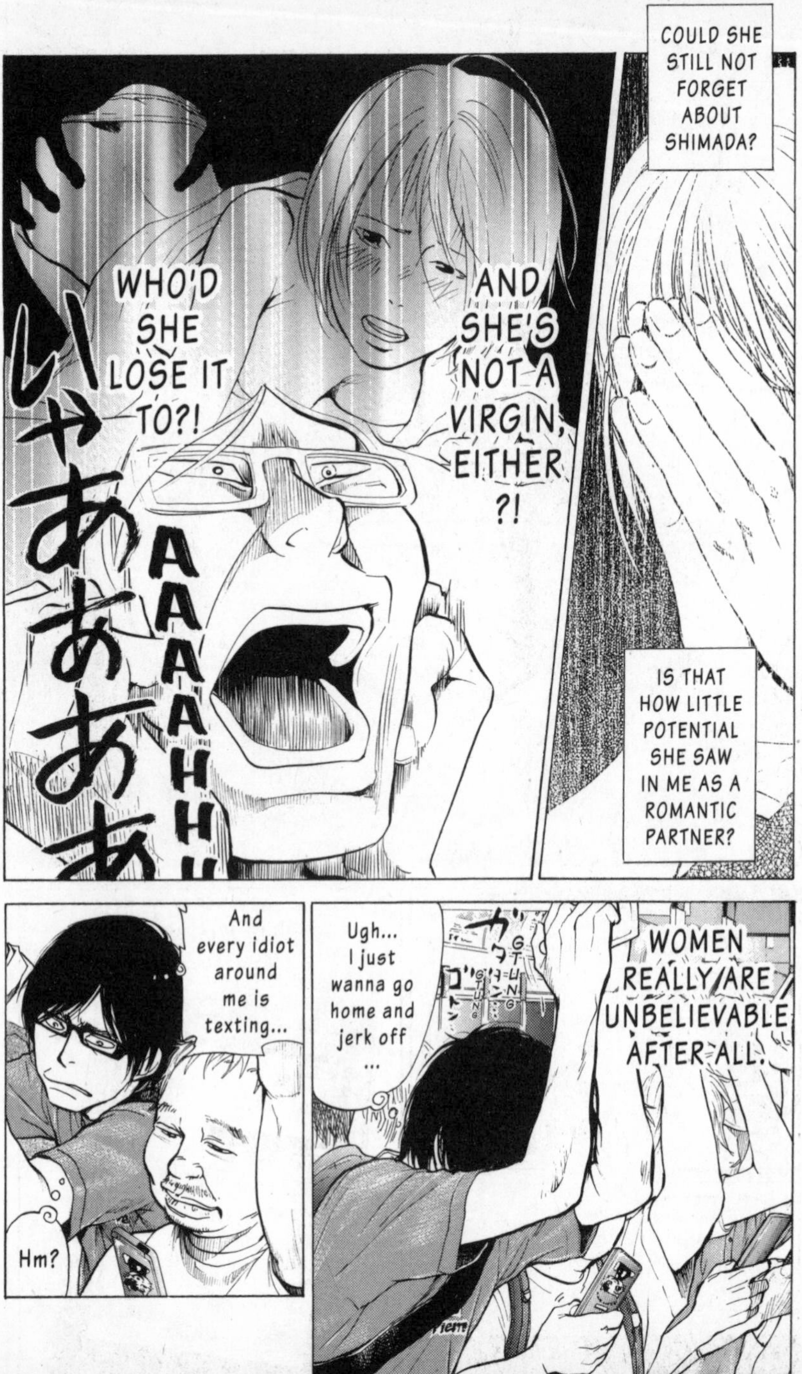
COULD SHE STILL NOT FORGET ABOUT SHIMADA?
IS THAT HOW LITTLE POTENTIAL SHE SAW IN ME AS A ROMANTIC PARTNER?
AND SHE'S NOT A VIRGIN, EITHER ?!
WHO'D SHE LOSE IT TO?!
いやあああ
AAAAHH
WOMEN REALLY ARE UNBELIEVABLE AFTER ALL.
ガタン
GTUNG
ゴトン
GTUNG
Ugh... I just wanna go home and jerk off ...
And every idiot around me is texting...
Hm?

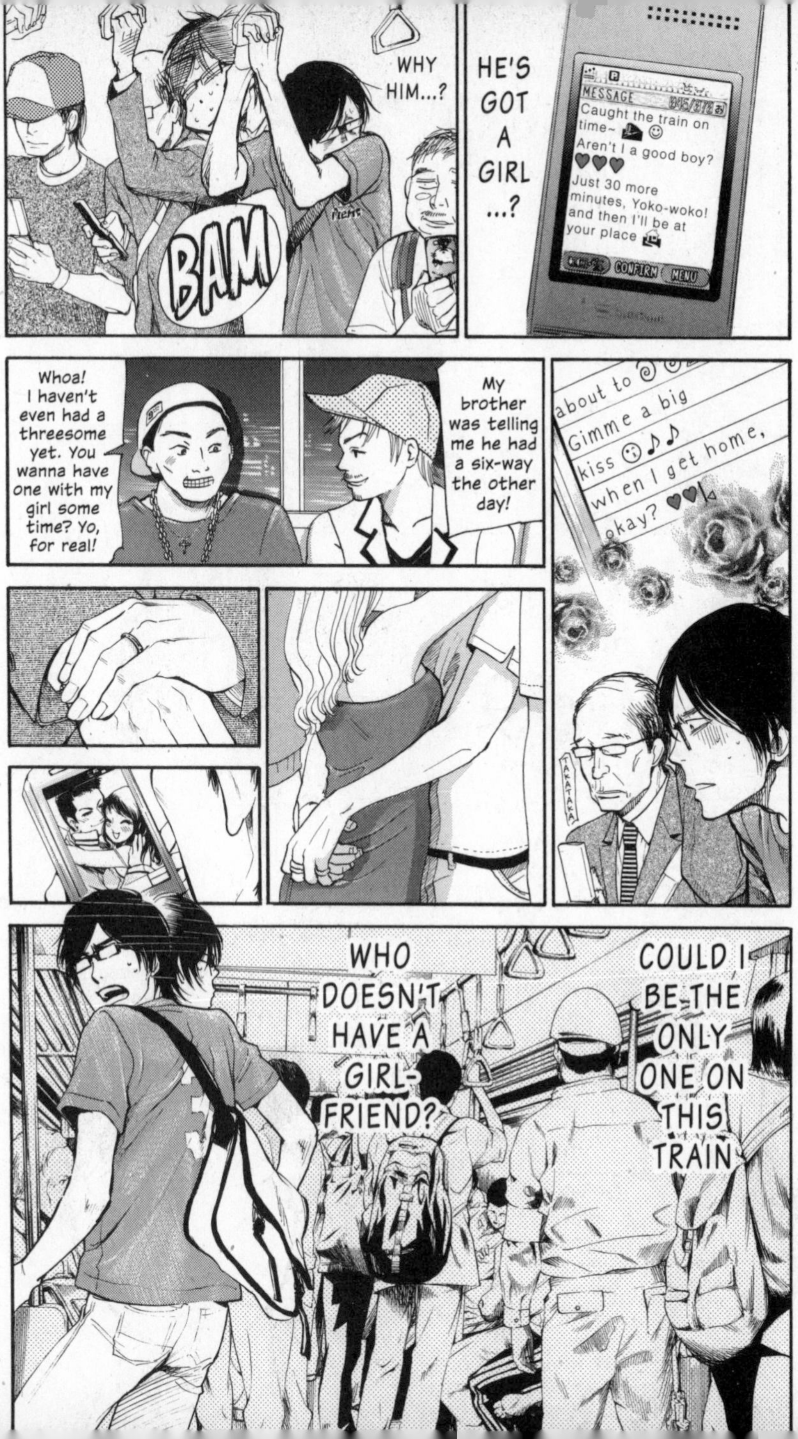
MESSAGE
Caught the train on time~ ☺
Aren't I a good boy? ♥♥♥
Just 30 more minutes, Yoko-woko! and then I'll be at your place
CONFIRM
MENU
HE'S GOT A GIRL ...?
WHY HIM...?
BAM
about to
Gimme a big kiss ♪♪
when I get home, okay? ♥♥
TAKATAKA
My brother was telling me he had a six-way the other day!
Whoa! I haven't even had a threesome yet. You wanna have one with my girl some time? Yo, for real!
COULD I BE THE ONLY ONE ON THIS TRAIN
WHO DOESN'T HAVE A GIRL-FRIEND?

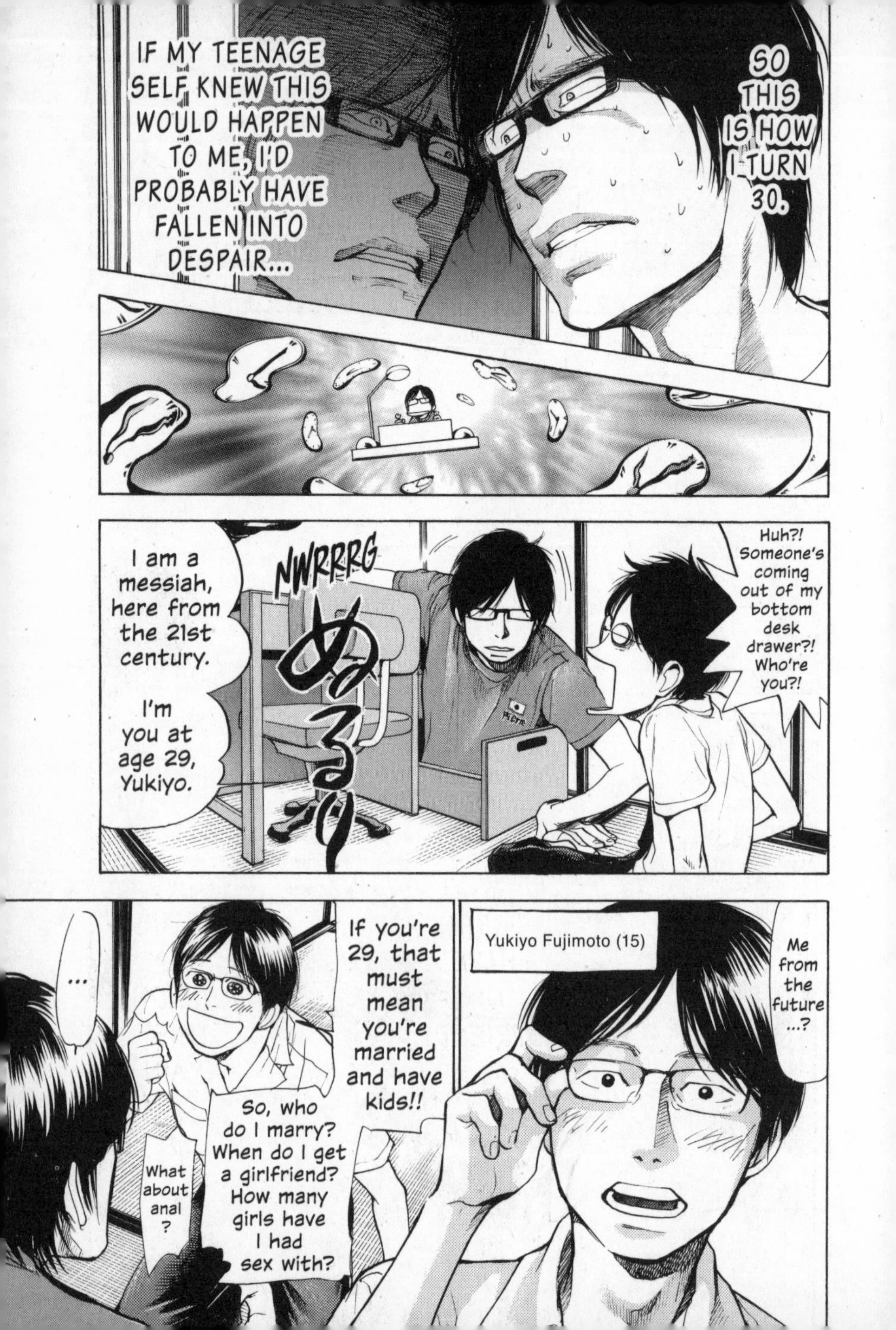
SO THIS IS HOW I TURN 30.
IF MY TEENAGE SELF KNEW THIS WOULD HAPPEN TO ME, I'D PROBABLY HAVE FALLEN INTO DESPAIR...
Huh?! Someone's coming out of my bottom desk drawer?! Who're you?!
NWRRRG
I am a messiah, here from the 21st century.
I'm you at age 29, Yukiyo.
めるり
Yukiyo Fujimoto (15)
Me from the future ...?
If you're 29, that must mean you're married and have kids!!
So, who do I marry? When do I get a girlfriend? How many girls have I had sex with?
...
What about anal ?

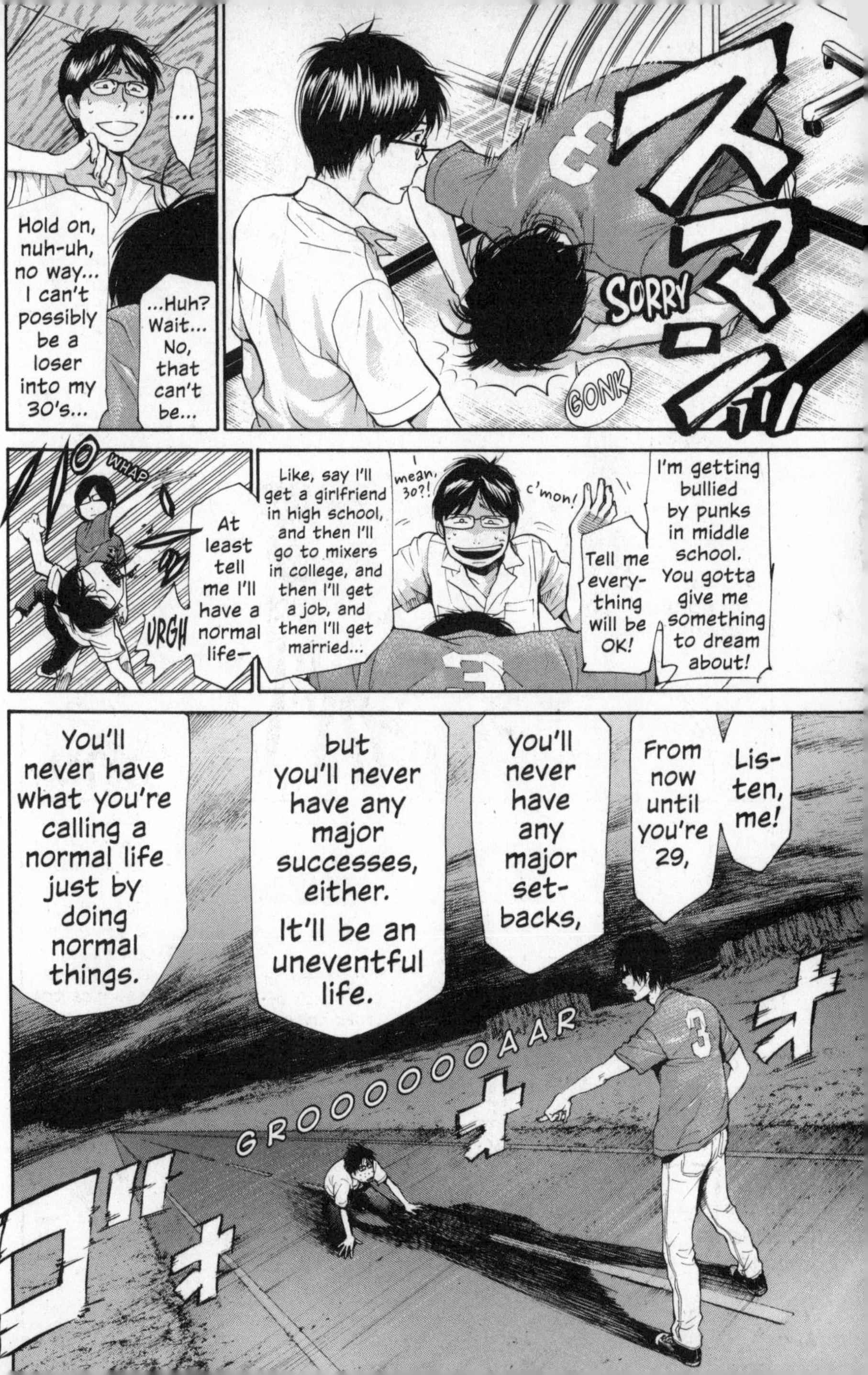
SORRY
GONK
...
...Huh? Wait... No, that can't be...
Hold on, nuh-uh, no way... I can't possibly be a loser into my 30's...
I'm getting bullied by punks in middle school. You gotta give me something to dream about!
Tell me every-thing will be OK!
c'mon!
I mean, 30?!
Like, say I'll get a girlfriend in high school, and then I'll go to mixers in college, and then I'll get a job, and then I'll get married...
At least tell me I'll have a normal life—
WHAP
URGH
Lis-ten, me!
From now until you're 29,
you'll never have any major set-backs,
but you'll never have any major successes, either.
It'll be an uneventful life.
You'll never have what you're calling a normal life just by doing normal things.
GROOOOOOOAAR

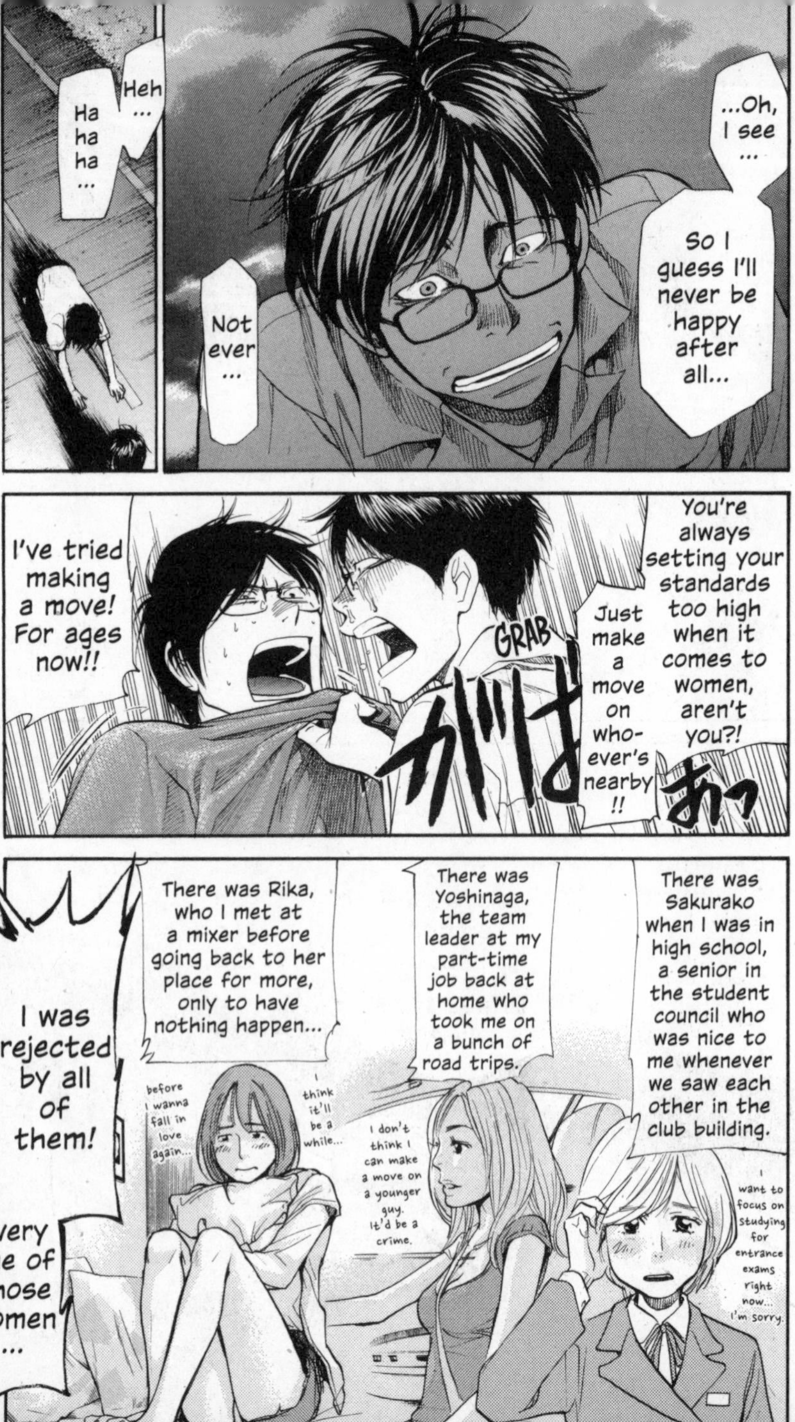
...Oh, I see...
So I guess I'll never be happy after all...
Not ever...
Heh...
Ha ha ha...
You're always setting your standards too high when it comes to women, aren't you?!
Just make a move on who-ever's nearby!!
GRAB
I've tried making a move! For ages now!!
There was Sakurako when I was in high school, a senior in the student council who was nice to me whenever we saw each other in the club building.
I want to focus on studying for entrance exams right now... I'm sorry.
There was Yoshinaga, the team leader at my part-time job back at home who took me on a bunch of road trips.
I don't think I can make a move on a younger guy. It'd be a crime.
There was Rika, who I met at a mixer before going back to her place for more, only to have nothing happen...
I think it'll be a while...
before I wanna fall in love again...
I was rejected by all of them!
Every one of those women...

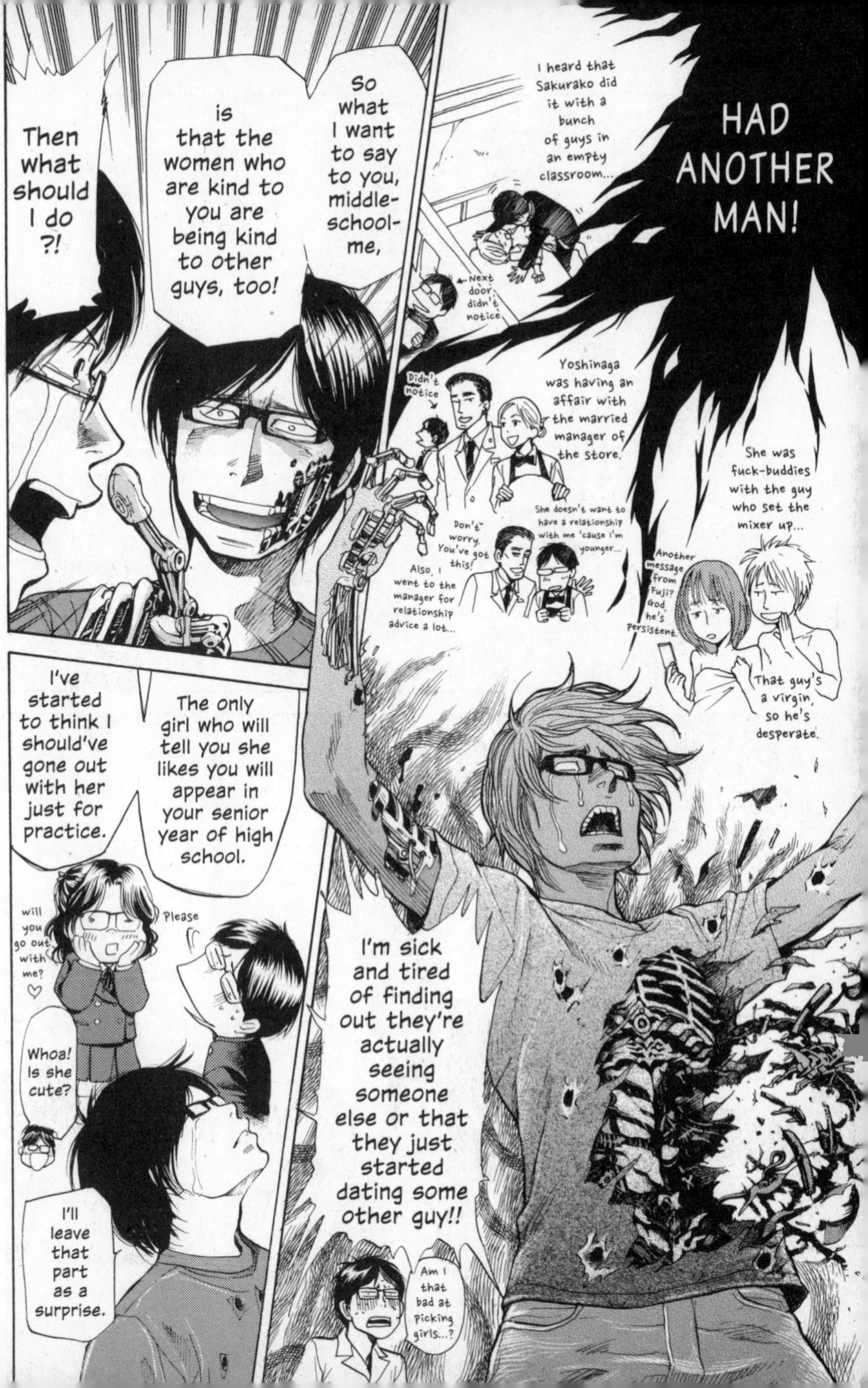

HAD ANOTHER MAN!
I heard that Sakurako did it with a bunch of guys in an empty classroom...
Next door didn't notice
Yoshinaga was having an affair with the married manager of the store.
Didn't notice
She was fuck-buddies with the guy who set the mixer up...
Another message from Fuji? God, he's persistent.
That guy's a virgin, so he's desperate.
She doesn't want to have a relationship with me 'cause I'm younger...
Don't worry. You've got this!
Also, I went to the manager for relationship advice a lot...
I'm sick and tired of finding out they're actually seeing someone else or that they just started dating some other guy!!
Am I that bad at picking girls...?
So what I want to say to you, middle-school-me,
is that the women who are kind to you are being kind to other guys, too!
Then what should I do?!
The only girl who will tell you she likes you will appear in your senior year of high school.
I've started to think I should've gone out with her just for practice.
Please
will you go out with me? ♡
Whoa! Is she cute?
I'll leave that part as a surprise.

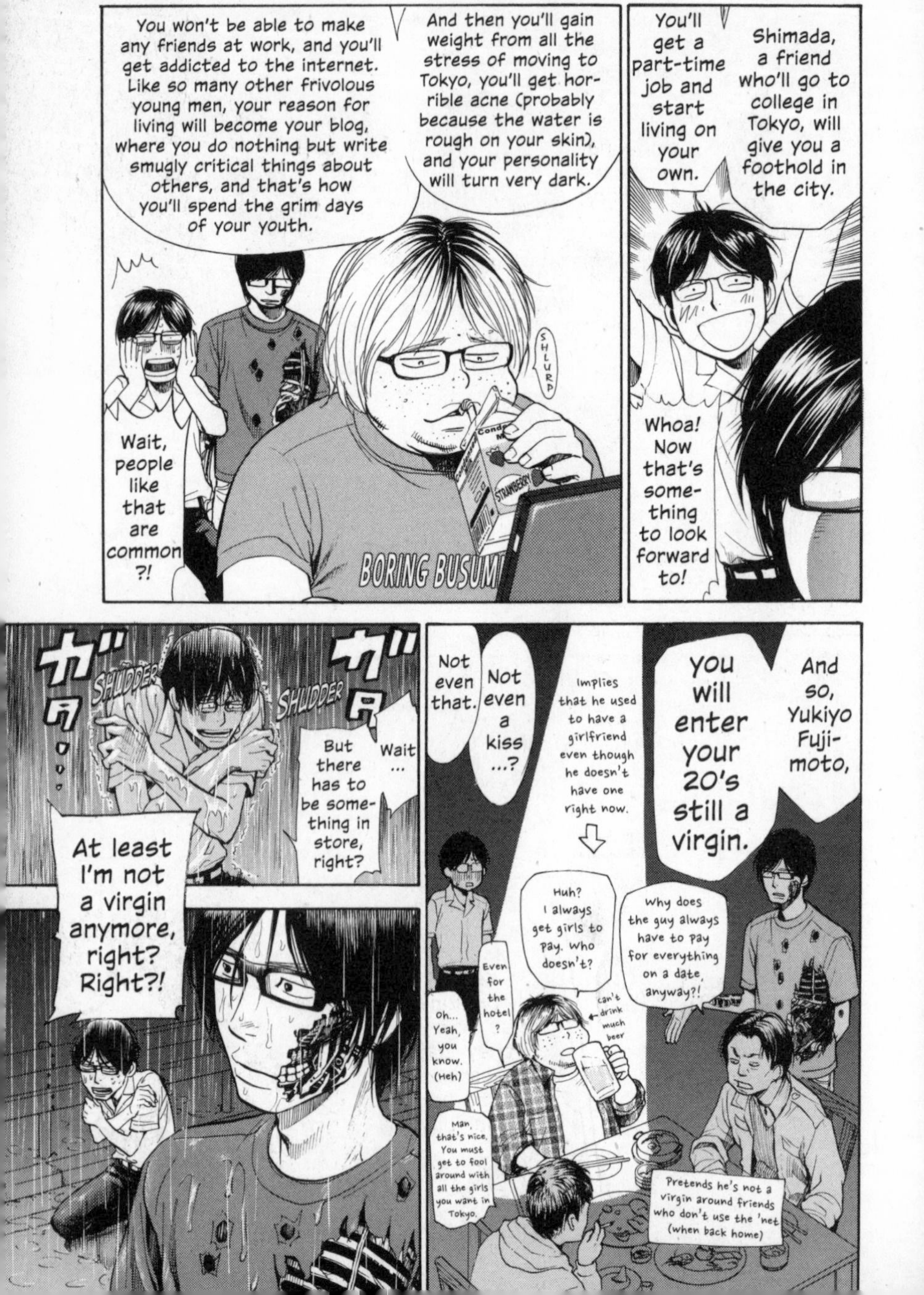
Shimada, a friend who'll go to college in Tokyo, will give you a foothold in the city.
You'll get a part-time job and start living on your own.
Whoa! Now that's something to look forward to!
You won't be able to make any friends at work, and you'll get addicted to the internet. Like so many other frivolous young men, your reason for living will become your blog, where you do nothing but write smugly critical things about others, and that's how you'll spend the grim days of your youth.
And then you'll gain weight from all the stress of moving to Tokyo, you'll get horrible acne (probably because the water is rough on your skin), and your personality will turn very dark.
SHLURP
STRAWBERRY
BORING BUSUMI
Wait, people like that are common?!
And so, Yukiyo Fujimoto,
you will enter your 20's still a virgin.
Implies that he used to have a girlfriend even though he doesn't have one right now.
Not even a kiss ...?
Not even that.
Why does the guy always have to pay for everything on a date, anyway?!
Huh? I always get girls to pay. Who doesn't?
Even for the hotel?
can't drink much beer
Oh... Yeah, you know. (Heh)
Man, that's nice. You must get to fool around with all the girls you want in Tokyo.
Pretends he's not a virgin around friends who don't use the 'net (when back home)
Wait ...
But there has to be something in store, right?
ガタ
SHUDDER
ガタ
SHUDDER
At least I'm not a virgin anymore, right? Right?!

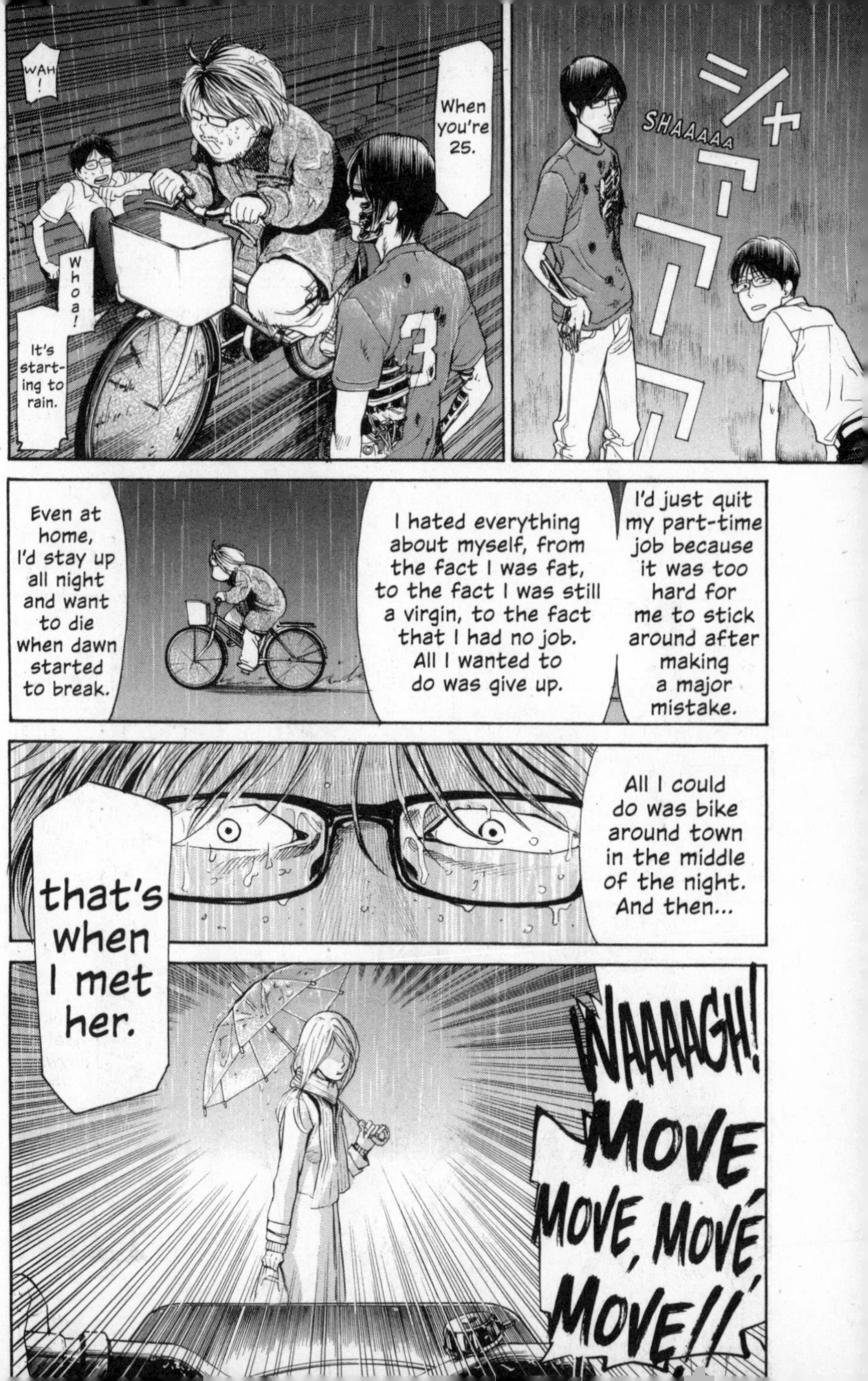
SHAAAAA
When you're 25.
WAH!
Whoa!
It's starting to rain.
I'd just quit my part-time job because it was too hard for me to stick around after making a major mistake.
I hated everything about myself, from the fact I was fat, to the fact I was still a virgin, to the fact that I had no job. All I wanted to do was give up.
Even at home, I'd stay up all night and want to die when dawn started to break.
All I could do was bike around town in the middle of the night. And then...
that's when I met her.
WAAAAGH! MOVE
MOVE, MOVE, MOVE!!

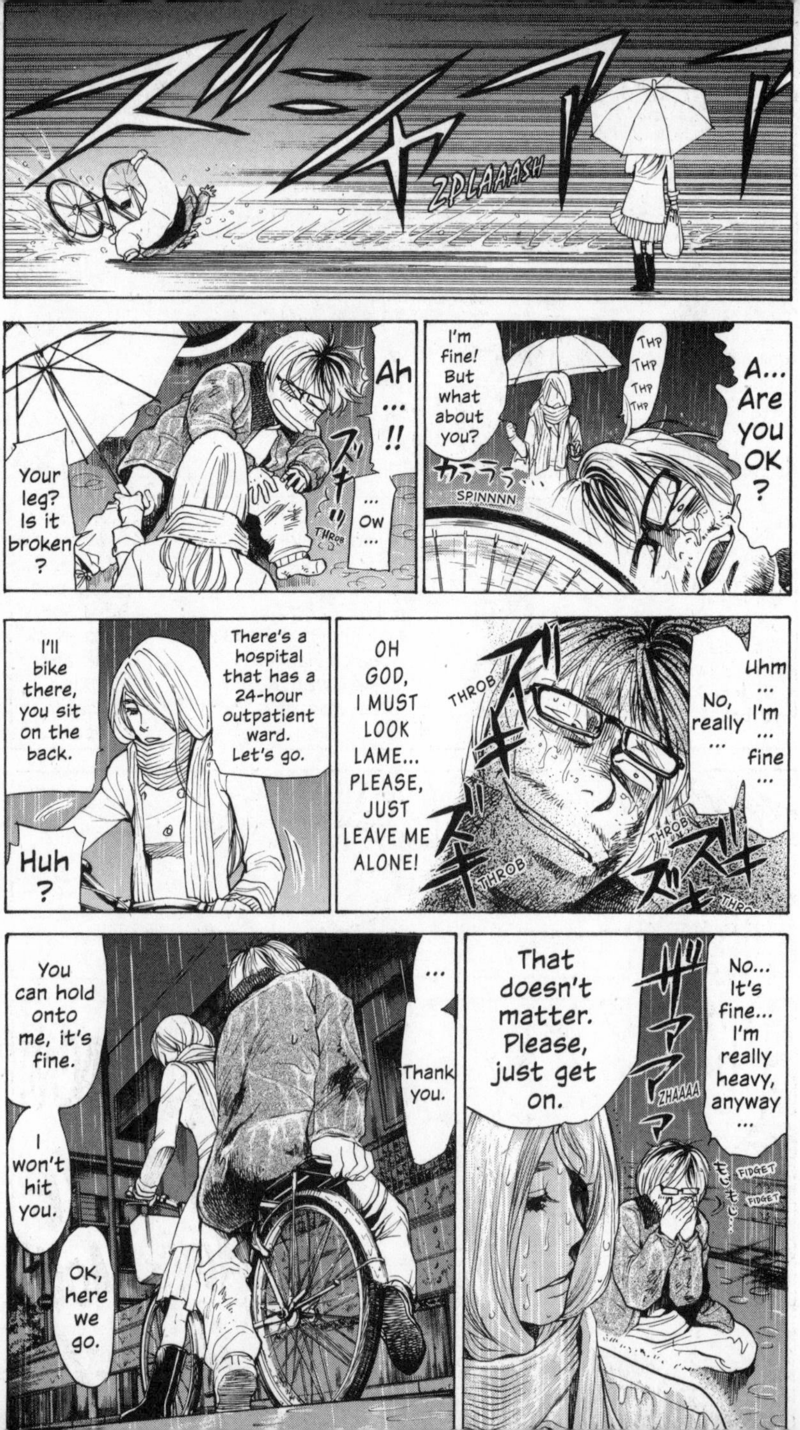
ZPLAAASH
A... Are you OK?
THP THP THP THP
I'm fine! But what about you?
SPINNNN
Ah ...!!
... Ow ...
THROB
Your leg? Is it broken?
Uhm ... I'm ... fine ...
No, really ...
THROB
THROB
THROB
OH GOD, I MUST LOOK LAME... PLEASE, JUST LEAVE ME ALONE!
There's a hospital that has a 24-hour outpatient ward. Let's go.
I'll bike there, you sit on the back.
Huh?
No... It's fine... I'm really heavy, anyway ...
ZHAAAA
That doesn't matter. Please, just get on.
FIDGET
FIDGET
...
Thank you.
You can hold onto me, it's fine.
I won't hit you.
OK, here we go.

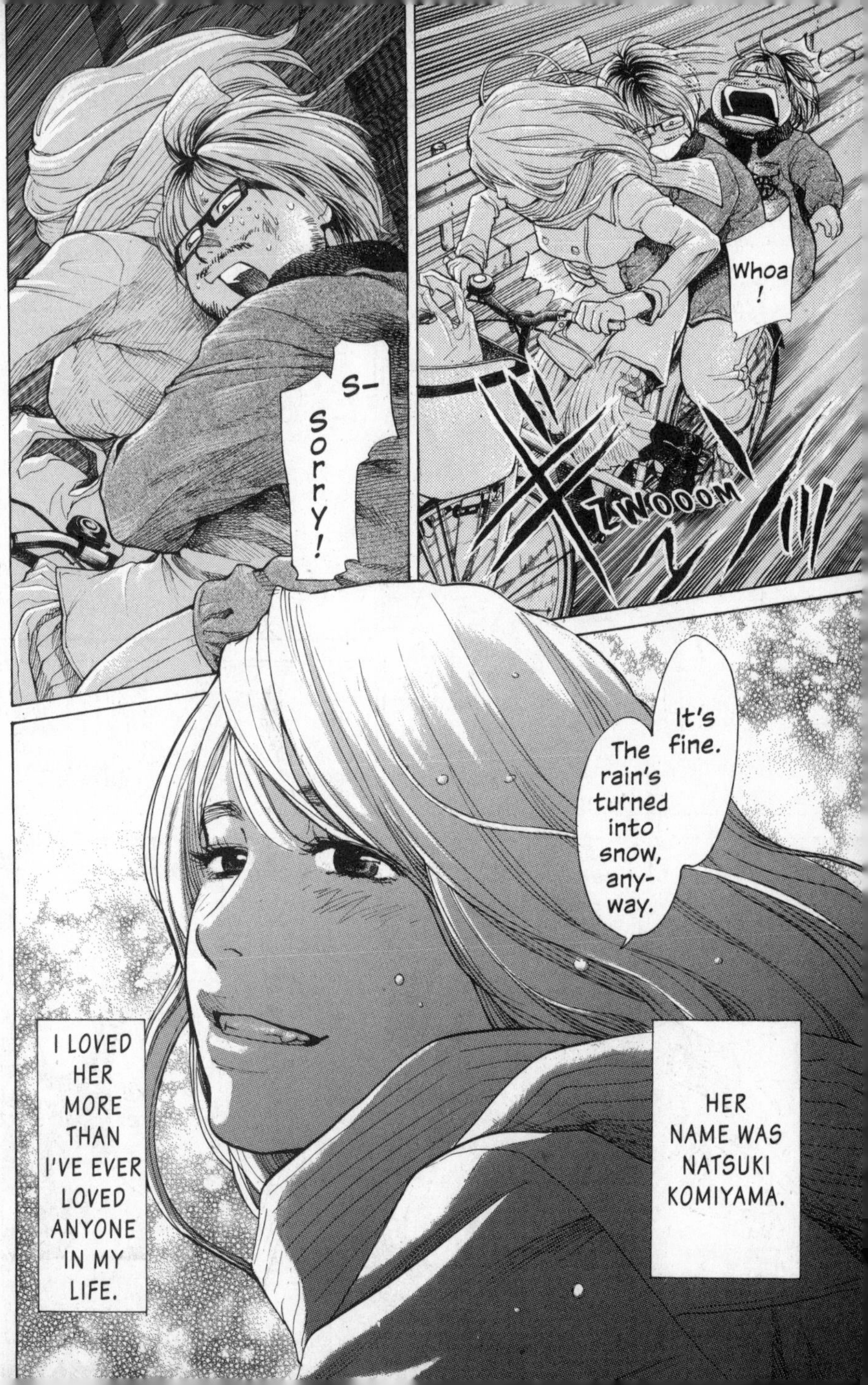
Whoa!
ZWOOOM
S-Sorry!
It's fine. The rain's turned into snow, anyway.
HER NAME WAS NATSUKI KOMIYAMA.
I LOVED HER MORE THAN I'VE EVER LOVED ANYONE IN MY LIFE.

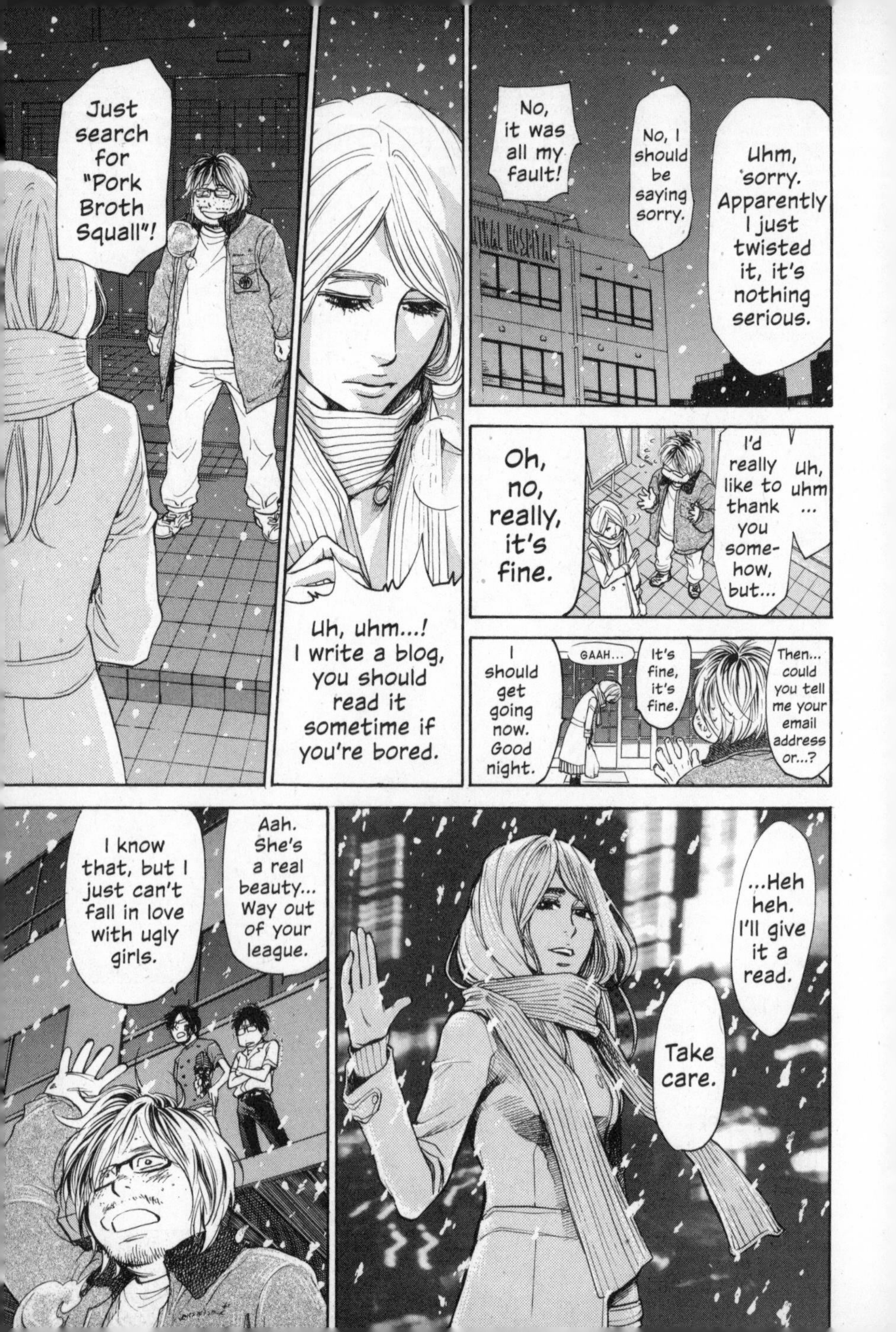

Uhm, sorry. Apparently I just twisted it, it's nothing serious.
No, I should be saying sorry.
No, it was all my fault!
Uh, uhm ...
I'd really like to thank you somehow, but...
Oh, no, really, it's fine.
Then... could you tell me your email address or...?
It's fine, it's fine.
GAAH...
I should get going now. Good night.
Uh, uhm...! I write a blog, you should read it sometime if you're bored.
Just search for "Pork Broth Squall"!
...Heh heh. I'll give it a read.
Take care.
Aah. She's a real beauty... Way out of your league.
I know that, but I just can't fall in love with ugly girls.

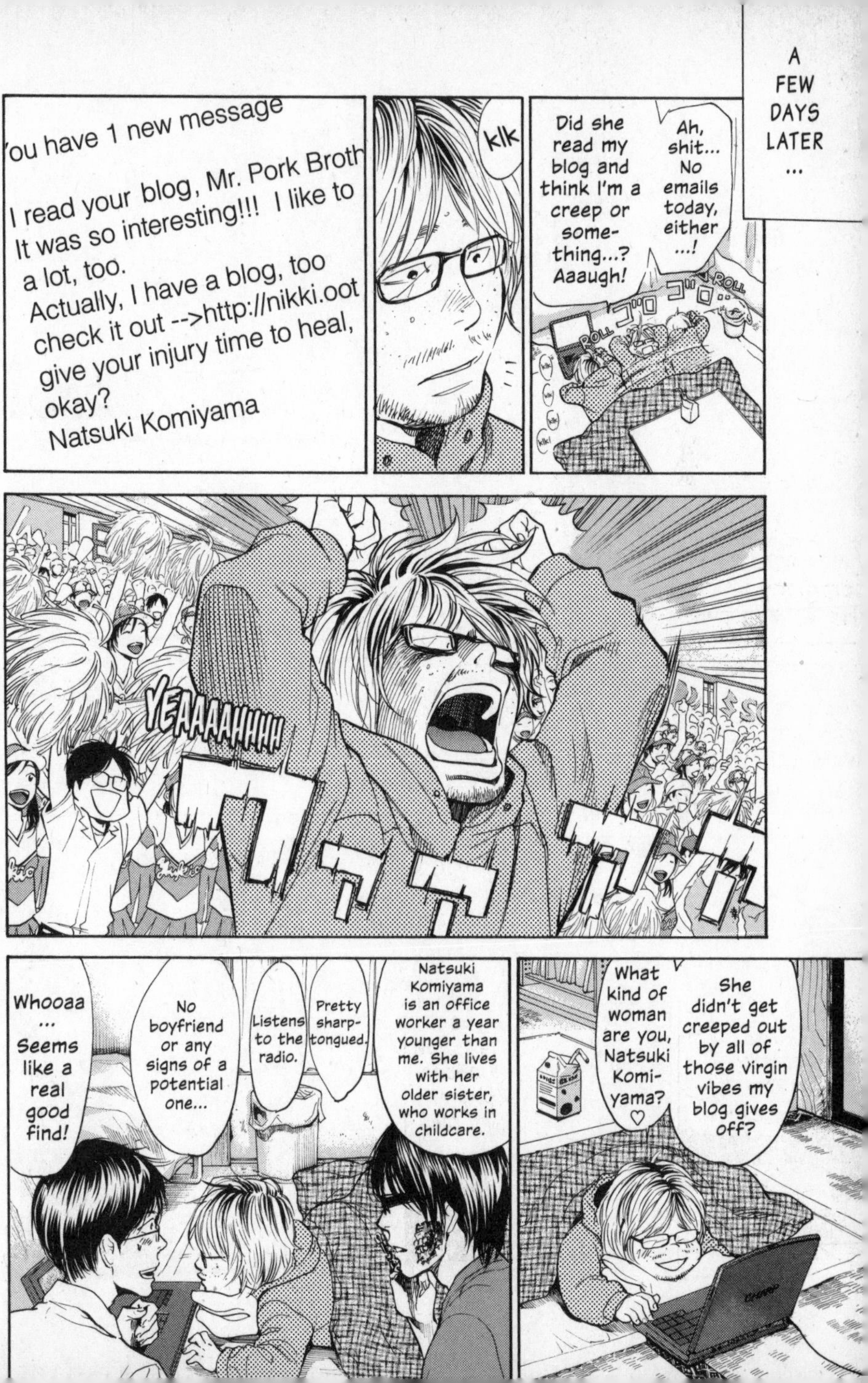
A FEW DAYS LATER ...
Ah, shit... No emails today, either ...!
Did she read my blog and think I'm a creep or some-thing...? Aaaugh!
ROLL
ROLL
klk
klk
'ou have 1 new message
I read your blog, Mr. Pork Broth
It was so interesting!!! I like to
a lot, too.
Actually, I have a blog, too
check it out -->http://nikki.oot
give your injury time to heal,
okay?
Natsuki Komiyama
YEAAAAHHHH
She didn't get creeped out by all of those virgin vibes my blog gives off?
What kind of woman are you, Natsuki Komi-yama? ♡
Natsuki Komiyama is an office worker a year younger than me. She lives with her older sister, who works in childcare.
Pretty sharp-tongued.
Listens to the radio.
No boyfriend or any signs of a potential one...
Whooaa ... Seems like a real good find!

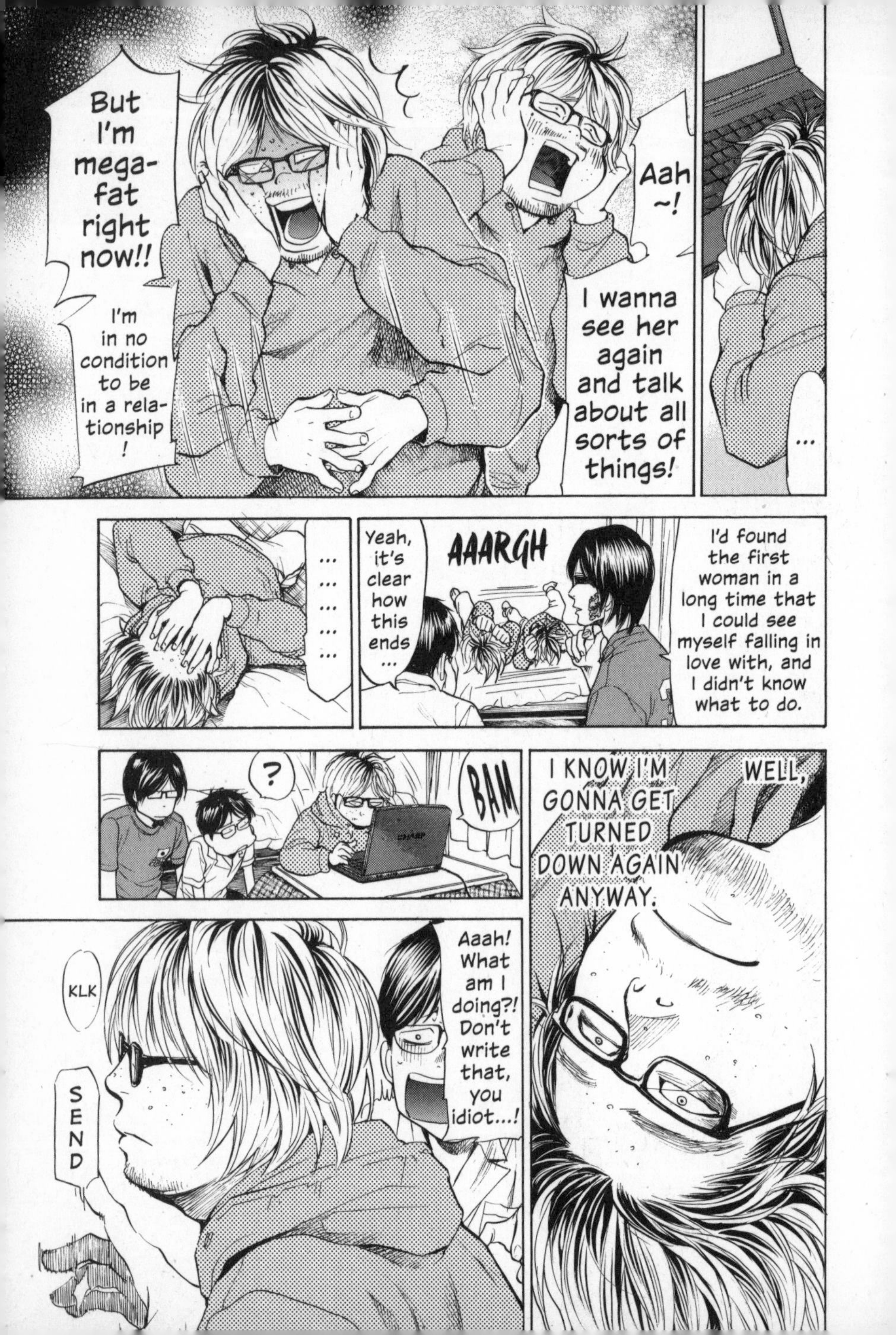
...
Aah ~!
I wanna see her again and talk about all sorts of things!
But I'm mega-fat right now!!
I'm in no condition to be in a relationship!
I'd found the first woman in a long time that I could see myself falling in love with, and I didn't know what to do.
AAARGH
Yeah, it's clear how this ends ...
... ...
WELL,
I KNOW I'M GONNA GET TURNED DOWN AGAIN ANYWAY.
BAM
?
Aaah! What am I doing?! Don't write that, you idiot...!
KLK
SEND

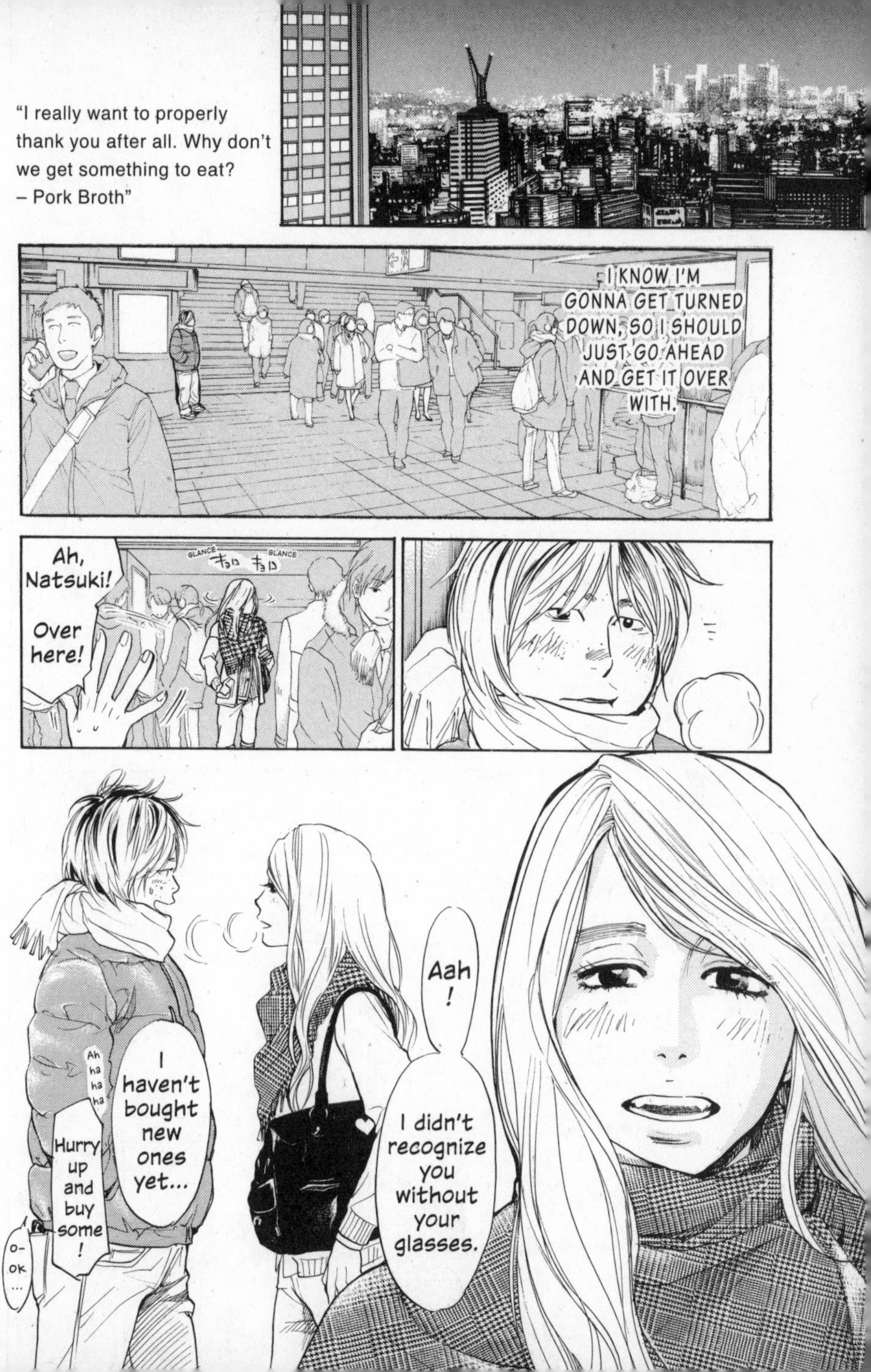
"I really want to properly thank you after all. Why don't we get something to eat? – Pork Broth"
I KNOW I'M GONNA GET TURNED DOWN, SO I SHOULD JUST GO AHEAD AND GET IT OVER WITH.
GLANCE
GLANCE
Ah, Natsuki!
Over here!
Aah!
I didn't recognize you without your glasses.
I haven't bought new ones yet...
Ah ha ha ha
Hurry up and buy some!
O-ok...

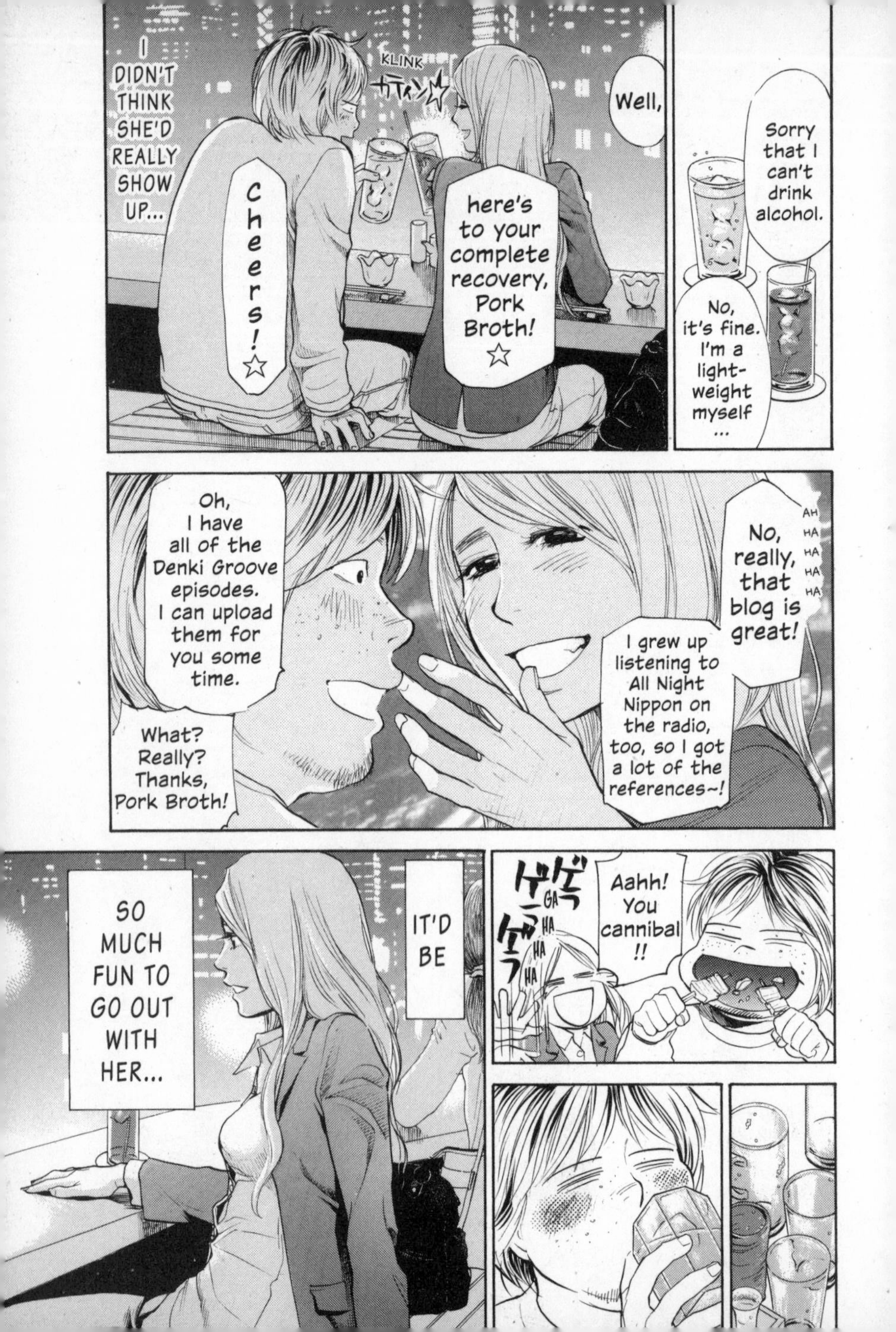
Sorry that I can't drink alcohol.
No, it's fine. I'm a light-weight myself...
Well,
here's to your complete recovery, Pork Broth! ☆
KLINK
カティン☆
Cheers!☆
I DIDN'T THINK SHE'D REALLY SHOW UP...
No, really, that blog is great!
AH HA HA HA HA
I grew up listening to All Night Nippon on the radio, too, so I got a lot of the references~!
Oh, I have all of the Denki Groove episodes. I can upload them for you some time.
What? Really? Thanks, Pork Broth!
Aahh! You cannibal!!
GA HA HA HA
IT'D BE
SO MUCH FUN TO GO OUT WITH HER...

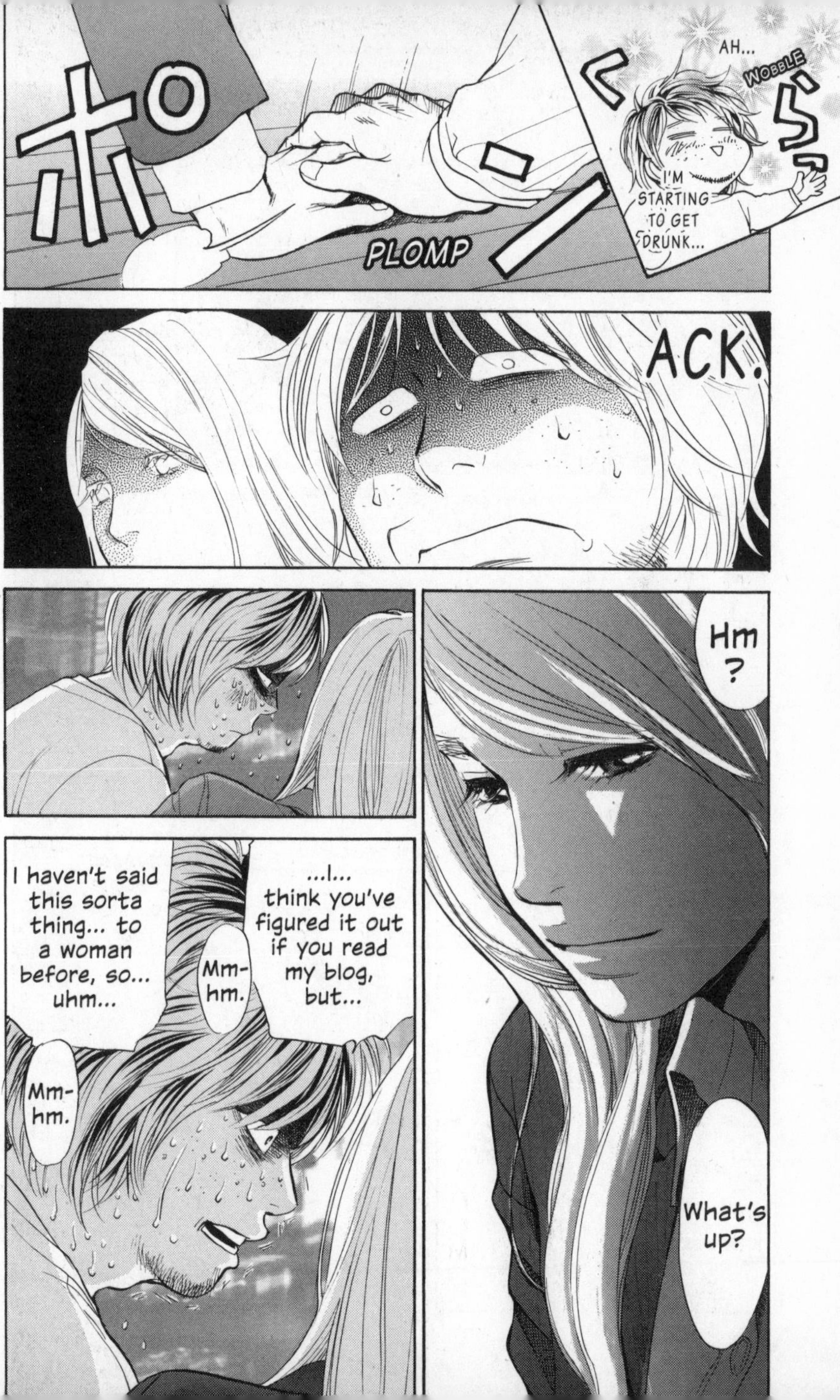
AH...
WOBBLE
I'M STARTING TO GET DRUNK...
PLOMP
ACK.
Hm?
What's up?
...I... think you've figured it out if you read my blog, but...
Mm-hm.
I haven't said this sorta thing... to a woman before, so... uhm...
Mm-hm.

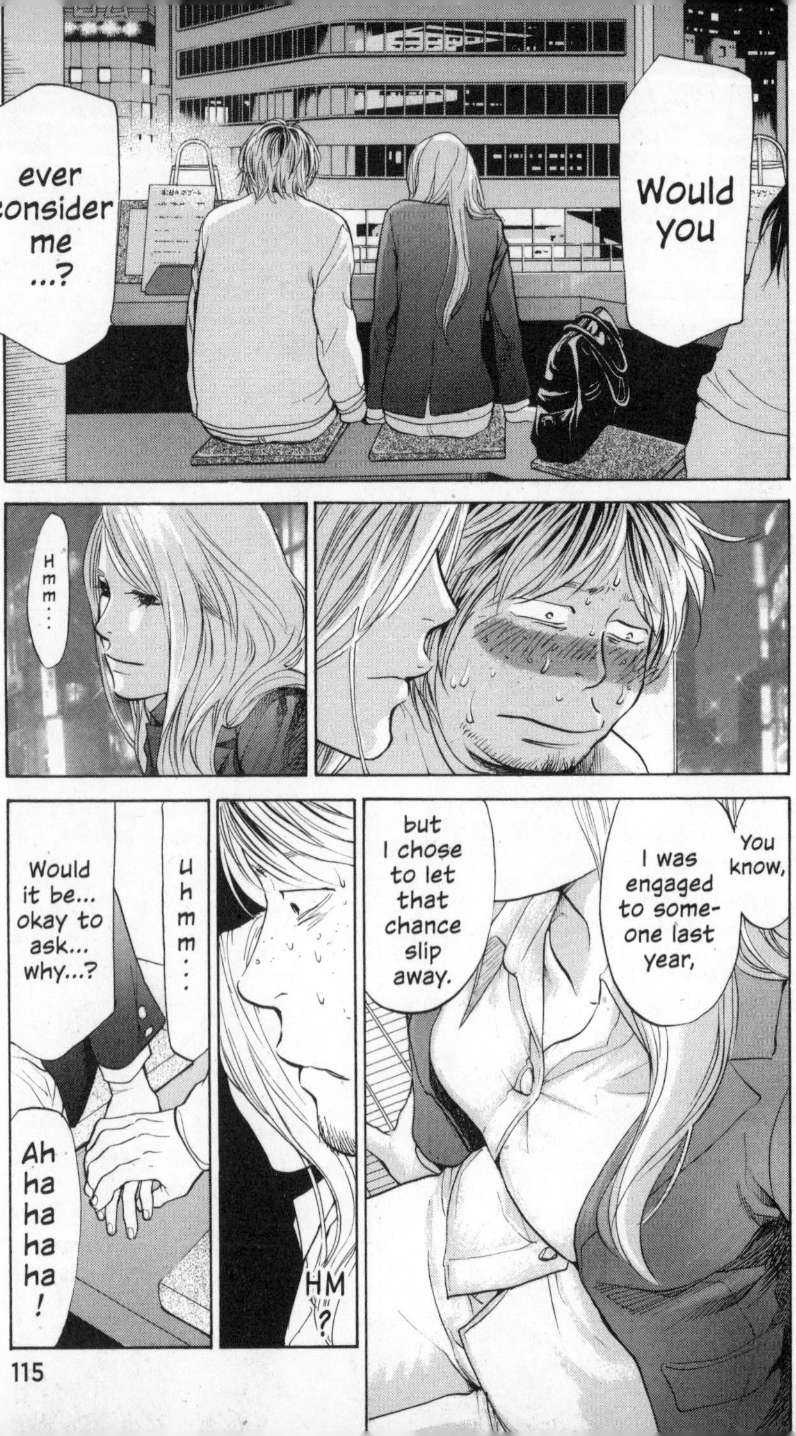
Would you
ever consider me ...?
Hmm...
You know,
I was engaged to some-one last year,
but I chose to let that chance slip away.
HM?
Uhmm...
Would it be... okay to ask... why...?
Ah ha ha ha ha!

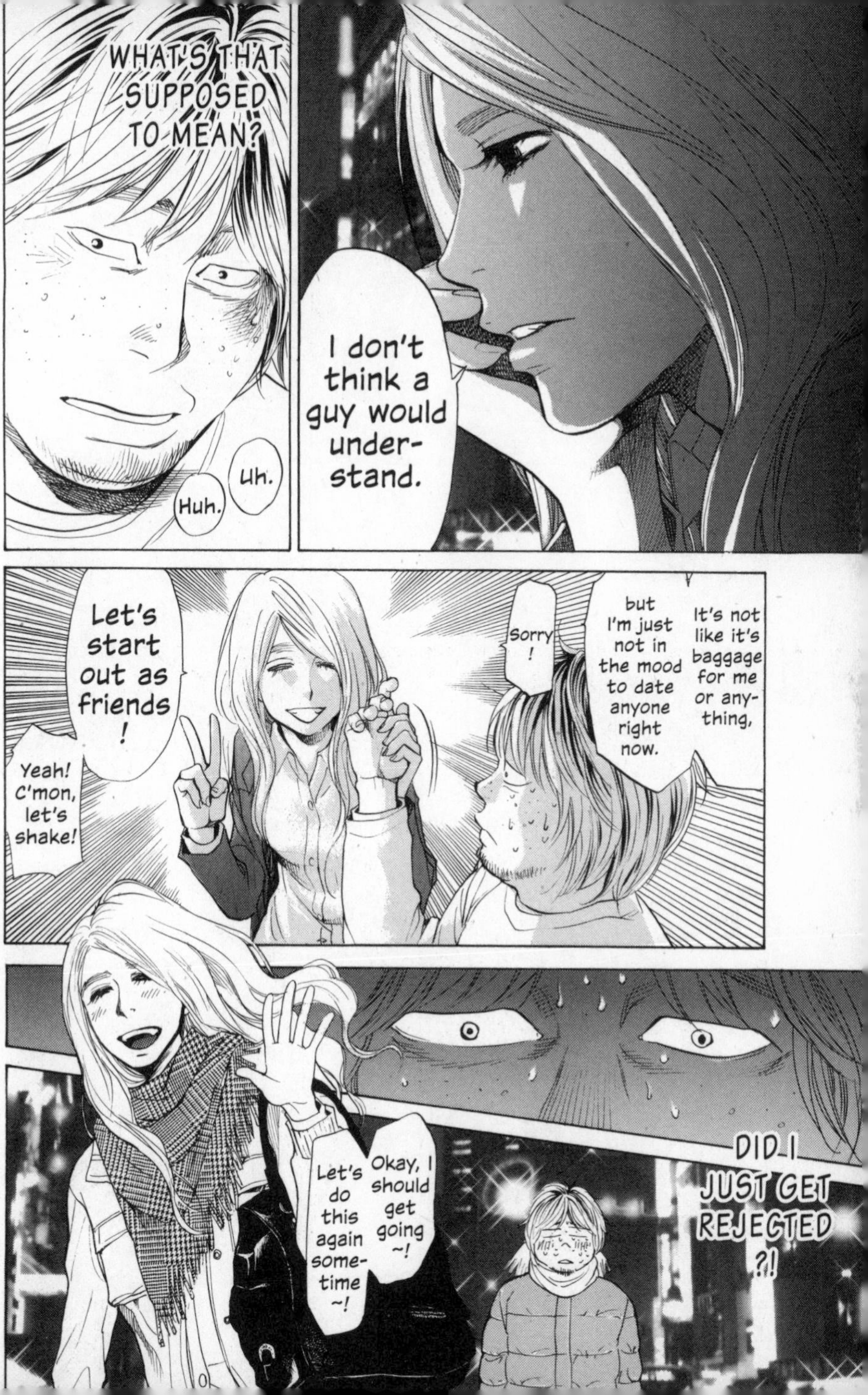
I don't think a guy would under-stand.
WHAT'S THAT SUPPOSED TO MEAN?
Uh.
Huh.
It's not like it's baggage for me or any-thing,
but I'm just not in the mood to date anyone right now.
Sorry!
Let's start out as friends!
Yeah! C'mon, let's shake!
DID I JUST GET REJECTED?!
Okay, I should get going~!
Let's do this again some-time~!

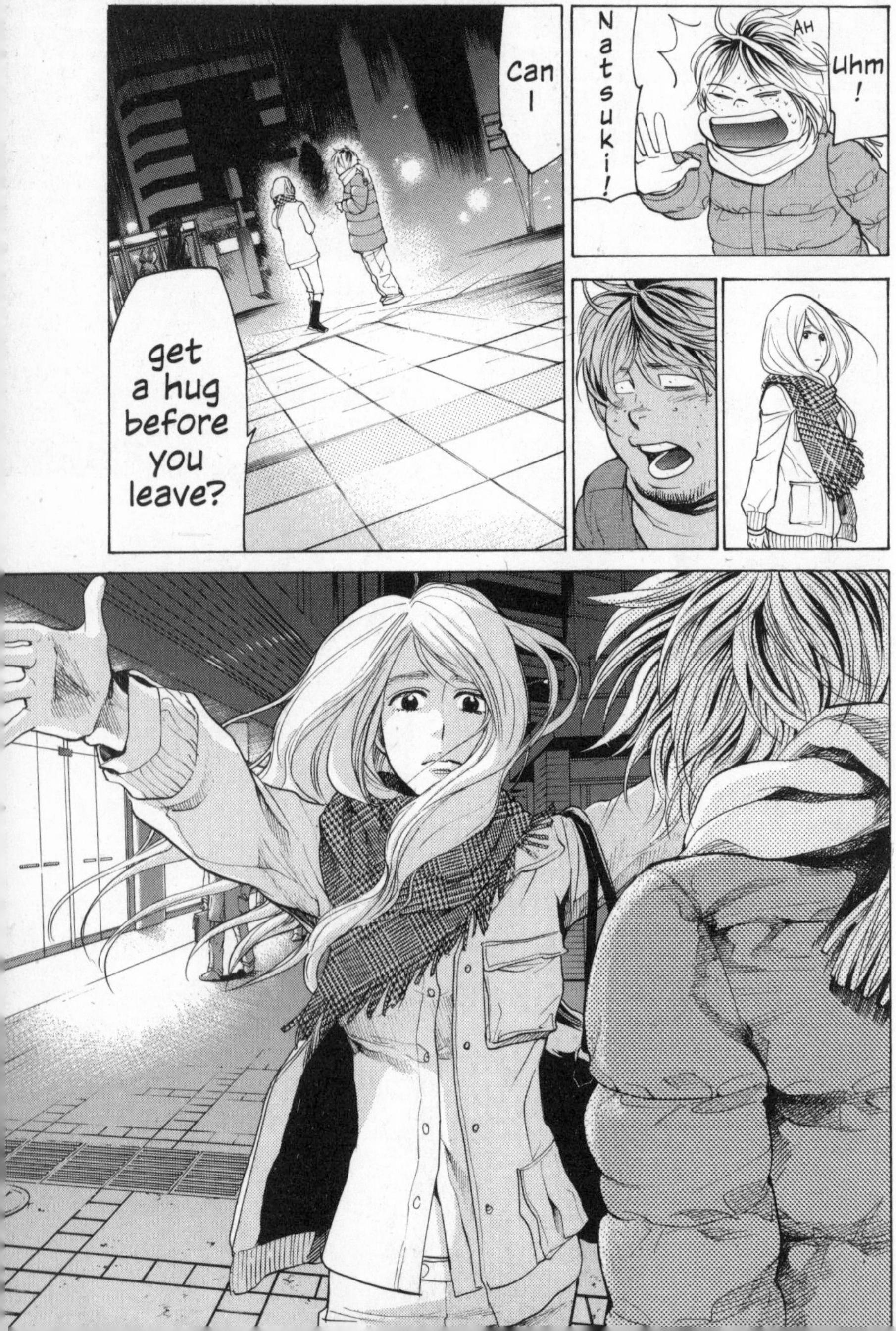
Uhm!
AH
Natsuki!
Can I
get a hug before you leave?

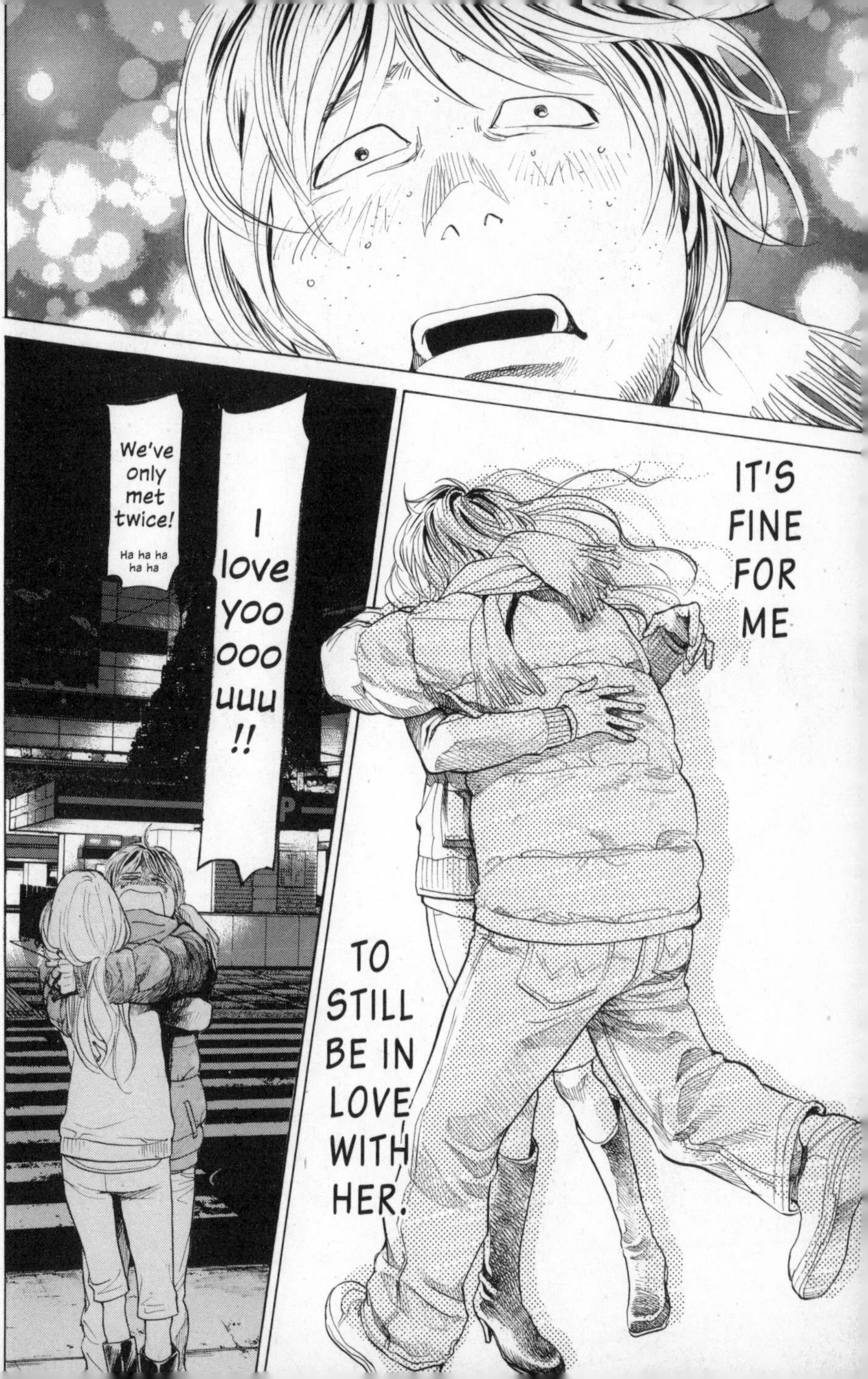
IT'S FINE FOR ME
TO STILL BE IN LOVE WITH HER.
I love yoooooouuu!!
We've only met twice!
Ha ha ha ha ha

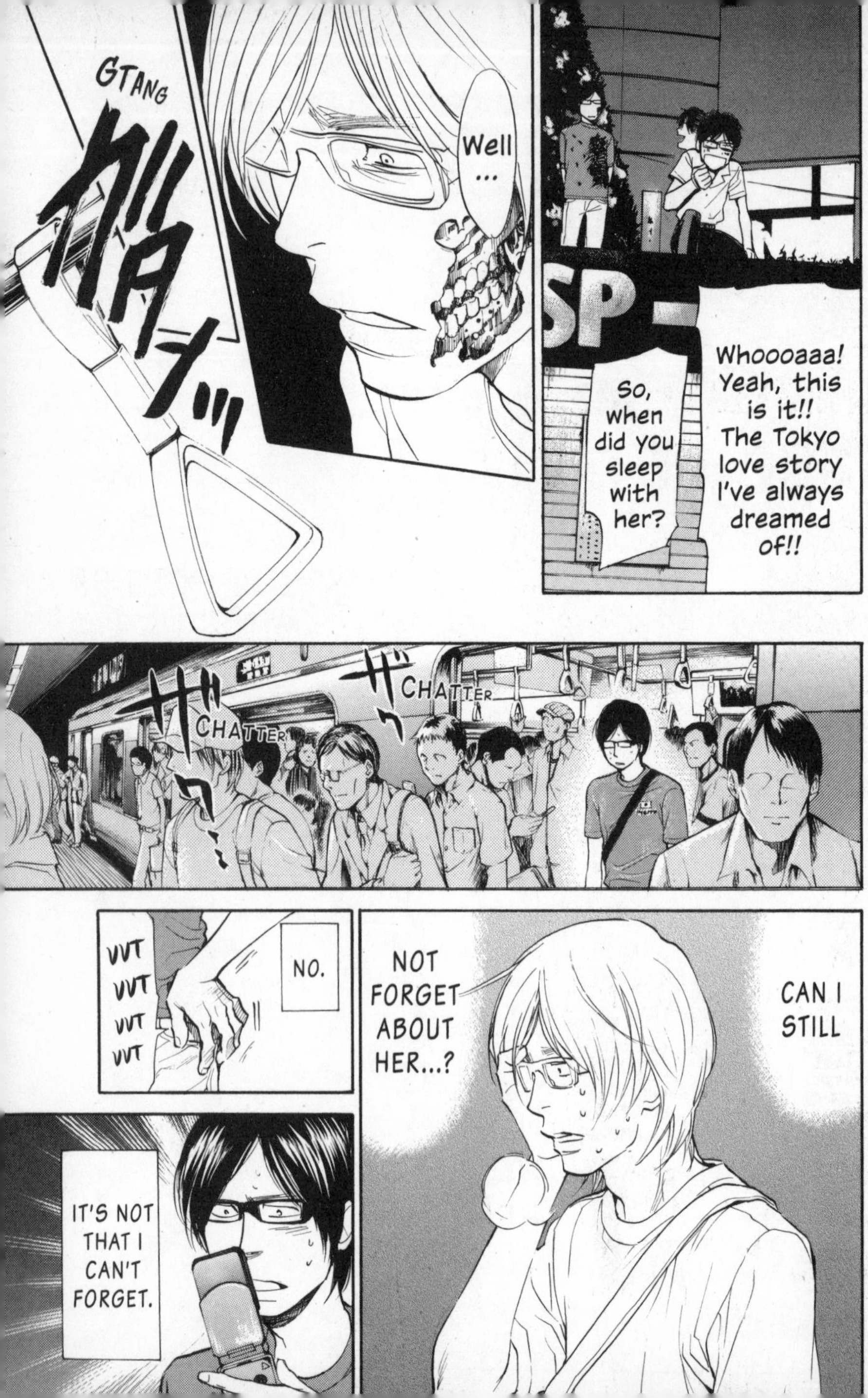
Whoooaaa! Yeah, this is it!! The Tokyo love story I've always dreamed of!!
So, when did you sleep with her?
Well ...
GTANG
CHATTER
CHATTER
CAN I STILL
NOT FORGET ABOUT HER...?
NO.
VVT VVT VVT VVT
IT'S NOT THAT I CAN'T FORGET.

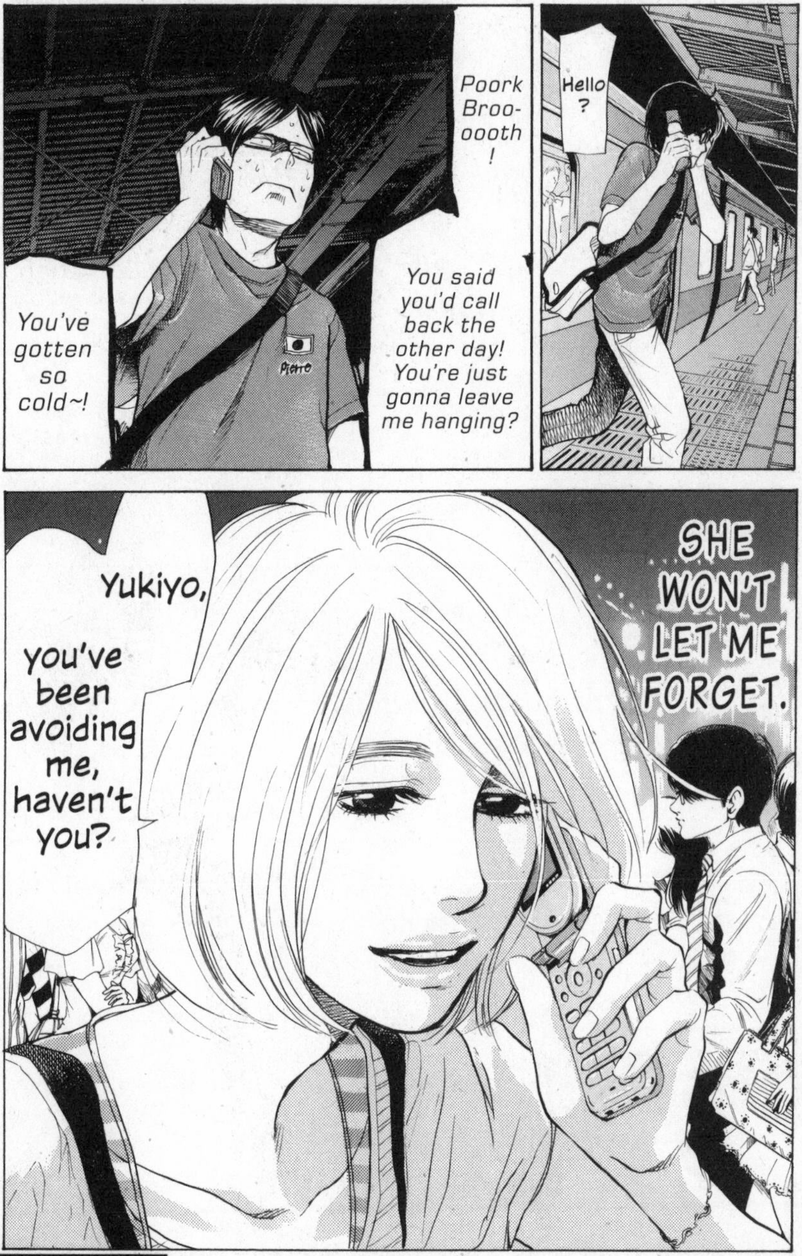
Hello?
Poork Broo-oooth!
You said you'd call back the other day! You're just gonna leave me hanging?
You've gotten so cold~!
SHE WON'T LET ME FORGET.
Yukiyo,
you've been avoiding me, haven't you?

chapter 4 ♥ END

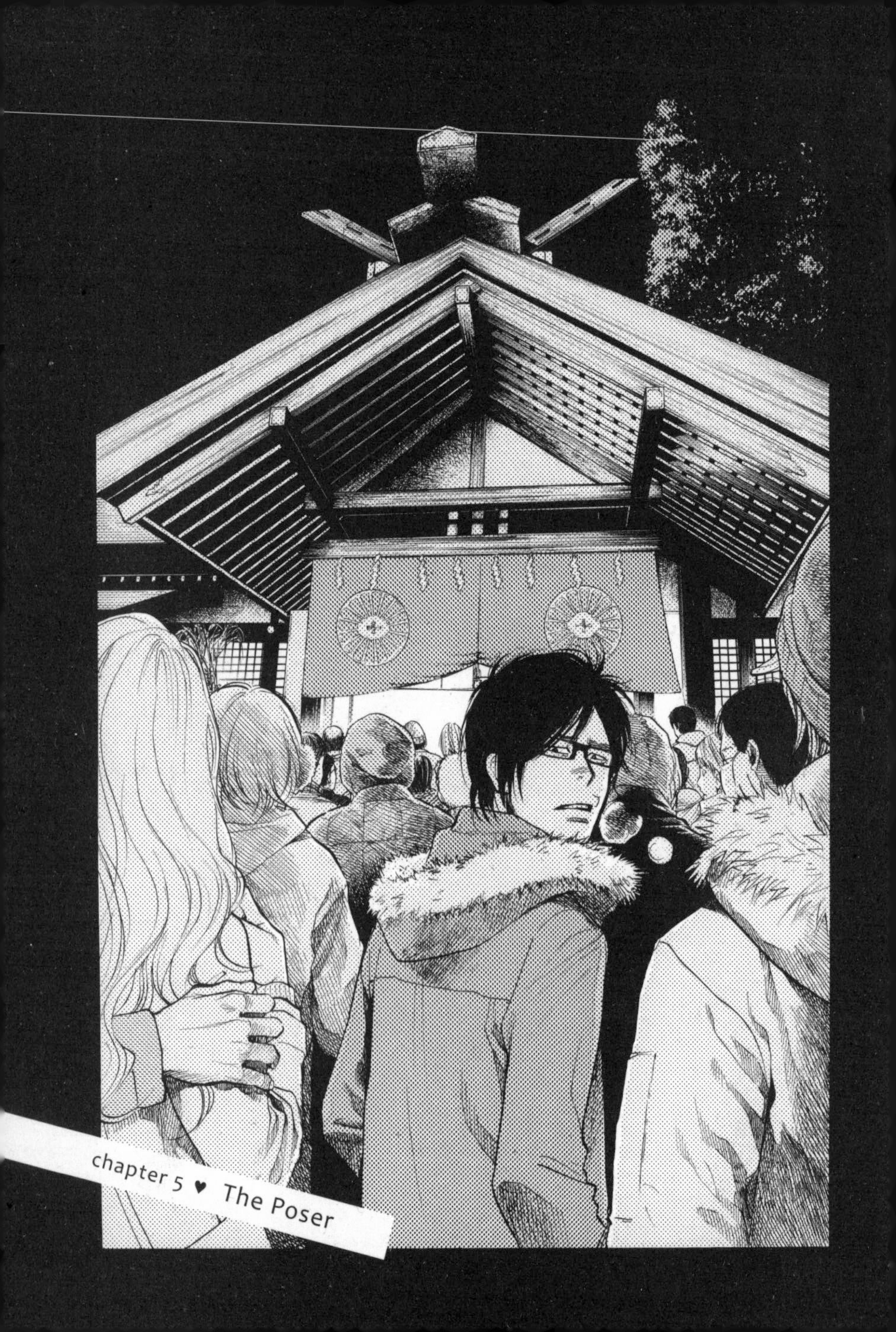
chapter 5 ♥ The Poser

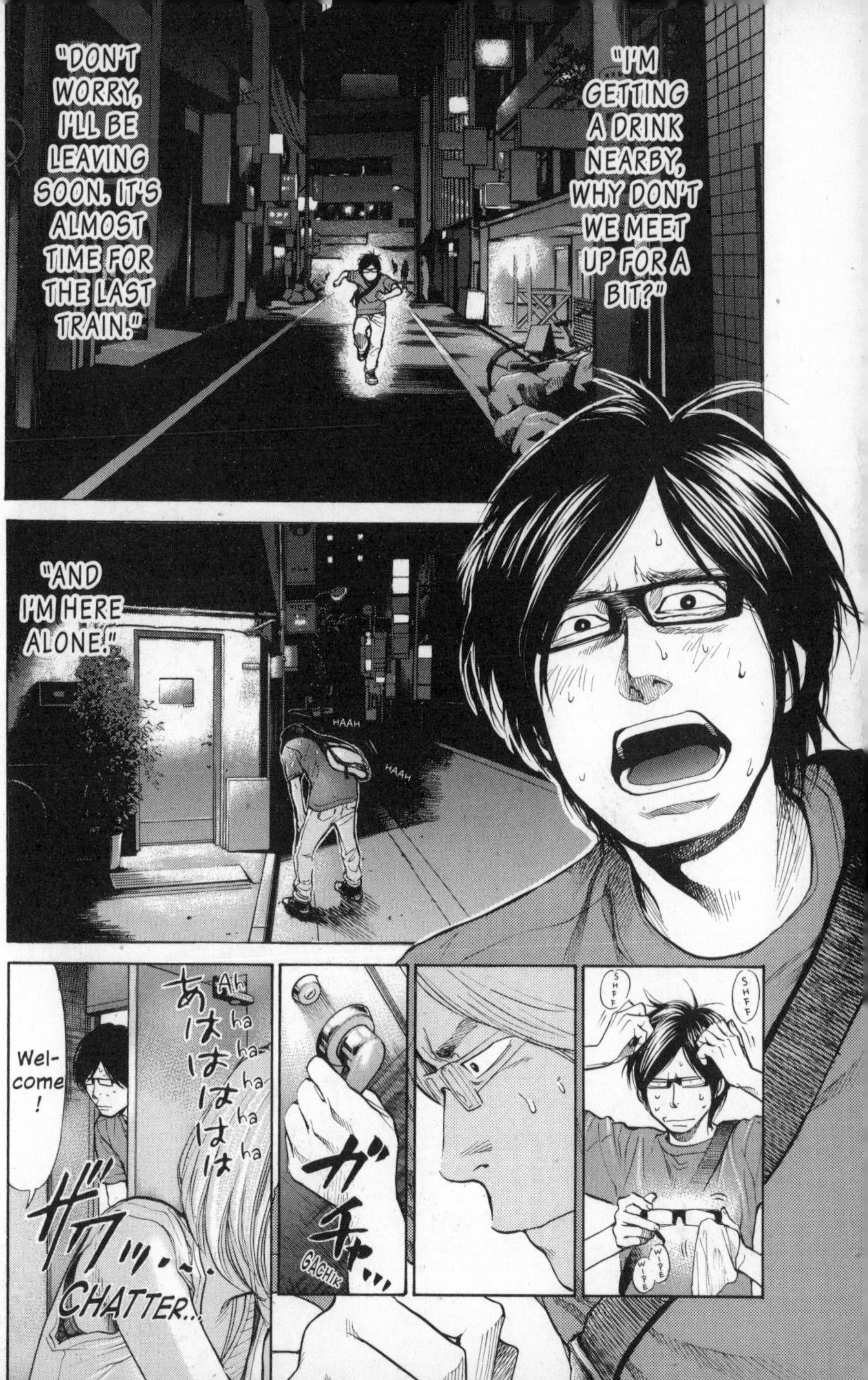
"I'M GETTING A DRINK NEARBY, WHY DON'T WE MEET UP FOR A BIT?"
"DON'T WORRY, I'LL BE LEAVING SOON. IT'S ALMOST TIME FOR THE LAST TRAIN."
"AND I'M HERE ALONE."
HAAH
HAAH
SHFF
SHFF
WIPE
WIPE
ガチャ…
GACHIK
あはははは
Ah ha ha ha ha ha ha
Wel-come!
ザワッ・・・
CHATTER...

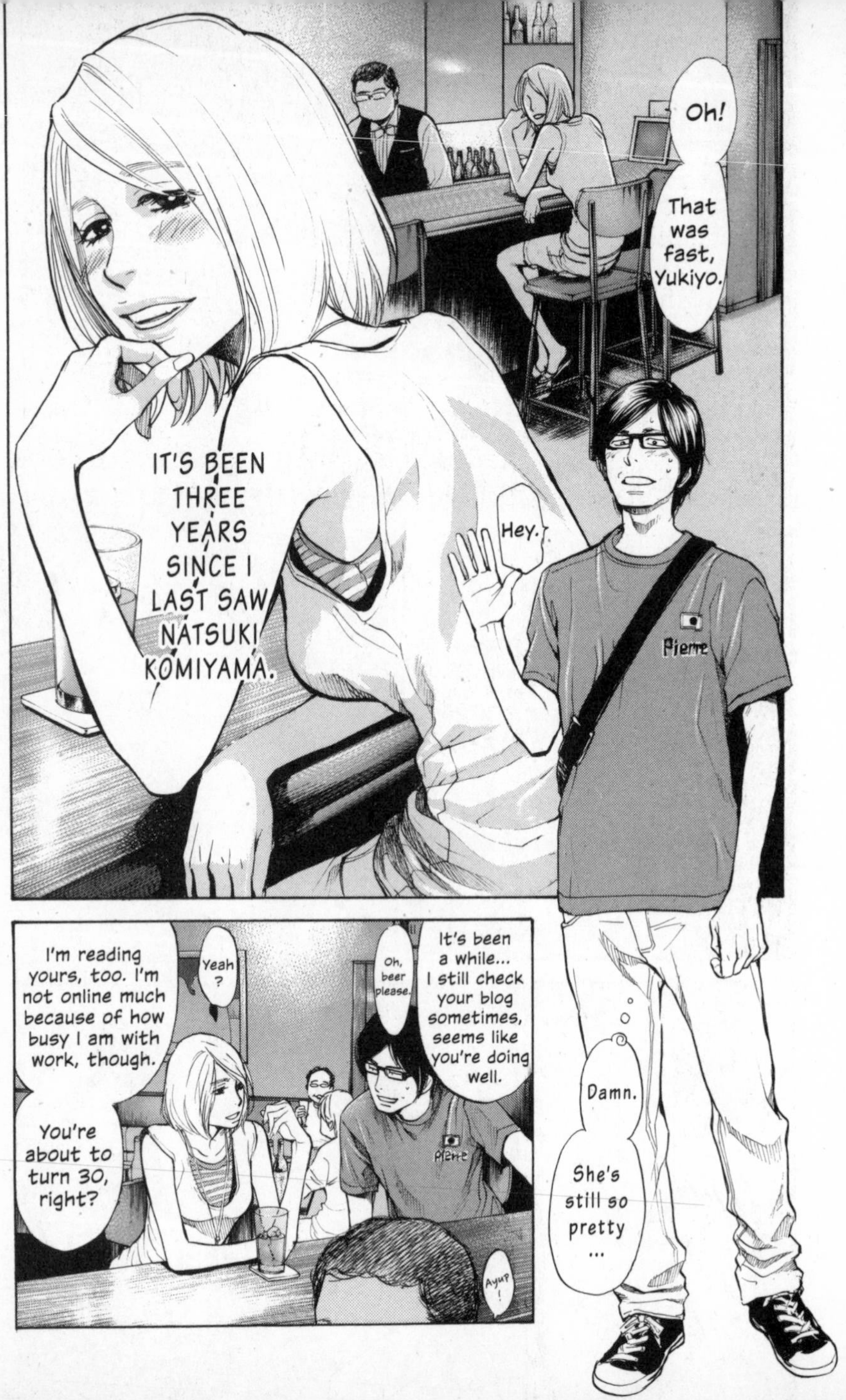
Oh!
That was fast, Yukiyo.
IT'S BEEN THREE YEARS SINCE I LAST SAW NATSUKI KOMIYAMA.
Hey.
Damn.
She's still so pretty ...
It's been a while... I still check your blog sometimes, seems like you're doing well.
Oh, beer please.
Yeah?
I'm reading yours, too. I'm not online much because of how busy I am with work, though.
You're about to turn 30, right?
Ayup!

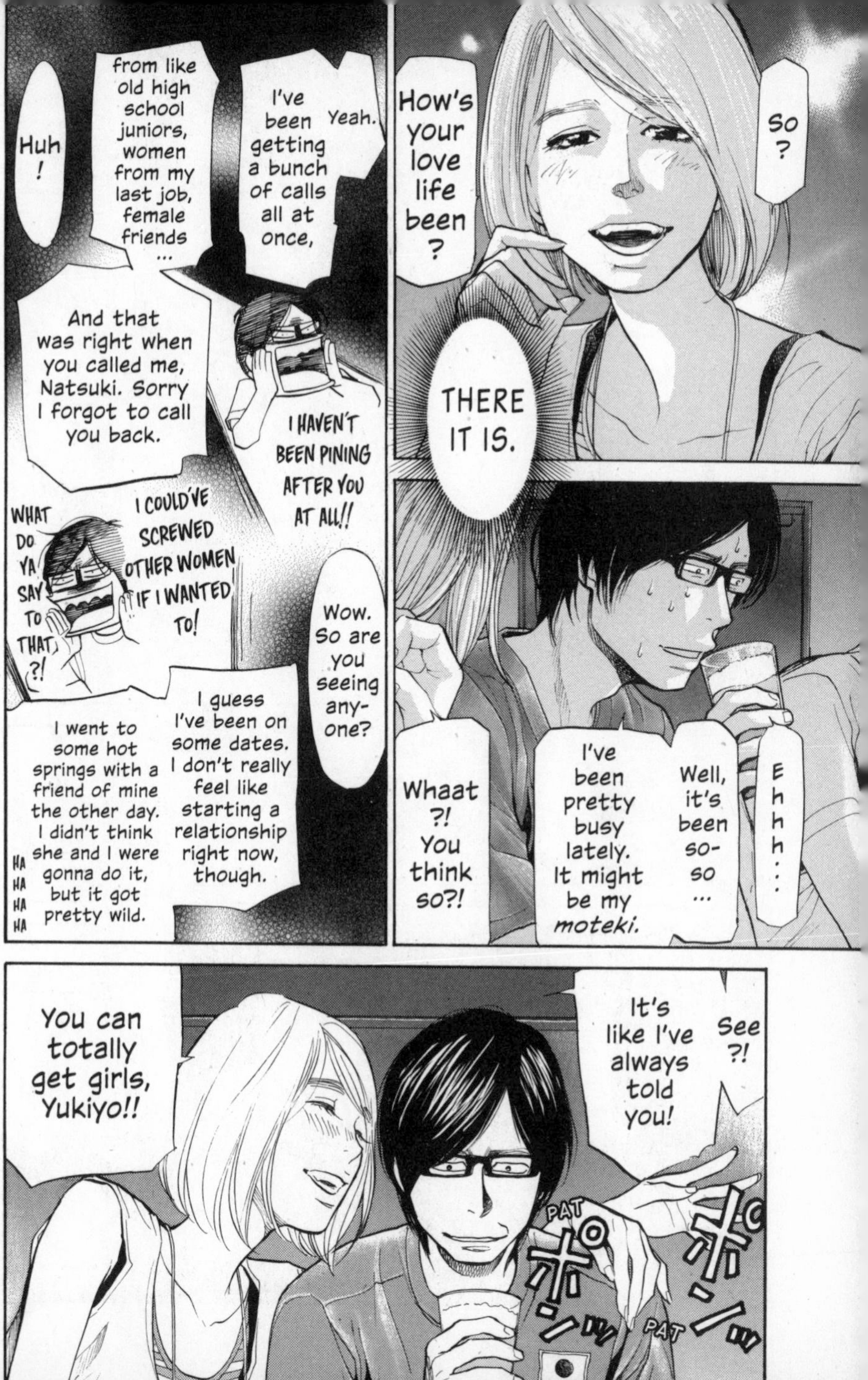
So?
How's your love life been?
THERE IT IS.
Ehhh...
Well, it's been so-so...
I've been pretty busy lately. It might be my *moteki*.
Whaat?! You think so?!
Yeah.
I've been getting a bunch of calls all at once,
from like old high school juniors, women from my last job, female friends...
Huh!
And that was right when you called me, Natsuki. Sorry I forgot to call you back.
I HAVEN'T BEEN PINING AFTER YOU AT ALL!!
I COULD'VE SCREWED OTHER WOMEN IF I WANTED TO!
WHAT DO YA SAY TO THAT?!
Wow. So are you seeing anyone?
I guess I've been on some dates. I don't really feel like starting a relationship right now, though.
I went to some hot springs with a friend of mine the other day. I didn't think she and I were gonna do it, but it got pretty wild.
HA HA HA HA
See?!
It's like I've always told you!
You can totally get girls, Yukiyo!!
PAT
PAT

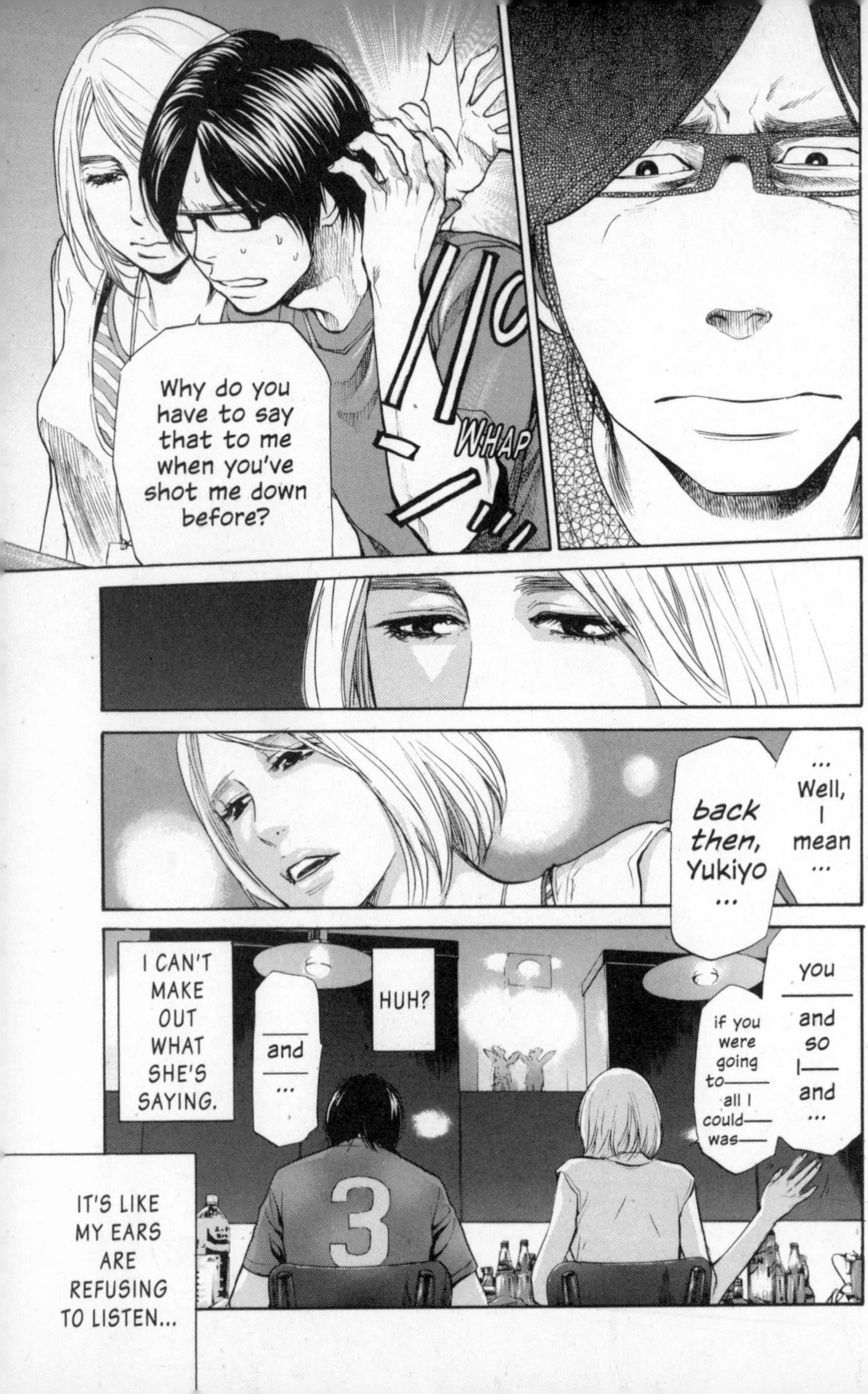
WHAP
Why do you have to say that to me when you've shot me down before?
... Well, I mean ...
back then, Yukiyo ...
you— and so I— and ...
if you were going to— all I could— was—
HUH?
—and— ...
I CAN'T MAKE OUT WHAT SHE'S SAYING.
IT'S LIKE MY EARS ARE REFUSING TO LISTEN...

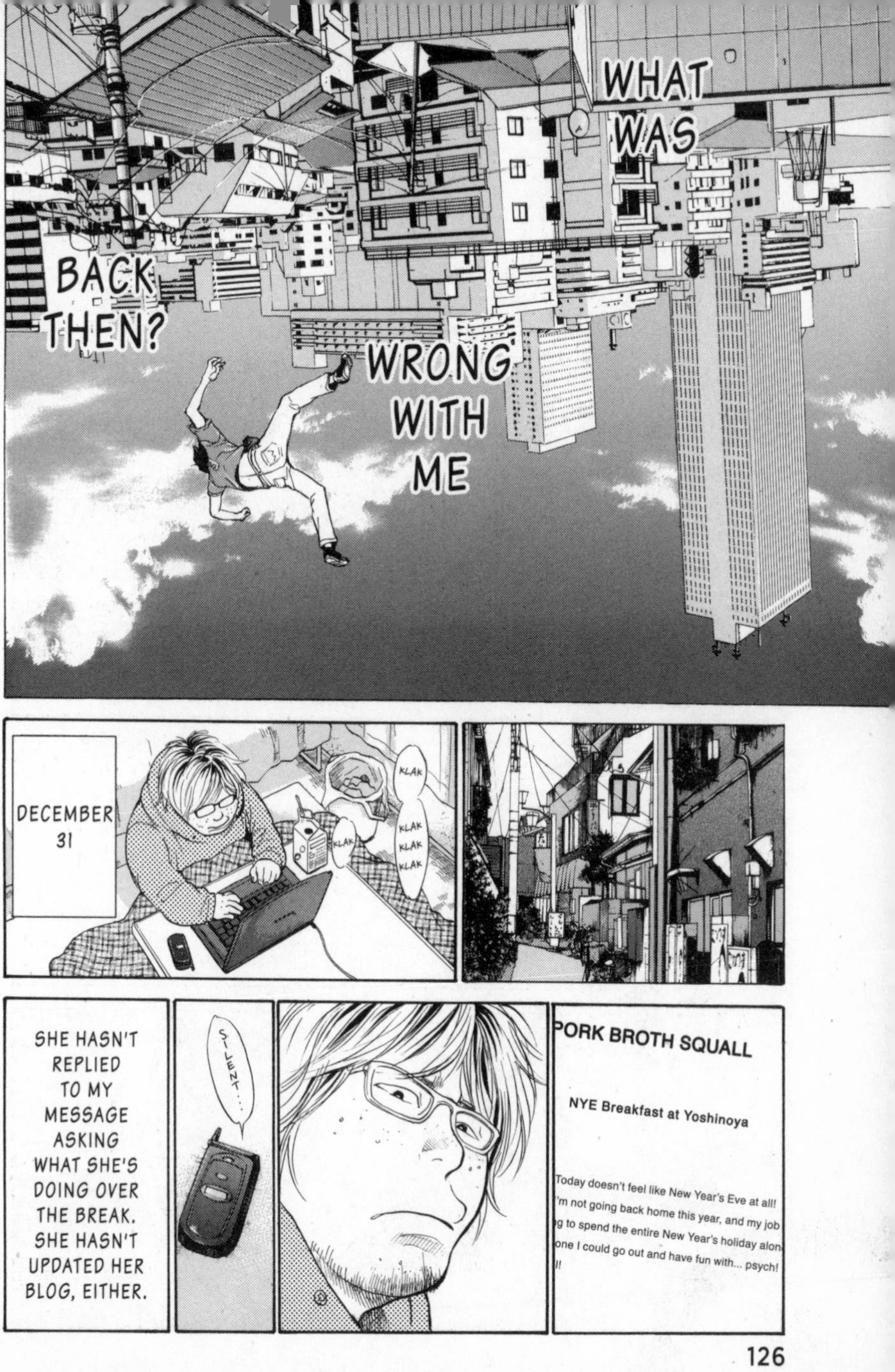
WHAT WAS
WRONG WITH ME
BACK THEN?
DECEMBER 31
KLAK
KLAK KLAK KLAK
KLAK
PORK BROTH SQUALL
NYE Breakfast at Yoshinoya
Today doesn't feel like New Year's Eve at all!
'm not going back home this year, and my job
g to spend the entire New Year's holiday alon
one I could go out and have fun with... psych!
l!
SILENT...
SHE HASN'T REPLIED TO MY MESSAGE ASKING WHAT SHE'S DOING OVER THE BREAK. SHE HASN'T UPDATED HER BLOG, EITHER.

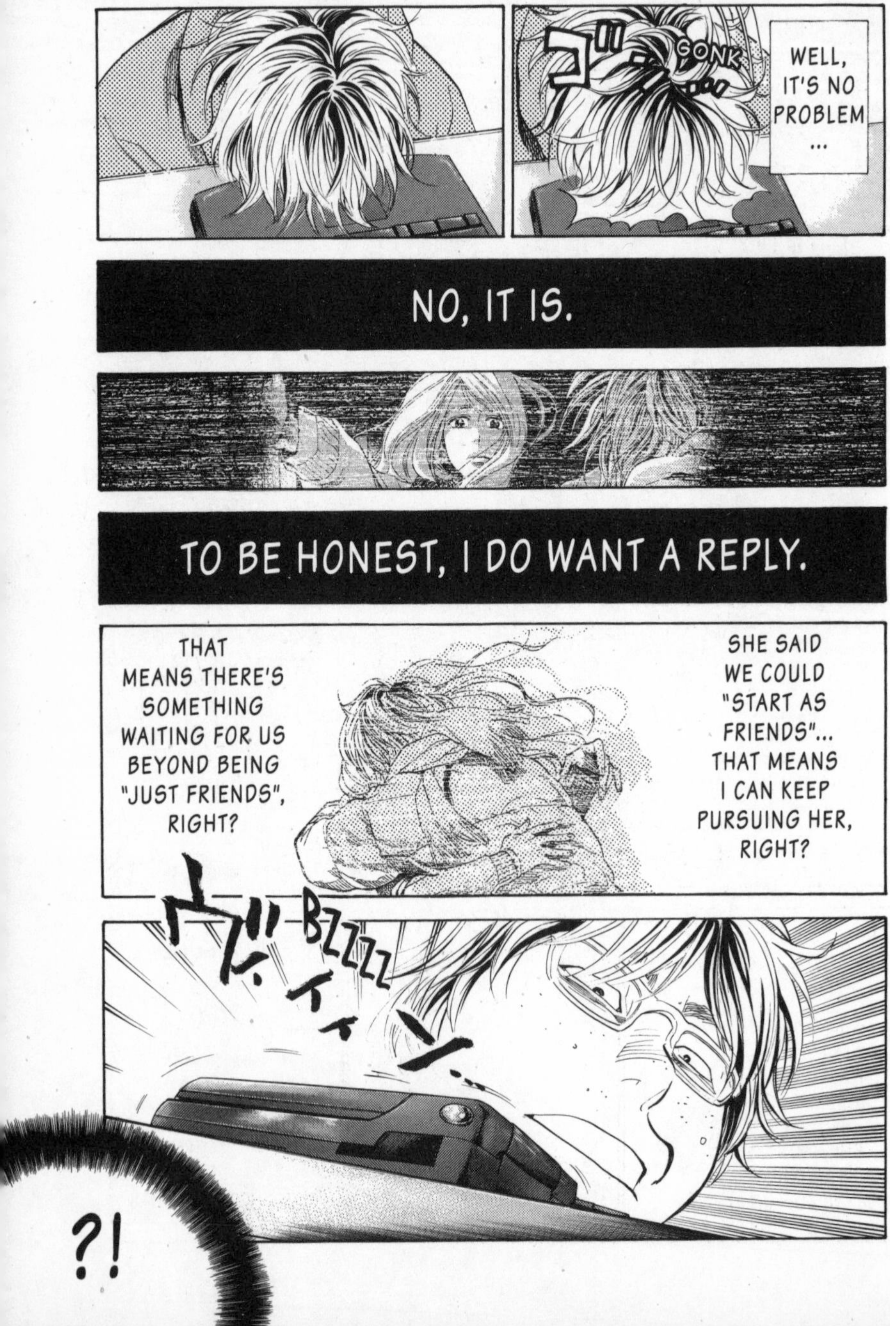
GONK
WELL, IT'S NO PROBLEM ...
NO, IT IS.
TO BE HONEST, I DO WANT A REPLY.
SHE SAID WE COULD "START AS FRIENDS"... THAT MEANS I CAN KEEP PURSUING HER, RIGHT?
THAT MEANS THERE'S SOMETHING WAITING FOR US BEYOND BEING "JUST FRIENDS", RIGHT?
BZZZZZ
?!

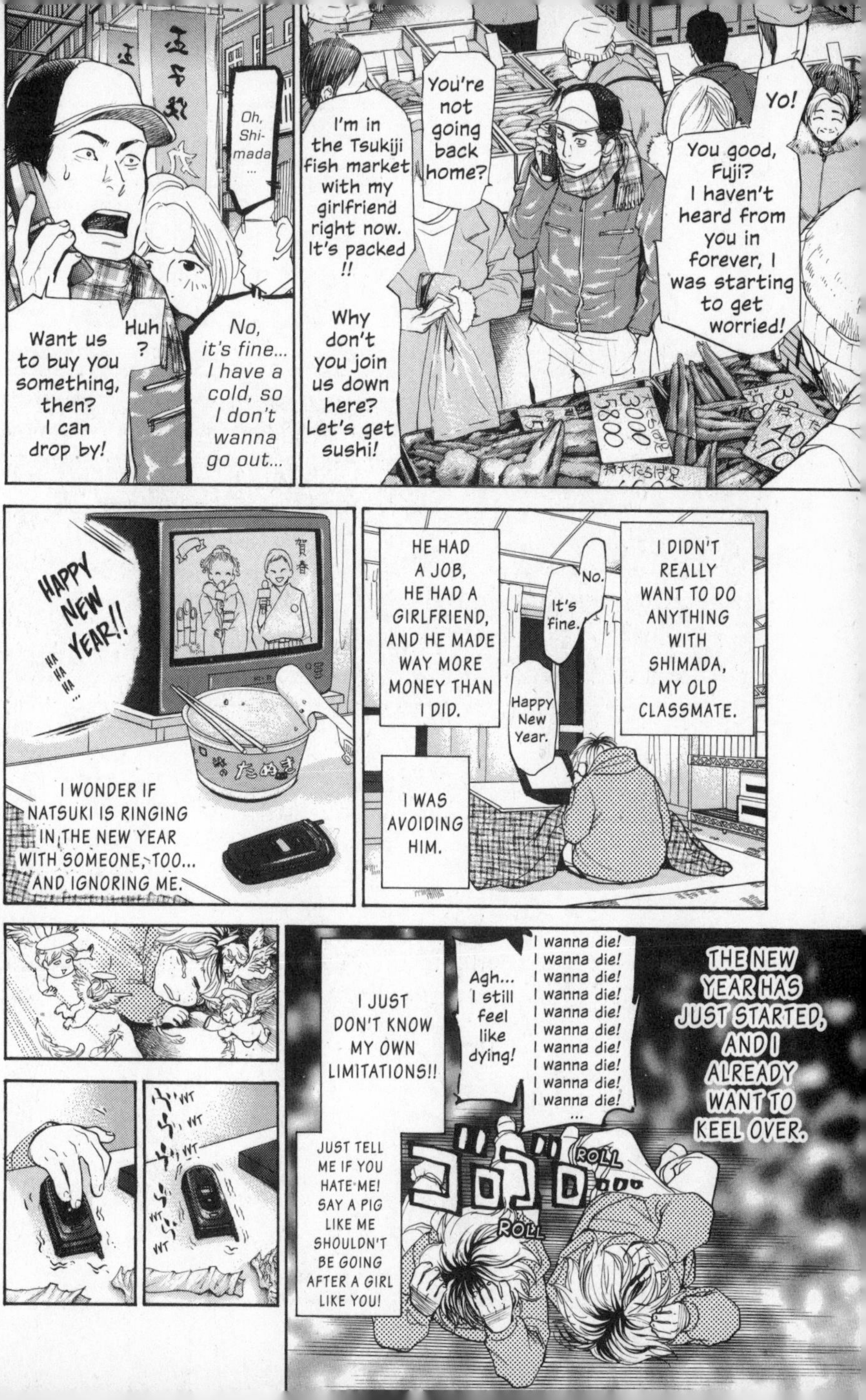
Yo!
You good, Fuji? I haven't heard from you in forever, I was starting to get worried!
You're not going back home?
I'm in the Tsukiji fish market with my girlfriend right now. It's packed!!
Why don't you join us down here? Let's get sushi!
Oh, Shimada...
No, it's fine... I have a cold, so I don't wanna go out...
Huh?
Want us to buy you something, then? I can drop by!
I DIDN'T REALLY WANT TO DO ANYTHING WITH SHIMADA, MY OLD CLASSMATE.
No.
It's fine.
HE HAD A JOB, HE HAD A GIRLFRIEND, AND HE MADE WAY MORE MONEY THAN I DID.
Happy New Year.
I WAS AVOIDING HIM.
HAPPY NEW YEAR!!
HA HA HA...
I WONDER IF NATSUKI IS RINGING IN THE NEW YEAR WITH SOMEONE, TOO... AND IGNORING ME.
THE NEW YEAR HAS JUST STARTED, AND I ALREADY WANT TO KEEL OVER.
I wanna die! I wanna die! I wanna die! I wanna die! I wanna die! I wanna die! I wanna die! I wanna die! I wanna die! I wanna die! ...
Agh... I still feel like dying!
I JUST DON'T KNOW MY OWN LIMITATIONS!!
ROLL
ROLL
JUST TELL ME IF YOU HATE ME! SAY A PIG LIKE ME SHOULDN'T BE GOING AFTER A GIRL LIKE YOU!
WT WT WT WT WT

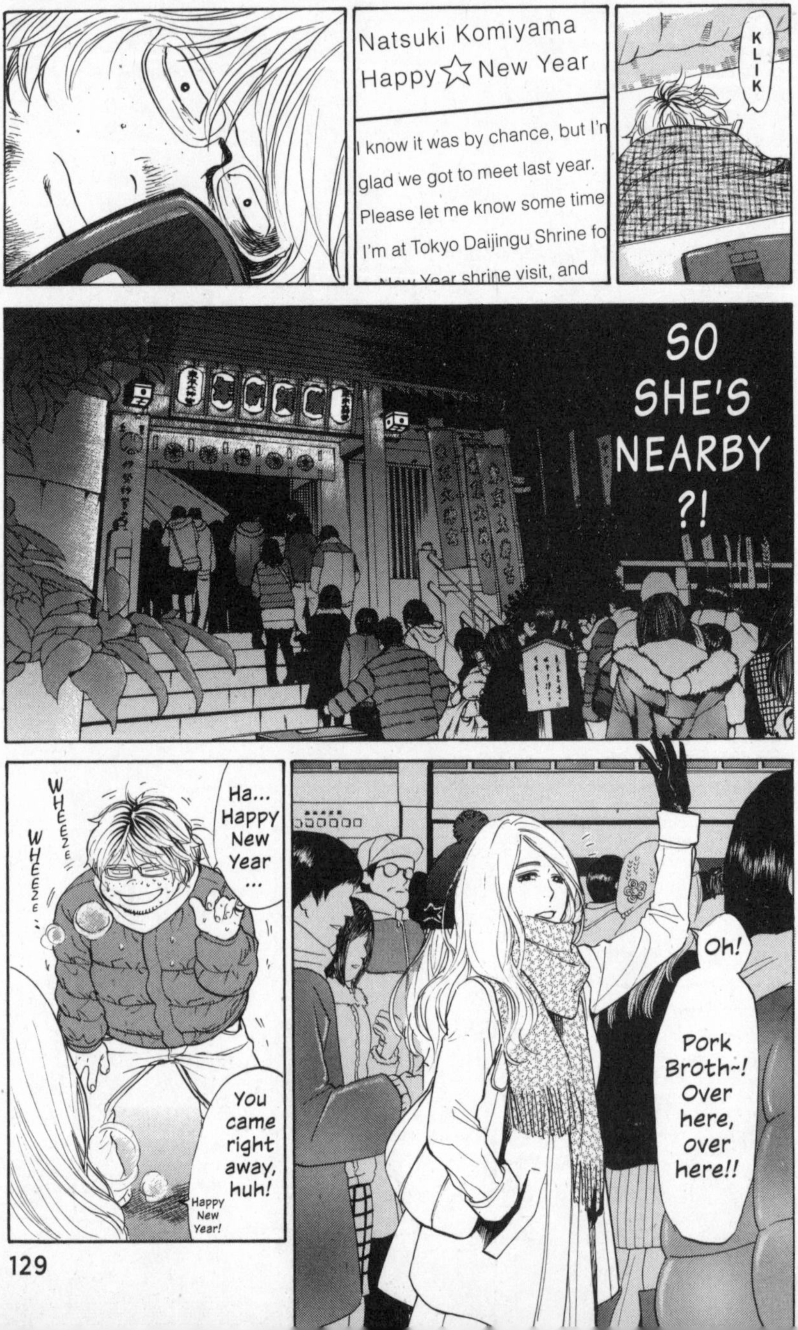
KLIK
Natsuki Komiyama
Happy☆New Year
I know it was by chance, but I'n
glad we got to meet last year.
Please let me know some time
I'm at Tokyo Daijingu Shrine fo
New Year shrine visit, and
SO SHE'S NEARBY ?!
Oh!
Pork Broth~! Over here, over here!!
WHEEZE
WHEEZE
Ha... Happy New Year ...
You came right away, huh!
Happy New Year!

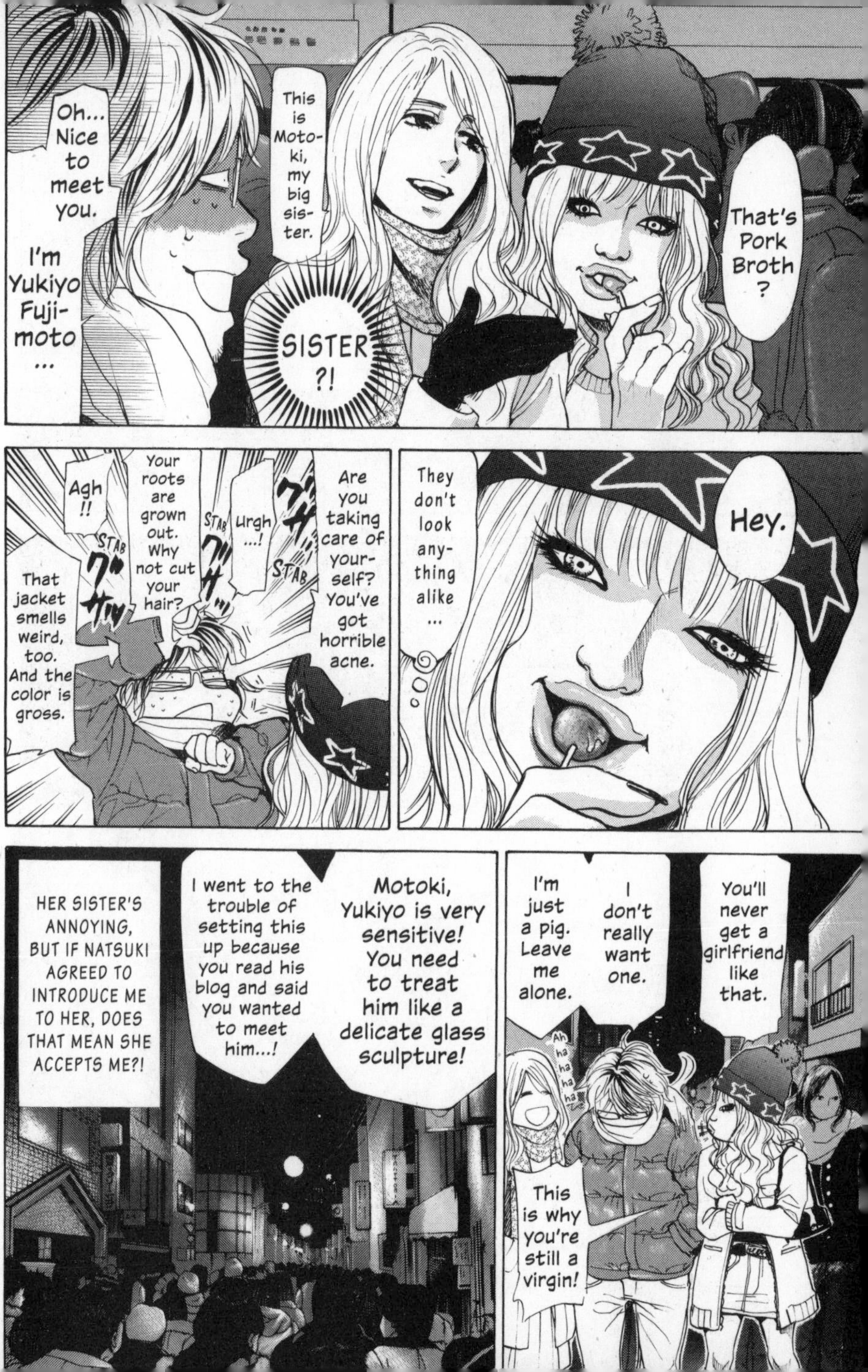
That's Pork Broth?
This is Moto-ki, my big sis-ter.
SISTER?!
Oh... Nice to meet you.
I'm Yukiyo Fuji-moto...
Hey.
They don't look any-thing alike...
Are you taking care of your-self? You've got horrible acne.
Urgh...!
STAB
STAB
Your roots are grown out. Why not cut your hair?
Agh!!
STAB
That jacket smells weird, too. And the color is gross.
You'll never get a girlfriend like that.
I don't really want one.
I'm just a pig. Leave me alone.
Ah ha ha ha ha
This is why you're still a virgin!
Motoki, Yukiyo is very sensitive! You need to treat him like a delicate glass sculpture!
I went to the trouble of setting this up because you read his blog and said you wanted to meet him...!
HER SISTER'S ANNOYING, BUT IF NATSUKI AGREED TO INTRODUCE ME TO HER, DOES THAT MEAN SHE ACCEPTS ME?!

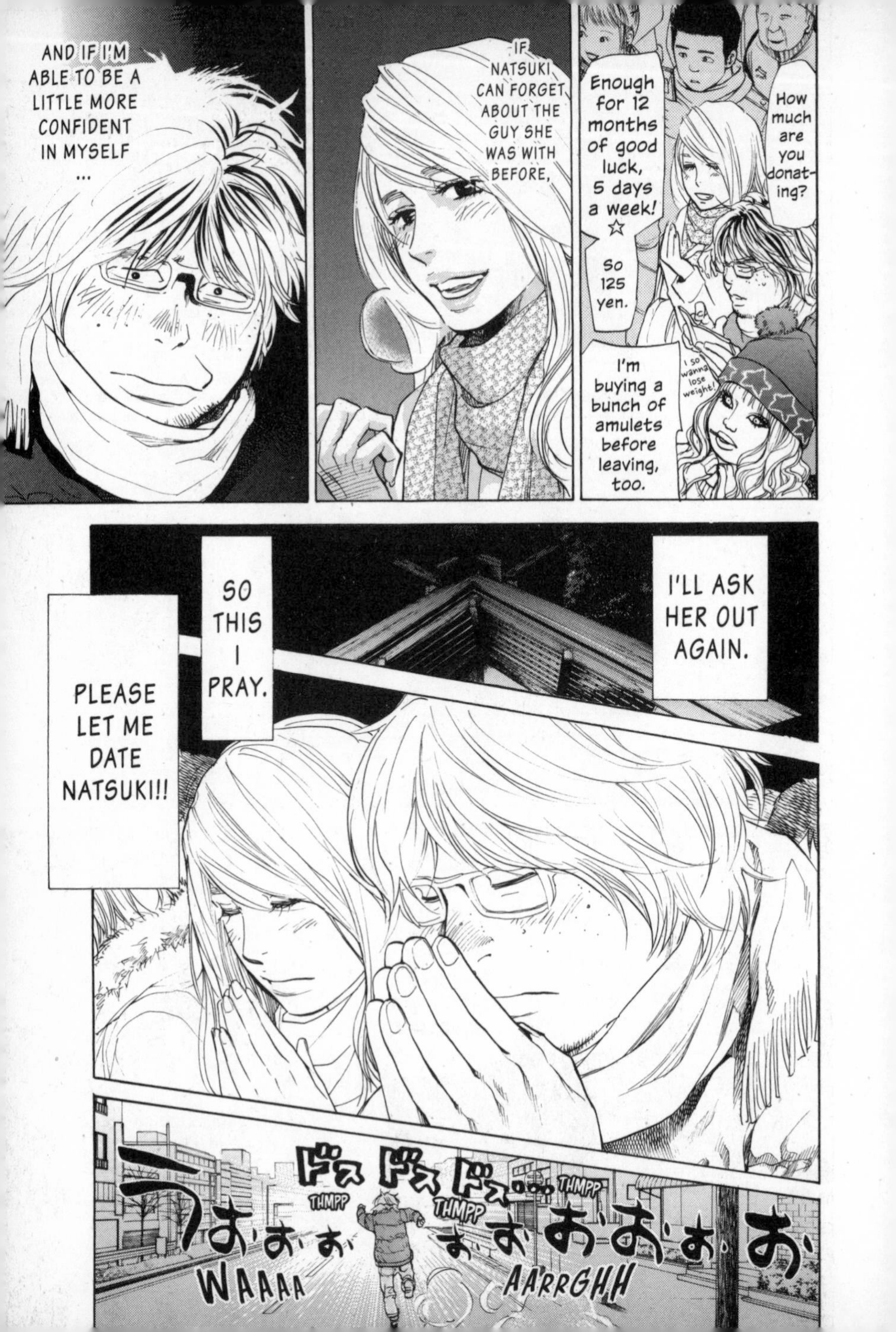
How much are you donating?
Enough for 12 months of good luck, 5 days a week! ☆
So 125 yen.
I so wanna lose weight!
I'm buying a bunch of amulets before leaving, too.
IF NATSUKI CAN FORGET ABOUT THE GUY SHE WAS WITH BEFORE,
AND IF I'M ABLE TO BE A LITTLE MORE CONFIDENT IN MYSELF ...
I'LL ASK HER OUT AGAIN.
SO THIS I PRAY.
PLEASE LET ME DATE NATSUKI!!
ドスドスドス…
THMPP
THMPP
THMPP
WAAAA
AARRGHH

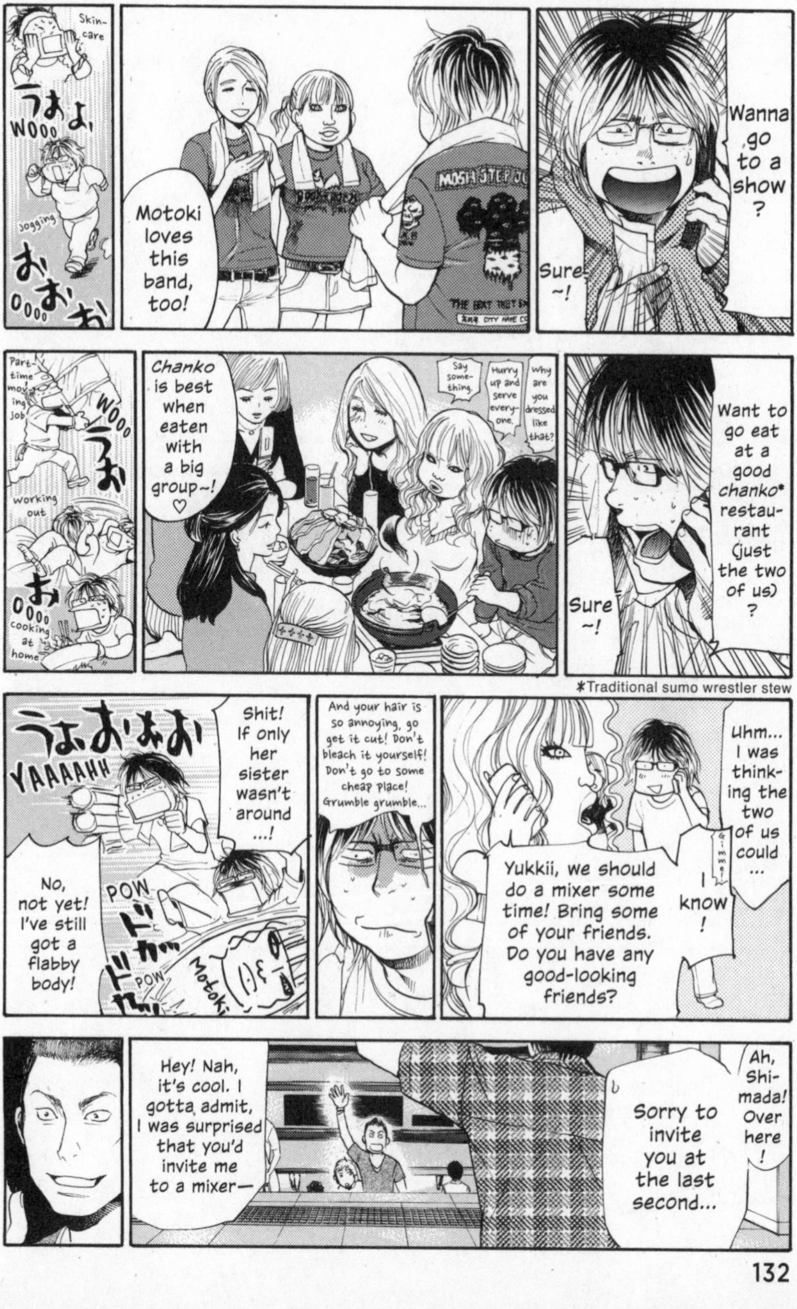
Wanna go to a show?
Sure~!
Motoki loves this band, too!
Skin-care
WOOO
jogging
OOOO
Want to go eat at a good chanko* restaurant (just the two of us)?
Sure~!
Chanko is best when eaten with a big group~! ♡
Say something.
Hurry up and serve everyone.
Why are you dressed like that?
Part-time moving job
WOOO
working out
OOOO
cooking at home
Uhm... I was thinking the two of us could...
Gimme!
I know!
Yukkii, we should do a mixer some time! Bring some of your friends. Do you have any good-looking friends?
And your hair is so annoying, go get it cut! Don't bleach it yourself! Don't go to some cheap place! Grumble grumble...
Shit! If only her sister wasn't around...!
YAAAAHH
No, not yet! I've still got a flabby body!
POW
POW
Motoki
Ah, Shimada! Over here!
Sorry to invite you at the last second...
Hey! Nah, it's cool. I gotta admit, I was surprised that you'd invite me to a mixer—

*Traditional sumo wrestler stew

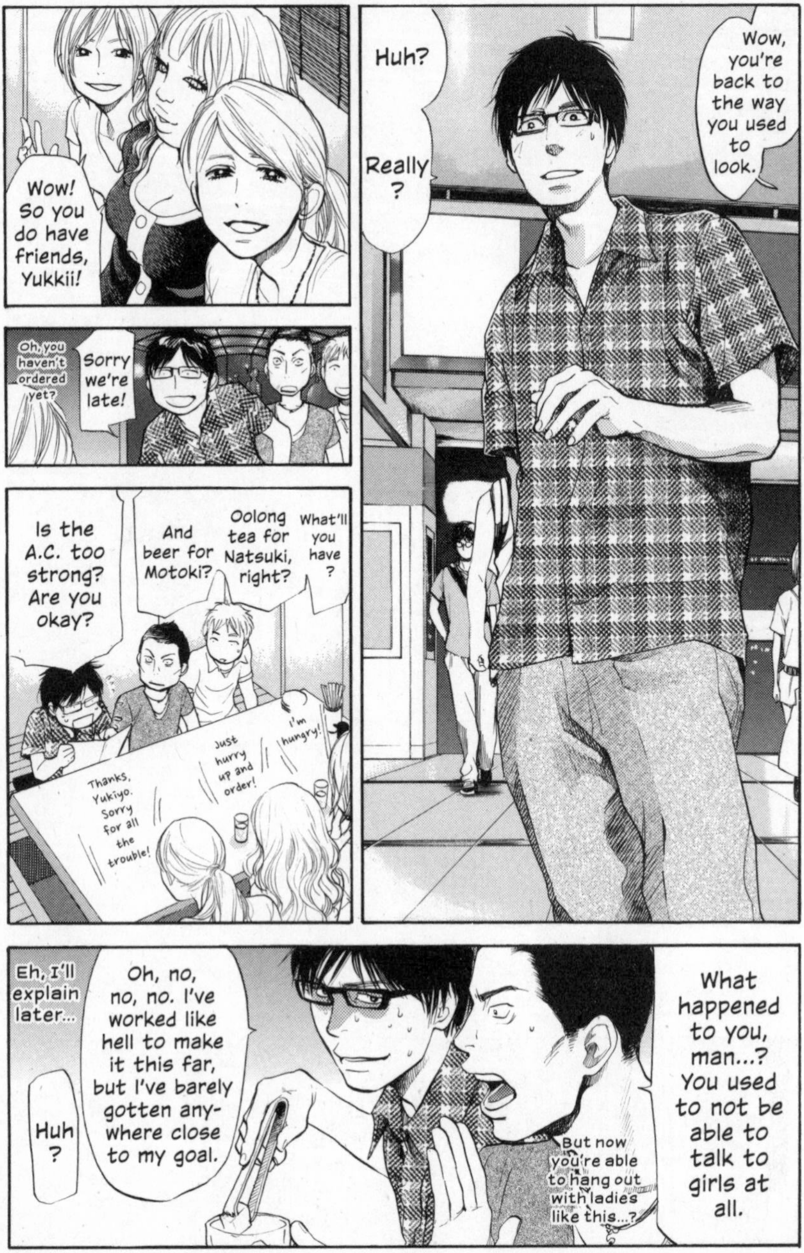
Wow, you're back to the way you used to look.
Huh?
Really?
Wow! So you do have friends, Yukkii!
Sorry we're late!
Oh, you haven't ordered yet?
What'll you have?
Oolong tea for Natsuki, right?
And beer for Motoki?
Is the A.C. too strong? Are you okay?
I'm hungry!
Just hurry up and order!
Thanks, Yukiyo. Sorry for all the trouble!
What happened to you, man...? You used to not be able to talk to girls at all.
But now you're able to hang out with ladies like this...?
Oh, no, no, no. I've worked like hell to make it this far, but I've barely gotten any-where close to my goal.
Huh?
Eh, I'll explain later...

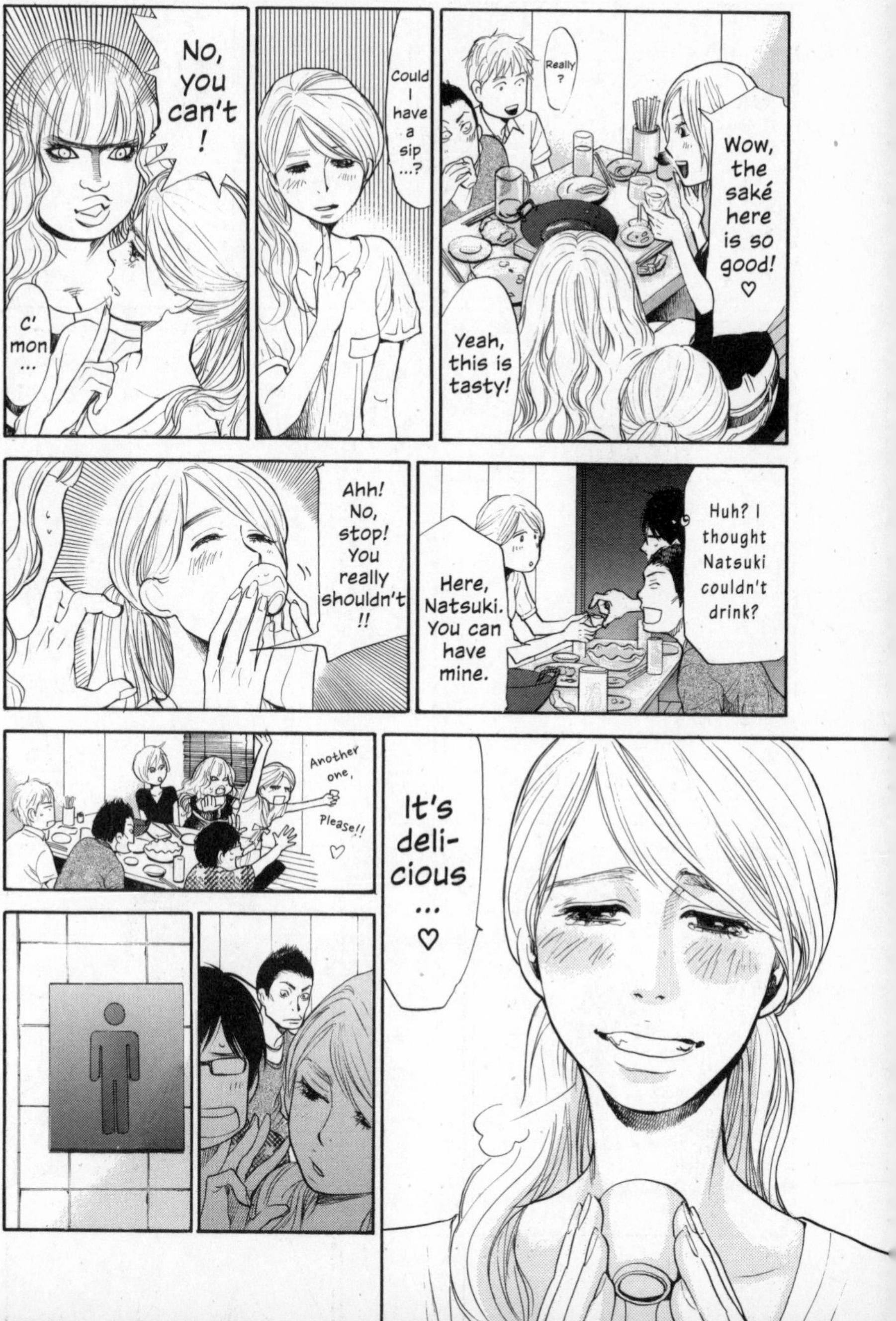
Wow, the saké here is so good! ♡
Really?
Yeah, this is tasty!
Could I have a sip ...?
No, you can't!
C'mon ...
Huh? I thought Natsuki couldn't drink?
Here, Natsuki. You can have mine.
Ahh! No, stop! You really shouldn't!!
It's delicious ... ♡
Another one, Please!! ♡

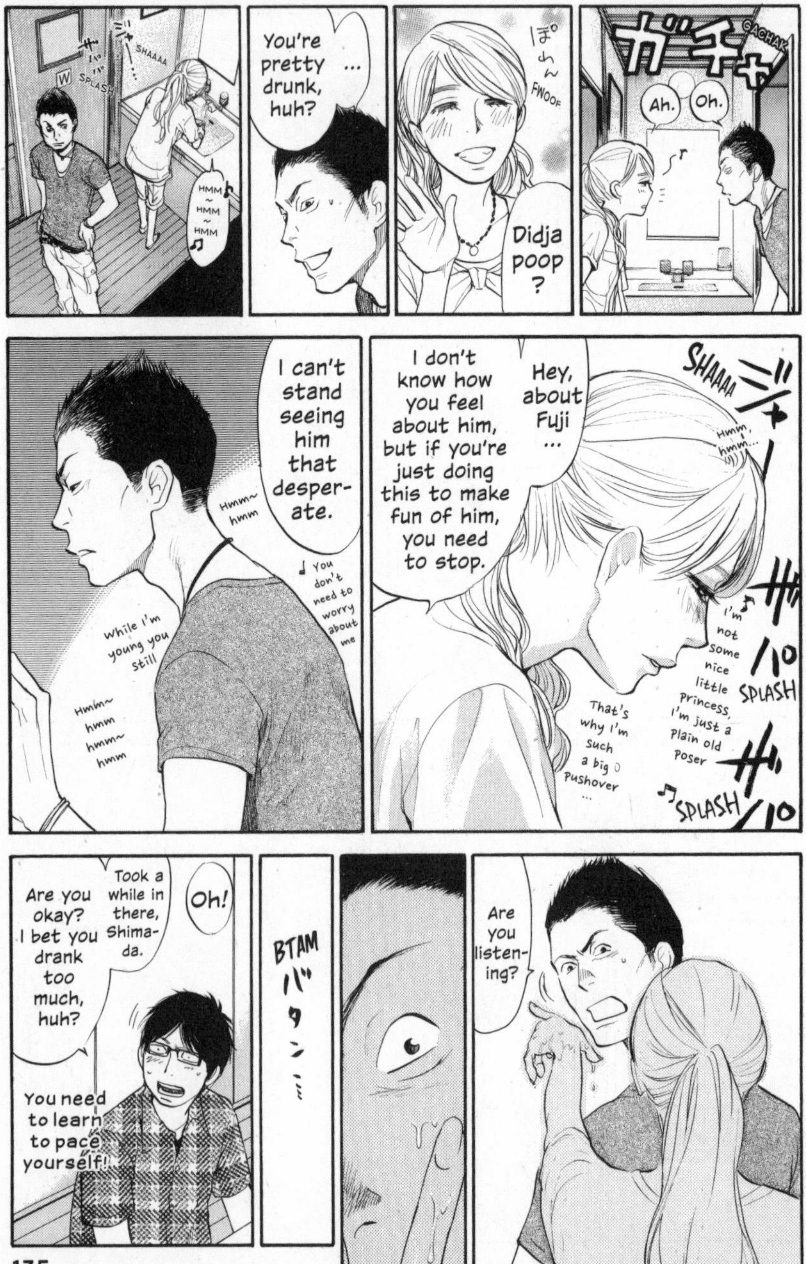
ガチャ
GACHAK
Oh.
Ah.
FWOOF
Didja poop?
You're pretty drunk, huh?
...
SHAAAA
SPLASH
HMM~ HMM~ HMM
SHAAAA
Hey, about Fuji ...
I don't know how you feel about him, but if you're just doing this to make fun of him, you need to stop.
Hmm, hmm...
I'm not some nice little Princess, I'm just a Plain old Poser
SPLASH
That's why I'm such a big pushover ...
SPLASH
I can't stand seeing him that desper-ate.
Hmm~ hmm
You don't need to worry about me
While I'm young you still
Hmm~ hmm hmm~ hmm
Are you listen-ing?
BTAM
バタン...
Oh!
Took a while in there, Shimada.
Are you okay? I bet you drank too much, huh?
You need to learn to pace yourself!

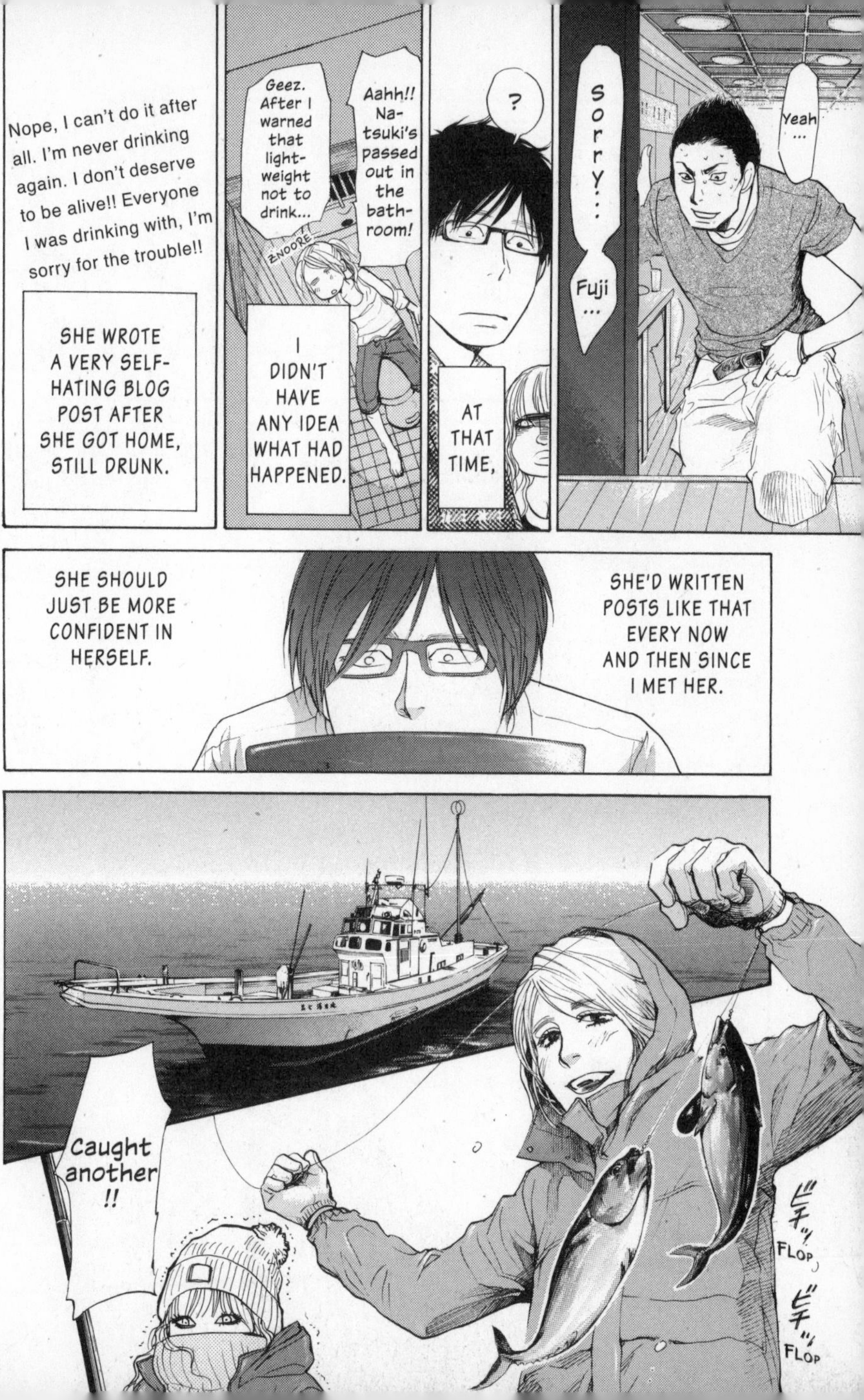
Yeah ...
Sorry...
Fuji ...
?
AT THAT TIME,
Aahh!! Natsuki's passed out in the bathroom!
Geez. After I warned that light-weight not to drink...
ZNOORE
I DIDN'T HAVE ANY IDEA WHAT HAD HAPPENED.
Nope, I can't do it after all. I'm never drinking again. I don't deserve to be alive!! Everyone I was drinking with, I'm sorry for the trouble!!
SHE WROTE A VERY SELF-HATING BLOG POST AFTER SHE GOT HOME, STILL DRUNK.
SHE'D WRITTEN POSTS LIKE THAT EVERY NOW AND THEN SINCE I MET HER.
SHE SHOULD JUST BE MORE CONFIDENT IN HERSELF.
Caught another!!
ビチッ
FLOP
ビチッ
FLOP

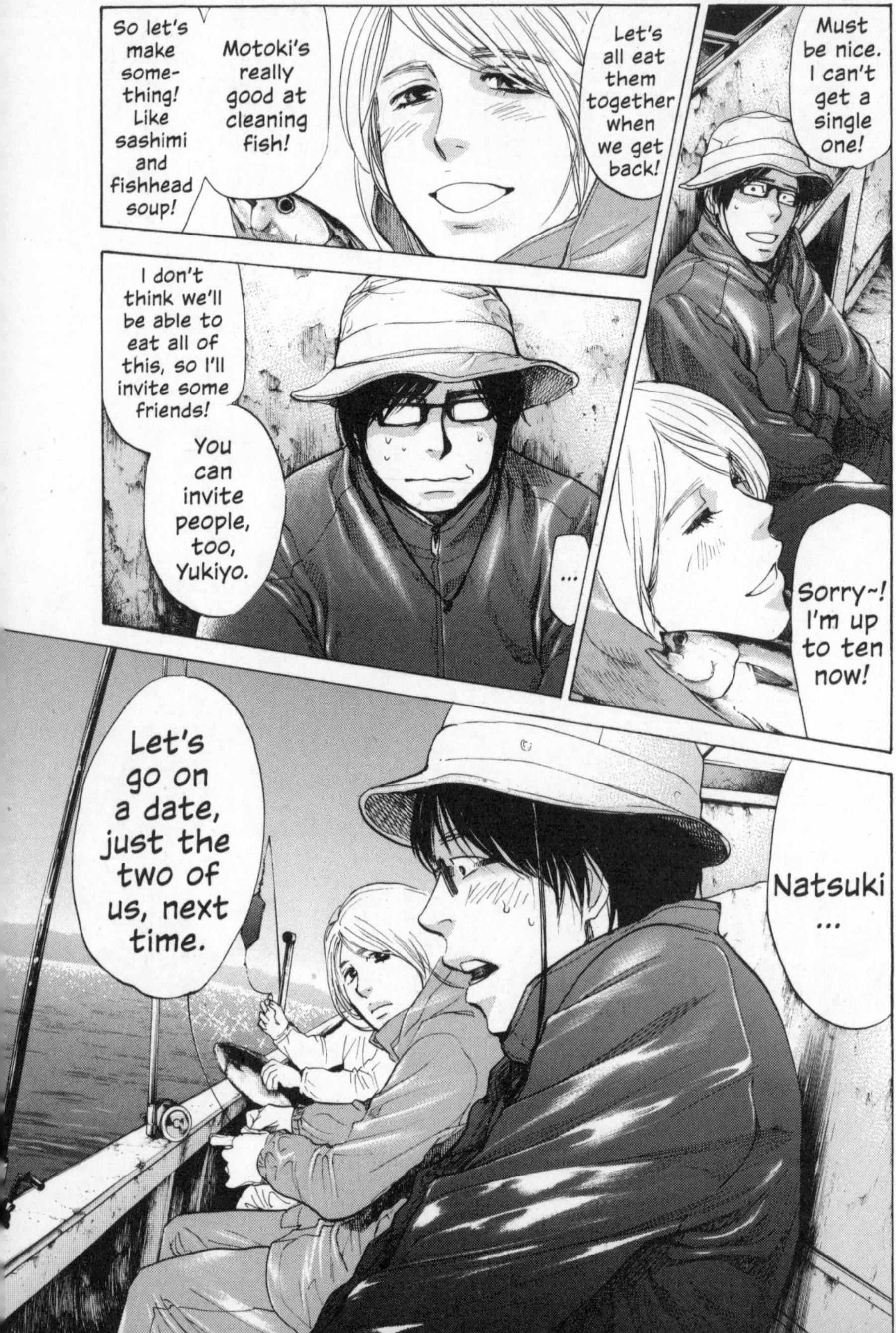
Must be nice. I can't get a single one!
Sorry~! I'm up to ten now!
Let's all eat them together when we get back!
Motoki's really good at cleaning fish!
So let's make some-thing! Like sashimi and fishhead soup!
I don't think we'll be able to eat all of this, so I'll invite some friends!
You can invite people, too, Yukiyo.
...
Natsuki ...
Let's go on a date, just the two of us, next time.

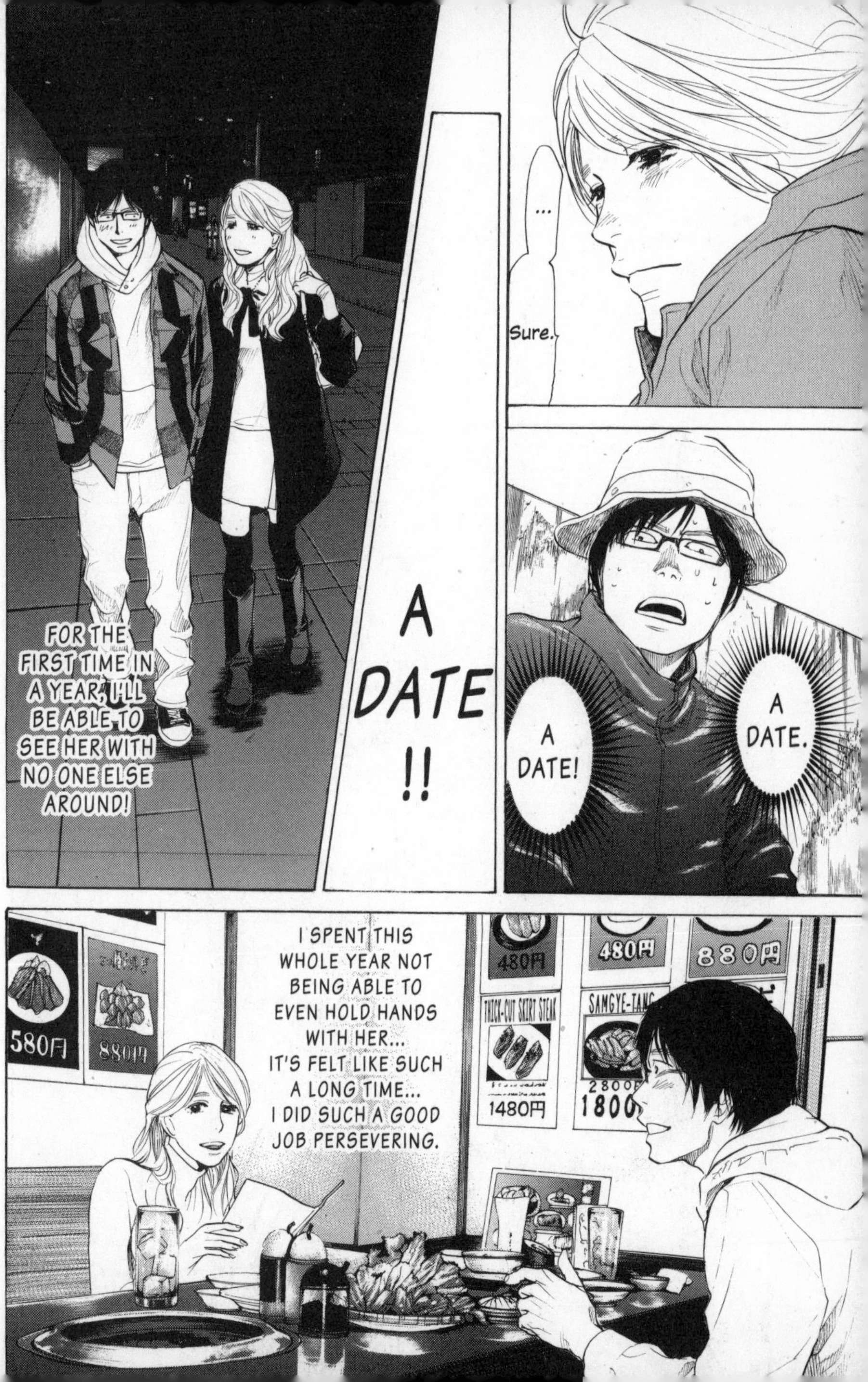
...
Sure.
A DATE.
A DATE!
A DATE !!
FOR THE FIRST TIME IN A YEAR, I'LL BE ABLE TO SEE HER WITH NO ONE ELSE AROUND!
880円
480円
480円
SAMGYE-TANG
THICK-CUT SKIRT STEAK
1480円
I SPENT THIS WHOLE YEAR NOT BEING ABLE TO EVEN HOLD HANDS WITH HER... IT'S FELT LIKE SUCH A LONG TIME... I DID SUCH A GOOD JOB PERSEVERING.
880円
580円

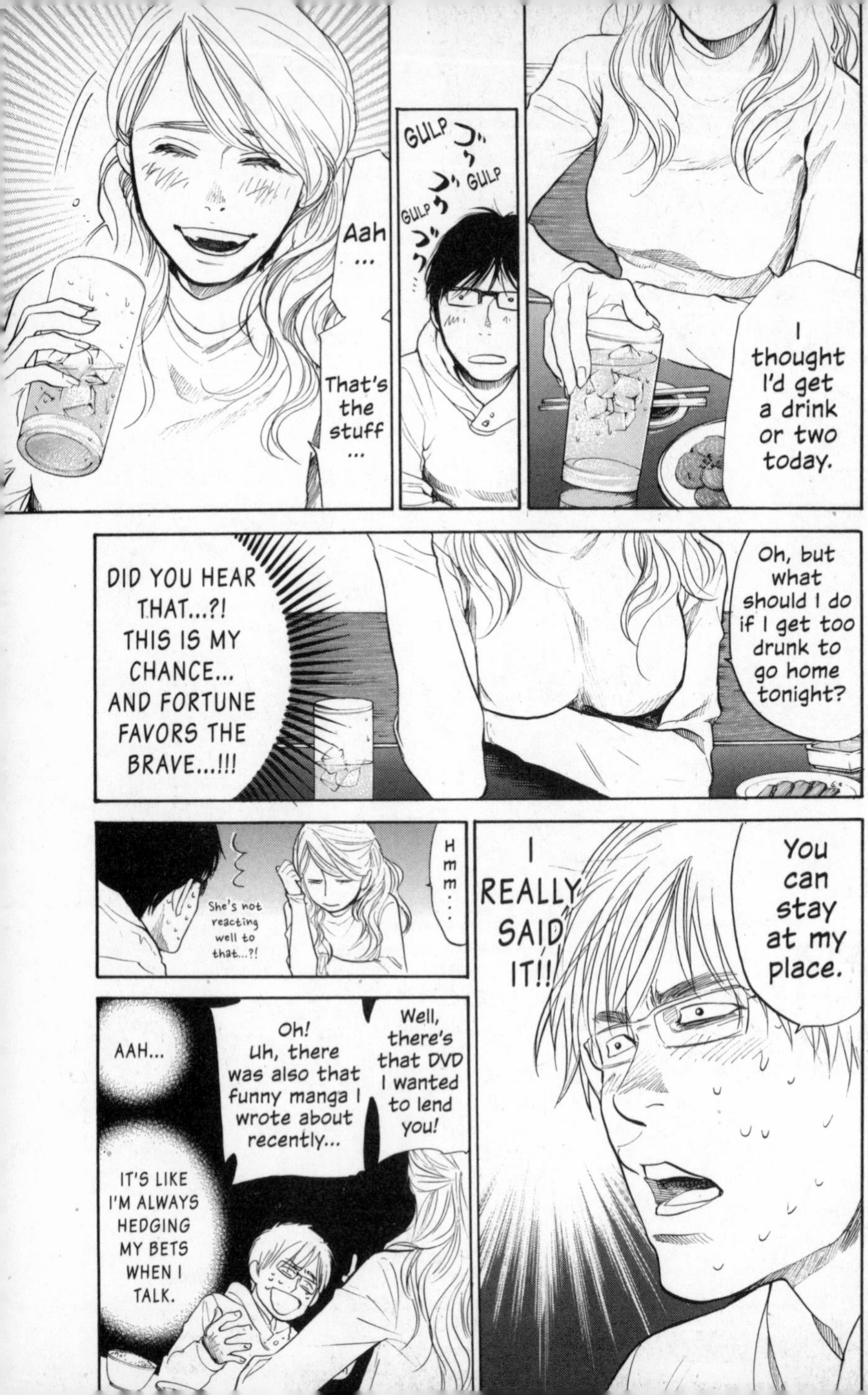
I thought I'd get a drink or two today.
GULP
GULP
GULP
Aah ...
That's the stuff ...
Oh, but what should I do if I get too drunk to go home tonight?
DID YOU HEAR THAT...?! THIS IS MY CHANCE... AND FORTUNE FAVORS THE BRAVE...!!!
You can stay at my place.
I REALLY SAID IT!!
Hmm...
She's not reacting well to that...?!
Well, there's that DVD I wanted to lend you!
Oh! Uh, there was also that funny manga I wrote about recently...
AAH...
IT'S LIKE I'M ALWAYS HEDGING MY BETS WHEN I TALK.

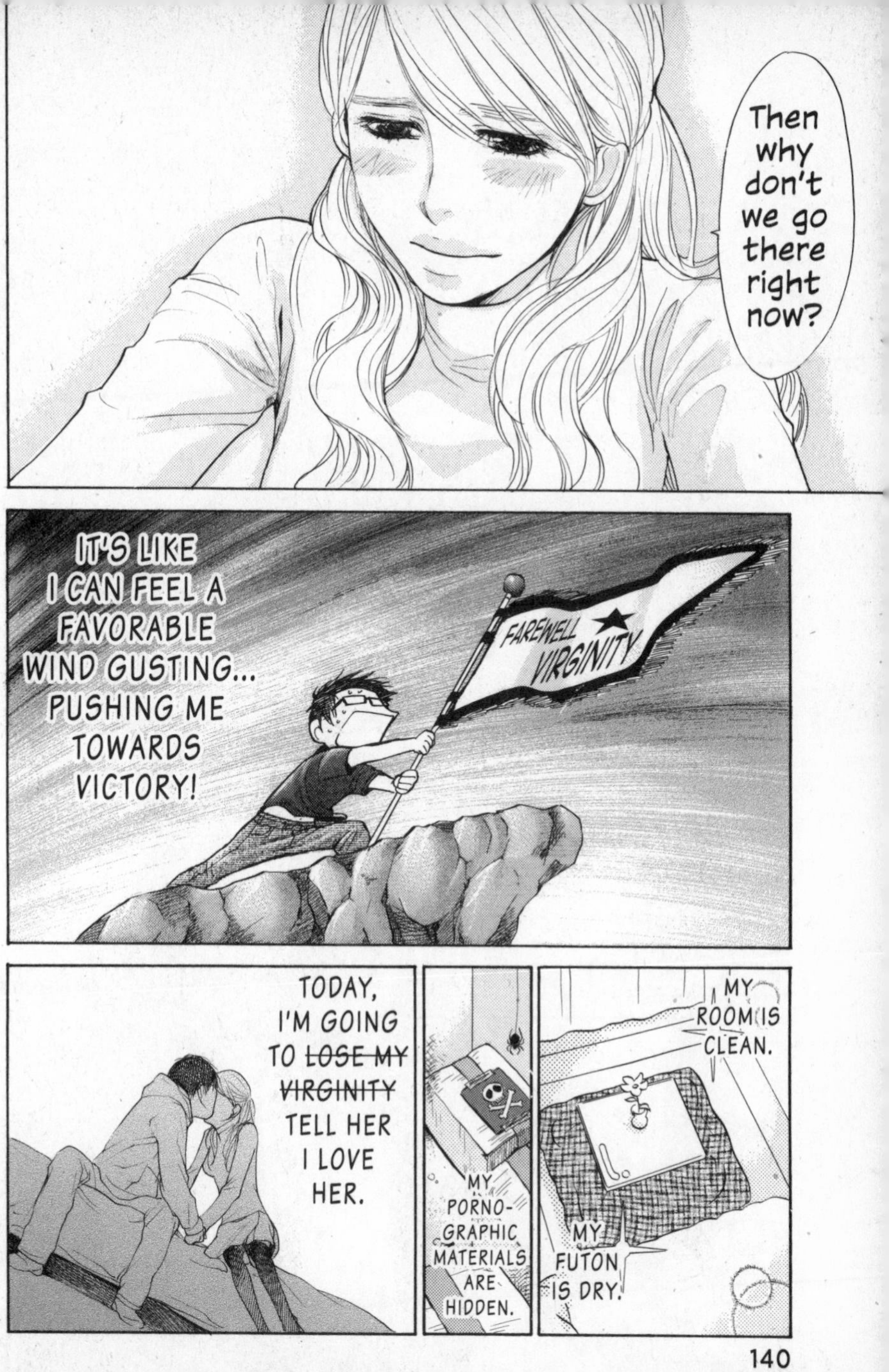
Then why don't we go there right now?
IT'S LIKE I CAN FEEL A FAVORABLE WIND GUSTING... PUSHING ME TOWARDS VICTORY!
FAREWELL ★ VIRGINITY
MY ROOM IS CLEAN.
MY FUTON IS DRY.
MY PORNO-GRAPHIC MATERIALS ARE HIDDEN.
TODAY, I'M GOING TO ~~LOSE MY VIRGINITY~~ TELL HER I LOVE HER.

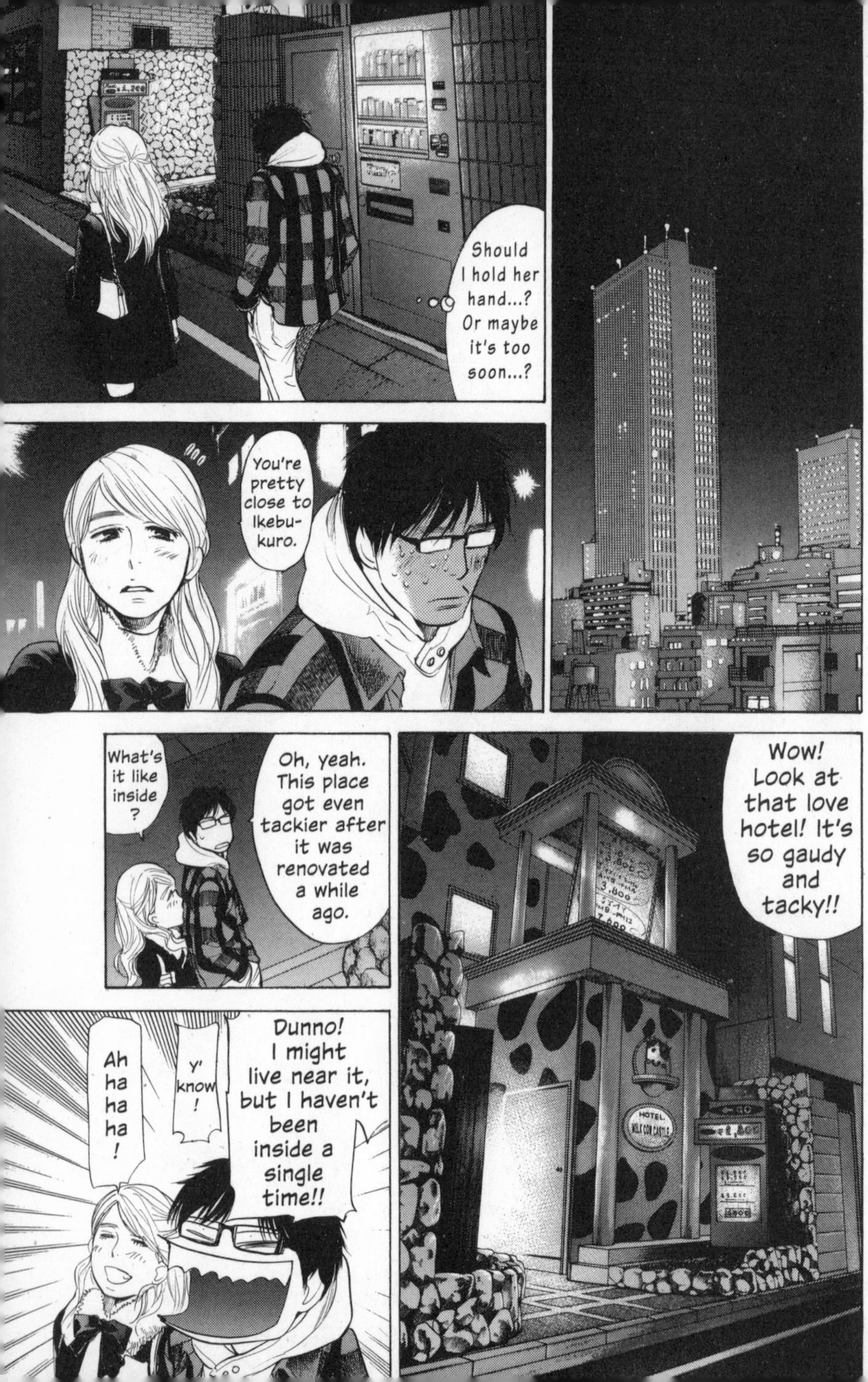
Should I hold her hand...? Or maybe it's too soon...?
You're pretty close to Ikebukuro.
Wow! Look at that love hotel! It's so gaudy and tacky!!
HOTEL
MILK COW CASTLE
Oh, yeah. This place got even tackier after it was renovated a while ago.
What's it like inside?
Dunno! I might live near it, but I haven't been inside a single time!!
Y' know!
Ah ha ha ha!

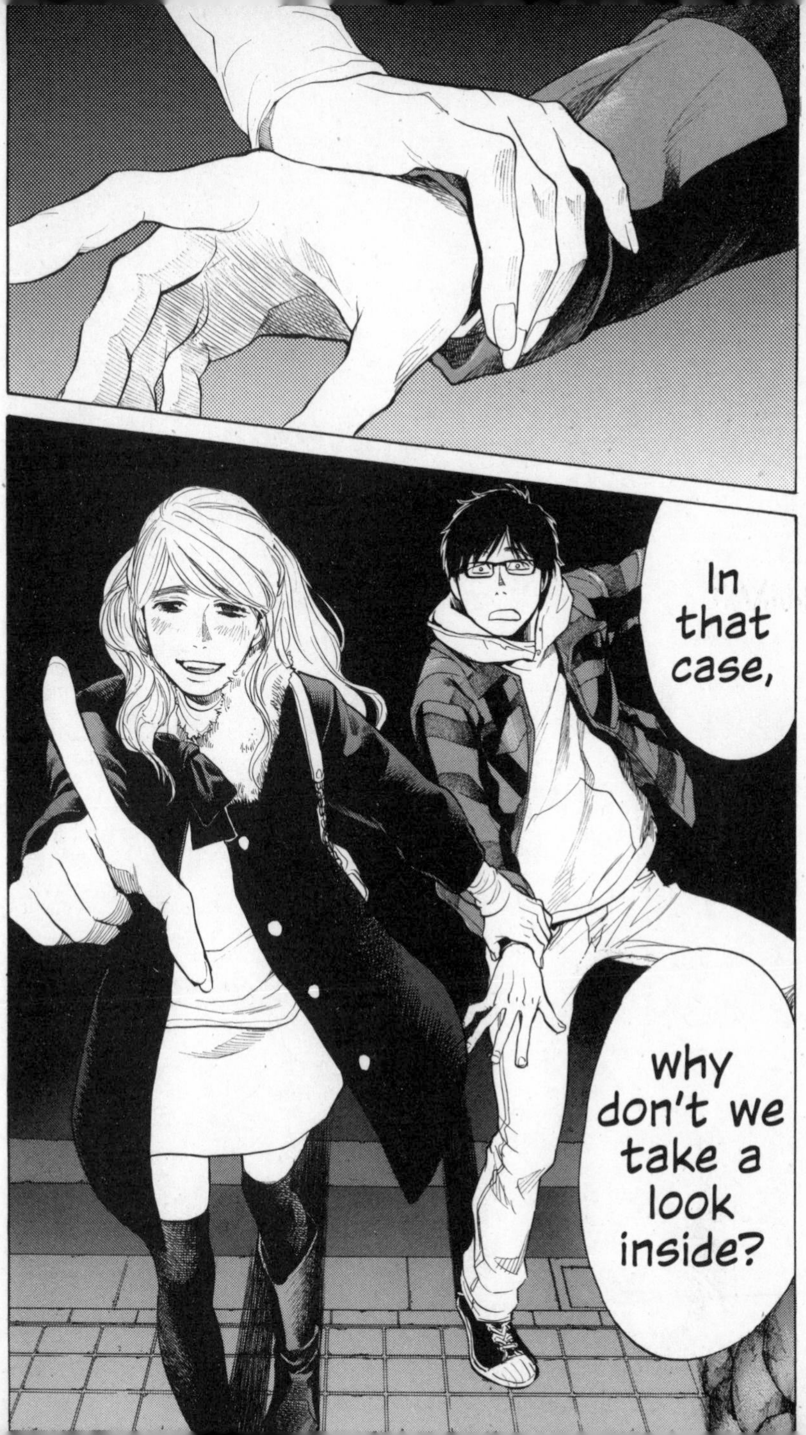
In that case,
why don't we take a look inside?

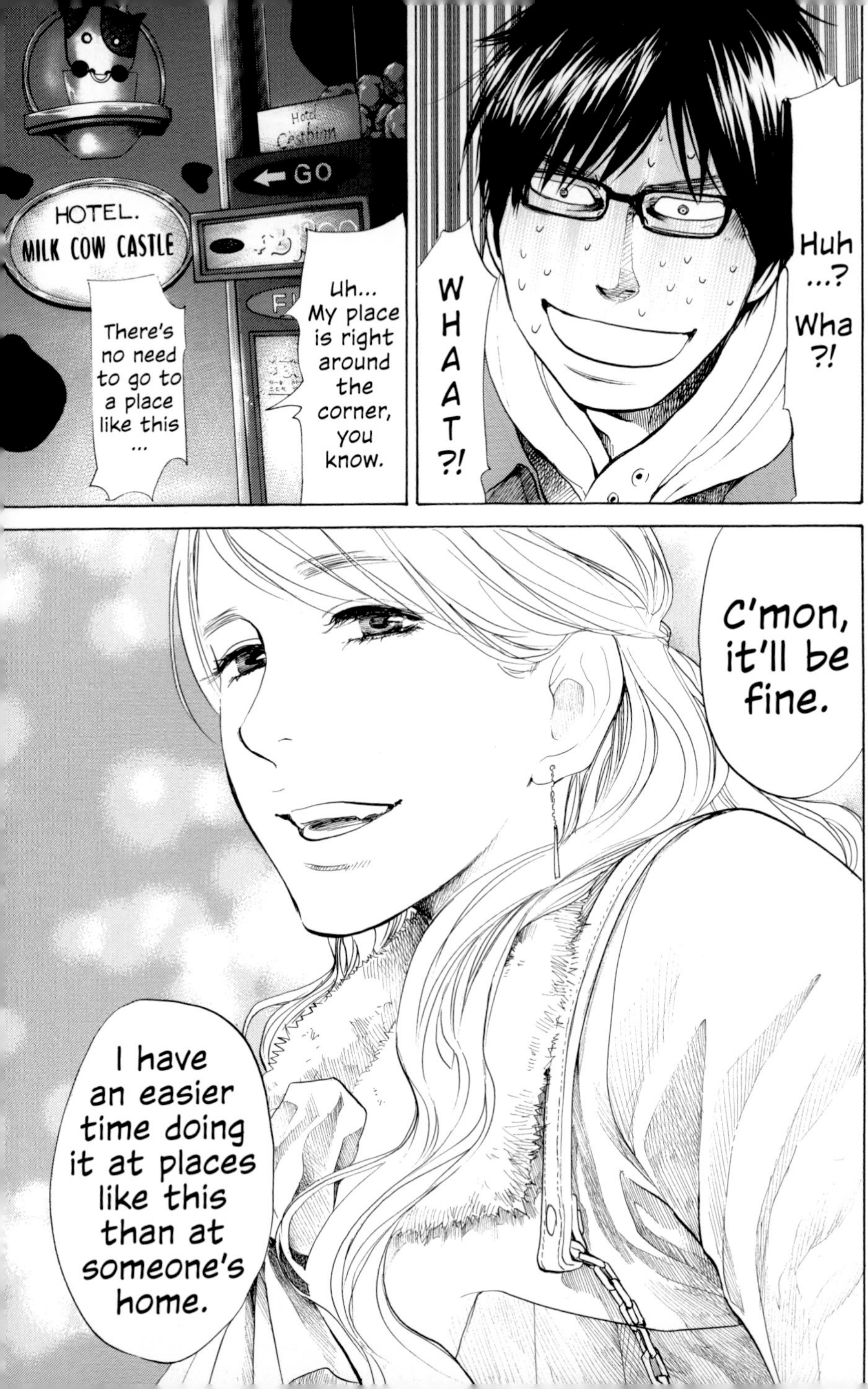
Huh ...? Wha ?!
WHAAT?!
Uh... My place is right around the corner, you know.
GO
HOTEL. MILK COW CASTLE
There's no need to go to a place like this ...
C'mon, it'll be fine.
I have an easier time doing it at places like this than at someone's home.

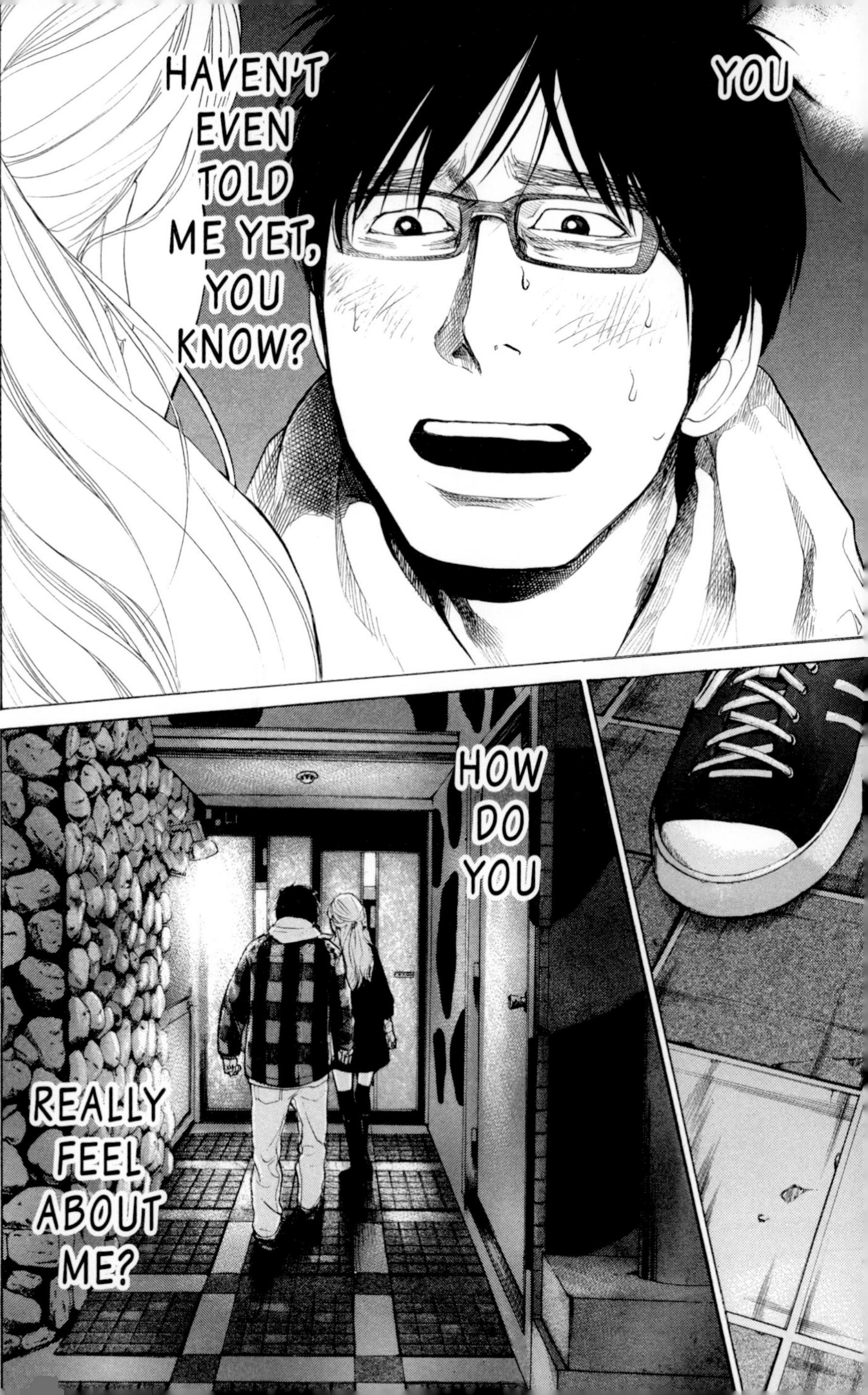
YOU
HAVEN'T EVEN TOLD ME YET, YOU KNOW?
HOW DO YOU
REALLY FEEL ABOUT ME?

chapter 5 ♥ END

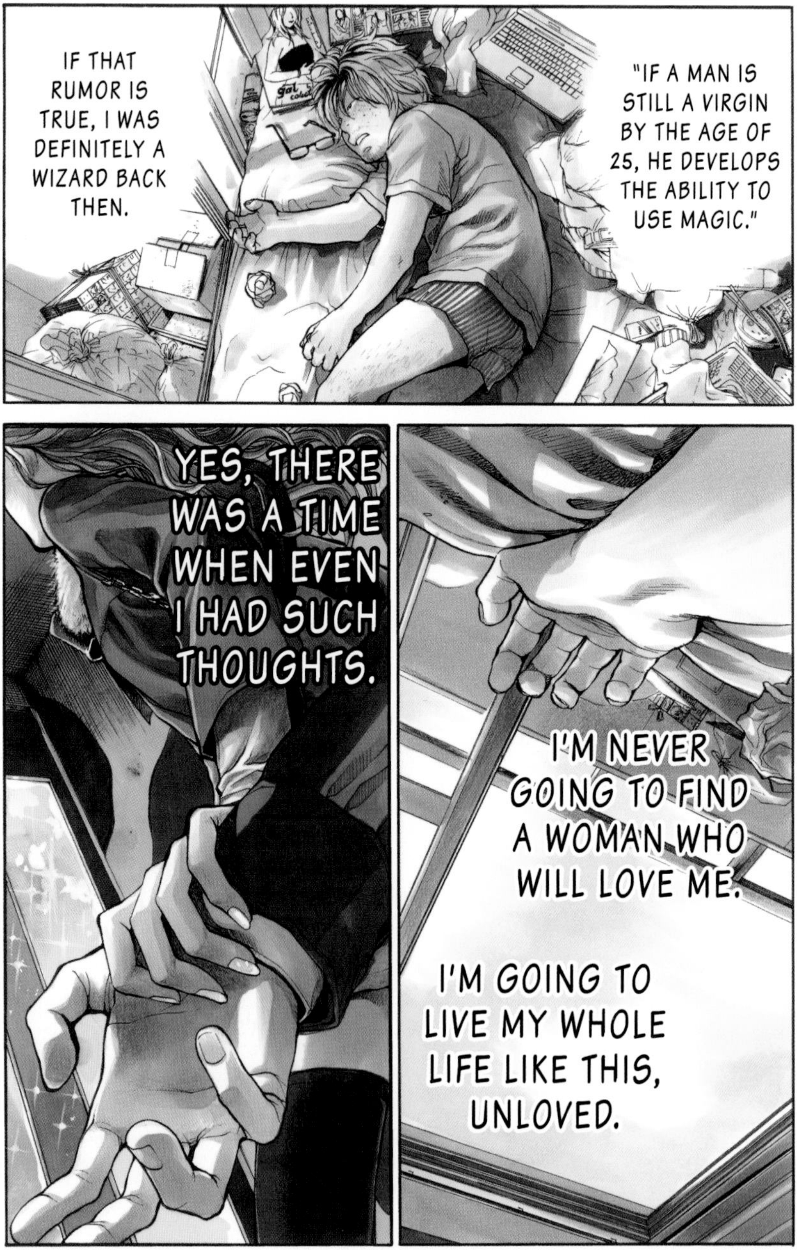
"IF A MAN IS STILL A VIRGIN BY THE AGE OF 25, HE DEVELOPS THE ABILITY TO USE MAGIC."
IF THAT RUMOR IS TRUE, I WAS DEFINITELY A WIZARD BACK THEN.
I'M NEVER GOING TO FIND A WOMAN WHO WILL LOVE ME.
I'M GOING TO LIVE MY WHOLE LIFE LIKE THIS, UNLOVED.
YES, THERE WAS A TIME WHEN EVEN I HAD SUCH THOUGHTS.

chapter 6 ♥ Late Night, High Speed

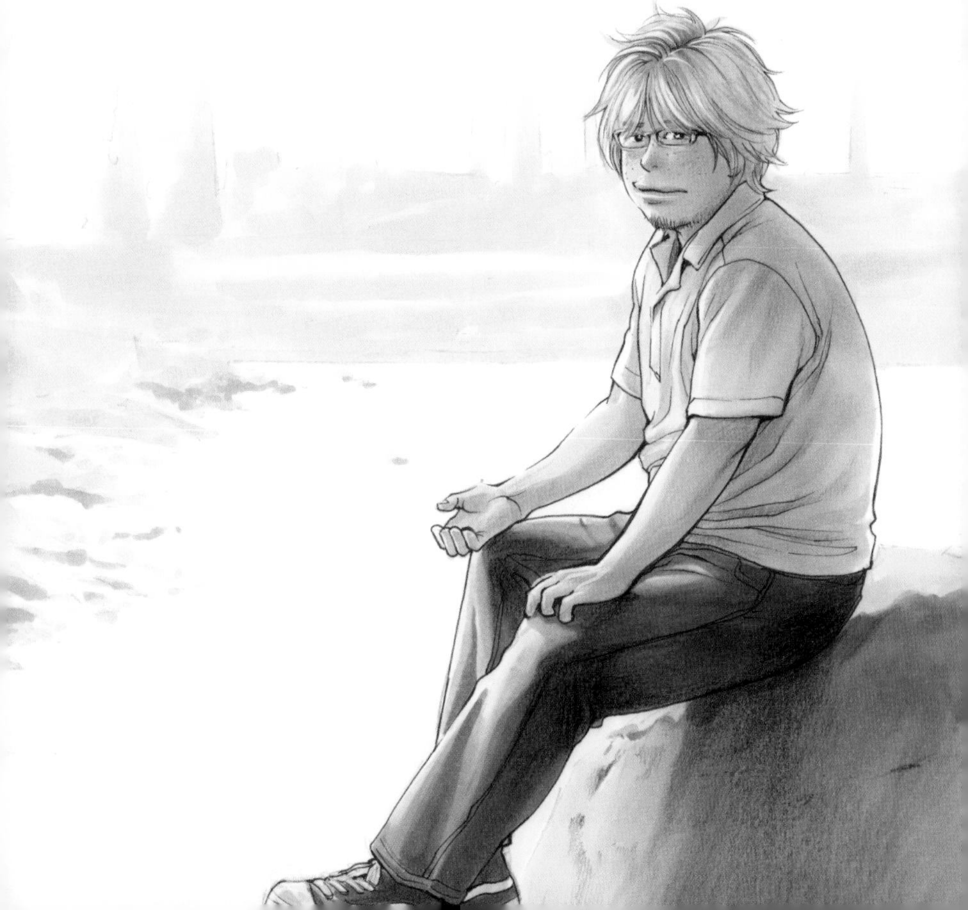

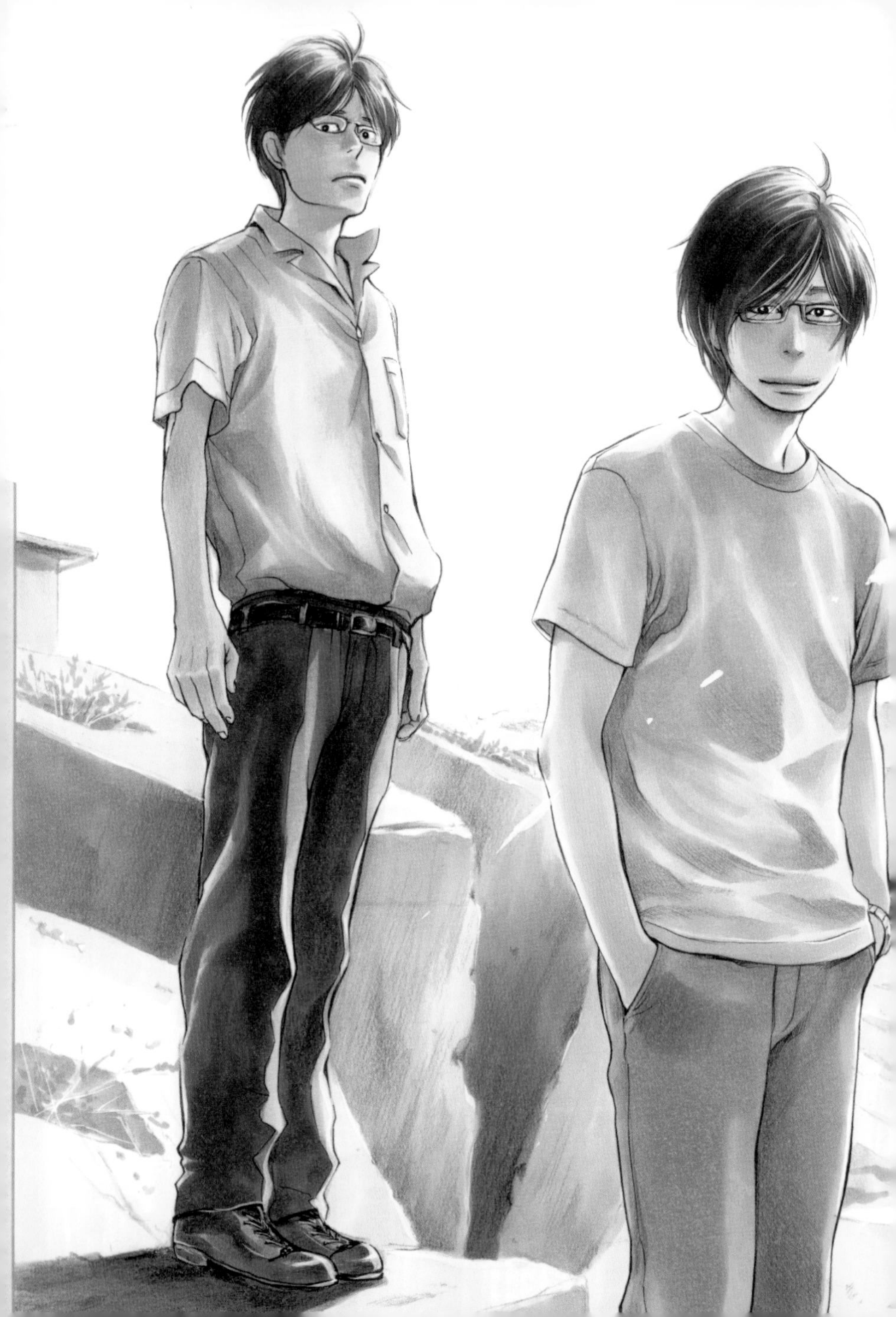

M o t e k i

M i t s u r o u   K u b o

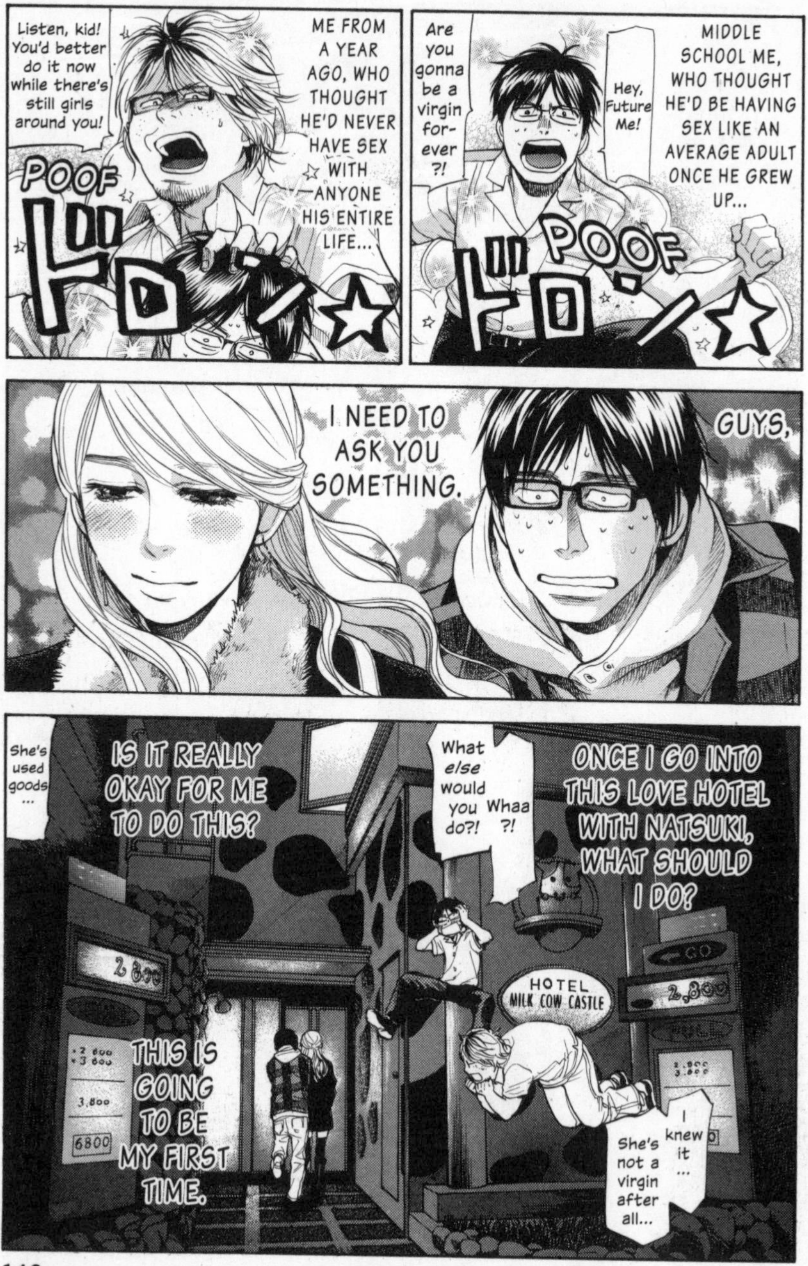

MIDDLE SCHOOL ME, WHO THOUGHT HE'D BE HAVING SEX LIKE AN AVERAGE ADULT ONCE HE GREW UP...
Hey, Future Me!
Are you gonna be a virgin forever?!
POOF
ME FROM A YEAR AGO, WHO THOUGHT HE'D NEVER HAVE SEX WITH ANYONE HIS ENTIRE LIFE...
Listen, kid! You'd better do it now while there's still girls around you!
POOF
GUYS,
I NEED TO ASK YOU SOMETHING.
ONCE I GO INTO THIS LOVE HOTEL WITH NATSUKI, WHAT SHOULD I DO?
Whaa ?!
What else would you do?!
HOTEL MILK COW CASTLE
I knew it...
She's not a virgin after all...
IS IT REALLY OKAY FOR ME TO DO THIS?
She's used goods...
THIS IS GOING TO BE MY FIRST TIME.

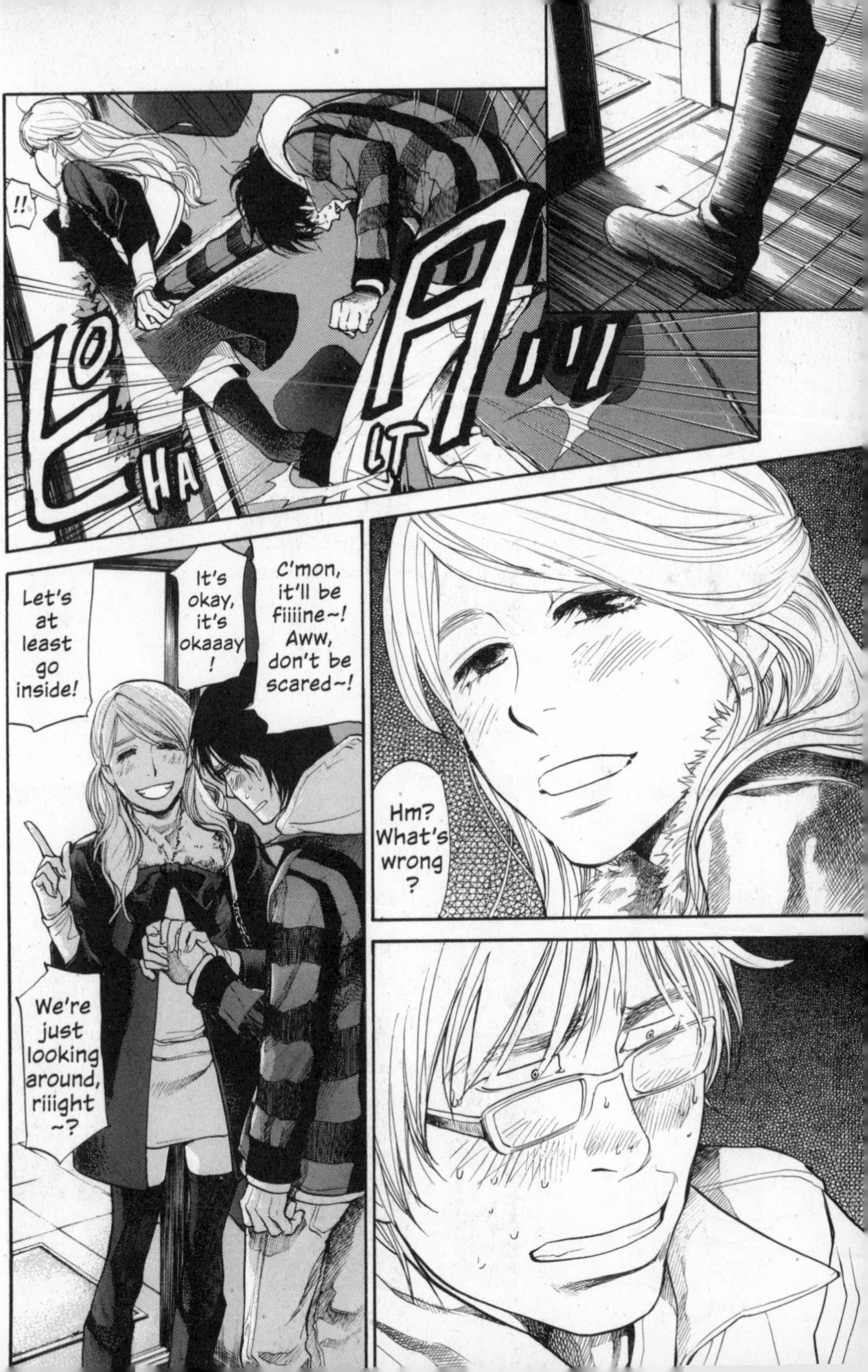
!!
Hm? What's wrong?
C'mon, it'll be fiiiine~! Aww, don't be scared~!
It's okay, it's okaaay!
Let's at least go inside!
We're just looking around, riiight~?

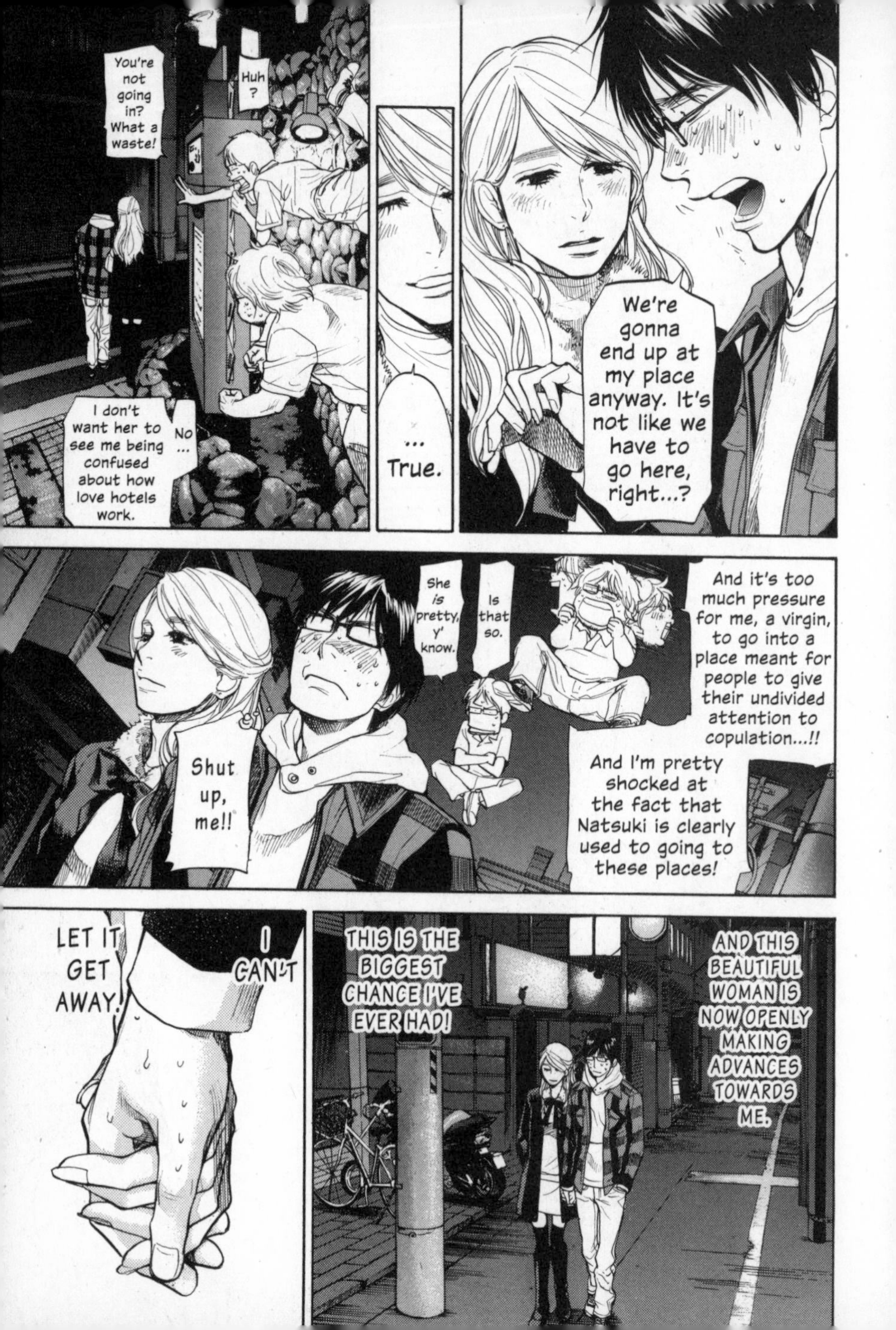
We're gonna end up at my place anyway. It's not like we have to go here, right...?
... True.
Huh?
You're not going in? What a waste!
No ...
I don't want her to see me being confused about how love hotels work.
And it's too much pressure for me, a virgin, to go into a place meant for people to give their undivided attention to copulation...!!
And I'm pretty shocked at the fact that Natsuki is clearly used to going to these places!
Is that so.
She is pretty, y' know.
Shut up, me!!
AND THIS BEAUTIFUL WOMAN IS NOW OPENLY MAKING ADVANCES TOWARDS ME.
THIS IS THE BIGGEST CHANCE I'VE EVER HAD!
I CAN'T
LET IT GET AWAY.

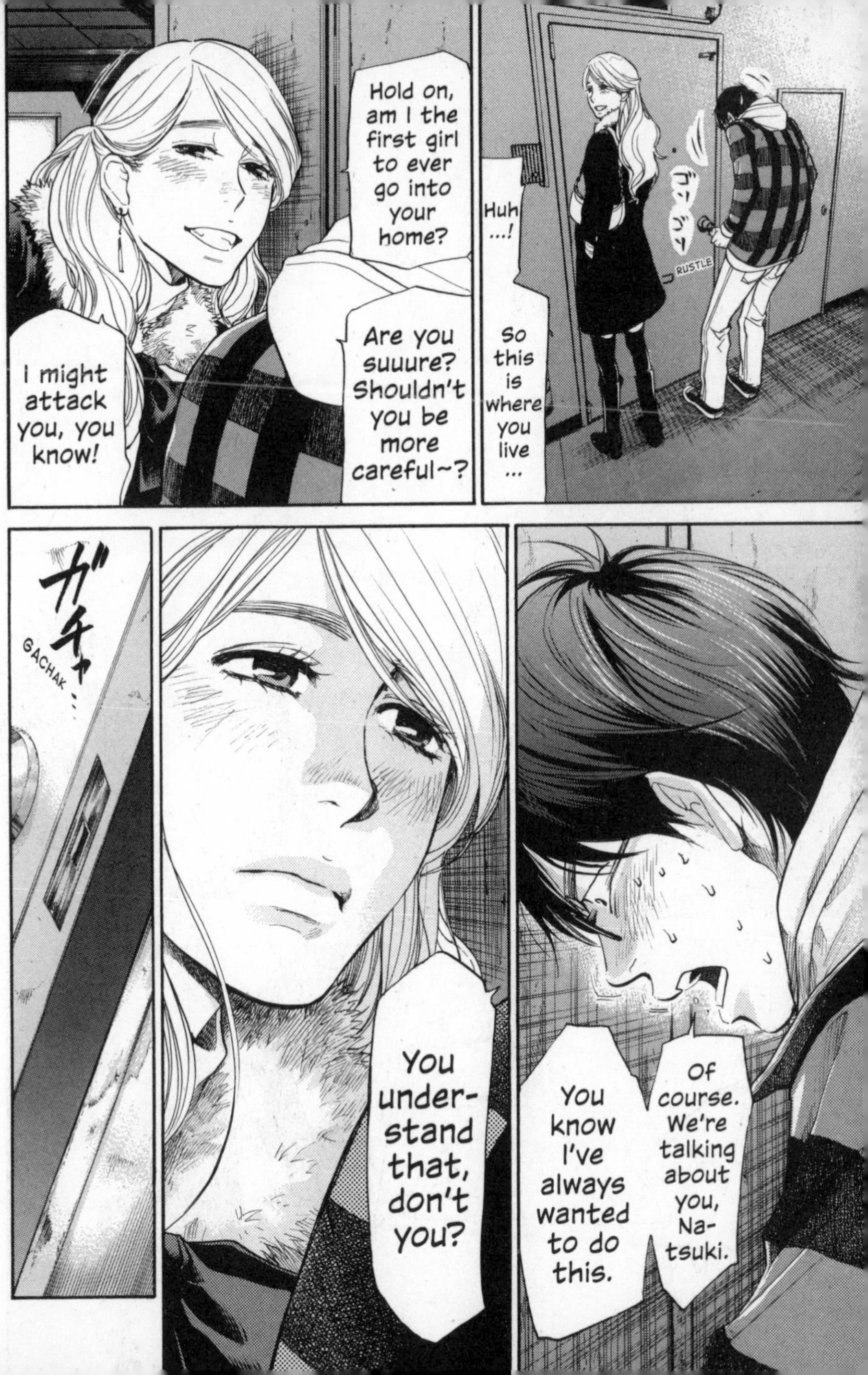
ゴソゴソ
RUSTLE
So this is where you live...
Hold on, am I the first girl to ever go into your home?
Huh...!
Are you suuure? Shouldn't you be more careful~?
I might attack you, you know!
Of course. We're talking about you, Na-tsuki.
You know I've always wanted to do this.
You under-stand that, don't you?
ガチャ
GACHAK

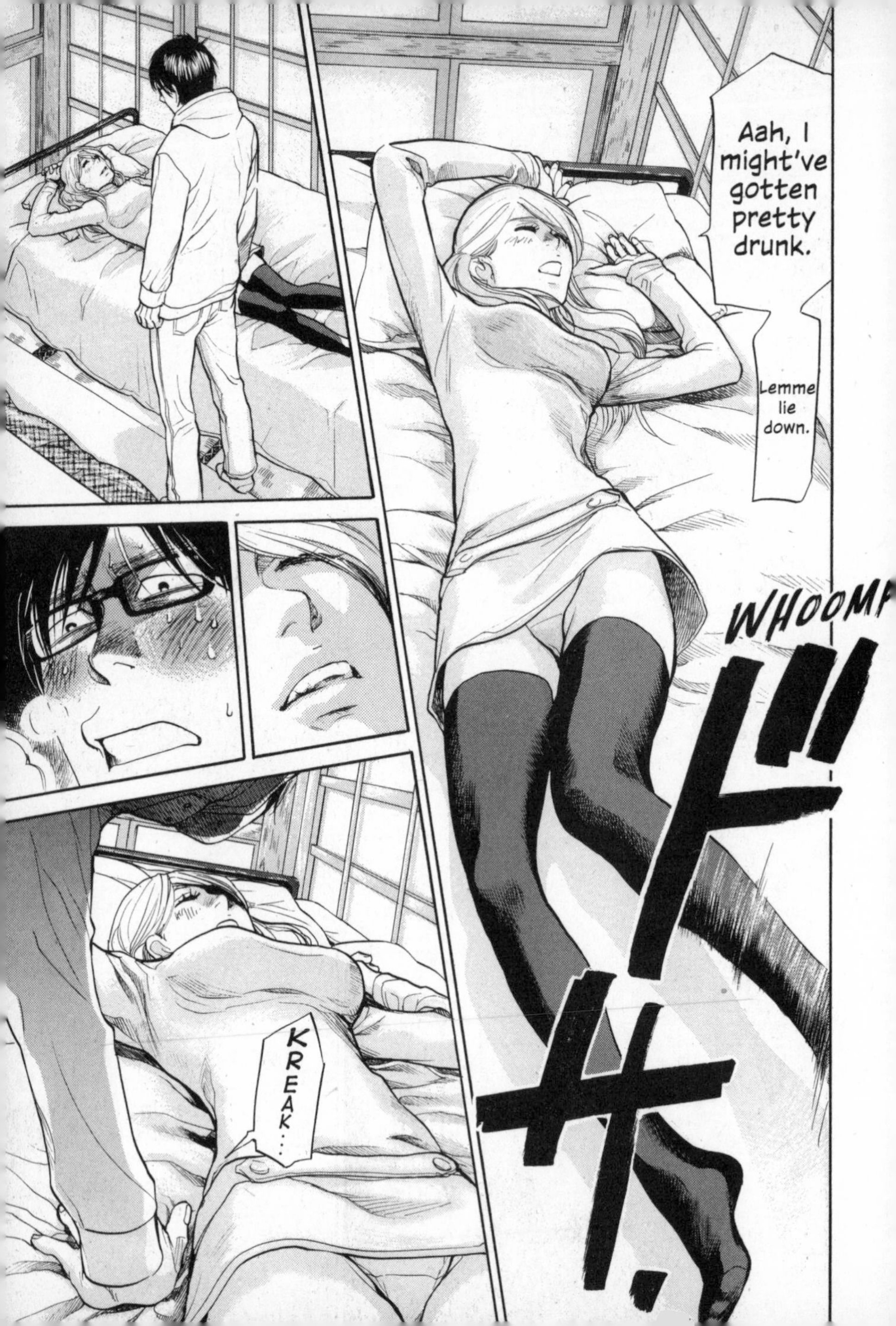
Aah, I might've gotten pretty drunk.
Lemme lie down.
WHOOMP
KREAK...

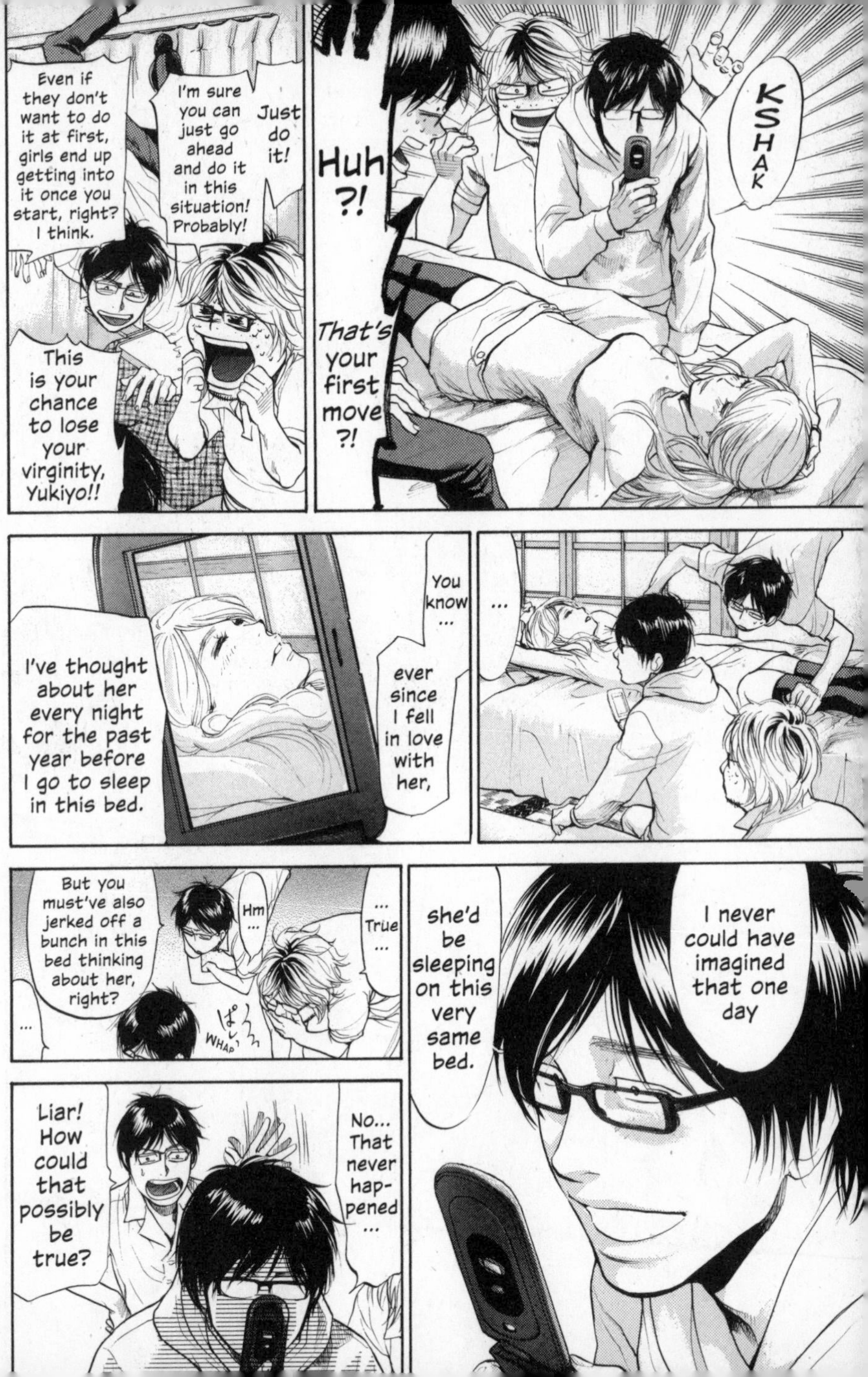
KSHAK
Huh ?!
That's your first move ?!
Just do it!
I'm sure you can just go ahead and do it in this situation! Probably!
Even if they don't want to do it at first, girls end up getting into it once you start, right? I think.
This is your chance to lose your virginity, Yukiyo!!
...
You know ...
ever since I fell in love with her,
I've thought about her every night for the past year before I go to sleep in this bed.
I never could have imagined that one day
she'd be sleeping on this very same bed.
... True ...
Hm ...
But you must've also jerked off a bunch in this bed thinking about her, right?
ぱし WHAP
...
No... That never hap-pened ...
Liar! How could that possibly be true?

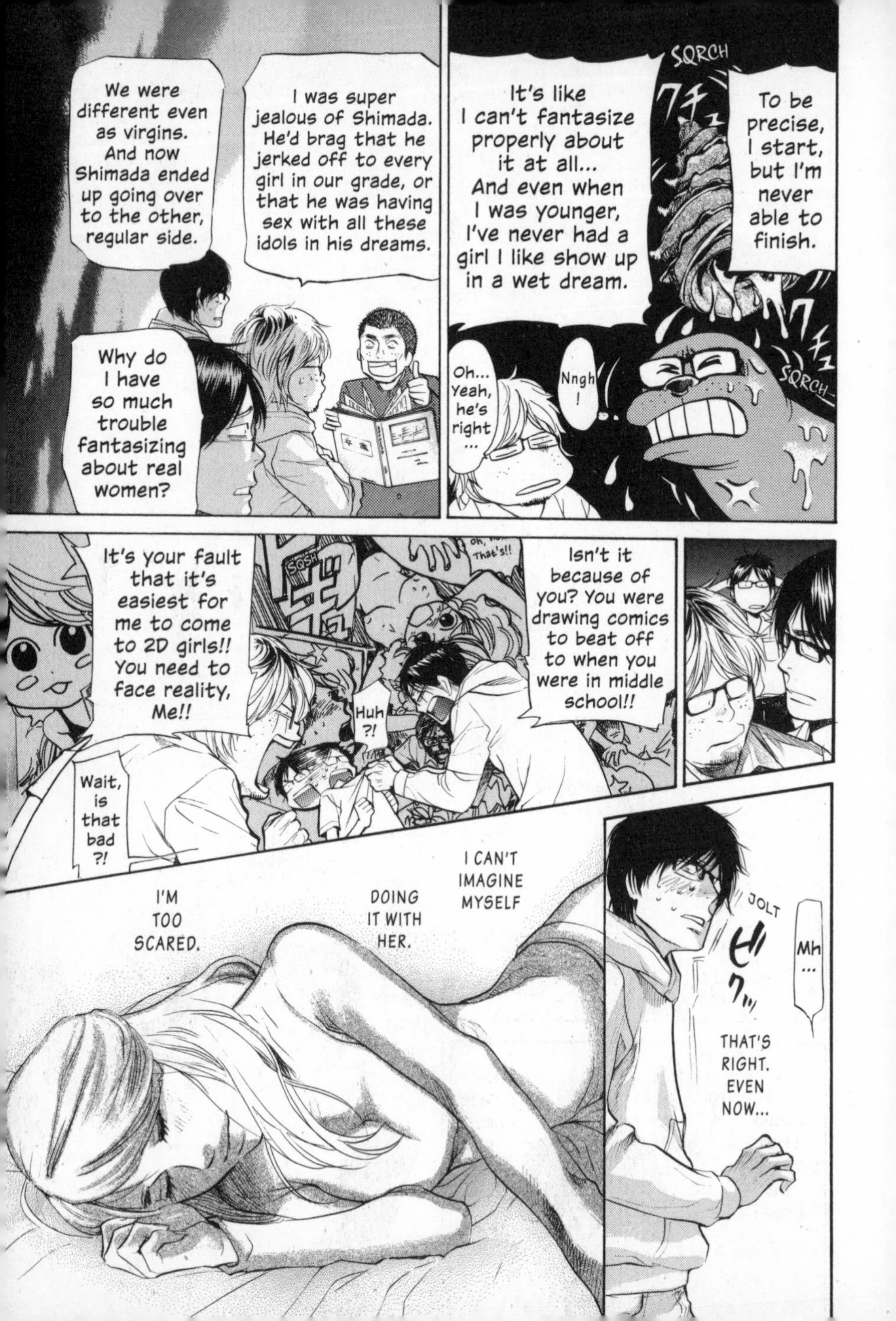
SQRCH
To be precise, I start, but I'm never able to finish.
It's like I can't fantasize properly about it at all... And even when I was younger, I've never had a girl I like show up in a wet dream.
SQRCH-
Nngh!
Oh... Yeah, he's right...
I was super jealous of Shimada. He'd brag that he jerked off to every girl in our grade, or that he was having sex with all these idols in his dreams.
We were different even as virgins. And now Shimada ended up going over to the other, regular side.
Why do I have so much trouble fantasizing about real women?
Isn't it because of you? You were drawing comics to beat off to when you were in middle school!!
SQSH
It's your fault that it's easiest for me to come to 2D girls!! You need to face reality, Me!!
Huh?!
Wait, is that bad?!
Mh...
JOLT
THAT'S RIGHT. EVEN NOW...
I CAN'T IMAGINE MYSELF
DOING IT WITH HER.
I'M TOO SCARED.

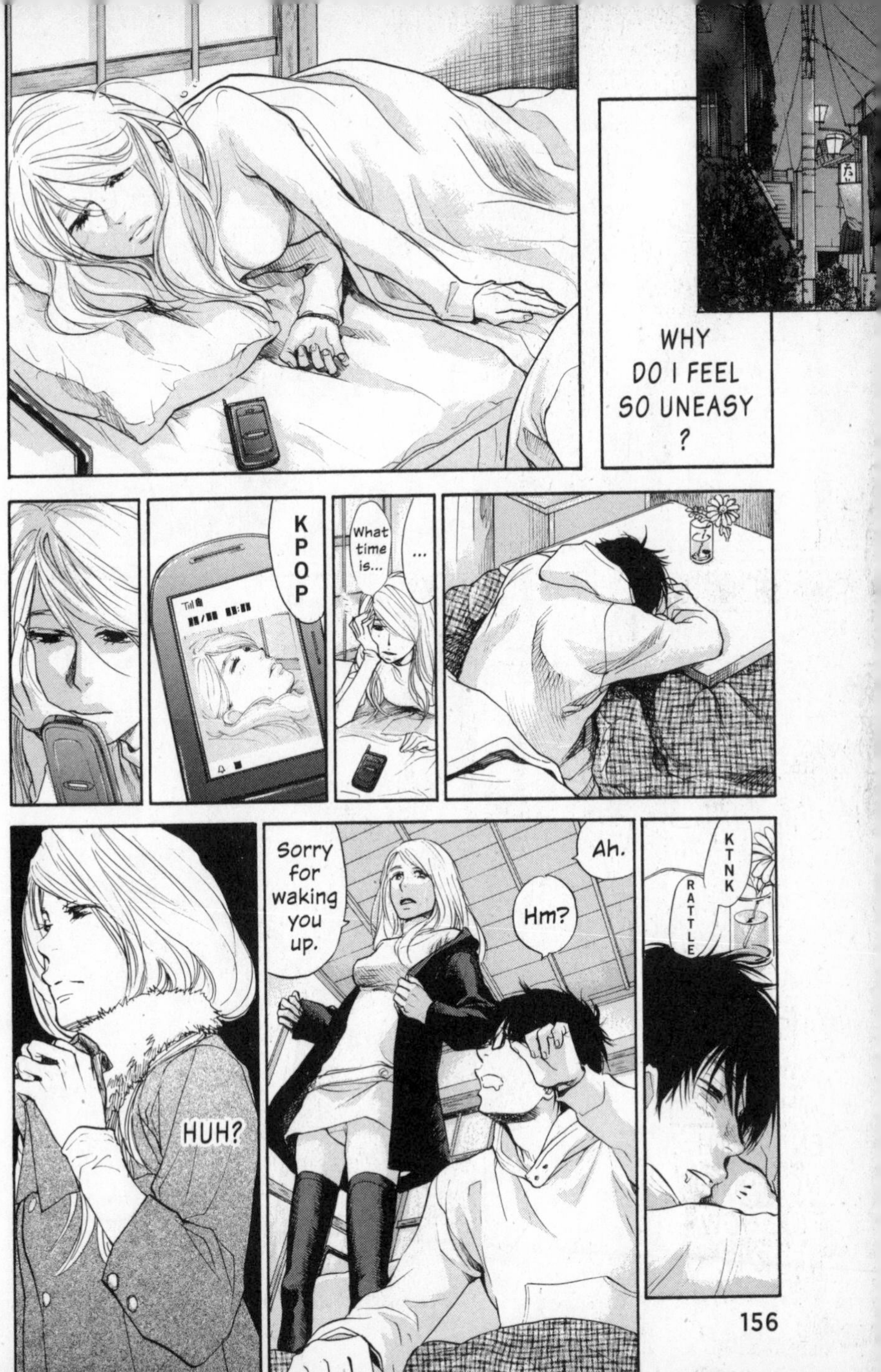
WHY DO I FEEL SO UNEASY ?
...
What time is...
KPOP
KTNK
RATTLE
Ah.
Hm?
Sorry for waking you up.
HUH?

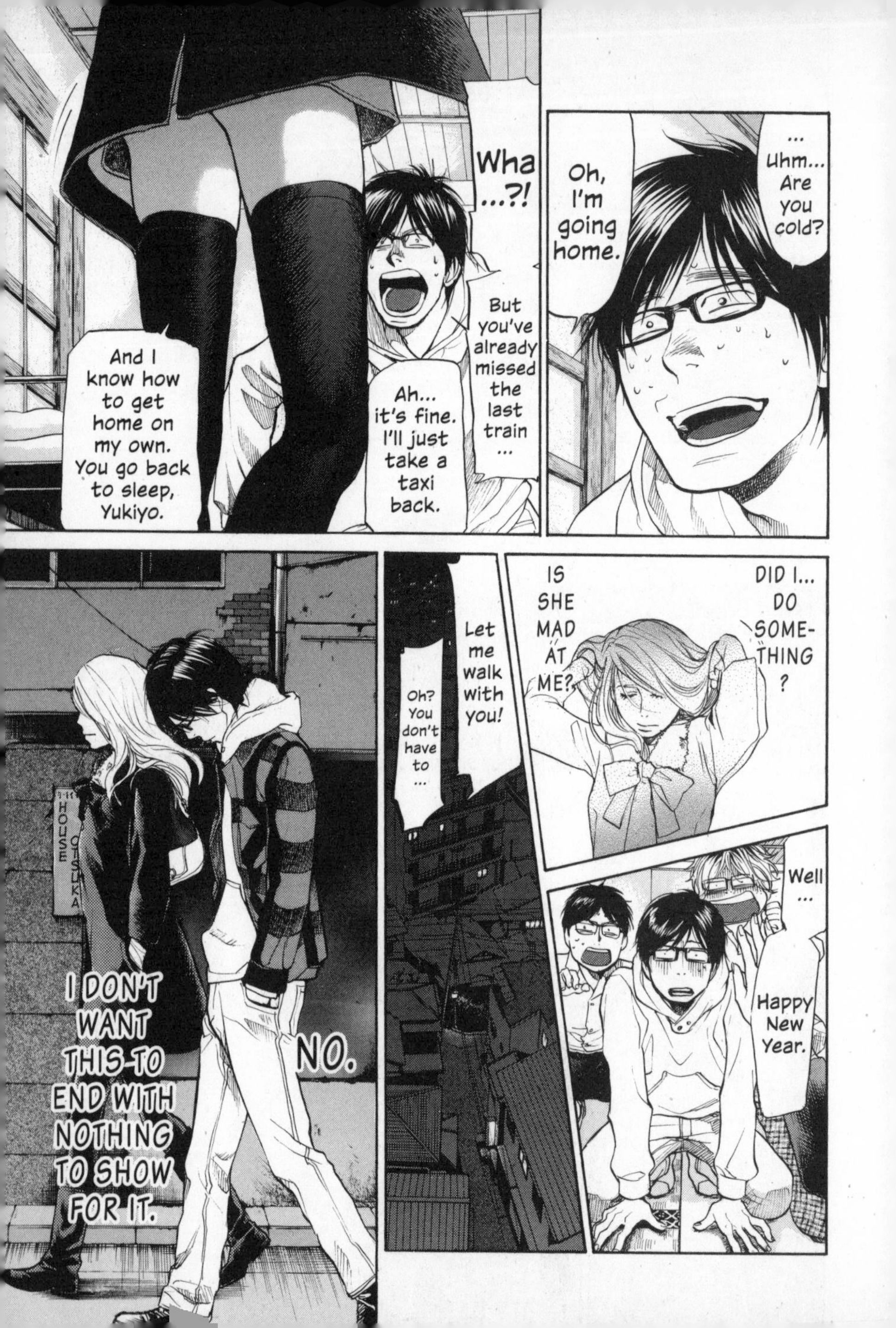
... Uhm... Are you cold?
Oh, I'm going home.
Wha...?!
But you've already missed the last train...
Ah... it's fine. I'll just take a taxi back.
And I know how to get home on my own. You go back to sleep, Yukiyo.
DID I... DO SOME-THING?
IS SHE MAD AT ME?
Well...
Happy New Year.
Let me walk with you!
Oh? You don't have to...
NO.
I DON'T WANT THIS TO END WITH NOTHING TO SHOW FOR IT.

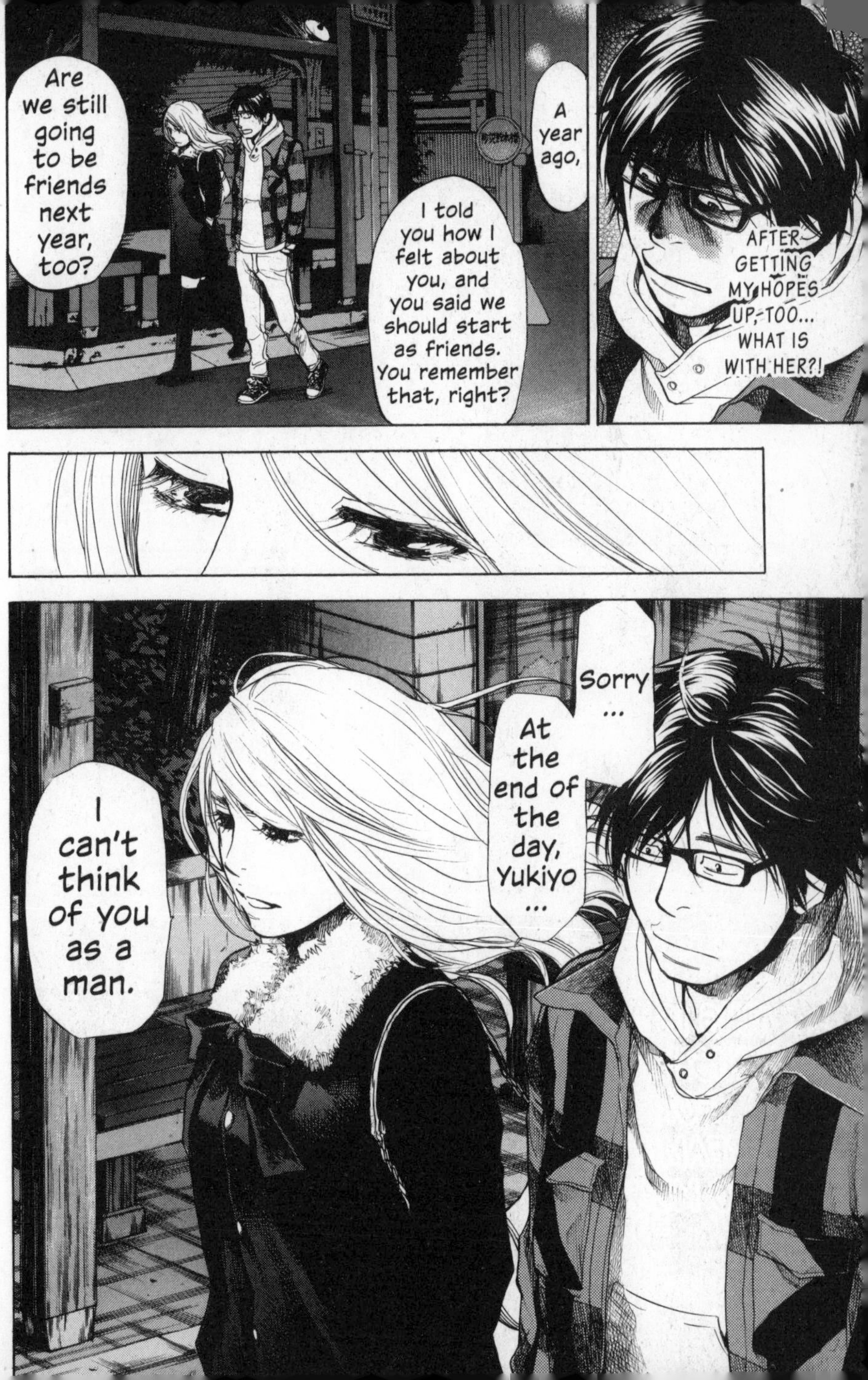
AFTER GETTING MY HOPES UP, TOO... WHAT IS WITH HER?!
A year ago,
I told you how I felt about you, and you said we should start as friends. You remember that, right?
Are we still going to be friends next year, too?
Sorry...
At the end of the day, Yukiyo...
I can't think of you as a man.

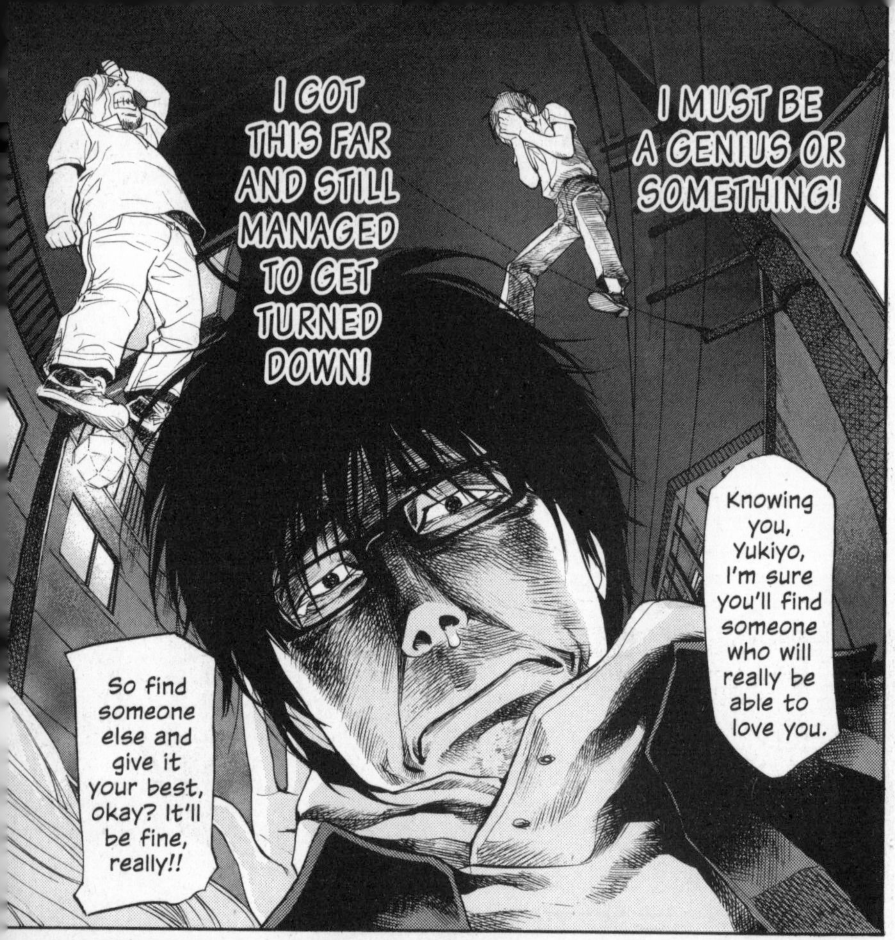
I MUST BE A GENIUS OR SOMETHING!
I GOT THIS FAR AND STILL MANAGED TO GET TURNED DOWN!
Knowing you, Yukiyo, I'm sure you'll find someone who will really be able to love you.
So find someone else and give it your best, okay? It'll be fine, really!!
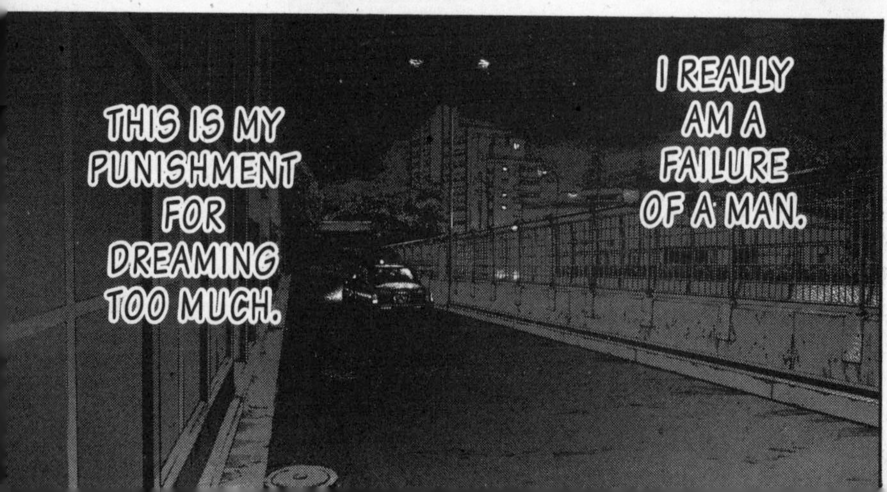
I REALLY AM A FAILURE OF A MAN.
THIS IS MY PUNISHMENT FOR DREAMING TOO MUCH.

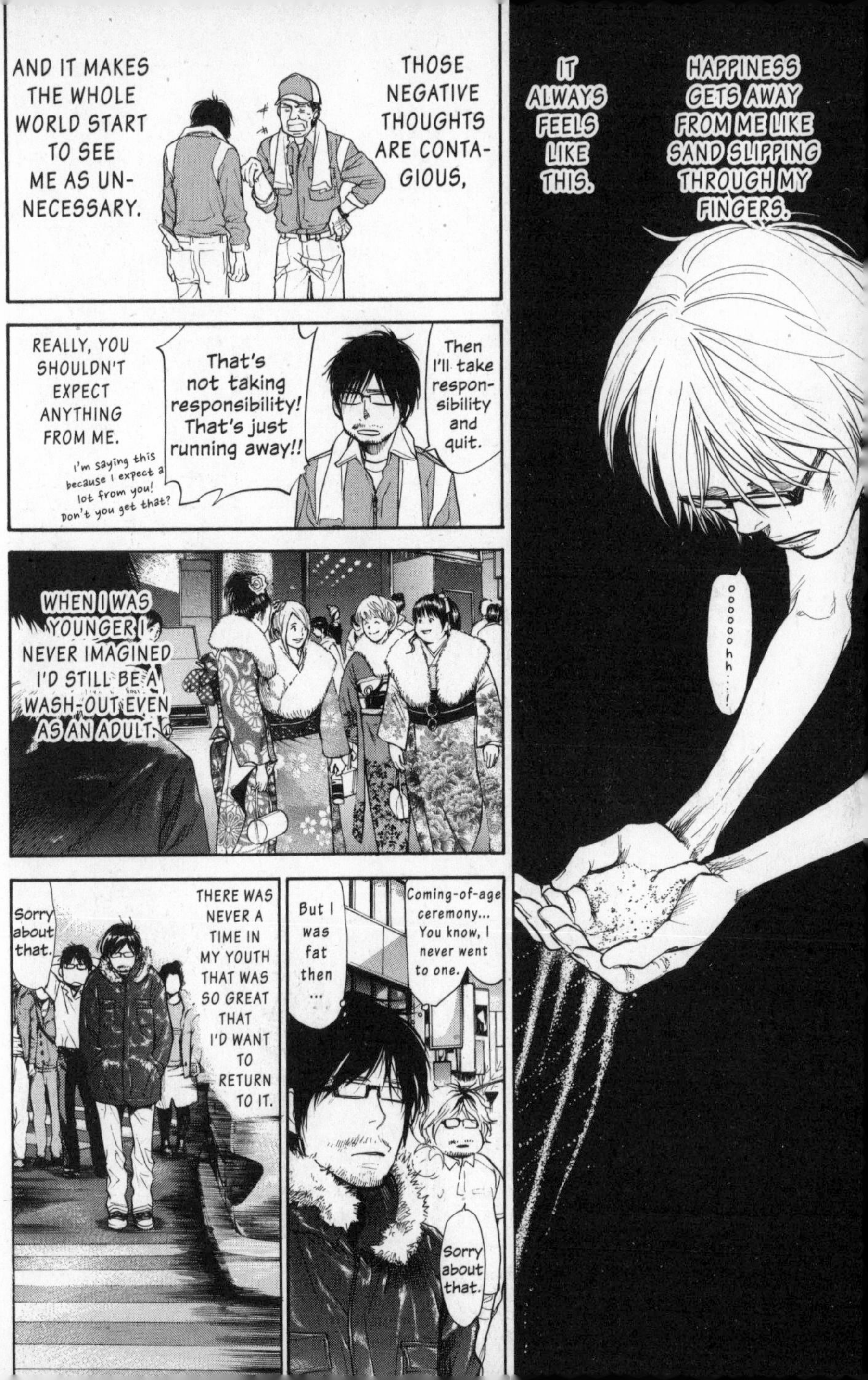
HAPPINESS GETS AWAY FROM ME LIKE SAND SLIPPING THROUGH MY FINGERS.
IT ALWAYS FEELS LIKE THIS.
ooooooh...!
THOSE NEGATIVE THOUGHTS ARE CONTAGIOUS,
AND IT MAKES THE WHOLE WORLD START TO SEE ME AS UNNECESSARY.
Then I'll take responsibility and quit.
That's not taking responsibility! That's just running away!!
I'm saying this because I expect a lot from you! Don't you get that?
REALLY, YOU SHOULDN'T EXPECT ANYTHING FROM ME.
WHEN I WAS YOUNGER I NEVER IMAGINED I'D STILL BE A WASH-OUT EVEN AS AN ADULT.
Coming-of-age ceremony... You know, I never went to one.
But I was fat then ...
Sorry about that.
THERE WAS NEVER A TIME IN MY YOUTH THAT WAS SO GREAT THAT I'D WANT TO RETURN TO IT.
Sorry about that.

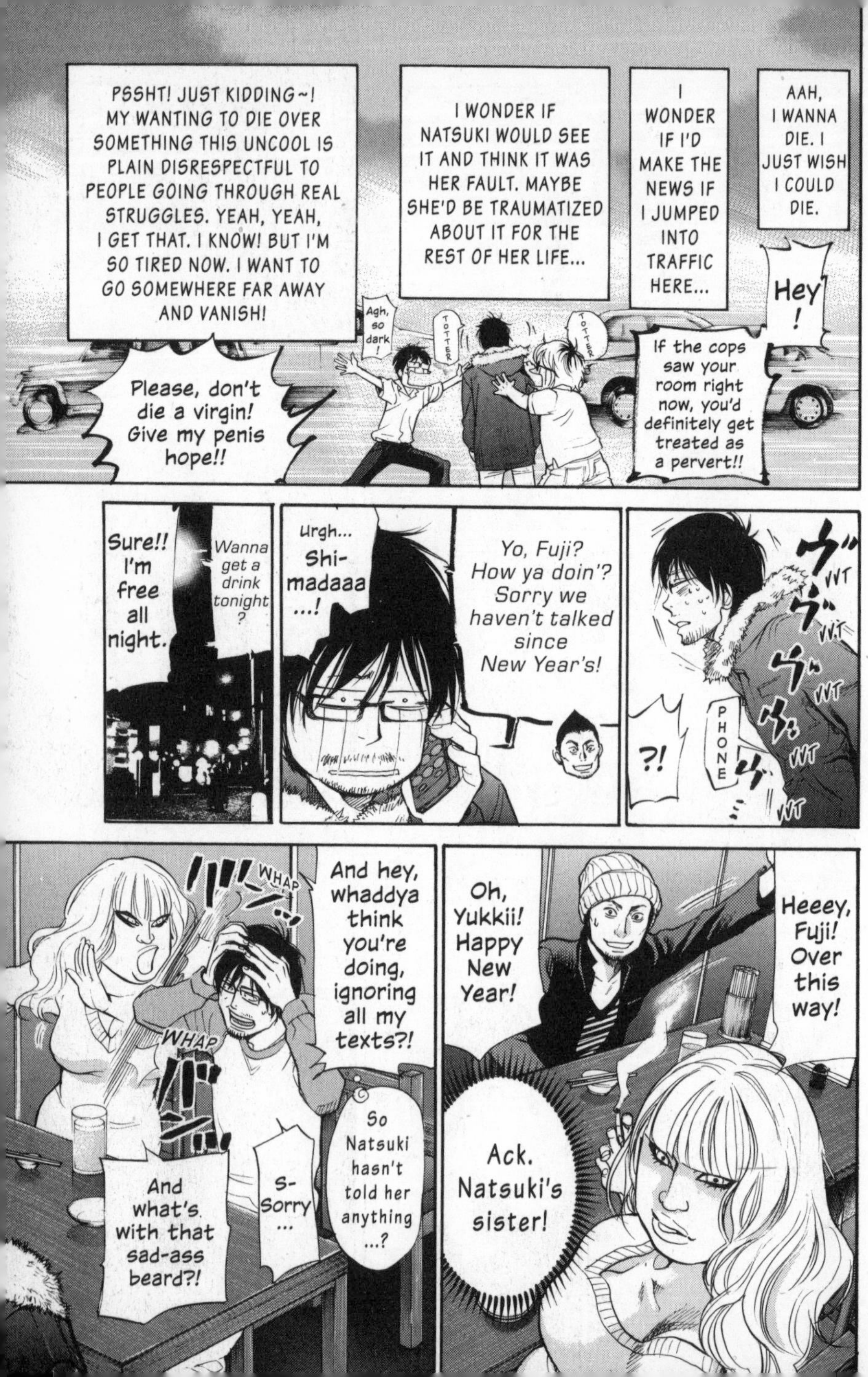
AAH, I WANNA DIE. I JUST WISH I COULD DIE.
I WONDER IF I'D MAKE THE NEWS IF I JUMPED INTO TRAFFIC HERE...
I WONDER IF NATSUKI WOULD SEE IT AND THINK IT WAS HER FAULT. MAYBE SHE'D BE TRAUMATIZED ABOUT IT FOR THE REST OF HER LIFE...
PSSHT! JUST KIDDING~! MY WANTING TO DIE OVER SOMETHING THIS UNCOOL IS PLAIN DISRESPECTFUL TO PEOPLE GOING THROUGH REAL STRUGGLES. YEAH, YEAH, I GET THAT. I KNOW! BUT I'M SO TIRED NOW. I WANT TO GO SOMEWHERE FAR AWAY AND VANISH!
Hey!
If the cops saw your room right now, you'd definitely get treated as a pervert!!
TOTTER
TOTTER
Agh, so dark!
Please, don't die a virgin! Give my penis hope!!
VVT
VVT
VVT
VVT
VVT
PHONE
?!
Yo, Fuji? How ya doin'? Sorry we haven't talked since New Year's!
Urgh... Shi-madaaa...!
Wanna get a drink tonight?
Sure!! I'm free all night.
Heeey, Fuji! Over this way!
Oh, Yukkii! Happy New Year!
Ack. Natsuki's sister!
And hey, whaddya think you're doing, ignoring all my texts?!
WHAP
WHAP
So Natsuki hasn't told her anything...?
S-Sorry...
And what's with that sad-ass beard?!

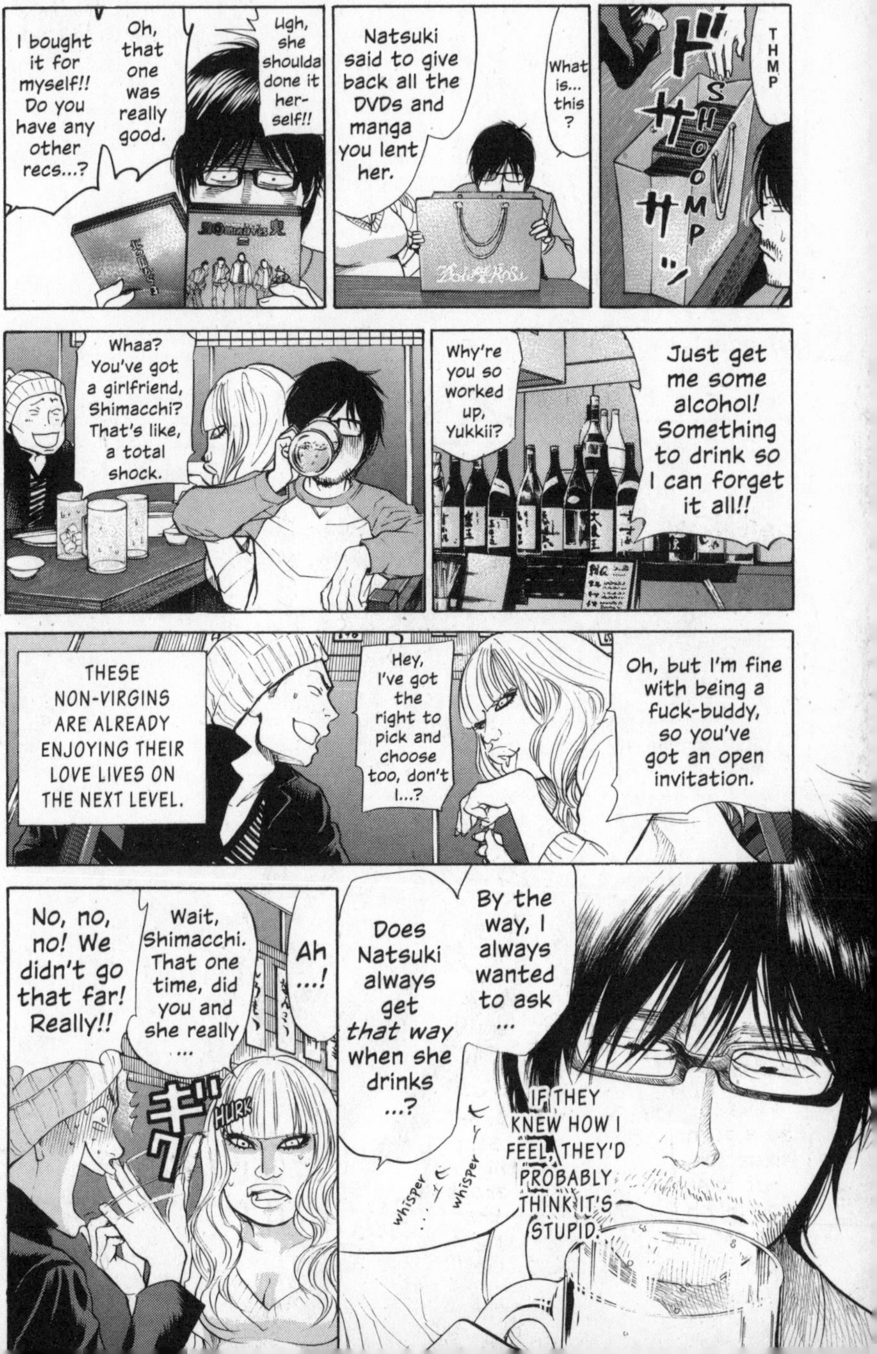
THMP
SHOOMP
What is... this?
Natsuki said to give back all the DVDs and manga you lent her.
Ugh, she shoulda done it her-self!!
Oh, that one was really good.
I bought it for myself!! Do you have any other recs...?
Just get me some alcohol! Something to drink so I can forget it all!!
Why're you so worked up, Yukkii?
Whaa? You've got a girlfriend, Shimacchi? That's like, a total shock.
Oh, but I'm fine with being a fuck-buddy, so you've got an open invitation.
Hey, I've got the right to pick and choose too, don't I...?
THESE NON-VIRGINS ARE ALREADY ENJOYING THEIR LOVE LIVES ON THE NEXT LEVEL.
By the way, I always wanted to ask...
Does Natsuki always get *that way* when she drinks...?
whisper
whisper
IF THEY KNEW HOW I FEEL, THEY'D PROBABLY THINK IT'S STUPID.
Ah...!
Wait, Shimacchi. That one time, did you and she really...
No, no, no! We didn't go that far! Really!!
HURK

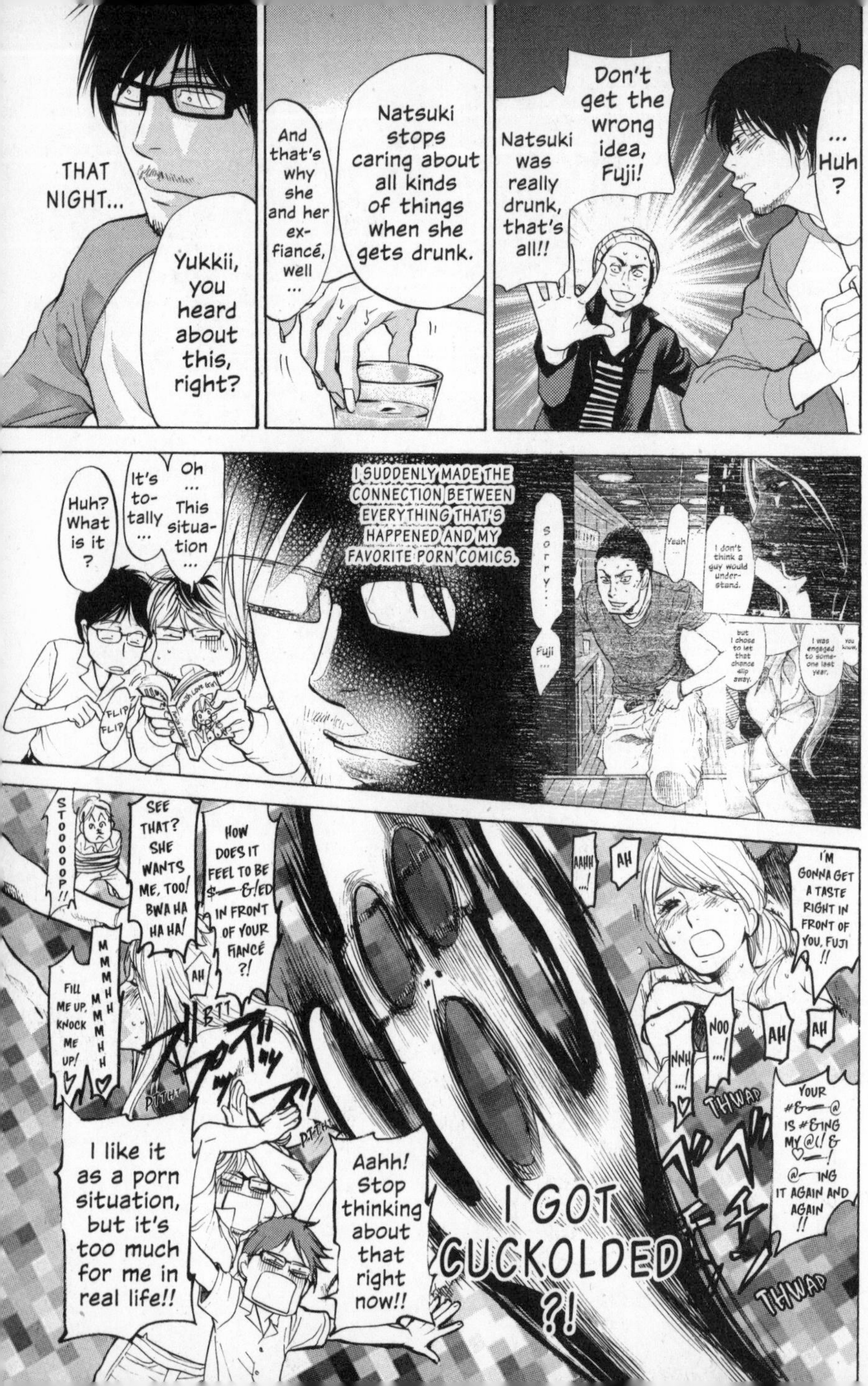
... Huh?
Don't get the wrong idea, Fuji!
Natsuki was really drunk, that's all!!
Natsuki stops caring about all kinds of things when she gets drunk.
And that's why she and her ex-fiancé, well ...
THAT NIGHT...
Yukkii, you heard about this, right?
I don't think a guy would understand.
Yeah ...
you know,
I was engaged to someone last year.
but I chose to let that chance slip away.
sorry... Fuji ...
I SUDDENLY MADE THE CONNECTION BETWEEN EVERYTHING THAT'S HAPPENED AND MY FAVORITE PORN COMICS.
Oh ... This situation ...
It's totally ...
Huh? What is it ?
FLIP FLIP
I'M GONNA GET A TASTE RIGHT IN FRONT OF YOU, FUJI !!
AH
AAHH ...!
AH
AH
NOO ...!
NNH ...! ♡
THWAP
YOUR #&—@ IS #&ING MY @(! & ♡—! @—ING IT AGAIN AND AGAIN !!
THWAP
I GOT CUCKOLDED ?!
HOW DOES IT FEEL TO BE $—&!ED IN FRONT OF YOUR FIANCÉ ?!
SEE THAT? SHE WANTS ME, TOO! BWA HA HA HA!
STOOOOOOP!!
AH
MMMMHH MMMMHH ♡
FILL ME UP, KNOCK ME UP! ♡
BTT
PTTHT
Aahh! Stop thinking about that right now!!
I like it as a porn situation, but it's too much for me in real life!!

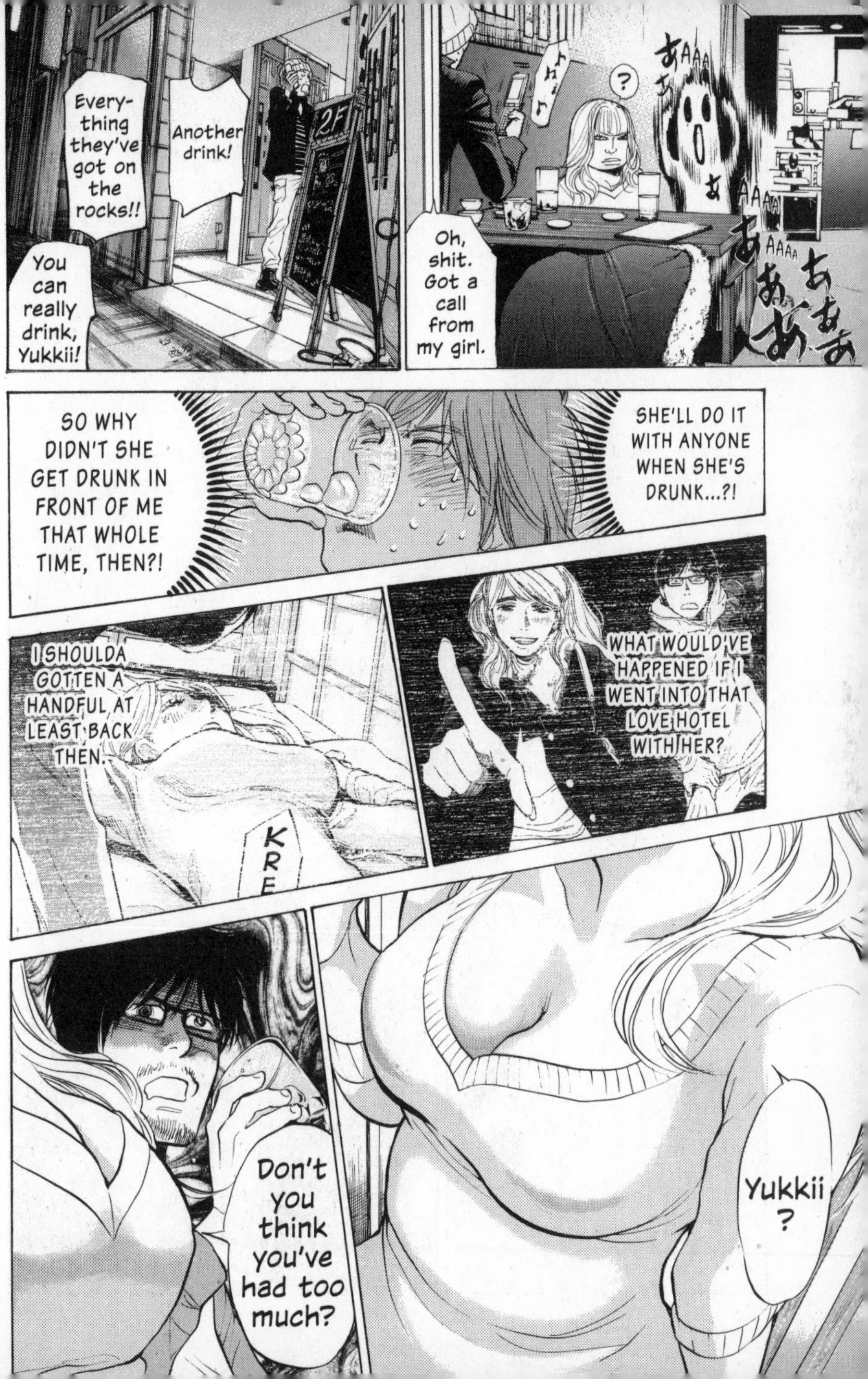

AAAA
?
Oh, shit. Got a call from my girl.
Another drink!
Everything they've got on the rocks!!
You can really drink, Yukkii!
SHE'LL DO IT WITH ANYONE WHEN SHE'S DRUNK...?!
SO WHY DIDN'T SHE GET DRUNK IN FRONT OF ME THAT WHOLE TIME, THEN?!
WHAT WOULD'VE HAPPENED IF I WENT INTO THAT LOVE HOTEL WITH HER?
I SHOULDA GOTTEN A HANDFUL AT LEAST BACK THEN.
KRE
Yukkii?
Don't you think you've had too much?

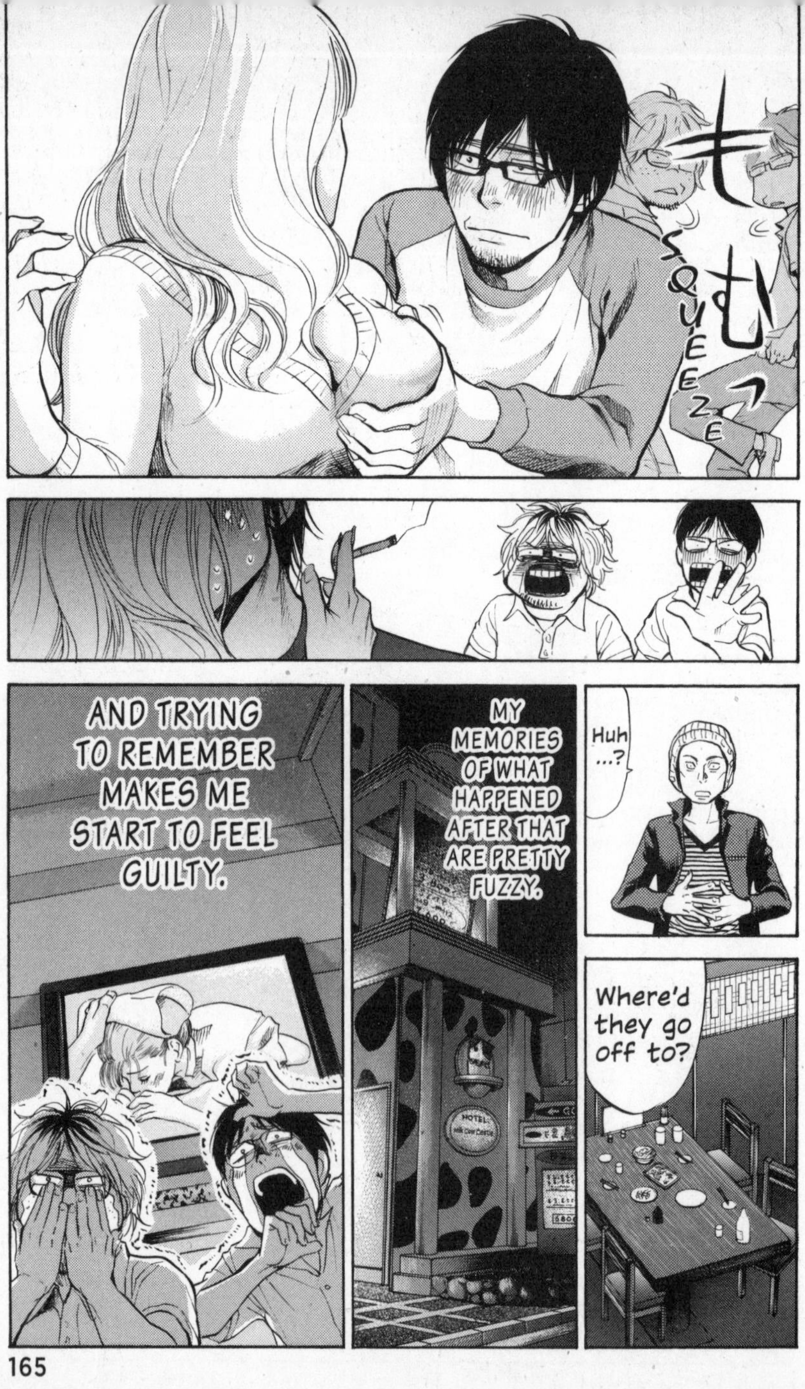
SQUEEZE
Huh ...?
Where'd they go off to?
MY MEMORIES OF WHAT HAPPENED AFTER THAT ARE PRETTY FUZZY.
AND TRYING TO REMEMBER MAKES ME START TO FEEL GUILTY.

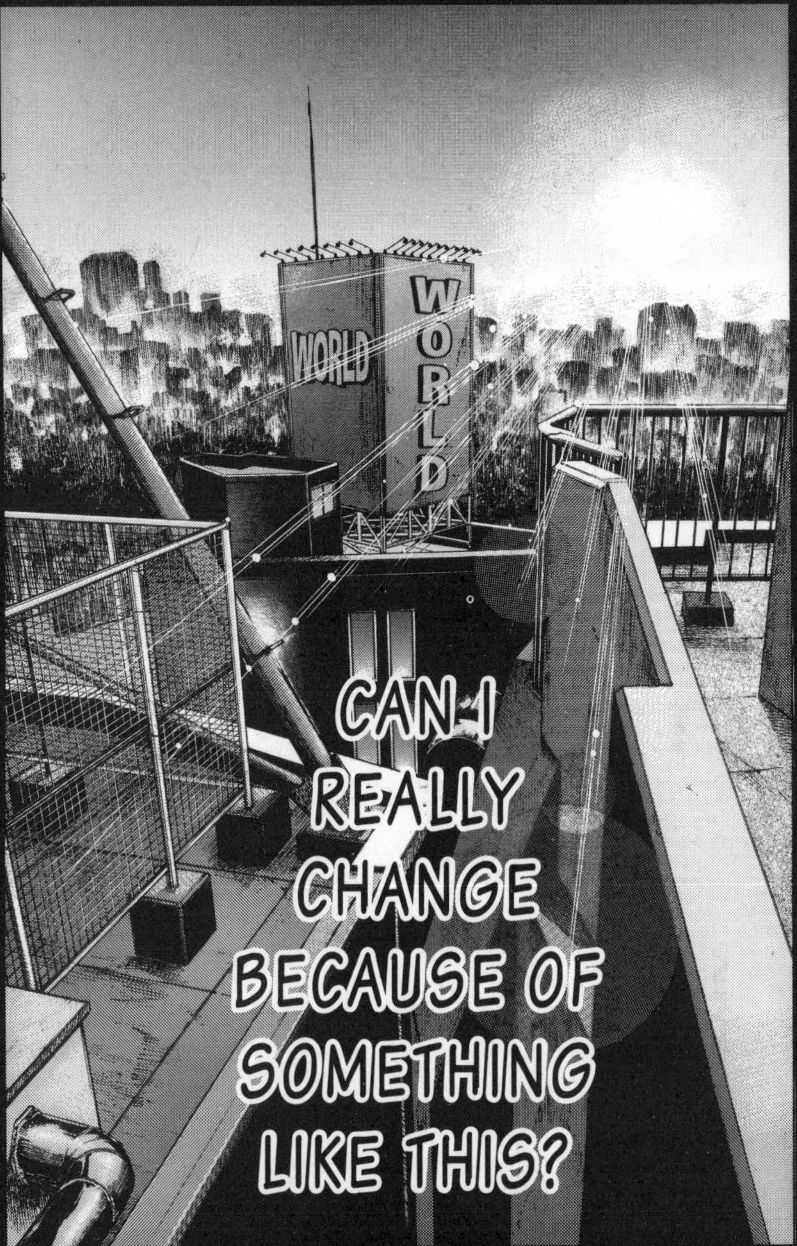
WORLD
WORLD
CAN I REALLY CHANGE BECAUSE OF SOMETHING LIKE THIS?

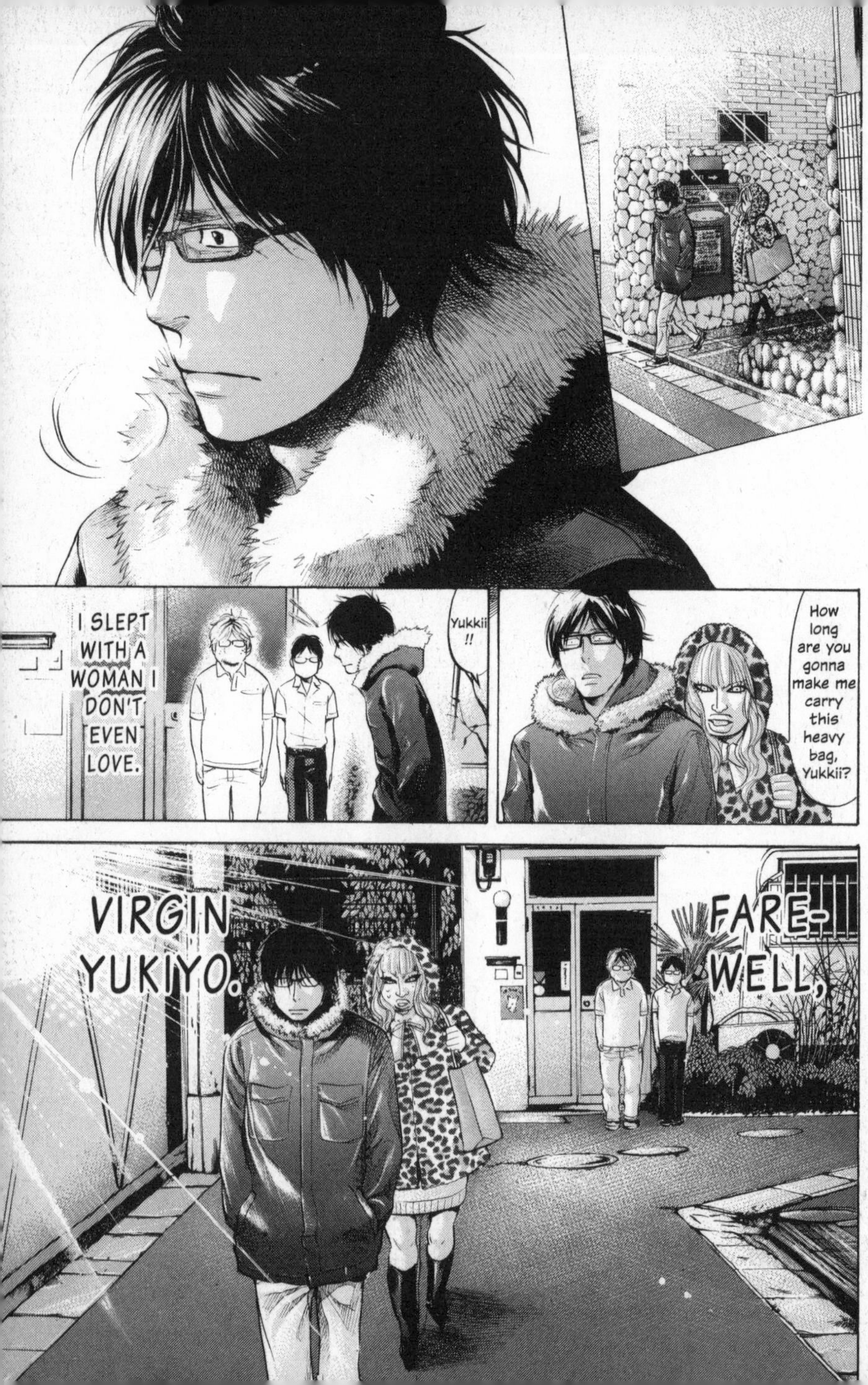
How long are you gonna make me carry this heavy bag, Yukkii?
Yukkii !!
I SLEPT WITH A WOMAN I DON'T EVEN LOVE.
FARE-WELL,
VIRGIN YUKIYO.

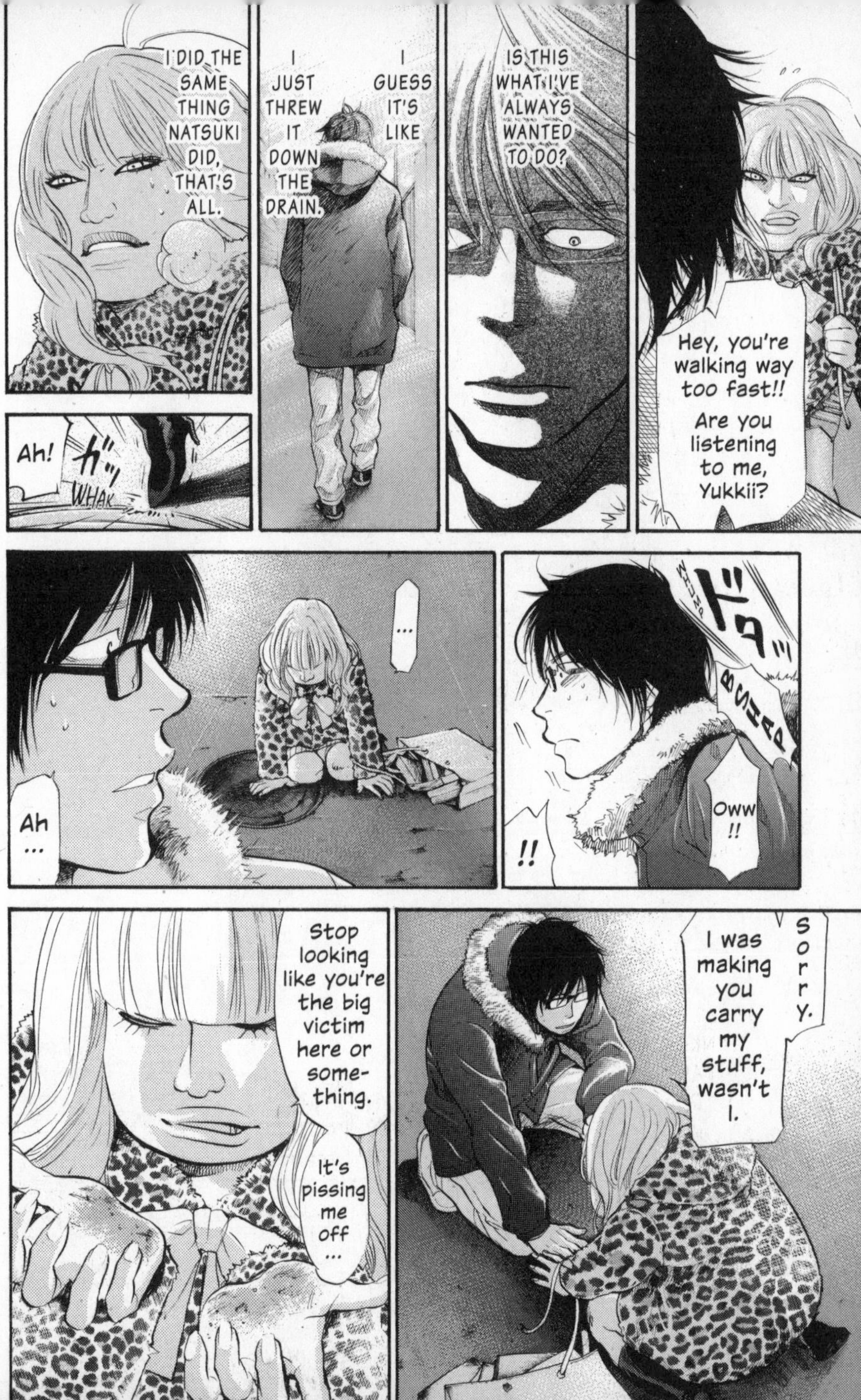
Hey, you're walking way too fast!!
Are you listening to me, Yukkii?
IS THIS WHAT I'VE ALWAYS WANTED TO DO?
I GUESS IT'S LIKE
I JUST THREW IT DOWN THE DRAIN.
I DID THE SAME THING NATSUKI DID, THAT'S ALL.
Ah!
ガッ
WHAK
ドタッ
BWHAP
Oww!!
!!
...
Ah ...
Sorry.
I was making you carry my stuff, wasn't I.
Stop looking like you're the big victim here or some-thing.
It's pissing me off ...

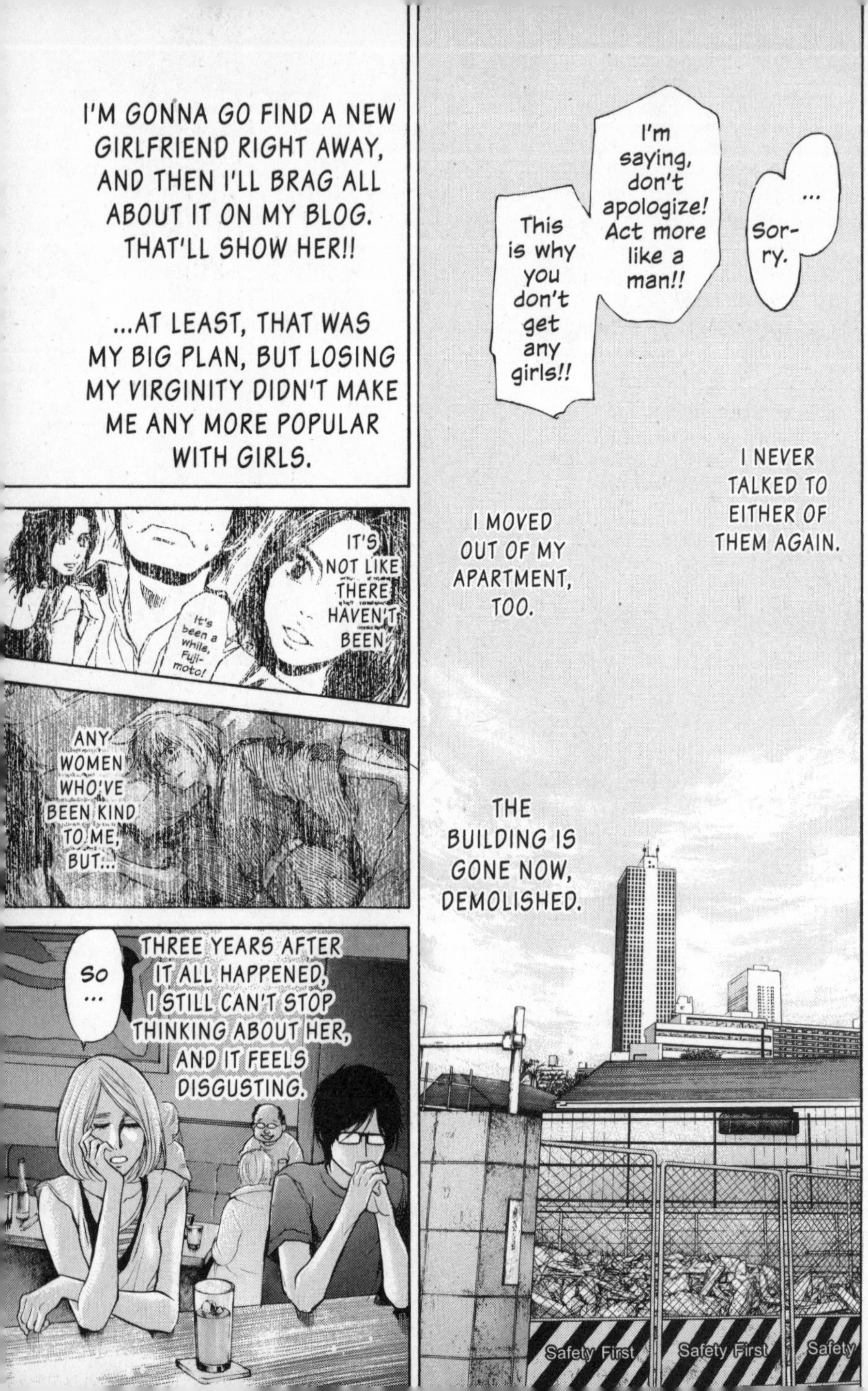
... Sor-ry.
I'm saying, don't apologize! Act more like a man!!
This is why you don't get any girls!!
I NEVER TALKED TO EITHER OF THEM AGAIN.
I MOVED OUT OF MY APARTMENT, TOO.
THE BUILDING IS GONE NOW, DEMOLISHED.
Safety First
Safety First
Safety
I'M GONNA GO FIND A NEW GIRLFRIEND RIGHT AWAY, AND THEN I'LL BRAG ALL ABOUT IT ON MY BLOG. THAT'LL SHOW HER!!
...AT LEAST, THAT WAS MY BIG PLAN, BUT LOSING MY VIRGINITY DIDN'T MAKE ME ANY MORE POPULAR WITH GIRLS.
IT'S NOT LIKE THERE HAVEN'T BEEN
It's been a while, Fuji-moto!
ANY WOMEN WHO'VE BEEN KIND TO ME, BUT...
THREE YEARS AFTER IT ALL HAPPENED, I STILL CAN'T STOP THINKING ABOUT HER, AND IT FEELS DISGUSTING.
So ...

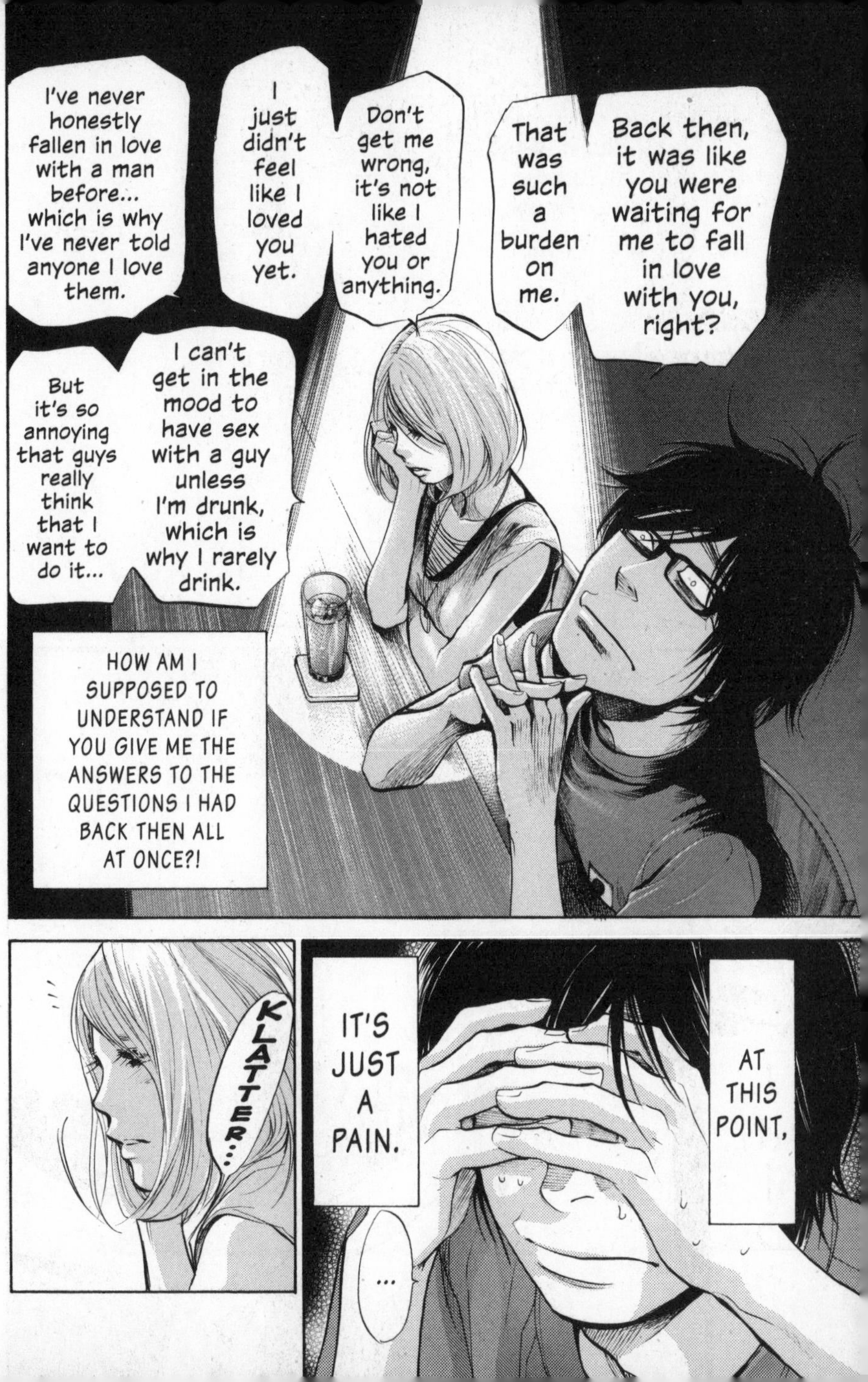
Back then, it was like you were waiting for me to fall in love with you, right?
That was such a burden on me.
Don't get me wrong, it's not like I hated you or anything.
I just didn't feel like I loved you yet.
I've never honestly fallen in love with a man before... which is why I've never told anyone I love them.
I can't get in the mood to have sex with a guy unless I'm drunk, which is why I rarely drink.
But it's so annoying that guys really think that I want to do it...
HOW AM I SUPPOSED TO UNDERSTAND IF YOU GIVE ME THE ANSWERS TO THE QUESTIONS I HAD BACK THEN ALL AT ONCE?!
AT THIS POINT,
IT'S JUST A PAIN.
...
KLATTER...

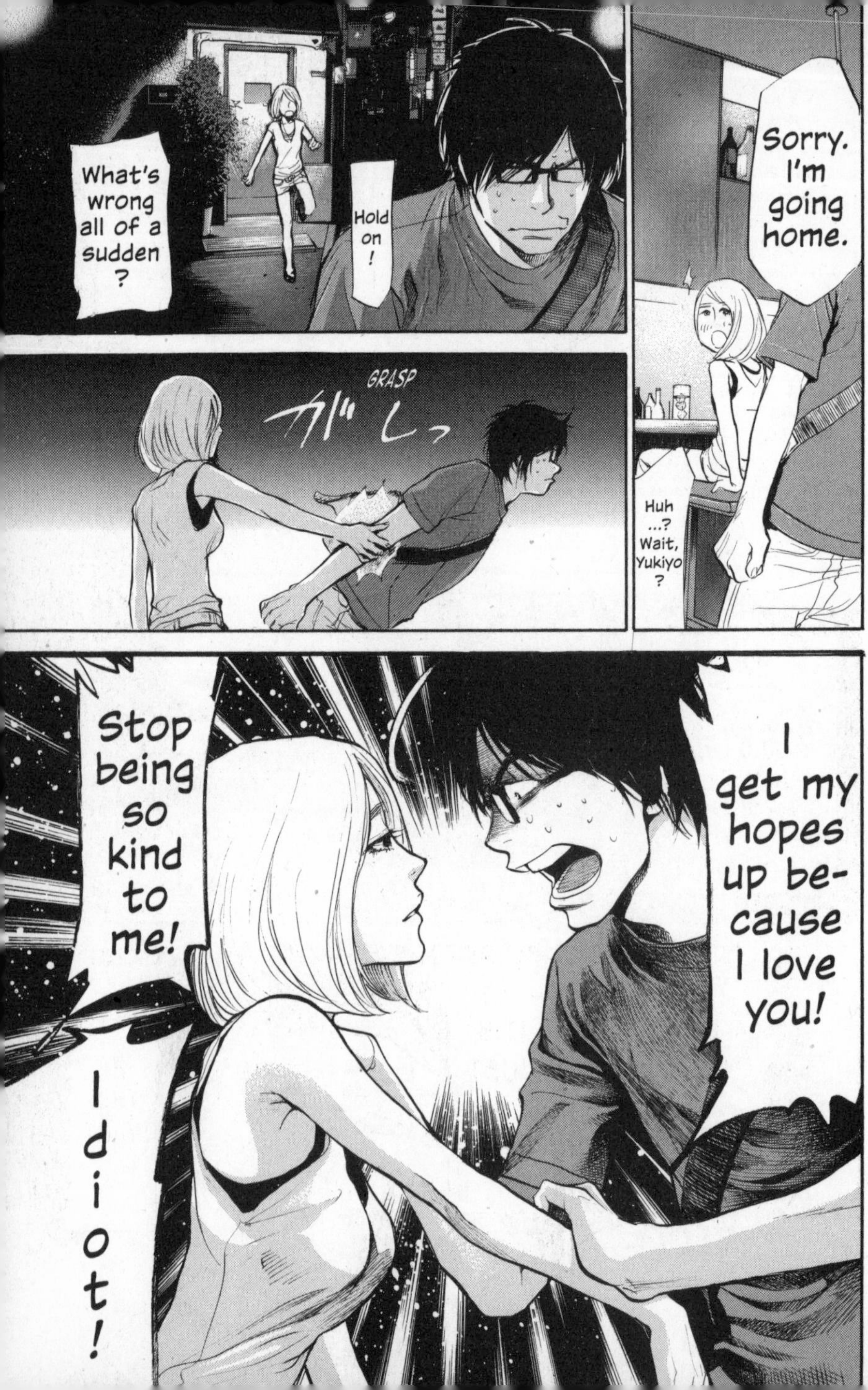
Sorry. I'm going home.
Huh...? Wait, Yukiyo?
Hold on!
What's wrong all of a sudden?
GRASP
I get my hopes up be-cause I love you!
Stop being so kind to me!
Idiot!

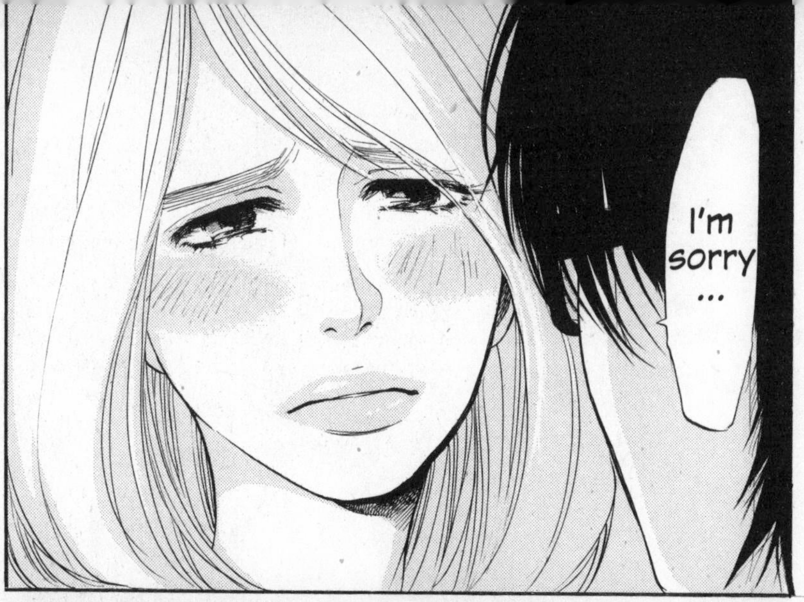
I'm sorry ...

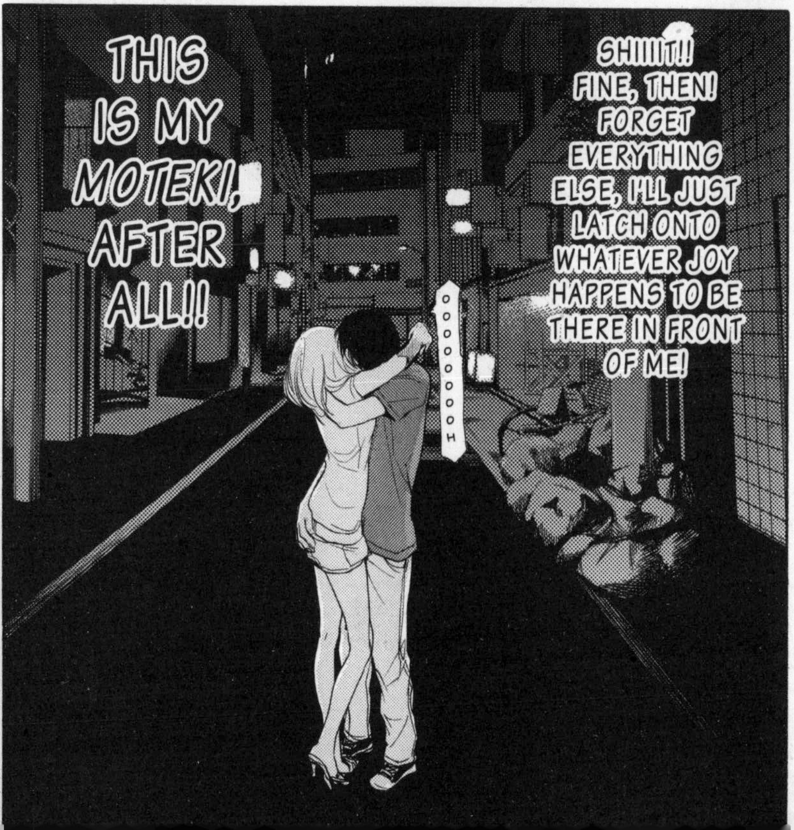
SHIIIIT!! FINE, THEN! FORGET EVERYTHING ELSE, I'LL JUST LATCH ONTO WHATEVER JOY HAPPENS TO BE THERE IN FRONT OF ME!
THIS IS MY MOTEKI, AFTER ALL!!
OOOOOOOOH

chapter 6 ♥ END

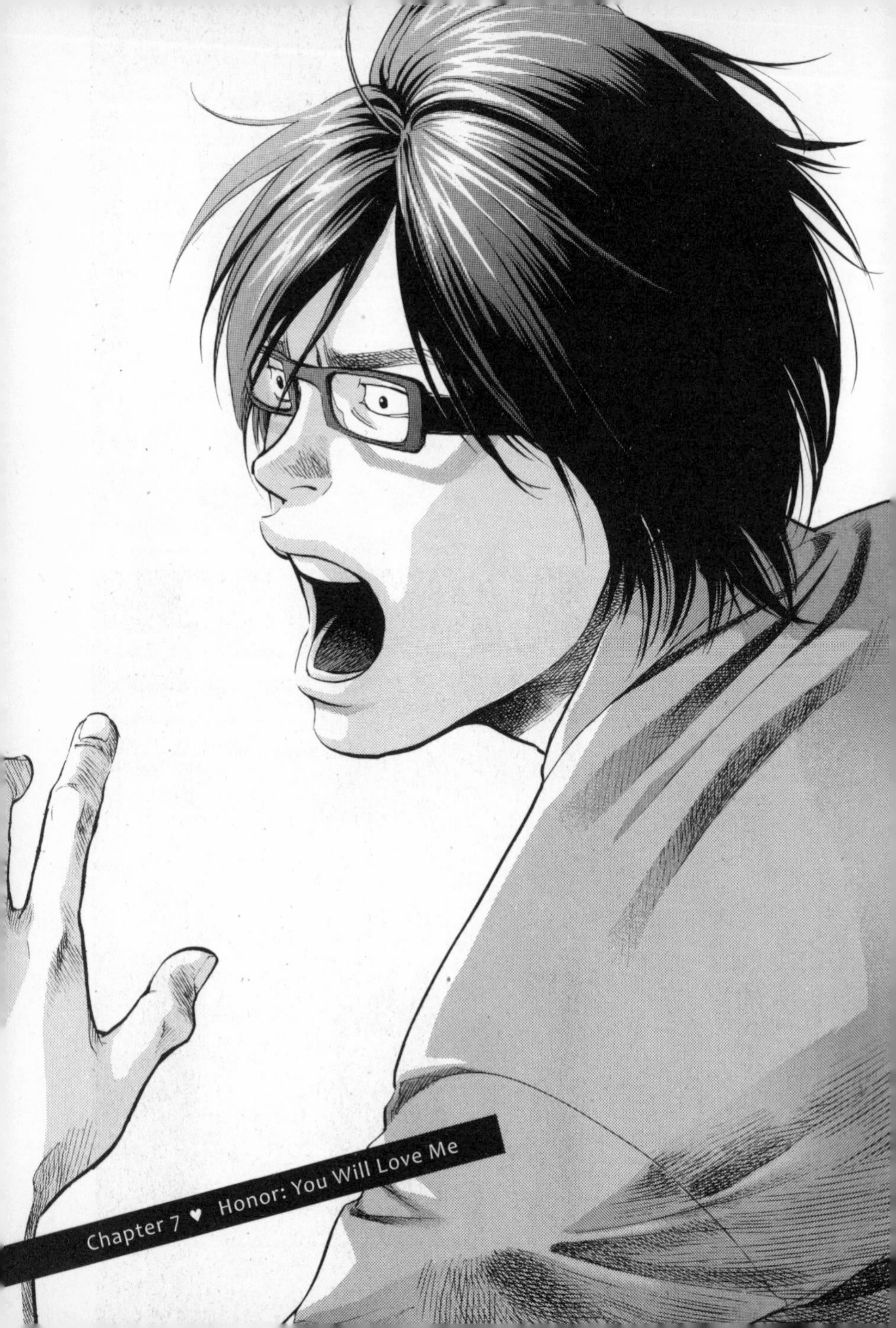
Chapter 7 ♥ Honor: You Will Love Me

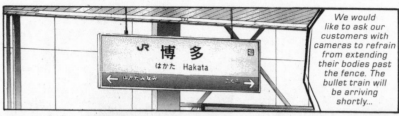

We would like to ask our customers with cameras to refrain from extending their bodies past the fence. The bullet train will be arriving shortly...
JR 博多
はかた Hakata
← はかたみなみ
こくら →
It's here!
SNAP
SNAP
SNAP
SNAP
SNAP
Please step back! Those in the rear, do not push forward !!
Please be careful !!
IT'S NOVEMBER NOW.

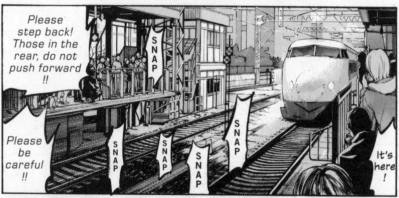

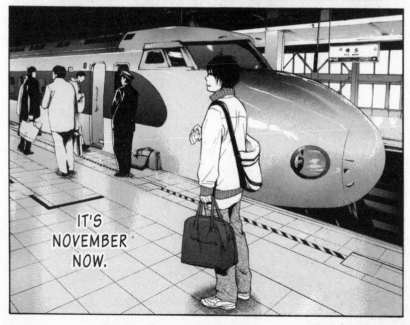

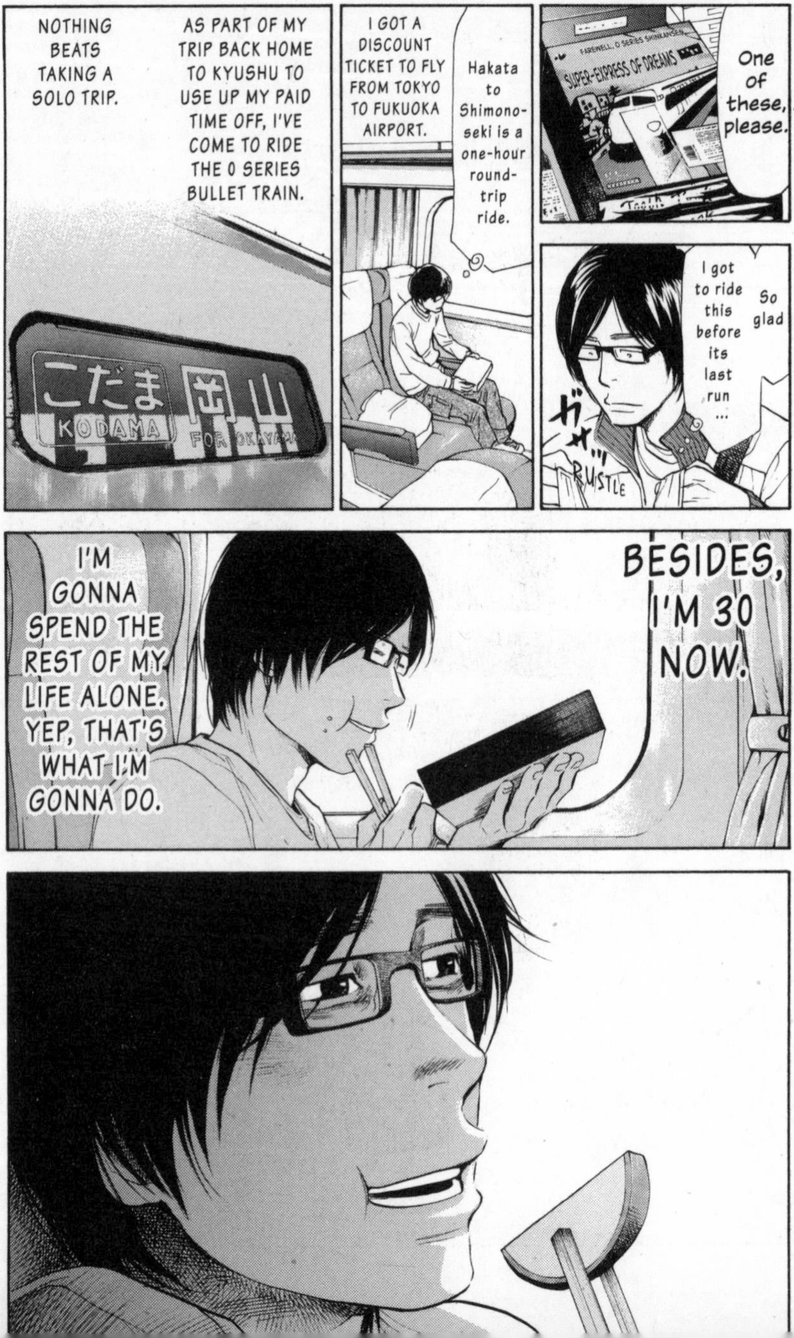
FAREWELL, 0 SERIES SHINKANSEN
SUPER-EXPRESS OF DREAMS
One of these, please.
So glad
I got to ride this before its last run ...
ガサ
RUSTLE
I GOT A DISCOUNT TICKET TO FLY FROM TOKYO TO FUKUOKA AIRPORT.
Hakata to Shimonoseki is a one-hour round-trip ride.
AS PART OF MY TRIP BACK HOME TO KYUSHU TO USE UP MY PAID TIME OFF, I'VE COME TO RIDE THE 0 SERIES BULLET TRAIN.
NOTHING BEATS TAKING A SOLO TRIP.
こだま 岡山
KODAMA
BESIDES, I'M 30 NOW.
I'M GONNA SPEND THE REST OF MY LIFE ALONE. YEP, THAT'S WHAT I'M GONNA DO.

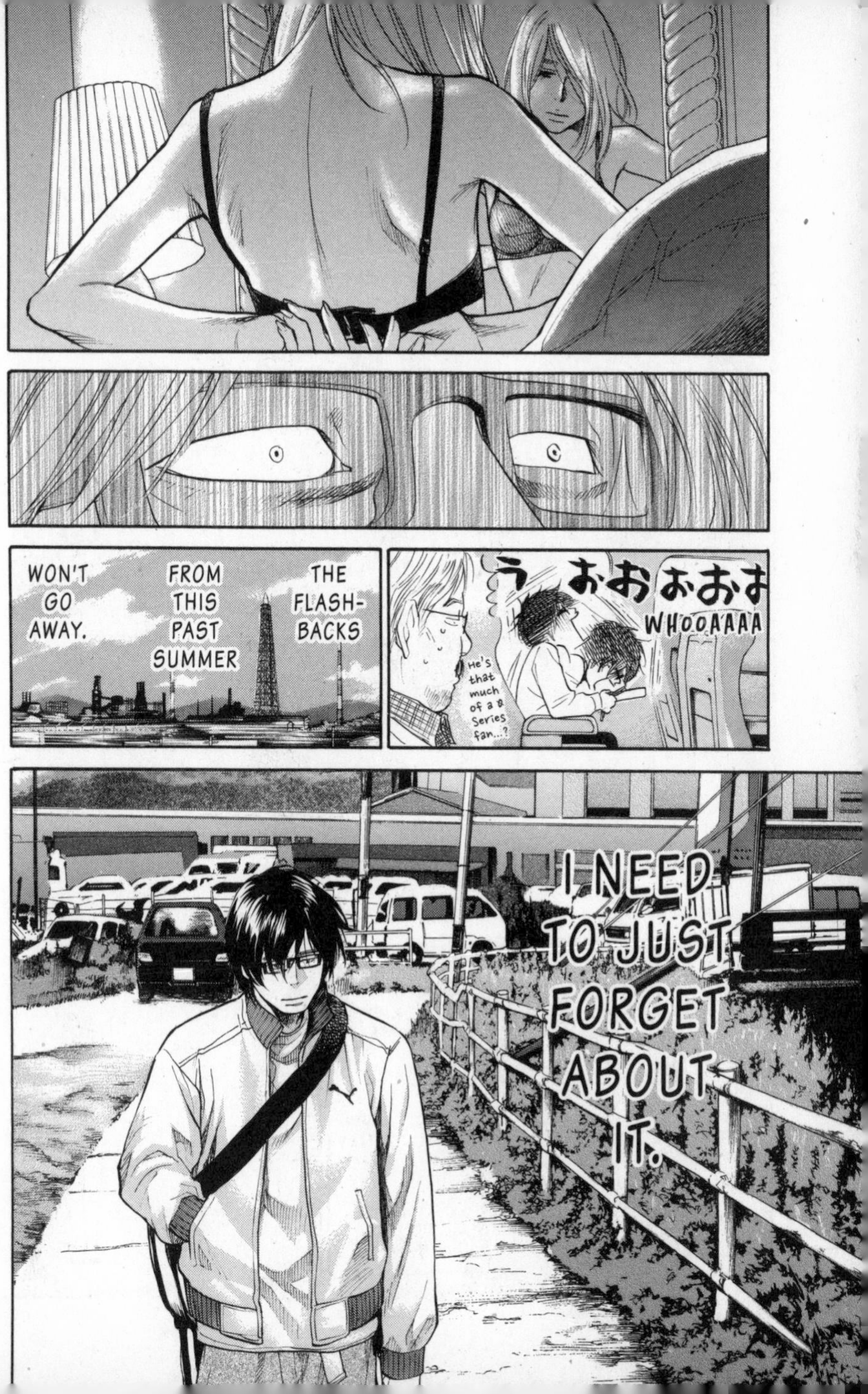
うおおぉお
WHOOAAAA
He's that much of a Series fan...?
THE FLASHBACKS
FROM THIS PAST SUMMER
WON'T GO AWAY.
I NEED TO JUST FORGET ABOUT IT.

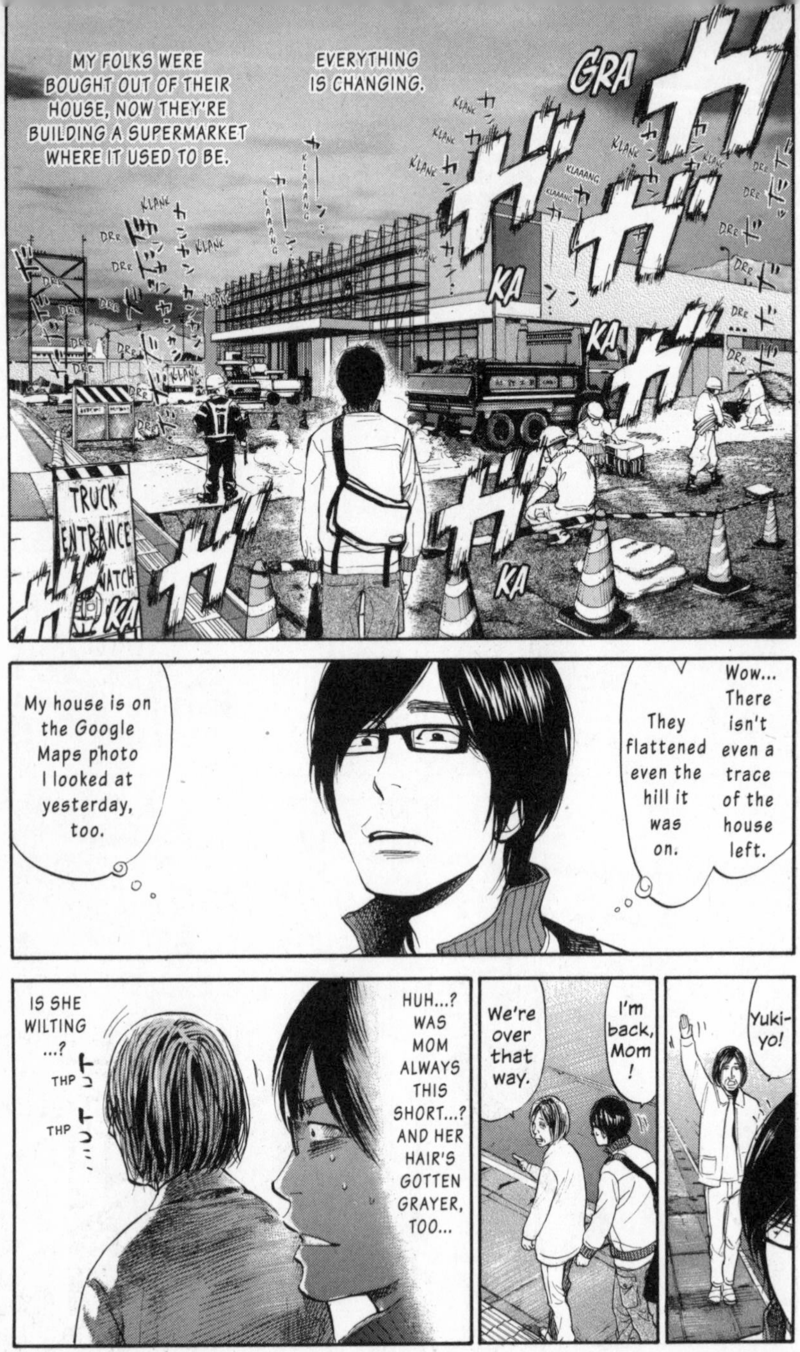
GRA
EVERYTHING IS CHANGING.
MY FOLKS WERE BOUGHT OUT OF THEIR HOUSE, NOW THEY'RE BUILDING A SUPERMARKET WHERE IT USED TO BE.
KLANK
KLAAANG
KA
DRR
TRUCK ENTRANCE
WATCH
KA
Wow... There isn't even a trace of the house left.
They flattened even the hill it was on.
My house is on the Google Maps photo I looked at yesterday, too.
Yuki-yo!
I'm back, Mom!
We're over that way.
HUH...? WAS MOM ALWAYS THIS SHORT...? AND HER HAIR'S GOTTEN GRAYER, TOO...
IS SHE WILTING ...?
THP
THP

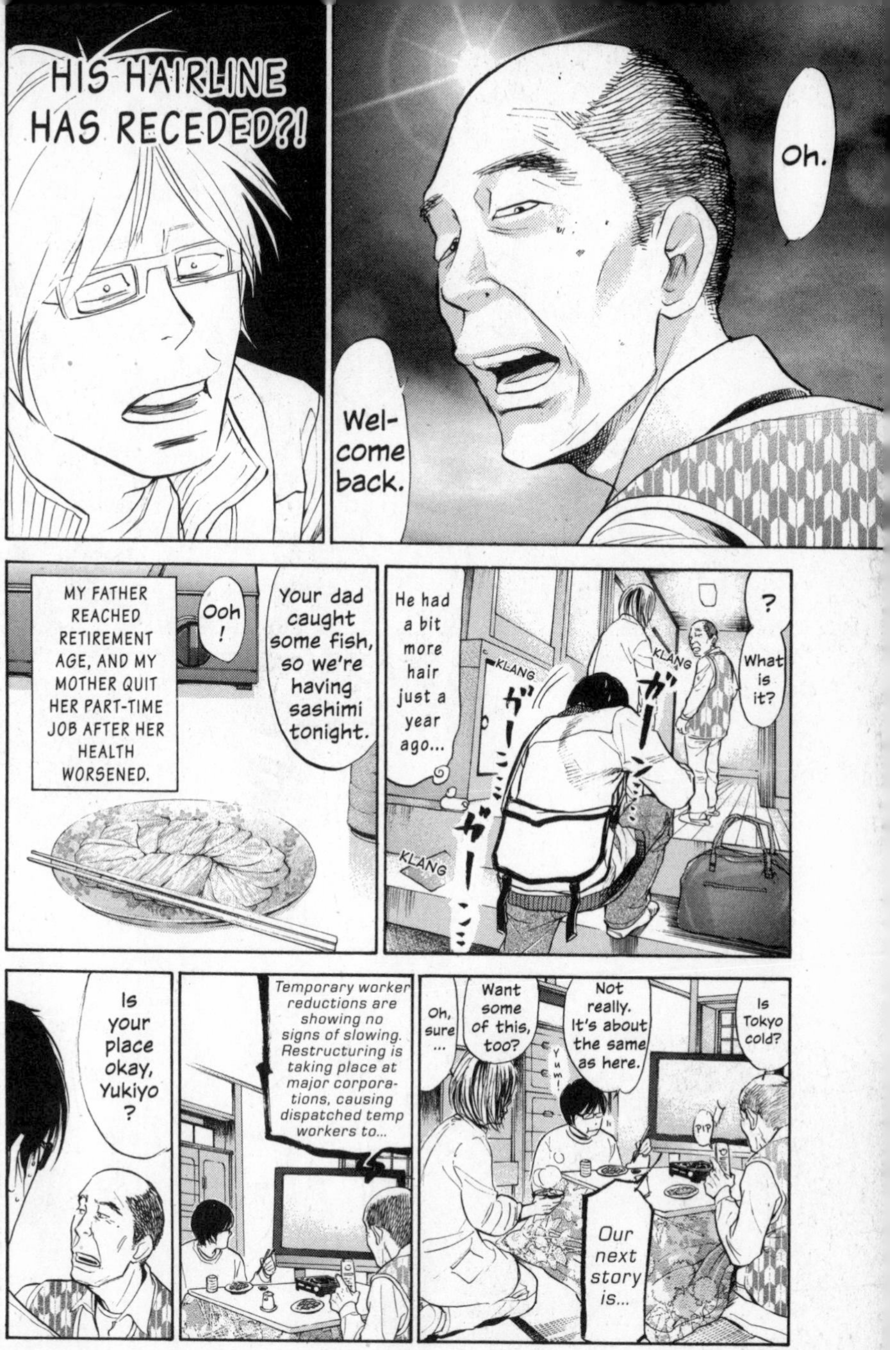
Oh.
Wel-come back.
HIS HAIRLINE HAS RECEDED?!
?
What is it?
KLANG
KLANG
KLANG
He had a bit more hair just a year ago...
Your dad caught some fish, so we're having sashimi tonight.
Ooh!
MY FATHER REACHED RETIREMENT AGE, AND MY MOTHER QUIT HER PART-TIME JOB AFTER HER HEALTH WORSENED.
Is Tokyo cold?
Not really. It's about the same as here.
Want some of this, too?
Oh, sure...
Yum!
PIP
Our next story is...
Temporary worker reductions are showing no signs of slowing. Restructuring is taking place at major corporations, causing dispatched temp workers to...
Is your place okay, Yukiyo?

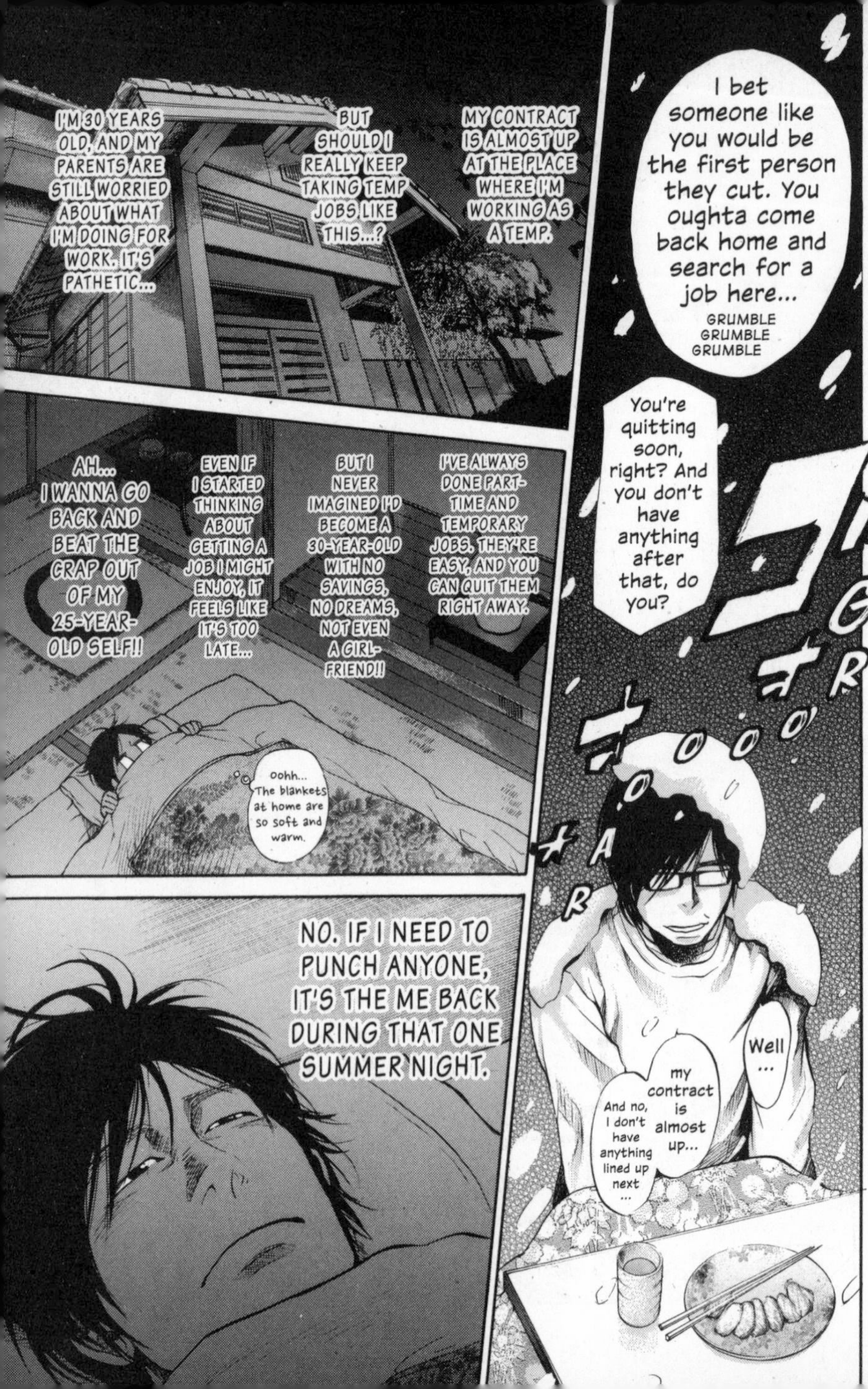
I bet someone like you would be the first person they cut. You oughta come back home and search for a job here...
GRUMBLE GRUMBLE GRUMBLE
You're quitting soon, right? And you don't have anything after that, do you?
GROOOOOAR
Well...
my contract is almost up...
And no, I don't have anything lined up next...
MY CONTRACT IS ALMOST UP AT THE PLACE WHERE I'M WORKING AS A TEMP.
BUT SHOULD I REALLY KEEP TAKING TEMP JOBS LIKE THIS...?
I'M 30 YEARS OLD, AND MY PARENTS ARE STILL WORRIED ABOUT WHAT I'M DOING FOR WORK. IT'S PATHETIC...
I'VE ALWAYS DONE PART-TIME AND TEMPORARY JOBS. THEY'RE EASY, AND YOU CAN QUIT THEM RIGHT AWAY.
BUT I NEVER IMAGINED I'D BECOME A 30-YEAR-OLD WITH NO SAVINGS, NO DREAMS, NOT EVEN A GIRL-FRIEND!!
EVEN IF I STARTED THINKING ABOUT GETTING A JOB I MIGHT ENJOY, IT FEELS LIKE IT'S TOO LATE...
AH... I WANNA GO BACK AND BEAT THE CRAP OUT OF MY 25-YEAR-OLD SELF!!
Oohh... The blankets at home are so soft and warm.
NO. IF I NEED TO PUNCH ANYONE, IT'S THE ME BACK DURING THAT ONE SUMMER NIGHT.

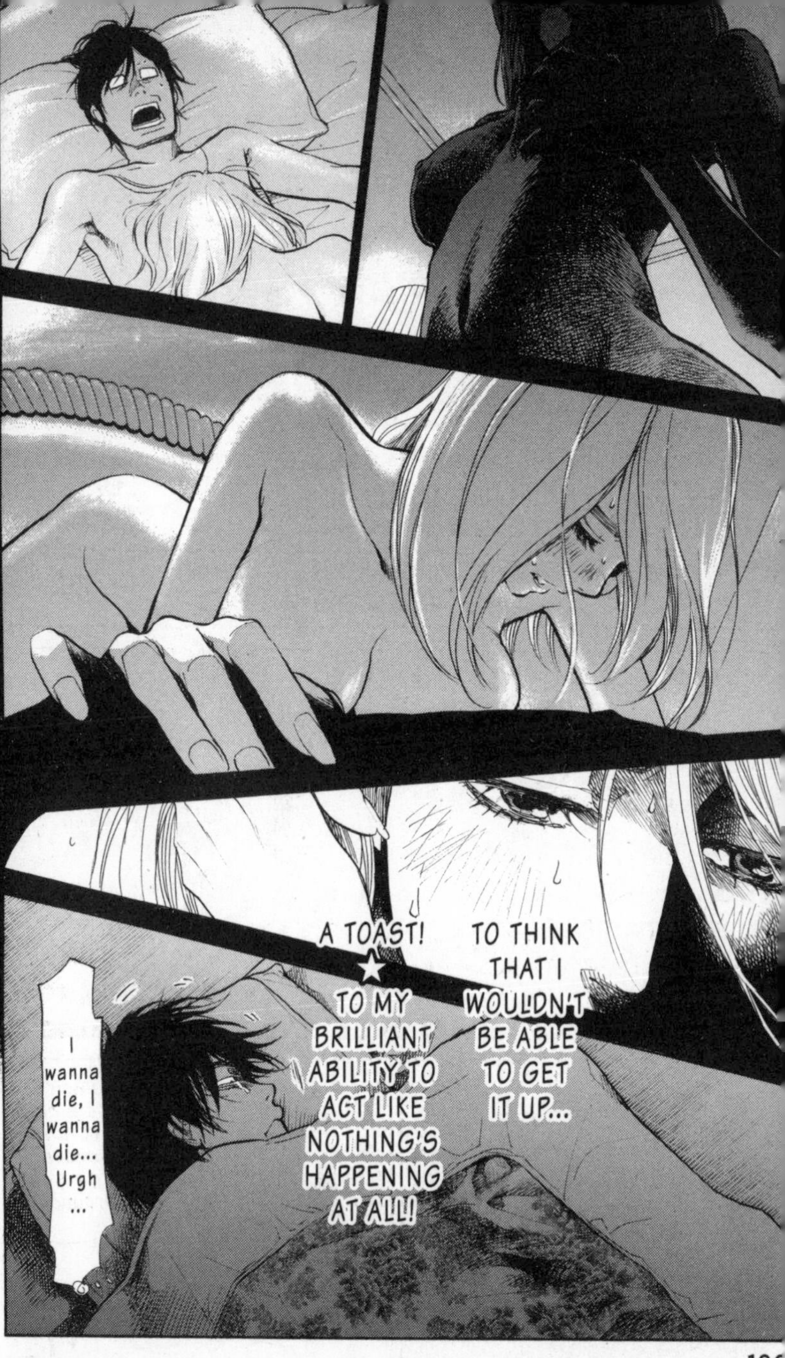
TO THINK THAT I WOULDN'T BE ABLE TO GET IT UP...
A TOAST! ★ TO MY BRILLIANT ABILITY TO ACT LIKE NOTHING'S HAPPENING AT ALL!
I wanna die, I wanna die... Urgh ...

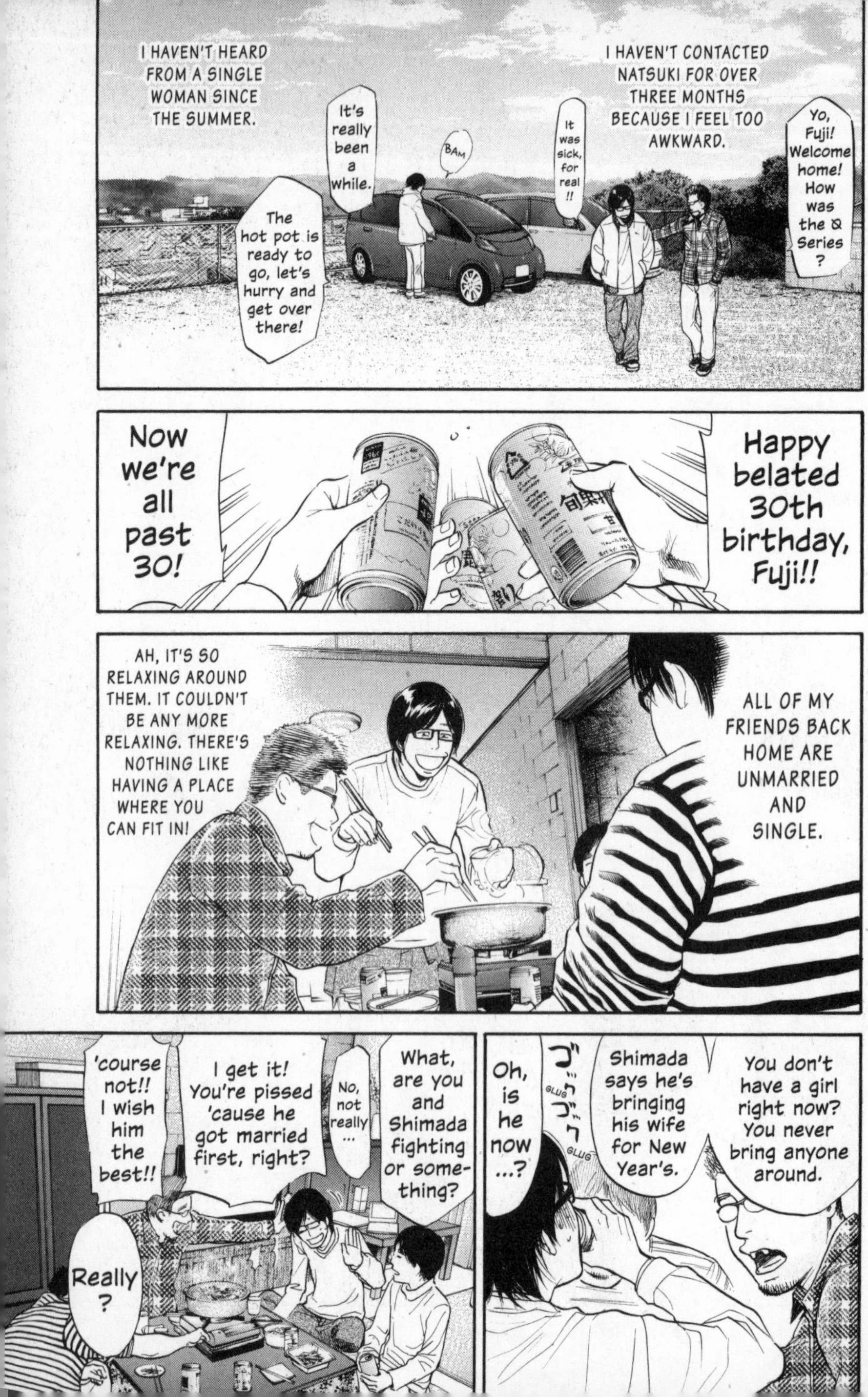
Yo, Fuji! Welcome home! How was the Q Series?
I HAVEN'T CONTACTED NATSUKI FOR OVER THREE MONTHS BECAUSE I FEEL TOO AWKWARD.
It was sick, for real!!
It's really been a while.
BAM
I HAVEN'T HEARD FROM A SINGLE WOMAN SINCE THE SUMMER.
The hot pot is ready to go, let's hurry and get over there!
Happy belated 30th birthday, Fuji!!
Now we're all past 30!
ALL OF MY FRIENDS BACK HOME ARE UNMARRIED AND SINGLE.
AH, IT'S SO RELAXING AROUND THEM. IT COULDN'T BE ANY MORE RELAXING. THERE'S NOTHING LIKE HAVING A PLACE WHERE YOU CAN FIT IN!
You don't have a girl right now? You never bring anyone around.
Shimada says he's bringing his wife for New Year's.
GLUG
GLUG
Oh, is he now...?
What, are you and Shimada fighting or something?
No, not really...
I get it! You're pissed 'cause he got married first, right?
'course not!! I wish him the best!!
Really?

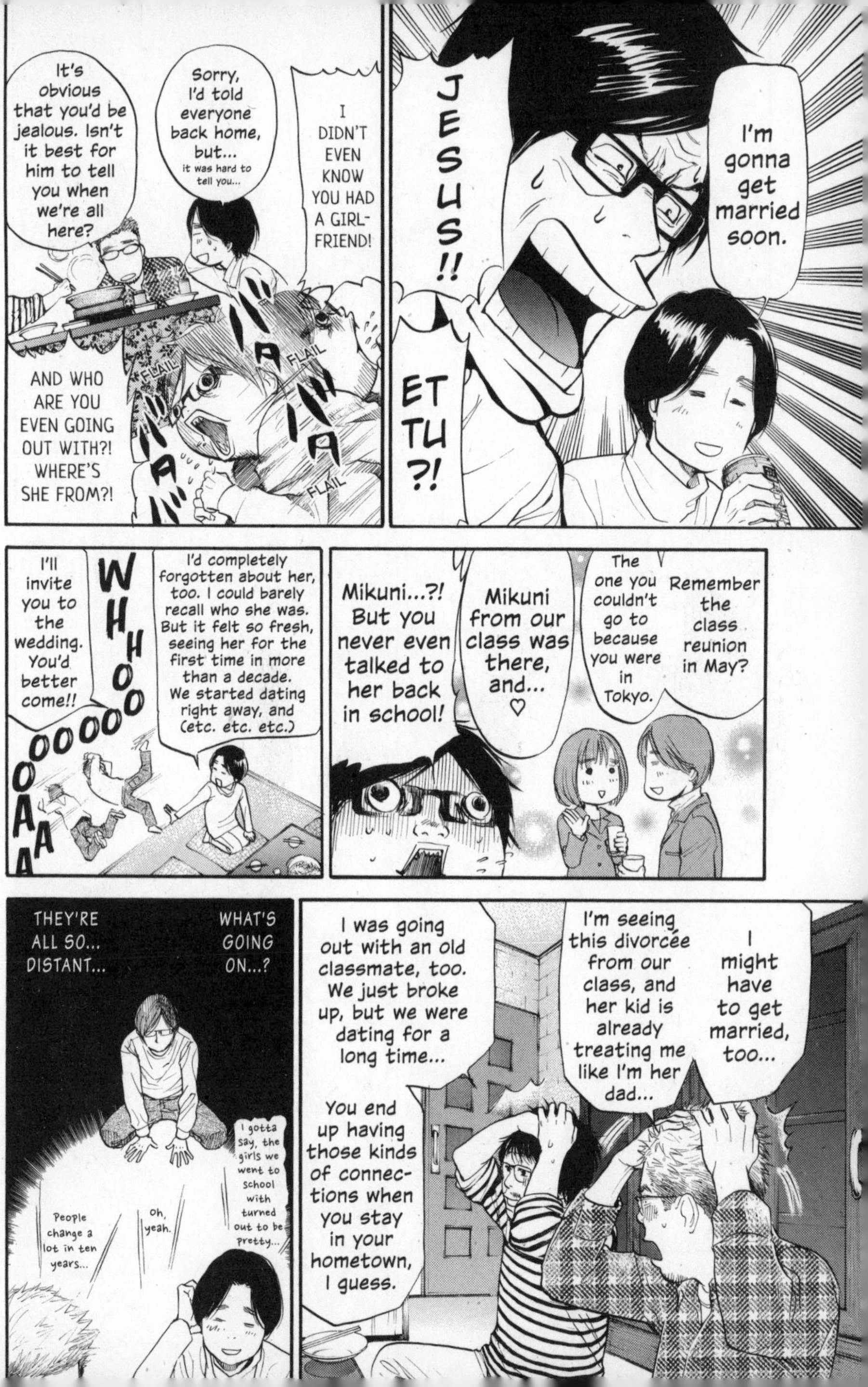
I'm gonna get married soon.
JESUS!!
ET TU?!
I DIDN'T EVEN KNOW YOU HAD A GIRL-FRIEND!
Sorry, I'd told everyone back home, but...
it was hard to tell you...
It's obvious that you'd be jealous. Isn't it best for him to tell you when we're all here?
FLAIL
FLAIL
FLAIL
AND WHO ARE YOU EVEN GOING OUT WITH?! WHERE'S SHE FROM?!
Remember the class reunion in May?
The one you couldn't go to because you were in Tokyo.
Mikuni from our class was there, and... ♡
Mikuni...?! But you never even talked to her back in school!
I'd completely forgotten about her, too. I could barely recall who she was. But it felt so fresh, seeing her for the first time in more than a decade. We started dating right away, and (etc. etc. etc.)
WHHOOOOOOOAAAA
I'll invite you to the wedding. You'd better come!!
I might have to get married, too...
I'm seeing this divorcée from our class, and her kid is already treating me like I'm her dad...
I was going out with an old classmate, too. We just broke up, but we were dating for a long time...
You end up having those kinds of connections when you stay in your hometown, I guess.
WHAT'S GOING ON...?
THEY'RE ALL SO... DISTANT...
I gotta say, the girls we went to school with turned out to be pretty...
Oh, yeah.
People change a lot in ten years...

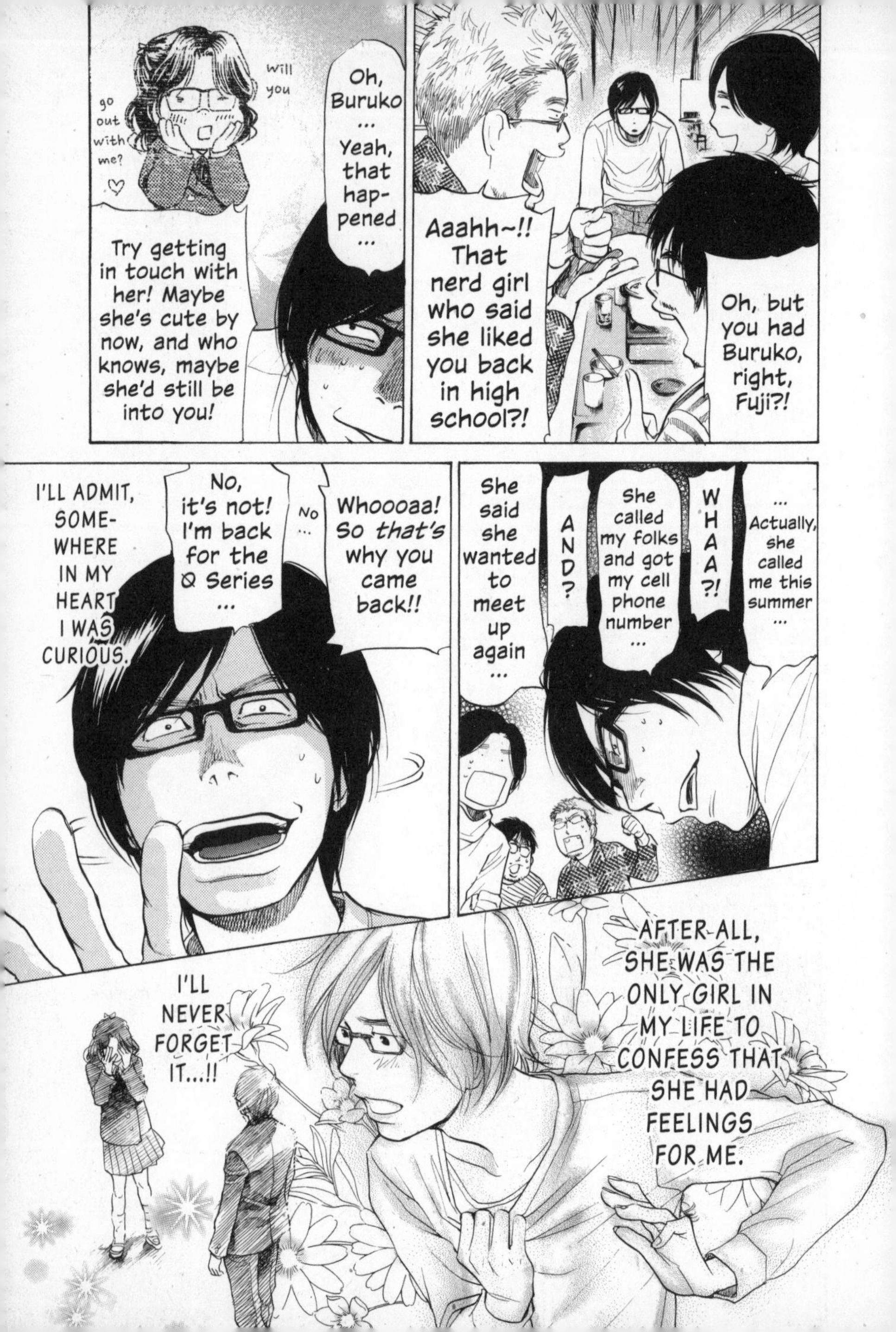

Oh, but you had Buruko, right, Fuji?!
Aaahh~!! That nerd girl who said she liked you back in high school?!
Oh, Buruko... Yeah, that hap-pened...
Will you go out with me? ♡
Try getting in touch with her! Maybe she's cute by now, and who knows, maybe she'd still be into you!
...Actually, she called me this summer...
WHAA?!
She called my folks and got my cell phone number...
AND?
She said she wanted to meet up again...
Whoooaa! So *that's* why you came back!!
No...
No, it's not! I'm back for the Q Series...
I'LL ADMIT, SOME-WHERE IN MY HEART I WAS CURIOUS.
AFTER ALL, SHE WAS THE ONLY GIRL IN MY LIFE TO CONFESS THAT SHE HAD FEELINGS FOR ME.
I'LL NEVER FORGET IT...!!

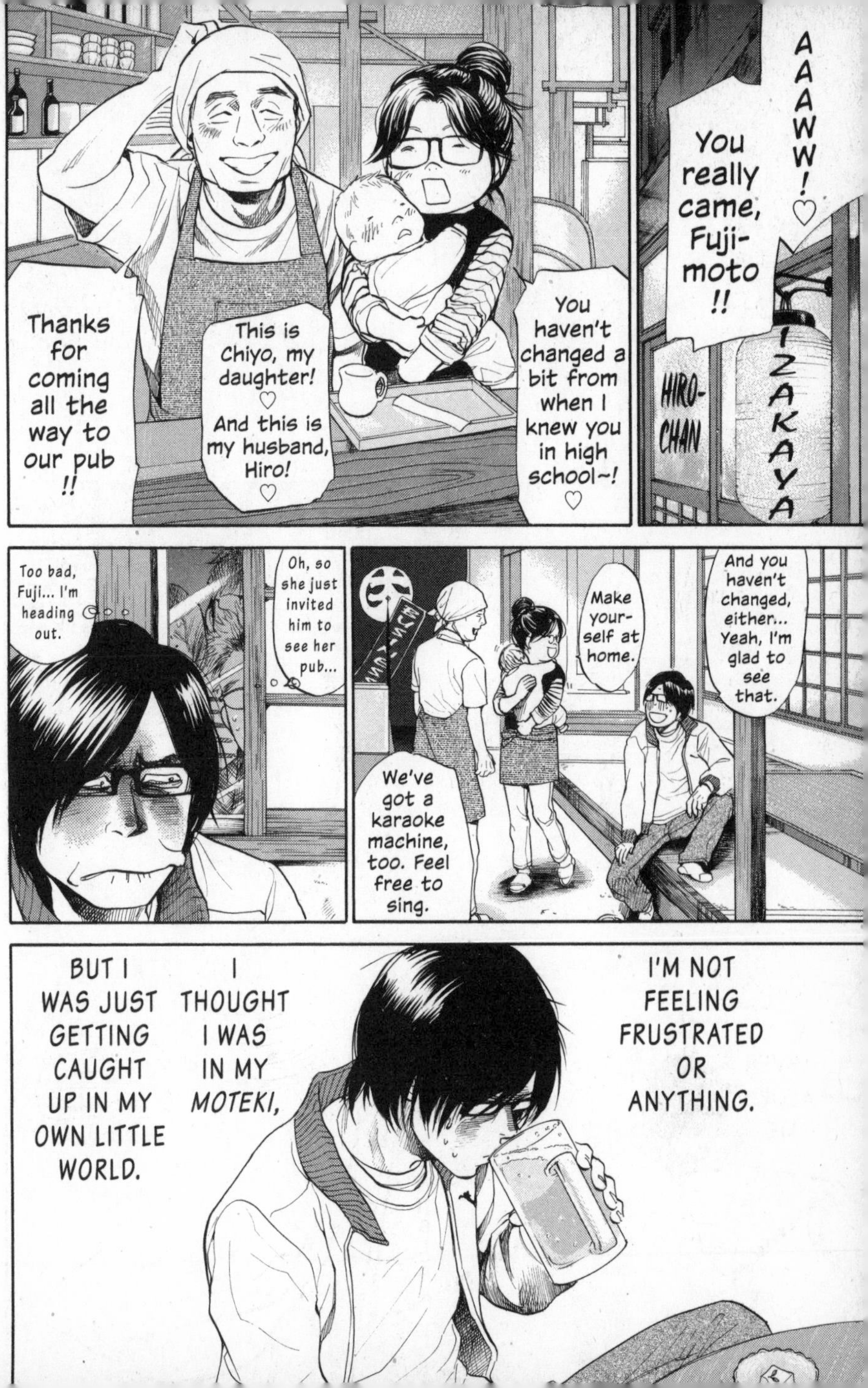
AAAWW! ♡
You really came, Fuji-moto!!
HIRO-CHAN
IZAKAYA
You haven't changed a bit from when I knew you in high school~! ♡
This is Chiyo, my daughter! ♡ And this is my husband, Hiro! ♡
Thanks for coming all the way to our pub!!
And you haven't changed, either... Yeah, I'm glad to see that.
Make your-self at home.
We've got a karaoke machine, too. Feel free to sing.
Oh, so she just invited him to see her pub...
Too bad, Fuji... I'm heading out.
I'M NOT FEELING FRUSTRATED OR ANYTHING.
I THOUGHT I WAS IN MY *MOTEKI*,
BUT I WAS JUST GETTING CAUGHT UP IN MY OWN LITTLE WORLD.

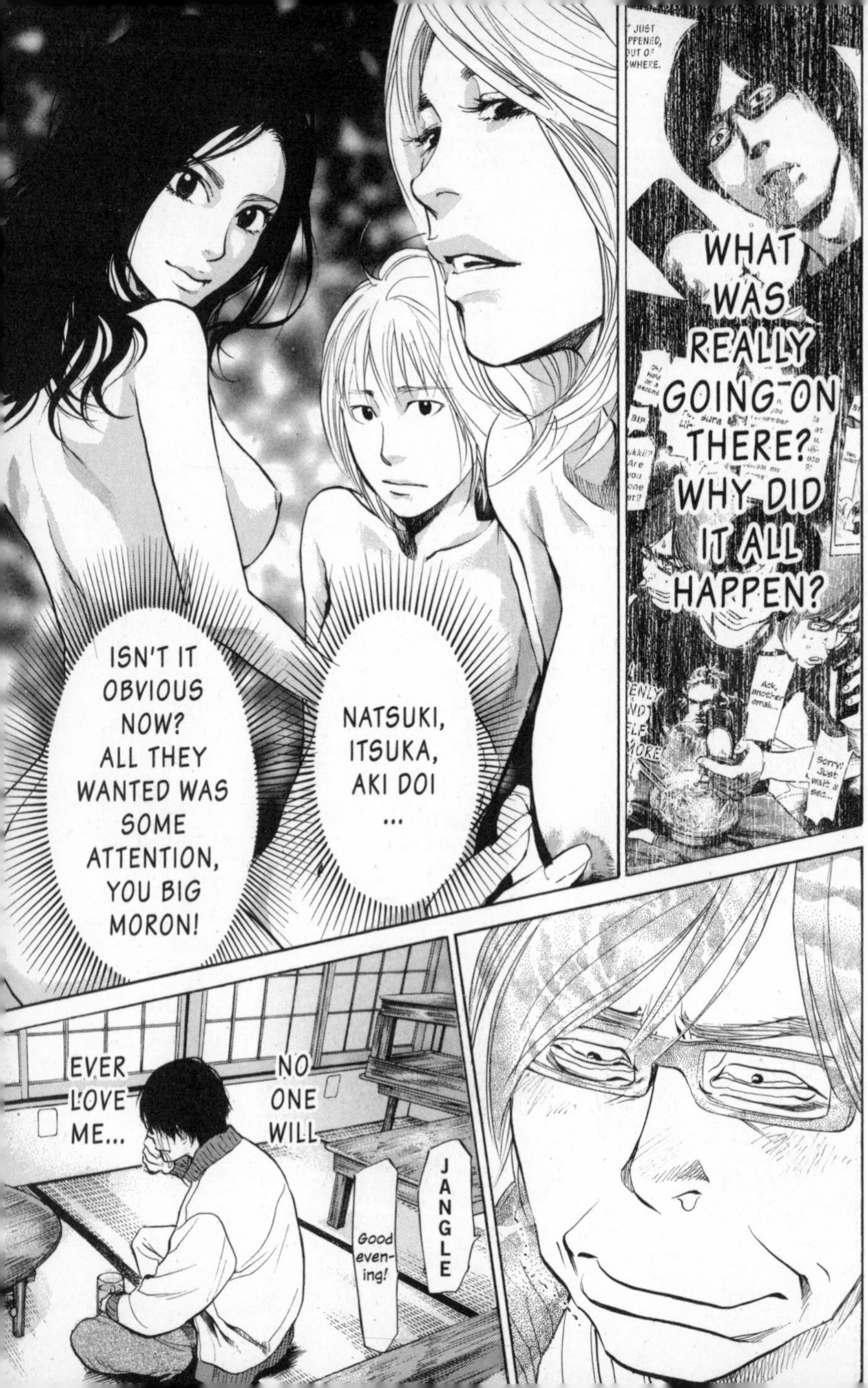
JUST PPENED, UT OF WHERE.
WHAT WAS REALLY GOING ON THERE? WHY DID IT ALL HAPPEN?
Ack, another email...
Sorry! Just wait a sec...
NATSUKI, ITSUKA, AKI DOI ...
ISN'T IT OBVIOUS NOW? ALL THEY WANTED WAS SOME ATTENTION, YOU BIG MORON!
JANGLE
Good even-ing!
NO ONE WILL
EVER LOVE ME...

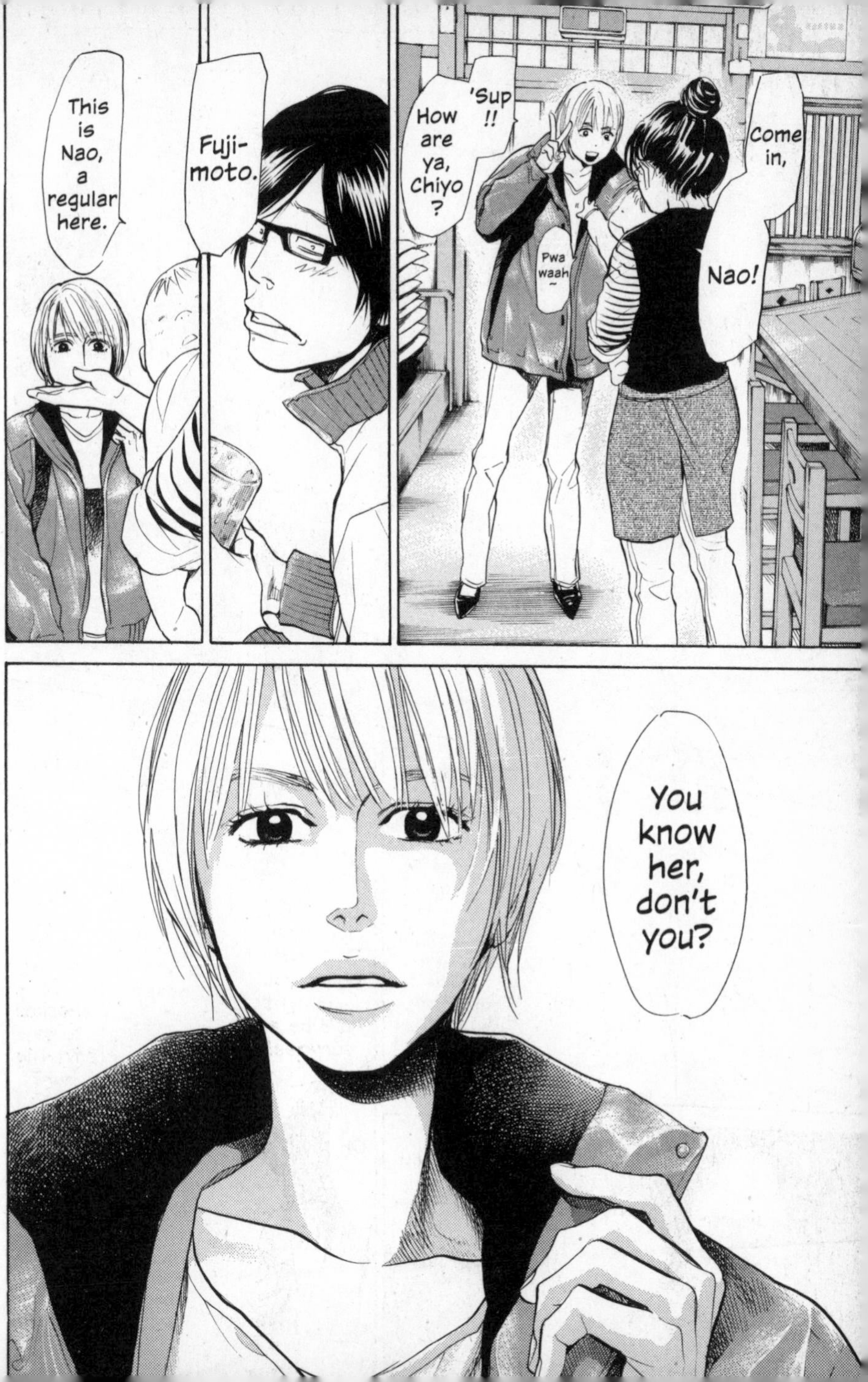
Come in, Nao!
'Sup!!
How are ya, Chiyo?
Pwa waah~
Fuji-moto.
This is Nao, a regular here.
You know her, don't you?

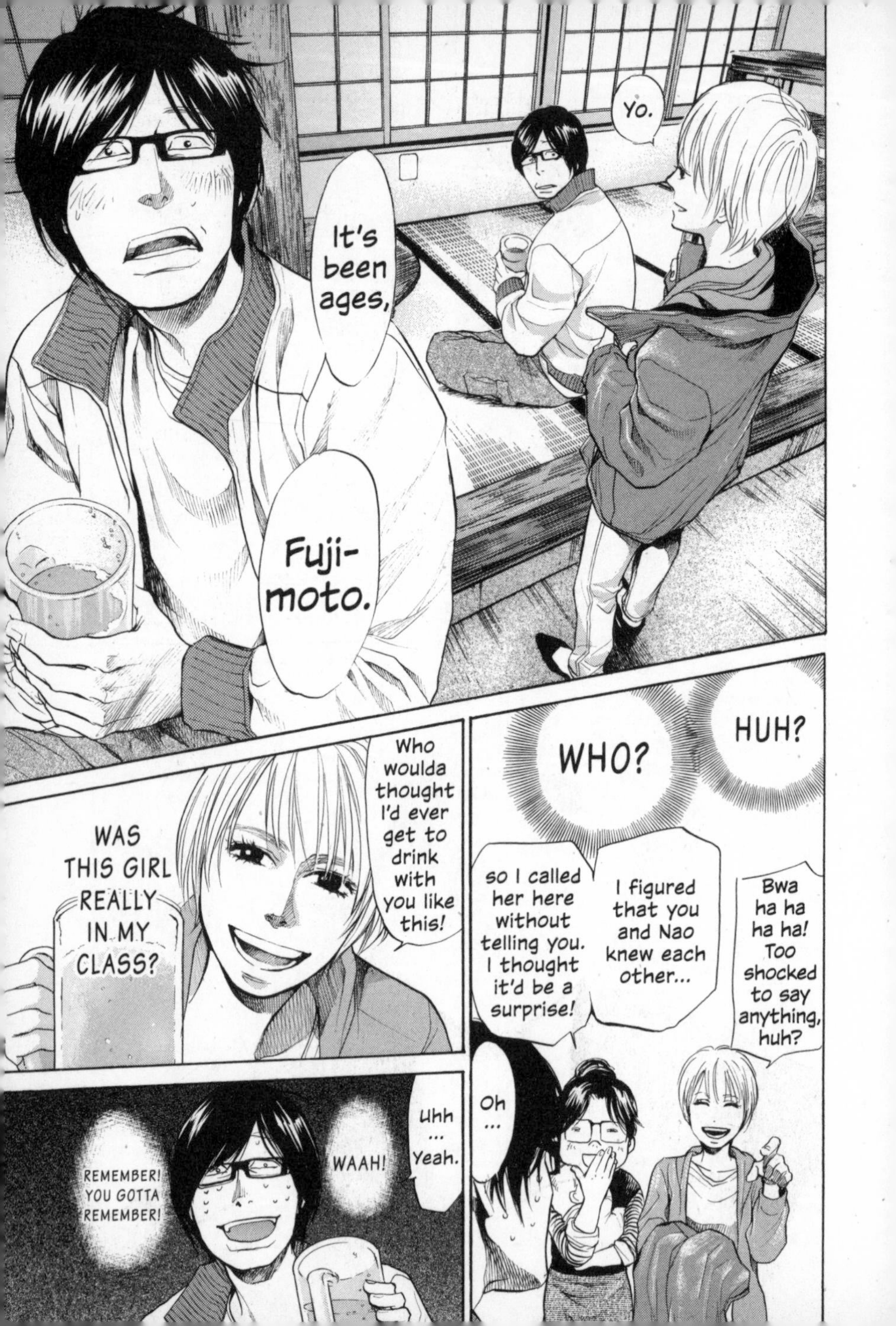

Yo.
It's been ages,
Fuji-moto.
HUH?
WHO?
Bwa ha ha ha ha! Too shocked to say anything, huh?
I figured that you and Nao knew each other...
so I called her here without telling you. I thought it'd be a surprise!
Oh ...
Who woulda thought I'd ever get to drink with you like this!
WAS THIS GIRL REALLY IN MY CLASS?
Uhh ... Yeah.
WAAH!
REMEMBER! YOU GOTTA REMEMBER!

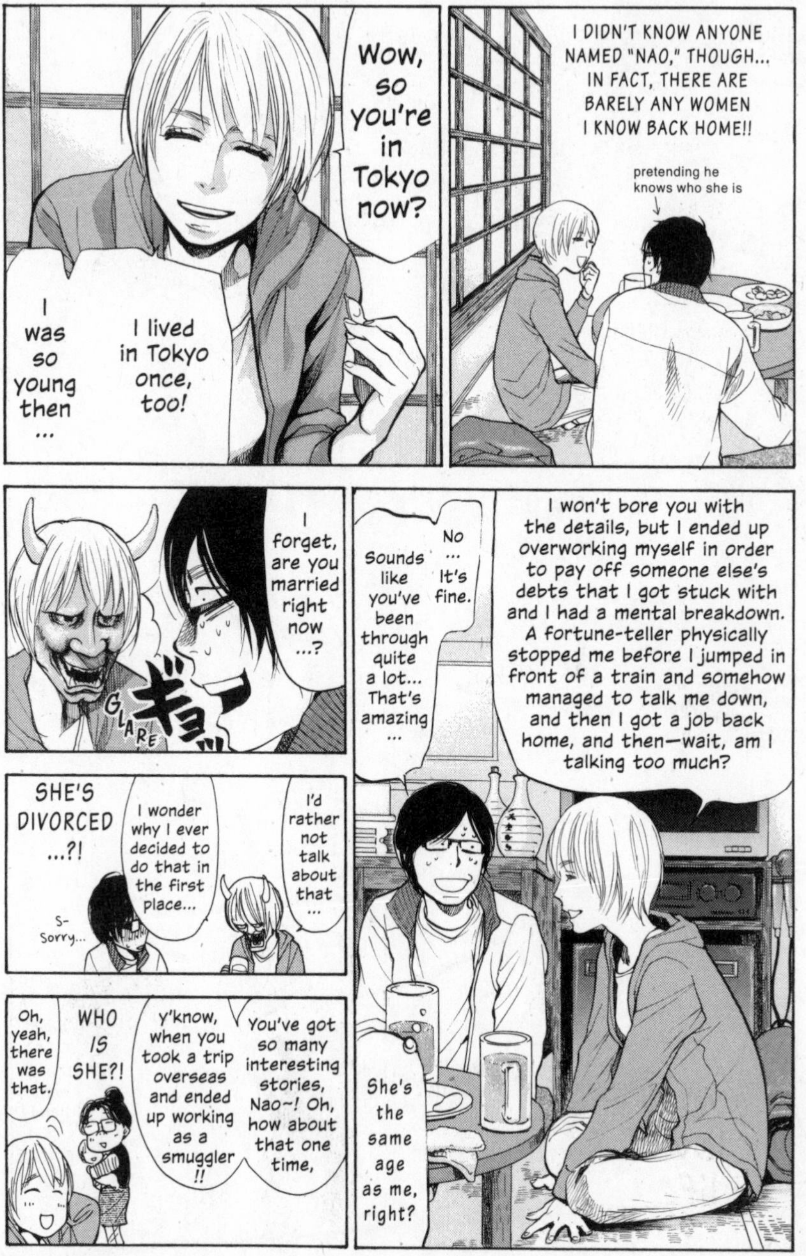
I DIDN'T KNOW ANYONE NAMED "NAO," THOUGH... IN FACT, THERE ARE BARELY ANY WOMEN I KNOW BACK HOME!!
pretending he knows who she is
Wow, so you're in Tokyo now?
I lived in Tokyo once, too!
I was so young then...
I won't bore you with the details, but I ended up overworking myself in order to pay off someone else's debts that I got stuck with and I had a mental breakdown. A fortune-teller physically stopped me before I jumped in front of a train and somehow managed to talk me down, and then I got a job back home, and then—wait, am I talking too much?
No... It's fine.
Sounds like you've been through quite a lot... That's amazing...
She's the same age as me, right?
I forget, are you married right now...?
GLARE
ギョ
I'd rather not talk about that...
I wonder why I ever decided to do that in the first place...
SHE'S DIVORCED...?!
S-Sorry...
You've got so many interesting stories, Nao~! Oh, how about that one time,
y'know, when you took a trip overseas and ended up working as a smuggler!!
WHO IS SHE?!
Oh, yeah, there was that.

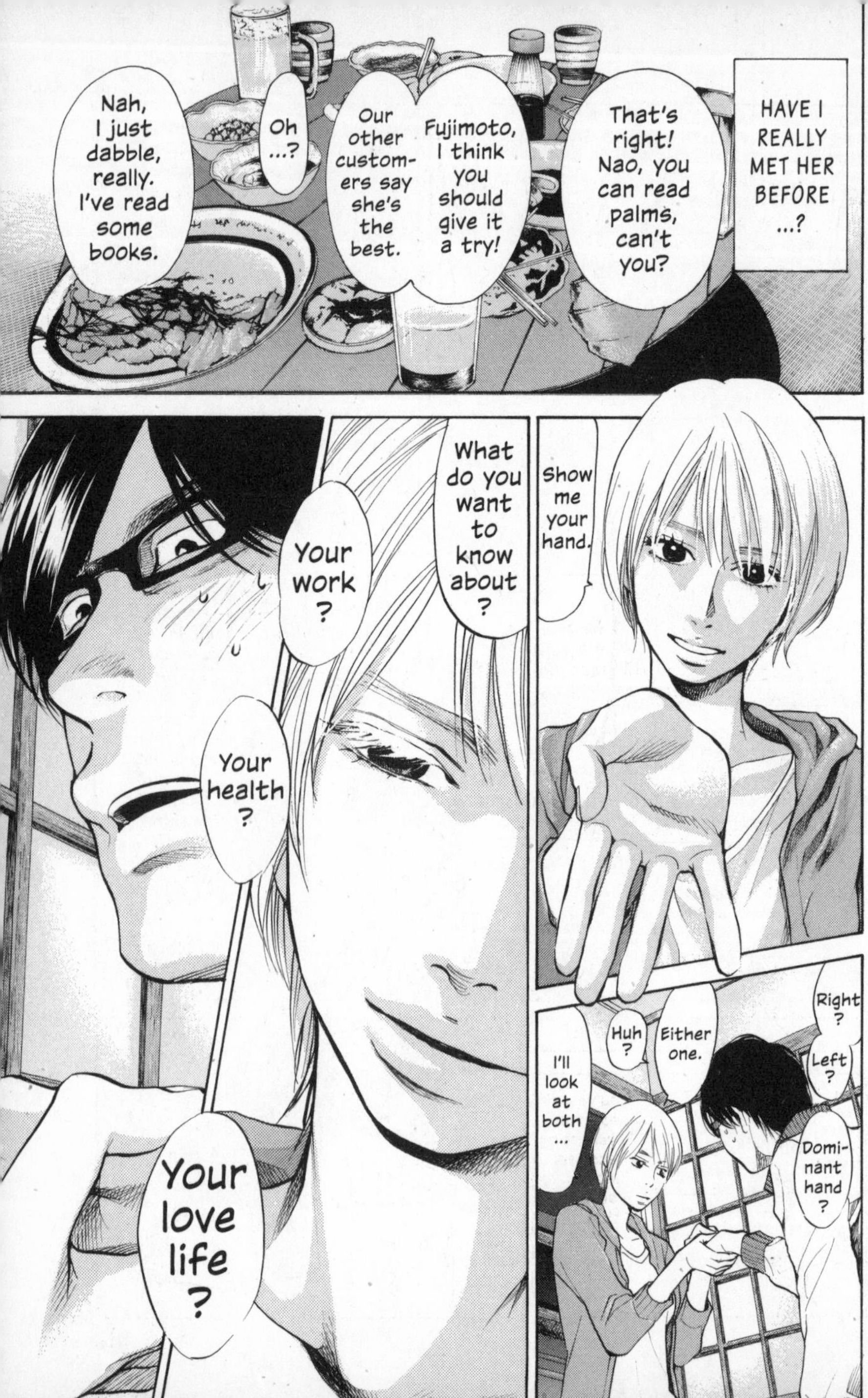
HAVE I REALLY MET HER BEFORE ...?
That's right! Nao, you can read palms, can't you?
Fujimoto, I think you should give it a try!
Our other customers say she's the best.
Oh ...?
Nah, I just dabble, really. I've read some books.
Show me your hand.
Right?
Left?
Dominant hand?
Either one.
Huh?
I'll look at both ...
What do you want to know about?
Your work?
Your health?
Your love life?

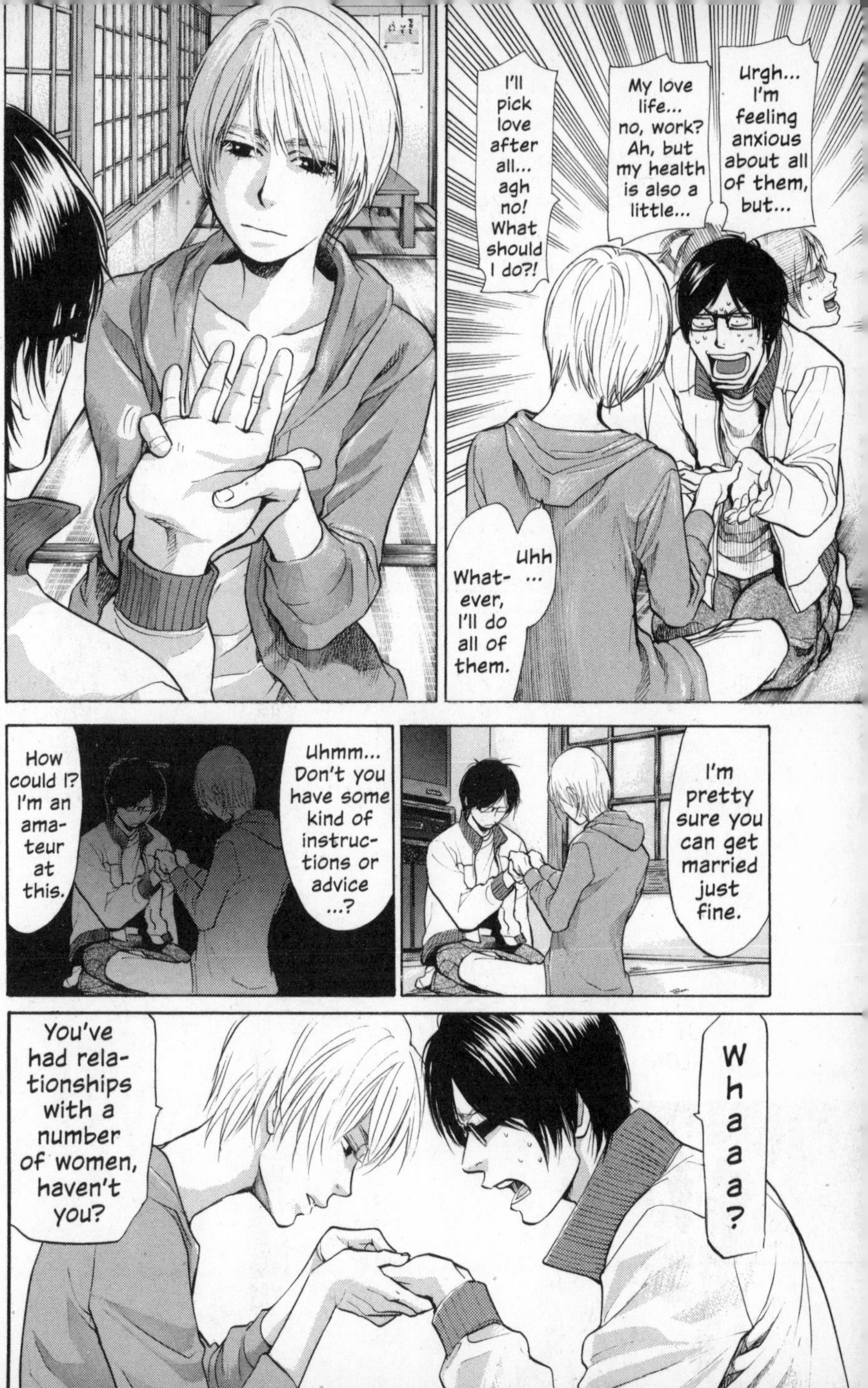
Urgh... I'm feeling anxious about all of them, but...
My love life... no, work? Ah, but my health is also a little...
I'll pick love after all... agh no! What should I do?!
Uhh ...
Whatever, I'll do all of them.
I'm pretty sure you can get married just fine.
Uhmm... Don't you have some kind of instructions or advice ...?
How could I? I'm an amateur at this.
Whaaaa?
You've had relationships with a number of women, haven't you?

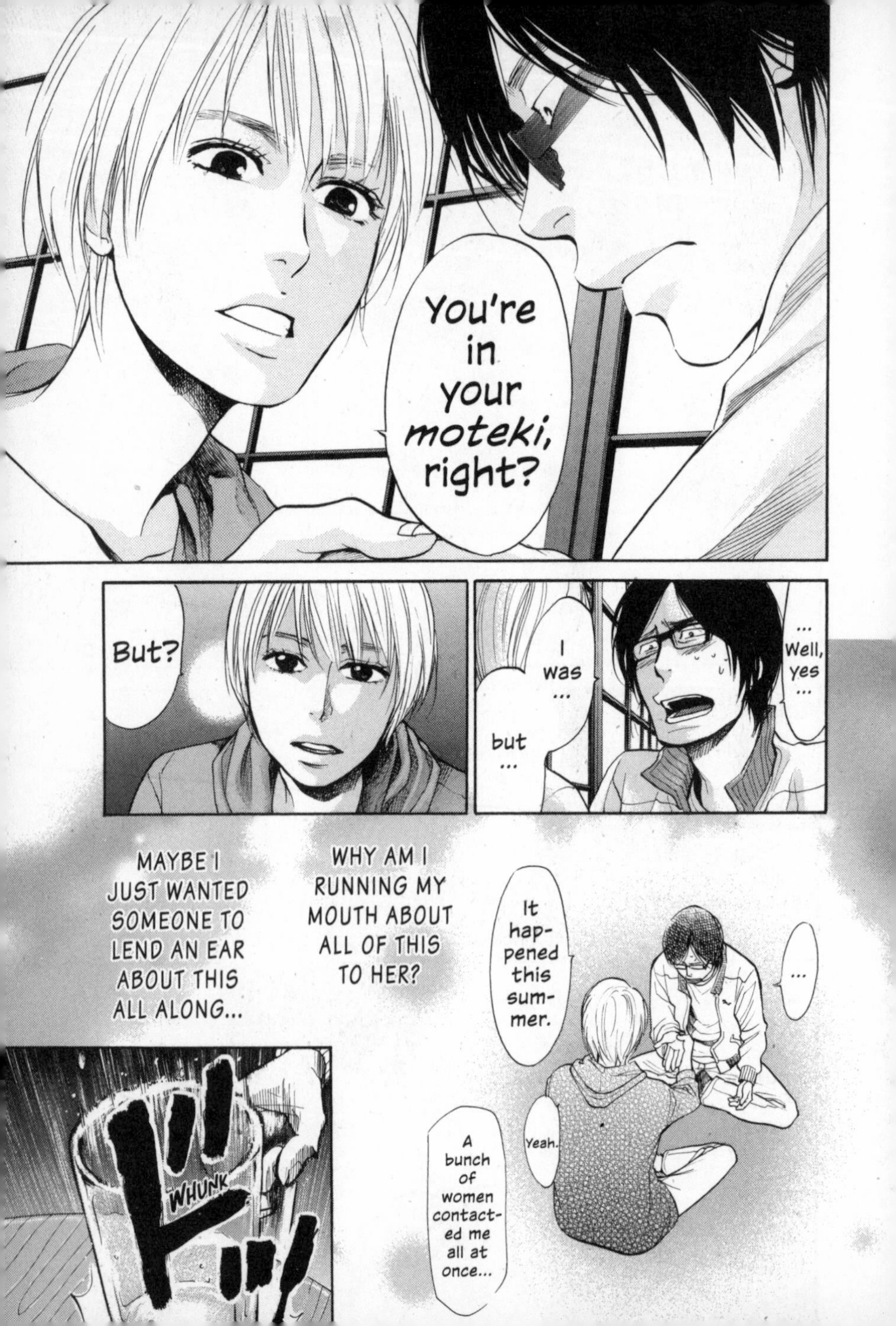
You're in your *moteki*, right?
... Well, yes ...
I was ... but ...
But?
...
It happened this summer.
WHY AM I RUNNING MY MOUTH ABOUT ALL OF THIS TO HER?
MAYBE I JUST WANTED SOMEONE TO LEND AN EAR ABOUT THIS ALL ALONG...
Yeah.
A bunch of women contacted me all at once...
WHUNK

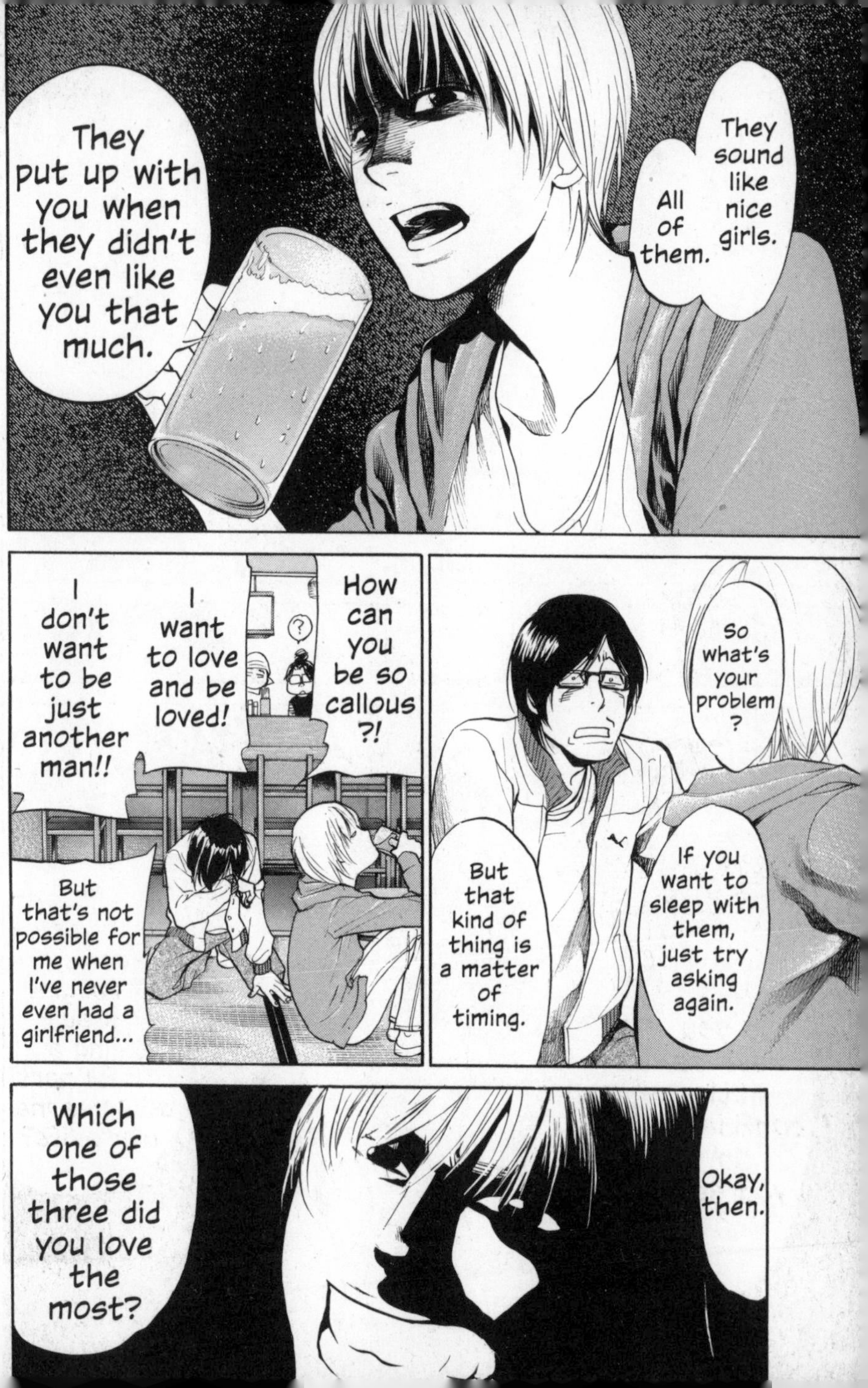
They sound like nice girls.
All of them.
They put up with you when they didn't even like you that much.
So what's your problem?
If you want to sleep with them, just try asking again.
But that kind of thing is a matter of timing.
How can you be so callous?!
I want to love and be loved!
I don't want to be just another man!!
But that's not possible for me when I've never even had a girlfriend...
Okay, then.
Which one of those three did you love the most?

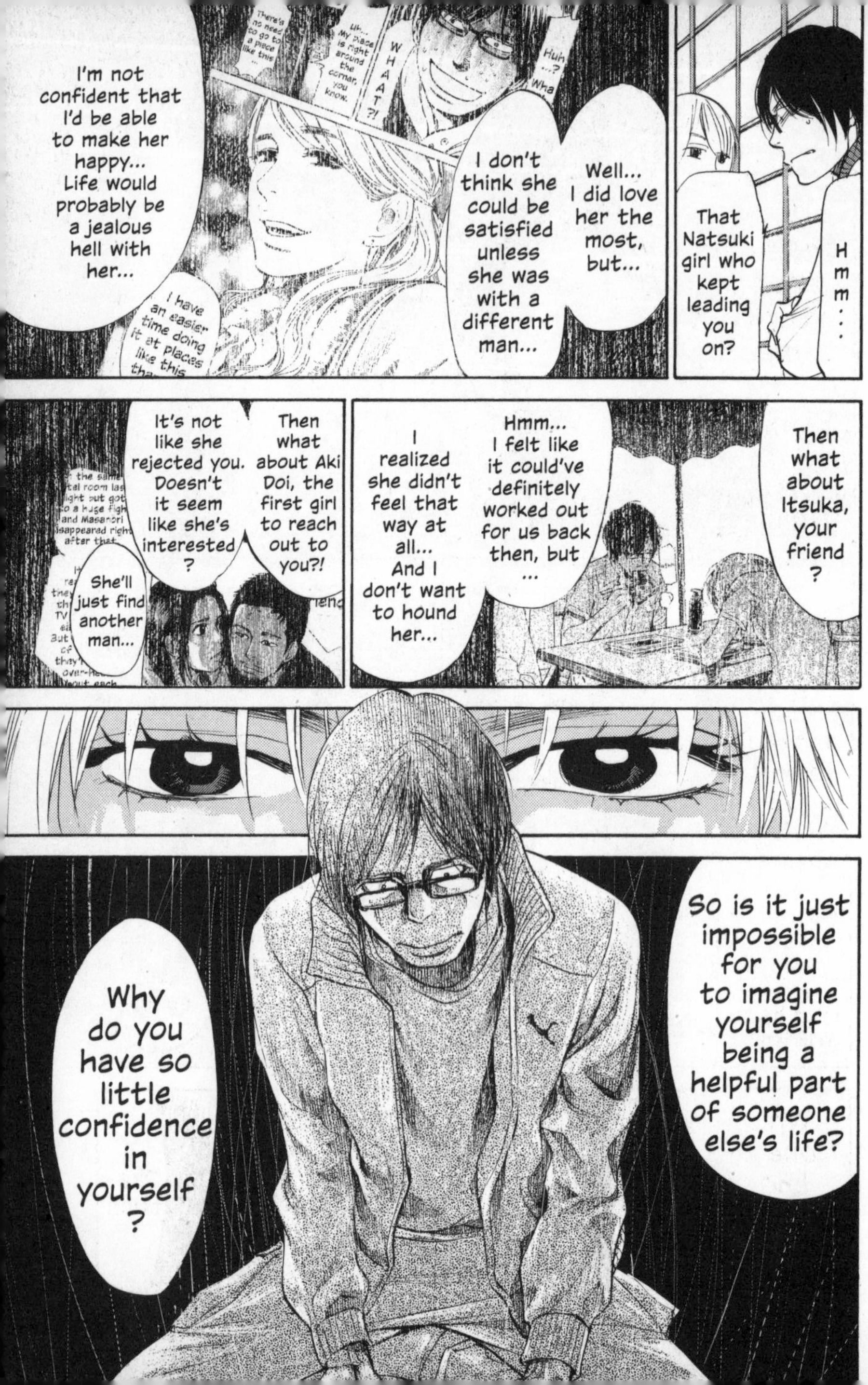
Hmm...
That Natsuki girl who kept leading you on?
Well... I did love her the most, but...
I don't think she could be satisfied unless she was with a different man...
Huh...? Wha
WHAAT?!
Uh... My place is right around the corner, you know.
There's no need to go to a place like this...
I'm not confident that I'd be able to make her happy... Life would probably be a jealous hell with her...
Then what about Itsuka, your friend?
Hmm... I felt like it could've definitely worked out for us back then, but...
I realized she didn't feel that way at all... And I don't want to hound her...
Then what about Aki Doi, the first girl to reach out to you?!
It's not like she rejected you. Doesn't it seem like she's interested?
She'll just find another man...
So is it just impossible for you to imagine yourself being a helpful part of someone else's life?
Why do you have so little confidence in yourself?

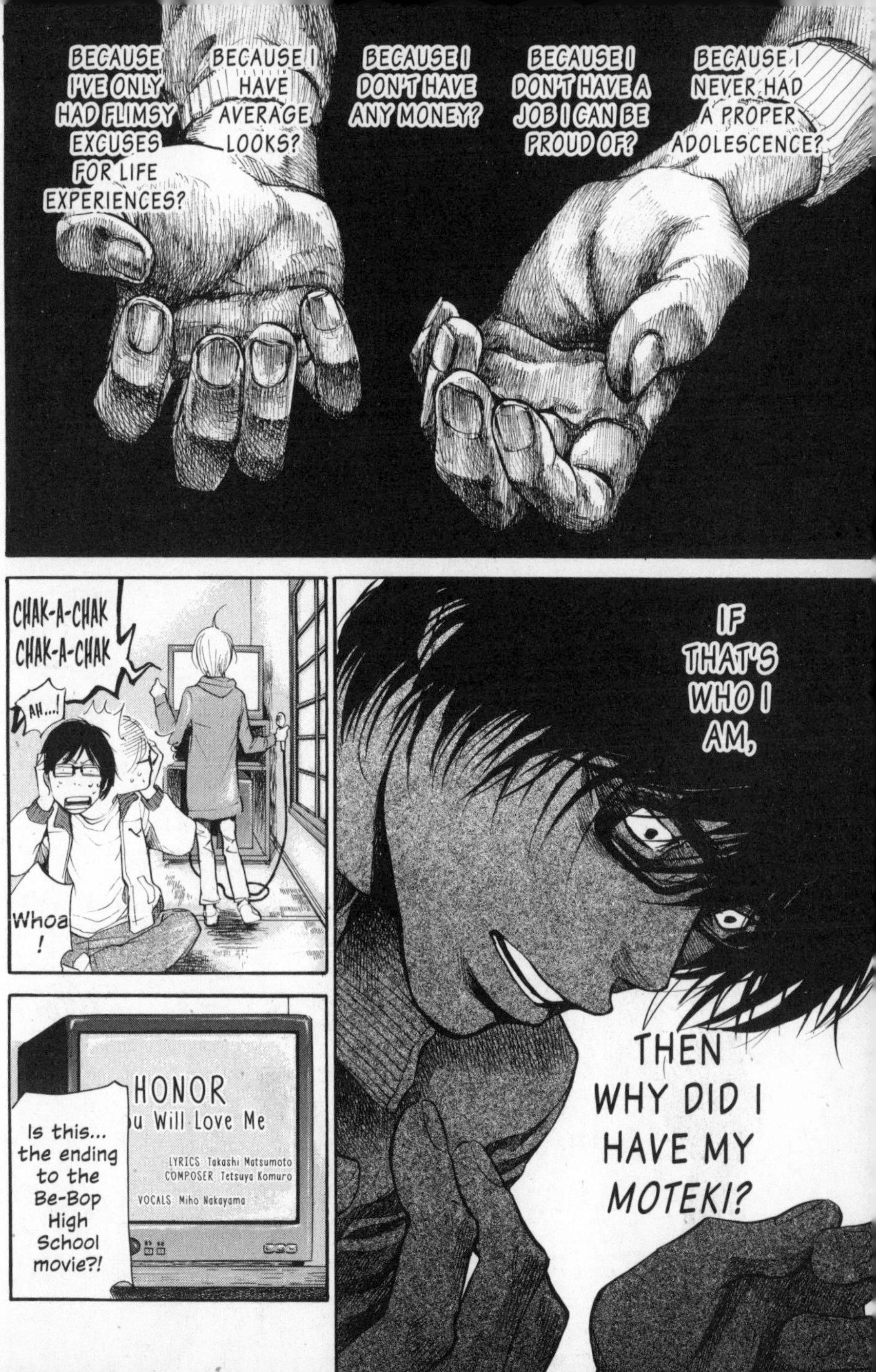
BECAUSE I NEVER HAD A PROPER ADOLESCENCE?
BECAUSE I DON'T HAVE A JOB I CAN BE PROUD OF?
BECAUSE I DON'T HAVE ANY MONEY?
BECAUSE I HAVE AVERAGE LOOKS?
BECAUSE I'VE ONLY HAD FLIMSY EXCUSES FOR LIFE EXPERIENCES?
IF THAT'S WHO I AM,
THEN WHY DID I HAVE MY *MOTEKI?*
CHAK-A-CHAK CHAK-A-CHAK
AH...!
Whoa!
HONOR
u Will Love Me
LYRICS Takashi Matsumoto
COMPOSER Tetsuya Komuro
VOCALS Miho Nakayama
Is this... the ending to the Be-Bop High School movie?!

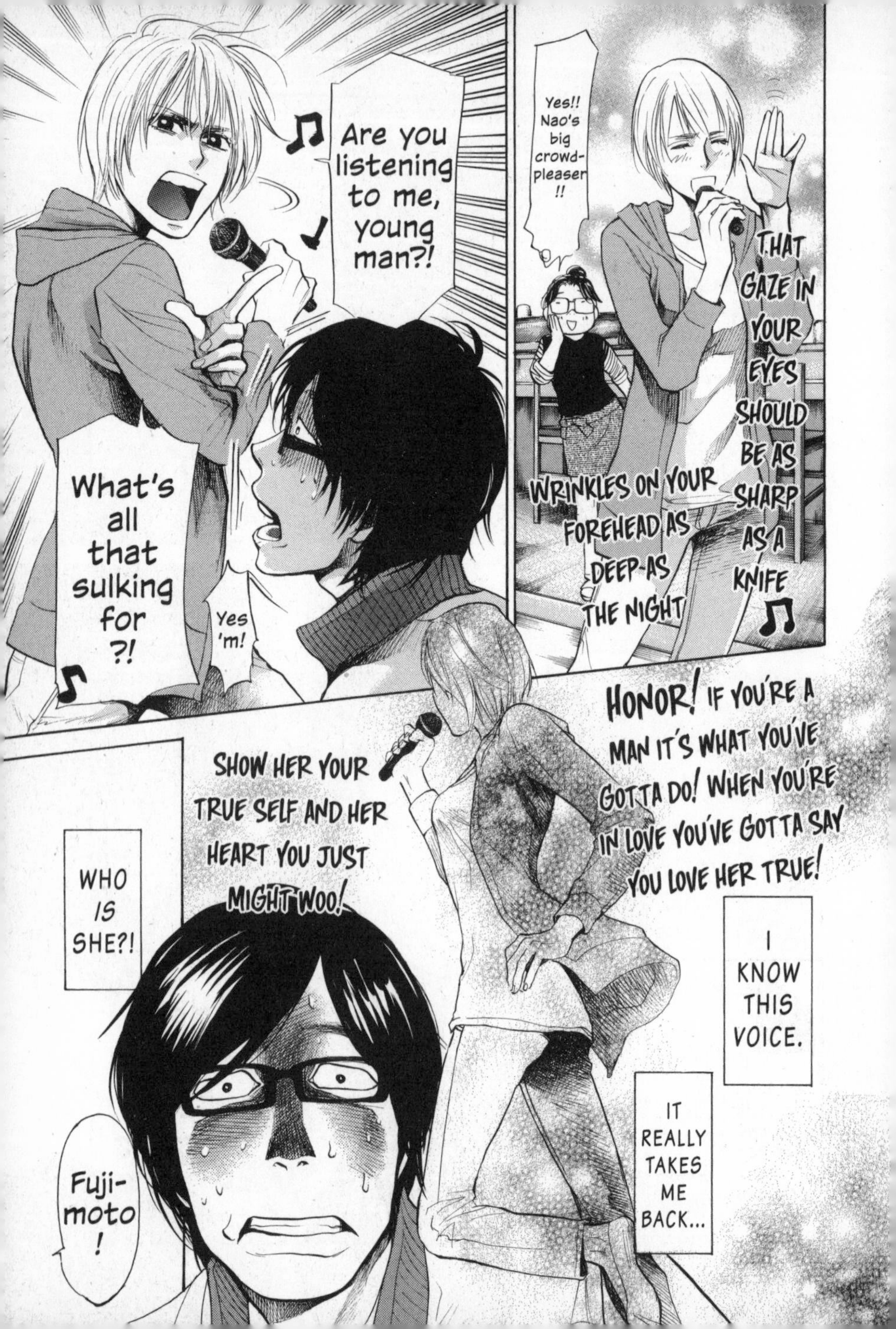
Yes!! Nao's big crowd-pleaser !!
THAT GAZE IN YOUR EYES SHOULD BE AS SHARP AS A KNIFE
WRINKLES ON YOUR FOREHEAD AS DEEP AS THE NIGHT
Are you listening to me, young man?!
What's all that sulking for ?!
Yes 'm!
HONOR! IF YOU'RE A MAN IT'S WHAT YOU'VE GOTTA DO! WHEN YOU'RE IN LOVE YOU'VE GOTTA SAY YOU LOVE HER TRUE!
SHOW HER YOUR TRUE SELF AND HER HEART YOU JUST MIGHT WOO!
I KNOW THIS VOICE.
WHO IS SHE?!
IT REALLY TAKES ME BACK...
Fuji-moto !

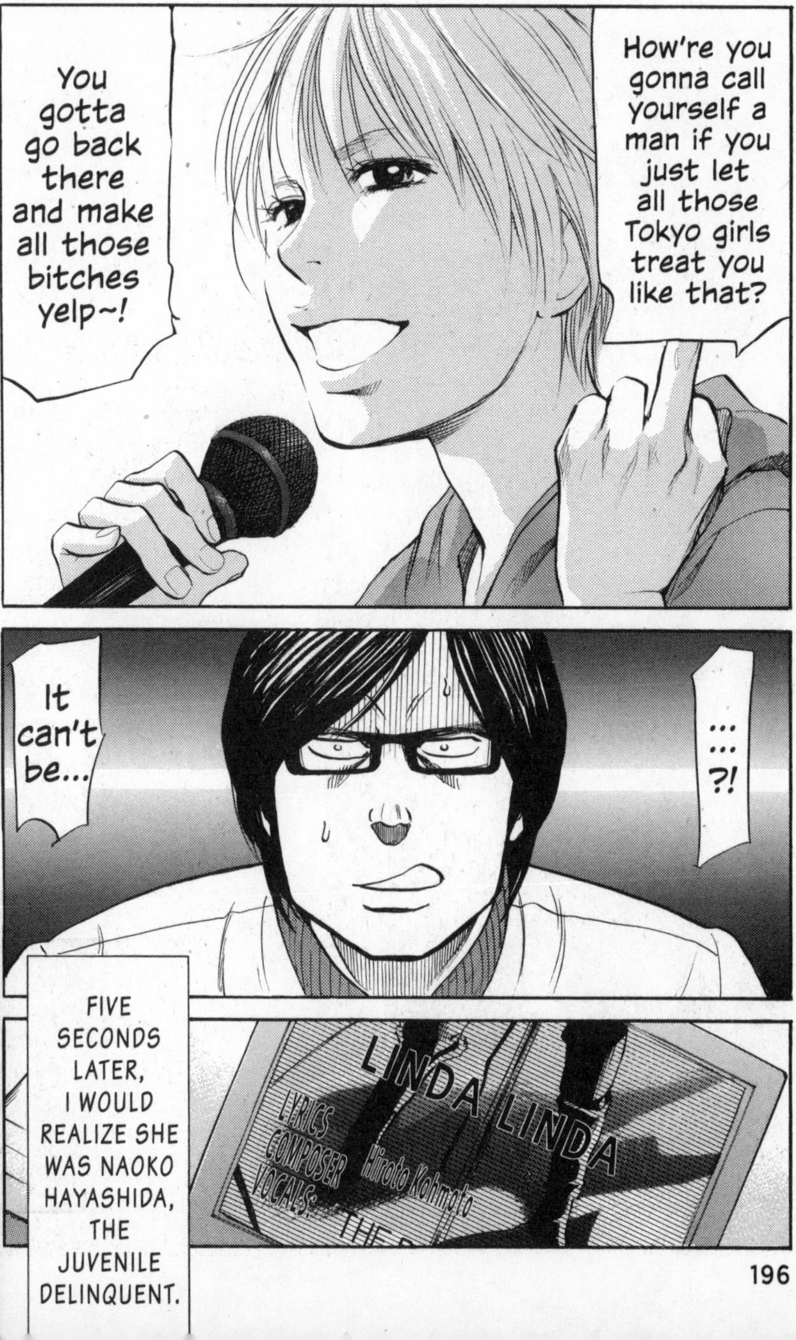
How're you gonna call yourself a man if you just let all those Tokyo girls treat you like that?
You gotta go back there and make all those bitches yelp~!
……?!
It can't be...
FIVE SECONDS LATER, I WOULD REALIZE SHE WAS NAOKO HAYASHIDA, THE JUVENILE DELINQUENT.
LINDA LINDA
LYRICS
COMPOSER Hiroto Kohmoto
VOCALS:

chapter 7 ♥ END

Moteki

Mitsurou Kubo

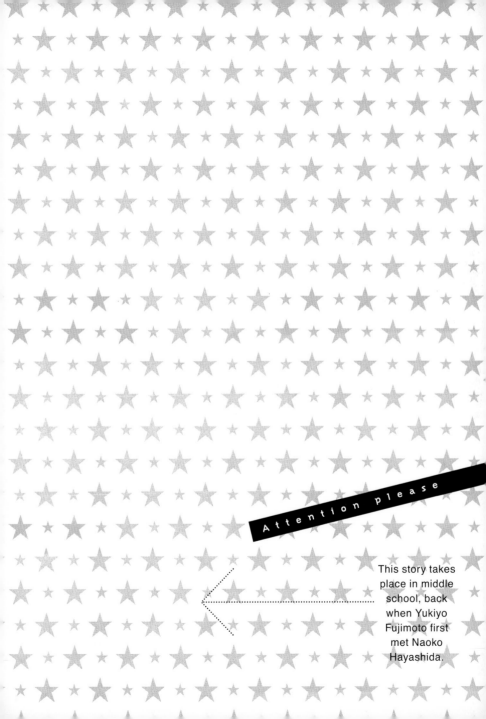

Attention please

This story takes place in middle school, back when Yukiyo Fujimoto first met Naoko Hayashida.

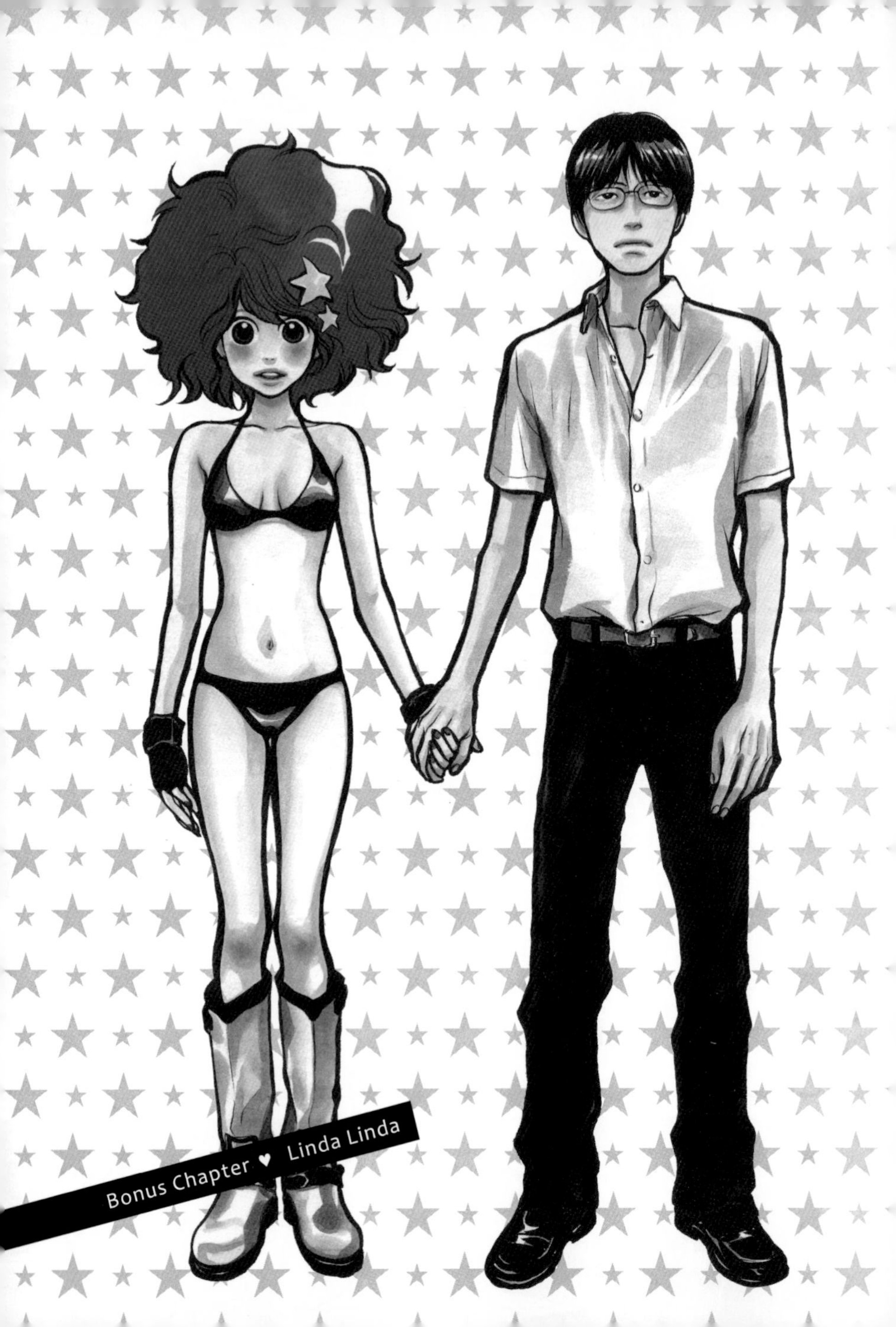
Bonus Chapter ♥ Linda Linda

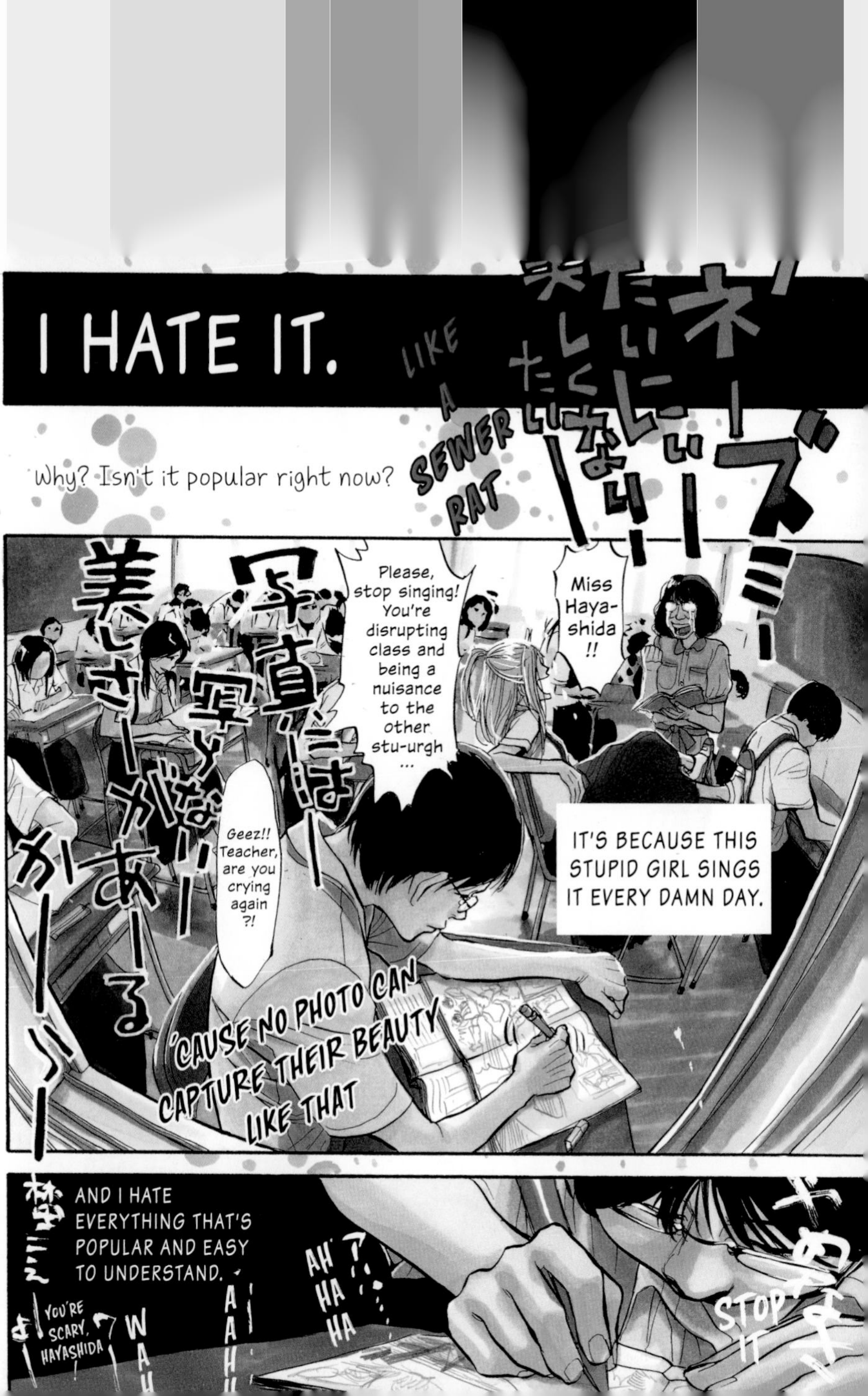
LIKE A SEWER RAT
I HATE IT.
Why? Isn't it popular right now?
Miss Haya-shida!!
Please, stop singing! You're disrupting class and being a nuisance to the other stu-urgh...
IT'S BECAUSE THIS STUPID GIRL SINGS IT EVERY DAMN DAY.
Geez!! Teacher, are you crying again?!
'CAUSE NO PHOTO CAN CAPTURE THEIR BEAUTY LIKE THAT
STOP IT
AH HA HA
AAAH
WAH
YOU'RE SCARY, HAYASHIDA!
AND I HATE EVERYTHING THAT'S POPULAR AND EASY TO UNDERSTAND.

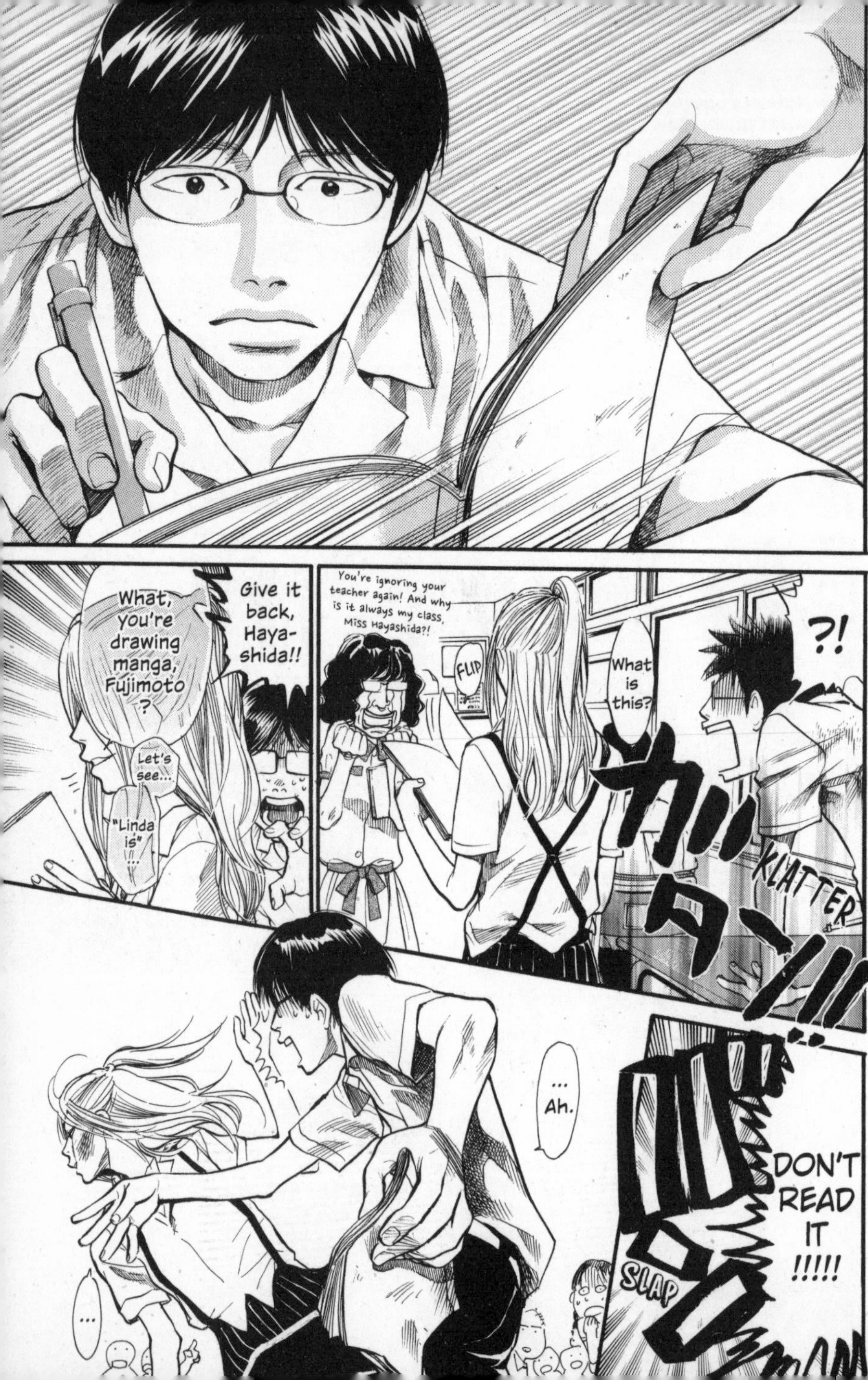
?!
What is this?
FLIP
You're ignoring your teacher again! And why is it always my class, Miss Hayashida?!
KLATTER
Give it back, Haya-shida!!
What, you're drawing manga, Fujimoto?
Let's see...
"Linda is"...
DON'T READ IT!!!!!
SLAP
... Ah.
...
...

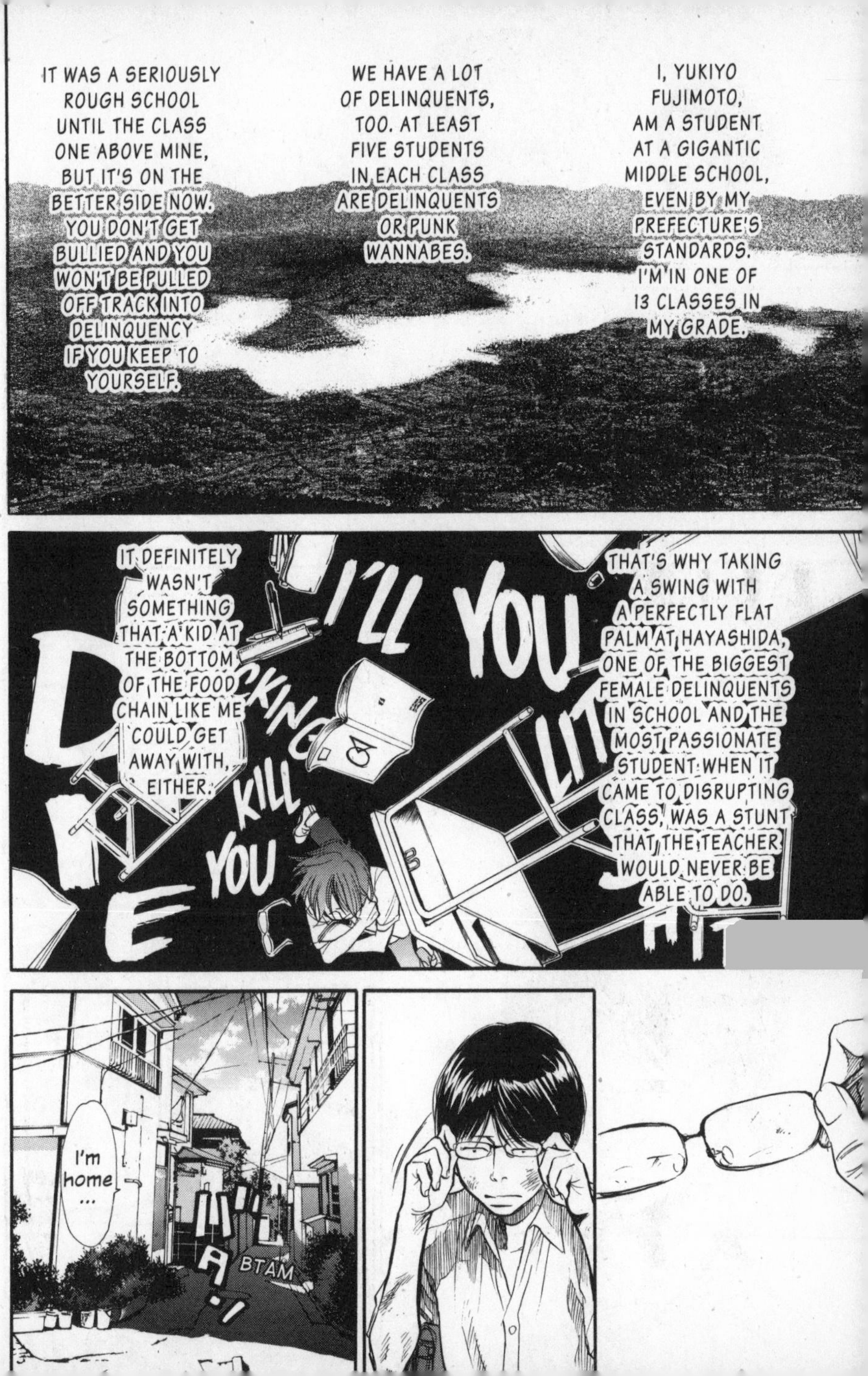
I, YUKIYO FUJIMOTO, AM A STUDENT AT A GIGANTIC MIDDLE SCHOOL, EVEN BY MY PREFECTURE'S STANDARDS. I'M IN ONE OF 13 CLASSES IN MY GRADE.
WE HAVE A LOT OF DELINQUENTS, TOO. AT LEAST FIVE STUDENTS IN EACH CLASS ARE DELINQUENTS OR PUNK WANNABES.
IT WAS A SERIOUSLY ROUGH SCHOOL UNTIL THE CLASS ONE ABOVE MINE, BUT IT'S ON THE BETTER SIDE NOW. YOU DON'T GET BULLIED AND YOU WON'T BE PULLED OFF TRACK INTO DELINQUENCY IF YOU KEEP TO YOURSELF.
THAT'S WHY TAKING A SWING WITH A PERFECTLY FLAT PALM AT HAYASHIDA, ONE OF THE BIGGEST FEMALE DELINQUENTS IN SCHOOL AND THE MOST PASSIONATE STUDENT WHEN IT CAME TO DISRUPTING CLASS, WAS A STUNT THAT THE TEACHER WOULD NEVER BE ABLE TO DO.
I'LL YOU
KILL YOU
IT DEFINITELY WASN'T SOMETHING THAT A KID AT THE BOTTOM OF THE FOOD CHAIN LIKE ME COULD GET AWAY WITH, EITHER.
I'm home ...
BTAM

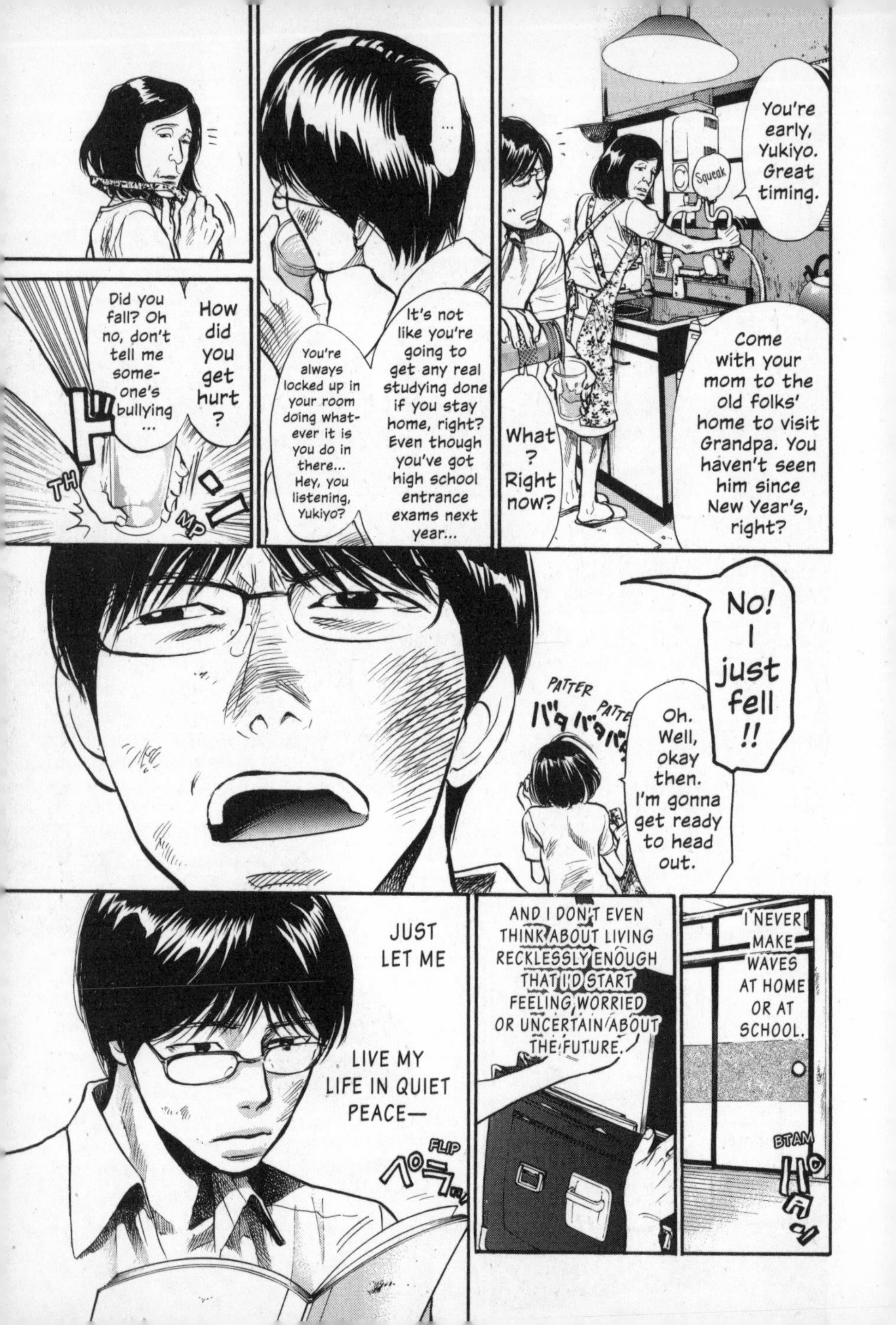
You're early, Yukiyo. Great timing.
Squeak
Come with your mom to the old folks' home to visit Grandpa. You haven't seen him since New Year's, right?
What? Right now?
...
It's not like you're going to get any real studying done if you stay home, right? Even though you've got high school entrance exams next year...
You're always locked up in your room doing whatever it is you do in there... Hey, you listening, Yukiyo?
How did you get hurt?
Did you fall? Oh no, don't tell me someone's bullying...
THUMP
No! I just fell!!
PATTER PATTER
Oh. Well, okay then. I'm gonna get ready to head out.
I NEVER MAKE WAVES AT HOME OR AT SCHOOL.
BTAM
AND I DON'T EVEN THINK ABOUT LIVING RECKLESSLY ENOUGH THAT I'D START FEELING WORRIED OR UNCERTAIN ABOUT THE FUTURE.
JUST LET ME
LIVE MY LIFE IN QUIET PEACE—
FLIP

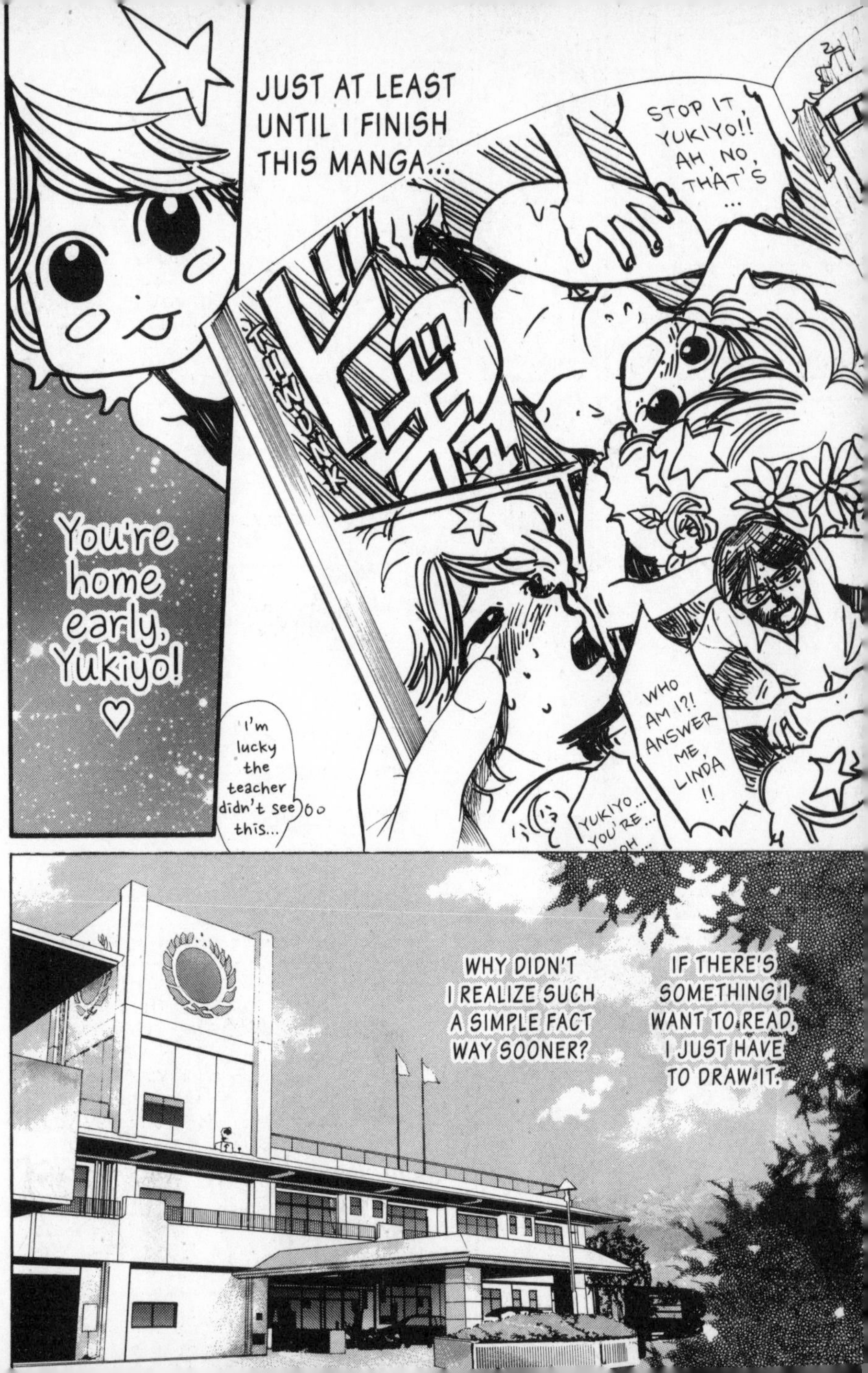
STOP IT YUKIYO!! AH, NO, THAT'S ...
JUST AT LEAST UNTIL I FINISH THIS MANGA...
WHO AM I?! ANSWER ME, LINDA !!
YUKIYO... YOU'RE... OH...
I'm lucky the teacher didn't see this...
You're home early, Yukiyo! ♡
IF THERE'S SOMETHING I WANT TO READ, I JUST HAVE TO DRAW IT.
WHY DIDN'T I REALIZE SUCH A SIMPLE FACT WAY SOONER?

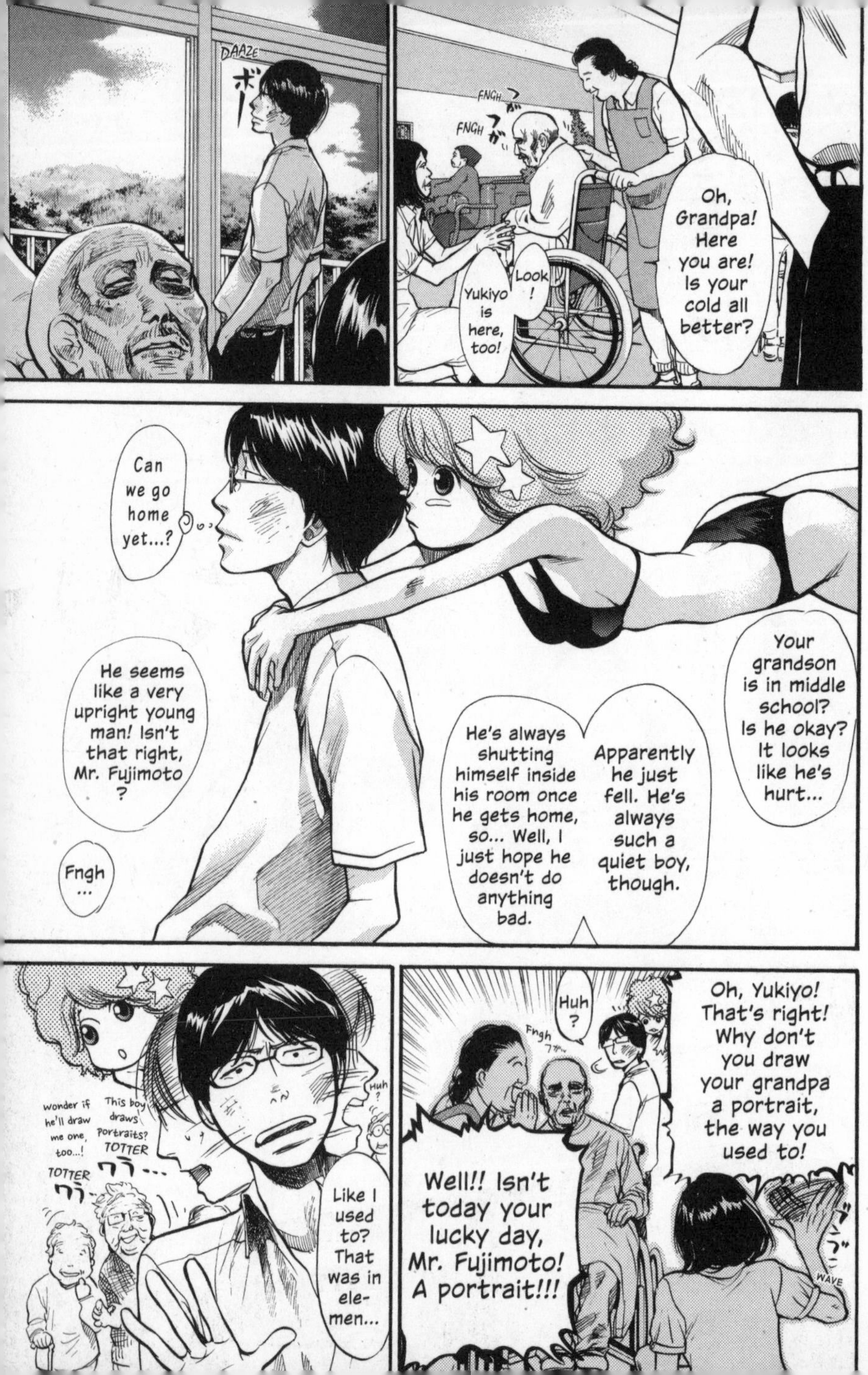
FNGH
FNGH
Oh, Grandpa! Here you are! Is your cold all better?
Look!
Yukiyo is here, too!
DAAZE
Your grandson is in middle school? Is he okay? It looks like he's hurt...
Apparently he just fell. He's always such a quiet boy, though.
He's always shutting himself inside his room once he gets home, so... Well, I just hope he doesn't do anything bad.
Can we go home yet...?
He seems like a very upright young man! Isn't that right, Mr. Fujimoto?
Fngh...
Oh, Yukiyo! That's right! Why don't you draw your grandpa a portrait, the way you used to!
Huh?
Fngh
WAVE
Well!! Isn't today your lucky day, Mr. Fujimoto! A portrait!!!
Huh?
Like I used to? That was in elemen...
This boy draws portraits?
wonder if he'll draw me one, too...!
TOTTER
TOTTER

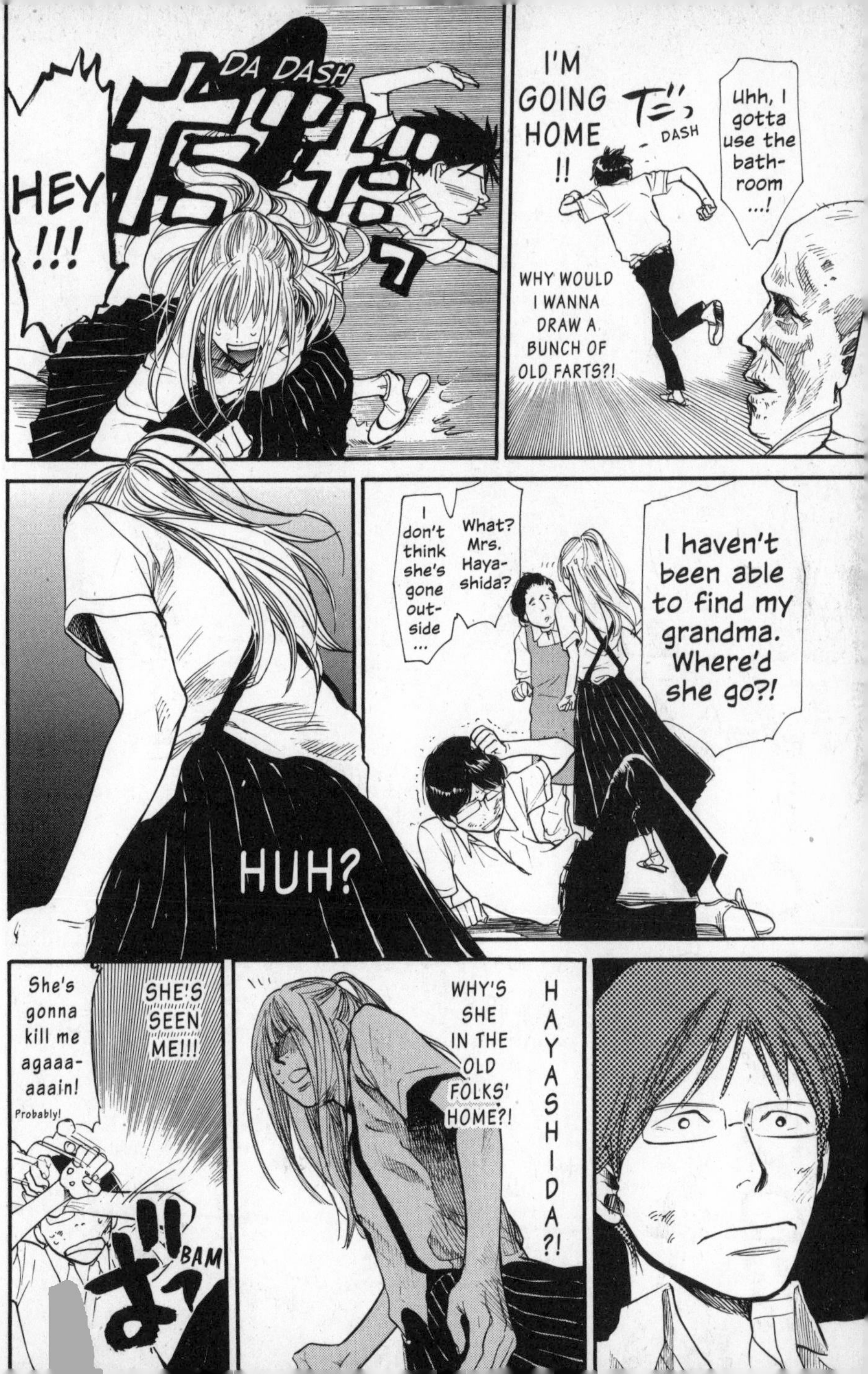

Uhh, I gotta use the bathroom...!
I'M GOING HOME!!
DASH
WHY WOULD I WANNA DRAW A BUNCH OF OLD FARTS?!
DA DASH
HEY!!!
I haven't been able to find my grandma. Where'd she go?!
What? Mrs. Hayashida?
I don't think she's gone outside...
HUH?
HAYASHIDA?!
WHY'S SHE IN THE OLD FOLKS' HOME?!
SHE'S SEEN ME!!!
She's gonna kill me agaaa-aaain!
Probably!
BAM

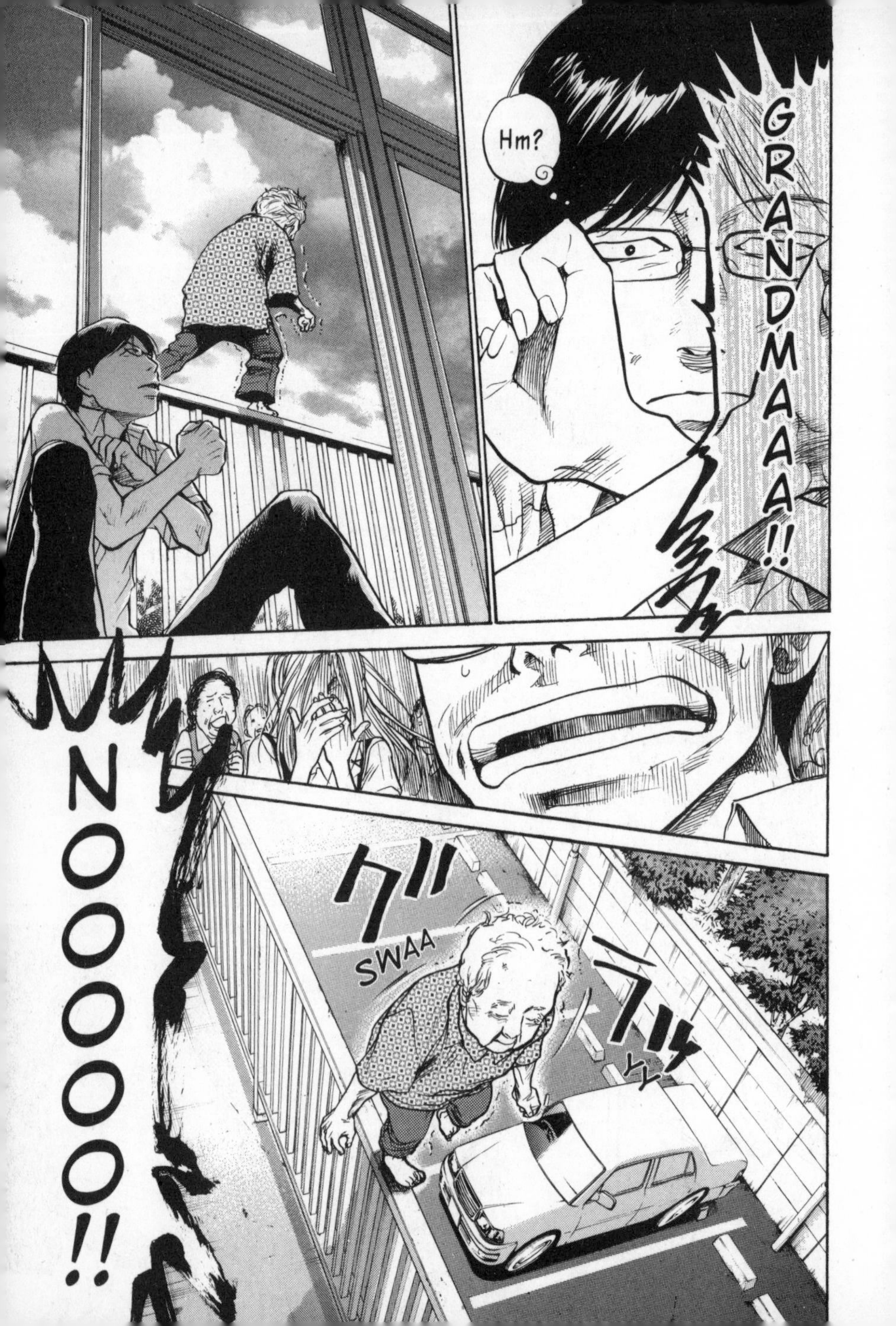
Hm?
GRANDMAAAA!!
NOOOOO!!
SWAA

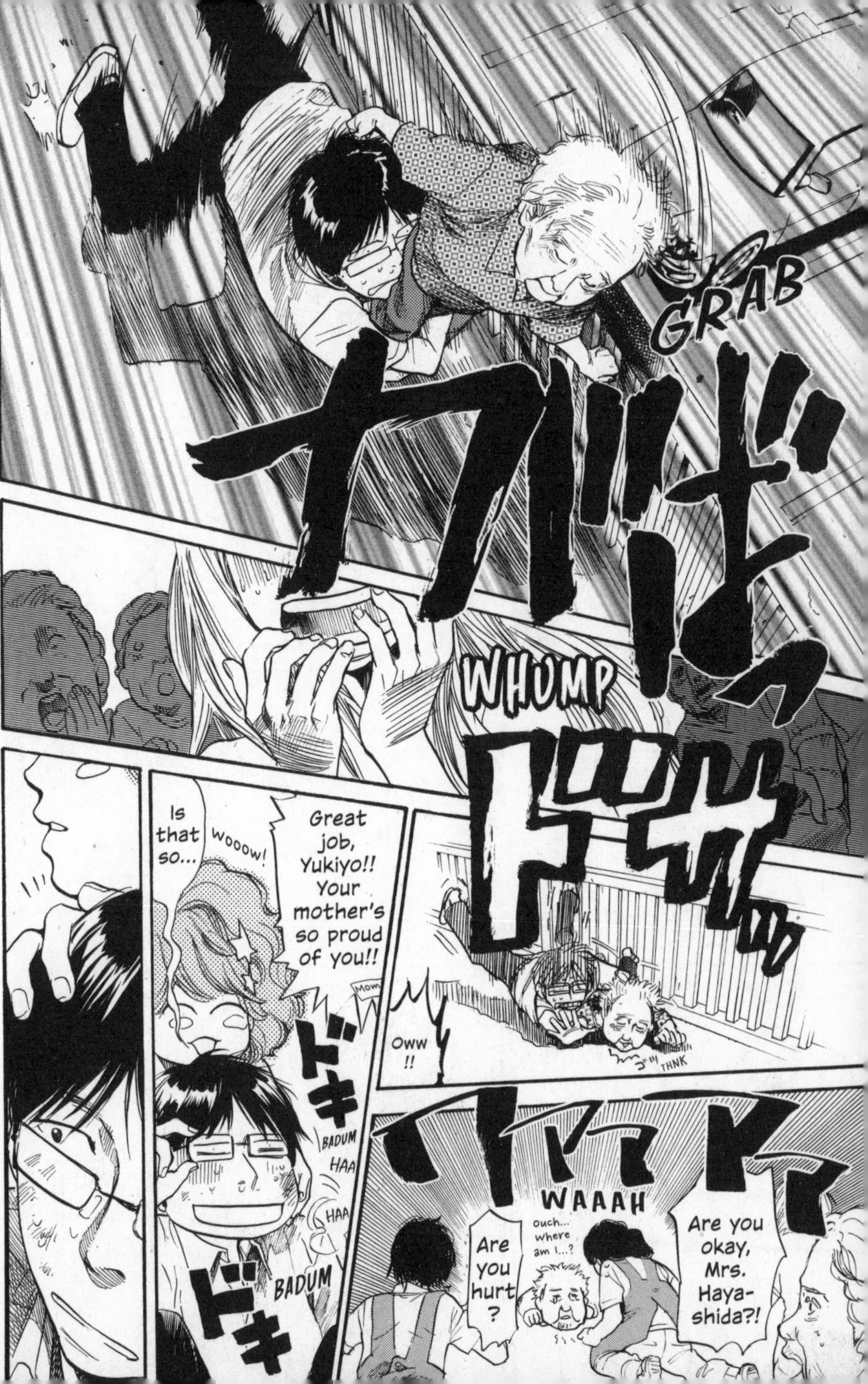
GRAB
WHUMP
Oww!!
THNK
Great job, Yukiyo!! Your mother's so proud of you!!
Wooow!
Is that so...
Mom
ドキ
BADUM
HAA
HAA
BADUM
ドキ
WAAAH
Are you okay, Mrs. Haya-shida?!
ouch... where am I...?
Are you hurt?

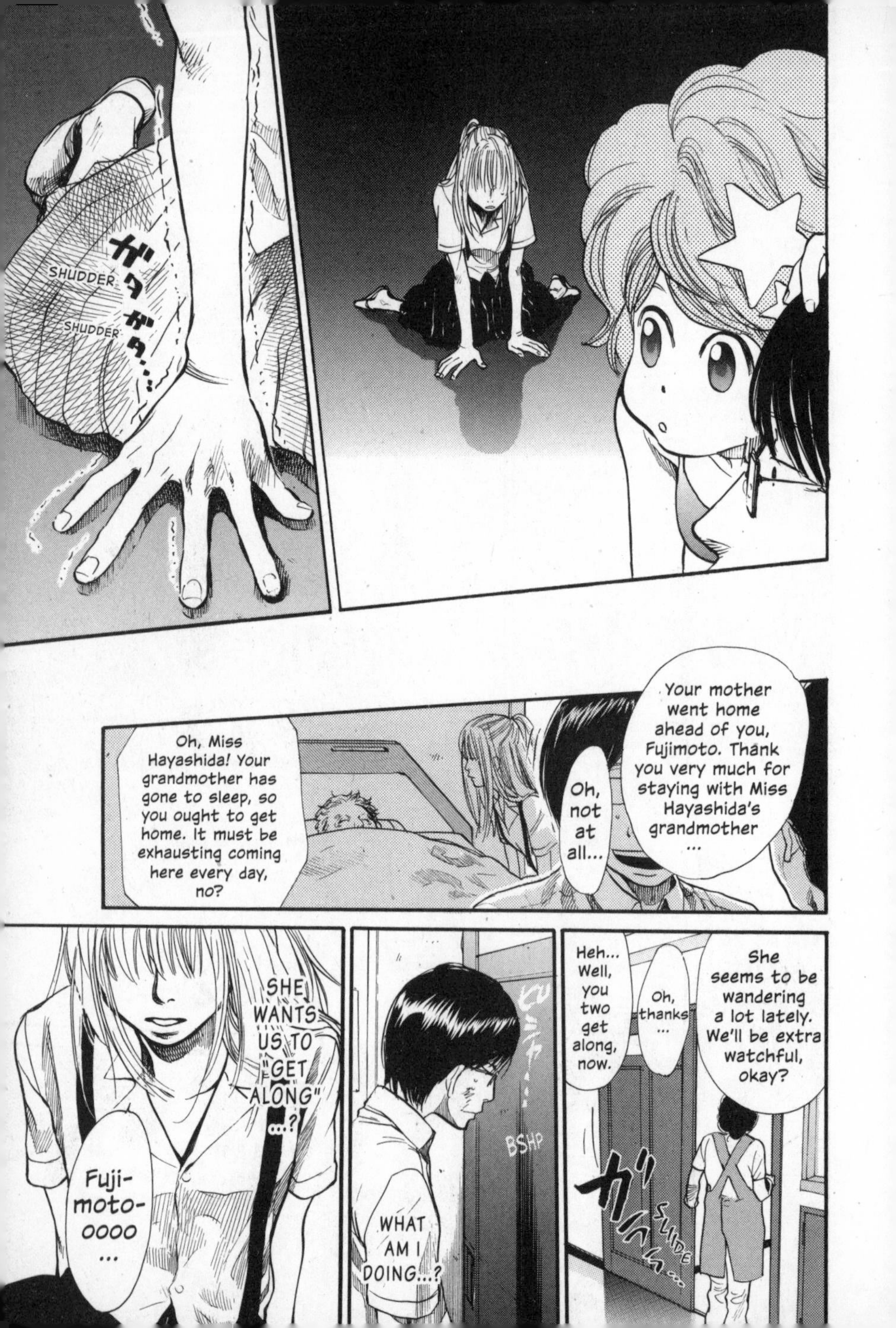
SHUDDER
SHUDDER
Your mother went home ahead of you, Fujimoto. Thank you very much for staying with Miss Hayashida's grandmother ...
Oh, not at all...
Oh, Miss Hayashida! Your grandmother has gone to sleep, so you ought to get home. It must be exhausting coming here every day, no?
She seems to be wandering a lot lately. We'll be extra watchful, okay?
Oh, thanks ...
Heh... Well, you two get along, now.
SLIDE
BSHP
WHAT AM I DOING...?
SHE WANTS US TO "GET ALONG" ...?
Fuji-moto-oooo ...

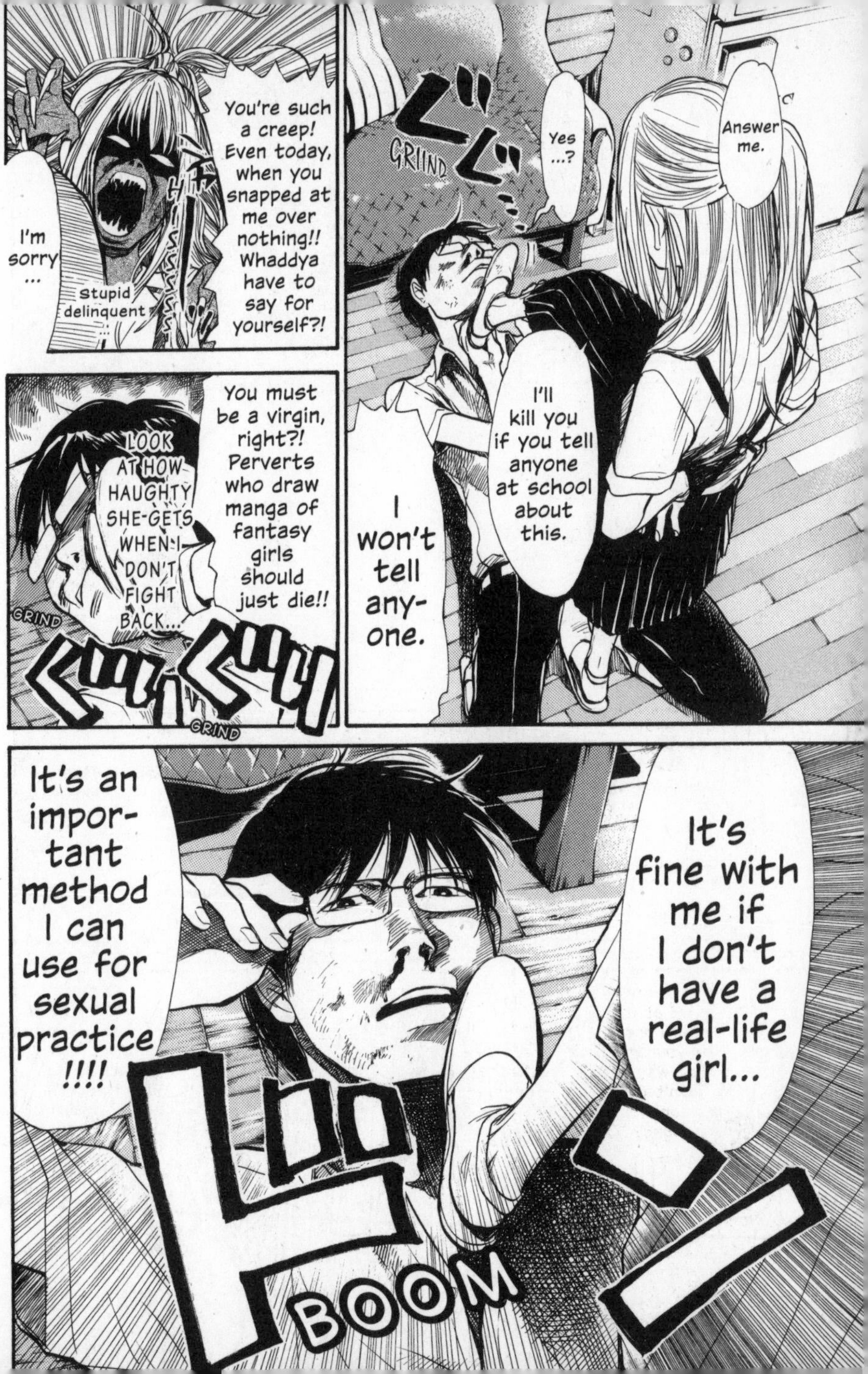

Answer me.
Yes ...?
GRIIND
I'll kill you if you tell anyone at school about this.
I won't tell any-one.
You're such a creep! Even today, when you snapped at me over nothing!! Whaddya have to say for yourself?!
Stupid delinquent ...
I'm sorry ...
You must be a virgin, right?! Perverts who draw manga of fantasy girls should just die!!
LOOK AT HOW HAUGHTY SHE-GETS WHEN I DON'T FIGHT BACK...
GRIND
GRIND
It's fine with me if I don't have a real-life girl...
It's an impor-tant method I can use for sexual practice !!!!
BOOM

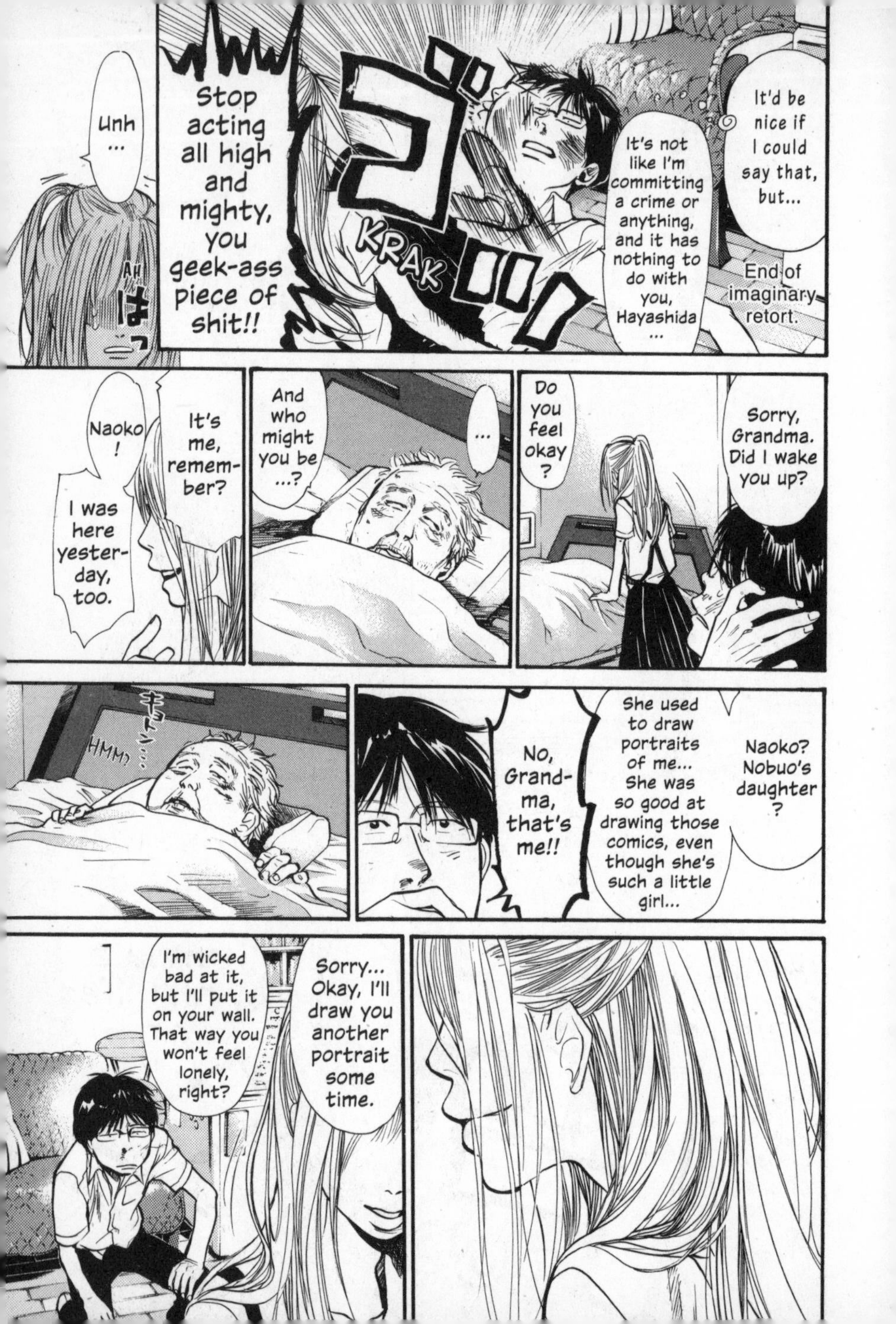
It'd be nice if I could say that, but...
It's not like I'm committing a crime or anything, and it has nothing to do with you, Hayashida ...
End of imaginary retort.
Stop acting all high and mighty, you geek-ass piece of shit!!
KRAK
Unh ...
AH
はっ
Sorry, Grandma. Did I wake you up?
Do you feel okay ?
...
And who might you be ...?
Naoko !
It's me, remember?
I was here yesterday, too.
Naoko? Nobuo's daughter ?
She used to draw portraits of me... She was so good at drawing those comics, even though she's such a little girl...
No, Grandma, that's me!!
キョトン...
HMM?
Sorry... Okay, I'll draw you another portrait some time.
I'm wicked bad at it, but I'll put it on your wall. That way you won't feel lonely, right?

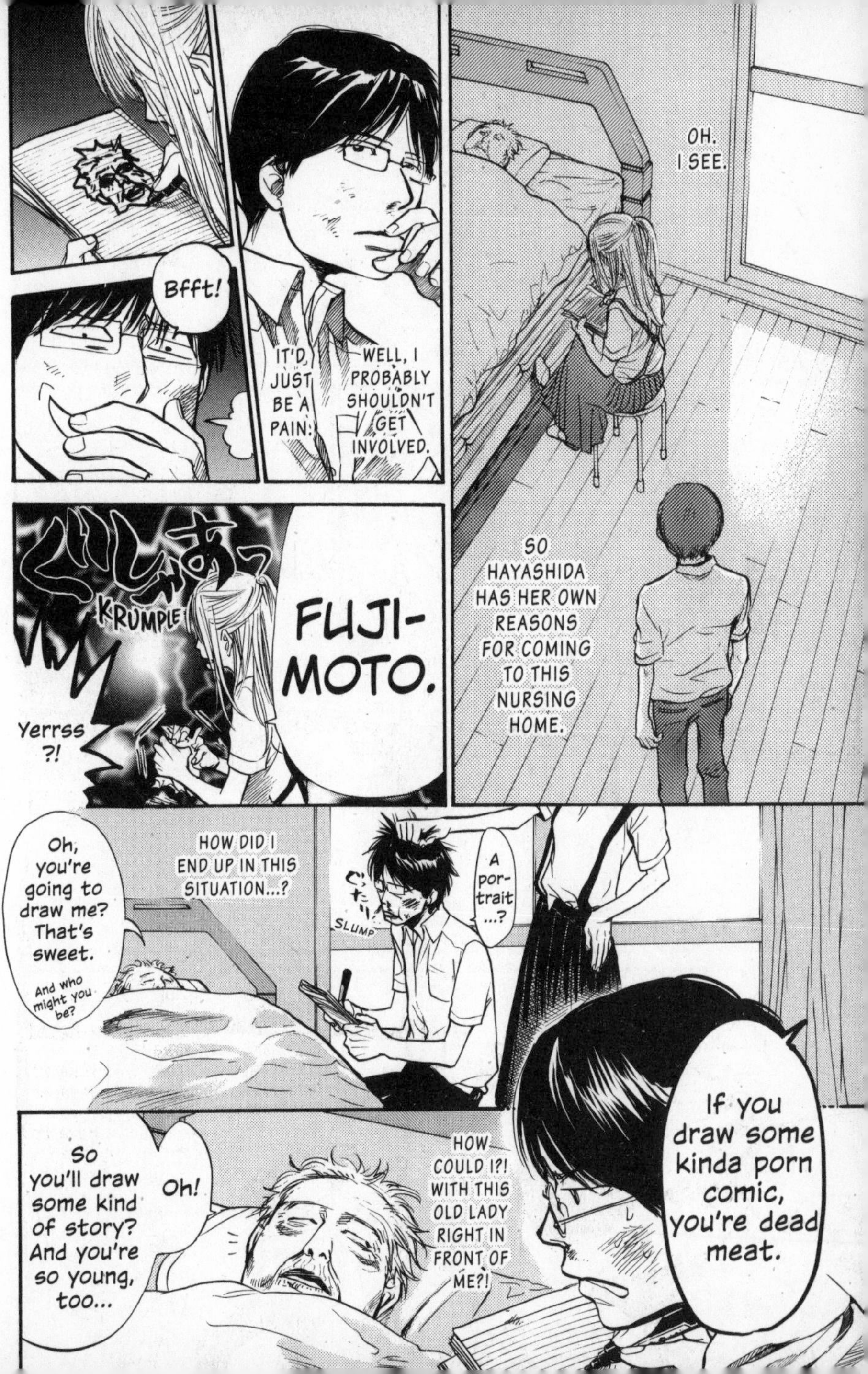
OH. I SEE.
SO HAYASHIDA HAS HER OWN REASONS FOR COMING TO THIS NURSING HOME.
WELL, I PROBABLY SHOULDN'T GET INVOLVED.
IT'D JUST BE A PAIN.
Bfft!
FUJI-MOTO.
KRUMPLE
Yerrss ?!
A portrait ...?
SLUMP
HOW DID I END UP IN THIS SITUATION...?
Oh, you're going to draw me? That's sweet.
And who might you be?
If you draw some kinda porn comic, you're dead meat.
HOW COULD I?! WITH THIS OLD LADY RIGHT IN FRONT OF ME?!
Oh!
So you'll draw some kind of story? And you're so young, too...

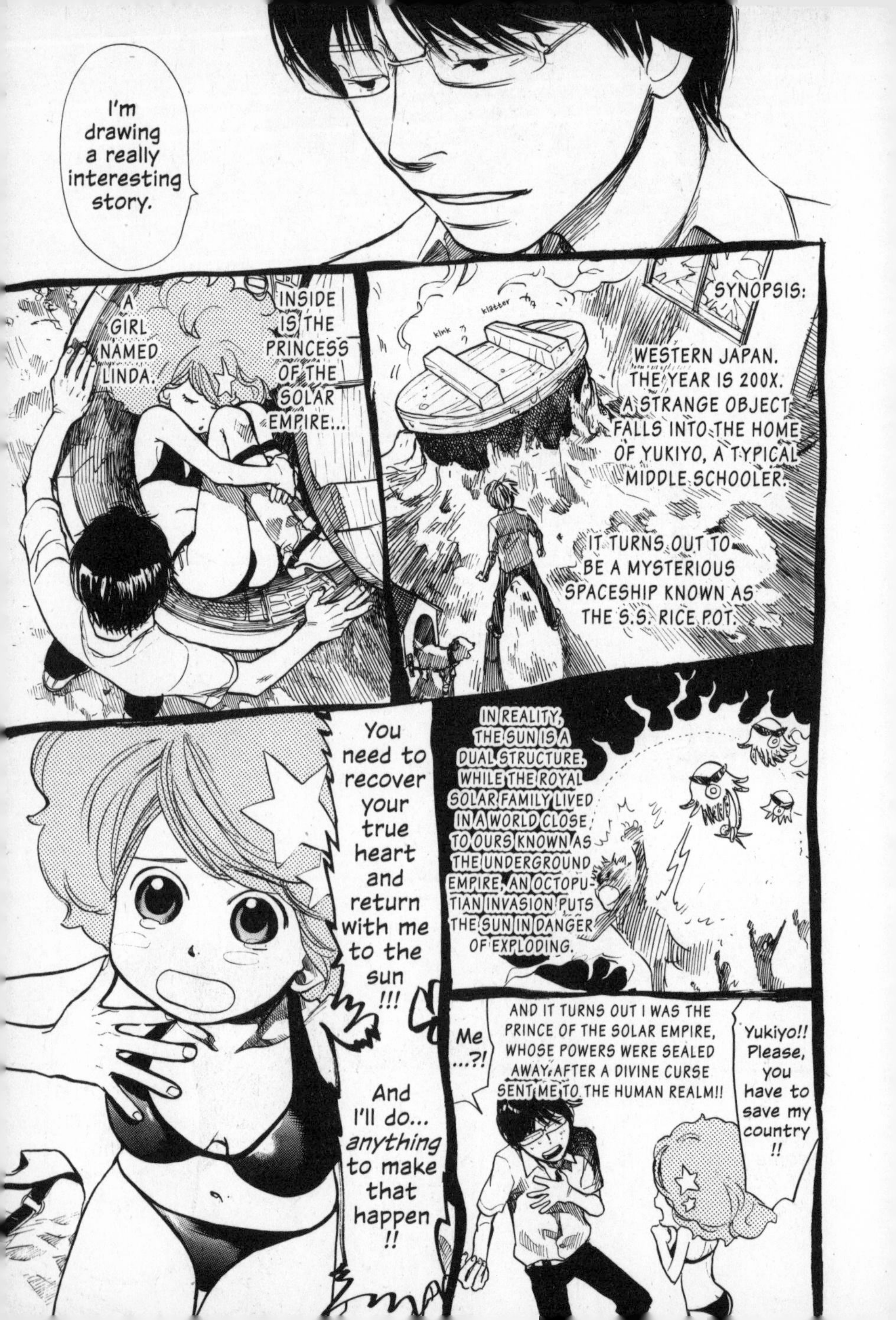
I'm drawing a really interesting story.
SYNOPSIS:
klatter
klink
WESTERN JAPAN. THE YEAR IS 200X. A STRANGE OBJECT FALLS INTO THE HOME OF YUKIYO, A TYPICAL MIDDLE SCHOOLER.
IT TURNS OUT TO BE A MYSTERIOUS SPACESHIP KNOWN AS THE S.S. RICE POT.
INSIDE IS THE PRINCESS OF THE SOLAR EMPIRE...
A GIRL NAMED LINDA.
IN REALITY, THE SUN IS A DUAL STRUCTURE. WHILE THE ROYAL SOLAR FAMILY LIVED IN A WORLD CLOSE TO OURS KNOWN AS THE UNDERGROUND EMPIRE, AN OCTOPUTIAN INVASION PUTS THE SUN IN DANGER OF EXPLODING.
Yukiyo!! Please, you have to save my country!!
AND IT TURNS OUT I WAS THE PRINCE OF THE SOLAR EMPIRE, WHOSE POWERS WERE SEALED AWAY AFTER A DIVINE CURSE SENT ME TO THE HUMAN REALM!!
Me...?!
You need to recover your true heart and return with me to the sun!!!
And I'll do... *anything* to make that happen!!

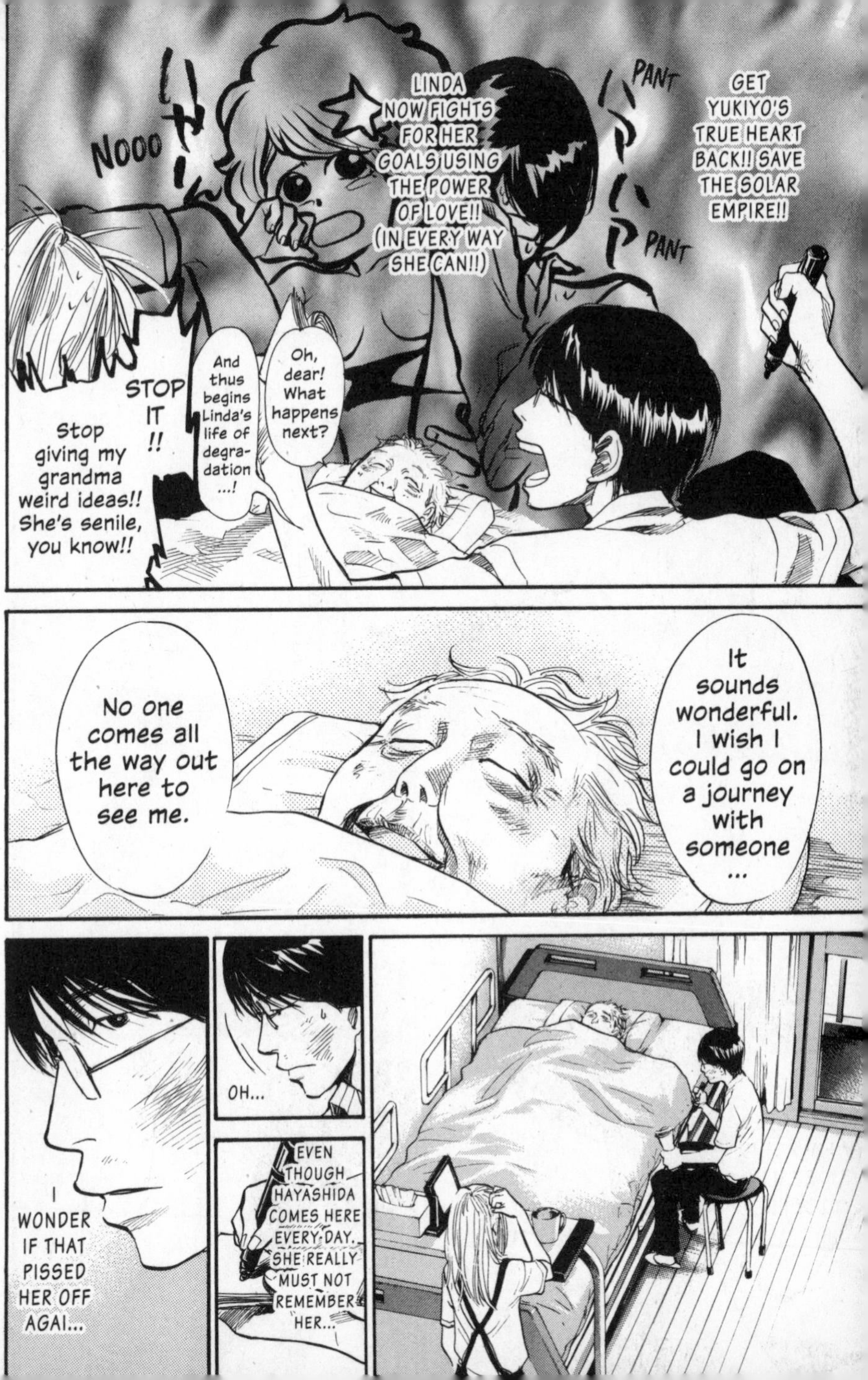
GET YUKIYO'S TRUE HEART BACK!! SAVE THE SOLAR EMPIRE!!
PANT
PANT
LINDA NOW FIGHTS FOR HER GOALS USING THE POWER OF LOVE!! (IN EVERY WAY SHE CAN!!)
NOOO
Oh, dear! What happens next?
And thus begins Linda's life of degradation ...!
STOP IT !!
Stop giving my grandma weird ideas!! She's senile, you know!!
It sounds wonderful. I wish I could go on a journey with someone ...
No one comes all the way out here to see me.
OH...
EVEN THOUGH HAYASHIDA COMES HERE EVERY DAY, SHE REALLY MUST NOT REMEMBER HER...
I WONDER IF THAT PISSED HER OFF AGAI...

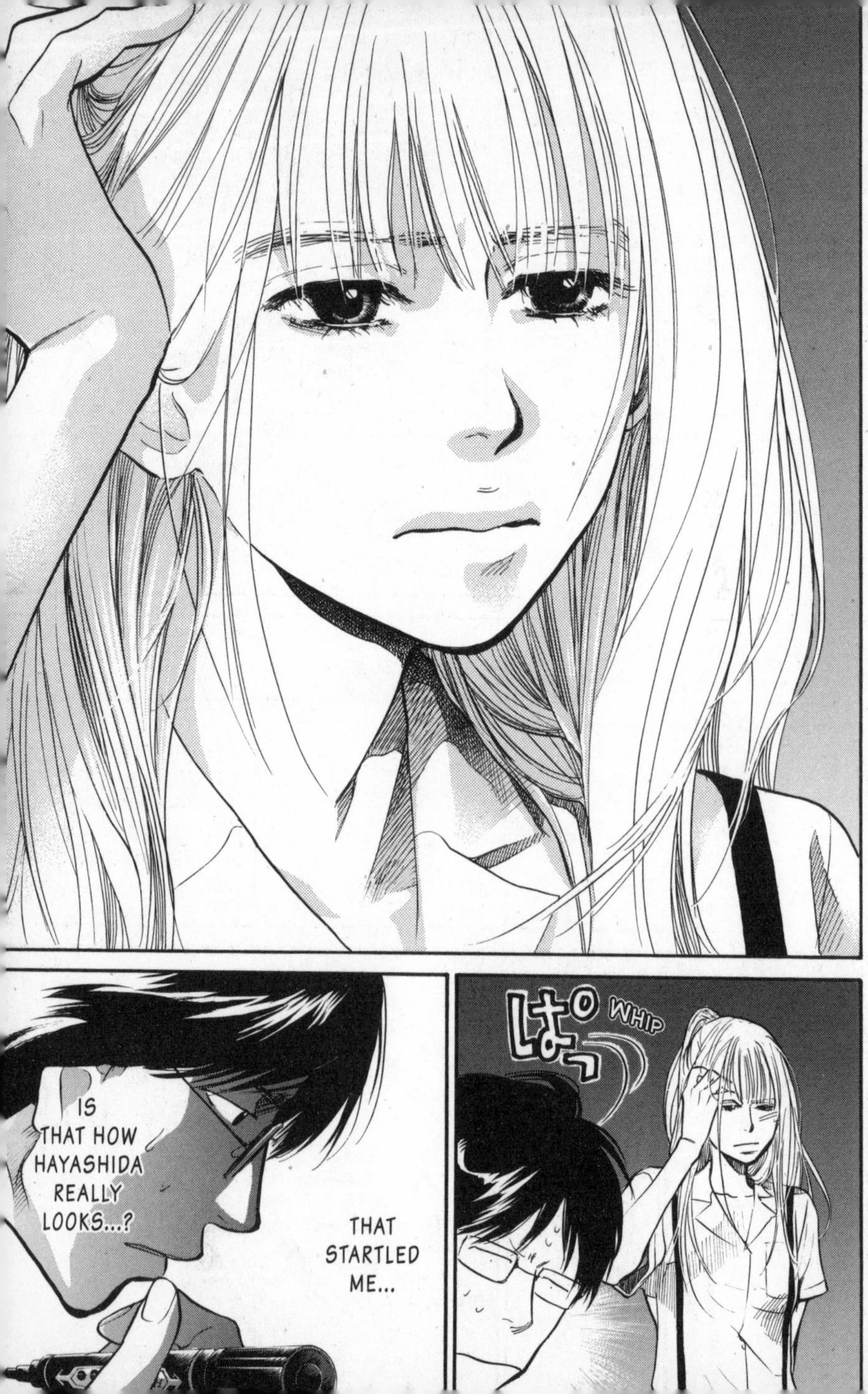
はっ
WHIP
THAT STARTLED ME...
IS THAT HOW HAYASHIDA REALLY LOOKS...?

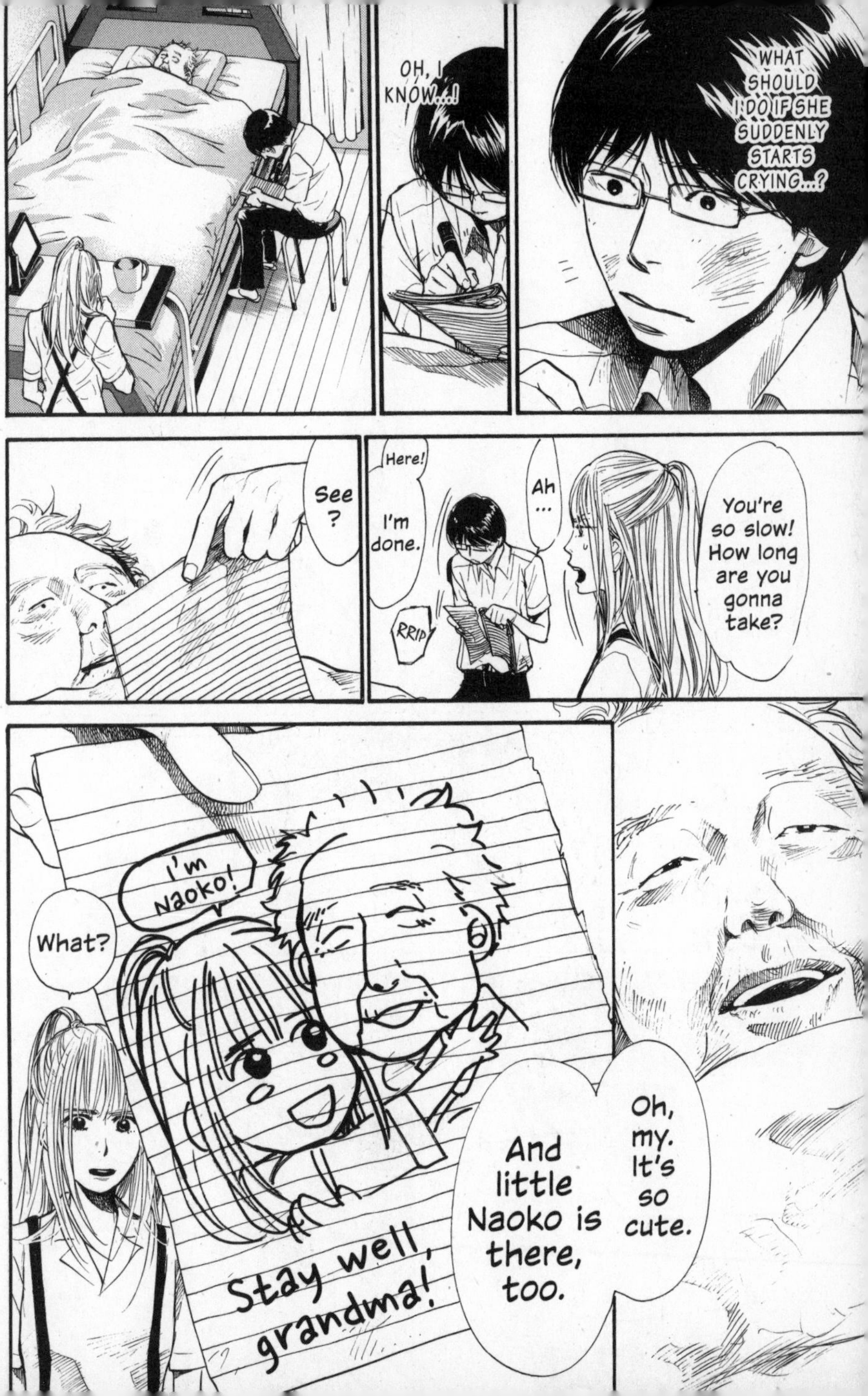
WHAT SHOULD I DO IF SHE SUDDENLY STARTS CRYING...?
OH, I KNOW...!
You're so slow! How long are you gonna take?
Ah ...
Here!
I'm done.
RRIP
See ?
Oh, my. It's so cute.
And little Naoko is there, too.
Stay well, grandma!
I'm Naoko!
What?

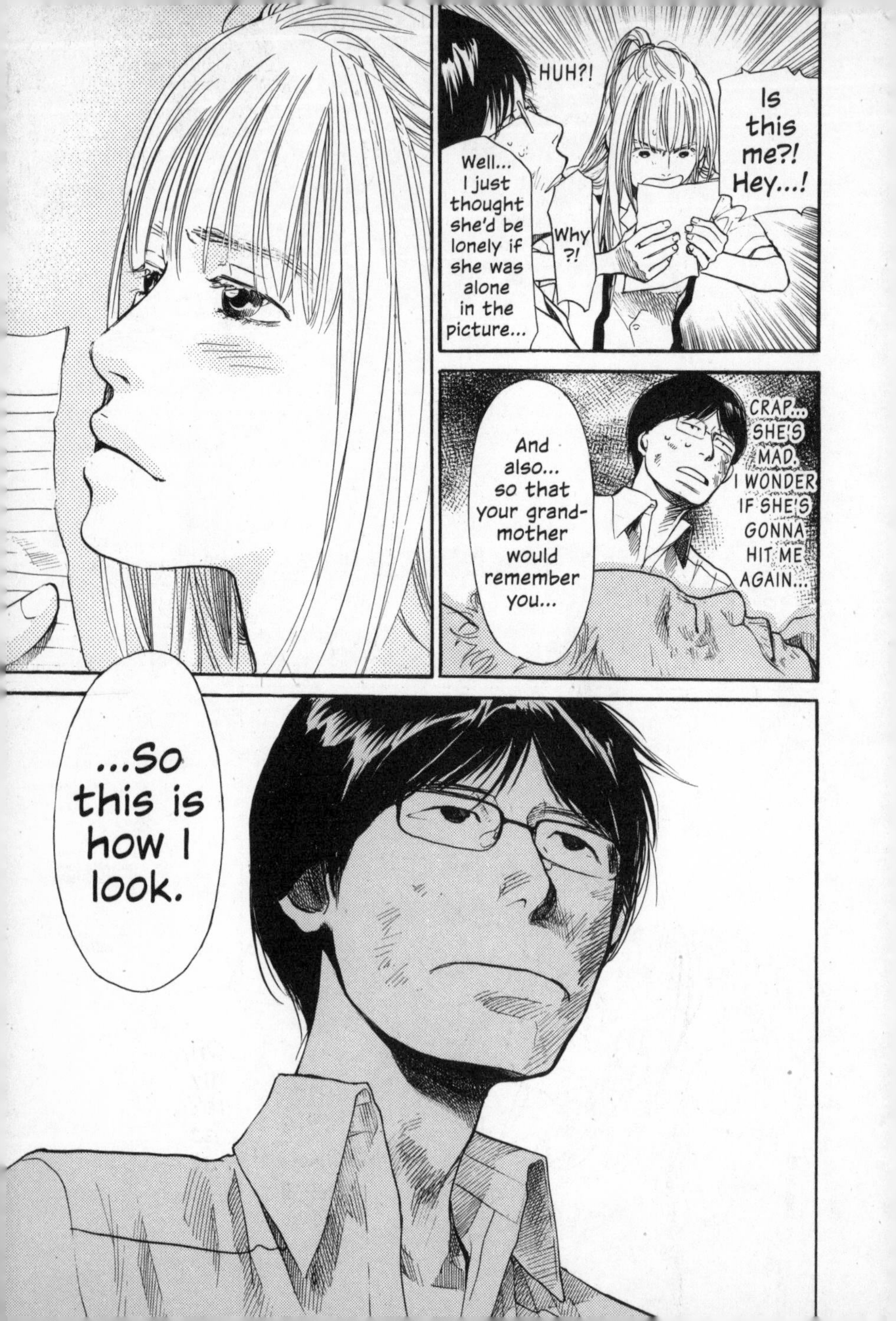
Is this me?! Hey...!
HUH?!
Why ?!
Well... I just thought she'd be lonely if she was alone in the picture...
CRAP... SHE'S MAD. I WONDER IF SHE'S GONNA HIT ME AGAIN...
And also... so that your grand-mother would remember you...
...So this is how I look.

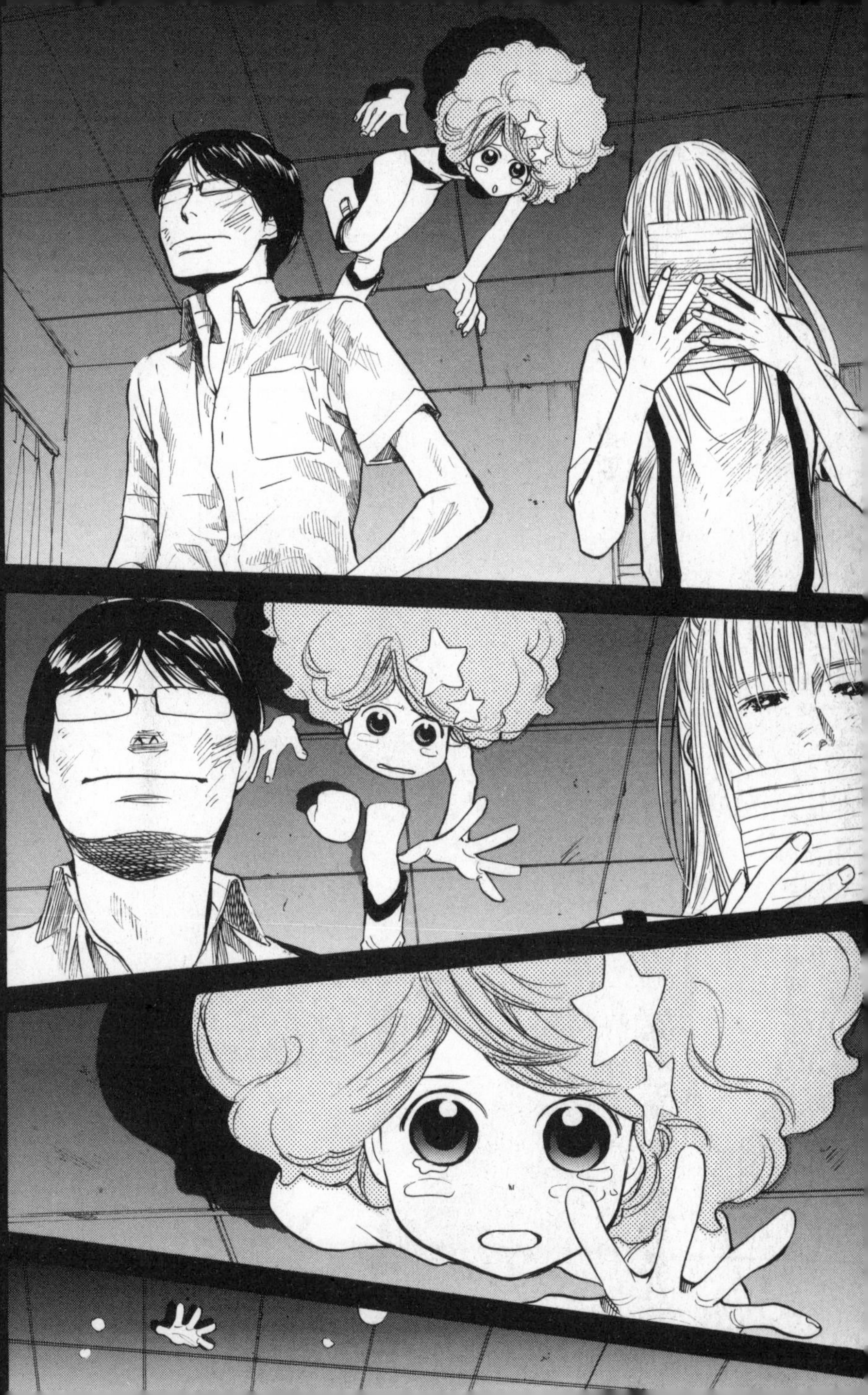

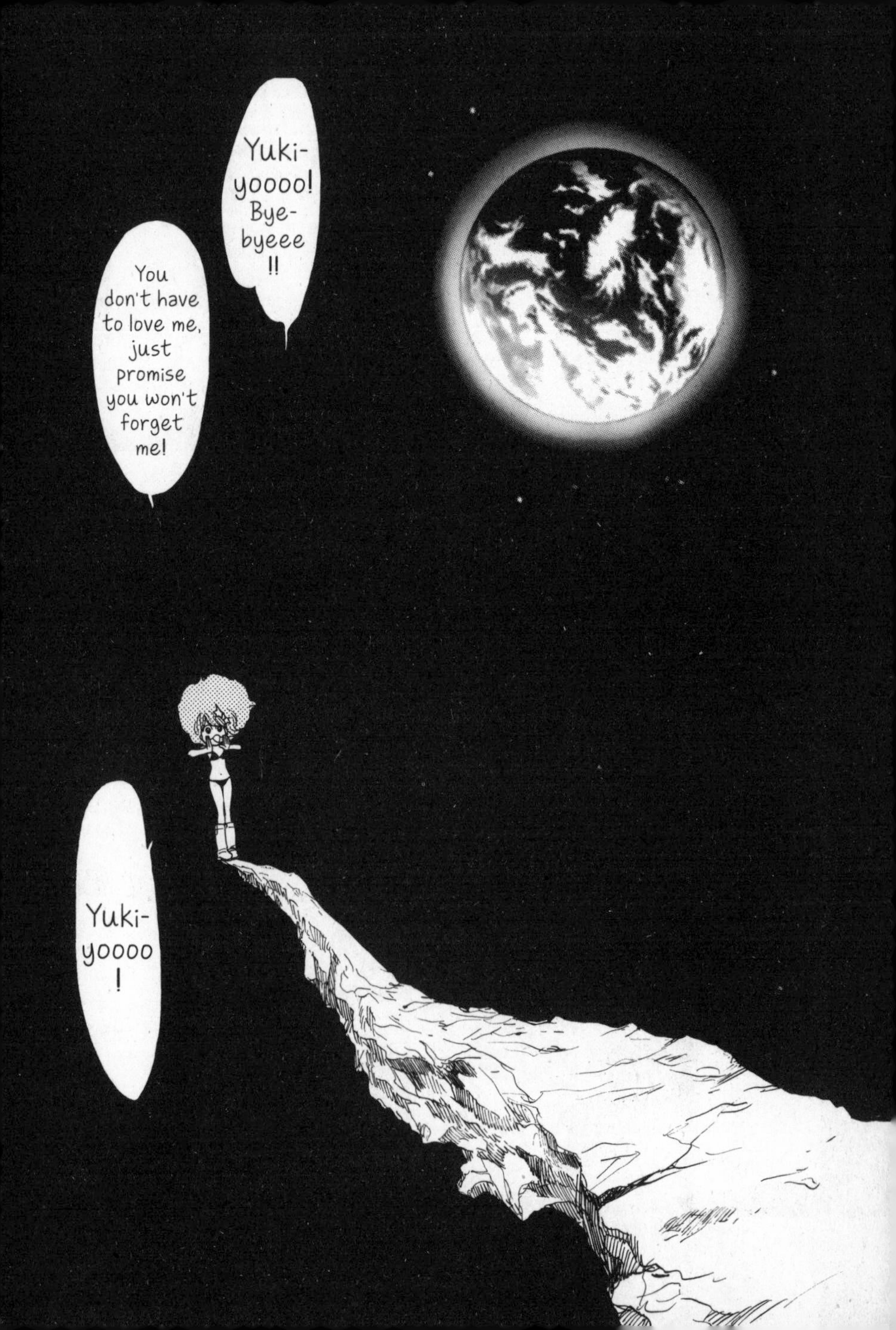
Yuki-yoooo! Bye-byeee !!
You don't have to love me, just promise you won't forget me!
Yuki-yoooo !

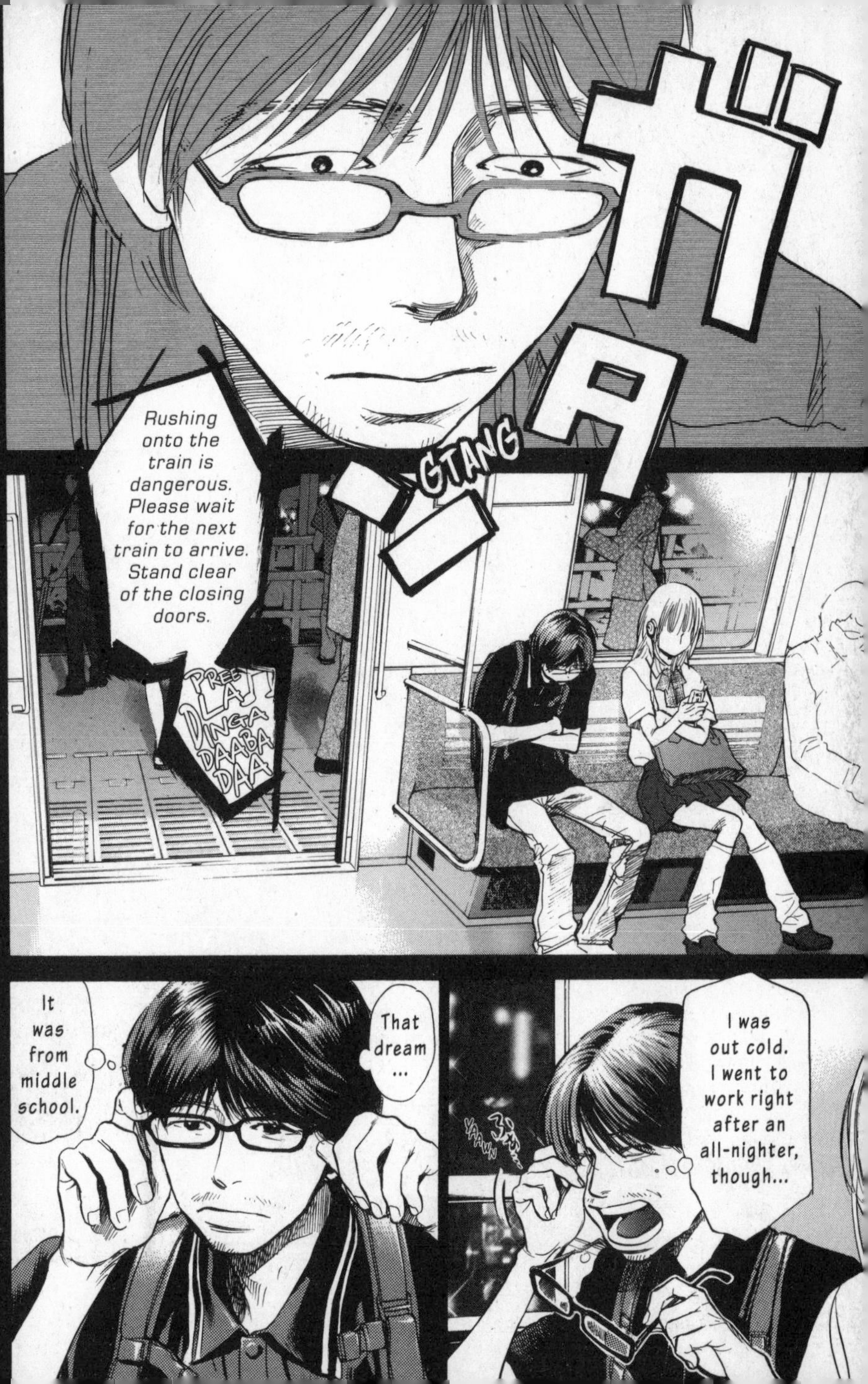
ガタ
GTANG
Rushing onto the train is dangerous. Please wait for the next train to arrive. Stand clear of the closing doors.
PREE LA DINGA DAABA DAA
I was out cold. I went to work right after an all-nighter, though...
YAAWN
That dream...
It was from middle school.

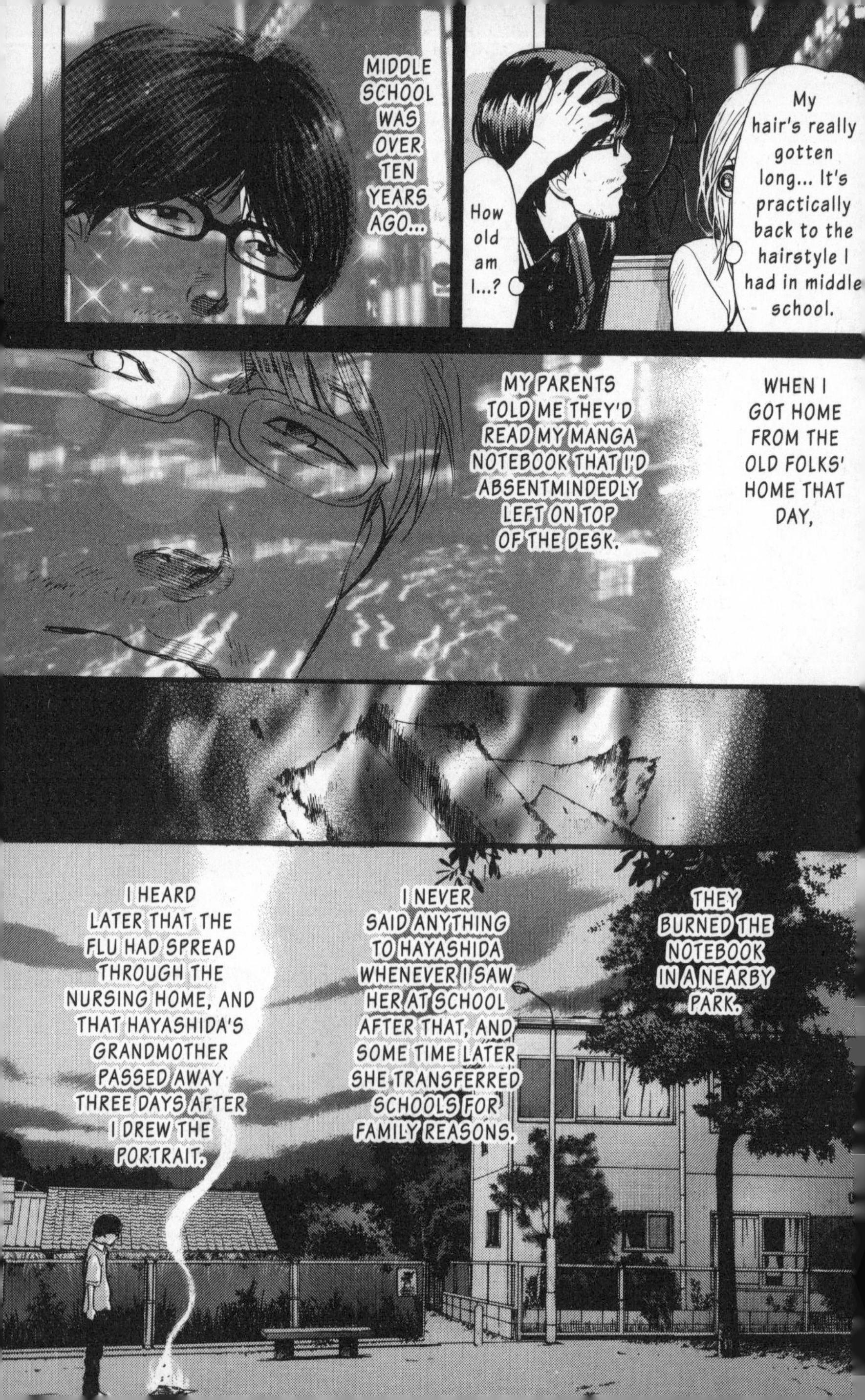
My hair's really gotten long... It's practically back to the hairstyle I had in middle school.
How old am I...?
MIDDLE SCHOOL WAS OVER TEN YEARS AGO...
WHEN I GOT HOME FROM THE OLD FOLKS' HOME THAT DAY,
MY PARENTS TOLD ME THEY'D READ MY MANGA NOTEBOOK THAT I'D ABSENTMINDEDLY LEFT ON TOP OF THE DESK.
THEY BURNED THE NOTEBOOK IN A NEARBY PARK.
I NEVER SAID ANYTHING TO HAYASHIDA WHENEVER I SAW HER AT SCHOOL AFTER THAT, AND SOME TIME LATER SHE TRANSFERRED SCHOOLS FOR FAMILY REASONS.
I HEARD LATER THAT THE FLU HAD SPREAD THROUGH THE NURSING HOME, AND THAT HAYASHIDA'S GRANDMOTHER PASSED AWAY THREE DAYS AFTER I DREW THE PORTRAIT.

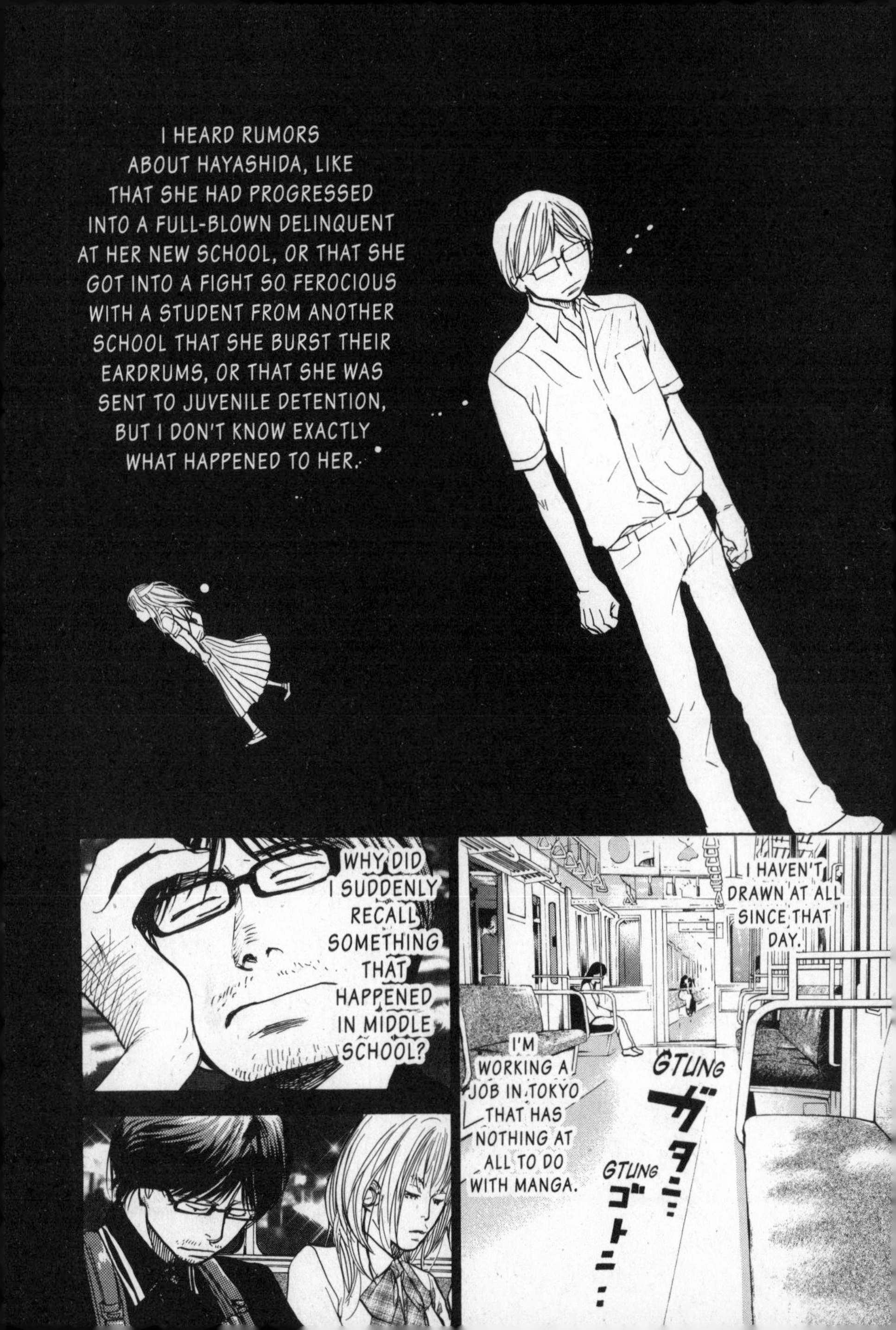
I HEARD RUMORS ABOUT HAYASHIDA, LIKE THAT SHE HAD PROGRESSED INTO A FULL-BLOWN DELINQUENT AT HER NEW SCHOOL, OR THAT SHE GOT INTO A FIGHT SO FEROCIOUS WITH A STUDENT FROM ANOTHER SCHOOL THAT SHE BURST THEIR EARDRUMS, OR THAT SHE WAS SENT TO JUVENILE DETENTION, BUT I DON'T KNOW EXACTLY WHAT HAPPENED TO HER.
I HAVEN'T DRAWN AT ALL SINCE THAT DAY.
I'M WORKING A JOB IN TOKYO THAT HAS NOTHING AT ALL TO DO WITH MANGA.
GTUNG
ガタン
GTUNG
ゴトン
WHY DID I SUDDENLY RECALL SOMETHING THAT HAPPENED IN MIDDLE SCHOOL?

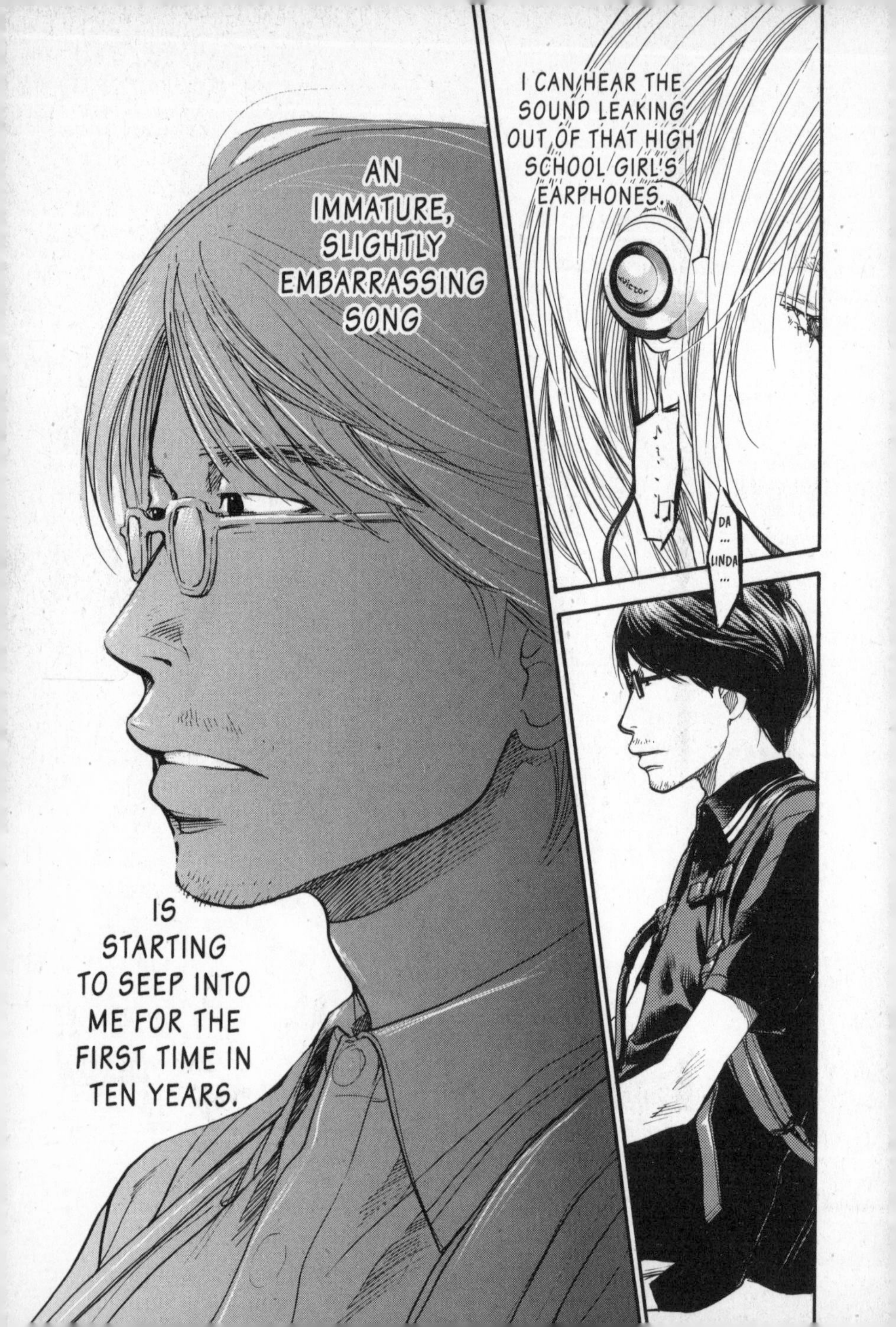
I CAN HEAR THE SOUND LEAKING OUT OF THAT HIGH SCHOOL GIRL'S EARPHONES.
DA ... LINDA ...
AN IMMATURE, SLIGHTLY EMBARRASSING SONG
IS STARTING TO SEEP INTO ME FOR THE FIRST TIME IN TEN YEARS.

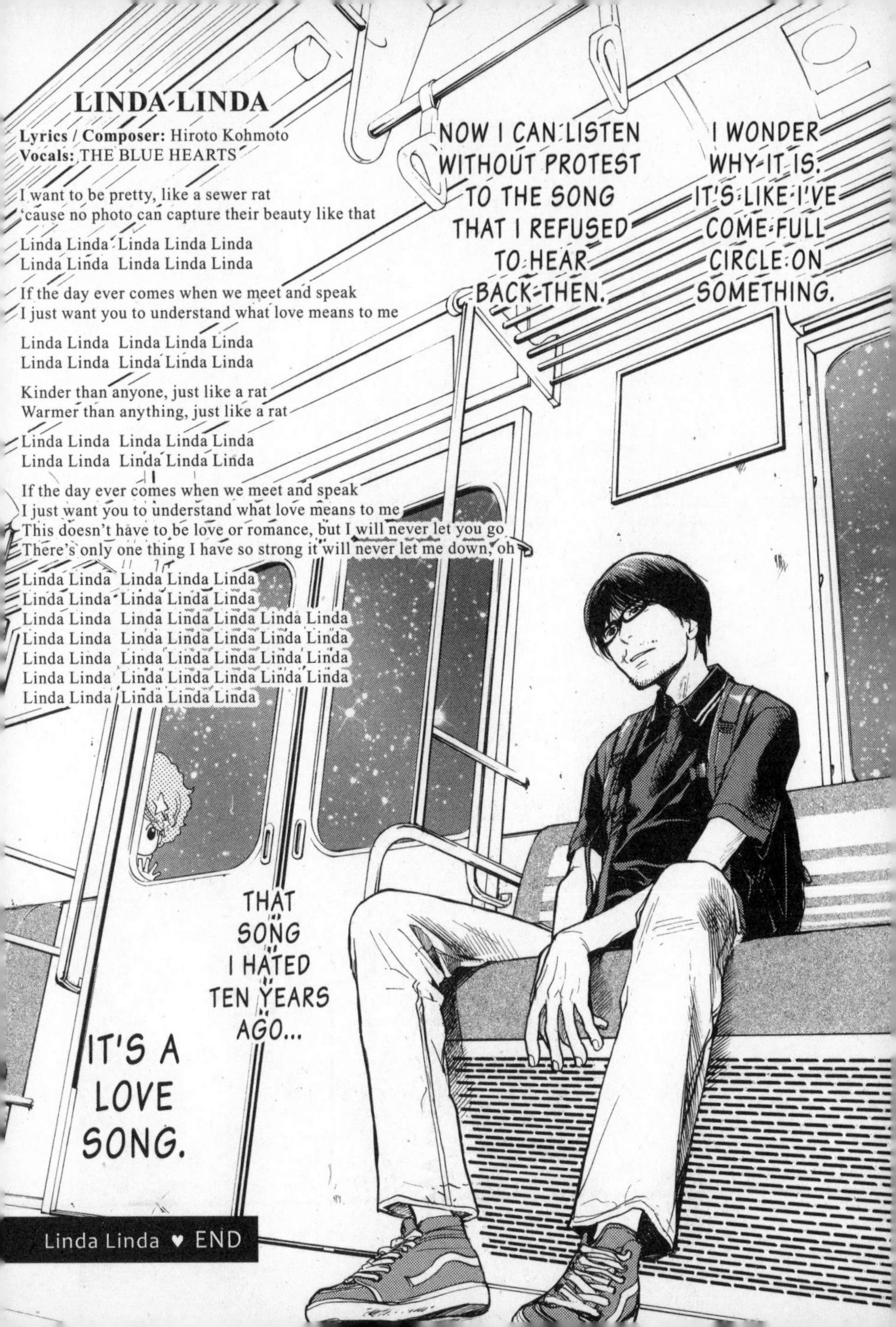

I WONDER WHY IT IS. IT'S LIKE I'VE COME FULL CIRCLE ON SOMETHING.
NOW I CAN LISTEN WITHOUT PROTEST TO THE SONG THAT I REFUSED TO HEAR BACK THEN.
LINDA LINDA
Lyrics / Composer: Hiroto Kohmoto
Vocals: THE BLUE HEARTS
I want to be pretty, like a sewer rat
'cause no photo can capture their beauty like that
Linda Linda Linda Linda Linda
Linda Linda Linda Linda Linda
If the day ever comes when we meet and speak
I just want you to understand what love means to me
Linda Linda Linda Linda Linda
Linda Linda Linda Linda Linda
Kinder than anyone, just like a rat
Warmer than anything, just like a rat
Linda Linda Linda Linda Linda
Linda Linda Linda Linda Linda
If the day ever comes when we meet and speak
I just want you to understand what love means to me
This doesn't have to be love or romance, but I will never let you go
There's only one thing I have so strong it will never let me down, oh
Linda Linda Linda Linda Linda
Linda Linda Linda Linda Linda
Linda Linda Linda Linda Linda Linda Linda
Linda Linda Linda Linda Linda Linda Linda
Linda Linda Linda Linda Linda Linda Linda
Linda Linda Linda Linda Linda Linda Linda
Linda Linda Linda Linda Linda
THAT SONG I HATED TEN YEARS AGO...
IT'S A LOVE SONG.
Linda Linda ♥ END

Motekis You Wouldn't Want to Read ①

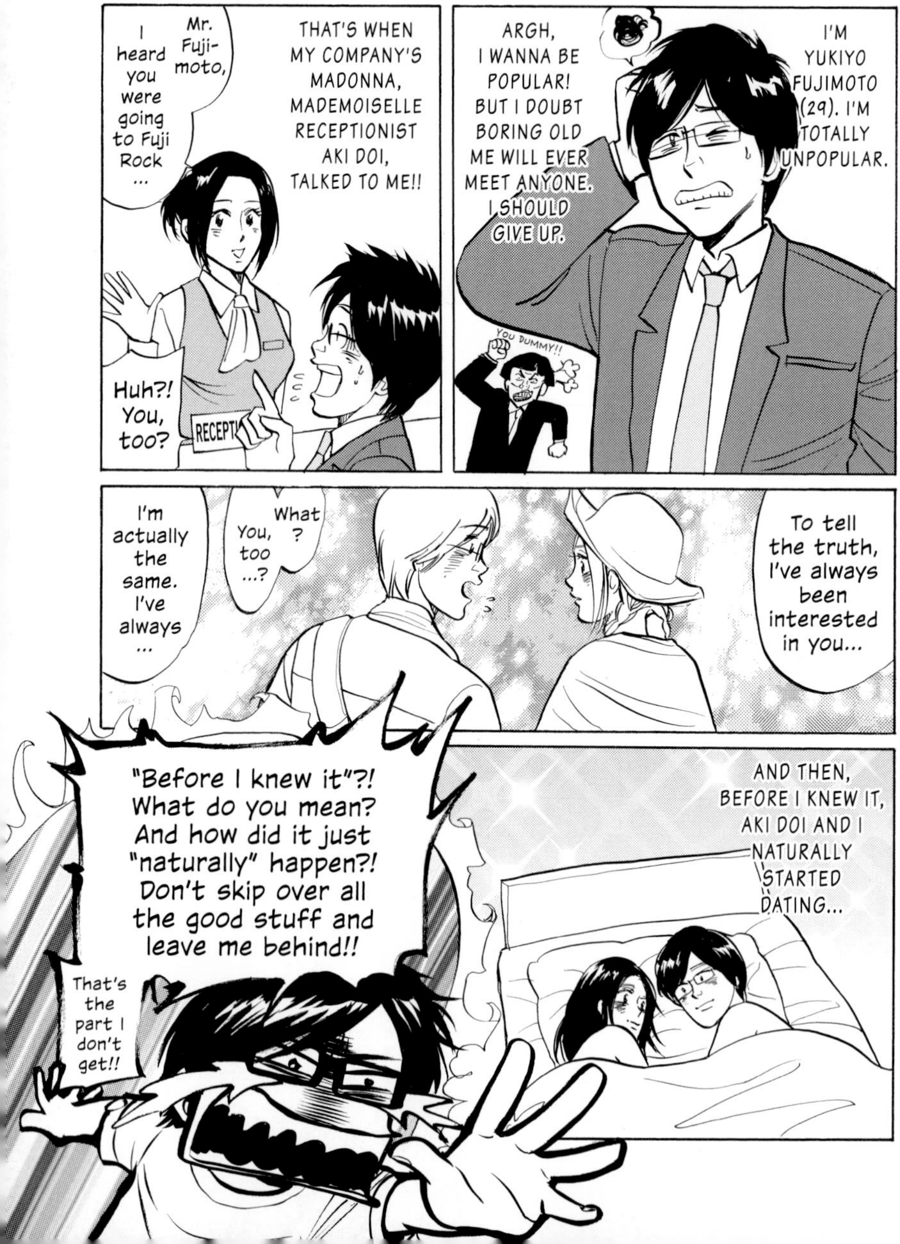

I'M YUKIYO FUJIMOTO (29). I'M TOTALLY UNPOPULAR.
ARGH, I WANNA BE POPULAR! BUT I DOUBT BORING OLD ME WILL EVER MEET ANYONE. I SHOULD GIVE UP.
YOU DUMMY!!
THAT'S WHEN MY COMPANY'S MADONNA, MADEMOISELLE RECEPTIONIST AKI DOI, TALKED TO ME!!
Mr. Fujimoto,
I heard you were going to Fuji Rock ...
RECEPTI
Huh?! You, too?
To tell the truth, I've always been interested in you...
What ?
You, too ...?
I'm actually the same. I've always ...
AND THEN, BEFORE I KNEW IT, AKI DOI AND I NATURALLY STARTED DATING...
"Before I knew it"?! What do you mean? And how did it just "naturally" happen?! Don't skip over all the good stuff and leave me behind!!
That's the part I don't get!!

Motekis You Wouldn't Want to Read ②

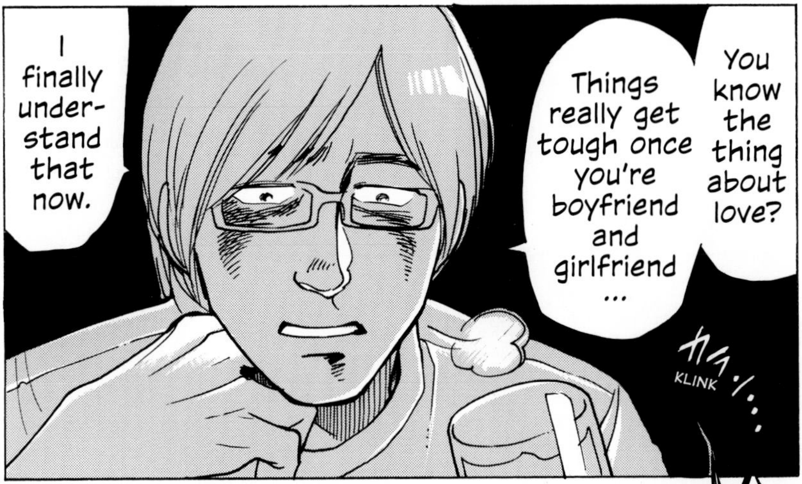
You know the thing about love?
Things really get tough once you're boyfriend and girlfriend…
KLINK
I finally under-stand that now.

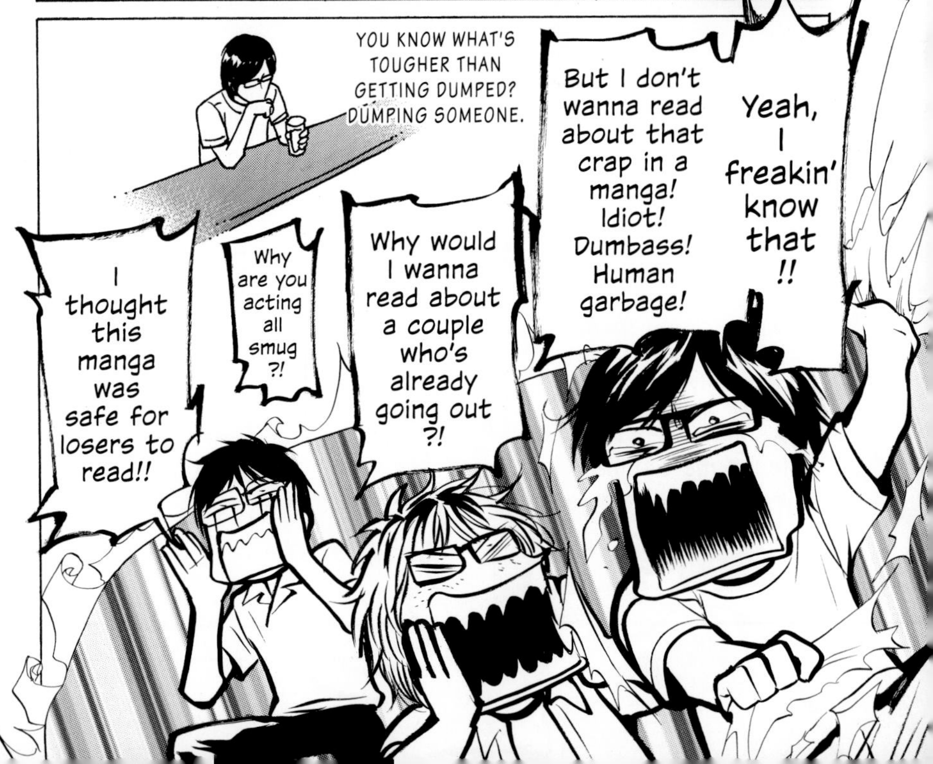
Yeah, I freakin' know that!!
But I don't wanna read about that crap in a manga! Idiot! Dumbass! Human garbage!
YOU KNOW WHAT'S TOUGHER THAN GETTING DUMPED? DUMPING SOMEONE.
Why would I wanna read about a couple who's already going out?!
Why are you acting all smug?!
I thought this manga was safe for losers to read!!

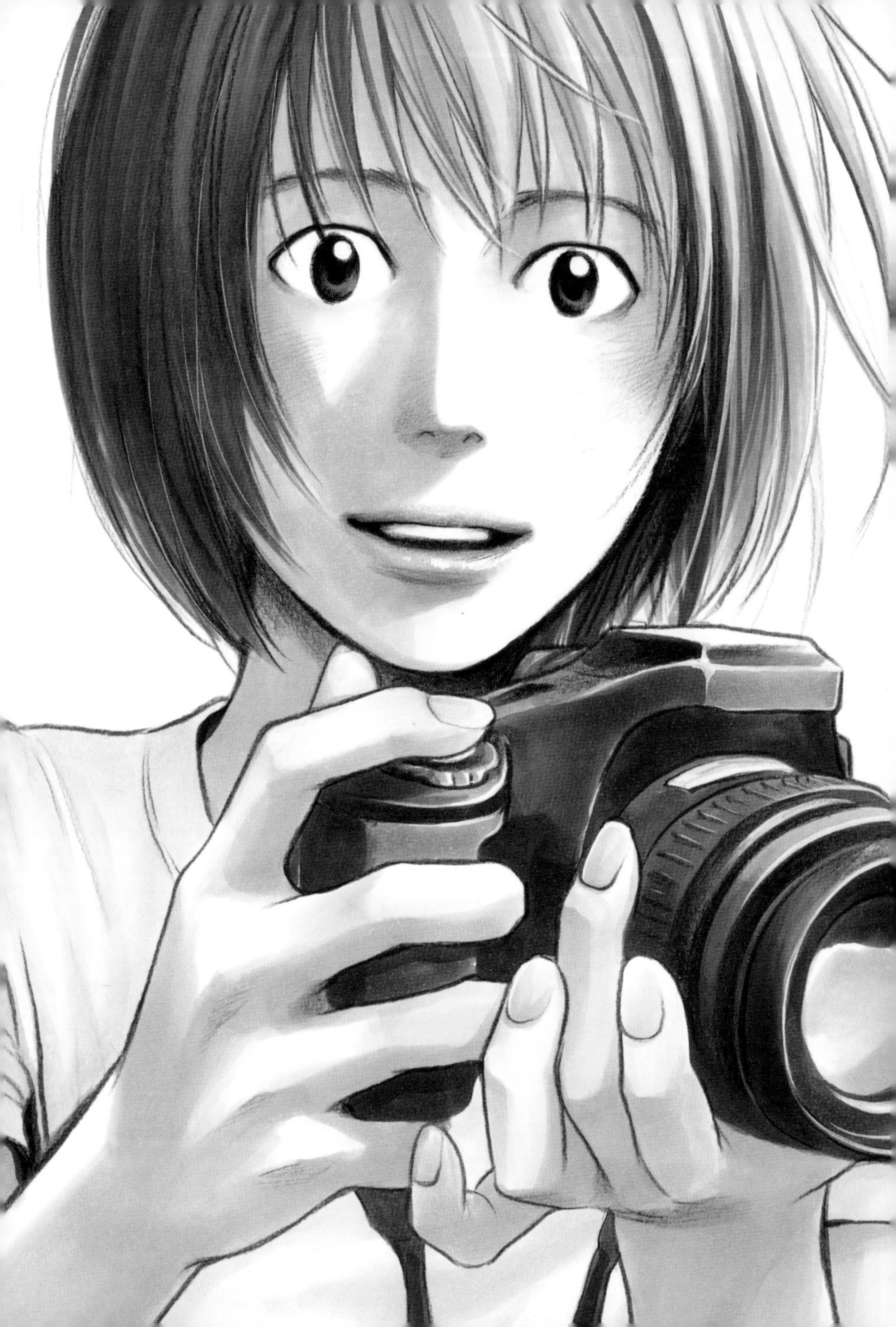

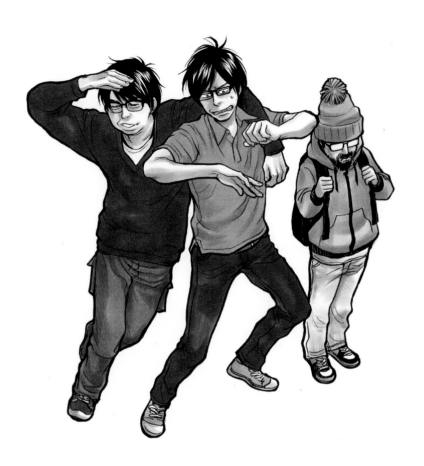

MOTEKI!

Love Strikes!

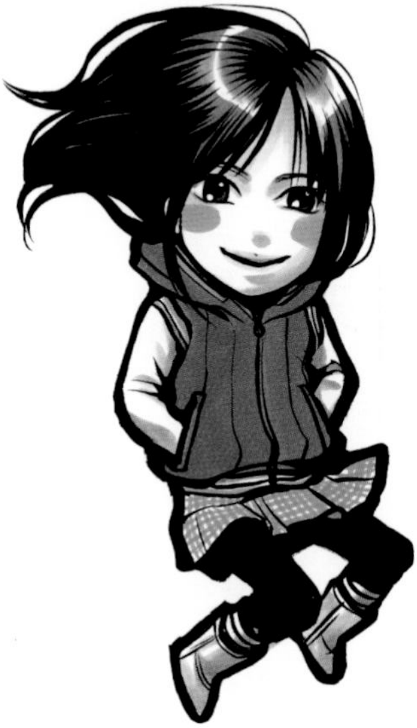

c o n t e n t s

♥

M o t e k i
M i t s u r o u
K u b o

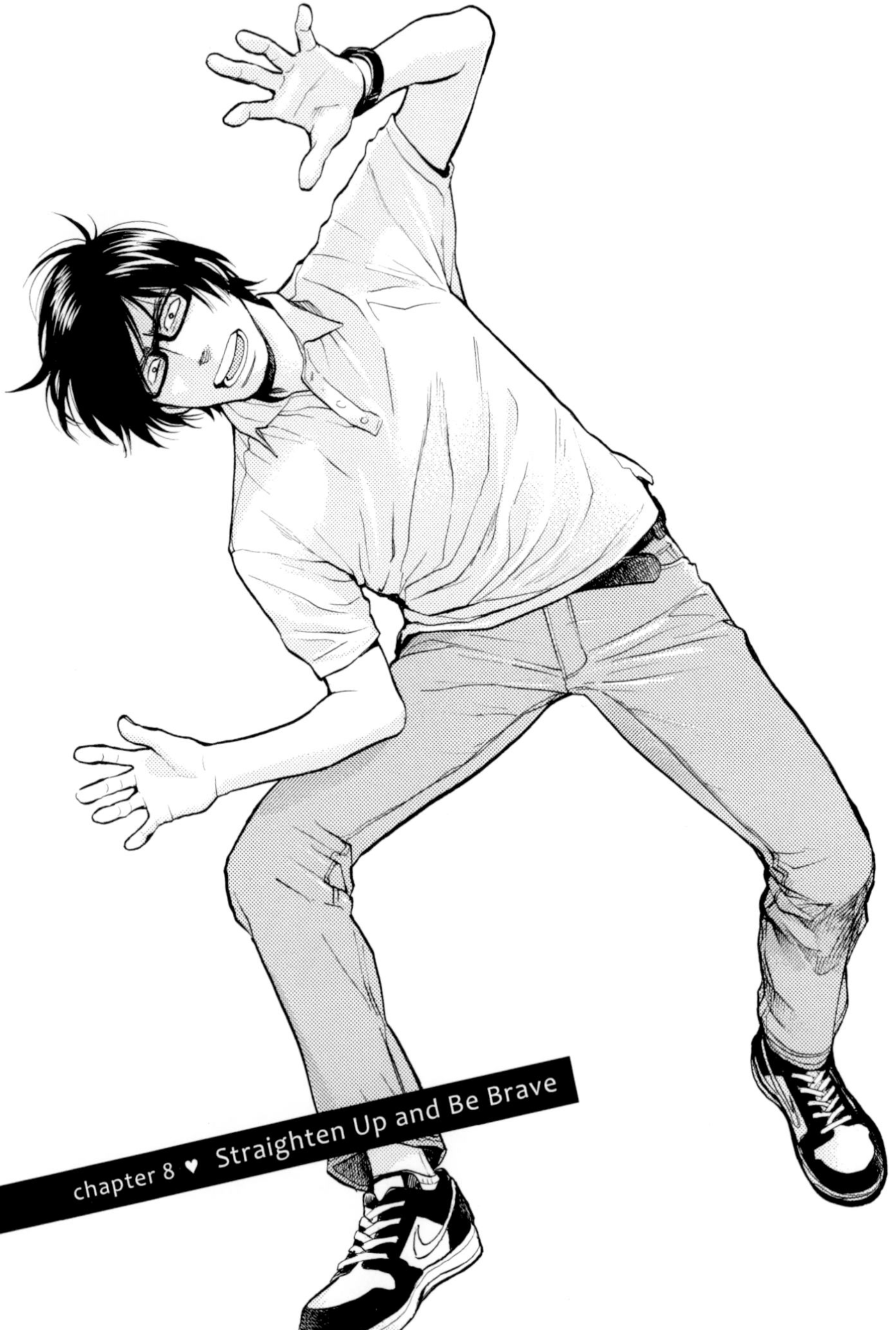

chapter 8 ♥ Straighten Up and Be Brave

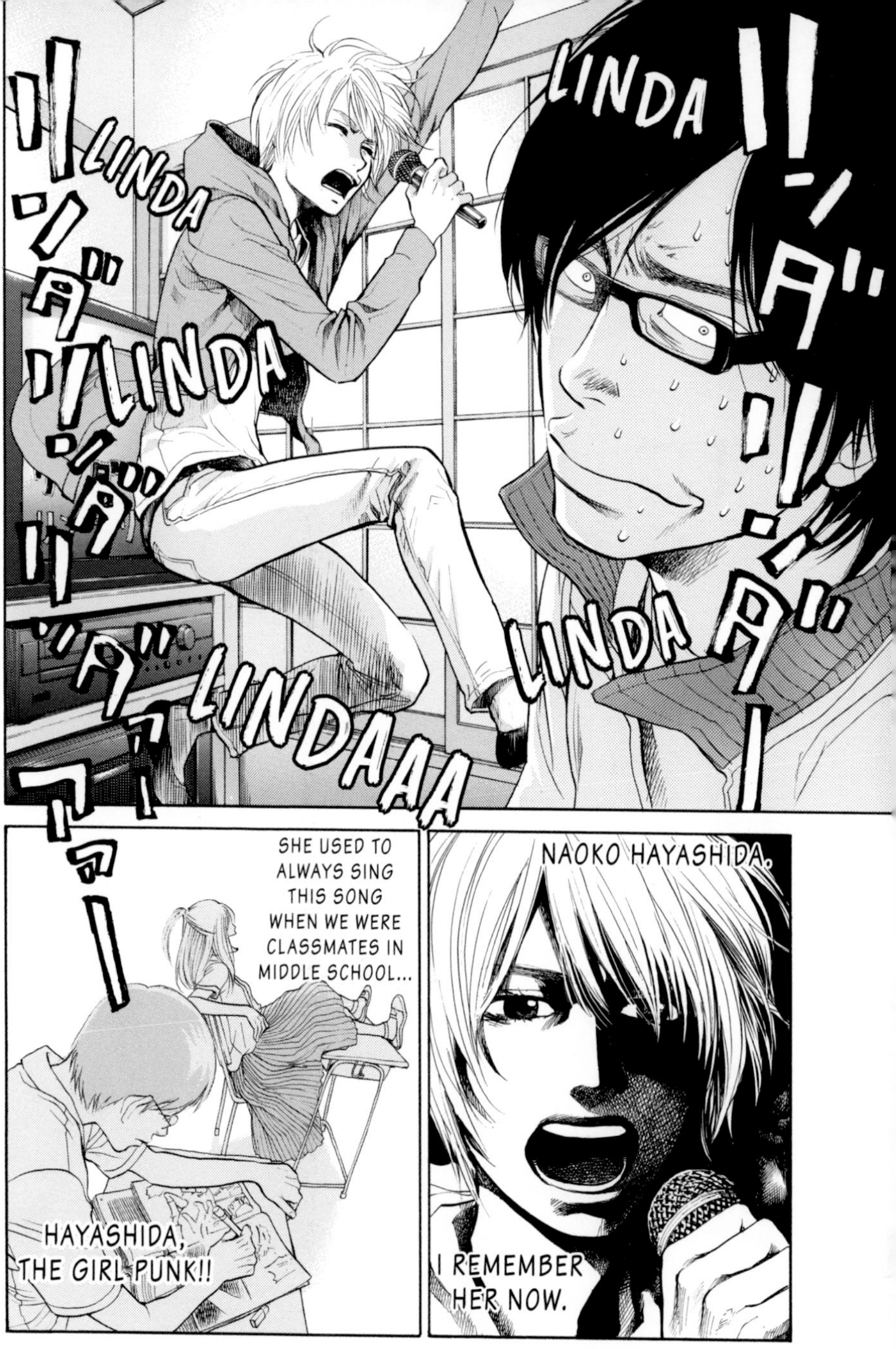
LINDA
LINDA
LINDA
LINDA
LINDA
LINDAAA
NAOKO HAYASHIDA.
I REMEMBER HER NOW.
SHE USED TO ALWAYS SING THIS SONG WHEN WE WERE CLASSMATES IN MIDDLE SCHOOL...
HAYASHIDA, THE GIRL PUNK!!

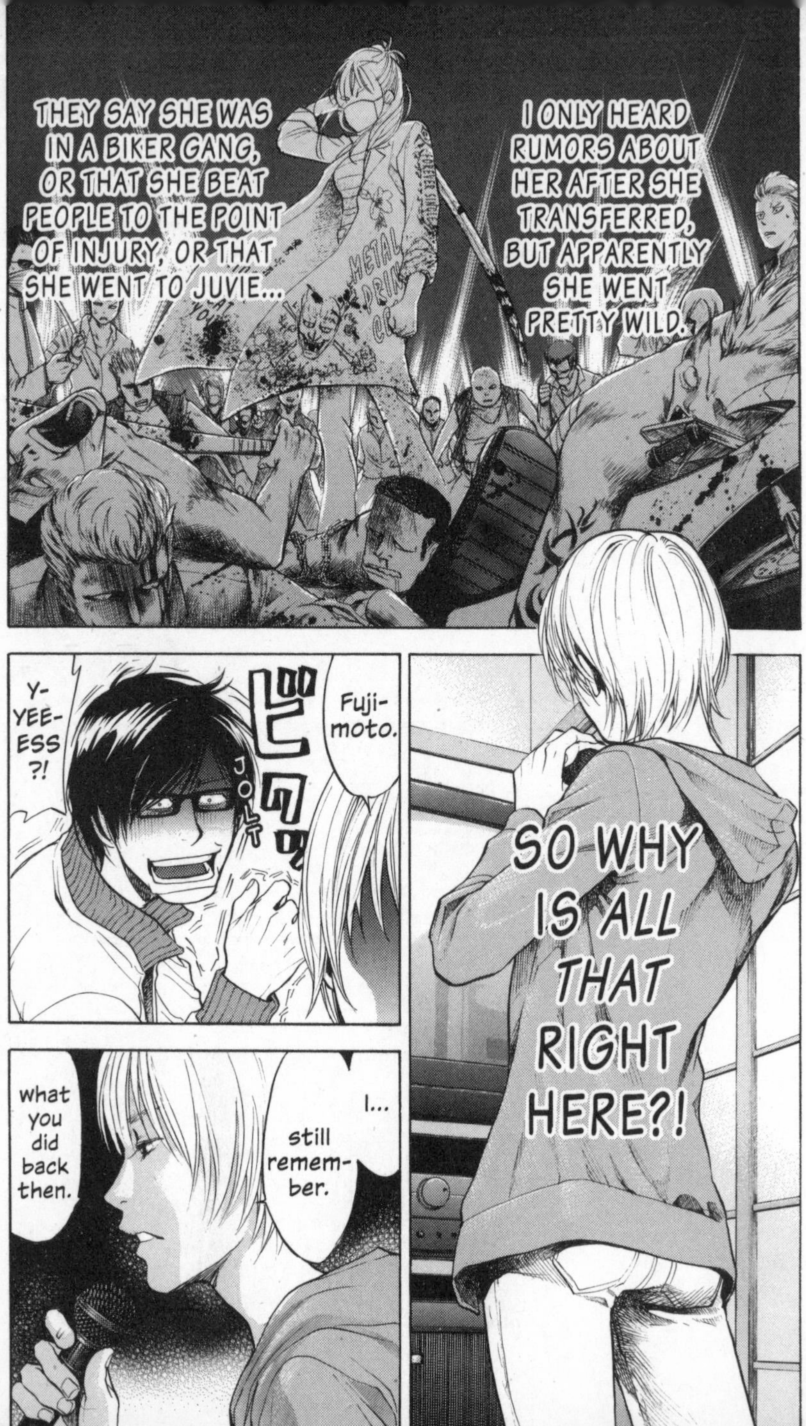
I ONLY HEARD RUMORS ABOUT HER AFTER SHE TRANSFERRED, BUT APPARENTLY SHE WENT PRETTY WILD.
THEY SAY SHE WAS IN A BIKER GANG, OR THAT SHE BEAT PEOPLE TO THE POINT OF INJURY, OR THAT SHE WENT TO JUVIE...
SO WHY IS ALL THAT RIGHT HERE?!
Fuji-moto.
JOLT
Y-YEEE-ESS ?!
I...
still remem-ber.
what you did back then.

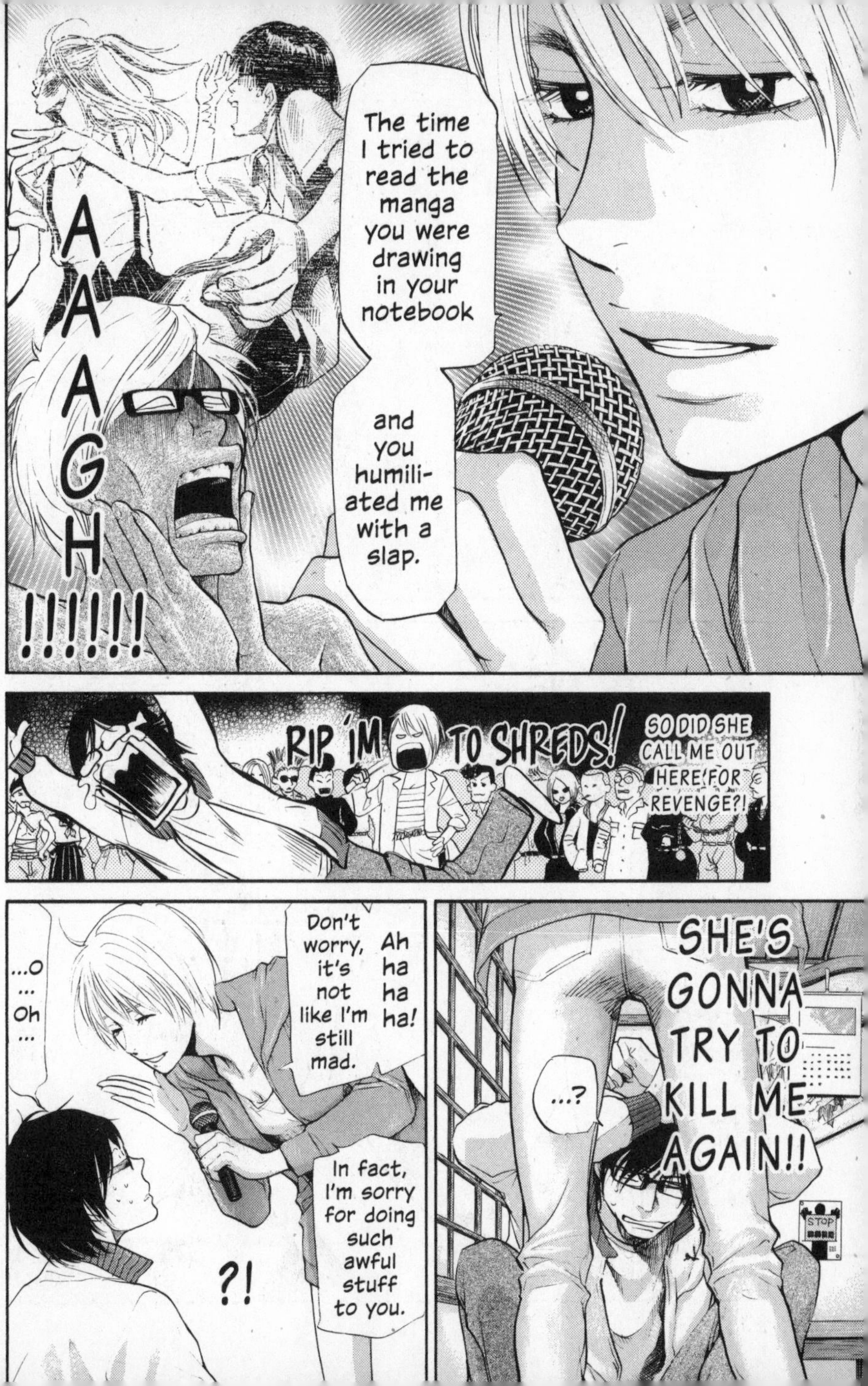
The time I tried to read the manga you were drawing in your notebook
and you humiliated me with a slap.
AAAGH!!!!!!
SO DID SHE CALL ME OUT HERE FOR REVENGE?!
RIP 'IM TO SHREDS!
SHE'S GONNA TRY TO KILL ME AGAIN!!
...?
Ah ha ha ha!
Don't worry, it's not like I'm still mad.
...o ... Oh ...
In fact, I'm sorry for doing such awful stuff to you.
?!

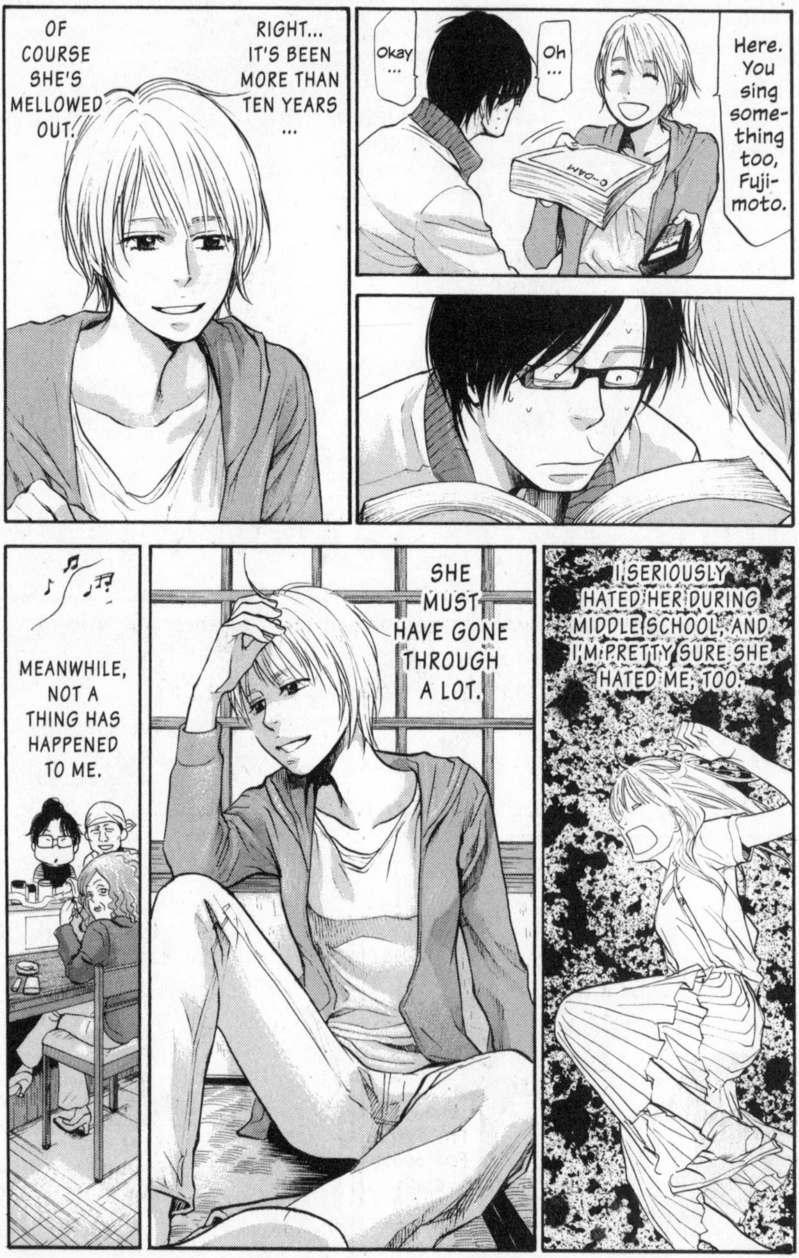

Here. You sing something too, Fujimoto.
Oh ...
Okay ...
RIGHT... IT'S BEEN MORE THAN TEN YEARS ...
OF COURSE SHE'S MELLOWED OUT.
I SERIOUSLY HATED HER DURING MIDDLE SCHOOL, AND I'M PRETTY SURE SHE HATED ME, TOO.
SHE MUST HAVE GONE THROUGH A LOT.
MEANWHILE, NOT A THING HAS HAPPENED TO ME.

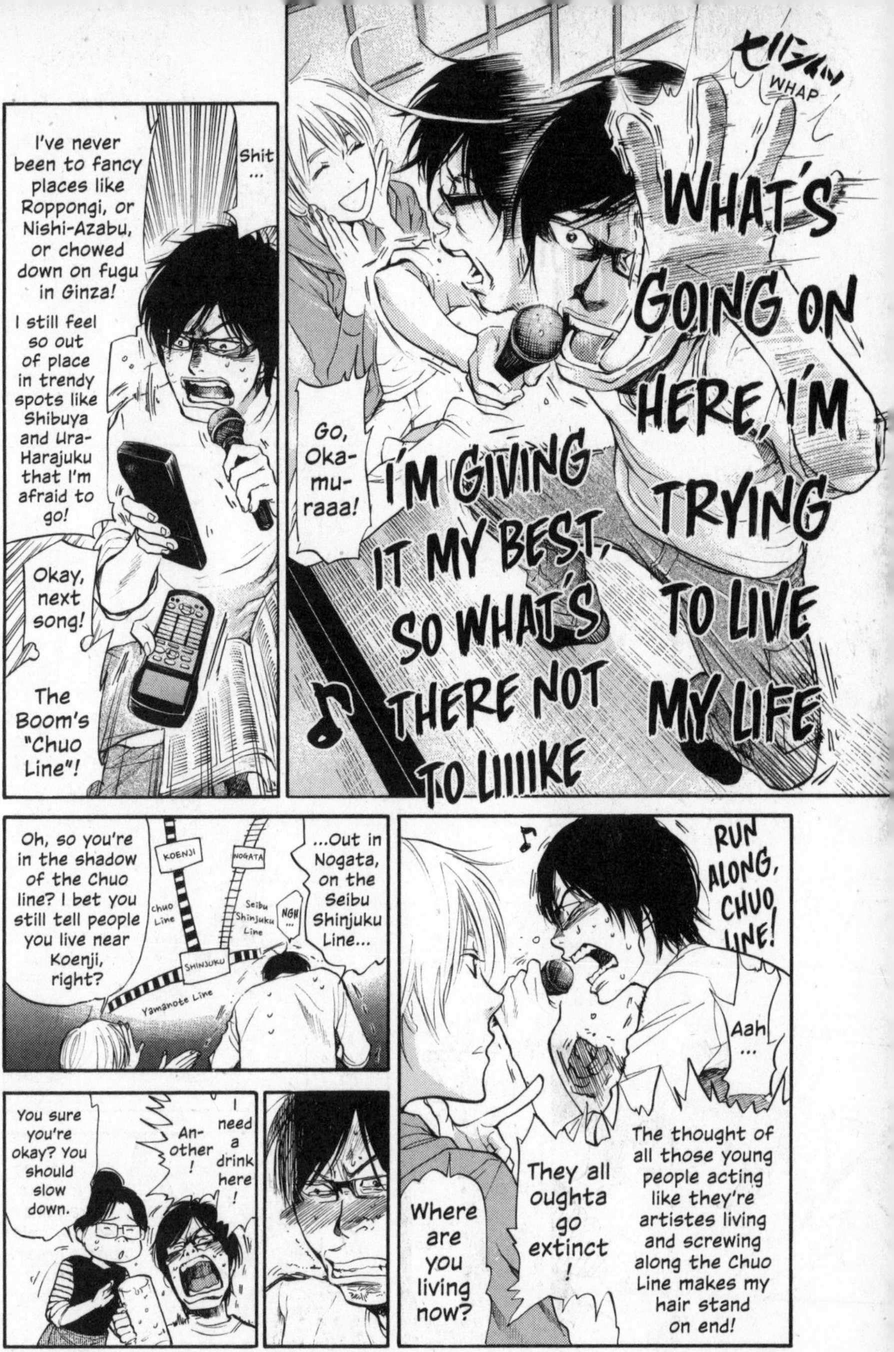
WHAP
WHAT'S GOING ON HERE, I'M TRYING TO LIVE MY LIFE
I'M GIVING IT MY BEST, SO WHAT'S THERE NOT TO LIIIIKE
Go, Oka-mu-raaa!
Shit ...
I've never been to fancy places like Roppongi, or Nishi-Azabu, or chowed down on fugu in Ginza!
I still feel so out of place in trendy spots like Shibuya and Ura-Harajuku that I'm afraid to go!
Okay, next song!
The Boom's "Chuo Line"!
RUN ALONG, CHUO LINE!
Aah ...
The thought of all those young people acting like they're artistes living and screwing along the Chuo Line makes my hair stand on end!
They all oughta go extinct!
Where are you living now?
...Out in Nogata, on the Seibu Shinjuku Line...
NGH ...
NOGATA
KOENJI
Seibu Shinjuku Line
Chuo Line
SHINJUKU
Yamanote Line
Oh, so you're in the shadow of the Chuo line? I bet you still tell people you live near Koenji, right?
I need a drink here!
An-other!
You sure you're okay? You should slow down.

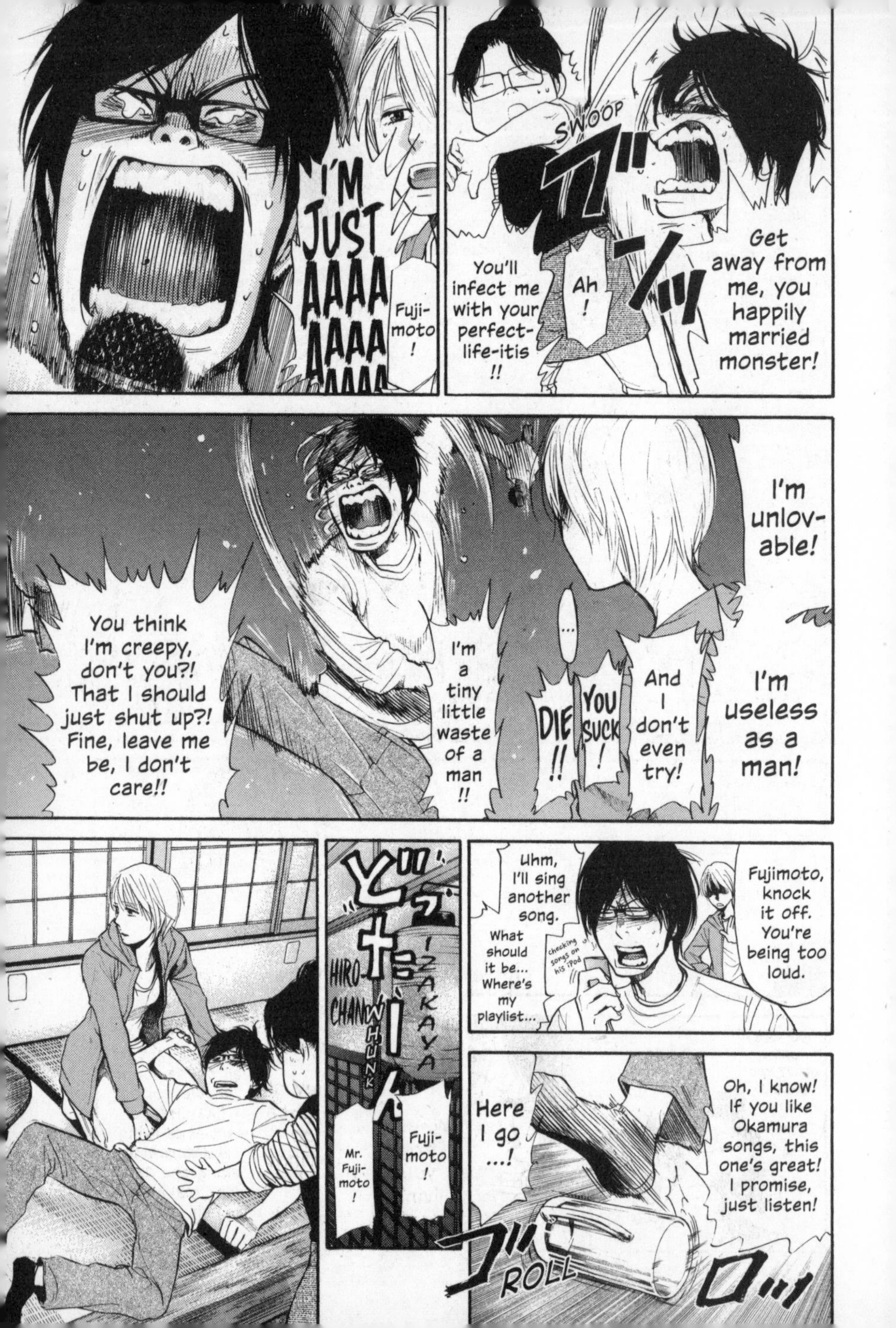
Get away from me, you happily married monster!
SWOOP
Ah!
You'll infect me with your perfect-life-itis!!
Fuji-moto!
I'M JUST AAAA AAAA AAAA
I'm unlov-able!
I'm useless as a man!
...
And I don't even try!
YOU SUCK!
DIE!!
I'm a tiny little waste of a man!!
You think I'm creepy, don't you?! That I should just shut up?! Fine, leave me be, I don't care!!
Fujimoto, knock it off. You're being too loud.
Uhm, I'll sing another song.
checking songs on his iPod
What should it be... Where's my playlist...
Oh, I know! If you like Okamura songs, this one's great! I promise, just listen!
Here I go ...!
ROLL
HIRO-CHAN
IZAKAYA
WHUNK
Fuji-moto!
Mr. Fuji-moto!

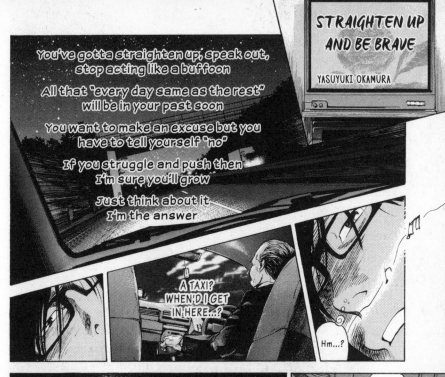

STRAIGHTEN UP AND BE BRAVE

YASUYUKI OKAMURA

You've gotta straighten up, speak out,
stop acting like a buffoon

All that "every day same as the rest"
will be in your past soon

You want to make an excuse but you
have to tell yourself "no"

If you struggle and push then
I'm sure you'll grow

Just think about it
I'm the answer

A TAXI?
WHEN'D I GET
IN HERE...?

Hm...?

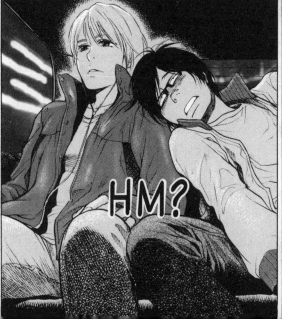

HM?

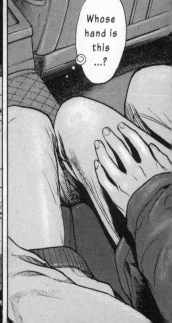

Whose
hand is
this
...?

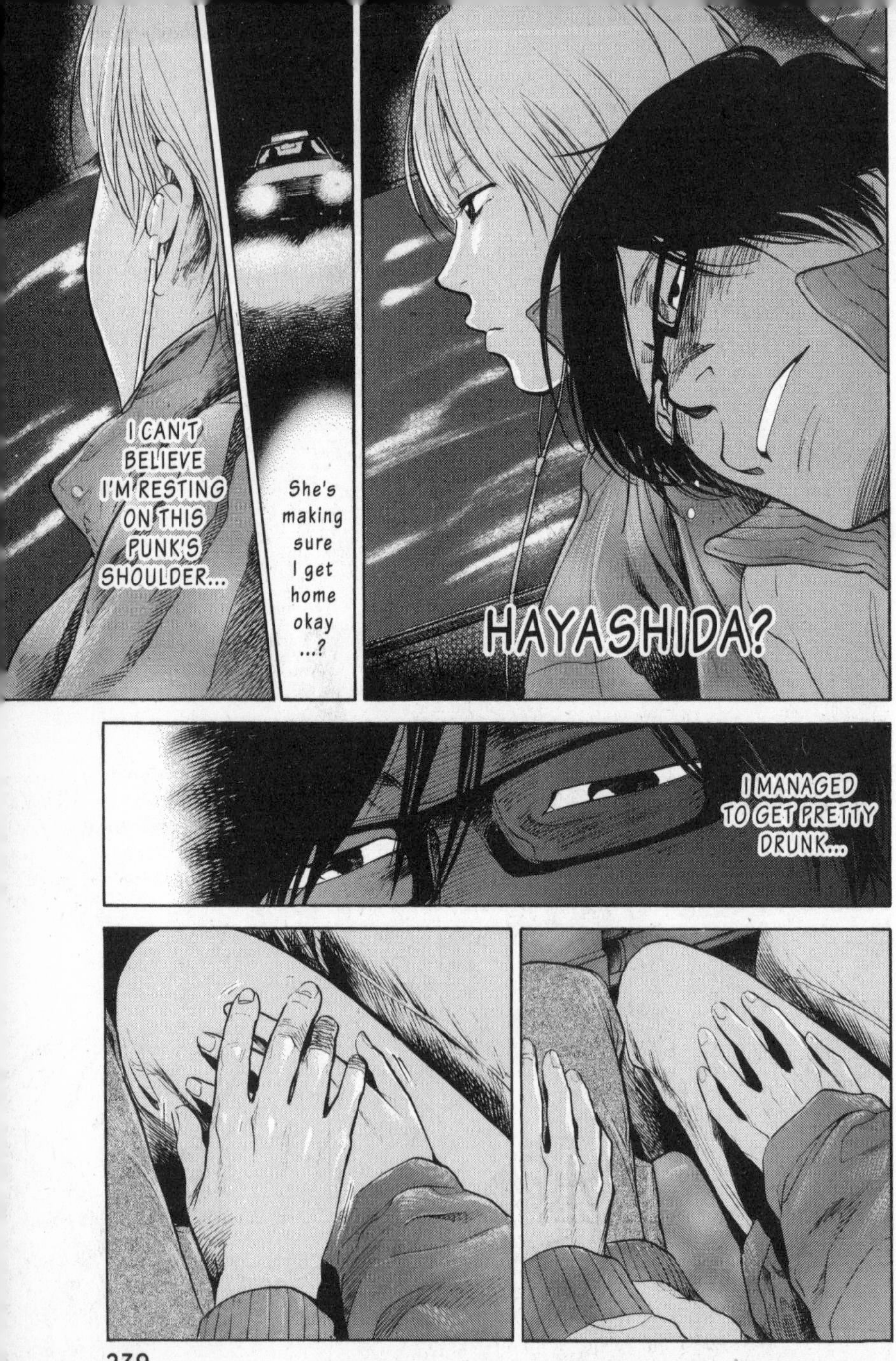
HAYASHIDA?
She's making sure I get home okay ...?
I CAN'T BELIEVE I'M RESTING ON THIS PUNK'S SHOULDER...
I MANAGED TO GET PRETTY DRUNK...

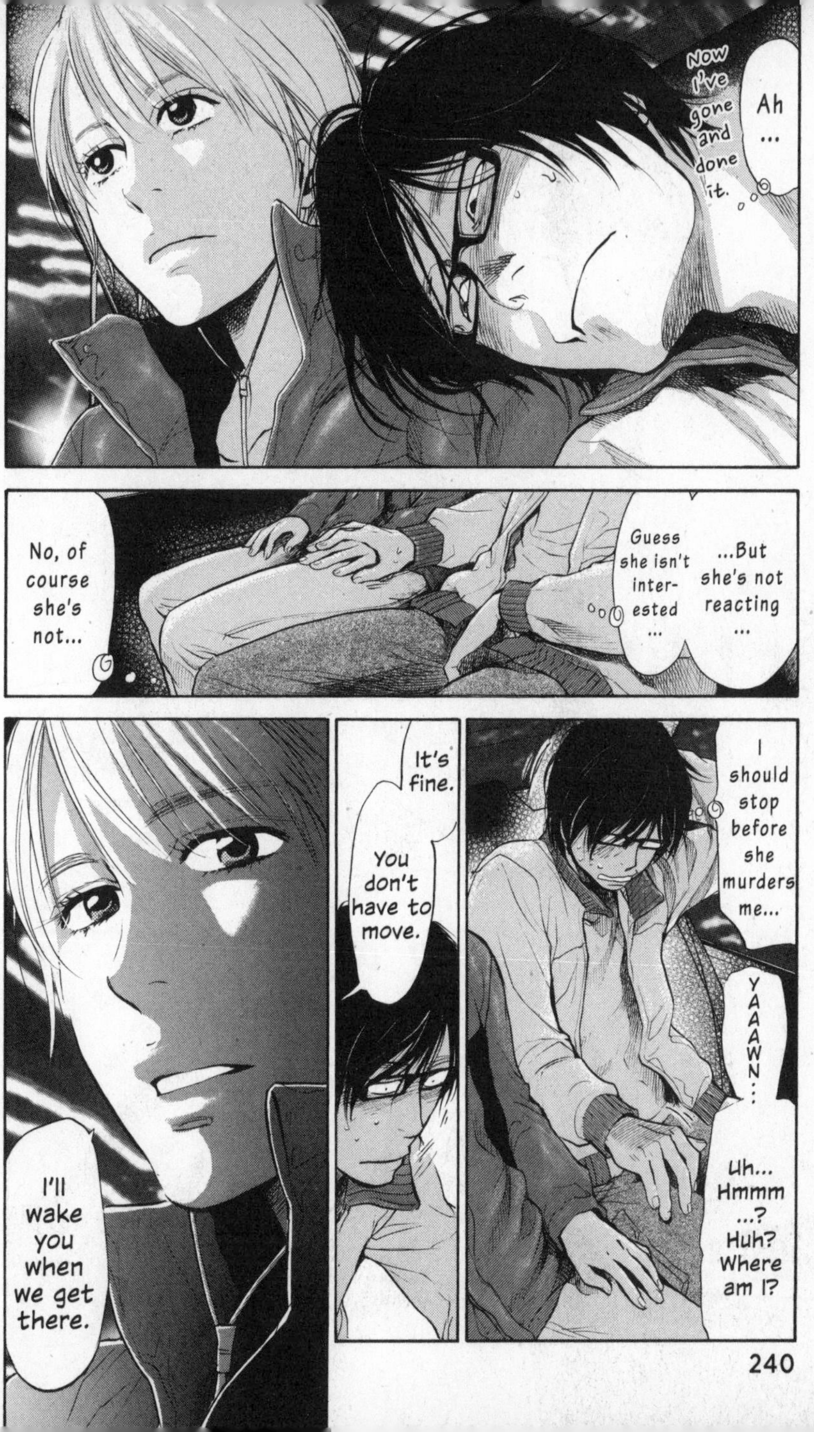
Ah ...
Now I've gone and done it.
...But she's not reacting ...
Guess she isn't inter-ested ...
No, of course she's not...
I should stop before she murders me...
YAAAWN...
Uh... Hmmm ...? Huh? Where am I?
It's fine.
You don't have to move.
I'll wake you when we get there.

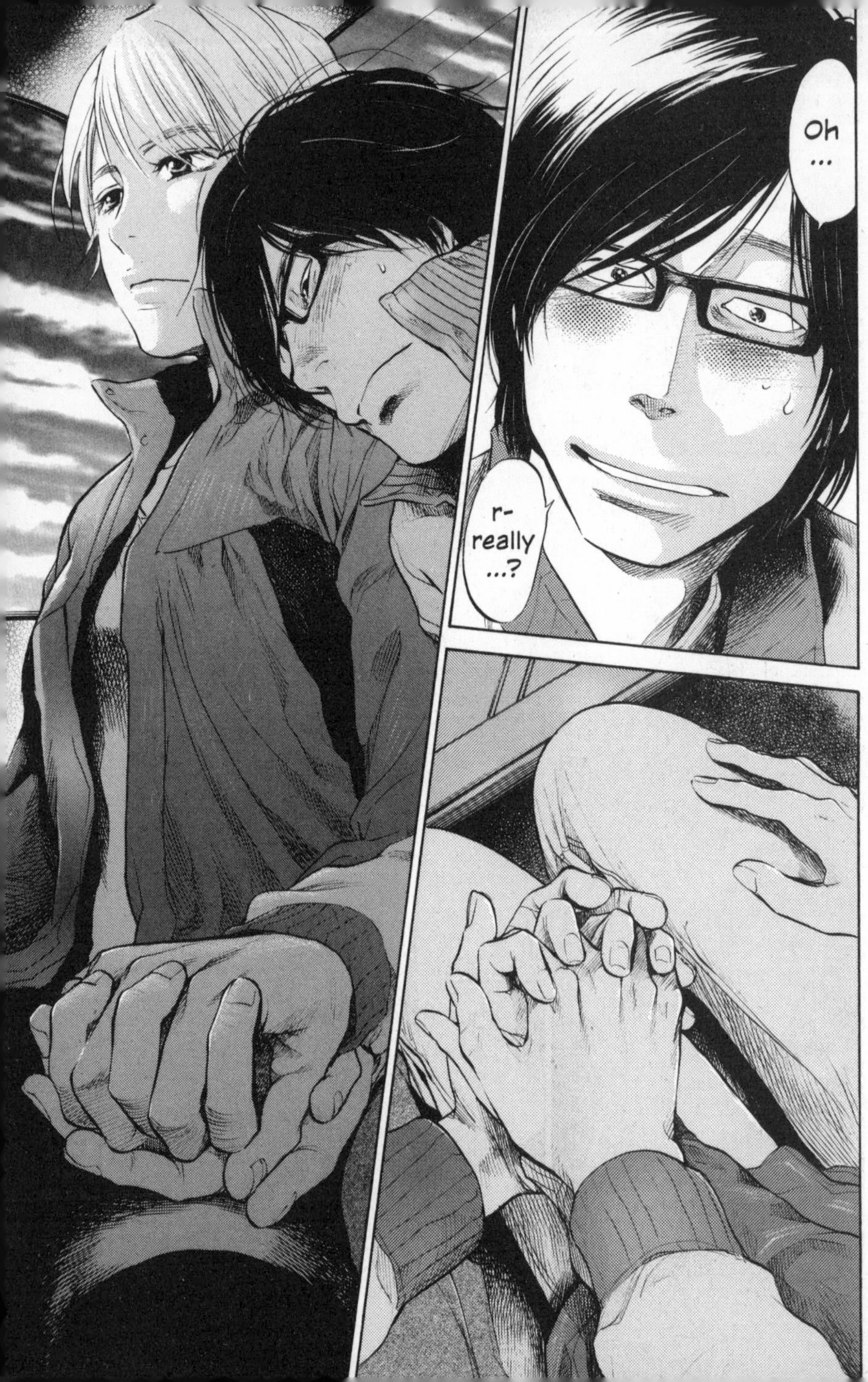
Oh ...
r- really ...?

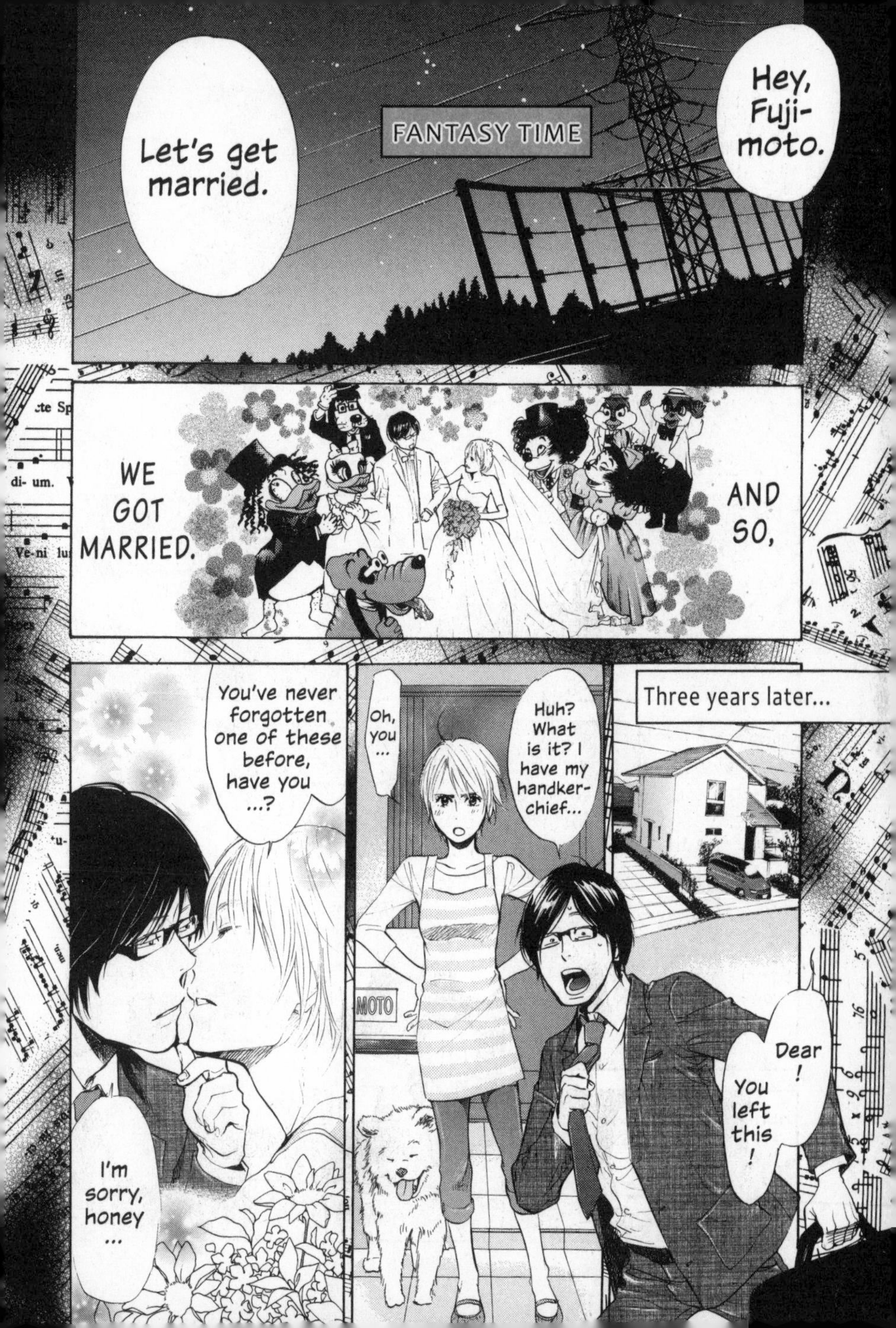
Hey, Fuji-moto.
FANTASY TIME
Let's get married.
AND SO,
WE GOT MARRIED.
Three years later...
Dear! You left this!
Huh? What is it? I have my handker-chief...
Oh, you ...
MOTO
You've never forgotten one of these before, have you ...?
I'm sorry, honey ...

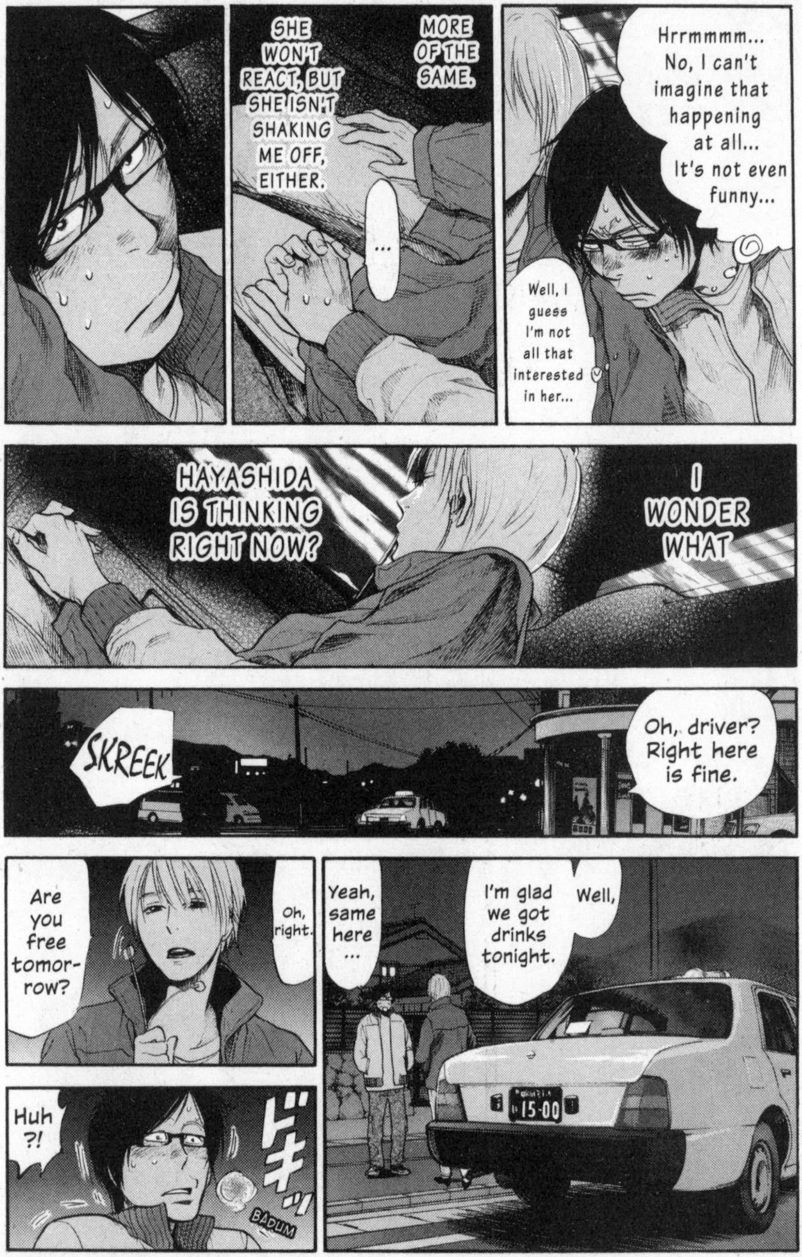
Hrrmmmm... No, I can't imagine that happening at all... It's not even funny...
Well, I guess I'm not all that interested in her...
MORE OF THE SAME.
SHE WON'T REACT, BUT SHE ISN'T SHAKING ME OFF, EITHER.
...
I WONDER WHAT
HAYASHIDA IS THINKING RIGHT NOW?
Oh, driver? Right here is fine.
SKREEK
Well,
I'm glad we got drinks tonight.
Yeah, same here ...
Are you free tomorrow?
Oh, right.
Huh ?!
ドキッ
BADUM

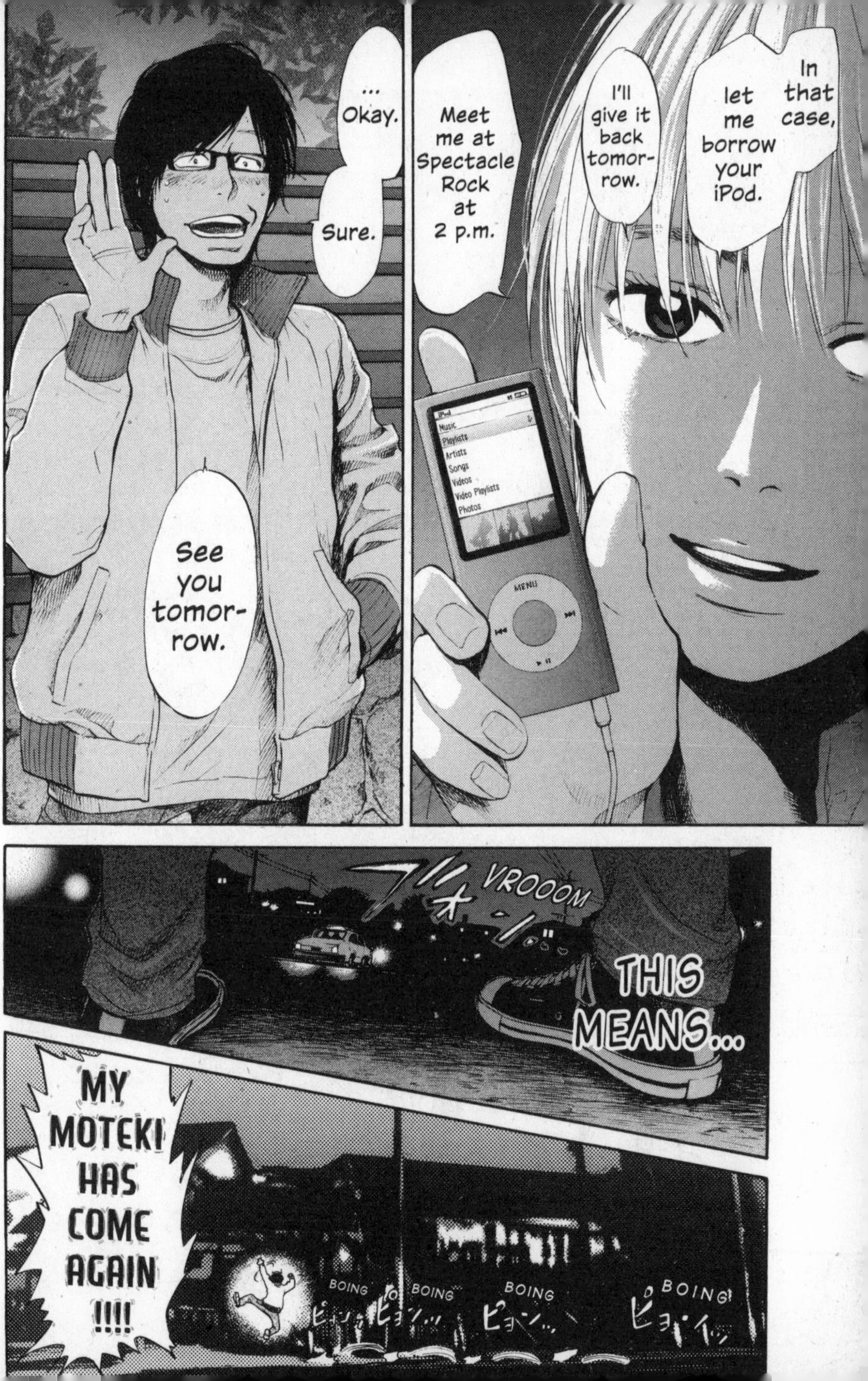
In that case, let me borrow your iPod.
I'll give it back tomorrow.
Meet me at Spectacle Rock at 2 p.m.
... Okay.
Sure.
See you tomorrow.
VROOOM
THIS MEANS...
MY MOTEKI HAS COME AGAIN!!!!
BOING
BOING
BOING
BOING

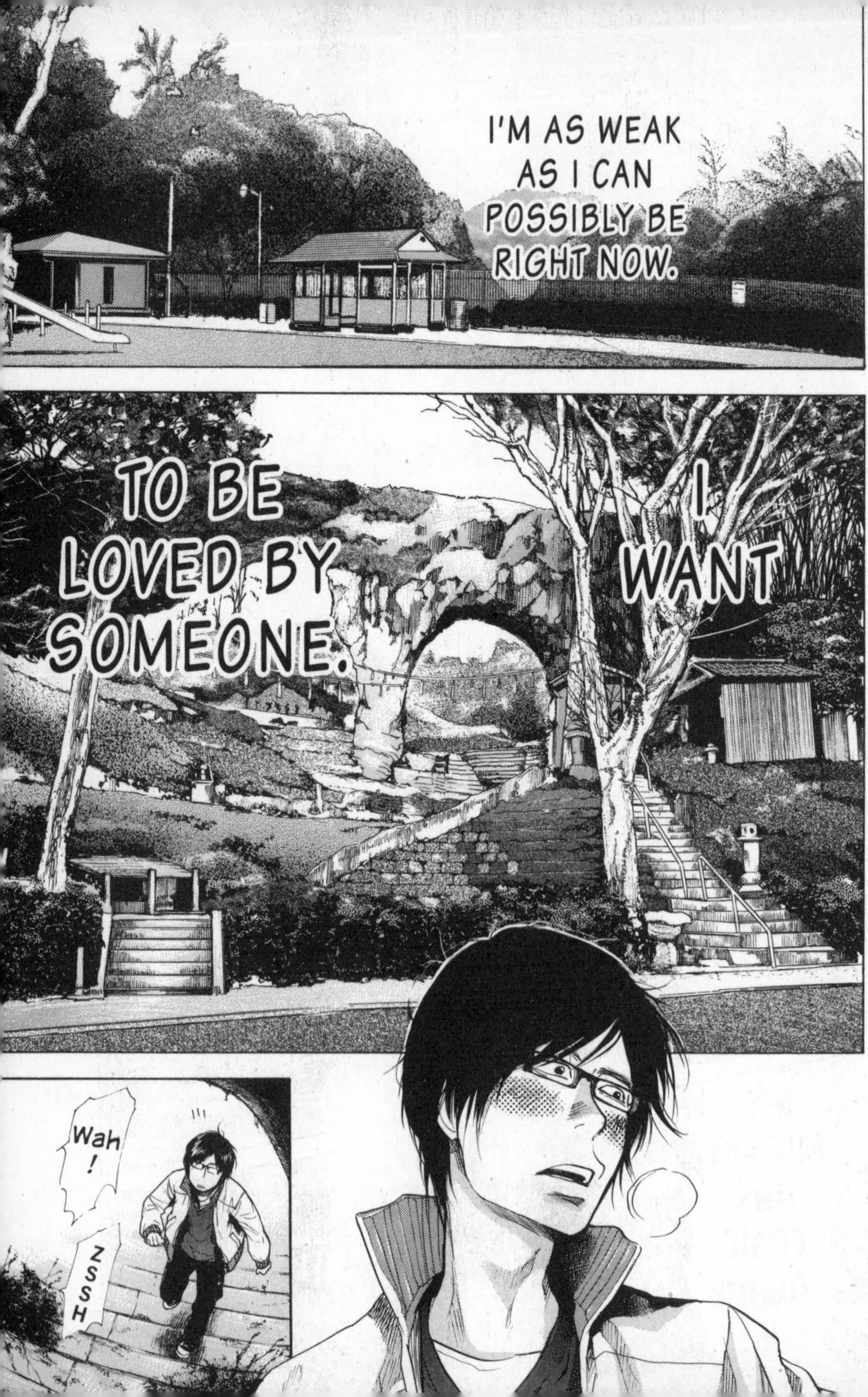
I'M AS WEAK AS I CAN POSSIBLY BE RIGHT NOW.
I WANT
TO BE LOVED BY SOMEONE.
Wah!
ZSSH

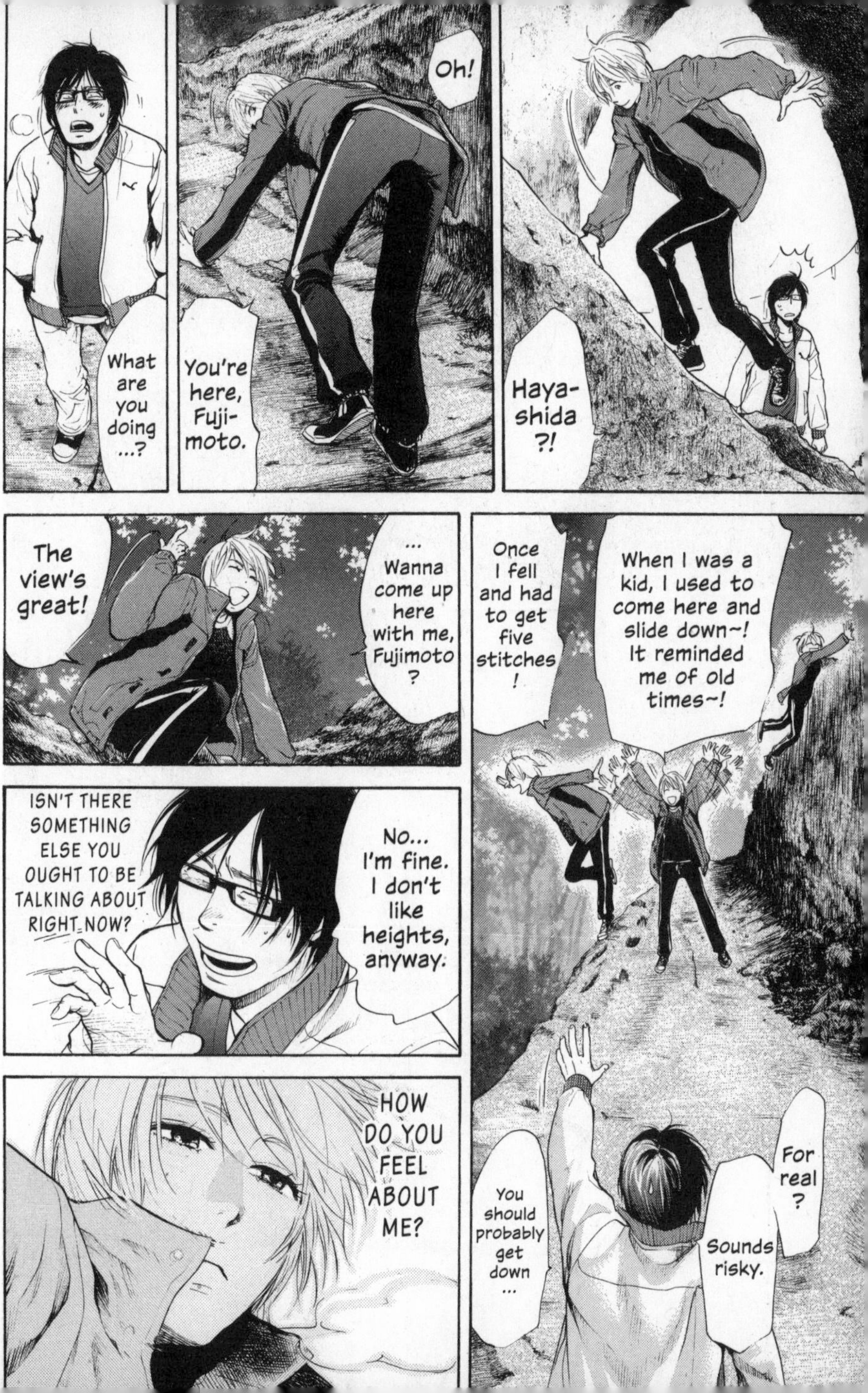
Haya-shida ?!
Oh!
You're here, Fuji-moto.
What are you doing ...?
When I was a kid, I used to come here and slide down~! It reminded me of old times~!
Once I fell and had to get five stitches !
For real ?
Sounds risky.
You should probably get down ...
... Wanna come up here with me, Fujimoto ?
The view's great!
No... I'm fine. I don't like heights, anyway.
ISN'T THERE SOMETHING ELSE YOU OUGHT TO BE TALKING ABOUT RIGHT NOW?
HOW DO YOU FEEL ABOUT ME?

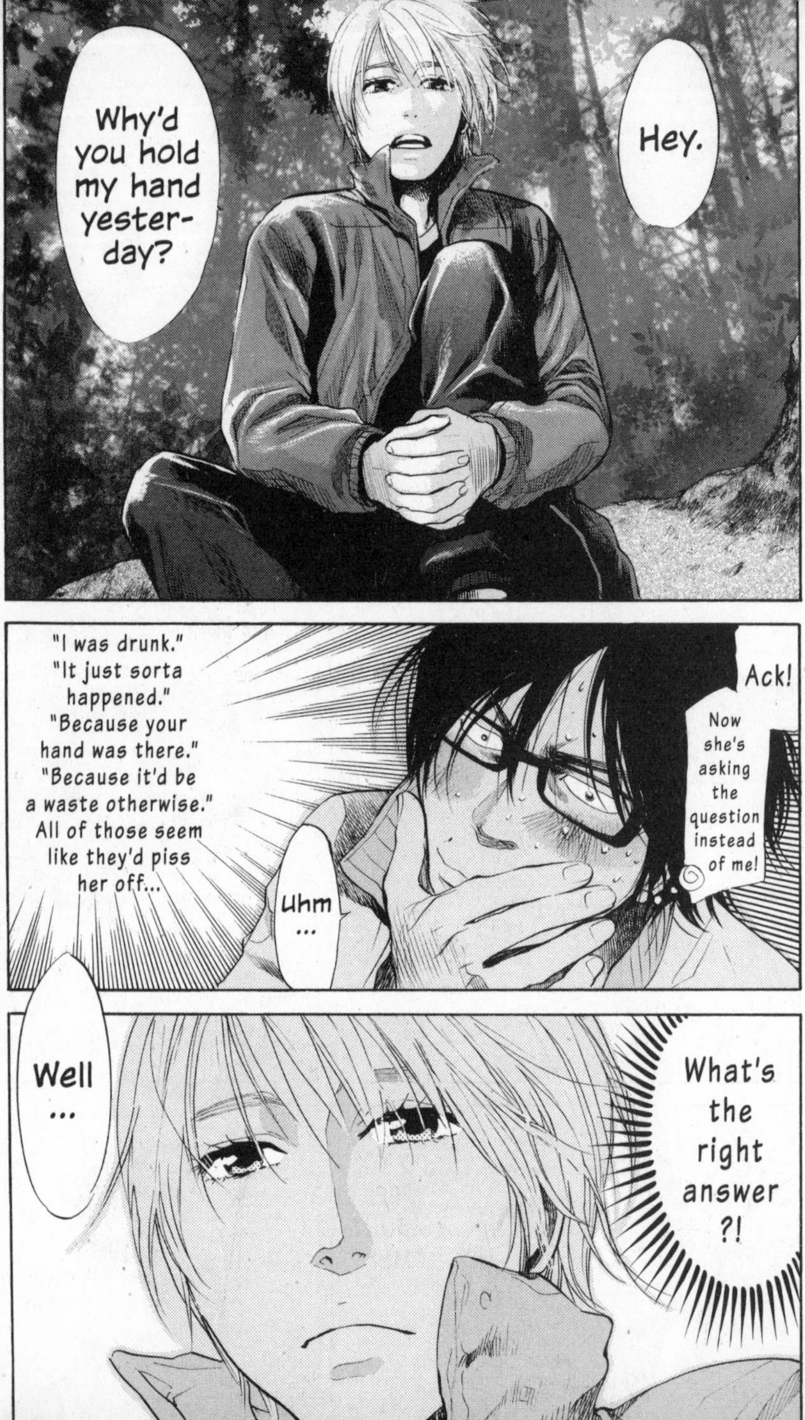
Hey.
Why'd you hold my hand yesterday?
Ack!
Now she's asking the question instead of me!
"I was drunk." "It just sorta happened." "Because your hand was there." "Because it'd be a waste otherwise." All of those seem like they'd piss her off...
Uhm ...
What's the right answer ?!
Well ...

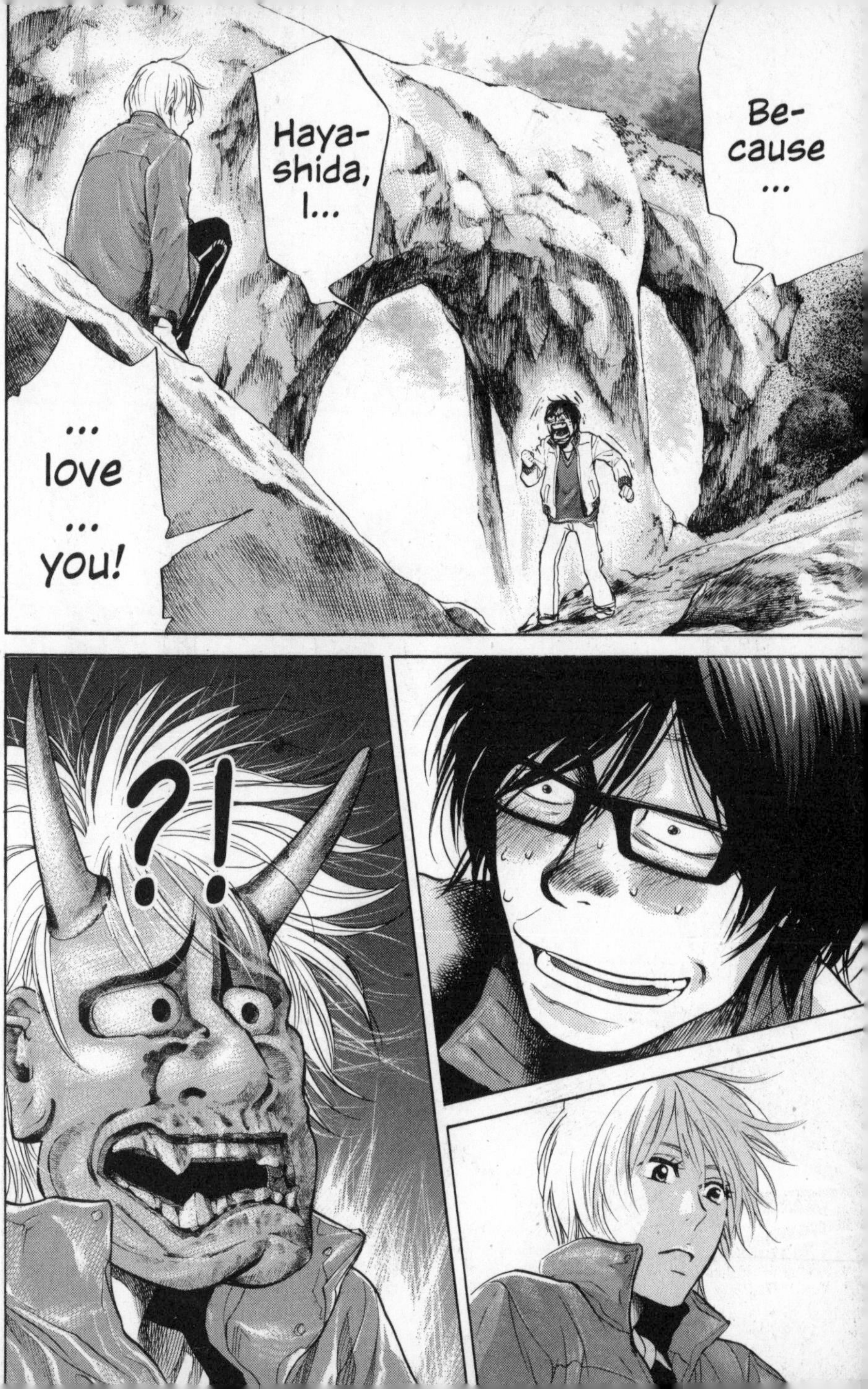
Be-
cause
...
Haya-
shida,
I...
... love
...
you!
?!

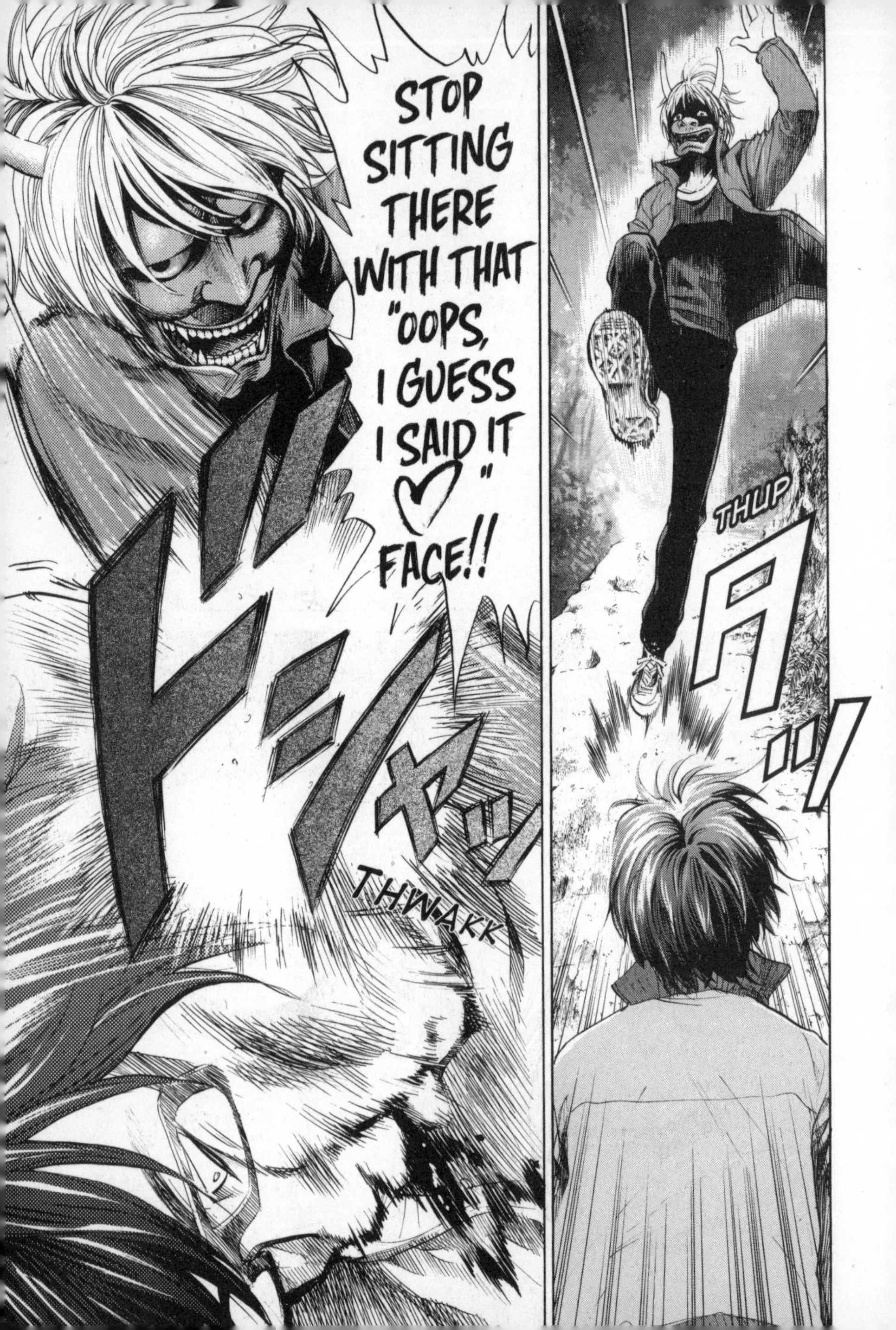
THUP
STOP SITTING THERE WITH THAT "OOPS, I GUESS I SAID IT ♥" FACE!!
THWAKK

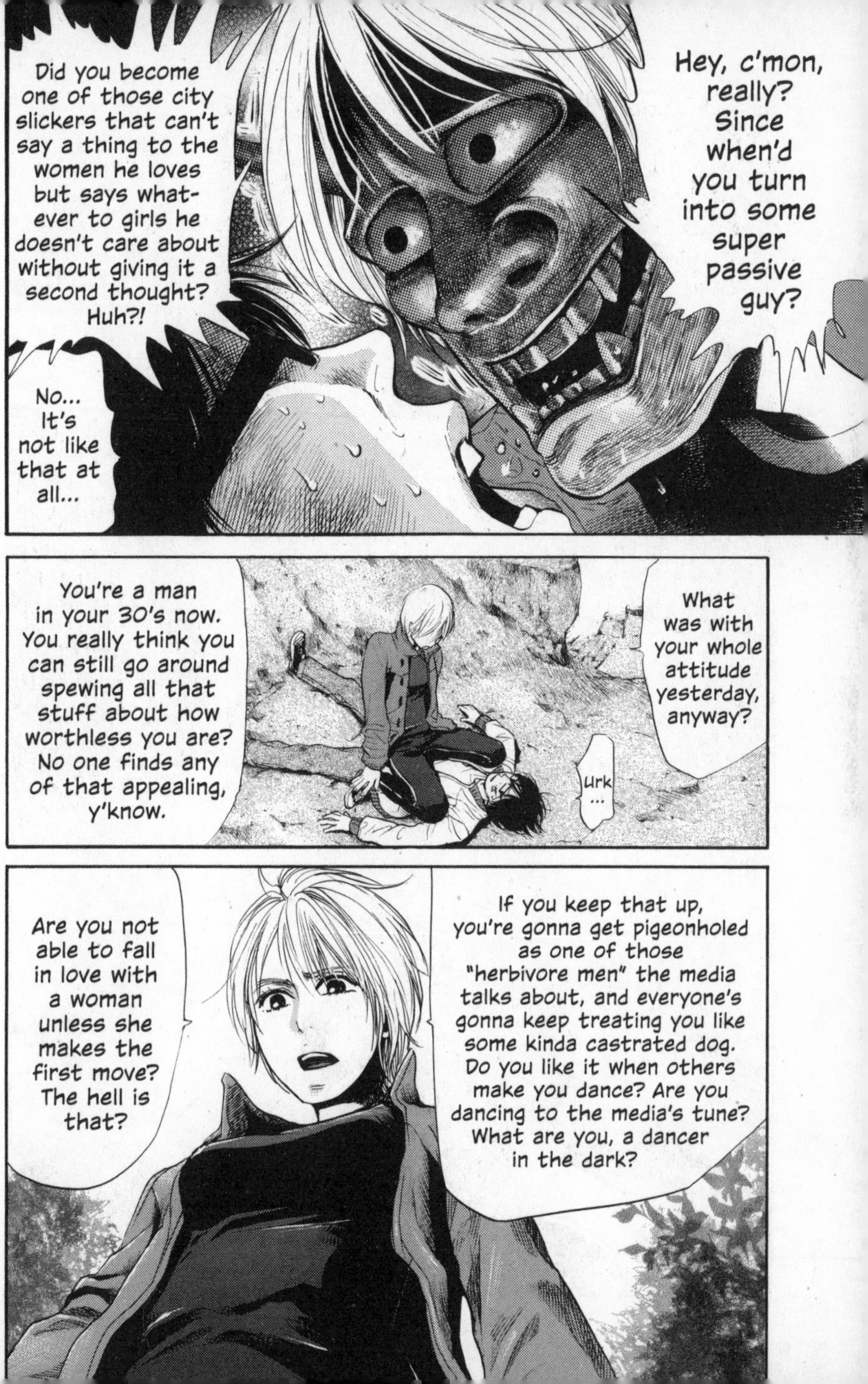
Hey, c'mon, really? Since when'd you turn into some super passive guy?
Did you become one of those city slickers that can't say a thing to the women he loves but says what-ever to girls he doesn't care about without giving it a second thought? Huh?!
No... It's not like that at all...
What was with your whole attitude yesterday, anyway?
Urk ...
You're a man in your 30's now. You really think you can still go around spewing all that stuff about how worthless you are? No one finds any of that appealing, y'know.
If you keep that up, you're gonna get pigeonholed as one of those "herbivore men" the media talks about, and everyone's gonna keep treating you like some kinda castrated dog. Do you like it when others make you dance? Are you dancing to the media's tune? What are you, a dancer in the dark?
Are you not able to fall in love with a woman unless she makes the first move? The hell is that?

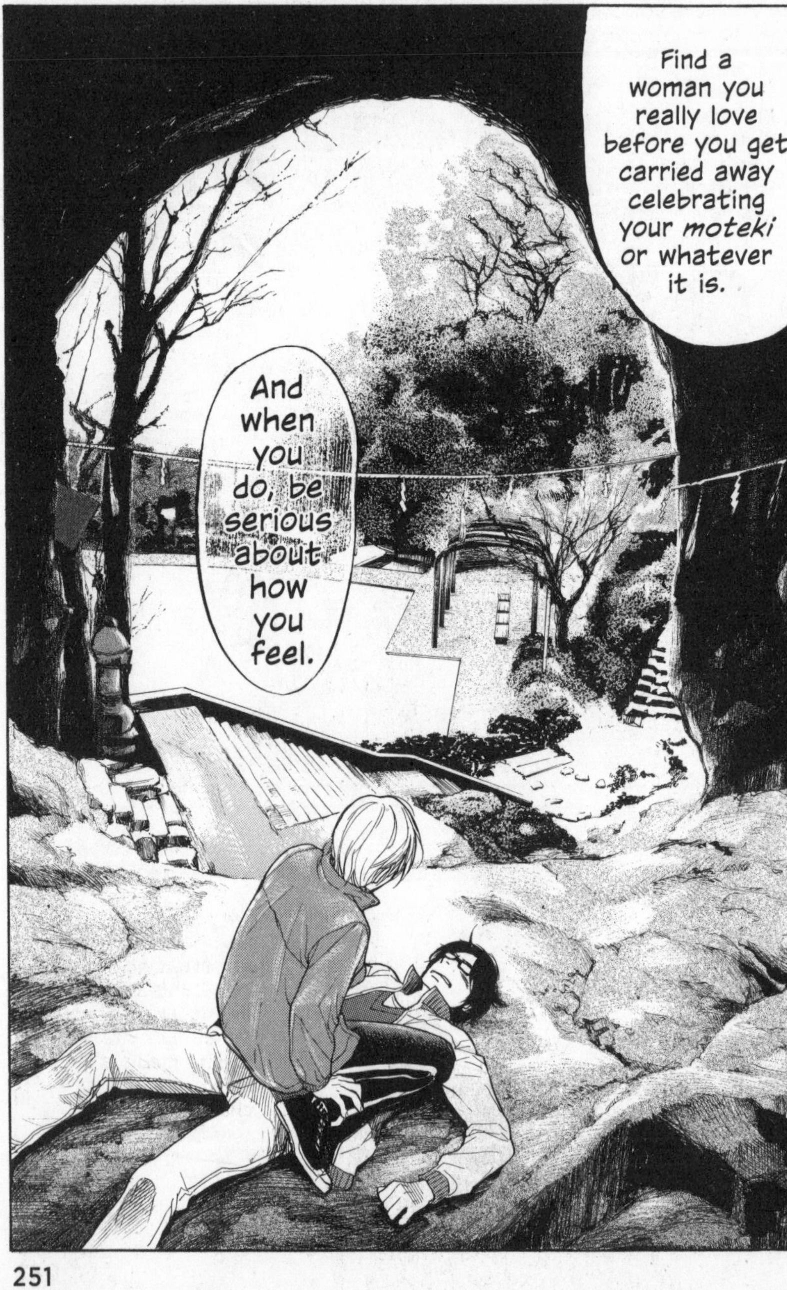
Find a woman you really love before you get carried away celebrating your *moteki* or whatever it is.
And when you do, be serious about how you feel.

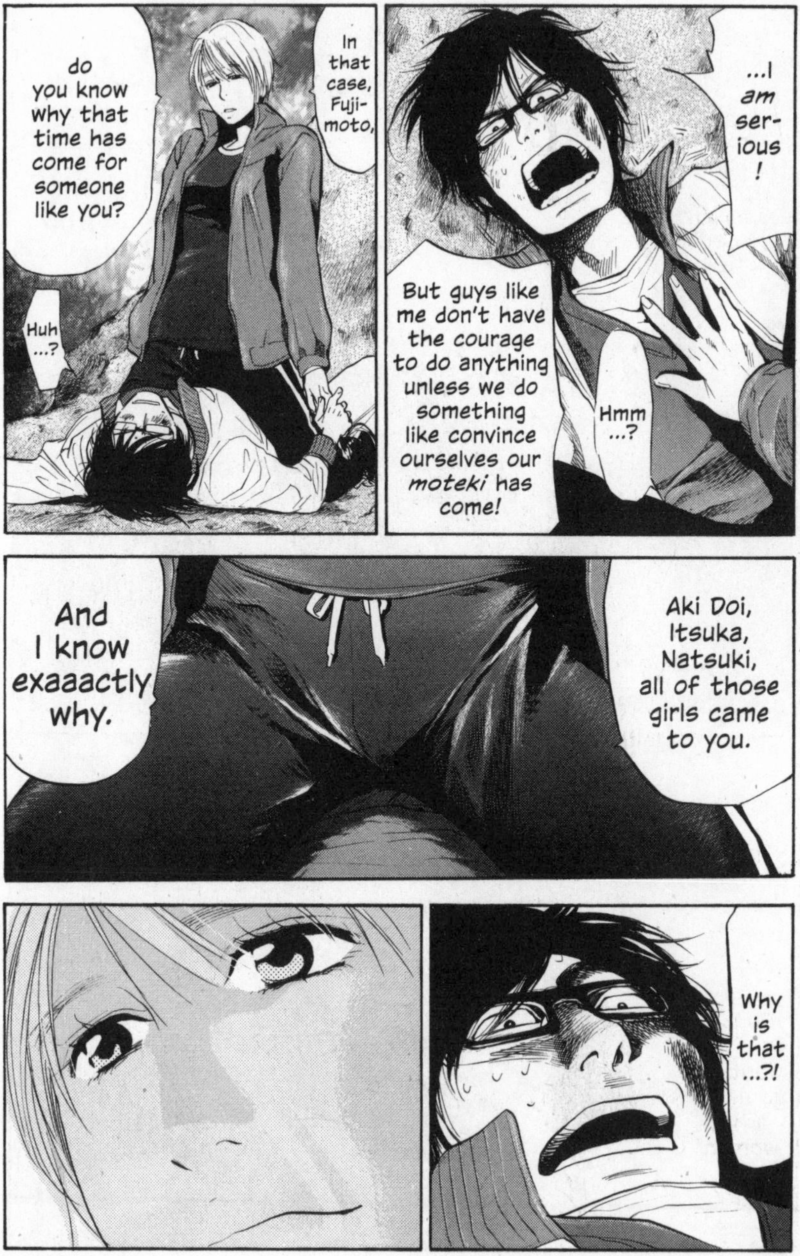
...I *am* serious!
But guys like me don't have the courage to do anything unless we do something like convince ourselves our *moteki* has come!
Hmm ...?
In that case, Fujimoto,
do you know why that time has come for someone like you?
Huh ...?
Aki Doi, Itsuka, Natsuki, all of those girls came to you.
And I know exaaactly why.
Why is that ...?!

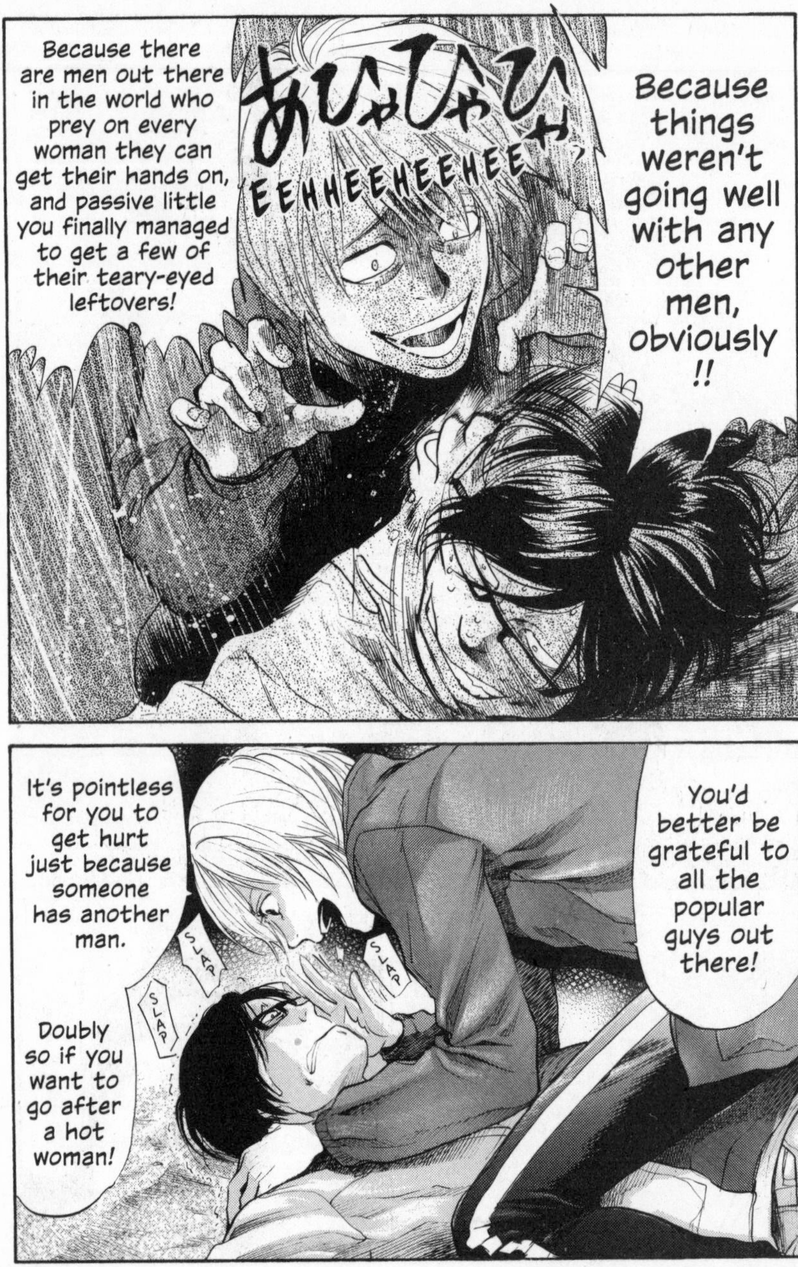
Because things weren't going well with any other men, obviously!!
あひゃひゃひゃ
EEHHEEHEEHEE
Because there are men out there in the world who prey on every woman they can get their hands on, and passive little you finally managed to get a few of their teary-eyed leftovers!
You'd better be grateful to all the popular guys out there!
SLAP
SLAP
SLAP
It's pointless for you to get hurt just because someone has another man.
Doubly so if you want to go after a hot woman!

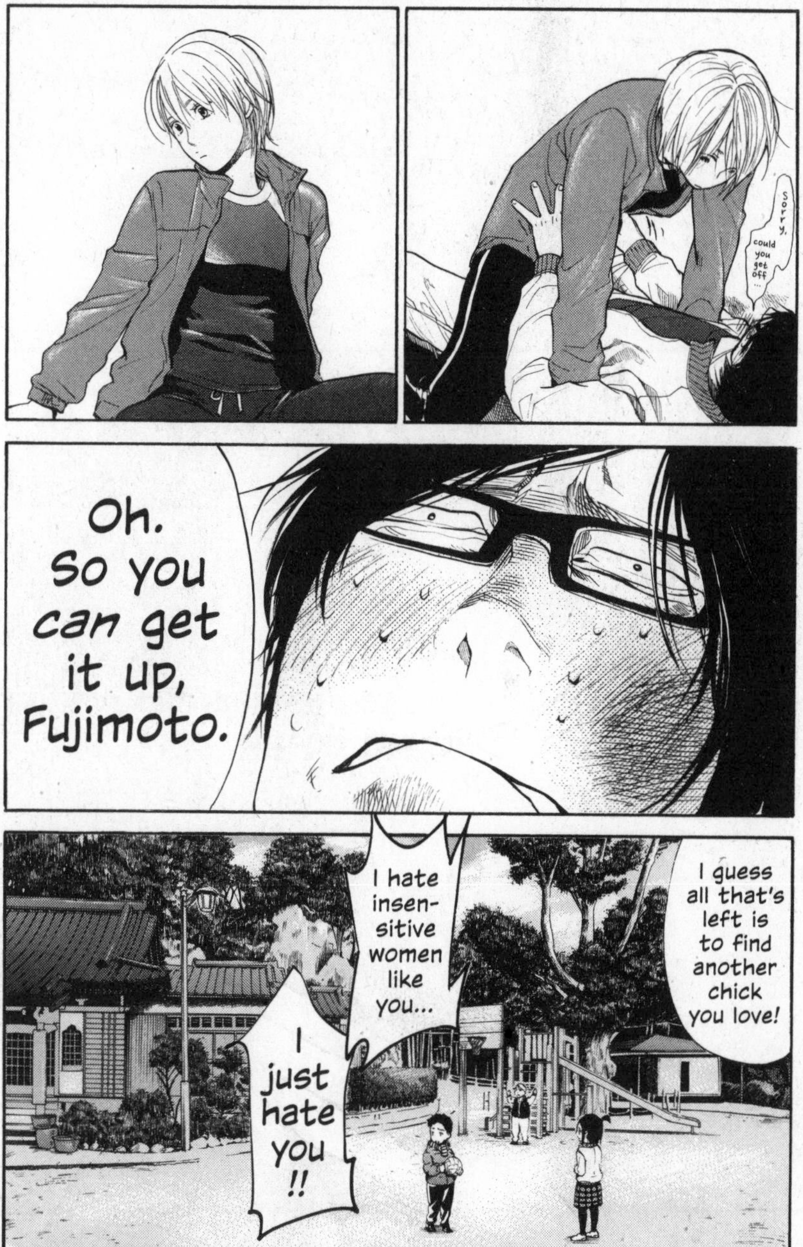
Sorry, could you get off...
Oh. So you can get it up, Fujimoto.
I guess all that's left is to find another chick you love!
I hate insensitive women like you...
I just hate you!!

chapter 8 ♥ END

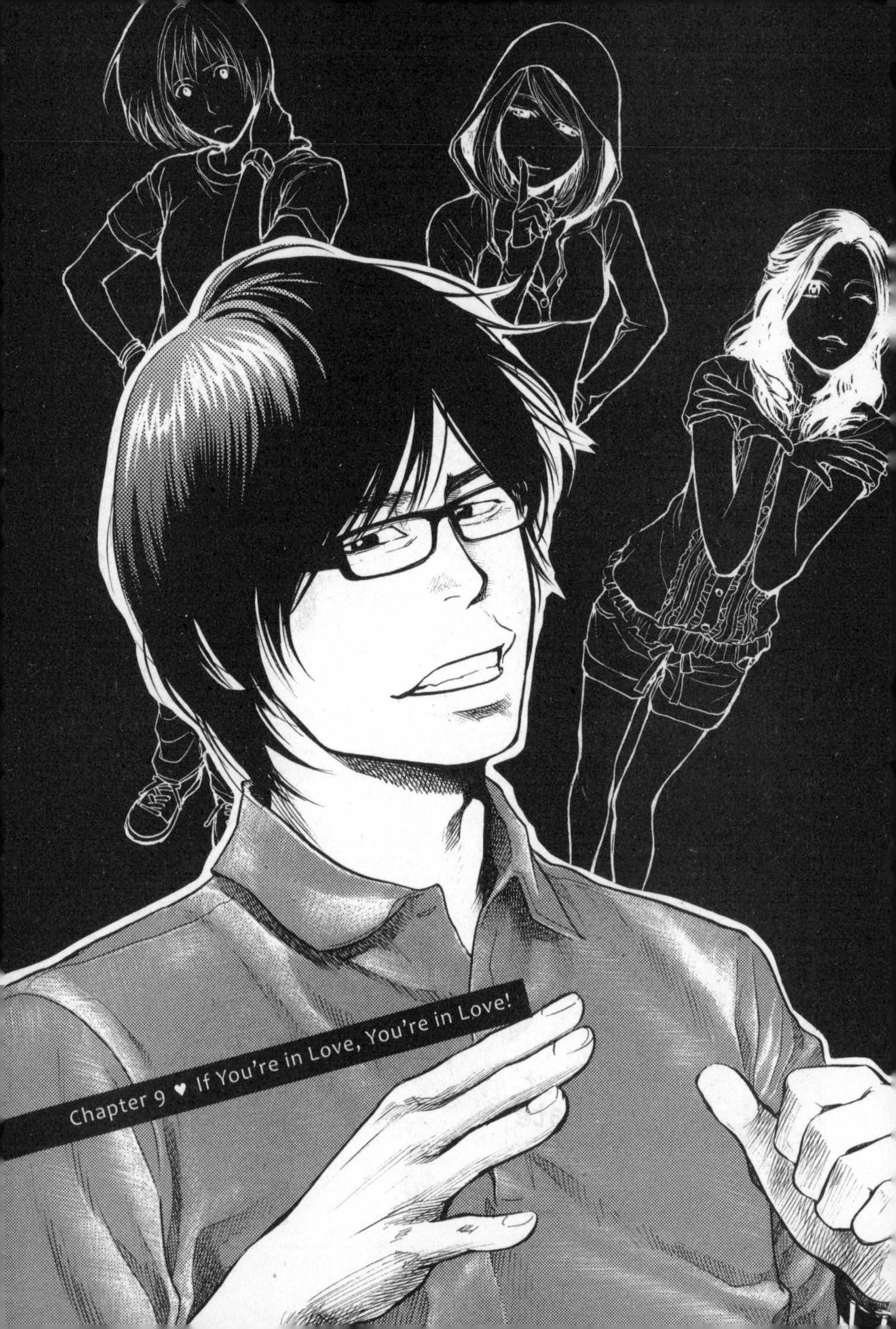
Chapter 9 ♥ If You're in Love, You're in Love!

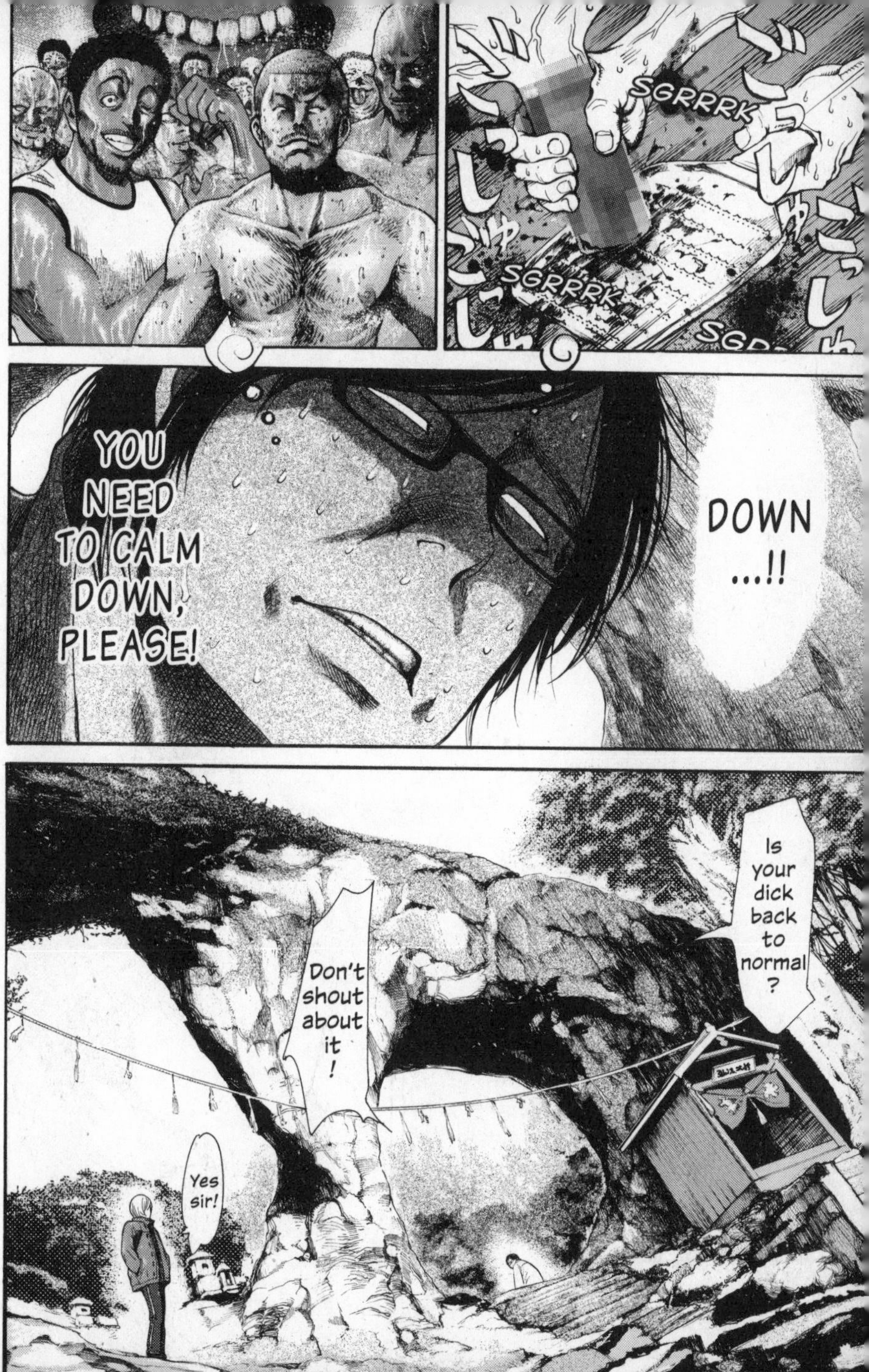
SGRRRK
SGRRRK
DOWN ...!!
YOU NEED TO CALM DOWN, PLEASE!
Is your dick back to normal?
Don't shout about it!
Yes sir!

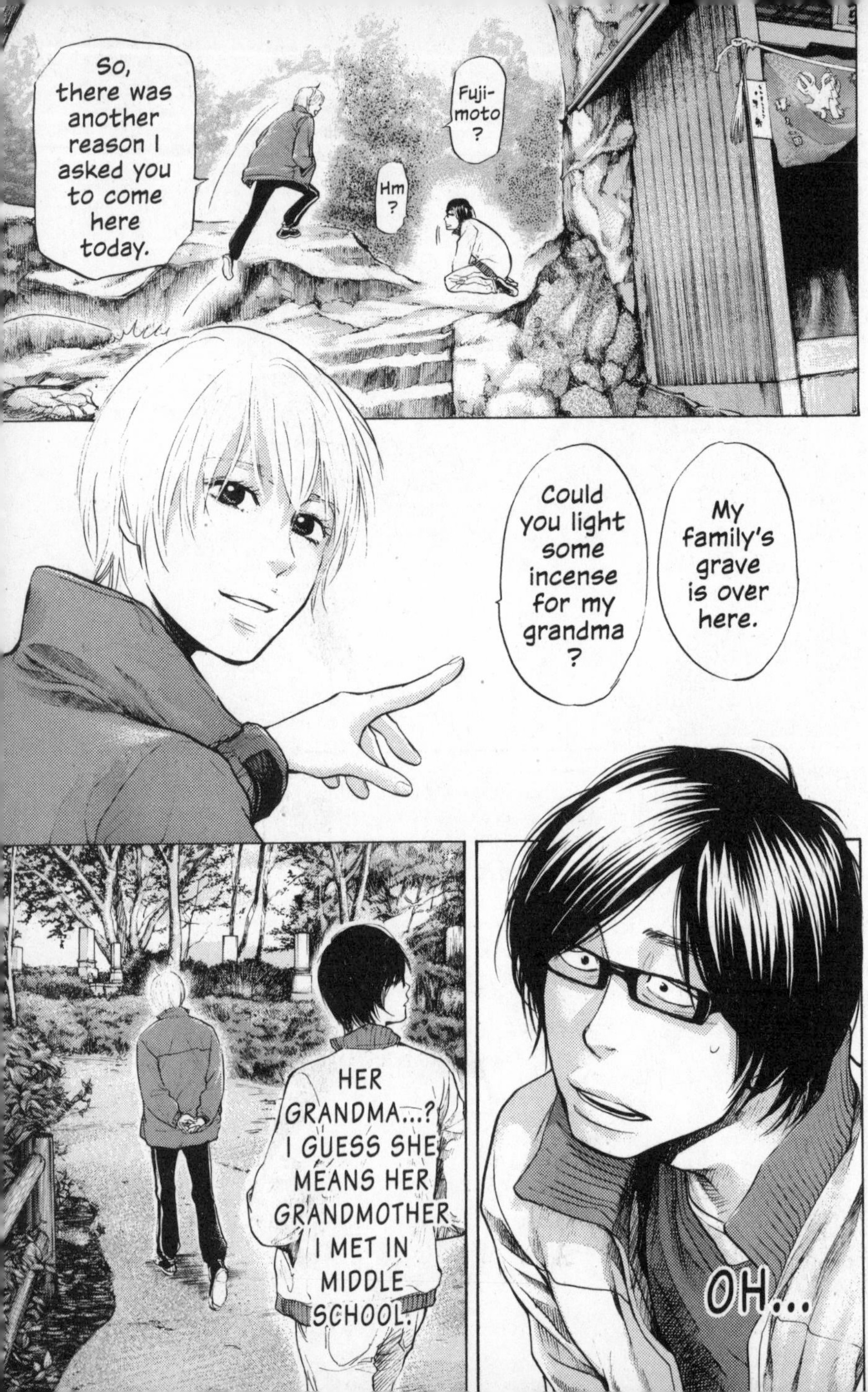
Fuji-moto?
Hm?
So, there was another reason I asked you to come here today.
My family's grave is over here.
Could you light some incense for my grandma?
OH...
HER GRANDMA...? I GUESS SHE MEANS HER GRANDMOTHER I MET IN MIDDLE SCHOOL.

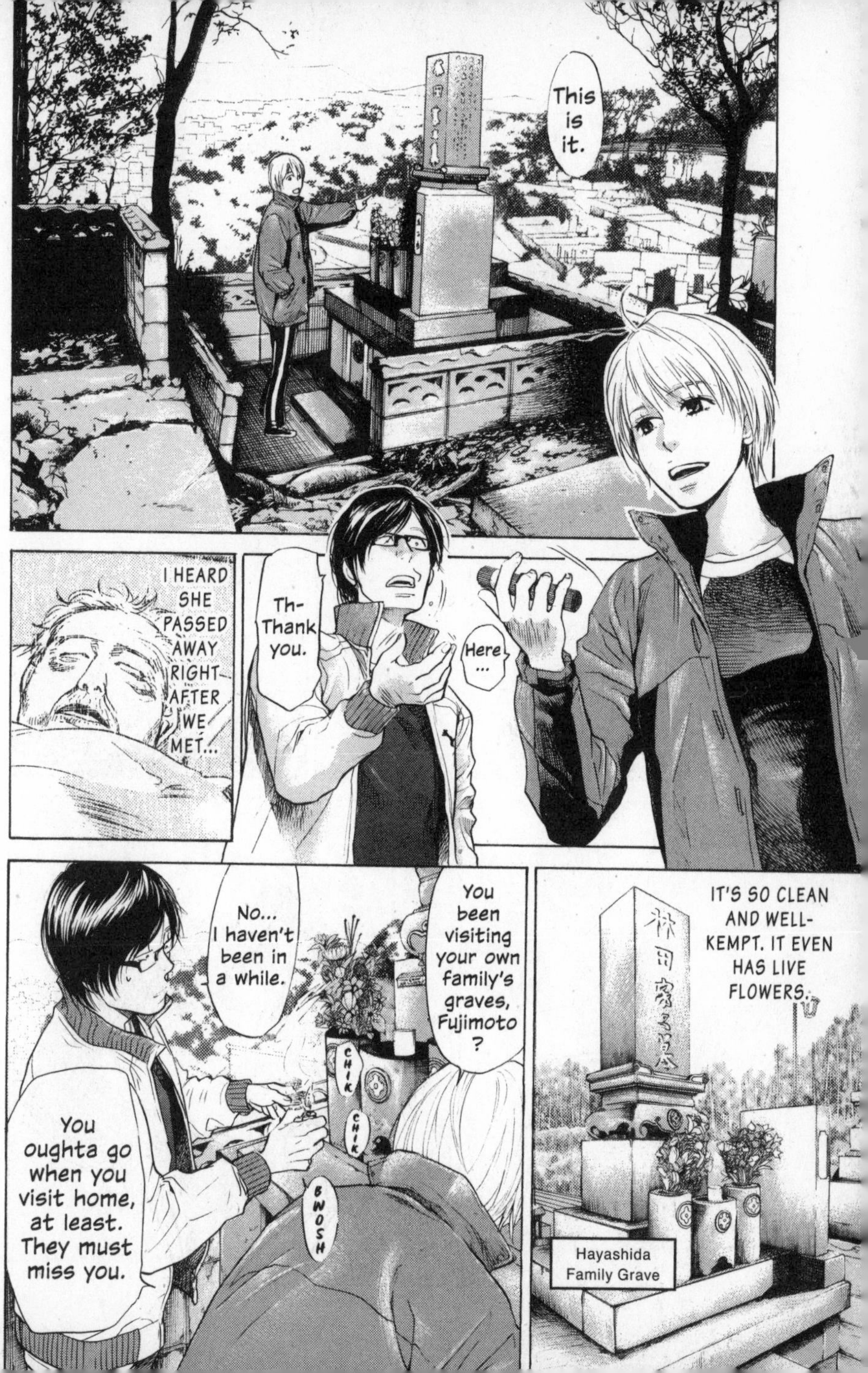
This is it.
Here...
Th-Thank you.
I HEARD SHE PASSED AWAY RIGHT AFTER WE MET...
IT'S SO CLEAN AND WELL-KEMPT. IT EVEN HAS LIVE FLOWERS.
Hayashida Family Grave
You been visiting your own family's graves, Fujimoto?
No... I haven't been in a while.
CHIK
CHIK
BWOSH
You oughta go when you visit home, at least. They must miss you.

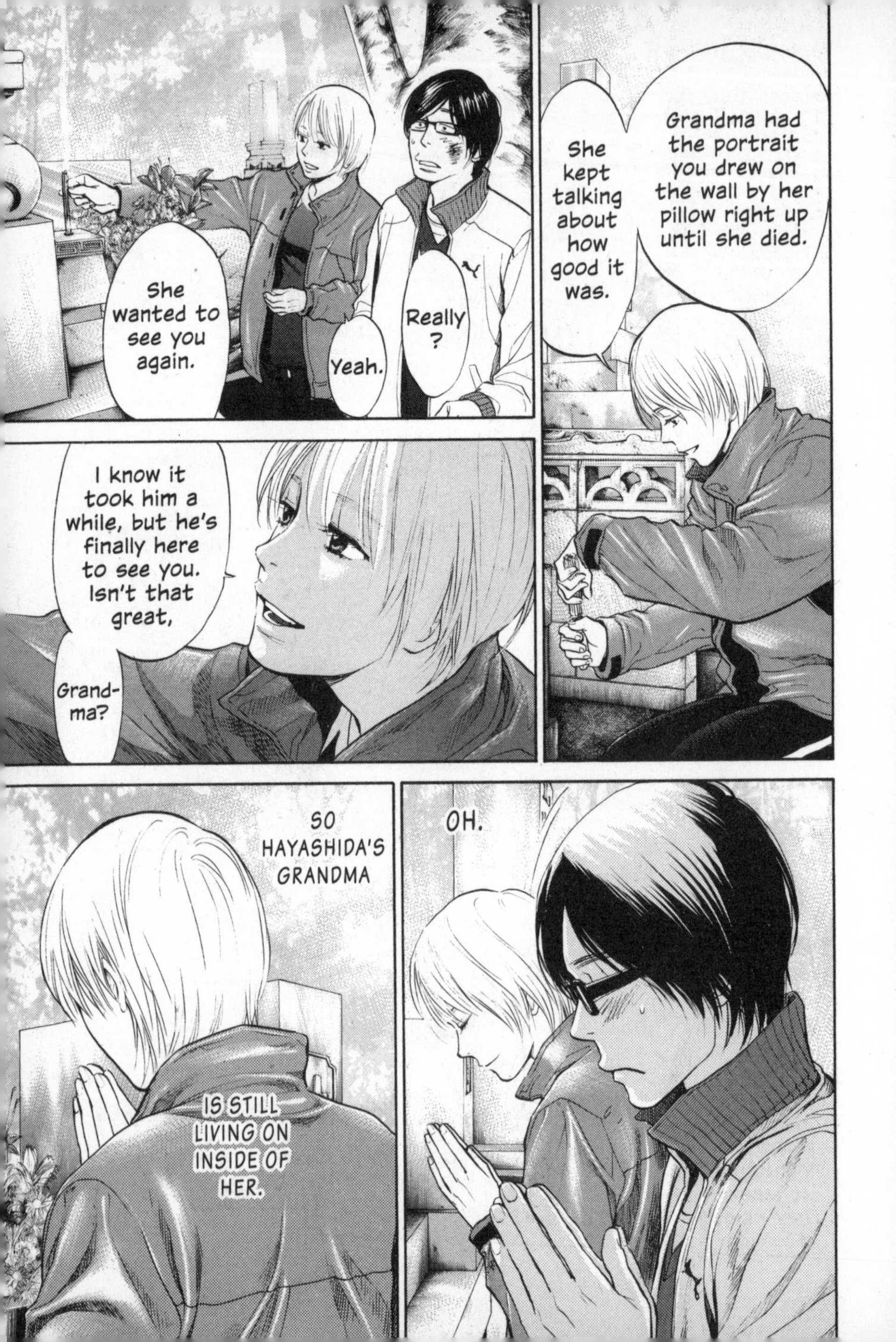
Grandma had the portrait you drew on the wall by her pillow right up until she died.
She kept talking about how good it was.
Really?
Yeah.
She wanted to see you again.
I know it took him a while, but he's finally here to see you. Isn't that great,
Grand-ma?
OH.
SO HAYASHIDA'S GRANDMA
IS STILL LIVING ON INSIDE OF HER.

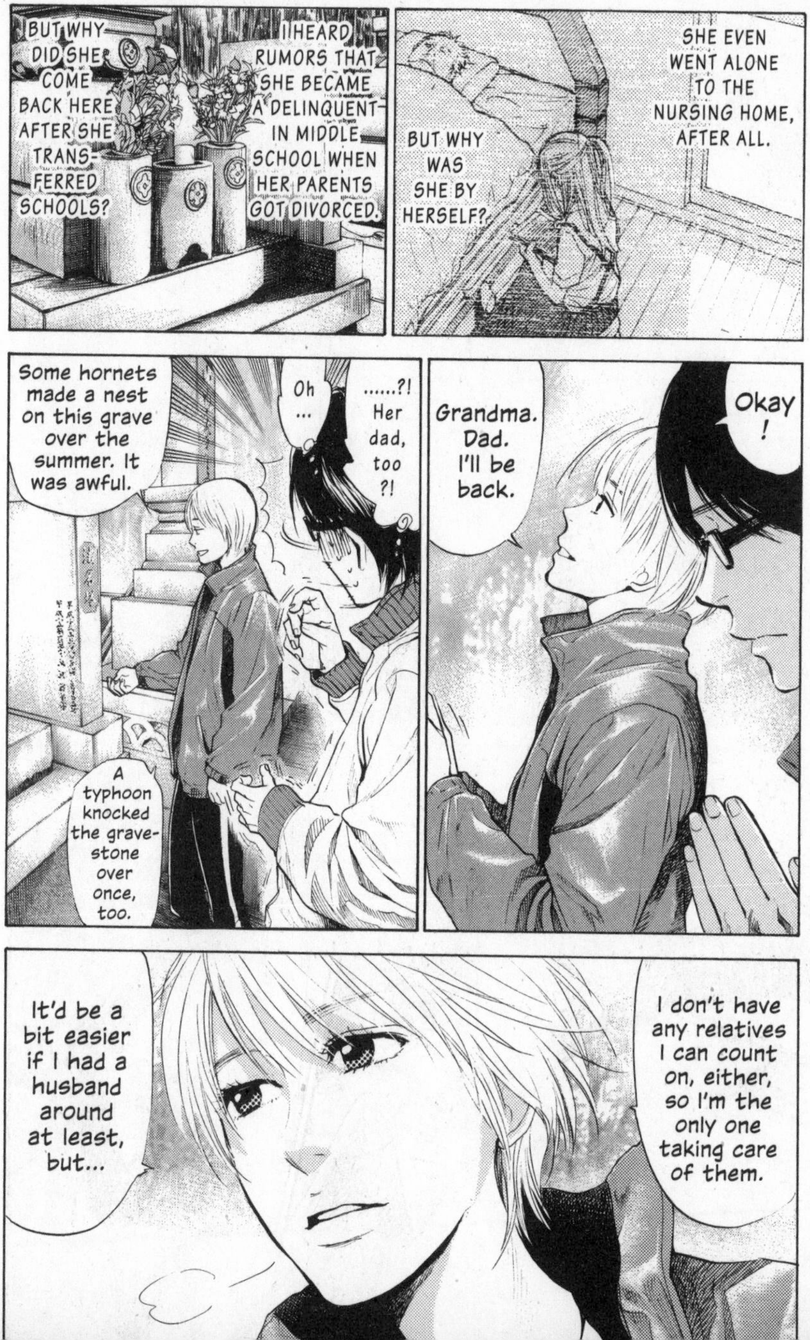
SHE EVEN WENT ALONE TO THE NURSING HOME, AFTER ALL.
BUT WHY WAS SHE BY HERSELF?
I HEARD RUMORS THAT SHE BECAME A DELINQUENT IN MIDDLE SCHOOL WHEN HER PARENTS GOT DIVORCED.
BUT WHY DID SHE COME BACK HERE AFTER SHE TRANS-FERRED SCHOOLS?
Okay!
Grandma. Dad. I'll be back.
......?! Her dad, too?!
Oh ...
Some hornets made a nest on this grave over the summer. It was awful.
A typhoon knocked the grave-stone over once, too.
I don't have any relatives I can count on, either, so I'm the only one taking care of them.
It'd be a bit easier if I had a husband around at least, but...

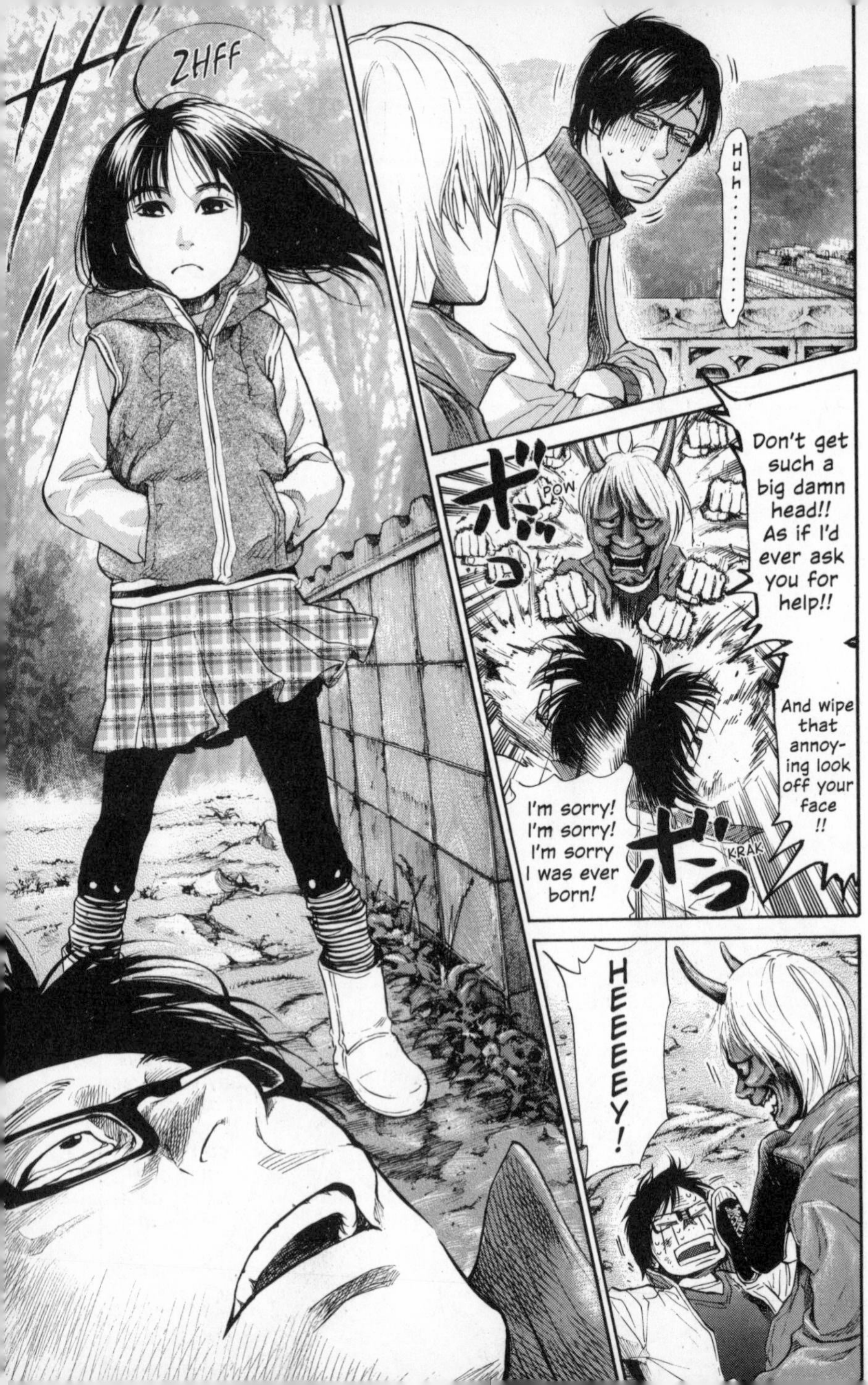
Huh........
Don't get such a big damn head!! As if I'd ever ask you for help!!
POW
And wipe that annoying look off your face !!
I'm sorry! I'm sorry! I'm sorry I was ever born!
KRAK
HEEEEEY!
ZHFF

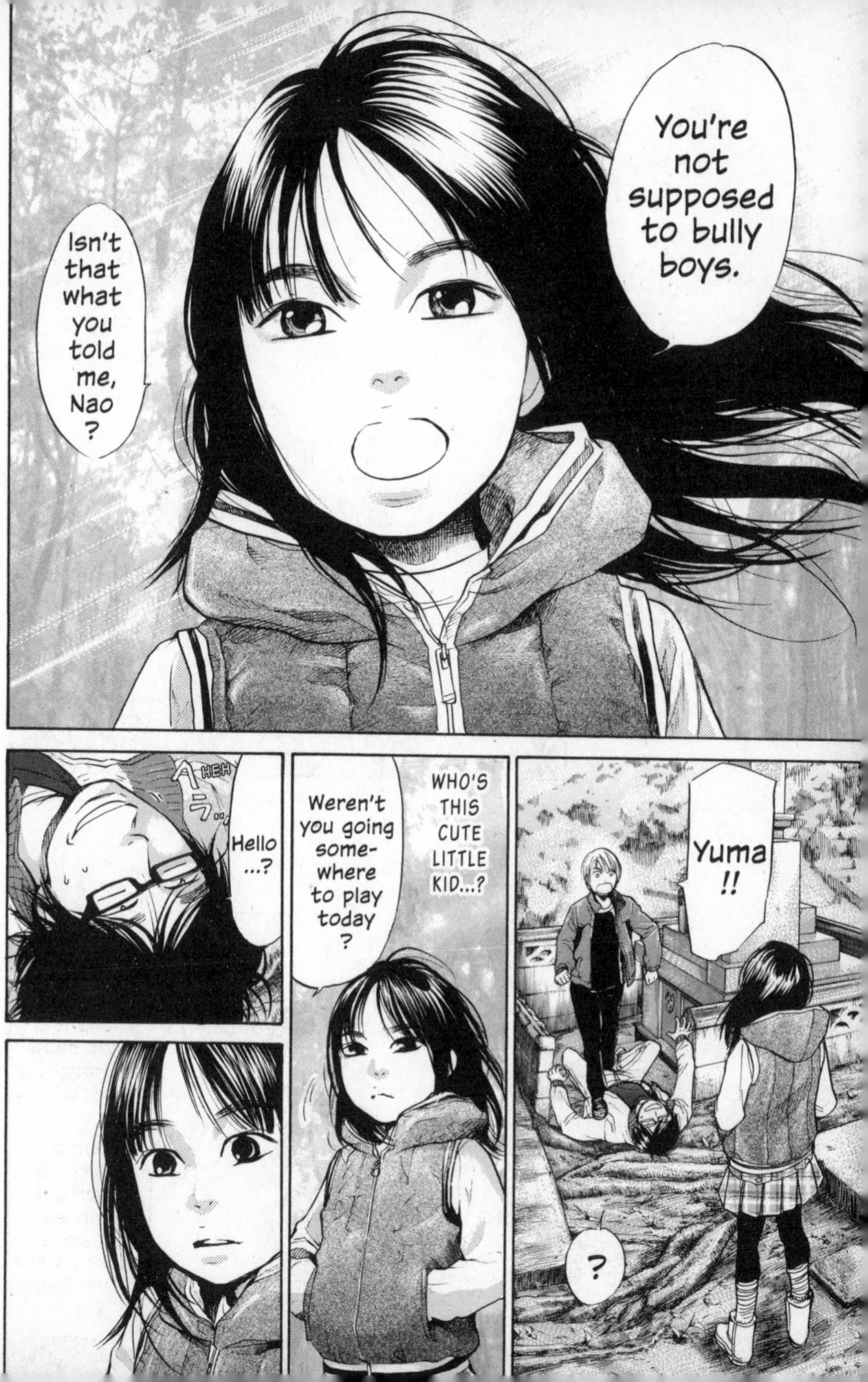
You're not supposed to bully boys.
Isn't that what you told me, Nao?
Yuma!!
?
WHO'S THIS CUTE LITTLE KID...?
Weren't you going some-where to play today?
HEH
Hello...?

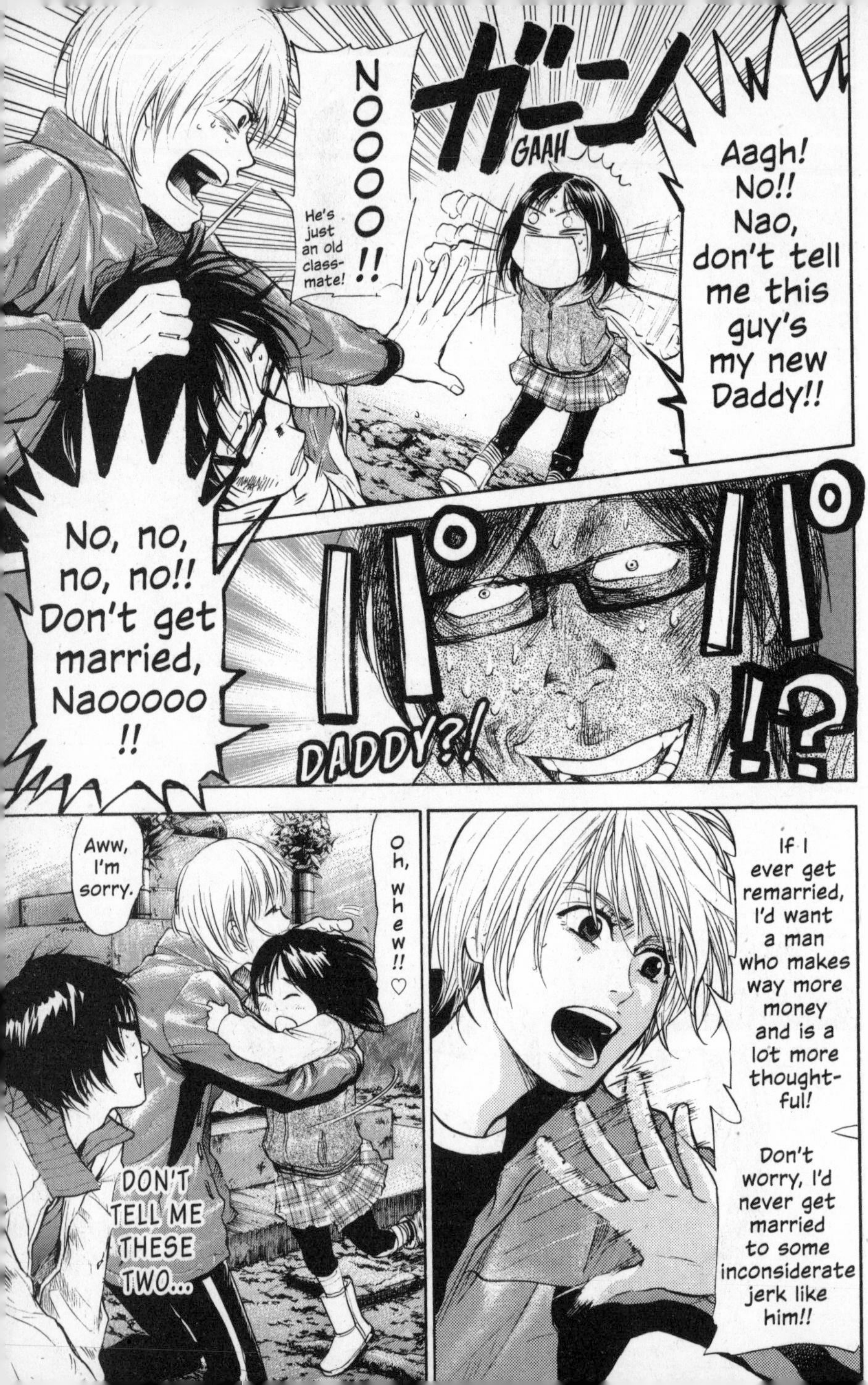
ガーン
GAAH
Aagh! No!! Nao, don't tell me this guy's my new Daddy!!
NOOOOO!!
He's just an old classmate!
パパ!?
DADDY?!
No, no, no, no!! Don't get married, Naoooooo!!
If I ever get remarried, I'd want a man who makes way more money and is a lot more thoughtful!
Don't worry, I'd never get married to some inconsiderate jerk like him!!
Oh, whew!! ♡
Aww, I'm sorry.
DON'T TELL ME THESE TWO...

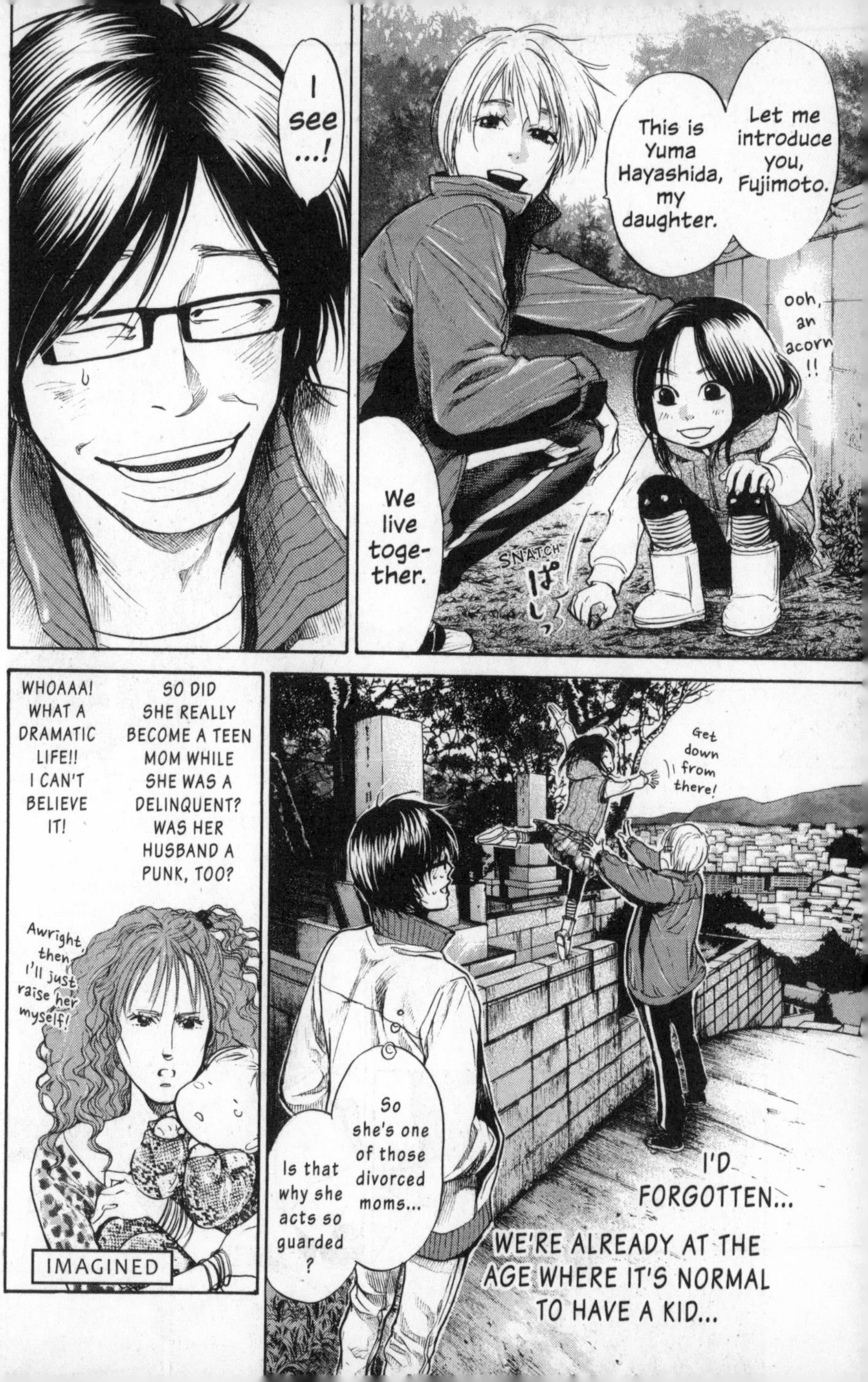
Let me introduce you, Fujimoto.
This is Yuma Hayashida, my daughter.
ooh, an acorn !!
We live toge-ther.
SNATCH
ぱしっ
I see ...!
Get down from there!
So she's one of those divorced moms...
Is that why she acts so guarded?
I'D FORGOTTEN...
WE'RE ALREADY AT THE AGE WHERE IT'S NORMAL TO HAVE A KID...
SO DID SHE REALLY BECOME A TEEN MOM WHILE SHE WAS A DELINQUENT? WAS HER HUSBAND A PUNK, TOO?
WHOAAA! WHAT A DRAMATIC LIFE!! I CAN'T BELIEVE IT!
Awright, then I'll just raise her myself!
IMAGINED

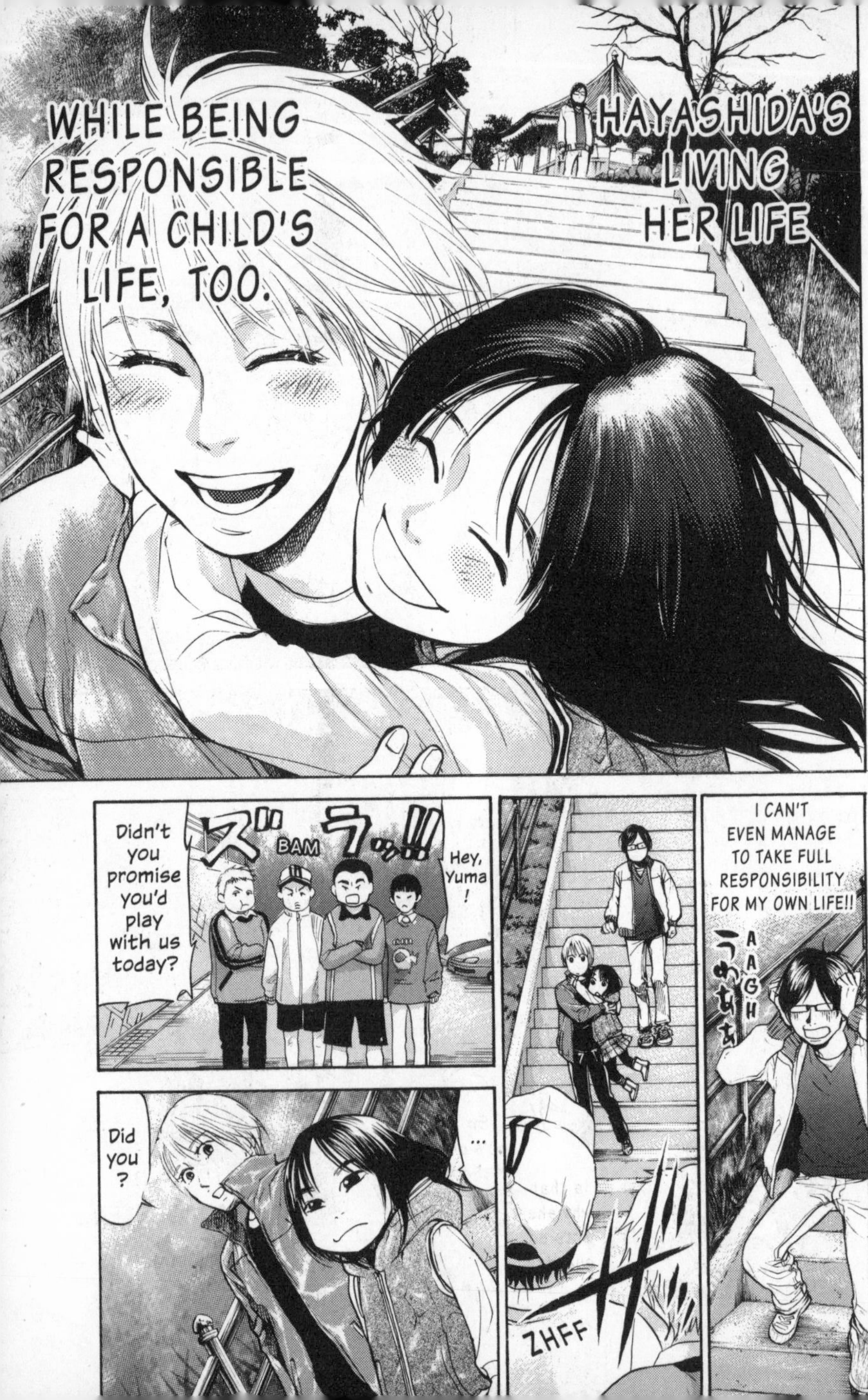
HAYASHIDA'S LIVING HER LIFE
WHILE BEING RESPONSIBLE FOR A CHILD'S LIFE, TOO.
I CAN'T EVEN MANAGE TO TAKE FULL RESPONSIBILITY FOR MY OWN LIFE!!
AAGH
Hey, Yuma!
BAM
Didn't you promise you'd play with us today?
ZHFF
...
Did you?

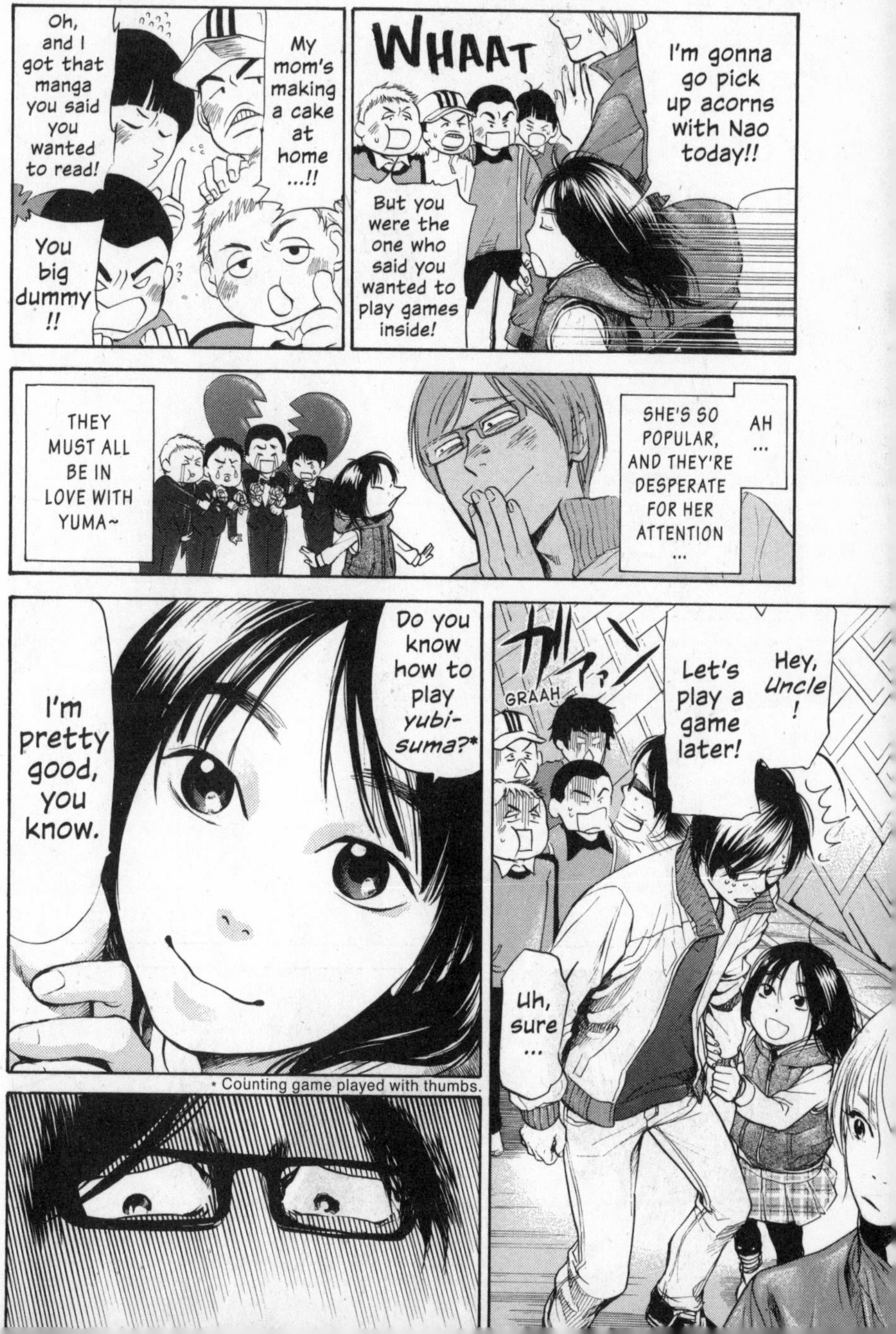
WHAAT
I'm gonna go pick up acorns with Nao today!!
But you were the one who said you wanted to play games inside!
My mom's making a cake at home ...!!
Oh, and I got that manga you said you wanted to read!
You big dummy !!
AH ...
SHE'S SO POPULAR, AND THEY'RE DESPERATE FOR HER ATTENTION ...
THEY MUST ALL BE IN LOVE WITH YUMA~
Hey, Uncle !
Let's play a game later!
GRAAH
Uh, sure ...
Do you know how to play yubi-suma?*
I'm pretty good, you know.

* Counting game played with thumbs.

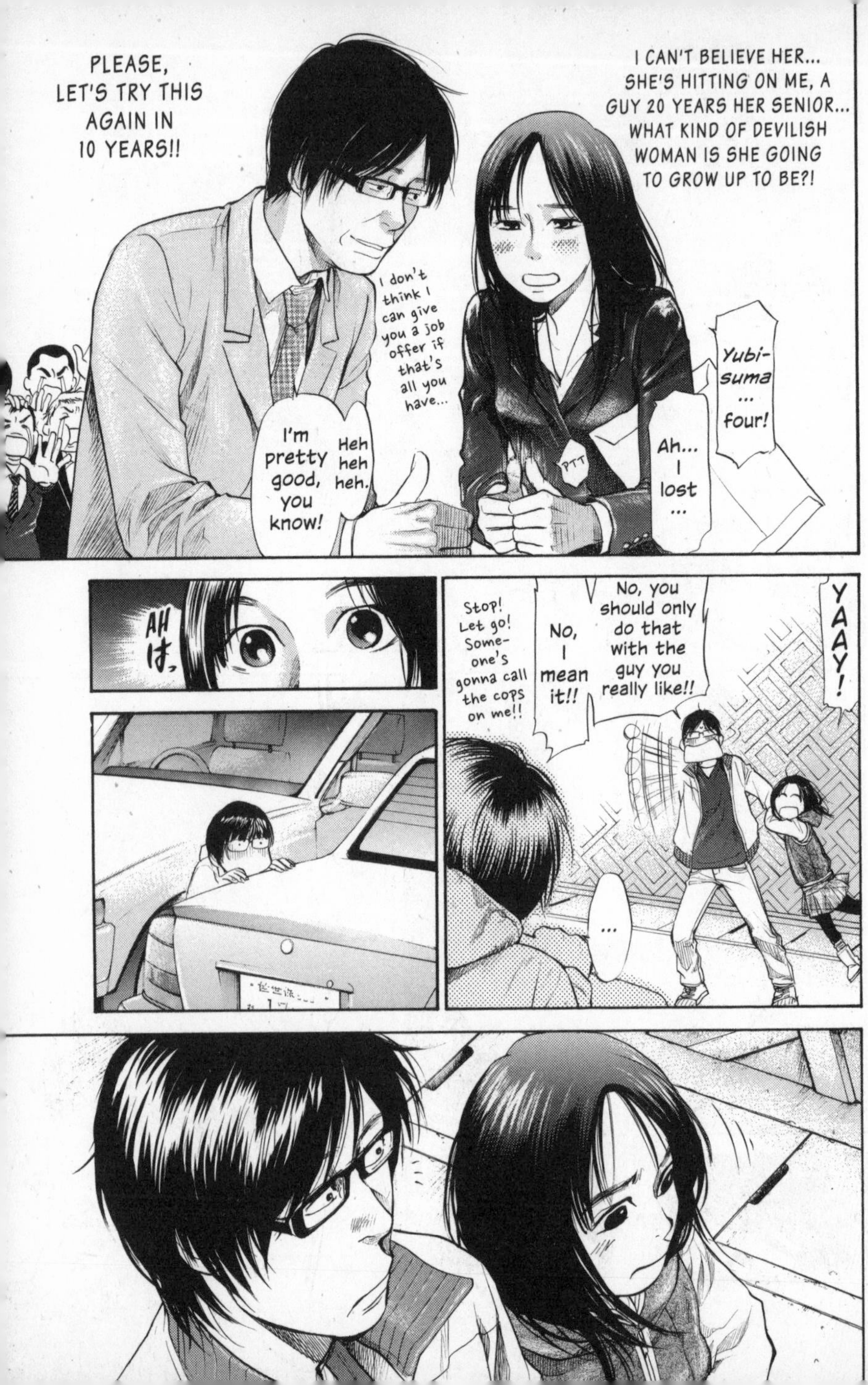
I CAN'T BELIEVE HER... SHE'S HITTING ON ME, A GUY 20 YEARS HER SENIOR... WHAT KIND OF DEVILISH WOMAN IS SHE GOING TO GROW UP TO BE?!
Yubi-suma ... four!
Ah... I lost ...
I don't think I can give you a job offer if that's all you have...
PTT
Heh heh heh.
I'm pretty good, you know!
PLEASE, LET'S TRY THIS AGAIN IN 10 YEARS!!
YAAAY!
No, you should only do that with the guy you really like!!
No, I mean it!!
Stop! Let go! Some-one's gonna call the cops on me!!
...
AH は

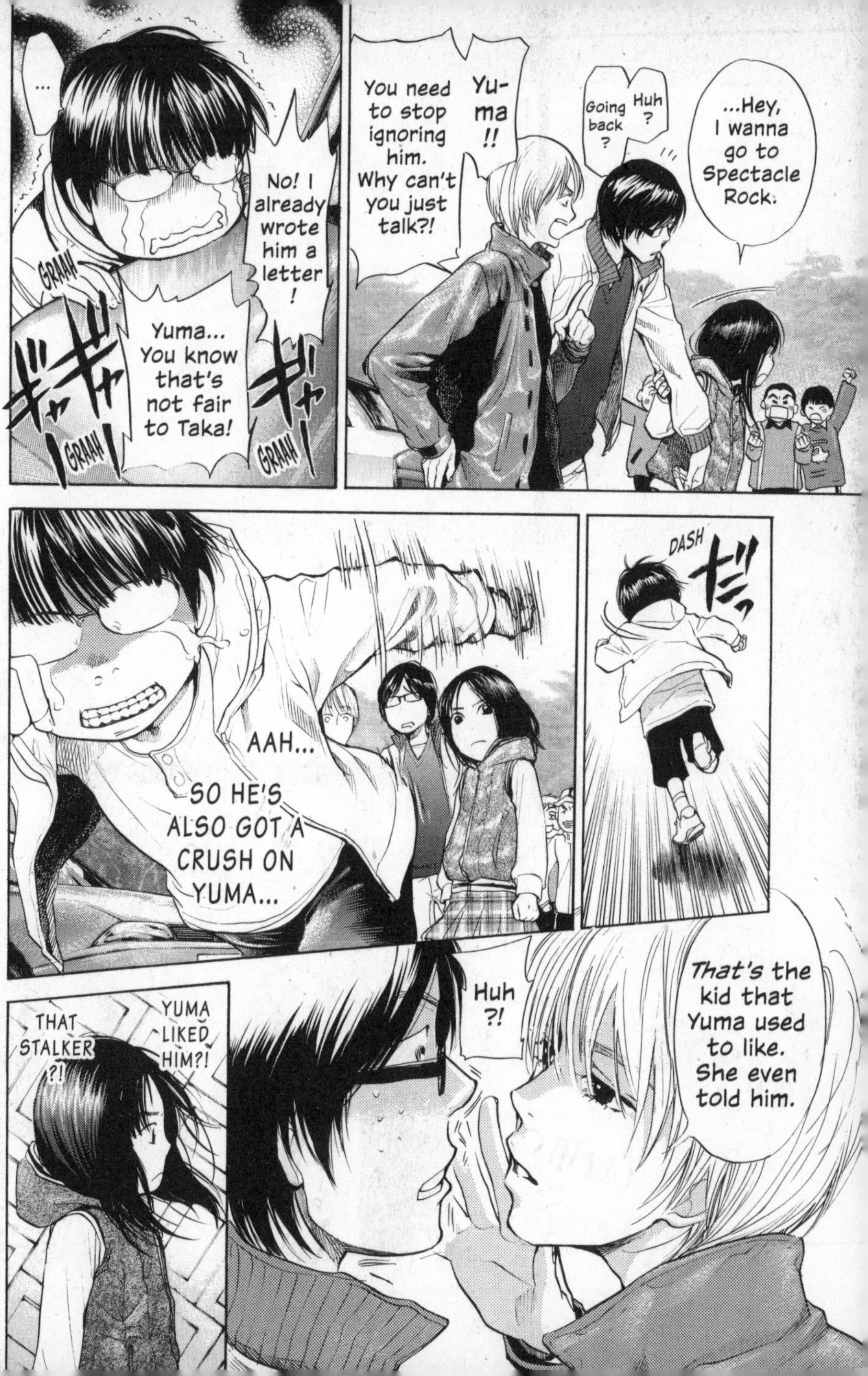

...Hey, I wanna go to Spectacle Rock.
Huh?
Going back?
Yu-ma!!
You need to stop ignoring him. Why can't you just talk?!
...
No! I already wrote him a letter!
Yuma... You know that's not fair to Taka!
GRAAH
GRAAH
GRAAH
DASH
AAH...
SO HE'S ALSO GOT A CRUSH ON YUMA...
That's the kid that Yuma used to like. She even told him.
Huh?!
YUMA LIKED HIM?!
THAT STALKER?!

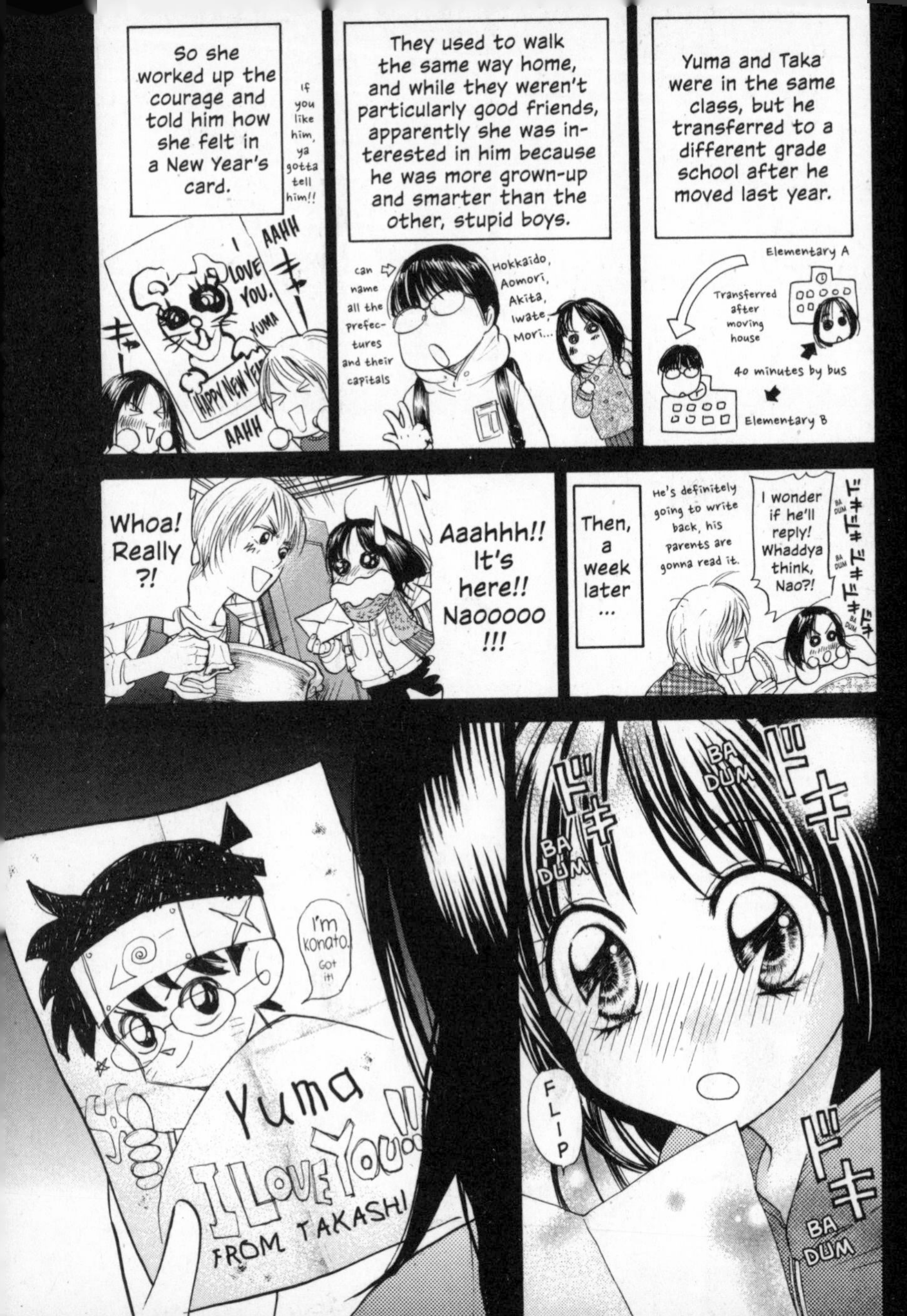
Yuma and Taka were in the same class, but he transferred to a different grade school after he moved last year.
Elementary A
Transferred after moving house
40 minutes by bus
Elementary B
They used to walk the same way home, and while they weren't particularly good friends, apparently she was interested in him because he was more grown-up and smarter than the other, stupid boys.
Hokkaido, Aomori, Akita, Iwate, Mori...
can name all the prefectures and their capitals
If you like him, ya gotta tell him!!
So she worked up the courage and told him how she felt in a New Year's card.
AAHH
I LOVE YOU. YUMA
HAPPY NEW YE
AAHH
BA DUM
BA DUM
BA DUM
I wonder if he'll reply! Whaddya think, Nao?!
He's definitely going to write back, his parents are gonna read it.
Then, a week later...
Aaahhh!! It's here!! Naoooooo!!!
Whoa! Really?!
BA DUM
BA DUM
FLIP
BA DUM
I'm Konato. Got it!
Yuma
I LOVE YOU!!
FROM TAKASHI

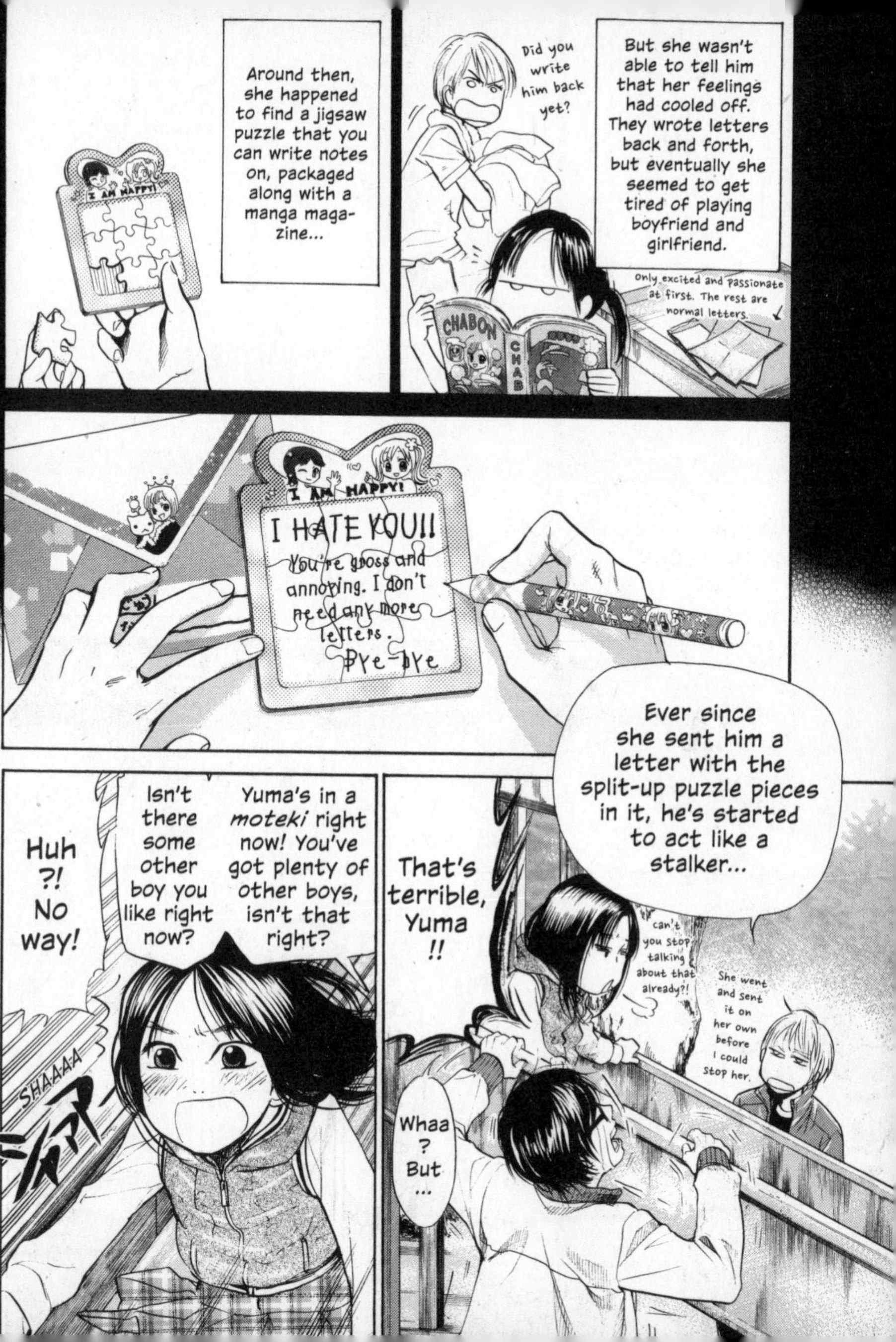

But she wasn't able to tell him that her feelings had cooled off. They wrote letters back and forth, but eventually she seemed to get tired of playing boyfriend and girlfriend.
Did you write him back yet?
Only excited and passionate at first. The rest are normal letters.
CHABON
Around then, she happened to find a jigsaw puzzle that you can write notes on, packaged along with a manga magazine...
I AM HAPPY!
I AM HAPPY!
I HATE YOU!!
You're gross and annoying. I don't need any more letters.
Bye-bye
Ever since she sent him a letter with the split-up puzzle pieces in it, he's started to act like a stalker...
can't you stop talking about that already?!
She went and sent it on her own before I could stop her.
That's terrible, Yuma!!
Whaa? But...
Yuma's in a *moteki* right now! You've got plenty of other boys, isn't that right?
Isn't there some other boy you like right now?
Huh?! No way!
SHAAAA

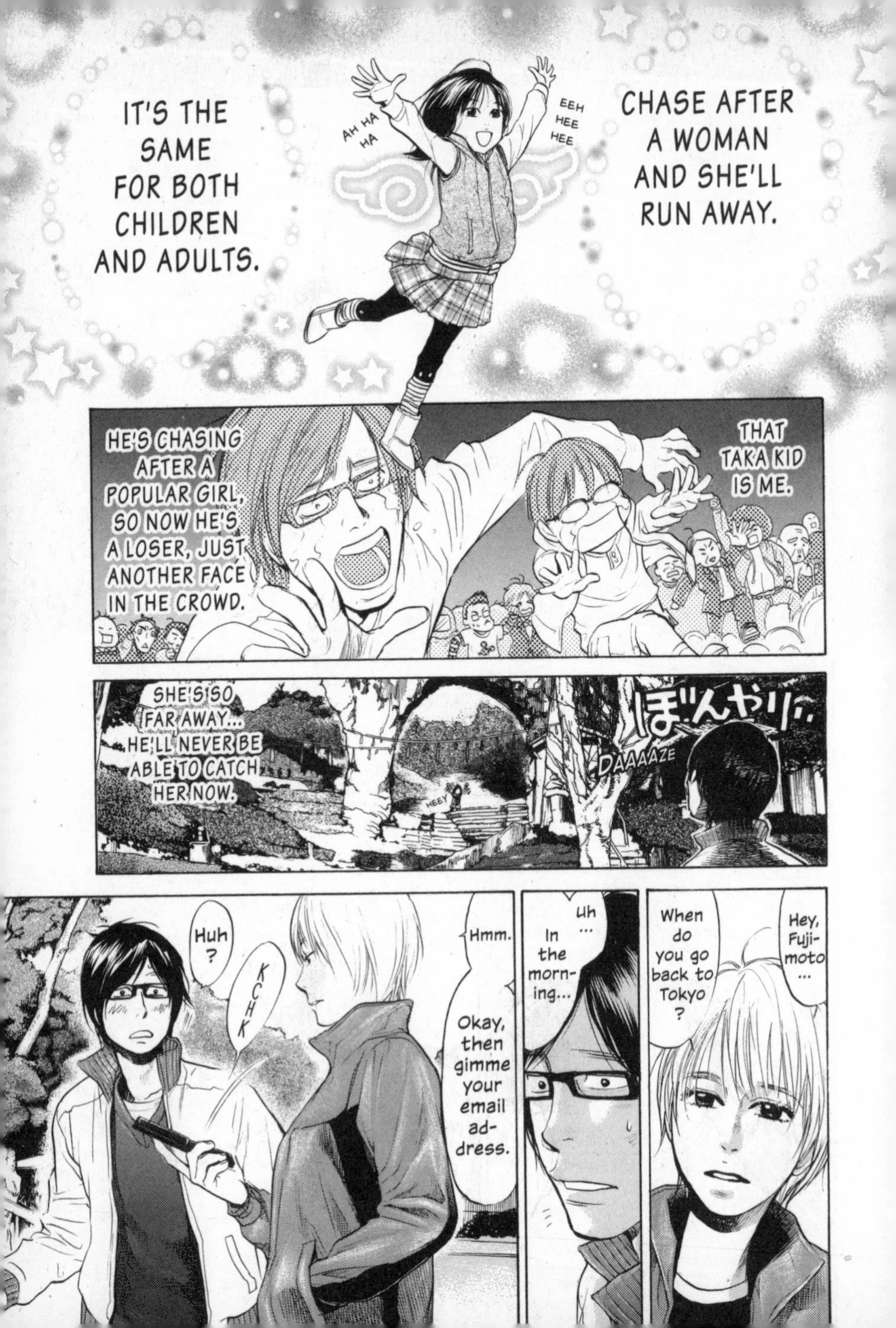
CHASE AFTER A WOMAN AND SHE'LL RUN AWAY.
EEH HEE HEE
AH HA HA
IT'S THE SAME FOR BOTH CHILDREN AND ADULTS.
THAT TAKA KID IS ME.
HE'S CHASING AFTER A POPULAR GIRL, SO NOW HE'S A LOSER, JUST ANOTHER FACE IN THE CROWD.
ぼんやり
DAAAAZE
HEEY
SHE'S SO FAR AWAY... HE'LL NEVER BE ABLE TO CATCH HER NOW.
Hey, Fuji-moto...
When do you go back to Tokyo?
Uh...
In the morn-ing...
Hmm.
Okay, then gimme your email ad-dress.
KCHK
Huh?

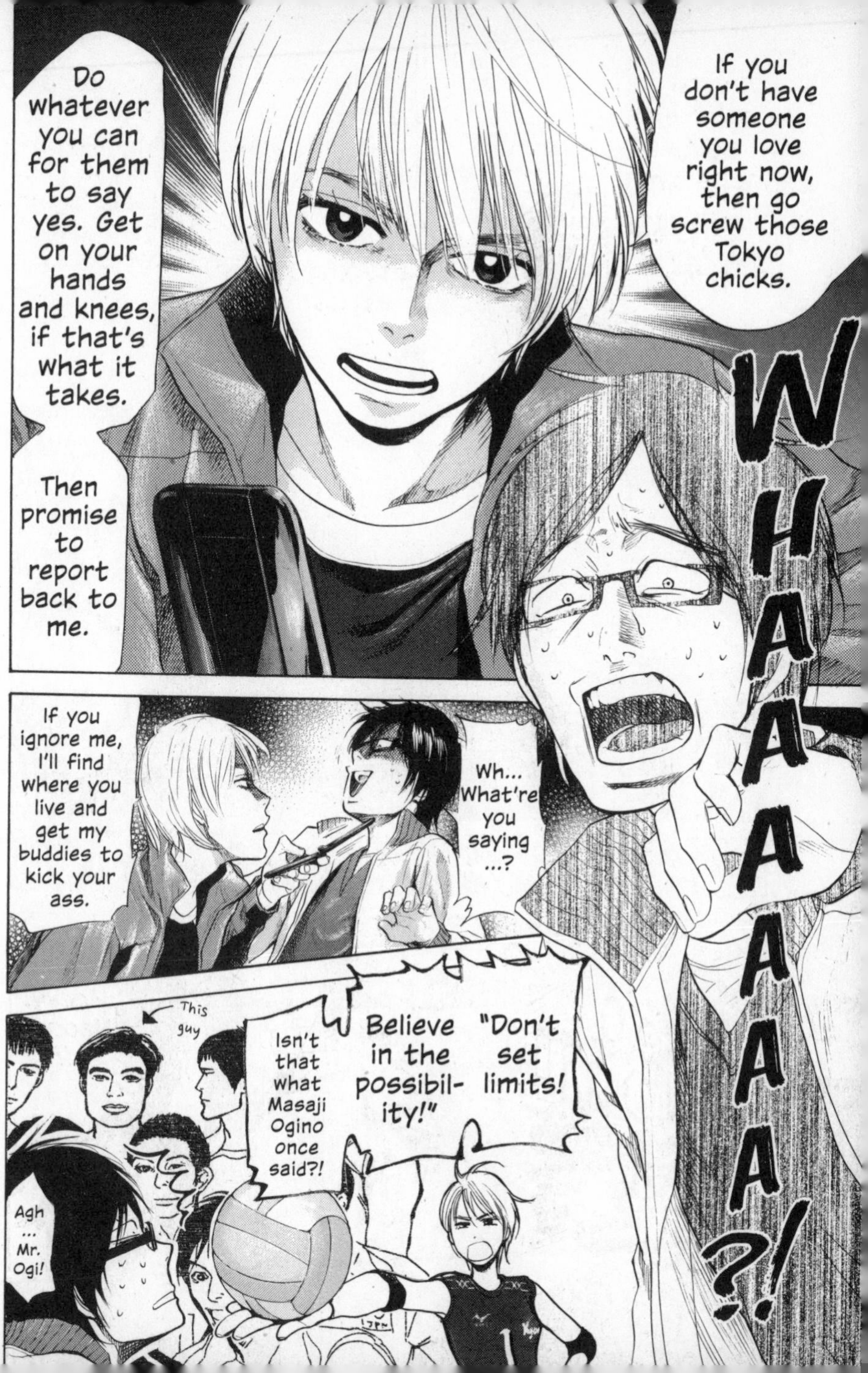
If you don't have someone you love right now, then go screw those Tokyo chicks.
Do whatever you can for them to say yes. Get on your hands and knees, if that's what it takes.
Then promise to report back to me.
If you ignore me, I'll find where you live and get my buddies to kick your ass.
Wh... What're you saying ...?
WHAAAAAAA?!
"Don't set limits!
Believe in the possibil-ity!"
Isn't that what Masaji Ogino once said?!
This guy
Agh ... Mr. Ogi!

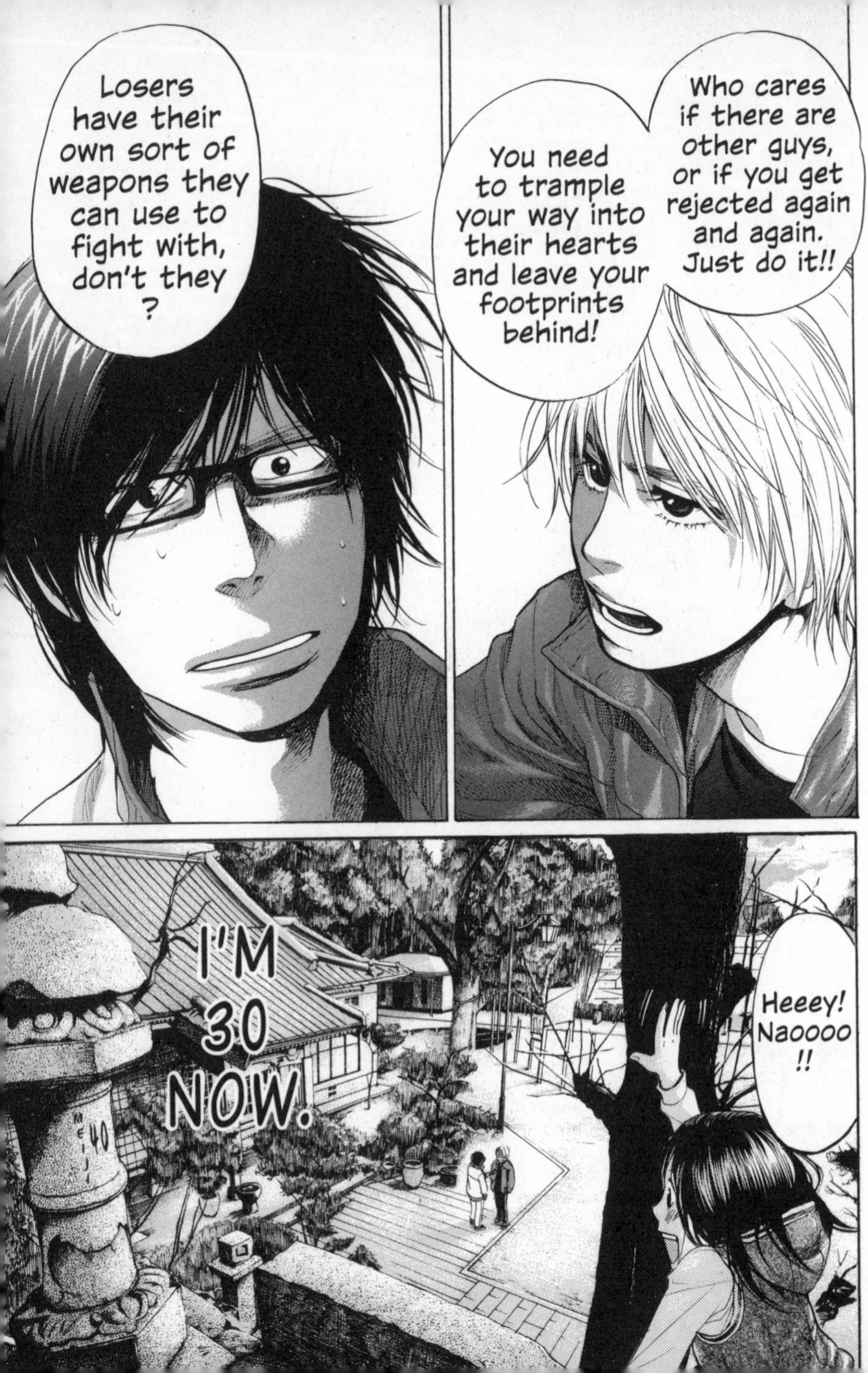
Who cares if there are other guys, or if you get rejected again and again. Just do it!!
You need to trample your way into their hearts and leave your footprints behind!
Losers have their own sort of weapons they can use to fight with, don't they ?
Heeey! Naoooo !!
I'M 30 NOW.
MEIJI 40

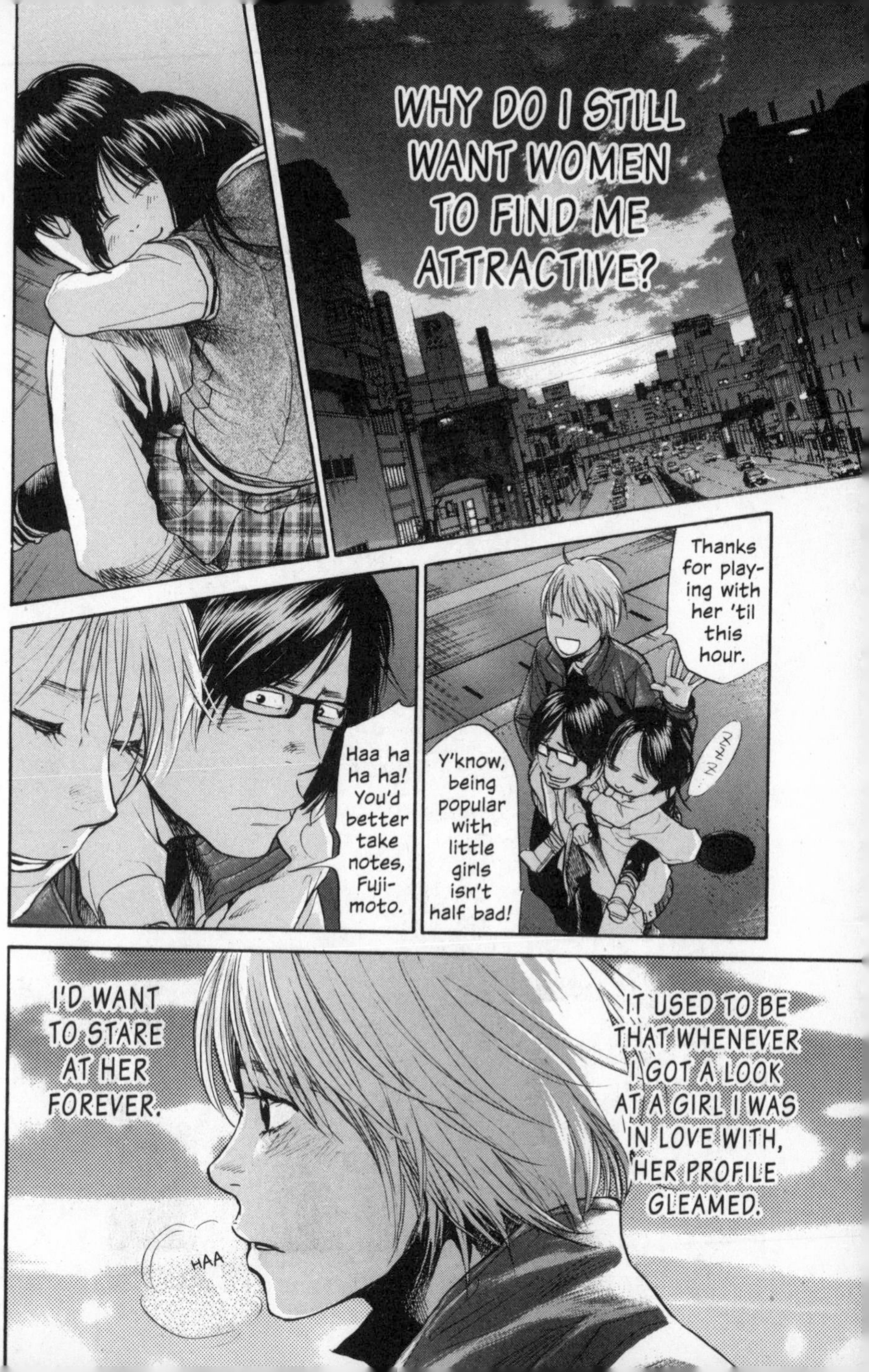
WHY DO I STILL WANT WOMEN TO FIND ME ATTRACTIVE?
Thanks for play-ing with her 'til this hour.
Y'know, being popular with little girls isn't half bad!
Haa ha ha ha! You'd better take notes, Fuji-moto.
IT USED TO BE THAT WHENEVER I GOT A LOOK AT A GIRL I WAS IN LOVE WITH, HER PROFILE GLEAMED.
I'D WANT TO STARE AT HER FOREVER.
HAA

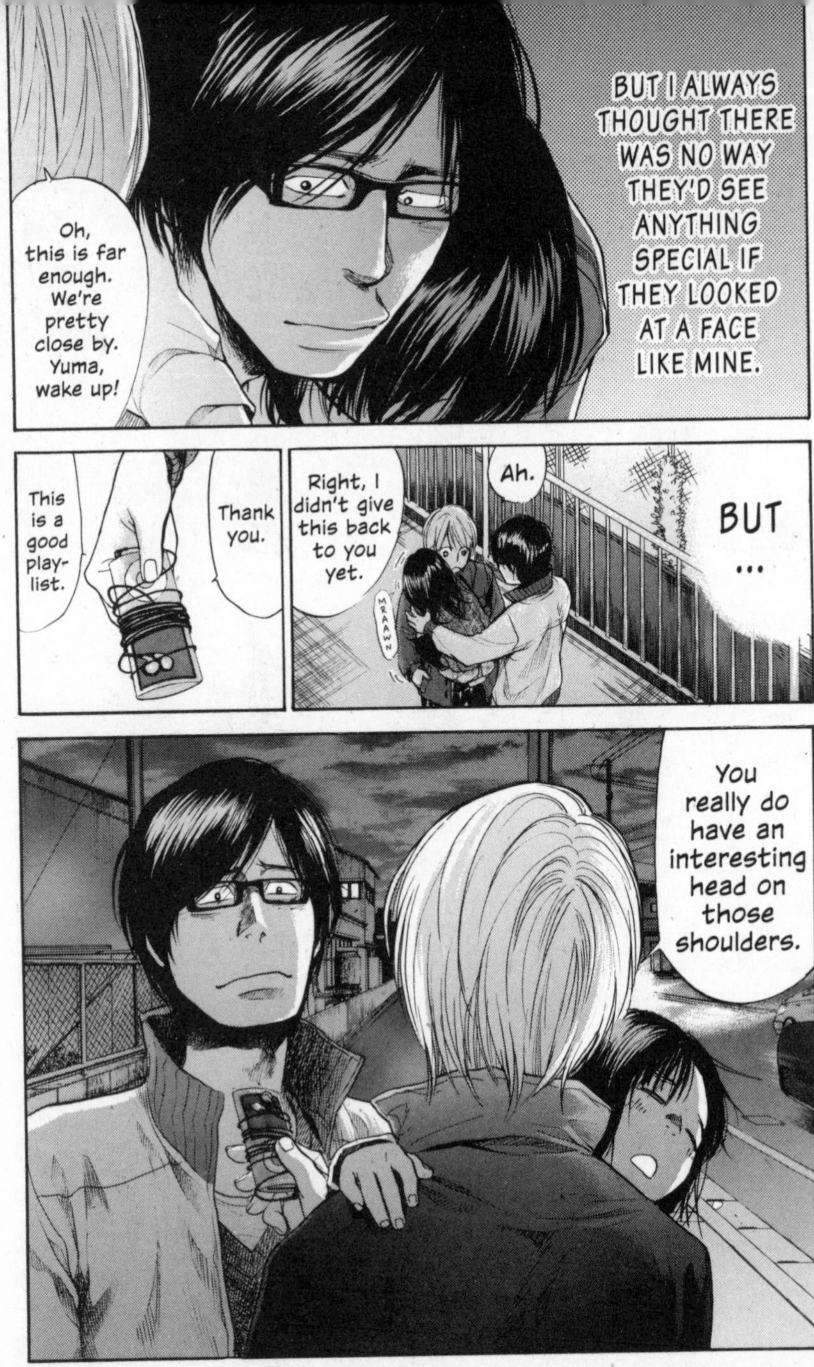
BUT I ALWAYS THOUGHT THERE WAS NO WAY THEY'D SEE ANYTHING SPECIAL IF THEY LOOKED AT A FACE LIKE MINE.
Oh, this is far enough. We're pretty close by. Yuma, wake up!
Ah.
Right, I didn't give this back to you yet.
MRAAWN
BUT ...
Thank you.
This is a good play-list.
You really do have an interesting head on those shoulders.

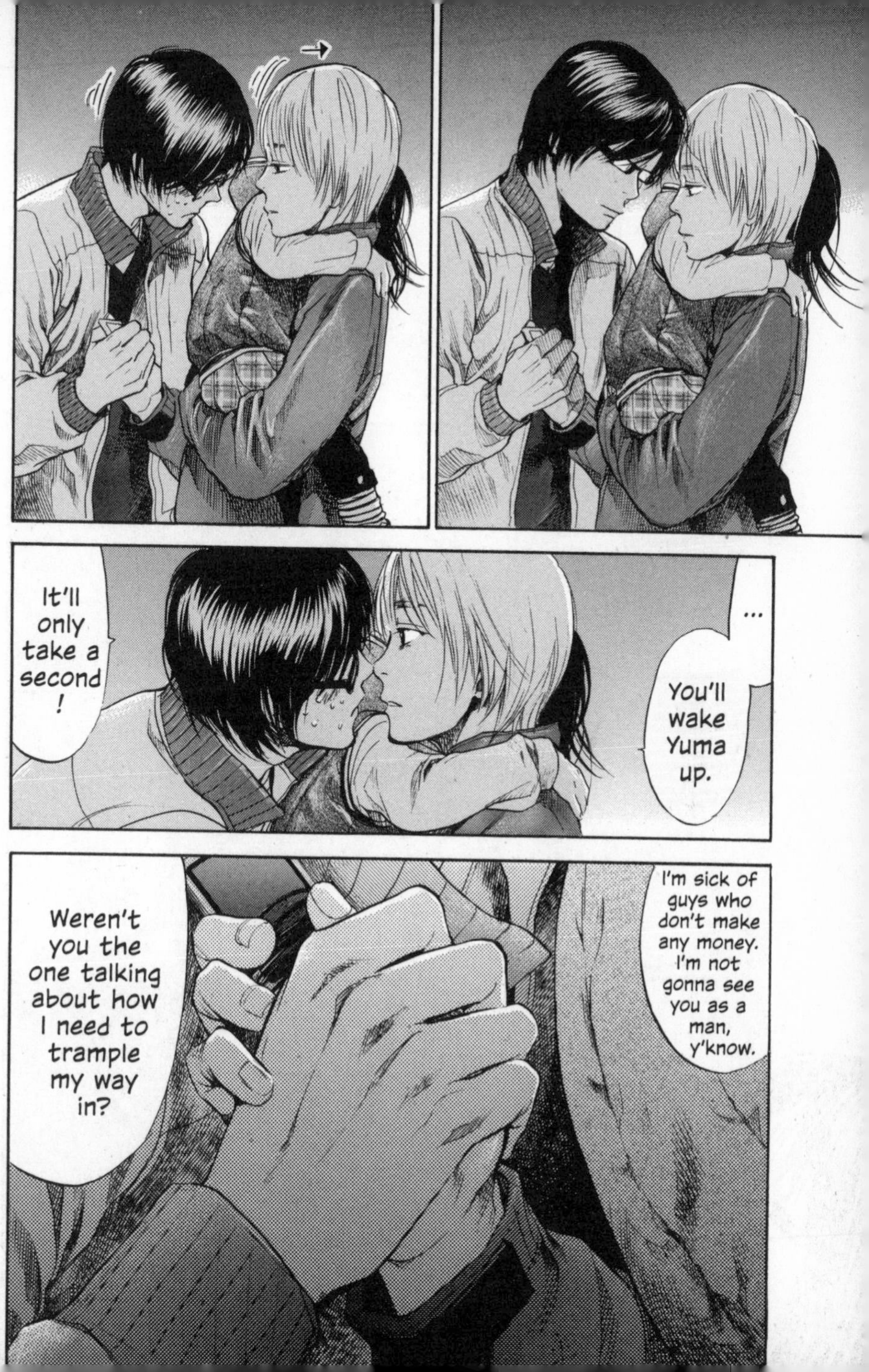
...
You'll wake Yuma up.
It'll only take a second!
I'm sick of guys who don't make any money. I'm not gonna see you as a man, y'know.
Weren't you the one talking about how I need to trample my way in?

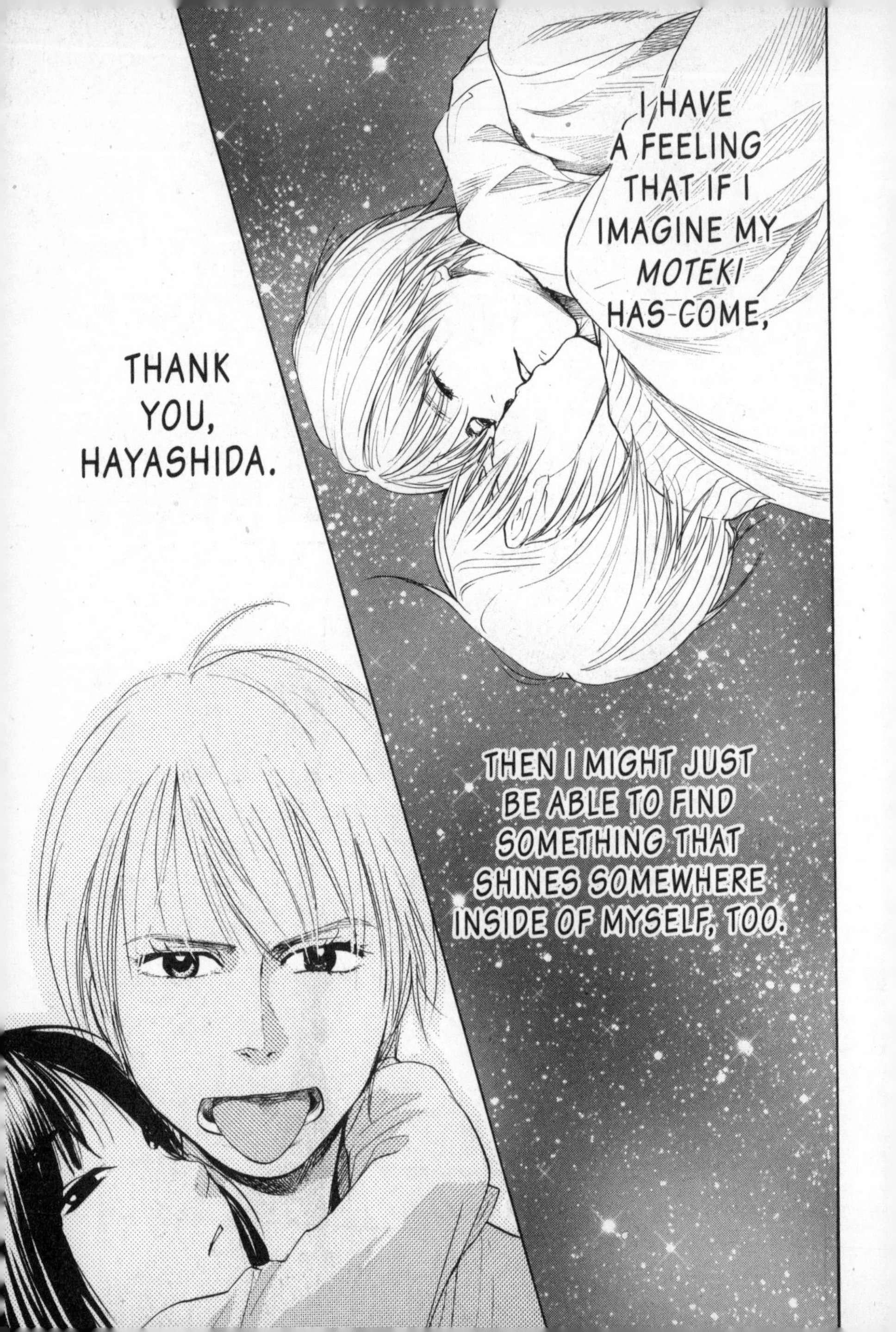
I HAVE A FEELING THAT IF I IMAGINE MY *MOTEKI* HAS COME,
THEN I MIGHT JUST BE ABLE TO FIND SOMETHING THAT SHINES SOMEWHERE INSIDE OF MYSELF, TOO.
THANK YOU, HAYASHIDA.

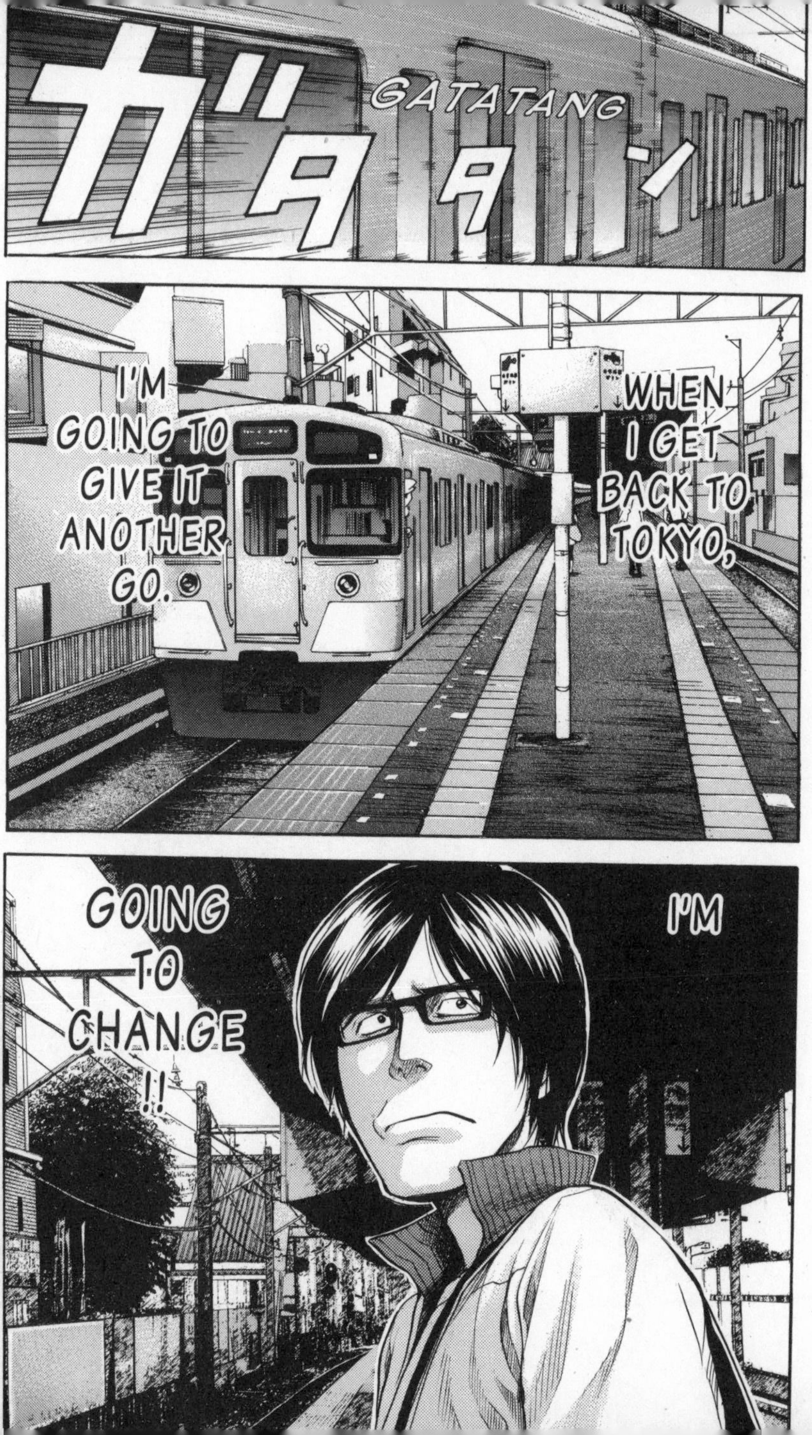
ガタターン
GATATANG
WHEN I GET BACK TO TOKYO,
I'M GOING TO GIVE IT ANOTHER GO.
I'M
GOING TO CHANGE !!

chapter 9 ♥ END

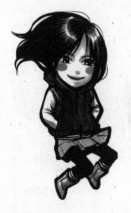

Moteki   Mitsurou Kubo

Moteki

Mitsurou Kubo

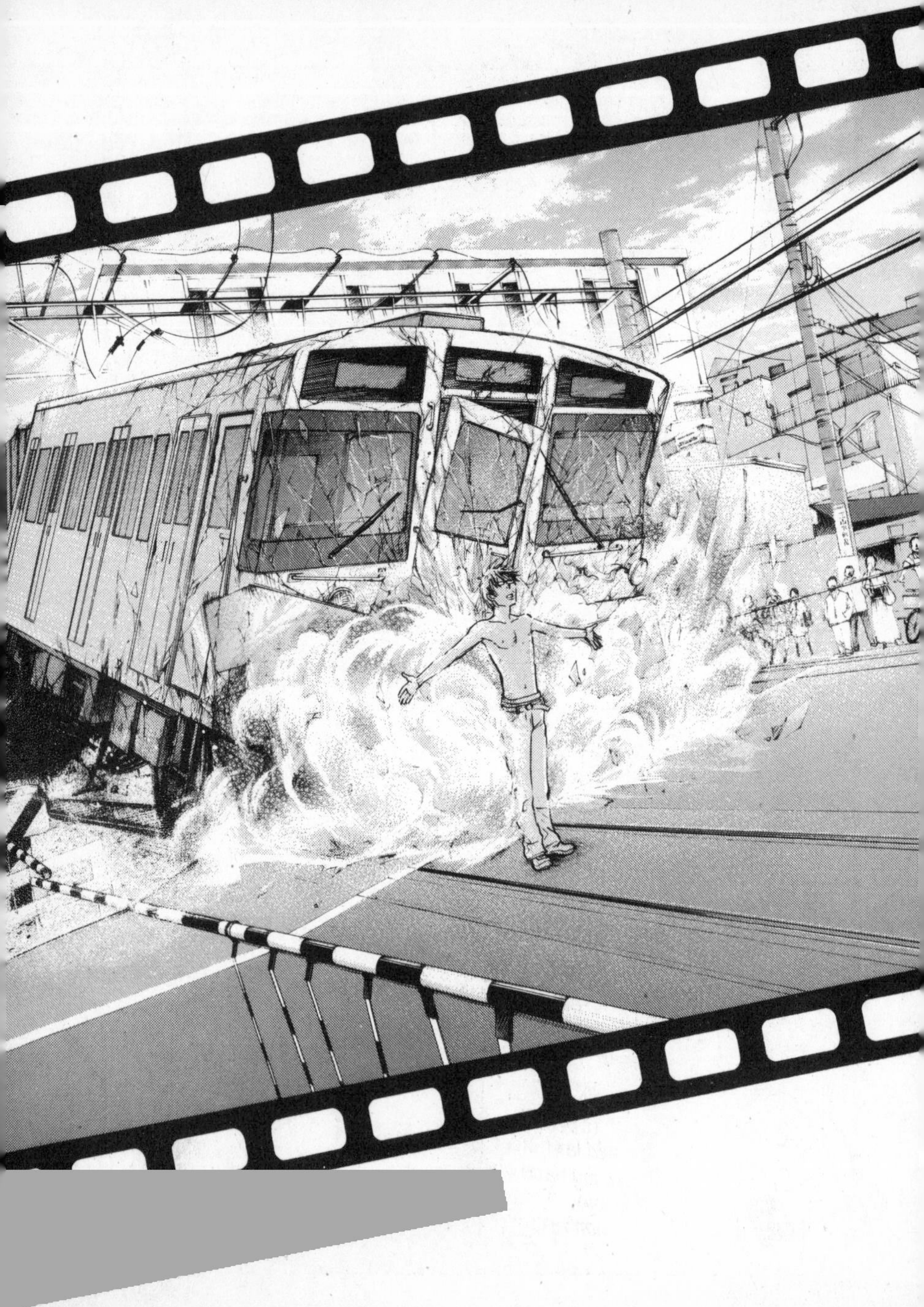

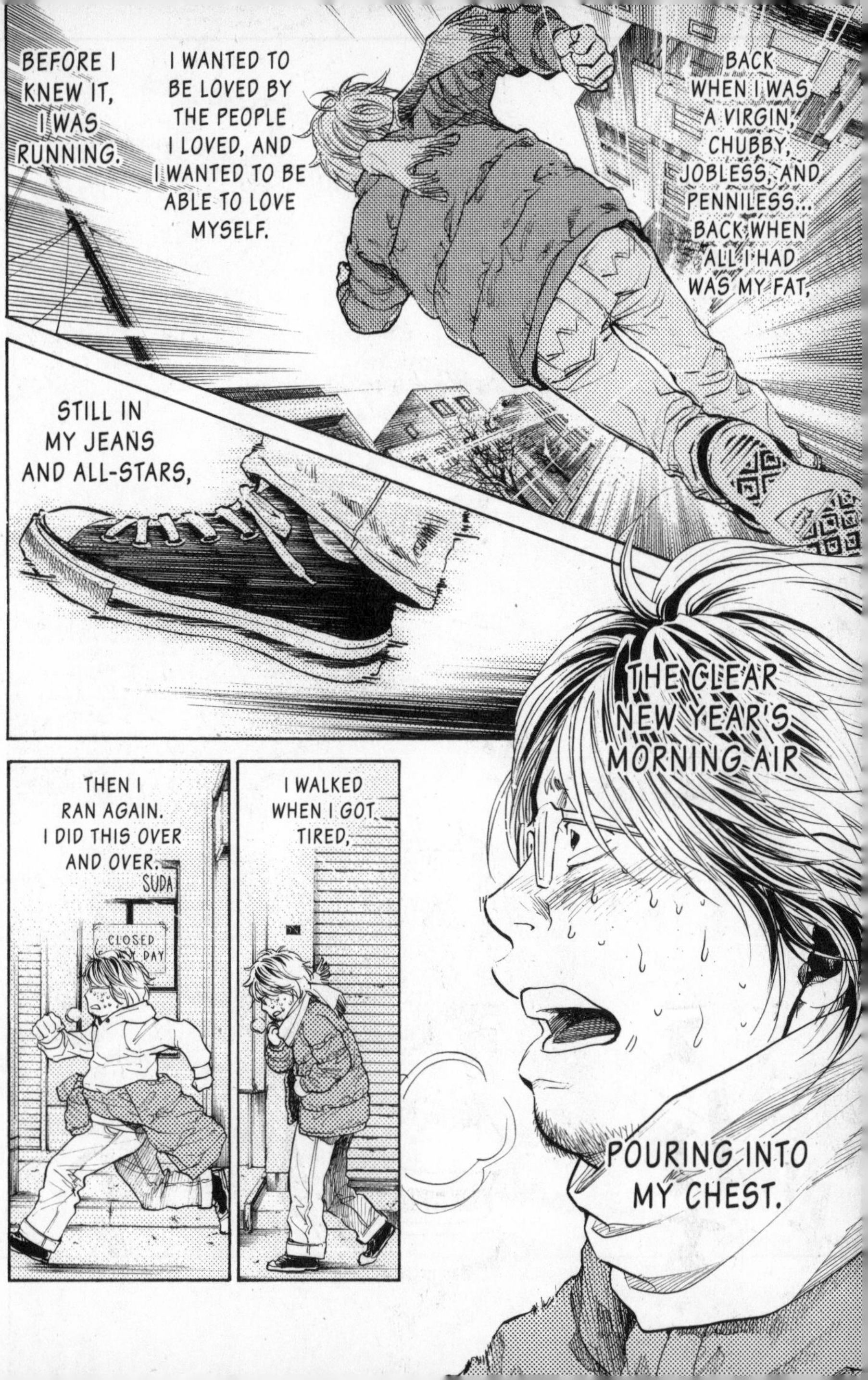
BACK WHEN I WAS A VIRGIN, CHUBBY, JOBLESS, AND PENNILESS... BACK WHEN ALL I HAD WAS MY FAT,
I WANTED TO BE LOVED BY THE PEOPLE I LOVED, AND I WANTED TO BE ABLE TO LOVE MYSELF.
BEFORE I KNEW IT, I WAS RUNNING.
THE CLEAR NEW YEAR'S MORNING AIR
POURING INTO MY CHEST.
STILL IN MY JEANS AND ALL-STARS,
I WALKED WHEN I GOT TIRED,
THEN I RAN AGAIN. I DID THIS OVER AND OVER.
SUDA
CLOSED

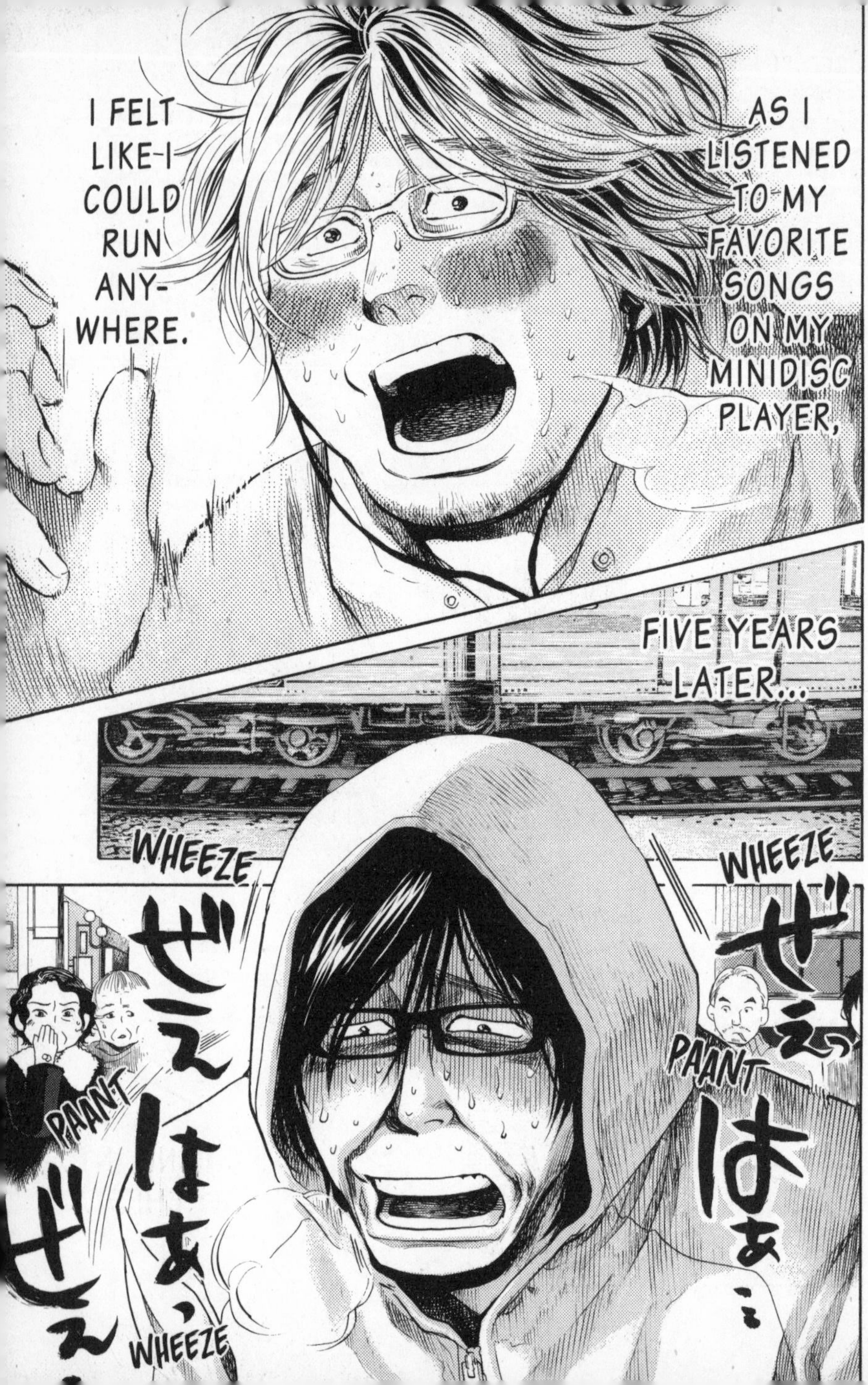
AS I LISTENED TO MY FAVORITE SONGS ON MY MINIDISC PLAYER,
I FELT LIKE I COULD RUN ANYWHERE.
FIVE YEARS LATER...
WHEEZE
ぜぇっ
PAANT
はぁ
WHEEZE
ぜぇ
PAANT
はぁっ
WHEEZE
ぜぇ

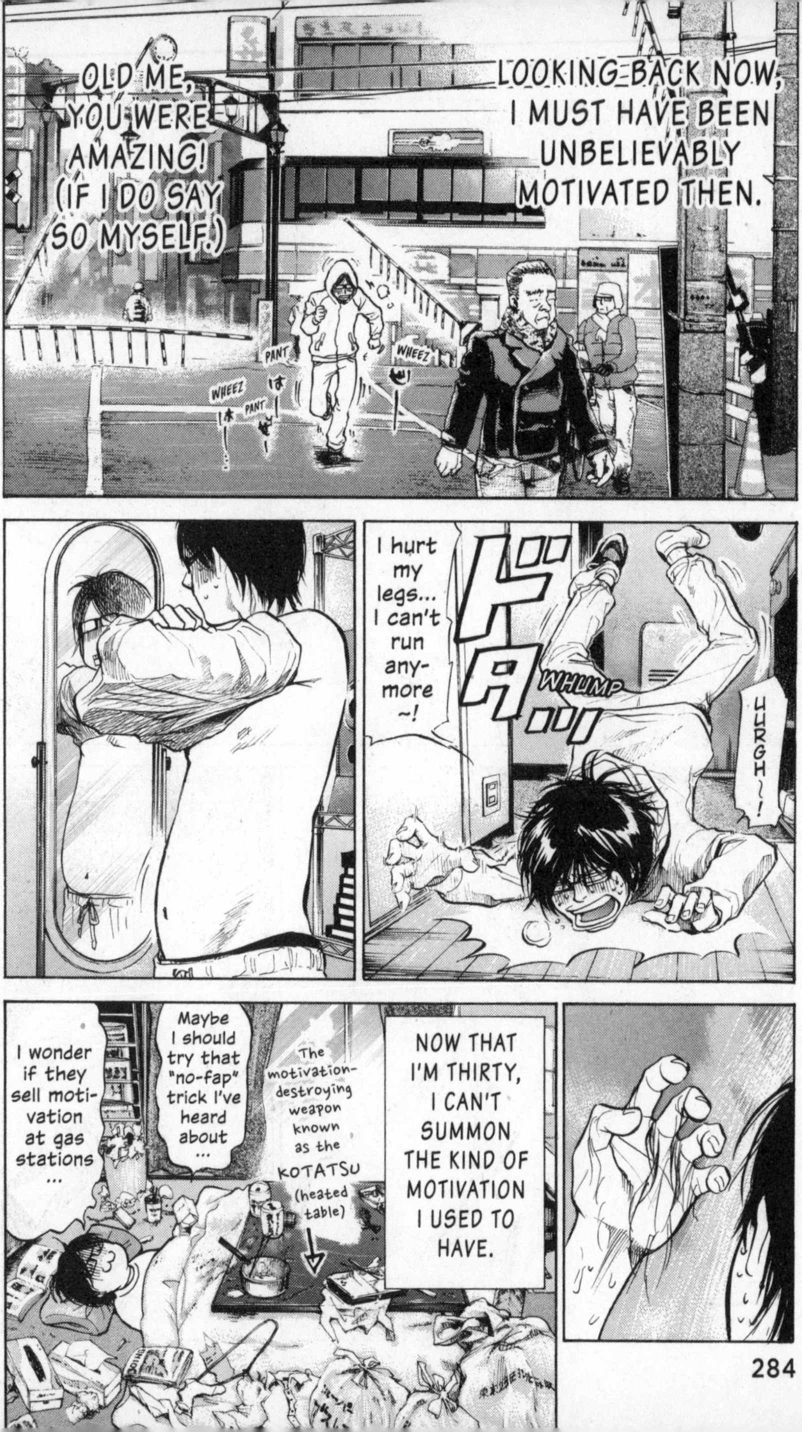
LOOKING BACK NOW, I MUST HAVE BEEN UNBELIEVABLY MOTIVATED THEN.
OLD ME, YOU WERE AMAZING! (IF I DO SAY SO MYSELF.)
WHEEZ
PANT
PANT
WHEEZ
I hurt my legs... I can't run any-more ~!
WHUMP
URGH~!
NOW THAT I'M THIRTY, I CAN'T SUMMON THE KIND OF MOTIVATION I USED TO HAVE.
The motivation-destroying weapon known as the KOTATSU (heated table)
Maybe I should try that "no-fap" trick I've heard about ...
I wonder if they sell moti-vation at gas stations ...

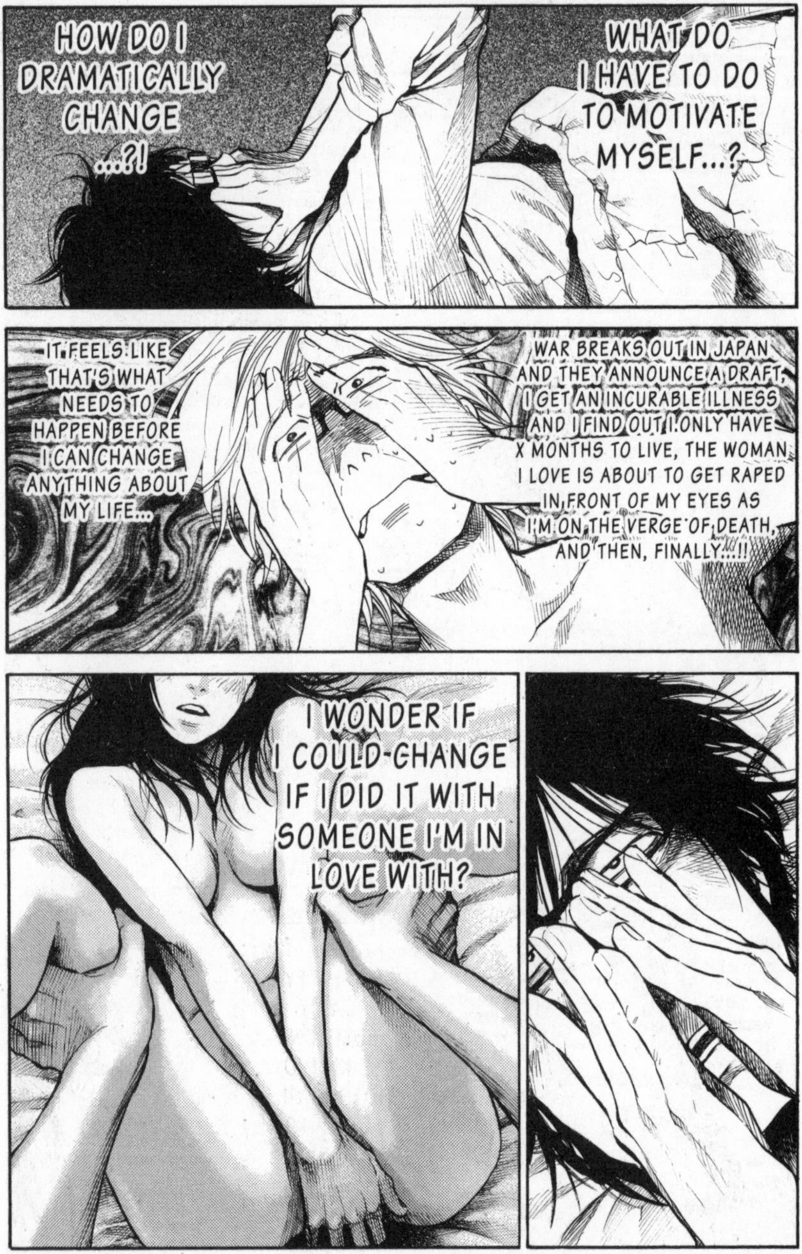
WHAT DO I HAVE TO DO TO MOTIVATE MYSELF...?
HOW DO I DRAMATICALLY CHANGE ...?!
WAR BREAKS OUT IN JAPAN AND THEY ANNOUNCE A DRAFT, I GET AN INCURABLE ILLNESS AND I FIND OUT I ONLY HAVE X MONTHS TO LIVE, THE WOMAN I LOVE IS ABOUT TO GET RAPED IN FRONT OF MY EYES AS I'M ON THE VERGE OF DEATH, AND THEN, FINALLY...!!
IT FEELS LIKE THAT'S WHAT NEEDS TO HAPPEN BEFORE I CAN CHANGE ANYTHING ABOUT MY LIFE...
I WONDER IF I COULD CHANGE IF I DID IT WITH SOMEONE I'M IN LOVE WITH?

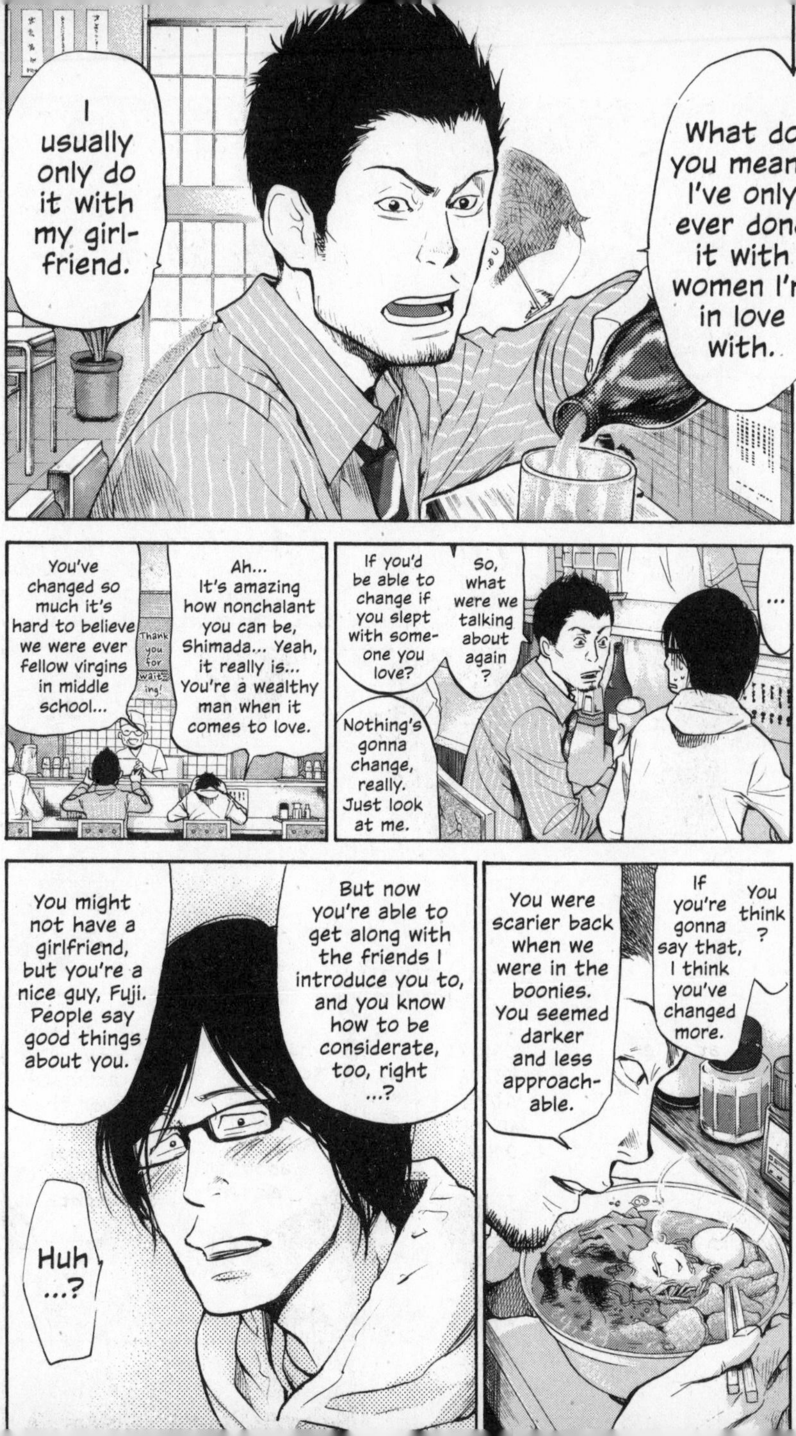
Huh? What do you mean? I've only ever done it with women I'm in love with.
I usually only do it with my girlfriend.
...
So, what were we talking about again?
If you'd be able to change if you slept with someone you love?
Nothing's gonna change, really. Just look at me.
Ah... It's amazing how nonchalant you can be, Shimada... Yeah, it really is... You're a wealthy man when it comes to love.
Thank you for wait-ing!
You've changed so much it's hard to believe we were ever fellow virgins in middle school...
You think?
If you're gonna say that, I think you've changed more.
You were scarier back when we were in the boonies. You seemed darker and less approachable.
But now you're able to get along with the friends I introduce you to, and you know how to be considerate, too, right...?
You might not have a girlfriend, but you're a nice guy, Fuji. People say good things about you.
Huh...?

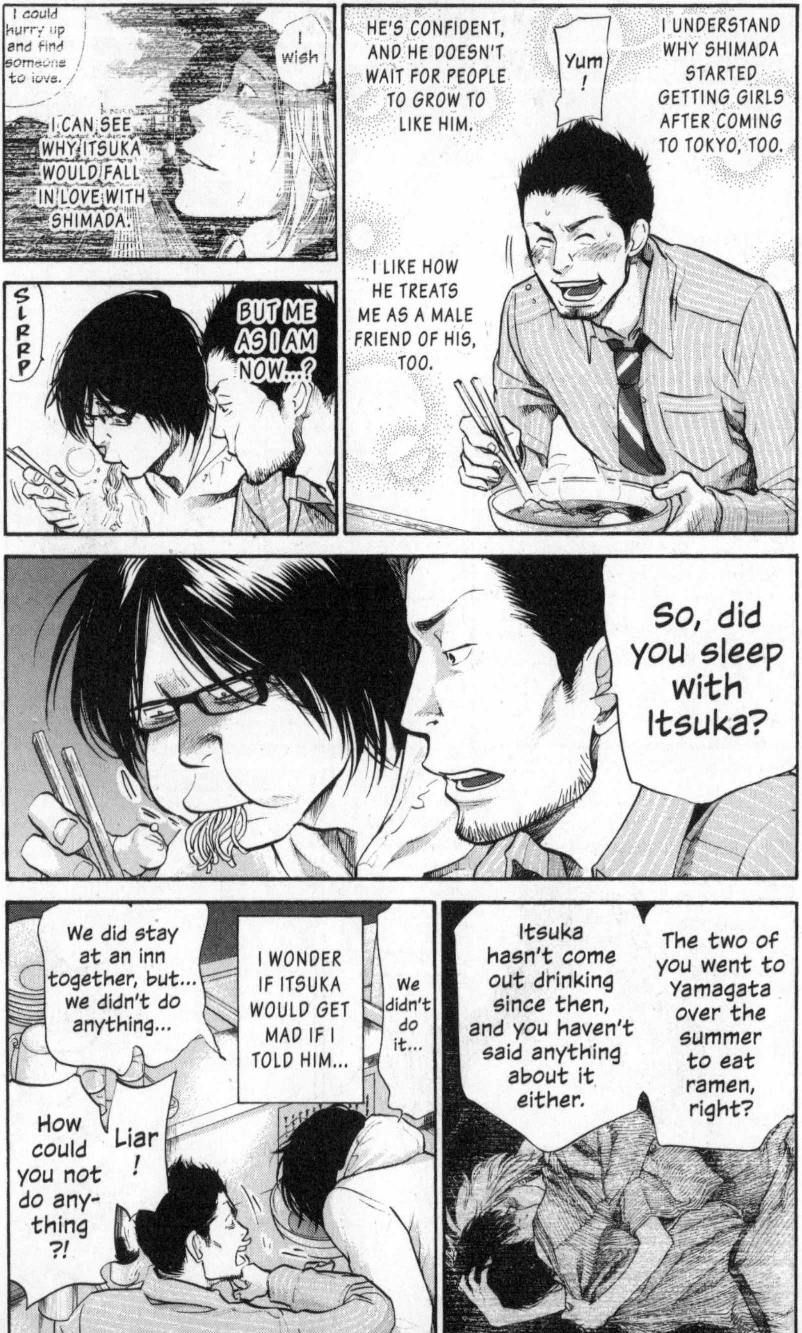
I UNDERSTAND WHY SHIMADA STARTED GETTING GIRLS AFTER COMING TO TOKYO, TOO.
Yum!
HE'S CONFIDENT, AND HE DOESN'T WAIT FOR PEOPLE TO GROW TO LIKE HIM.
I LIKE HOW HE TREATS ME AS A MALE FRIEND OF HIS, TOO.
I wish
I could hurry up and find someone to love.
I CAN SEE WHY ITSUKA WOULD FALL IN LOVE WITH SHIMADA.
BUT ME AS I AM NOW...?
SLRRP
So, did you sleep with Itsuka?
The two of you went to Yamagata over the summer to eat ramen, right?
Itsuka hasn't come out drinking since then, and you haven't said anything about it either.
We didn't do it...
I WONDER IF ITSUKA WOULD GET MAD IF I TOLD HIM...
We did stay at an inn together, but... we didn't do anything...
Liar!
How could you not do anything?!

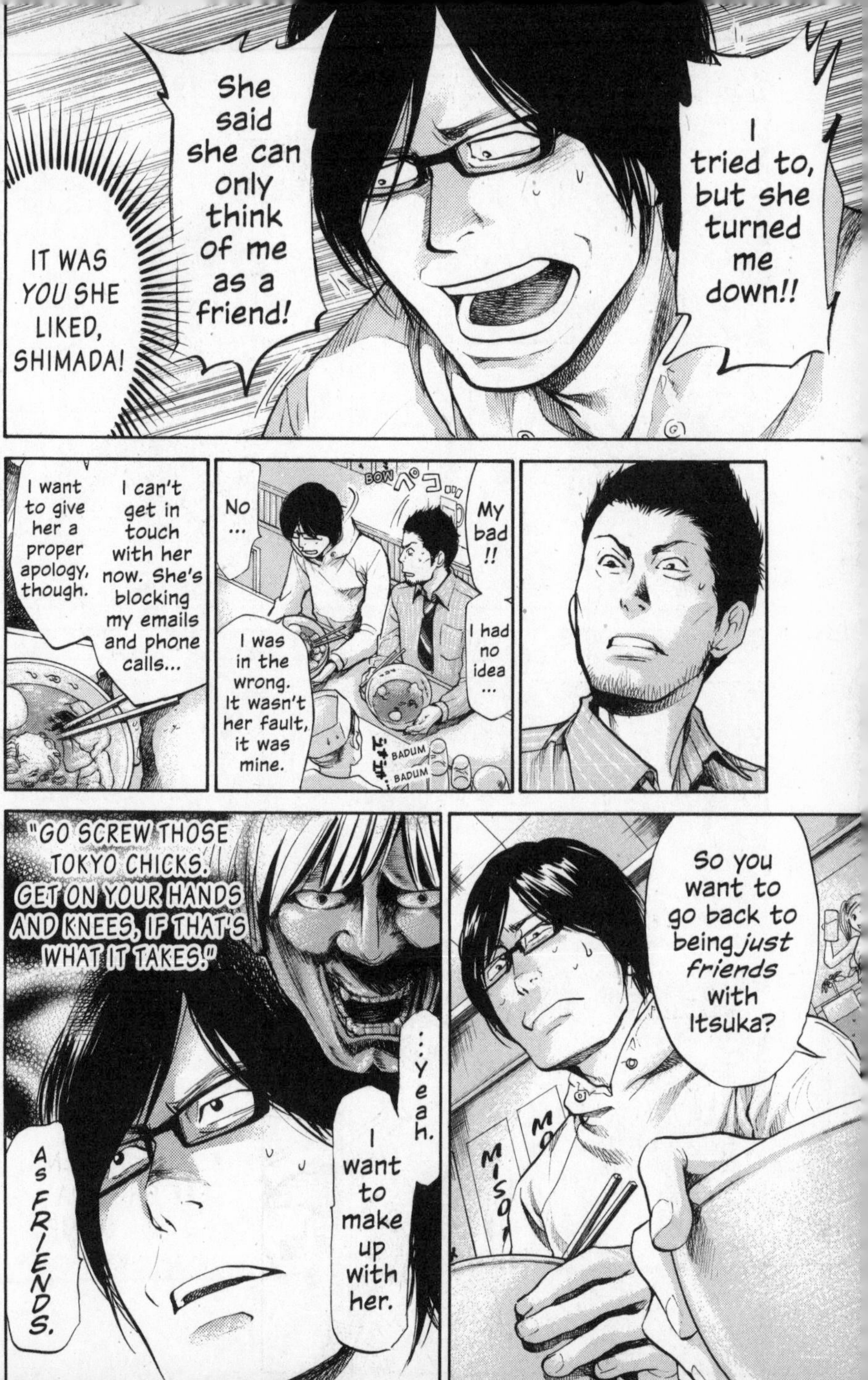
I tried to, but she turned me down!!
She said she can only think of me as a friend!
IT WAS *YOU* SHE LIKED, SHIMADA!
BOW
My bad!!
I had no idea...
No...
I was in the wrong. It wasn't her fault, it was mine.
BADUM
BADUM
I can't get in touch with her now. She's blocking my emails and phone calls...
I want to give her a proper apology, though.
So you want to go back to being *just friends* with Itsuka?
MISO
...Yeah.
I want to make up with her.
"GO SCREW THOSE TOKYO CHICKS. GET ON YOUR HANDS AND KNEES, IF THAT'S WHAT IT TAKES."
AS FRIENDS.

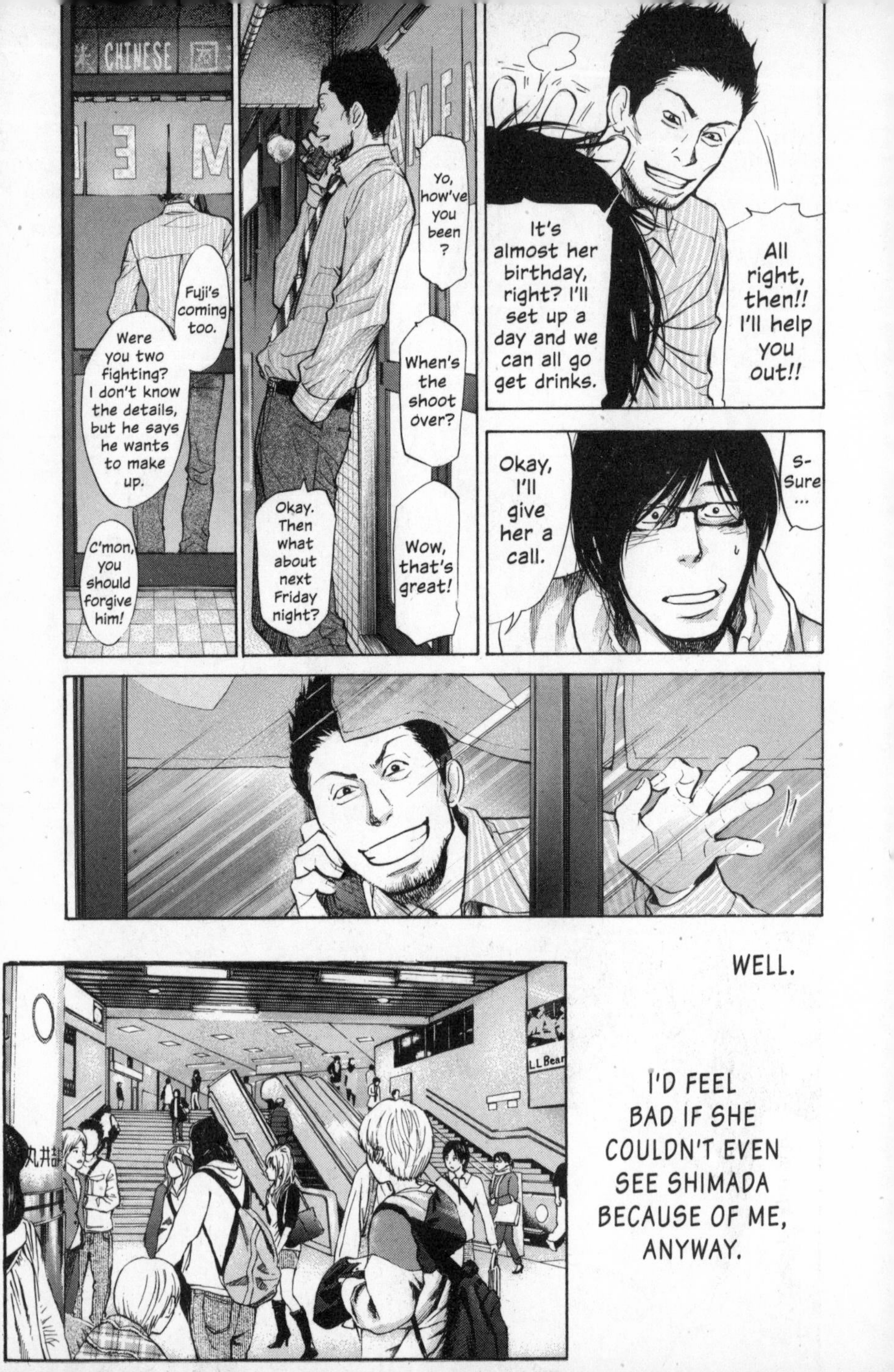
All right, then!! I'll help you out!!
It's almost her birthday, right? I'll set up a day and we can all go get drinks.
S-Sure...
Okay, I'll give her a call.
Yo, how've you been?
When's the shoot over?
Wow, that's great!
Okay. Then what about next Friday night?
CHINESE
Fuji's coming too.
Were you two fighting? I don't know the details, but he says he wants to make up.
C'mon, you should forgive him!
WELL.
I'D FEEL BAD IF SHE COULDN'T EVEN SEE SHIMADA BECAUSE OF ME, ANYWAY.

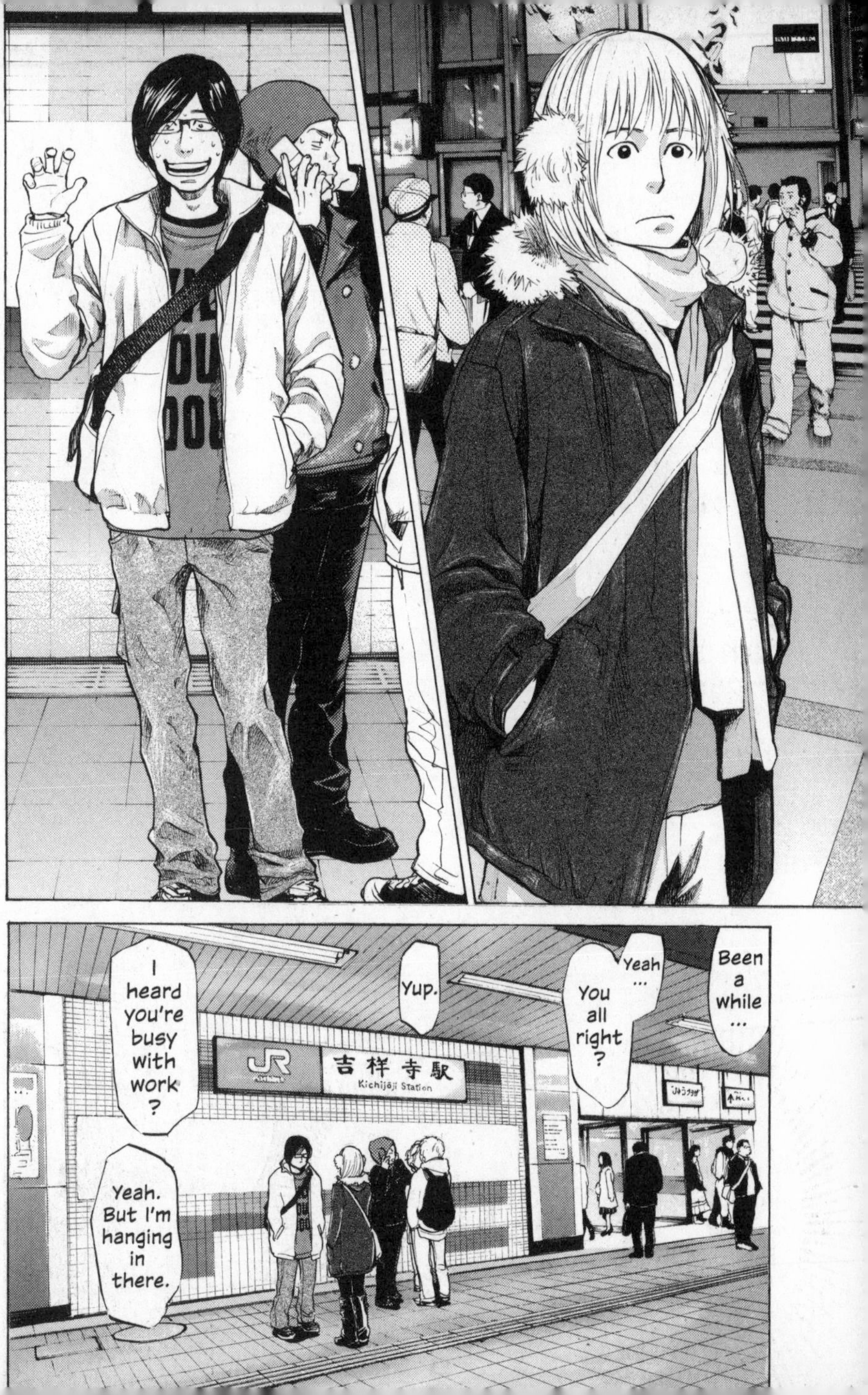
Been a while ...
Yeah ...
You all right?
Yup.
I heard you're busy with work?
JR
吉祥寺駅
Kichijōji Station
Yeah. But I'm hanging in there.

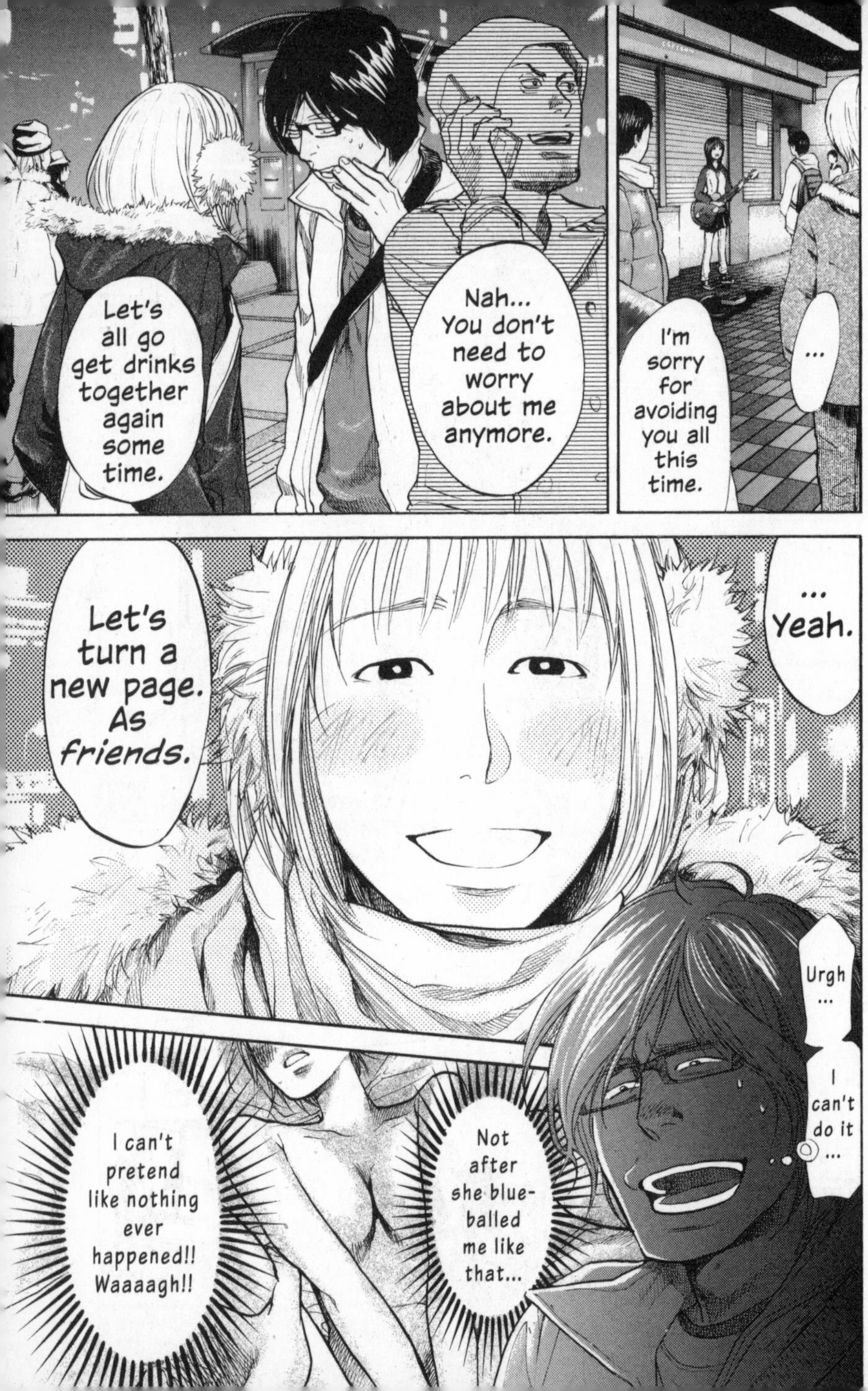
...
I'm sorry for avoiding you all this time.
Nah... You don't need to worry about me anymore.
Let's all go get drinks together again some time.
... Yeah.
Let's turn a new page. As *friends.*
Urgh ...
I can't do it ...
Not after she blue-balled me like that...
I can't pretend like nothing ever happened!! Waaaagh!!

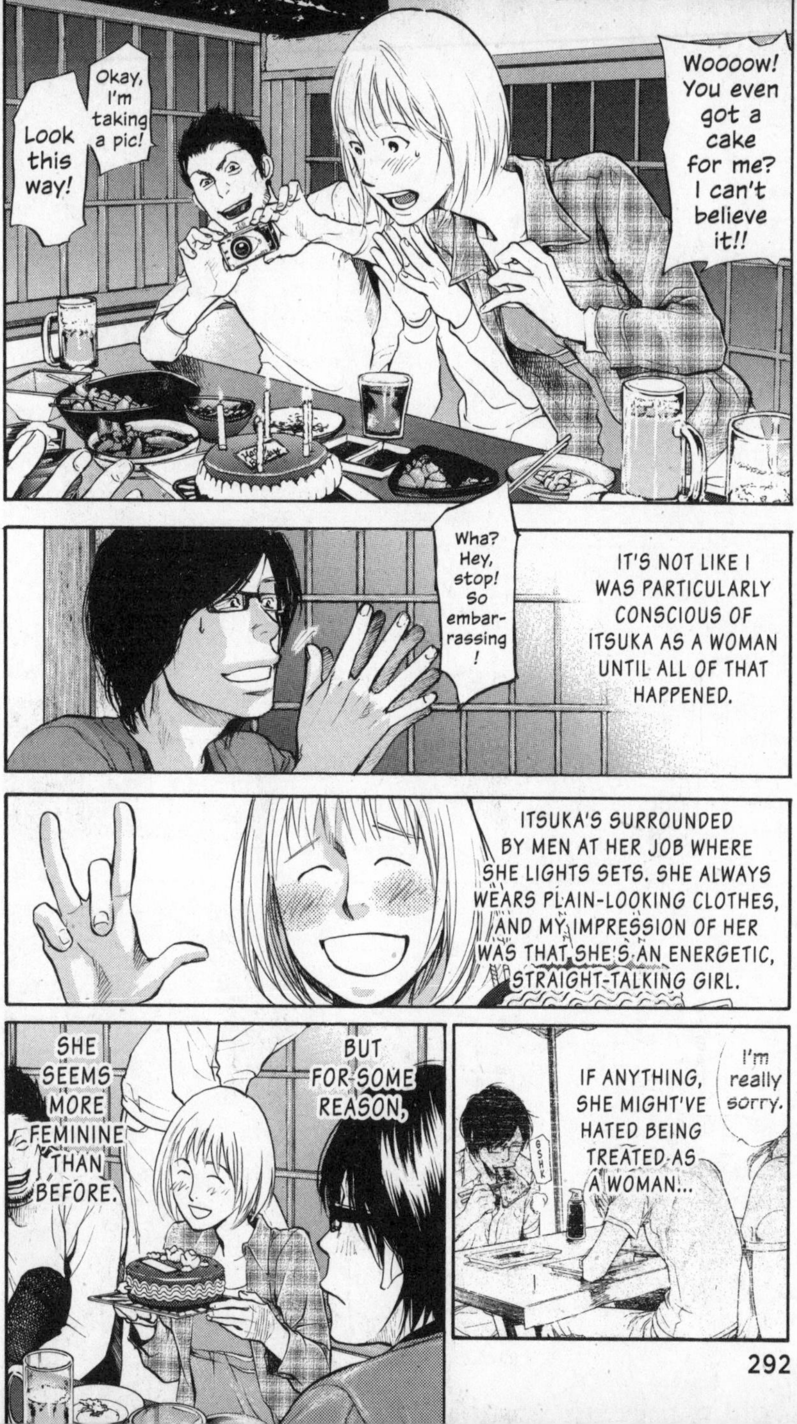
Wooooow! You even got a cake for me? I can't believe it!!
Okay, I'm taking a pic!
Look this way!
IT'S NOT LIKE I WAS PARTICULARLY CONSCIOUS OF ITSUKA AS A WOMAN UNTIL ALL OF THAT HAPPENED.
Wha? Hey, stop! So embarrassing!
ITSUKA'S SURROUNDED BY MEN AT HER JOB WHERE SHE LIGHTS SETS. SHE ALWAYS WEARS PLAIN-LOOKING CLOTHES, AND MY IMPRESSION OF HER WAS THAT SHE'S AN ENERGETIC, STRAIGHT-TALKING GIRL.
I'm really sorry.
IF ANYTHING, SHE MIGHT'VE HATED BEING TREATED AS A WOMAN...
GSHK
BUT FOR SOME REASON,
SHE SEEMS MORE FEMININE THAN BEFORE.

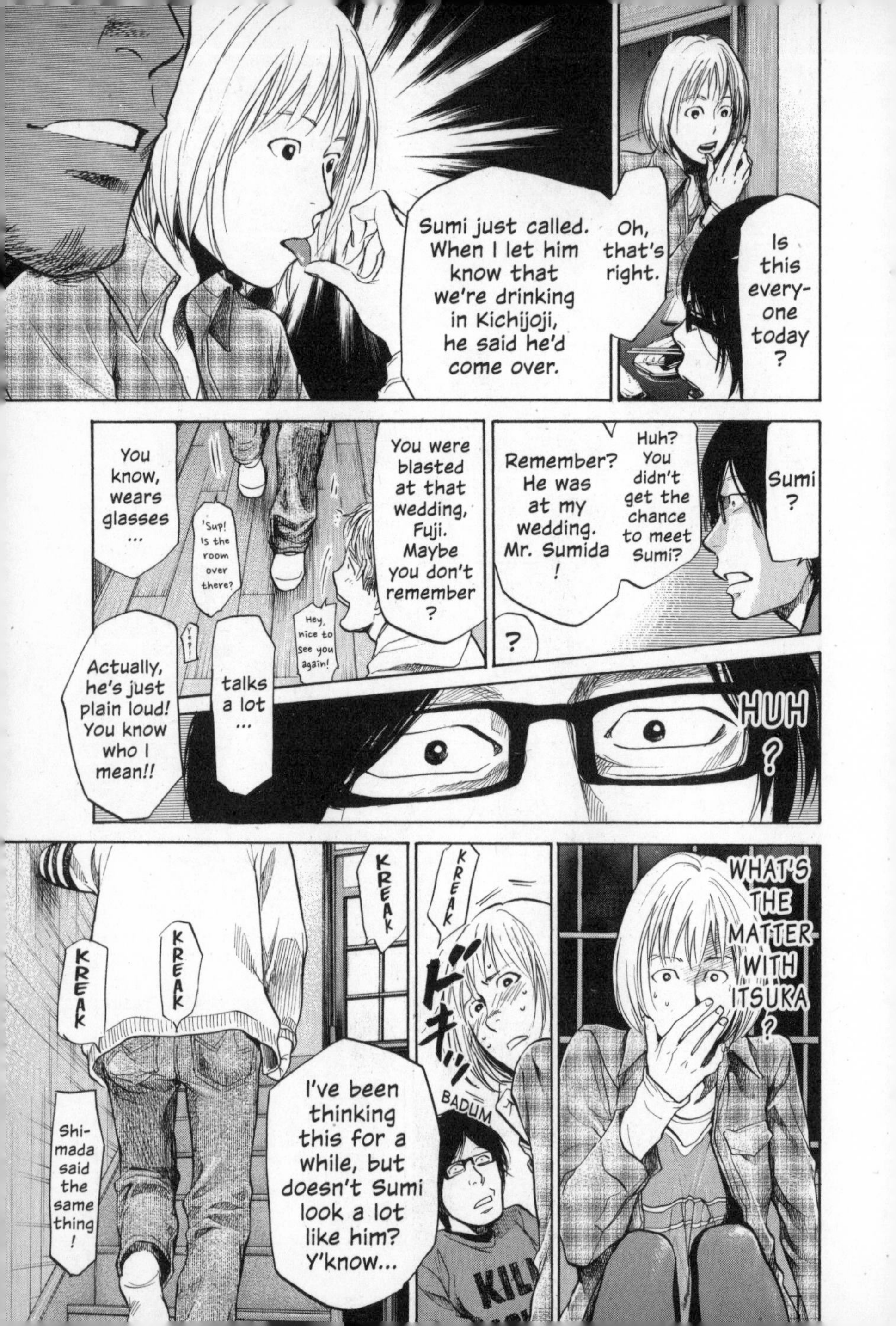
Is this every-one today?
Oh, that's right.
Sumi just called. When I let him know that we're drinking in Kichijoji, he said he'd come over.
Sumi?
Huh? You didn't get the chance to meet Sumi?
Remember? He was at my wedding. Mr. Sumida!
?
You were blasted at that wedding, Fuji. Maybe you don't remember?
You know, wears glasses...
'Sup! Is the room over there?
Hey, nice to see you again!
Yep!
talks a lot...
Actually, he's just plain loud! You know who I mean!!
HUH?
WHAT'S THE MATTER WITH ITSUKA?
KREAK
BADUM
I've been thinking this for a while, but doesn't Sumi look a lot like him? Y'know...
KREAK
KREAK
KREAK
Shi-mada said the same thing!

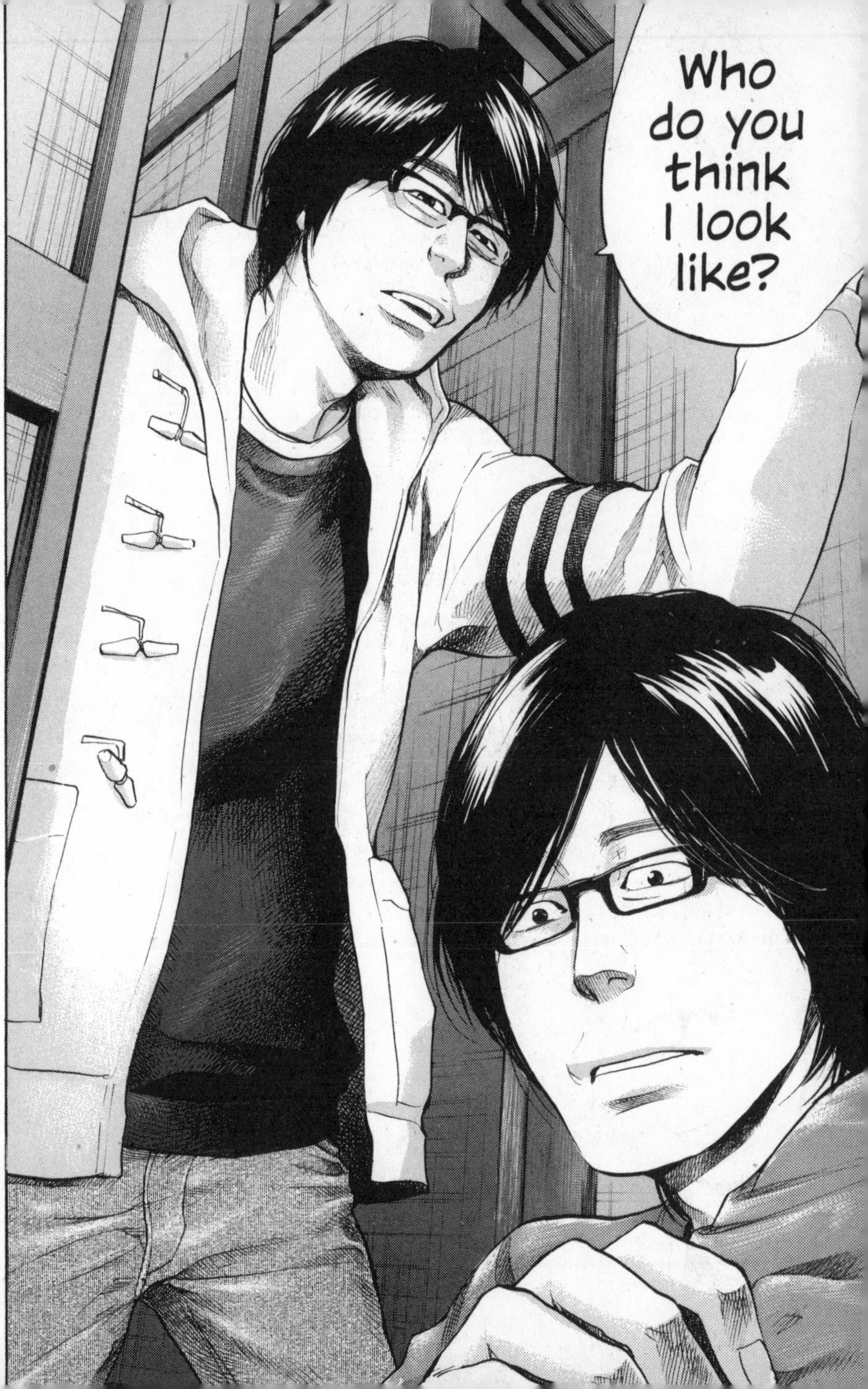
Who do you think I look like?

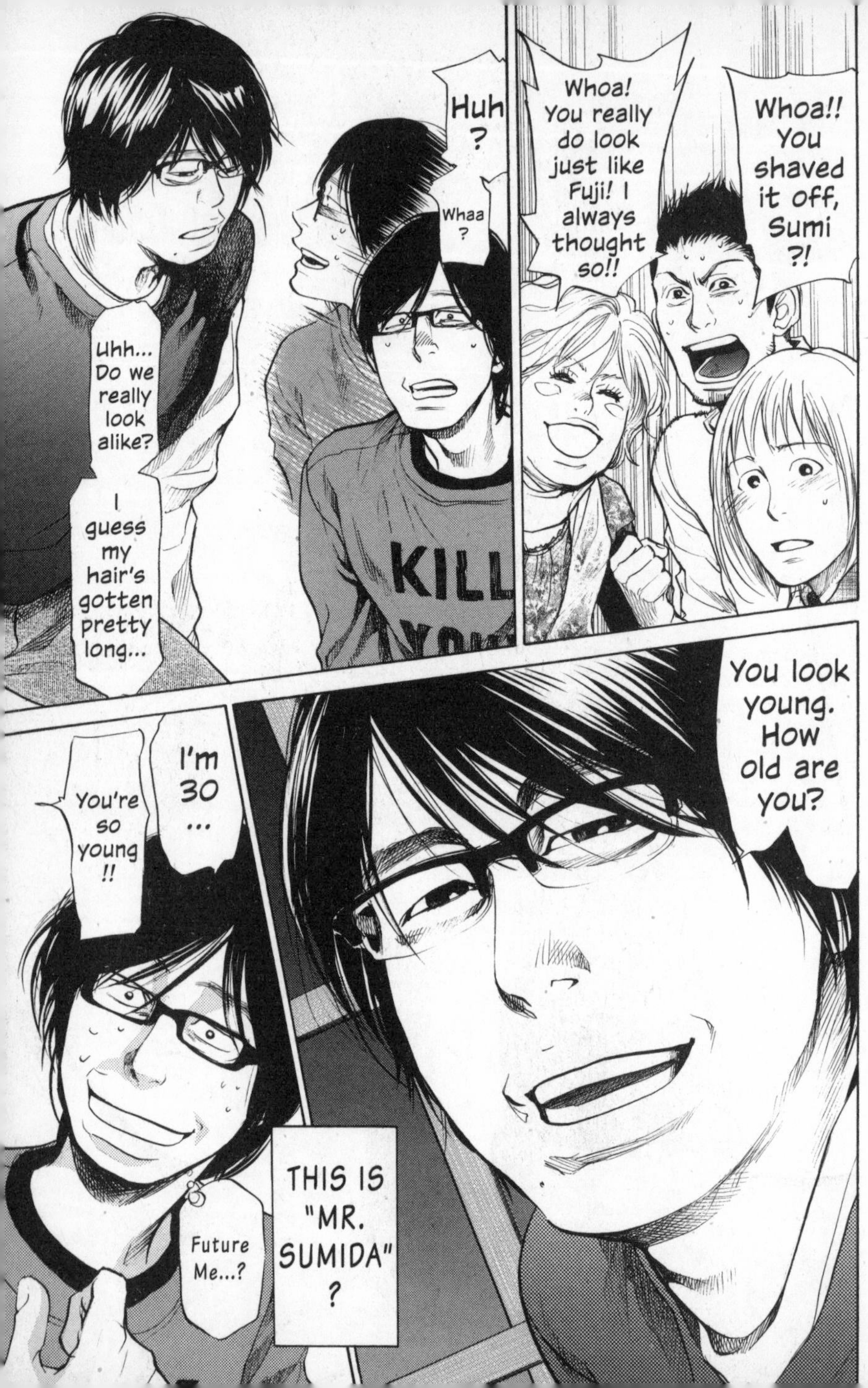
Whoa!! You shaved it off, Sumi?!
Whoa! You really do look just like Fuji! I always thought so!!
Huh?
Whaa?
Uhh... Do we really look alike?
I guess my hair's gotten pretty long...
You look young. How old are you?
THIS IS "MR. SUMIDA"?
I'm 30...
You're so young!!
Future Me...?

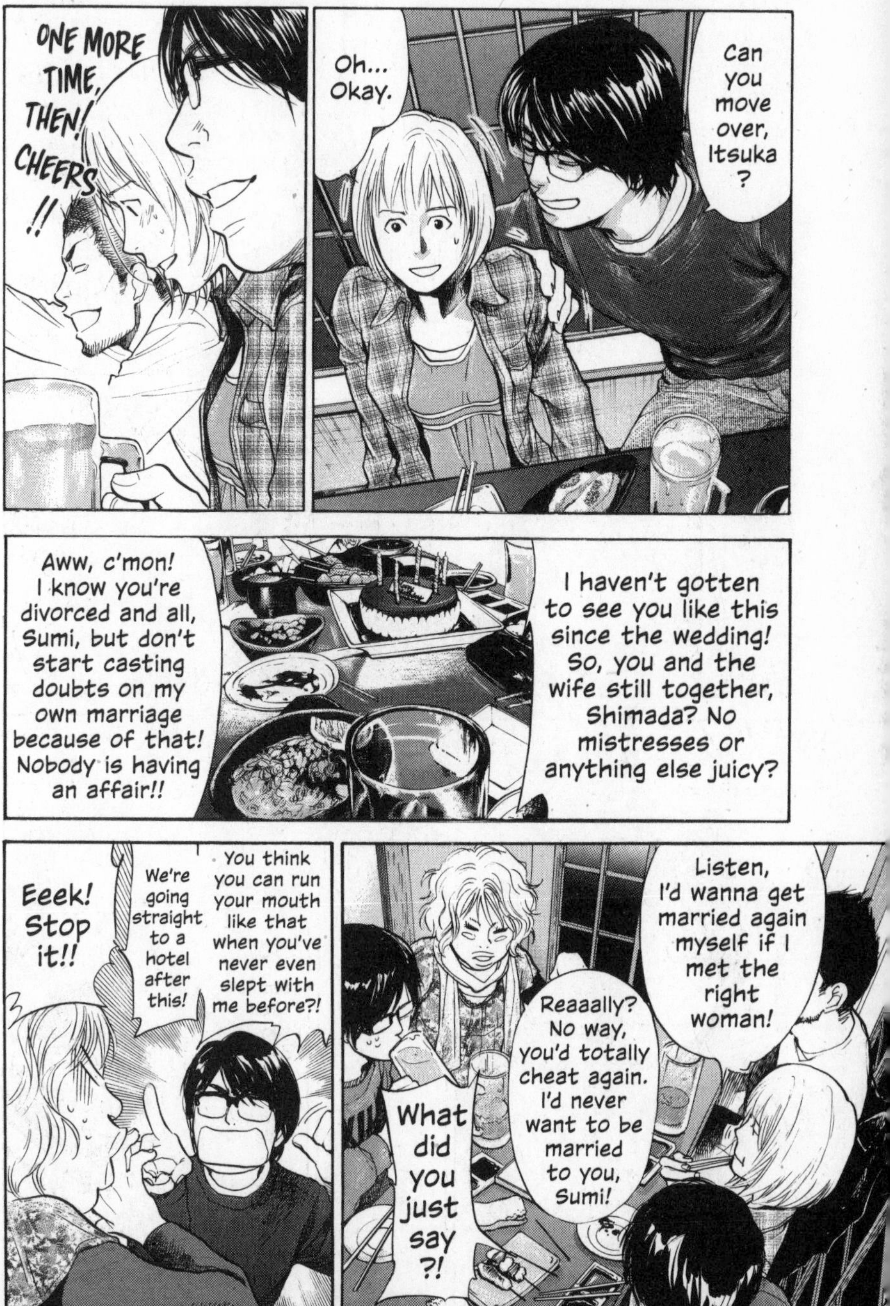
Can you move over, Itsuka?
Oh... Okay.
ONE MORE TIME, THEN! CHEERS!!
I haven't gotten to see you like this since the wedding! So, you and the wife still together, Shimada? No mistresses or anything else juicy?
Aww, c'mon! I know you're divorced and all, Sumi, but don't start casting doubts on my own marriage because of that! Nobody is having an affair!!
Listen, I'd wanna get married again myself if I met the right woman!
Reaaally? No way, you'd totally cheat again. I'd never want to be married to you, Sumi!
What did you just say?!
You think you can run your mouth like that when you've never even slept with me before?!
We're going straight to a hotel after this!
Eeek! Stop it!!

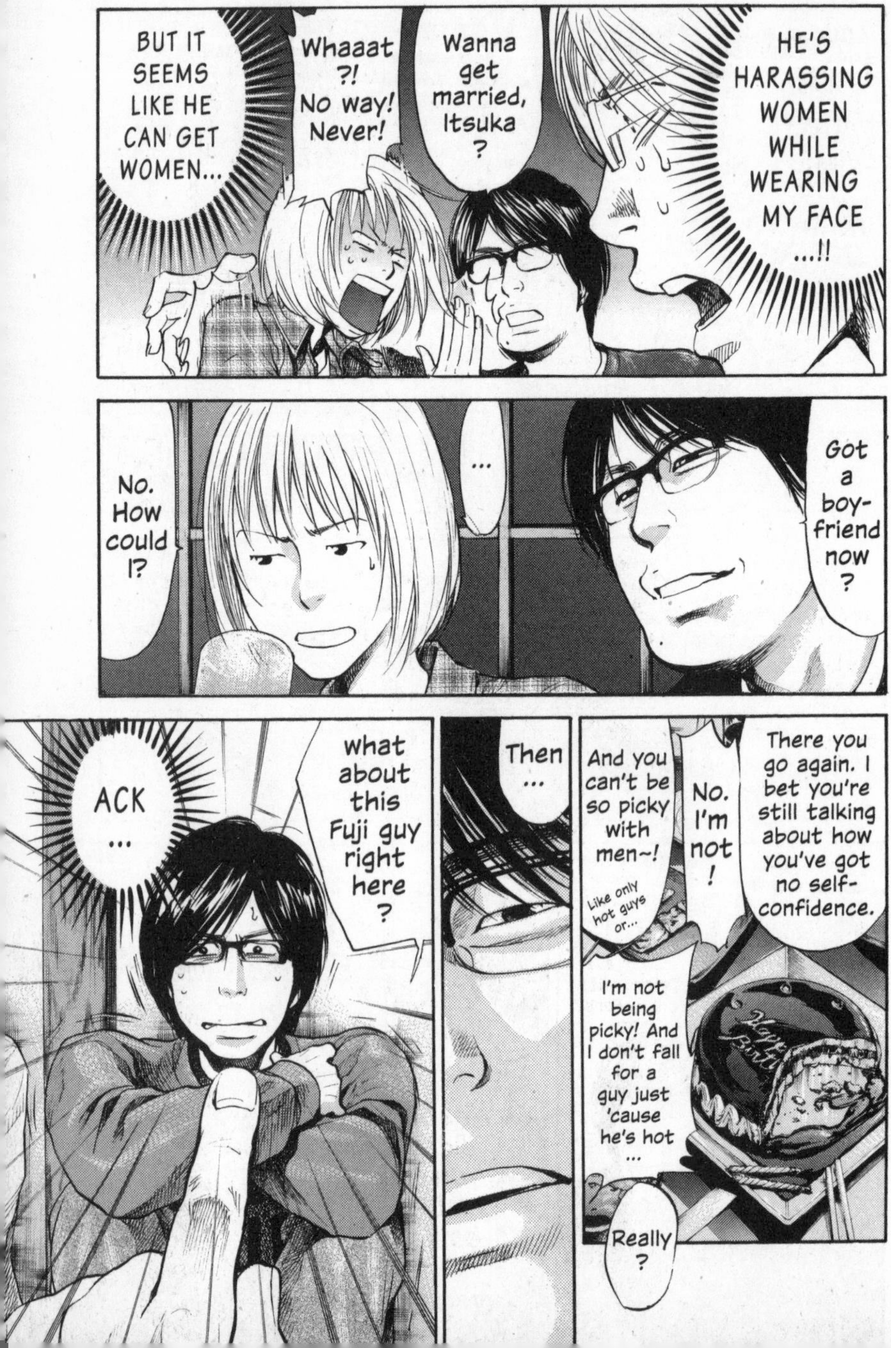
HE'S HARASSING WOMEN WHILE WEARING MY FACE ...!!
Wanna get married, Itsuka ?
Whaaat ?! No way! Never!
BUT IT SEEMS LIKE HE CAN GET WOMEN...
Got a boy-friend now ?
...
No. How could I?
There you go again. I bet you're still talking about how you've got no self-confidence.
No. I'm not !
And you can't be so picky with men~!
Like only hot guys or...
I'm not being picky! And I don't fall for a guy just 'cause he's hot ...
Really ?
Then ...
what about this Fuji guy right here ?
ACK ...

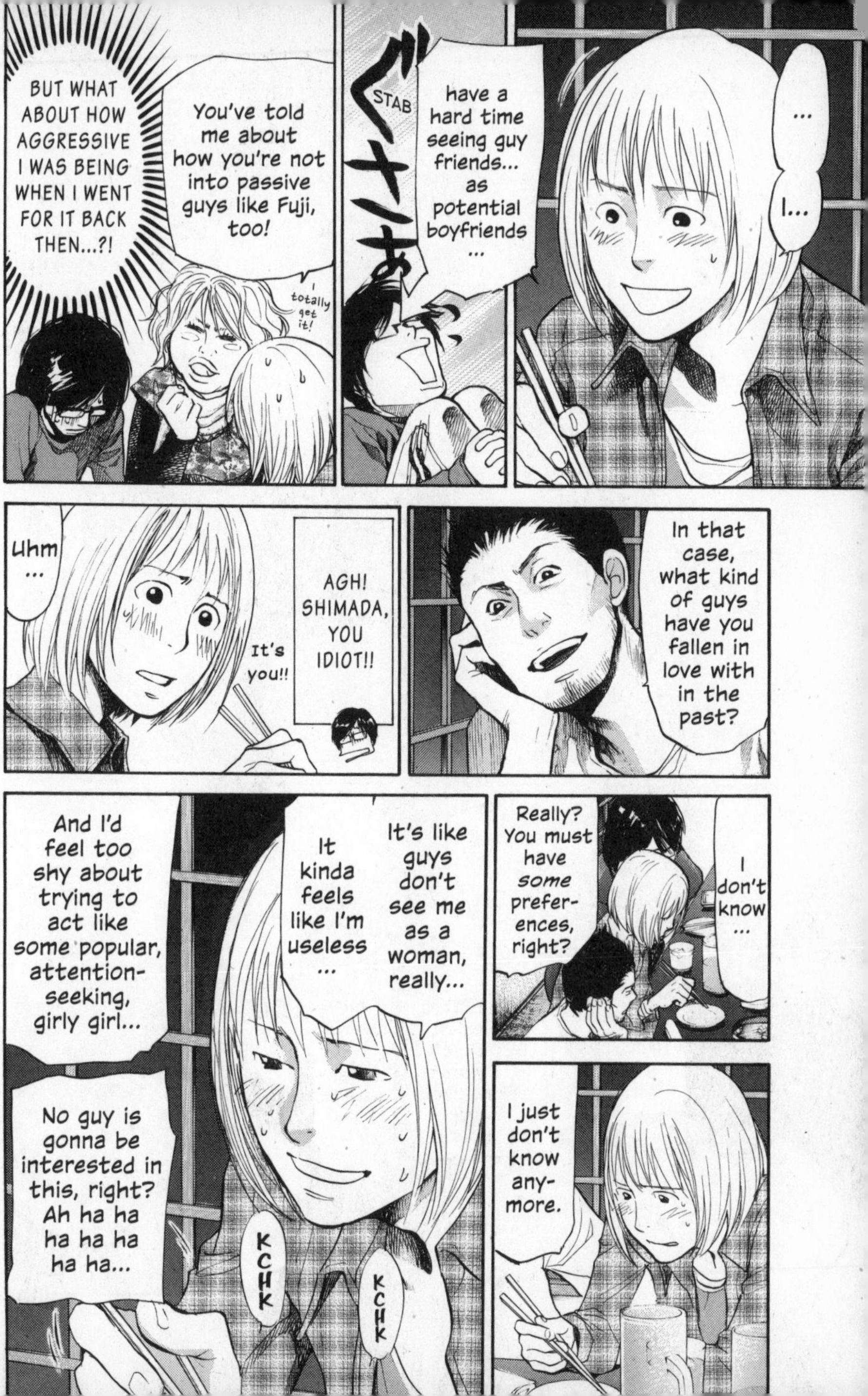
...
I...
STAB
have a hard time seeing guy friends... as potential boyfriends ...
You've told me about how you're not into passive guys like Fuji, too!
I totally get it!
BUT WHAT ABOUT HOW AGGRESSIVE I WAS BEING WHEN I WENT FOR IT BACK THEN...?!
In that case, what kind of guys have you fallen in love with in the past?
AGH! SHIMADA, YOU IDIOT!!
Uhm ...
It's you!!
I don't know ...
Really? You must have *some* preferences, right?
I just don't know anymore.
It's like guys don't see me as a woman, really...
It kinda feels like I'm useless ...
And I'd feel too shy about trying to act like some popular, attention-seeking, girly girl...
No guy is gonna be interested in this, right? Ah ha ha ha ha ha ha ha...
KCHK
KCHK

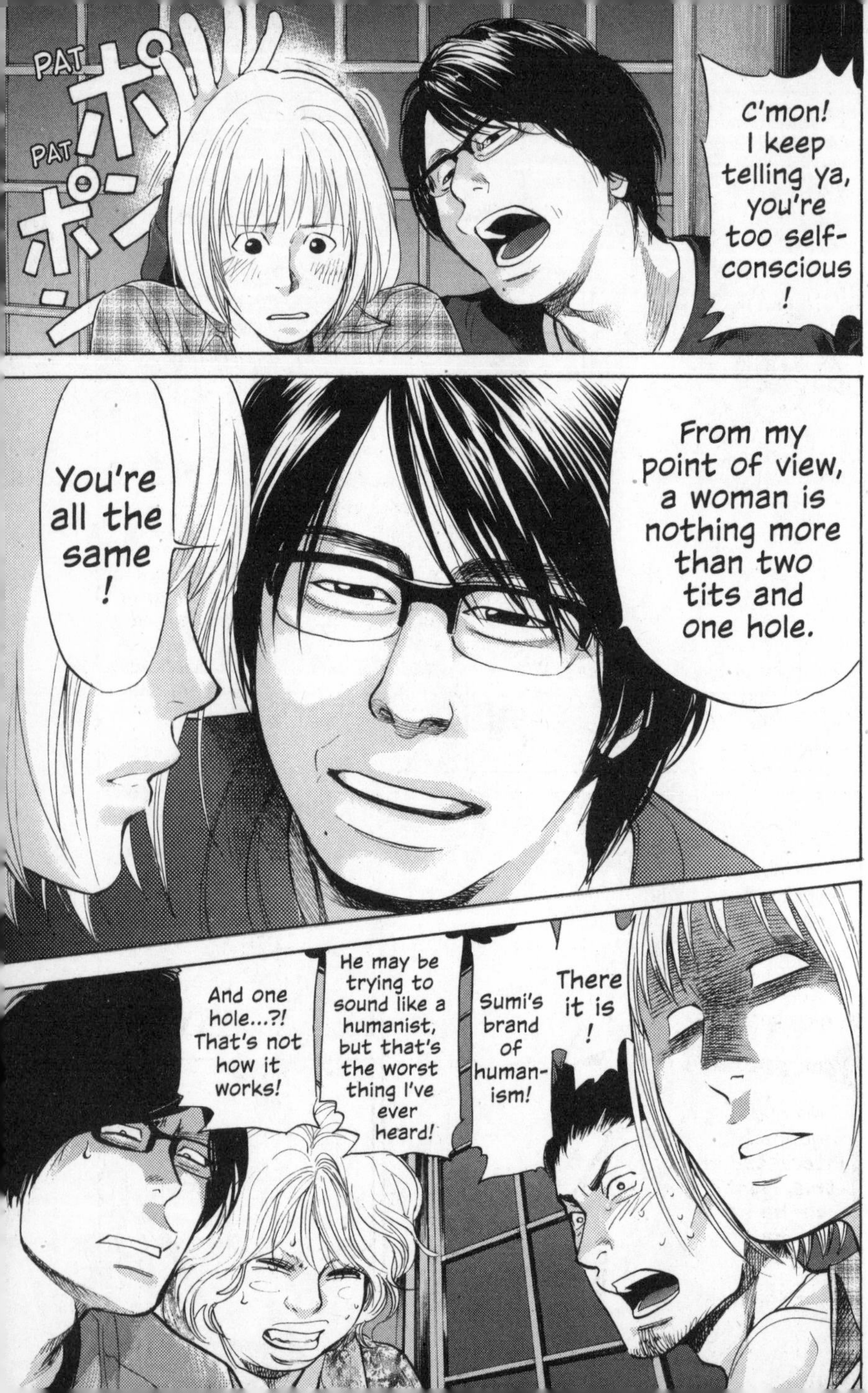
C'mon! I keep telling ya, you're too self-conscious!
PAT
PAT
From my point of view, a woman is nothing more than two tits and one hole.
You're all the same!
There it is!
Sumi's brand of humanism!
He may be trying to sound like a humanist, but that's the worst thing I've ever heard!
And one hole...?! That's not how it works!

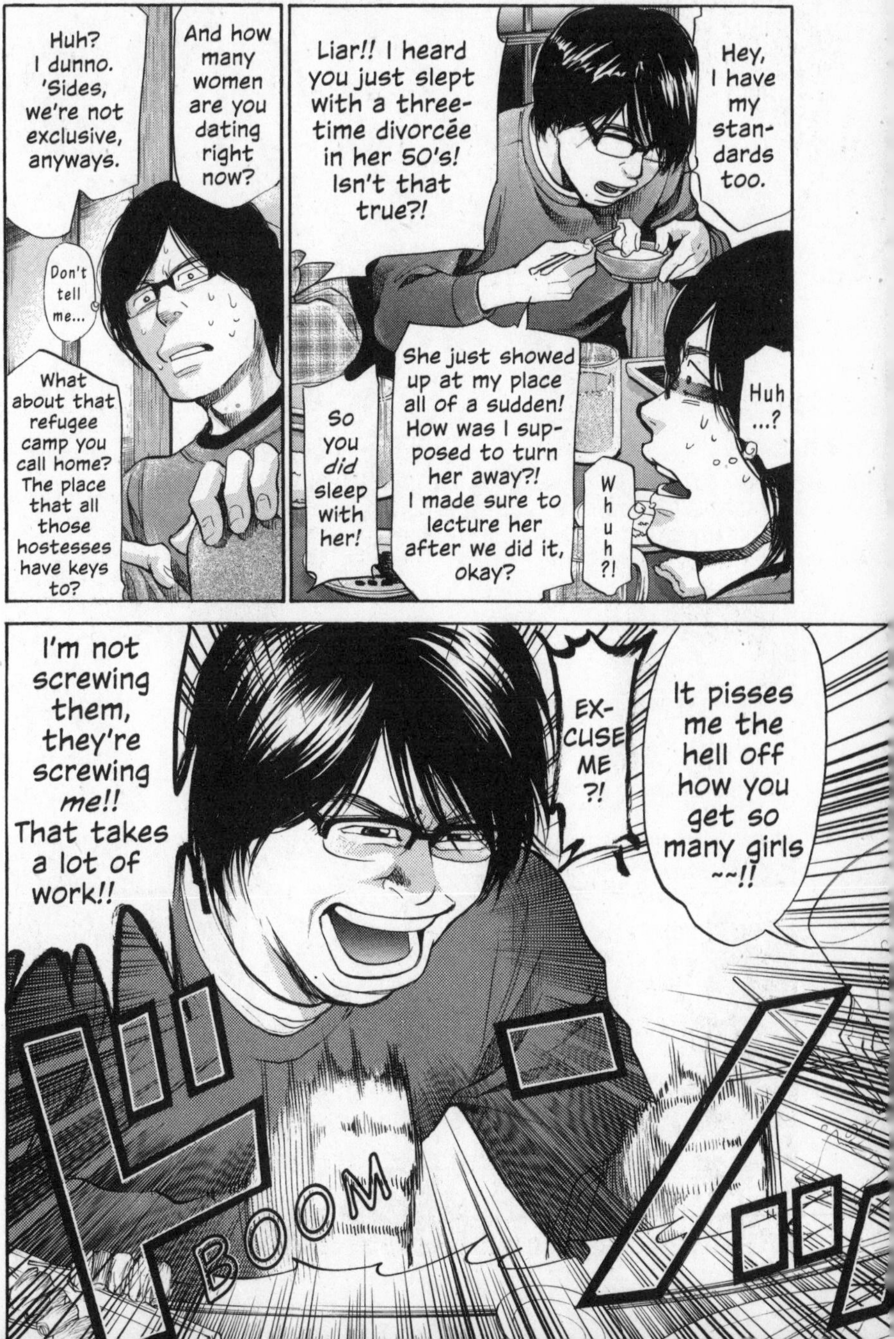
Hey, I have my standards too.
Liar!! I heard you just slept with a three-time divorcée in her 50's! Isn't that true?!
Huh ...?
Whuh?!
She just showed up at my place all of a sudden! How was I supposed to turn her away?! I made sure to lecture her after we did it, okay?
So you *did* sleep with her!
And how many women are you dating right now?
Huh? I dunno. 'Sides, we're not exclusive, anyways.
Don't tell me...
What about that refugee camp you call home? The place that all those hostesses have keys to?
It pisses me the hell off how you get so many girls ~~!!
EX-CUSE ME?!
I'm not screwing them, they're screwing *me*!! That takes a lot of work!!
BOOM

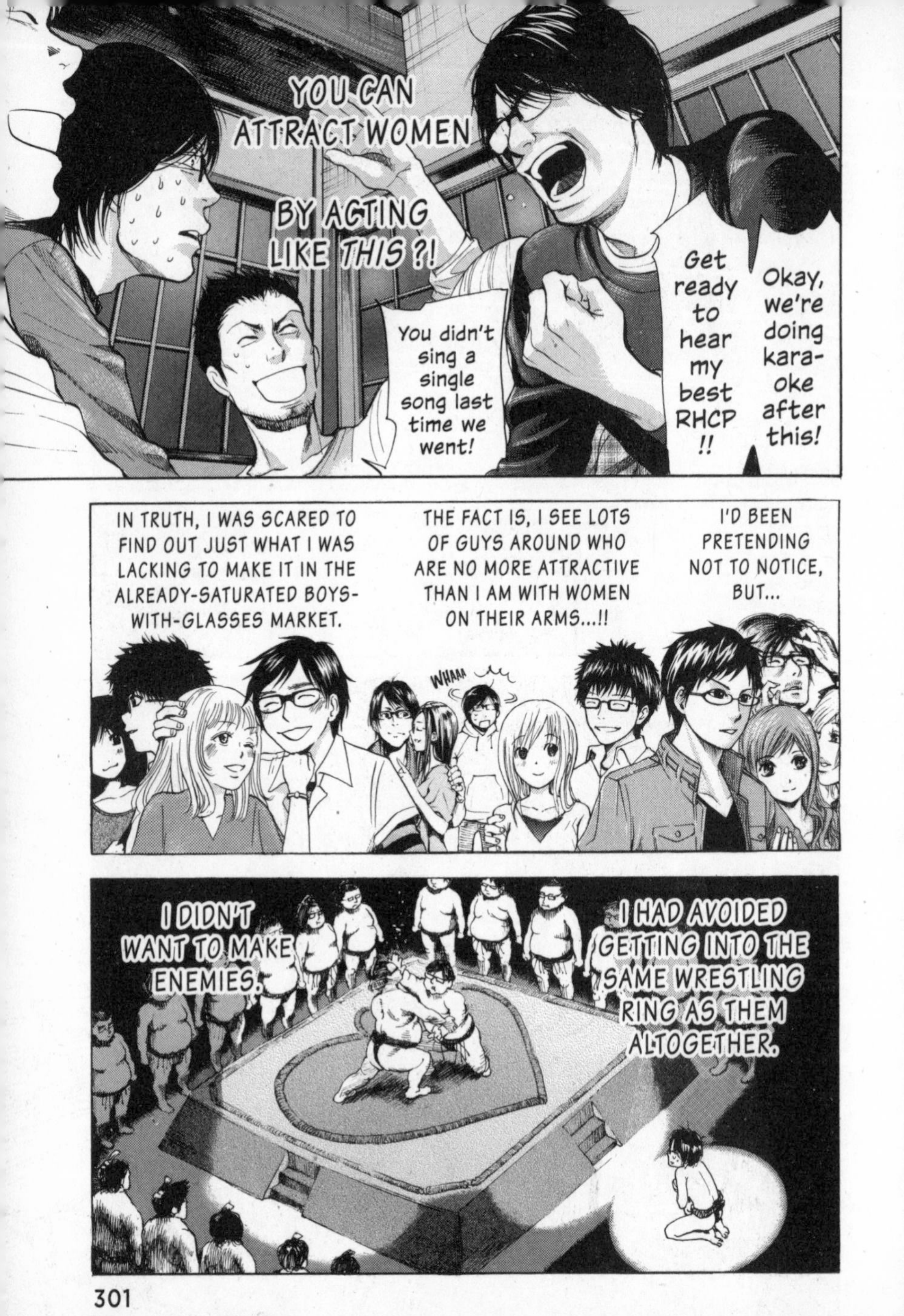
Okay, we're doing kara-oke after this!
Get ready to hear my best RHCP!!
You didn't sing a single song last time we went!
YOU CAN ATTRACT WOMEN BY ACTING LIKE *THIS*?!
I'D BEEN PRETENDING NOT TO NOTICE, BUT...
THE FACT IS, I SEE LOTS OF GUYS AROUND WHO ARE NO MORE ATTRACTIVE THAN I AM WITH WOMEN ON THEIR ARMS...!!
IN TRUTH, I WAS SCARED TO FIND OUT JUST WHAT I WAS LACKING TO MAKE IT IN THE ALREADY-SATURATED BOYS-WITH-GLASSES MARKET.
WHAAA
I HAD AVOIDED GETTING INTO THE SAME WRESTLING RING AS THEM ALTOGETHER.
I DIDN'T WANT TO MAKE ENEMIES.

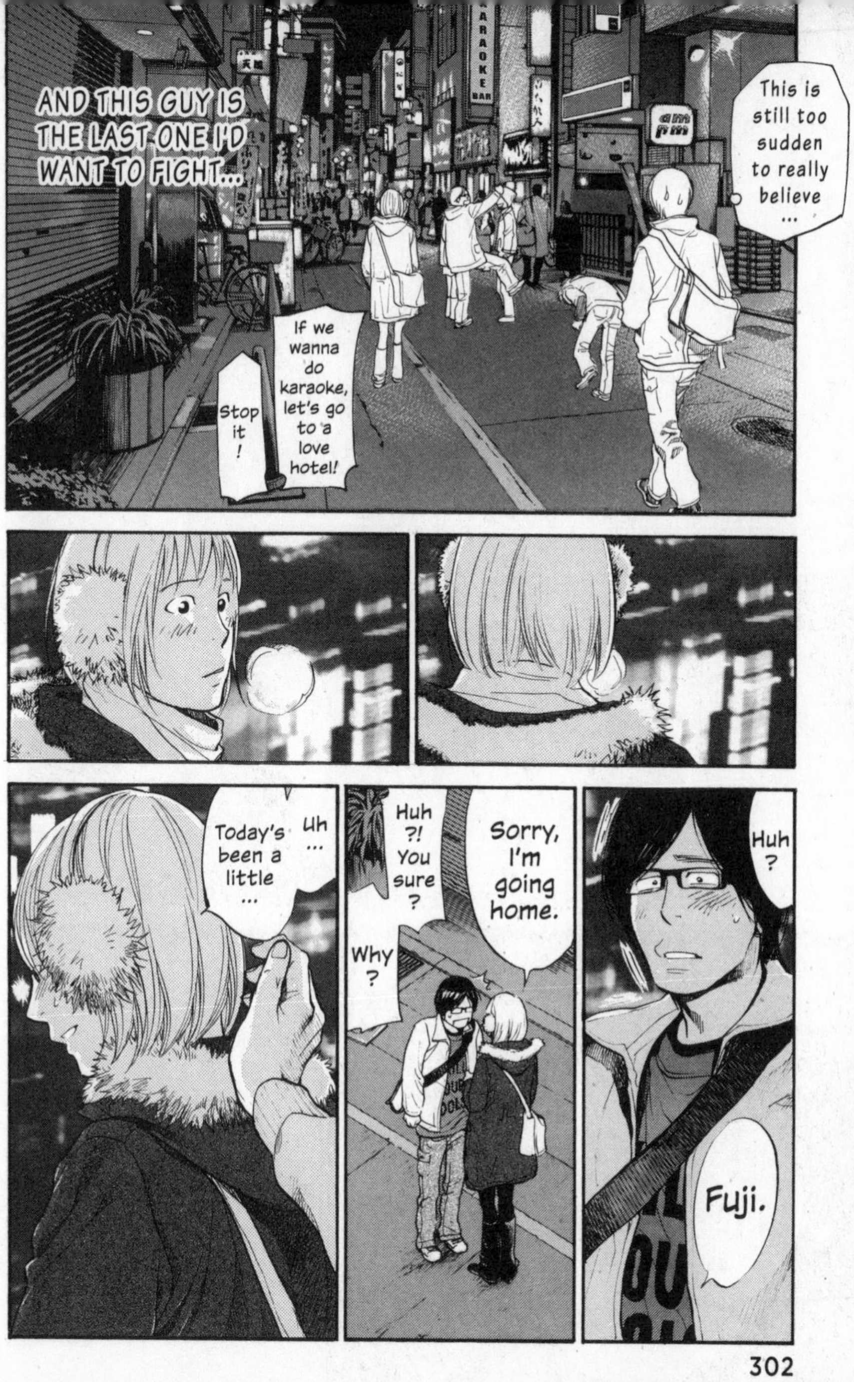
This is still too sudden to really believe ...
AND THIS GUY IS THE LAST ONE I'D WANT TO FIGHT...
If we wanna do karaoke, let's go to a love hotel!
Stop it!
Huh?
Fuji.
Sorry, I'm going home.
Huh?! You sure?
Why?
Uh ...
Today's been a little ...

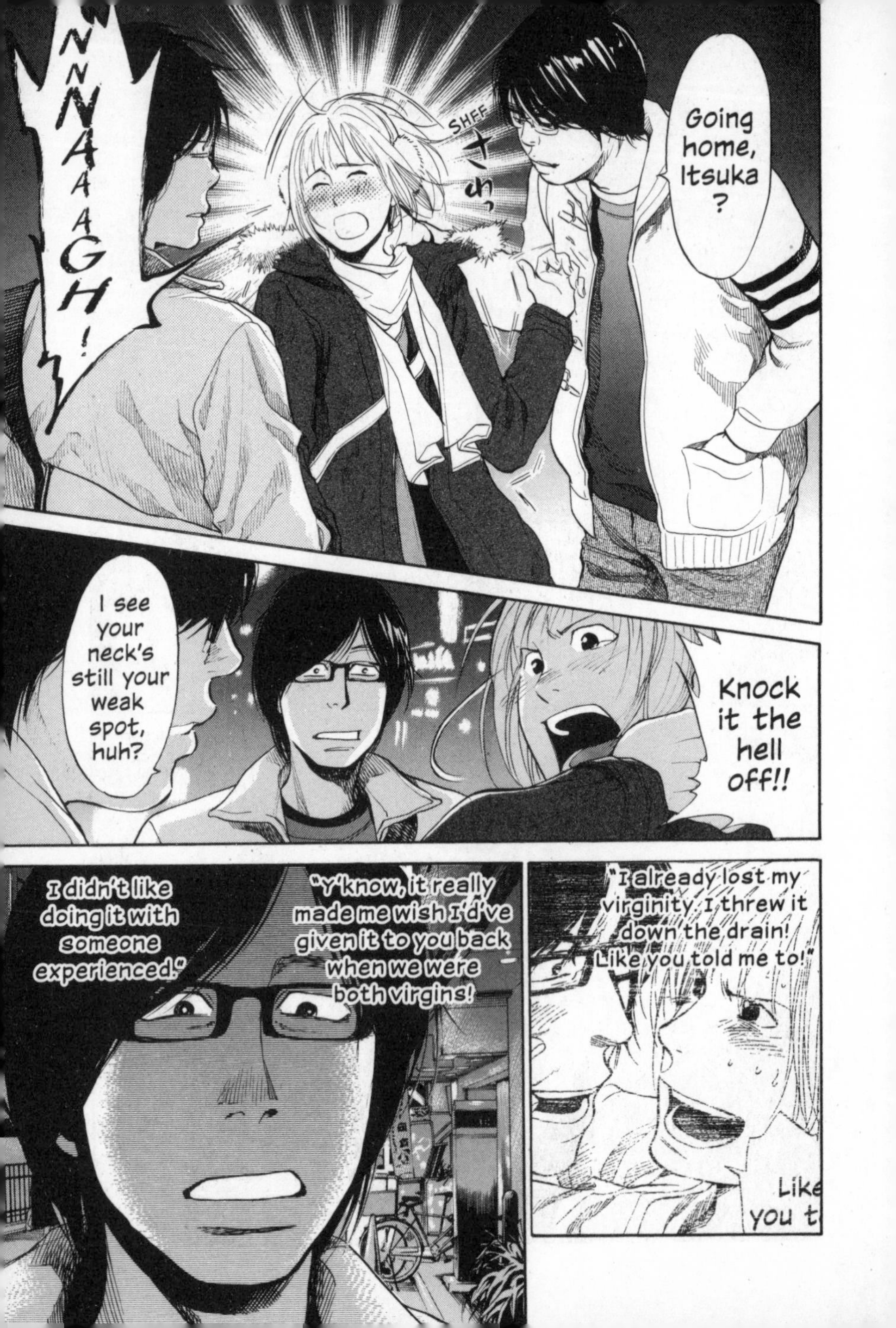
Going home, Itsuka?
SHFF
NNNNAAAAGH!
Knock it the hell off!!
I see your neck's still your weak spot, huh?
"I already lost my virginity. I threw it down the drain! Like you told me to!"
Like you t
"Y'know, it really made me wish I'd've given it to you back when we were both virgins!
I didn't like doing it with someone experienced."

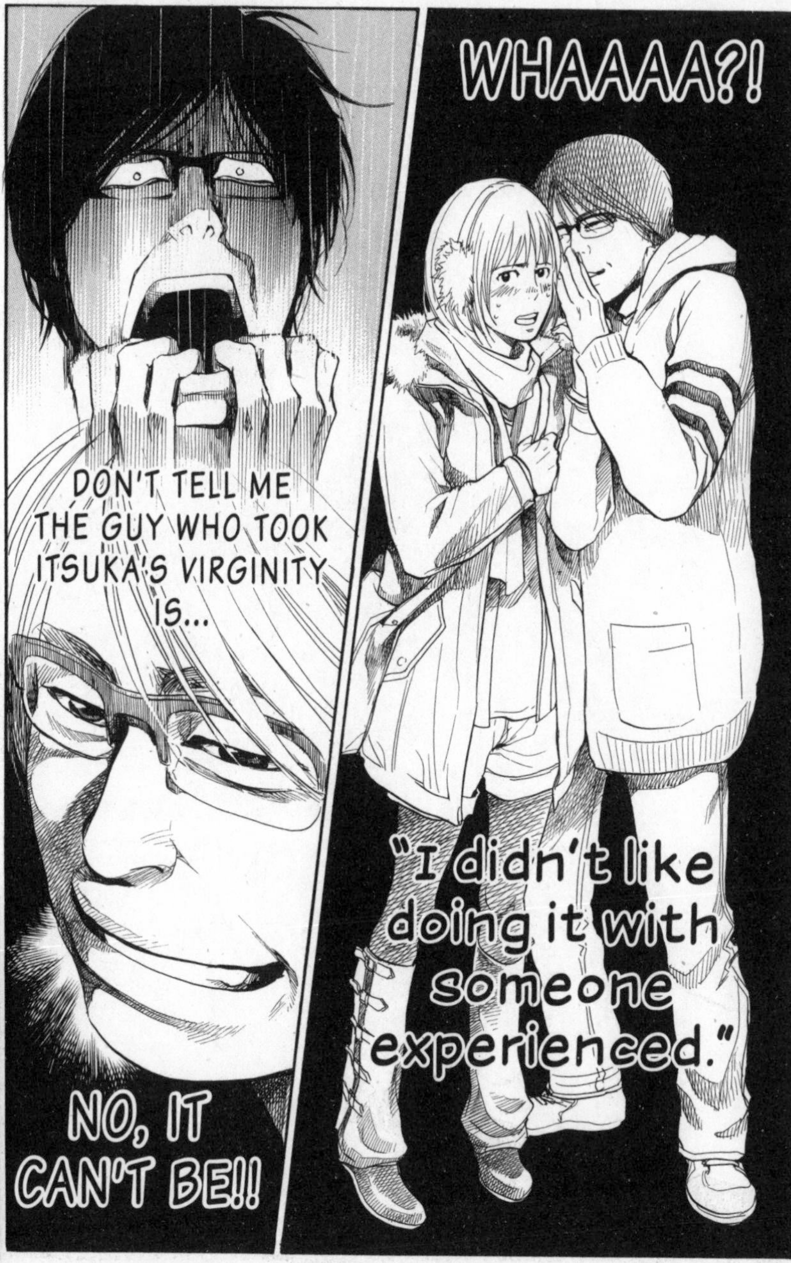
WHAAAA?!
"I didn't like doing it with someone experienced."
DON'T TELL ME THE GUY WHO TOOK ITSUKA'S VIRGINITY IS...
NO, IT CAN'T BE!!

chapter 10 ♥ END

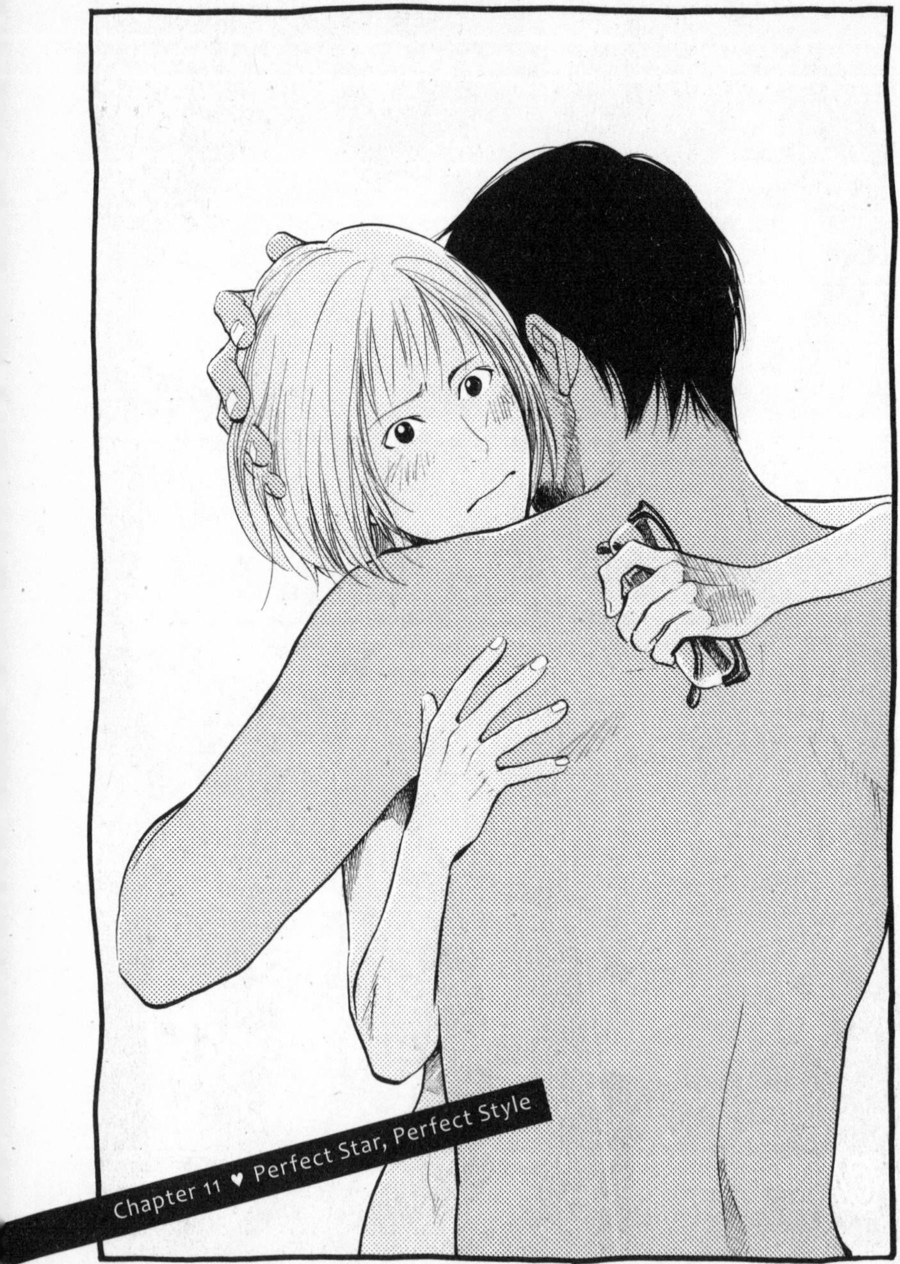
Chapter 11 ♥ Perfect Star, Perfect Style

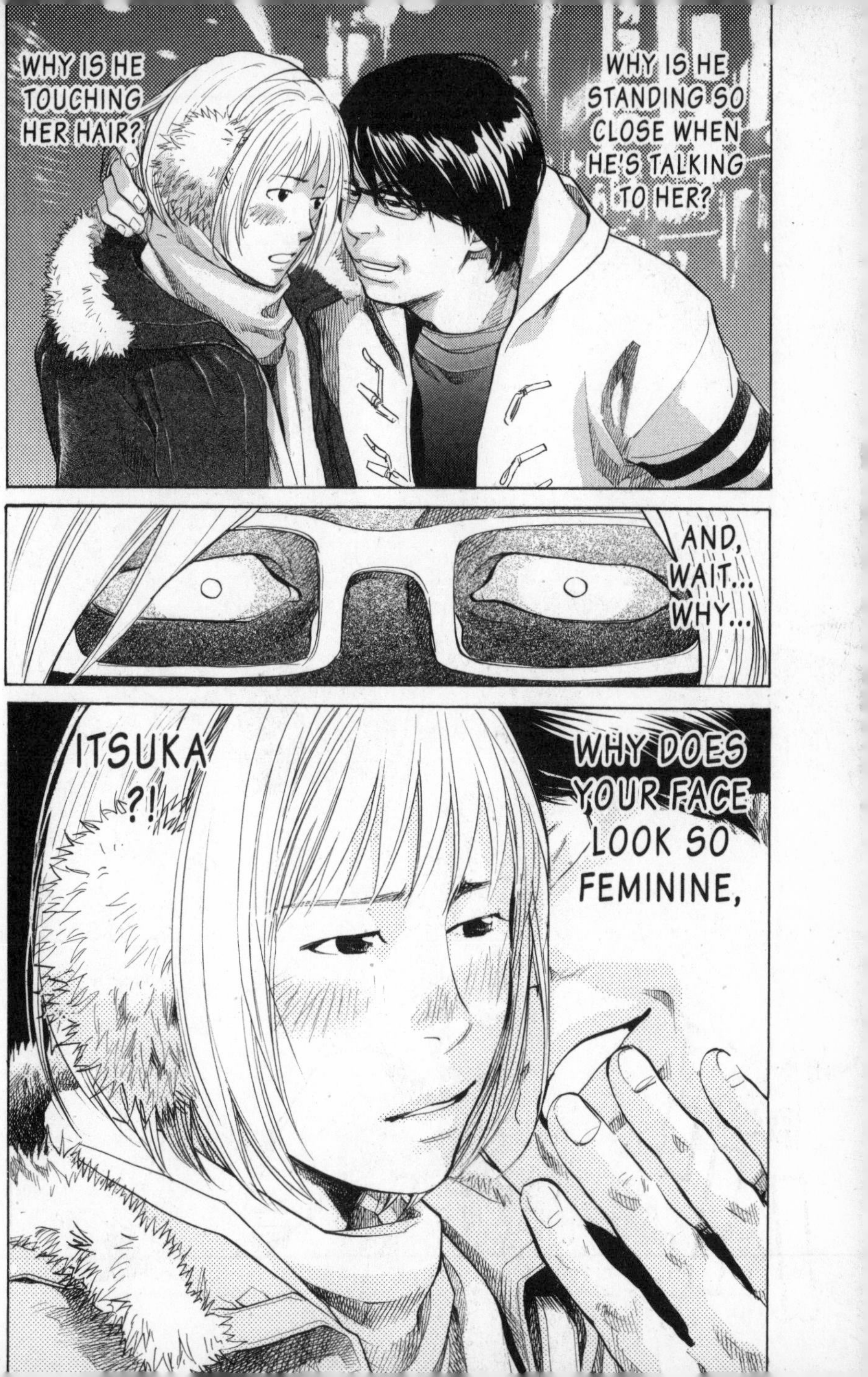
WHY IS HE STANDING SO CLOSE WHEN HE'S TALKING TO HER?
WHY IS HE TOUCHING HER HAIR?
AND, WAIT... WHY...
WHY DOES YOUR FACE LOOK SO FEMININE,
ITSUKA ?!

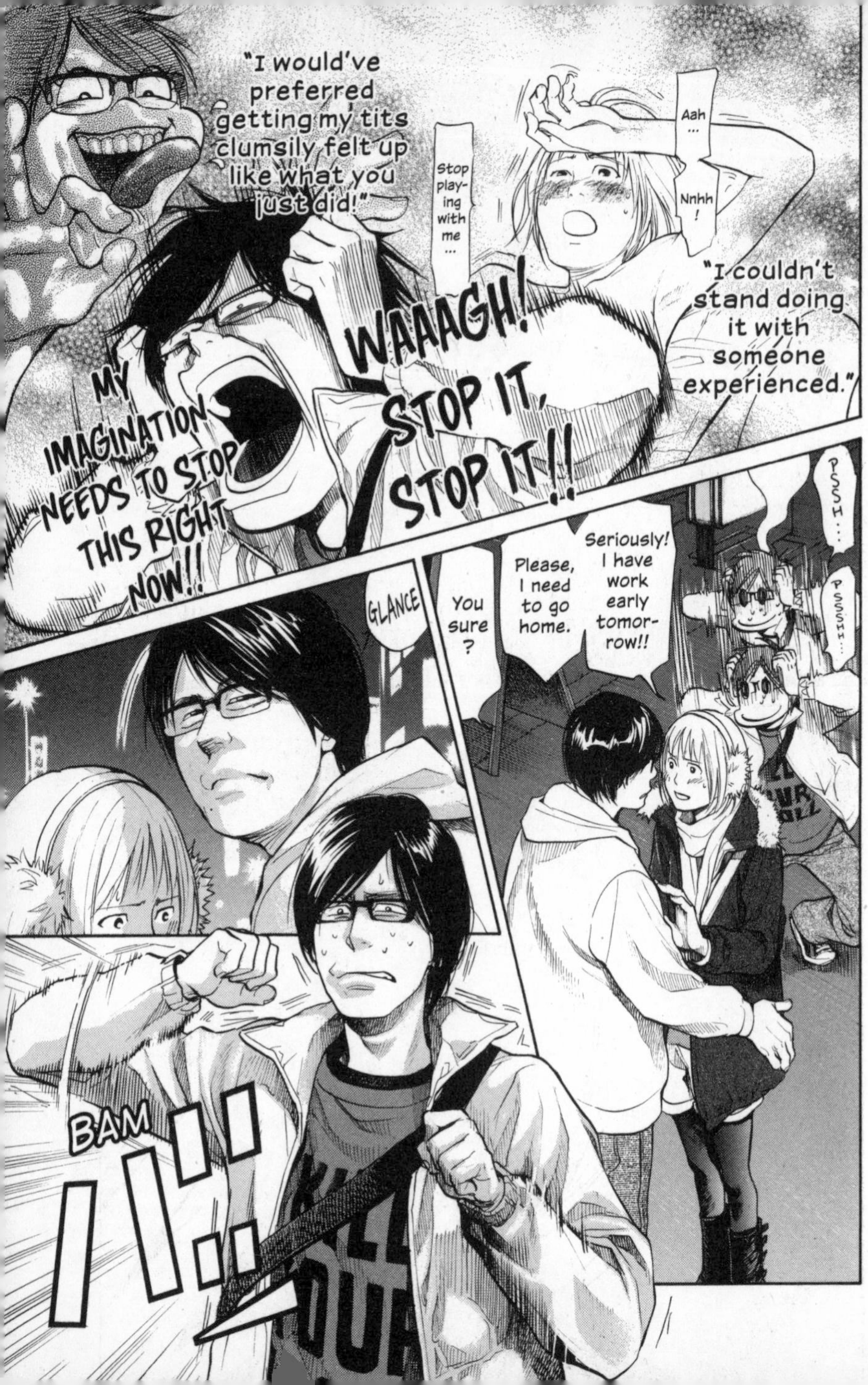
Aah...
Nnhh!
Stop playing with me...
"I would've preferred getting my tits clumsily felt up like what you just did!"
"I couldn't stand doing it with someone experienced."
WAAAGH! STOP IT, STOP IT!!
MY IMAGINATION NEEDS TO STOP THIS RIGHT NOW!!
PSSH...
PSSSH...
Seriously! I have work early tomorrow!!
Please, I need to go home.
You sure?
GLANCE
BAM

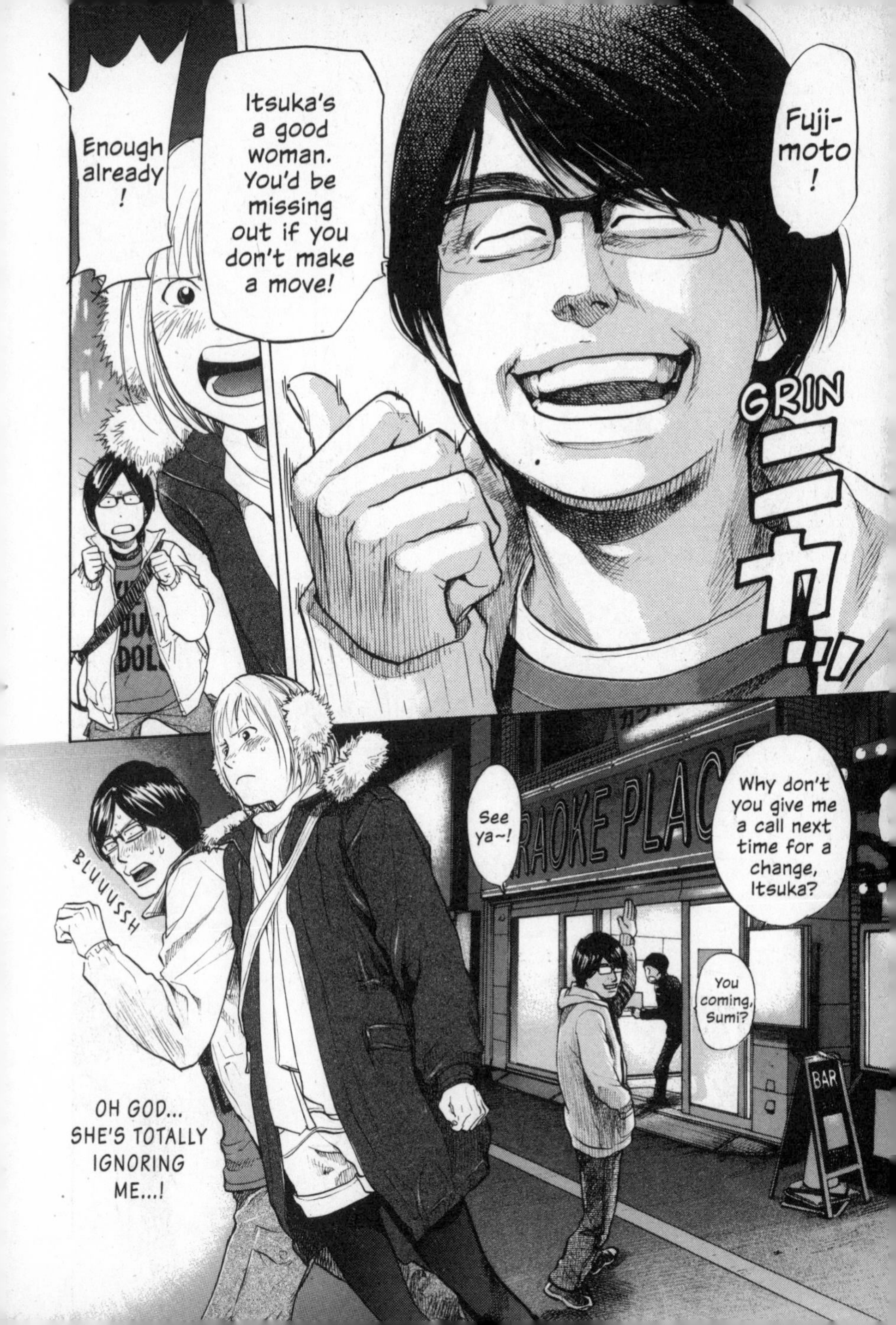
Fuji-moto!
Itsuka's a good woman. You'd be missing out if you don't make a move!
Enough already!
GRIN
ニヤッ
Why don't you give me a call next time for a change, Itsuka?
See ya~!
RAOKE PLAC
You coming, Sumi?
BAR
BLUUUSSH
OH GOD... SHE'S TOTALLY IGNORING ME...!

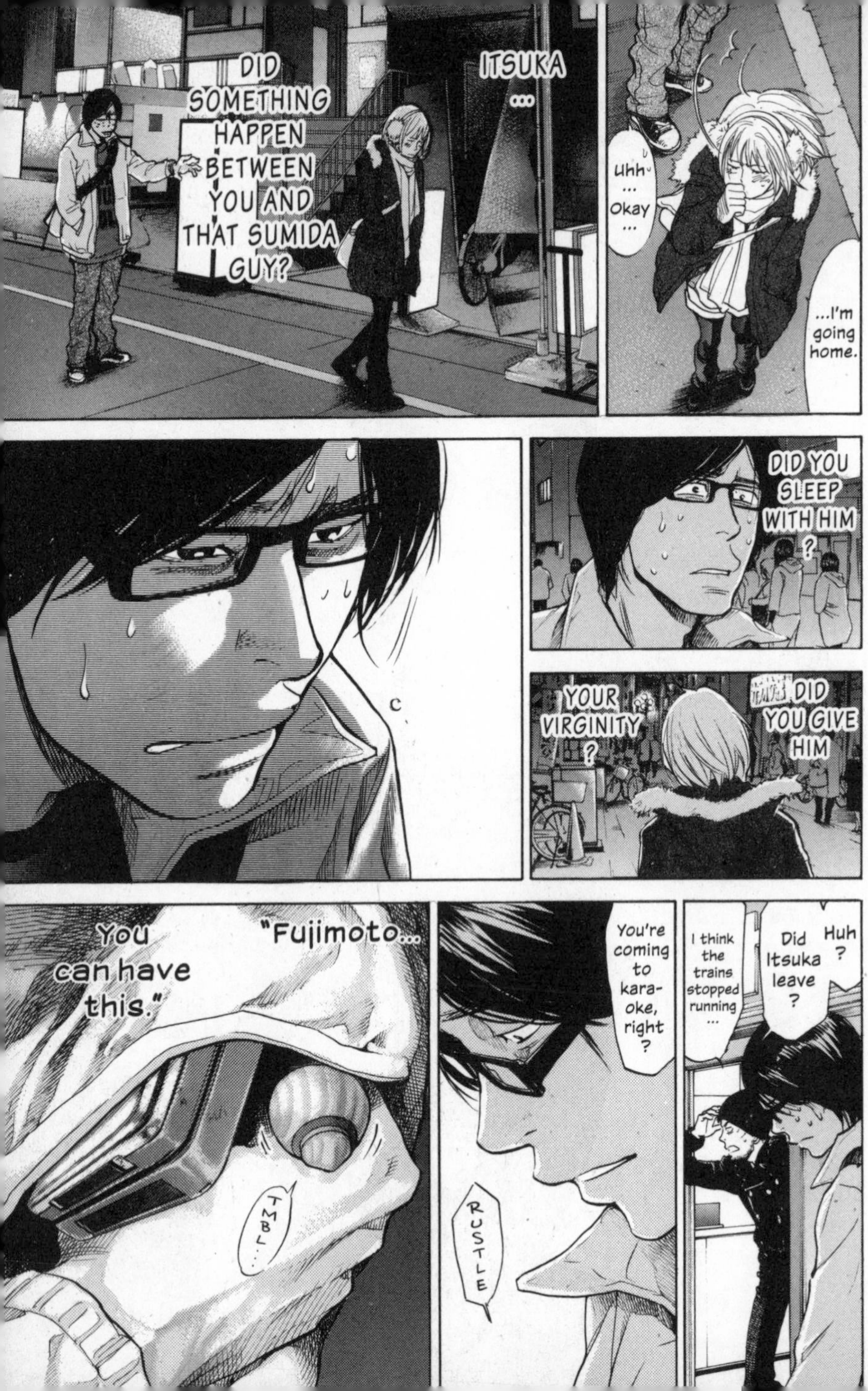
Uhh... Okay...
...I'm going home.
ITSUKA...
DID SOMETHING HAPPEN BETWEEN YOU AND THAT SUMIDA GUY?
DID YOU SLEEP WITH HIM?
DID YOU GIVE HIM
YOUR VIRGINITY?
Huh?
Did Itsuka leave?
I think the trains stopped running...
You're coming to karaoke, right?
RUSTLE
"Fujimoto...
You can have this."
TMBL...

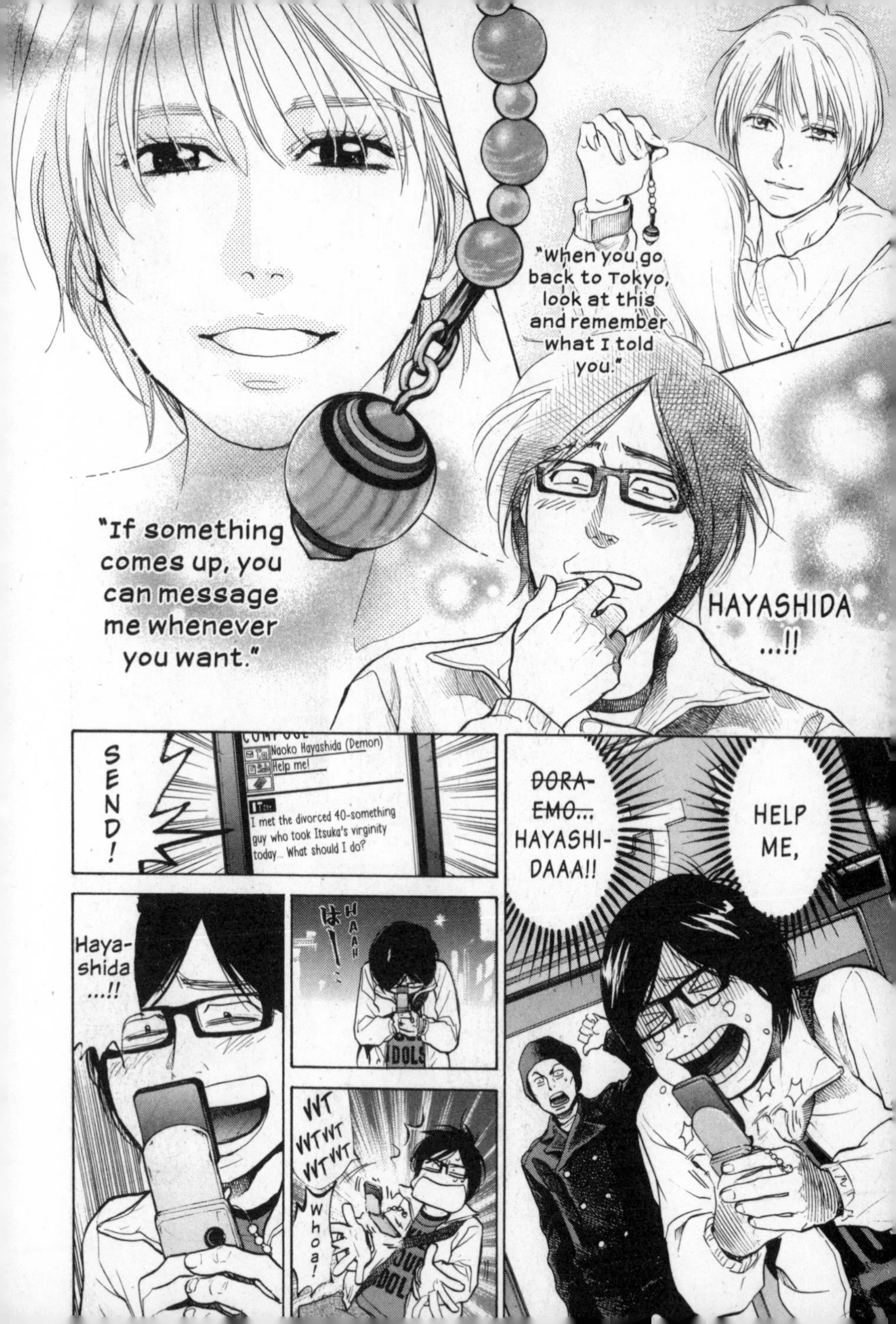
"When you go back to Tokyo, look at this and remember what I told you."
"If something comes up, you can message me whenever you want."
HAYASHIDA ...!!
HELP ME,
DORA-EMO... HAYASHI-DAAA!!
Naoko Hayashida (Demon)
Help me!
I met the divorced 40-something guy who took Itsuka's virginity today... What should I do?
SEND!
HAAAH
は－
WT WTWT WTWT WTWT
Whoa!
Hayashida ...!!

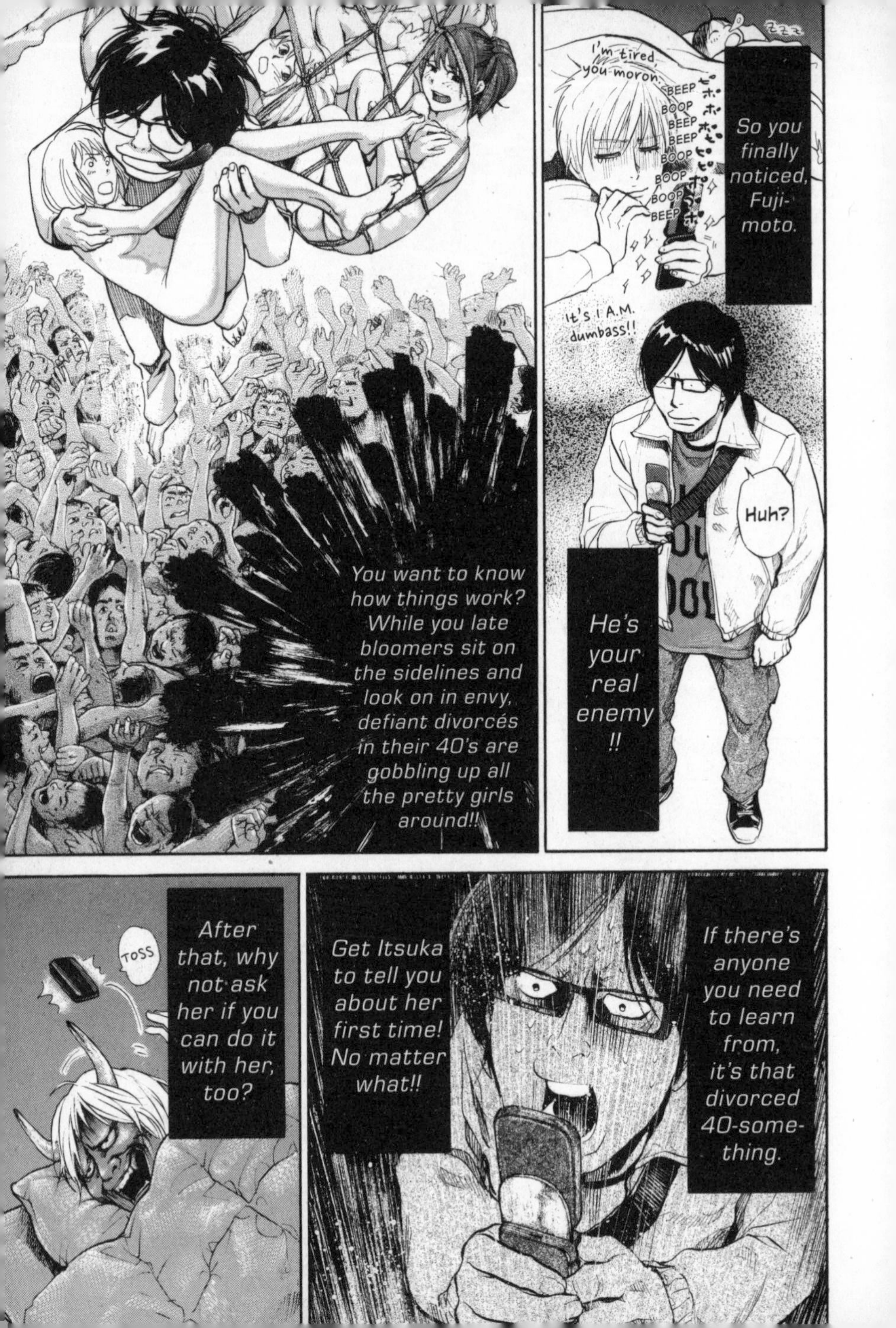
I'm tired, you moron.
BEEP BOOP BEEP BEEP BOOP BOOP BOOP BEEP
So you finally noticed, Fuji-moto.
It's 1 A.M. dumbass!!
Huh?
He's your real enemy !!
You want to know how things work? While you late bloomers sit on the sidelines and look on in envy, defiant divorcés in their 40's are gobbling up all the pretty girls around!!
If there's anyone you need to learn from, it's that divorced 40-some-thing.
Get Itsuka to tell you about her first time! No matter what!!
After that, why not ask her if you can do it with her, too?
TOSS

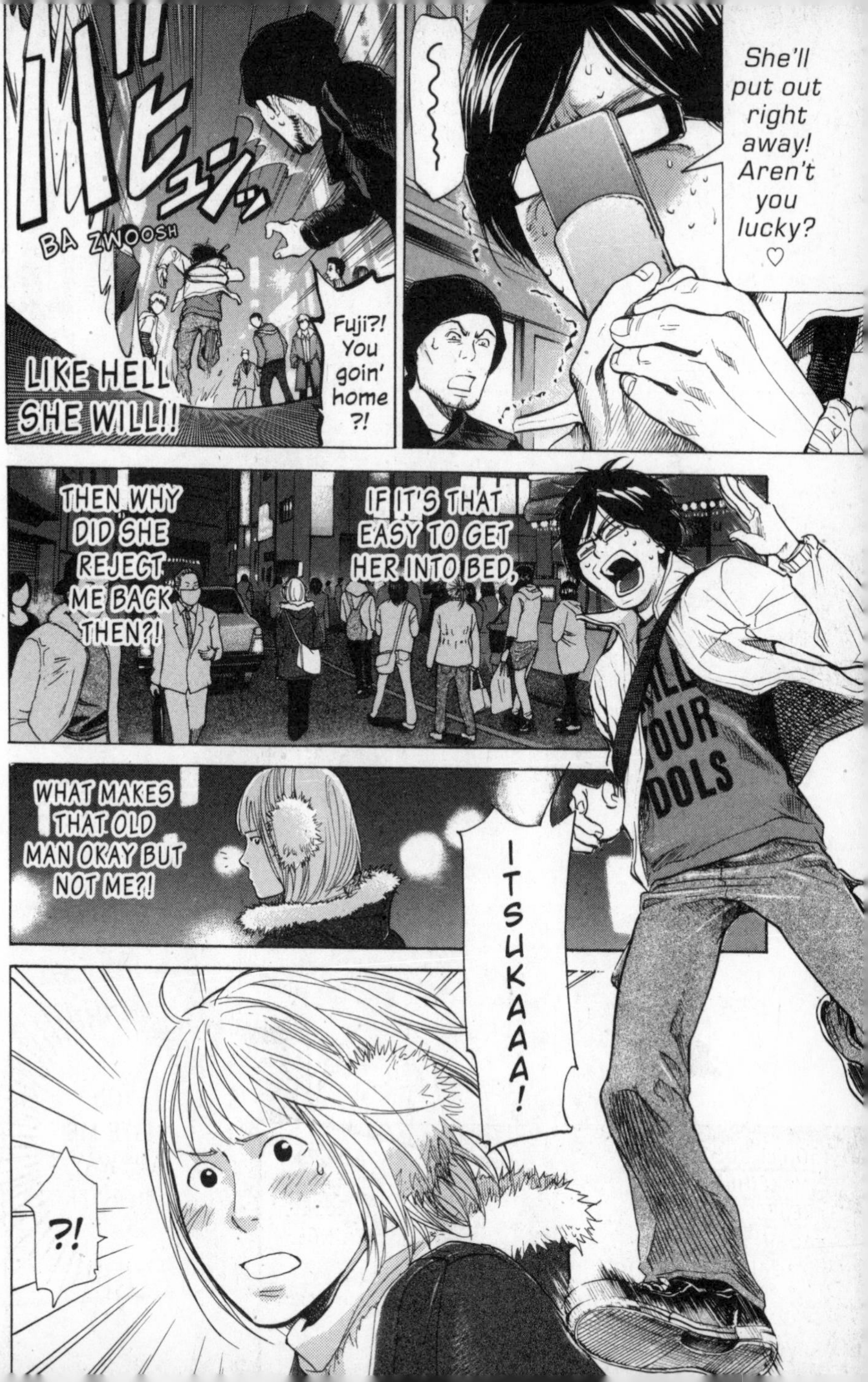
She'll put out right away! Aren't you lucky? ♡
ヒュンッ
BA ZWOOSH
Fuji?! You goin' home?!
LIKE HELL SHE WILL!!
IF IT'S THAT EASY TO GET HER INTO BED,
THEN WHY DID SHE REJECT ME BACK THEN?!
WHAT MAKES THAT OLD MAN OKAY BUT NOT ME?!
ITSUKAAAA!
?!

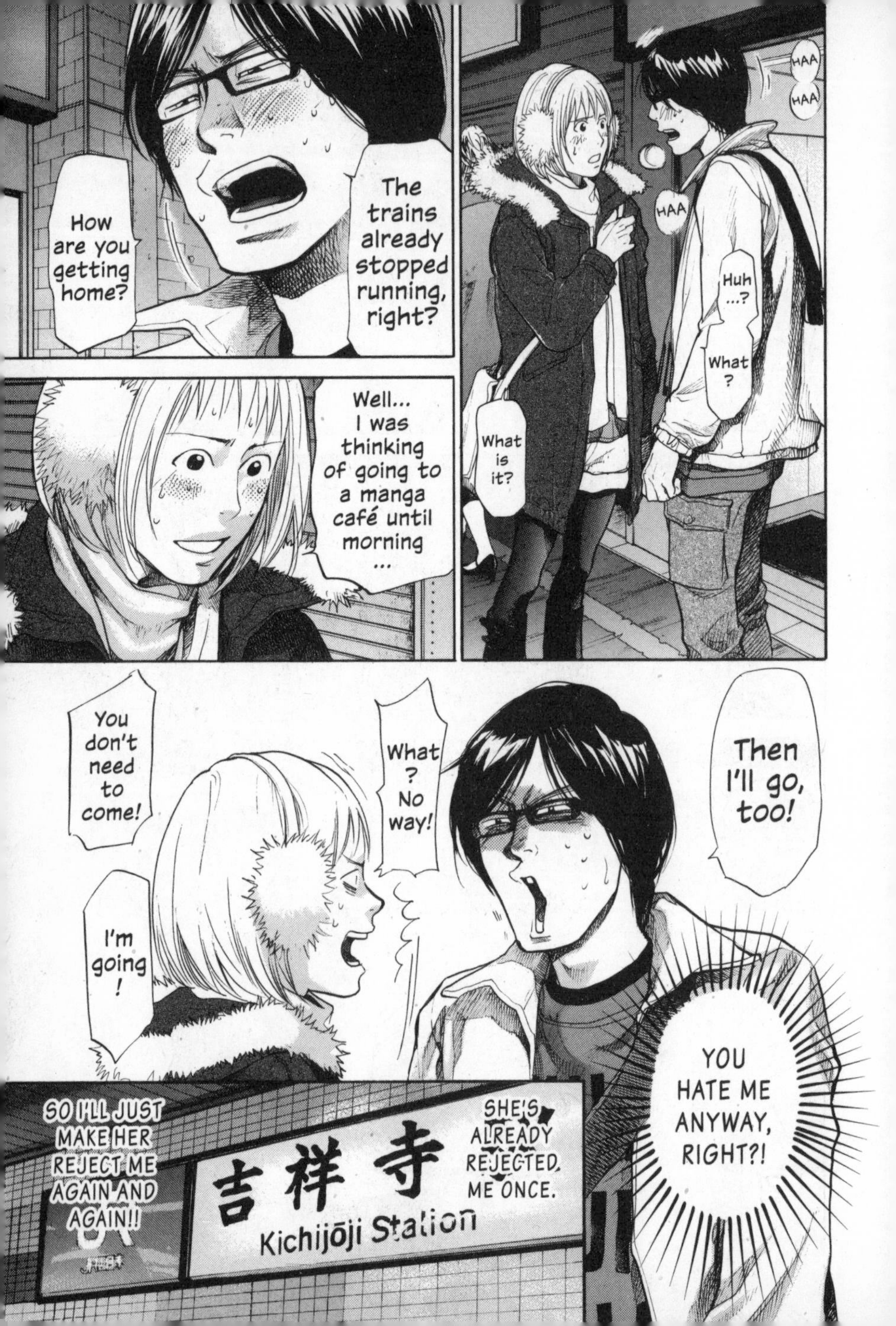
HAA
HAA
HAA
Huh ...?
What ?
What is it?
The trains already stopped running, right?
How are you getting home?
Well... I was thinking of going to a manga café until morning ...
Then I'll go, too!
What ? No way!
You don't need to come!
I'm going !
YOU HATE ME ANYWAY, RIGHT?!
SHE'S ALREADY REJECTED ME ONCE.
SO I'LL JUST MAKE HER REJECT ME AGAIN AND AGAIN!!
吉祥寺
Kichijōji Station

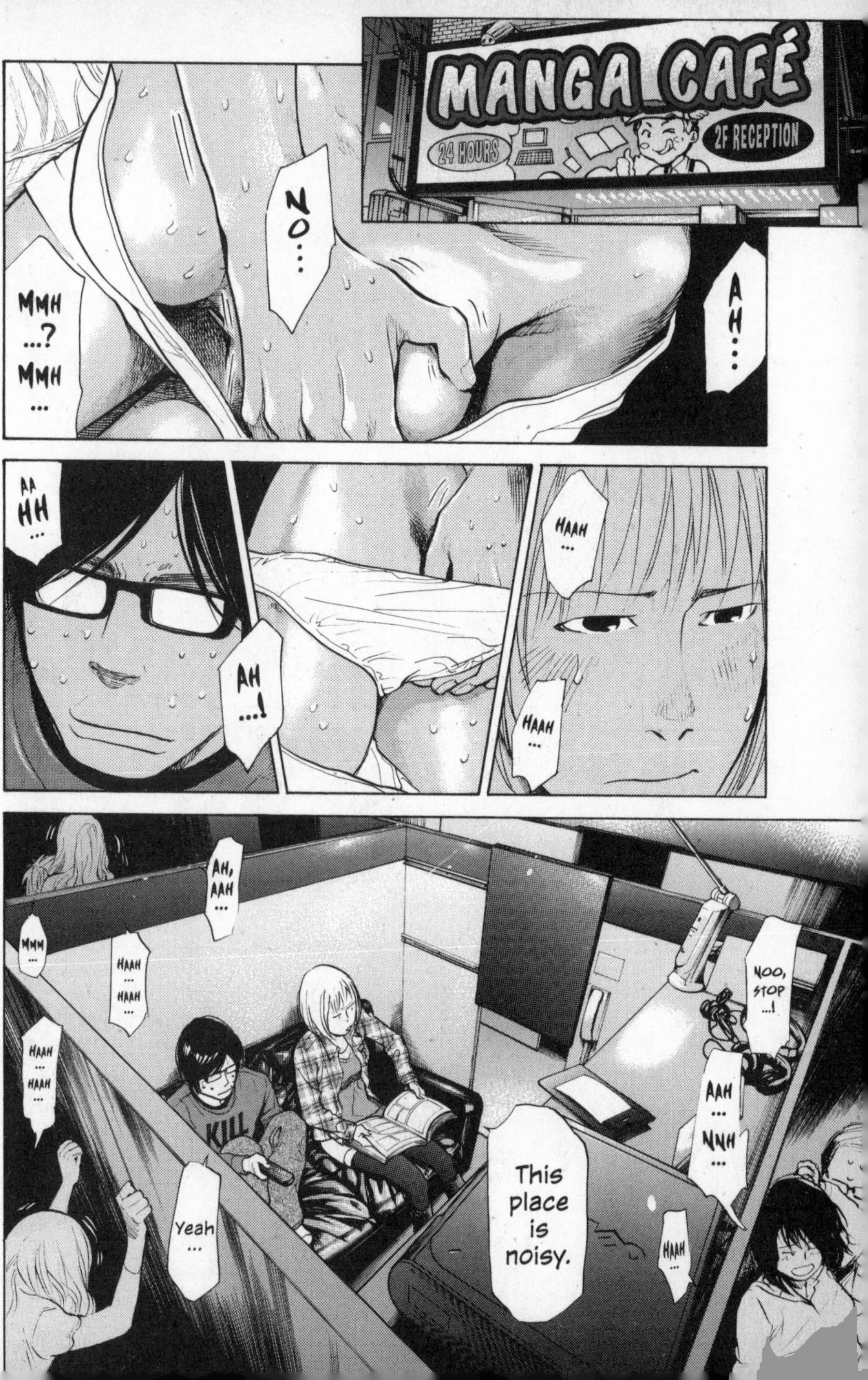
MANGA CAFÉ
24 HOURS
2F RECEPTION
AH...
NO...
MMH ...? MMH ...
HAAH ...
HAAH ...
AH ...!
AAHH ...
NOO, STOP ...!
AAH ... NNH ...
HAAH ...
This place is noisy.
Yeah ...
AH, AAH ...
HAAH ... HAAH ...
MMM ...
HAAH ... HAAH ...

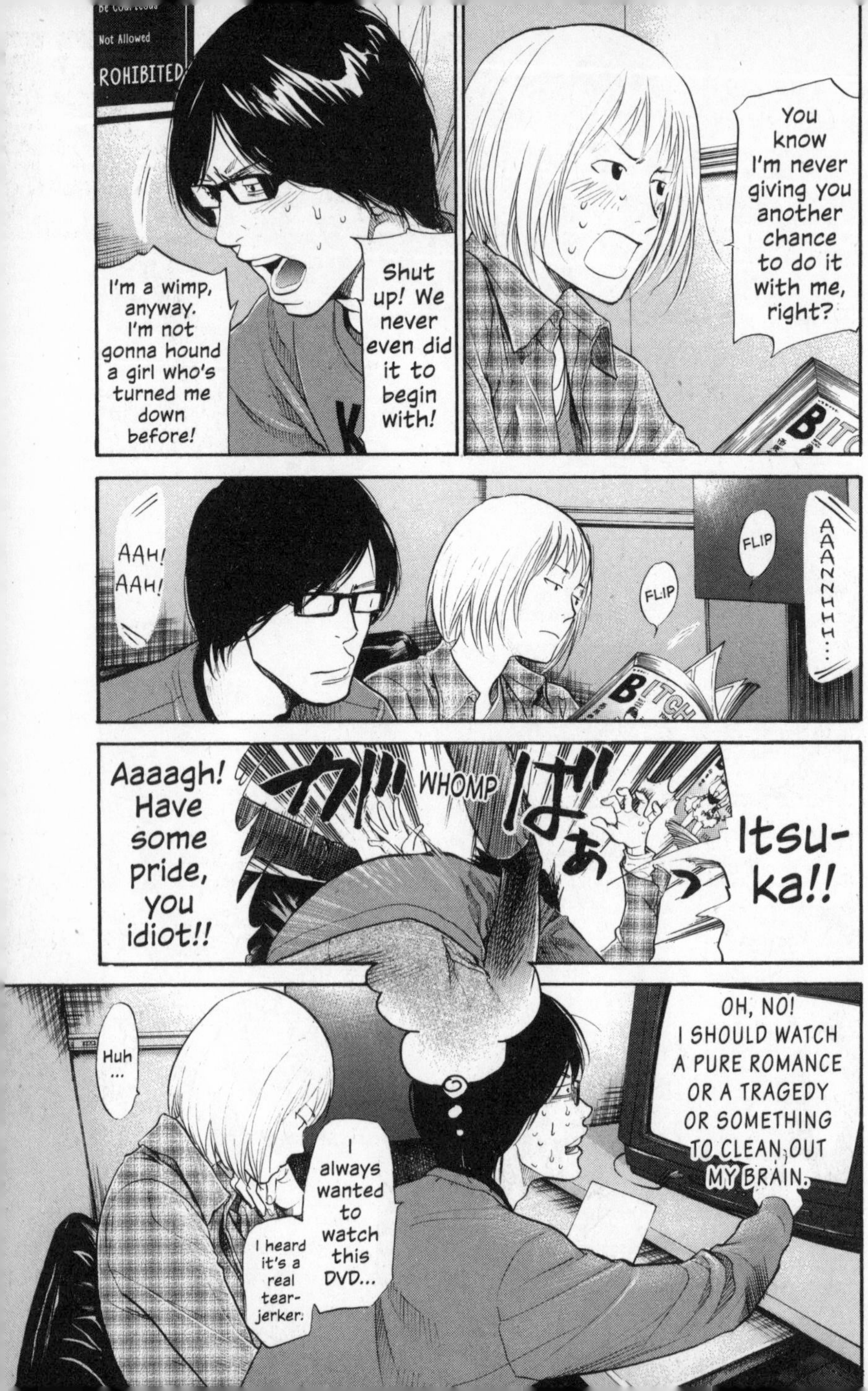
You know I'm never giving you another chance to do it with me, right?
Not Allowed
ROHIBITED
Shut up! We never even did it to begin with!
I'm a wimp, anyway. I'm not gonna hound a girl who's turned me down before!
AAAANNHHH...
FLIP
FLIP
AAH! AAH!
Itsu-ka!!
ばぁっ
WHOMP
ガ
Aaaagh! Have some pride, you idiot!!
OH, NO! I SHOULD WATCH A PURE ROMANCE OR A TRAGEDY OR SOMETHING TO CLEAN OUT MY BRAIN.
I always wanted to watch this DVD...
I heard it's a real tear-jerker.
Huh ...

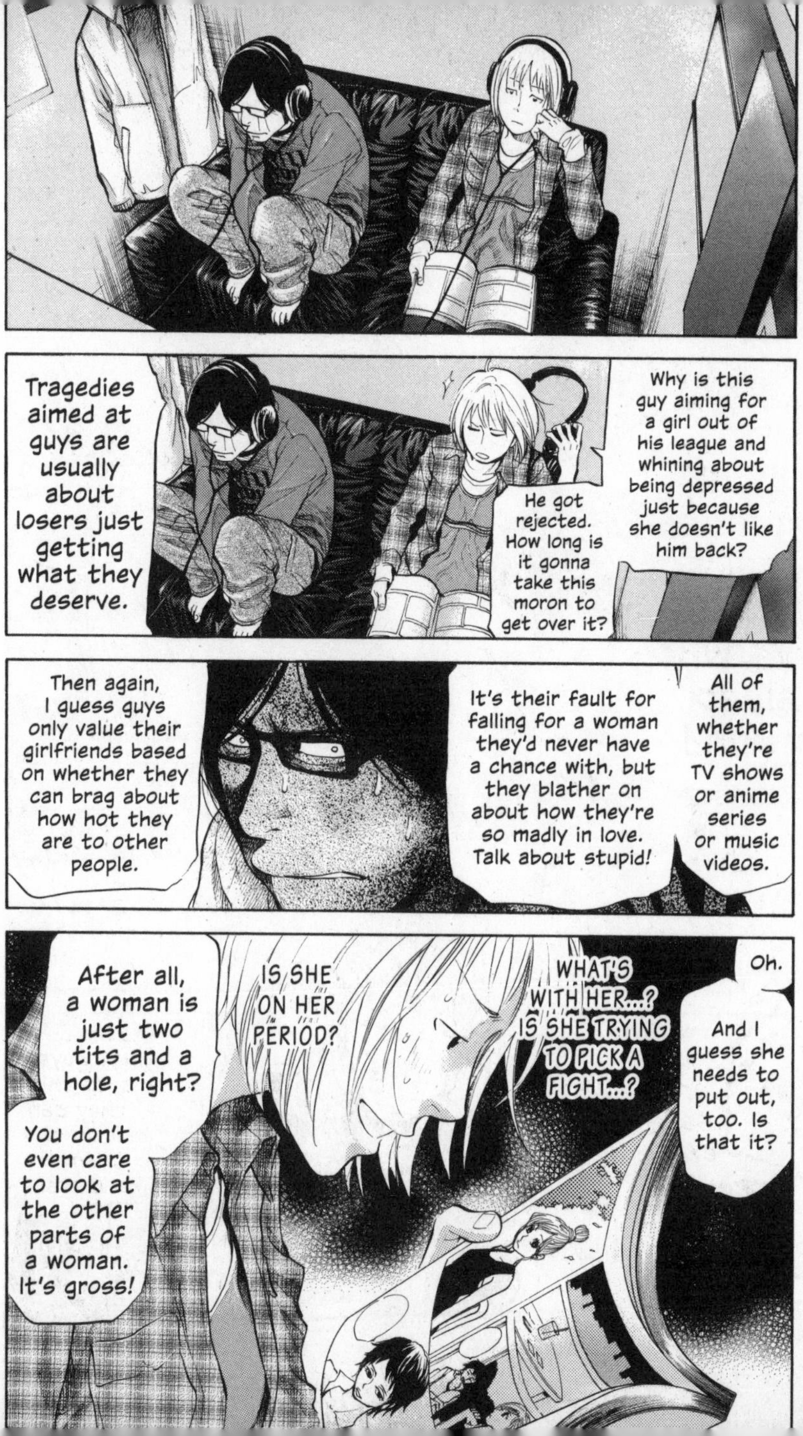
Why is this guy aiming for a girl out of his league and whining about being depressed just because she doesn't like him back?
He got rejected. How long is it gonna take this moron to get over it?
Tragedies aimed at guys are usually about losers just getting what they deserve.
All of them, whether they're TV shows or anime series or music videos.
It's their fault for falling for a woman they'd never have a chance with, but they blather on about how they're so madly in love. Talk about stupid!
Then again, I guess guys only value their girlfriends based on whether they can brag about how hot they are to other people.
Oh.
And I guess she needs to put out, too. Is that it?
WHAT'S WITH HER...? IS SHE TRYING TO PICK A FIGHT...?
IS SHE ON HER PERIOD?
After all, a woman is just two tits and a hole, right?
You don't even care to look at the other parts of a woman. It's gross!

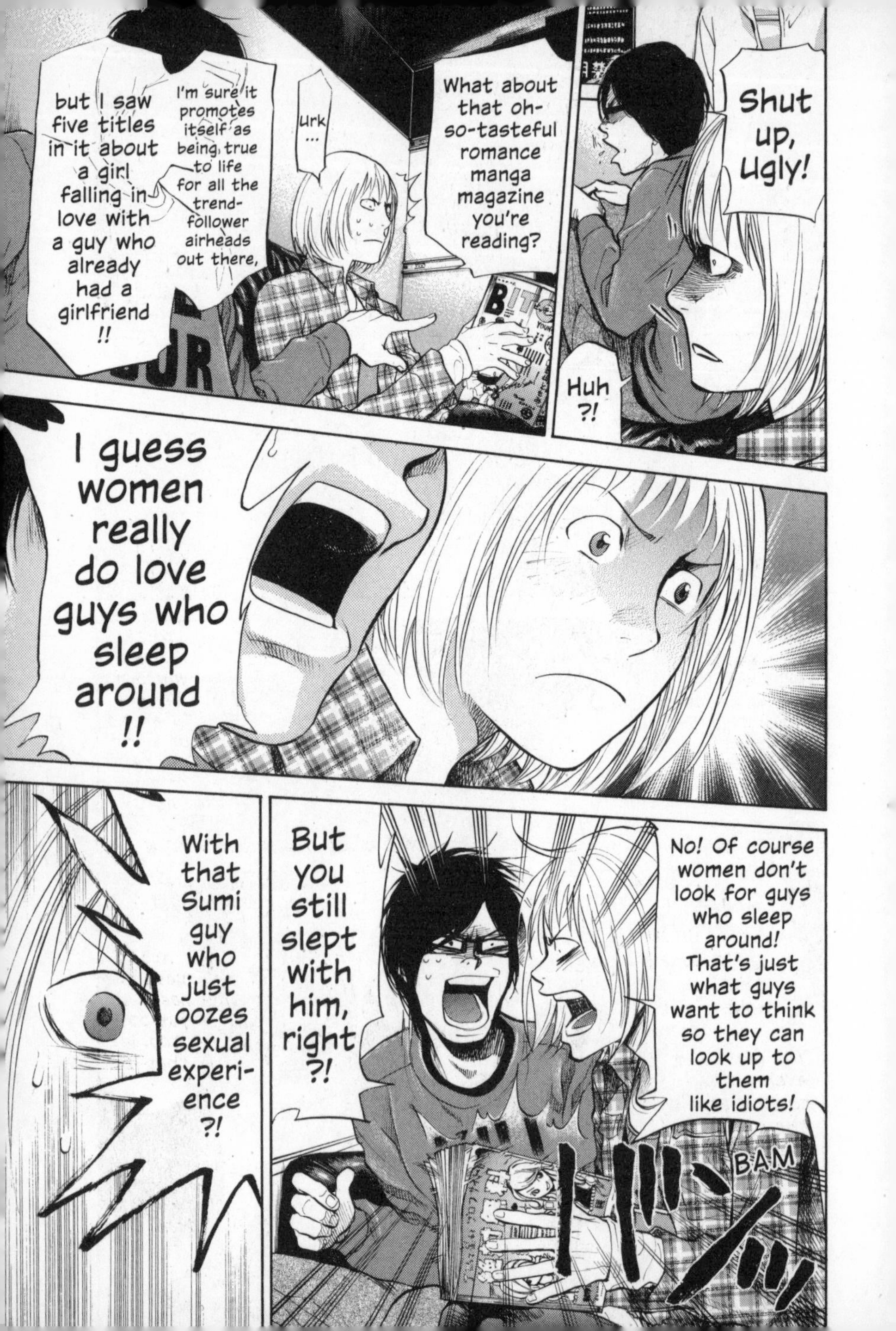
Shut up, Ugly!
Huh ?!
What about that oh-so-tasteful romance manga magazine you're reading?
Urk ...
I'm sure it promotes itself as being true to life for all the trend-follower airheads out there,
but I saw five titles in it about a girl falling in love with a guy who already had a girlfriend !!
I guess women really do love guys who sleep around !!
No! Of course women don't look for guys who sleep around! That's just what guys want to think so they can look up to them like idiots!
BAM
But you still slept with him, right ?!
With that Sumi guy who just oozes sexual experi-ence ?!

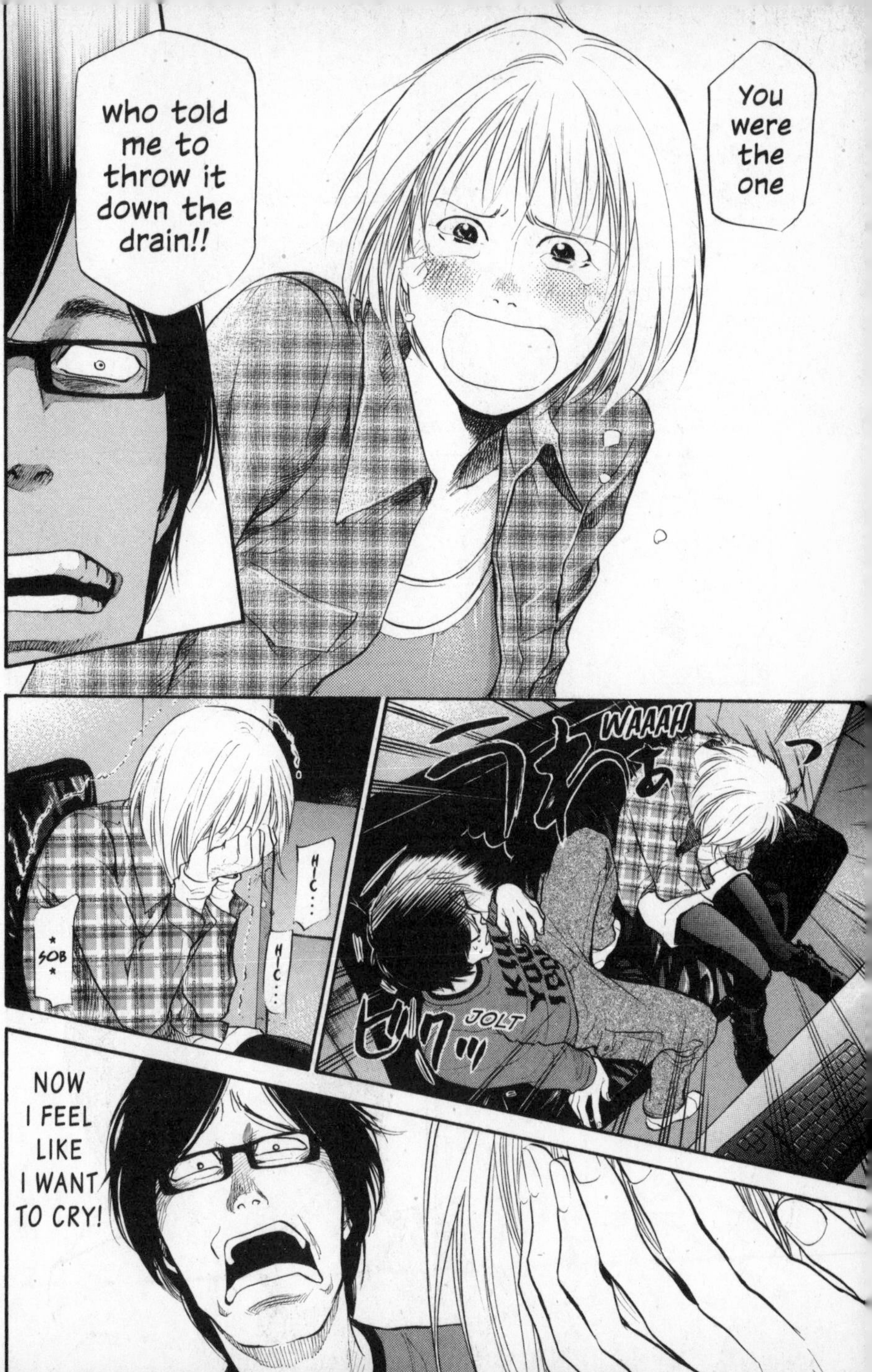
You were the one
who told me to throw it down the drain!!
WAAAH
JOLT
HIC...
HIC...
SOB
NOW I FEEL LIKE I WANT TO CRY!

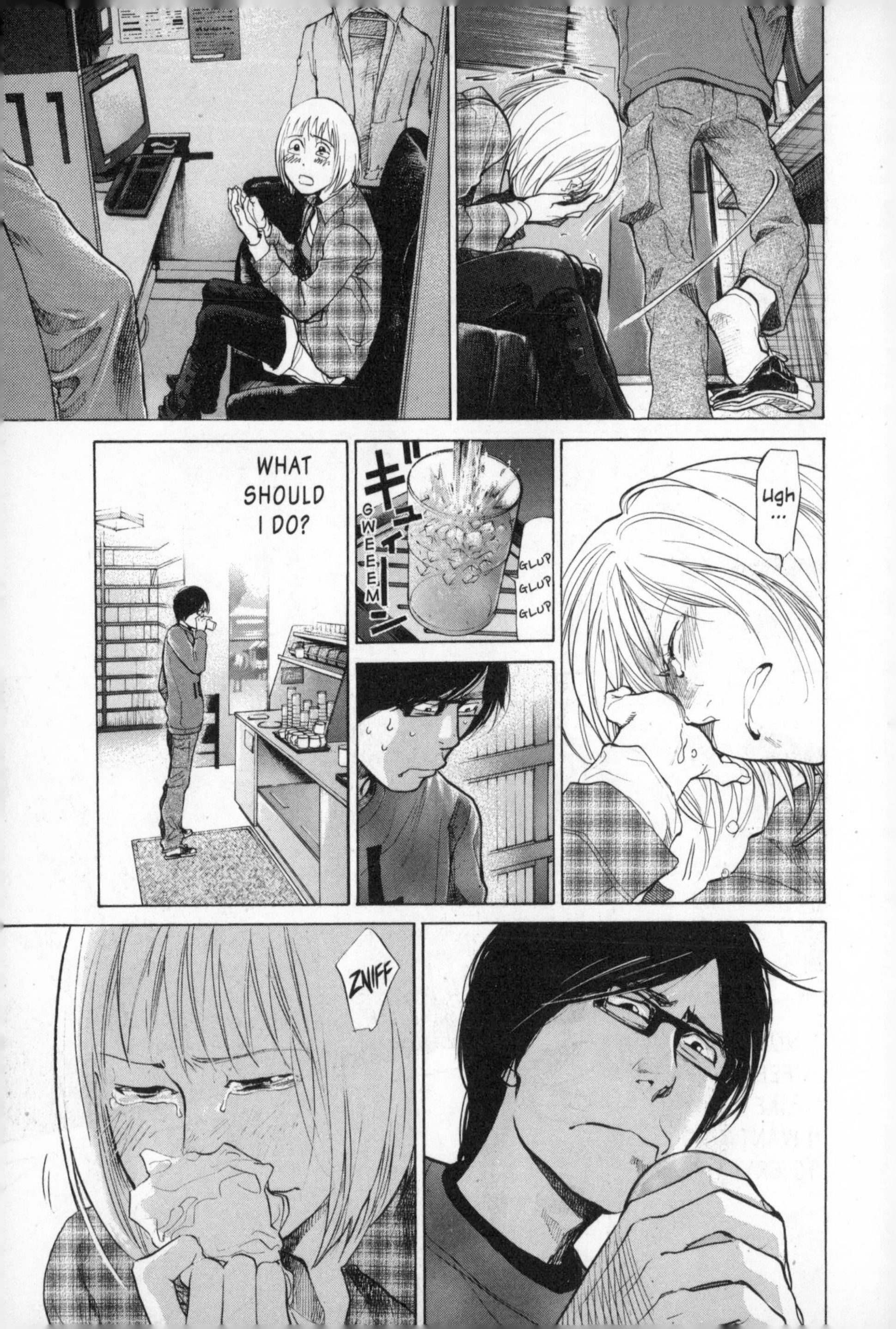
Ugh ...
ギュイー
GWEEEM
GLUP GLUP GLUP
WHAT SHOULD I DO?
ZNIFF

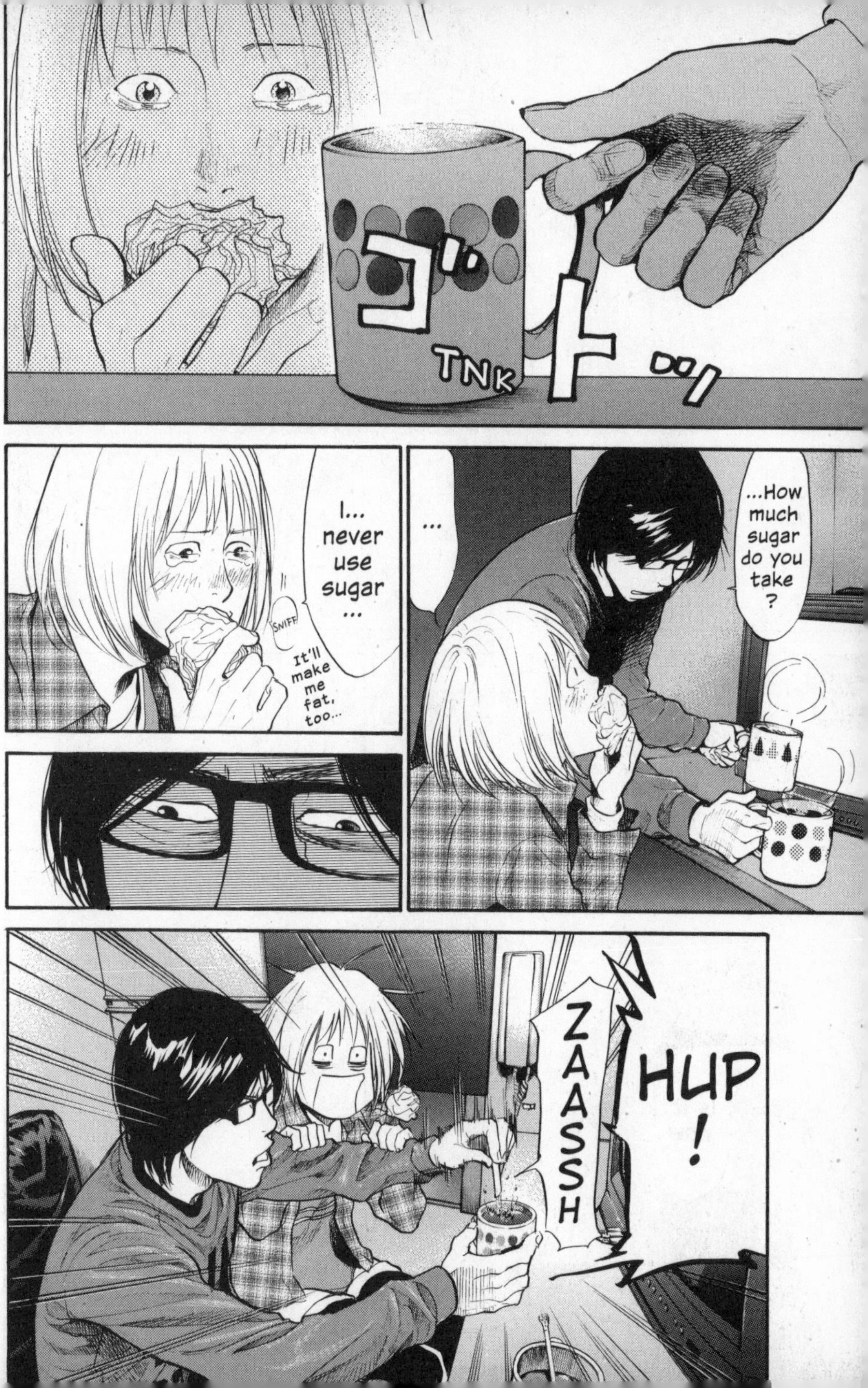
ゴトッ
TNK
...How much sugar do you take ?
...
I... never use sugar ...
SNIFF
It'll make me fat, too...
HUP !
ZAASSH

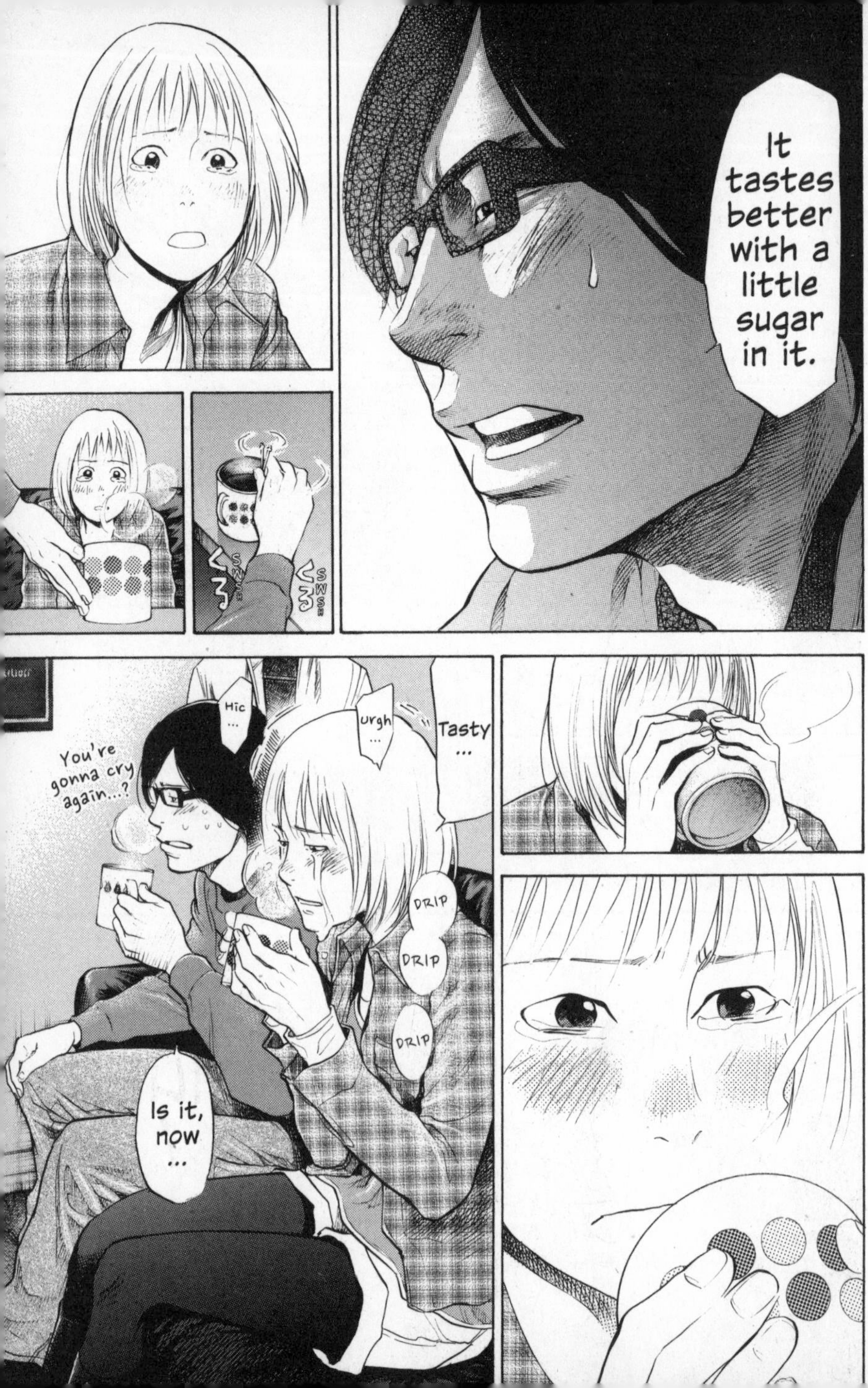
It tastes better with a little sugar in it.
くる SWSH
くる SWSH
Tasty ...
urgh ...
Hic ...
You're gonna cry again...?
DRIP
DRIP
DRIP
Is it, now ...

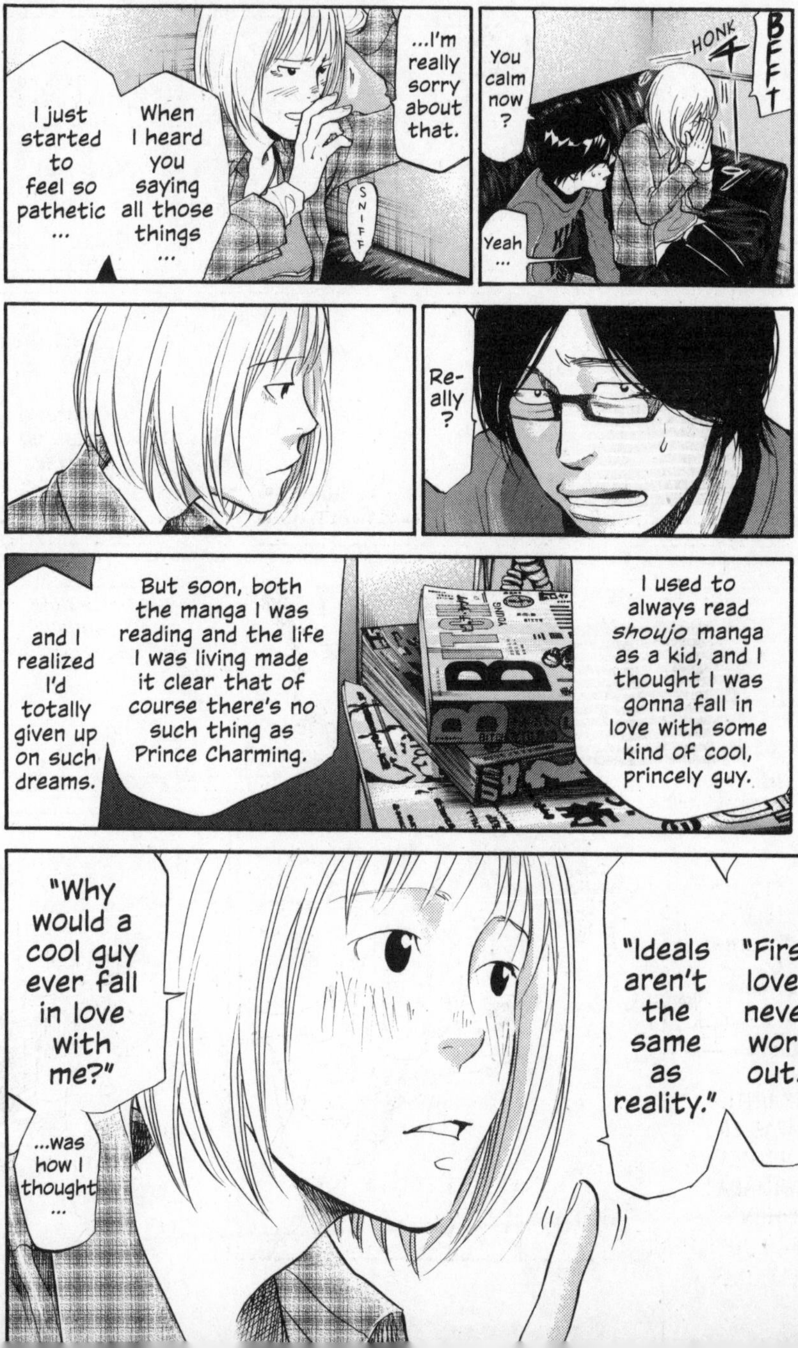
BFFT
HONK
You calm now?
Yeah...
...I'm really sorry about that.
SNIFF
When I heard you saying all those things...
I just started to feel so pathetic...
Re-ally?
I used to always read *shoujo* manga as a kid, and I thought I was gonna fall in love with some kind of cool, princely guy.
But soon, both the manga I was reading and the life I was living made it clear that of course there's no such thing as Prince Charming.
and I realized I'd totally given up on such dreams.
"First loves never work out."
"Ideals aren't the same as reality."
"Why would a cool guy ever fall in love with me?"
...was how I thought...

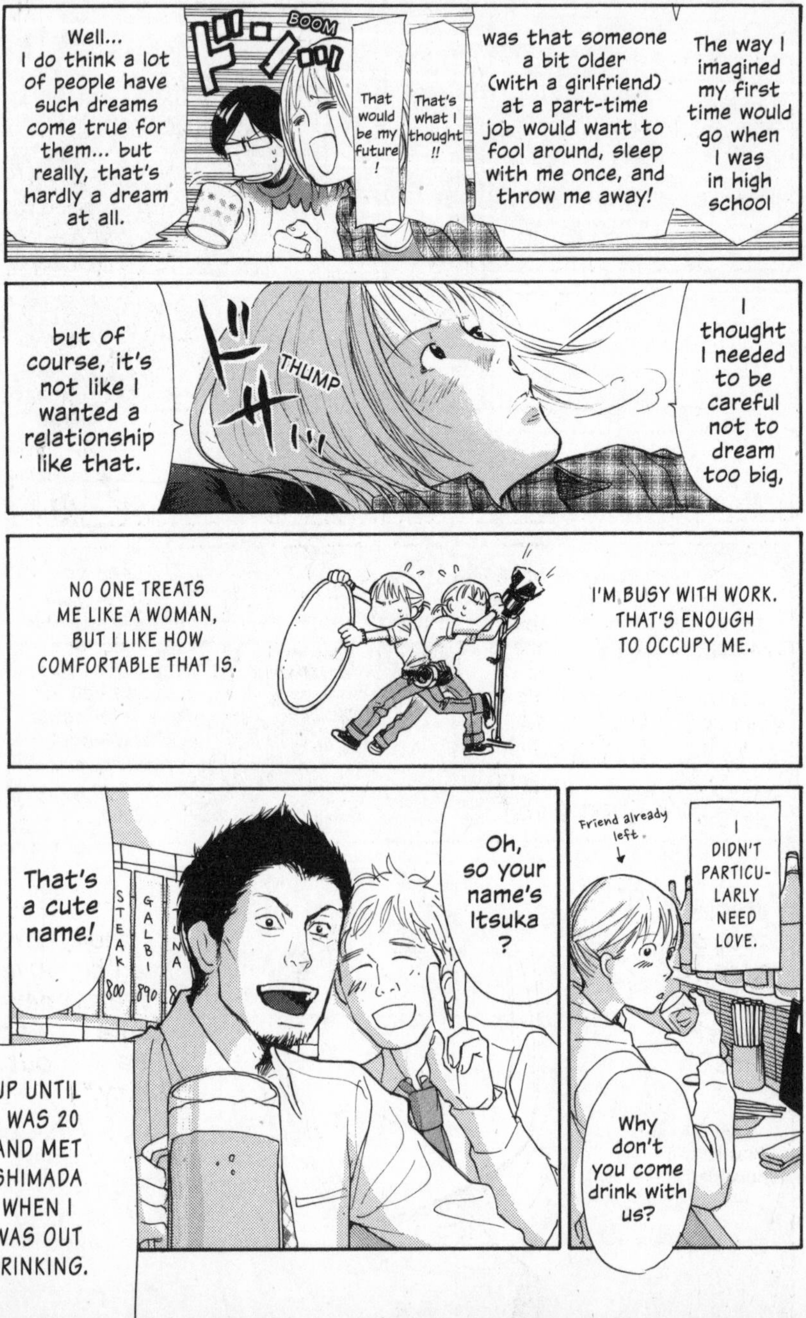
The way I imagined my first time would go when I was in high school
was that someone a bit older (with a girlfriend) at a part-time job would want to fool around, sleep with me once, and throw me away!
That's what I thought !!
That would be my future !
BOOM
Well... I do think a lot of people have such dreams come true for them... but really, that's hardly a dream at all.
I thought I needed to be careful not to dream too big,
THUMP
but of course, it's not like I wanted a relationship like that.
I'M BUSY WITH WORK. THAT'S ENOUGH TO OCCUPY ME.
NO ONE TREATS ME LIKE A WOMAN, BUT I LIKE HOW COMFORTABLE THAT IS.
I DIDN'T PARTICULARLY NEED LOVE.
Friend already left
Why don't you come drink with us?
Oh, so your name's Itsuka?
That's a cute name!
STEAK 800
GALBI 890
UP UNTIL I WAS 20 AND MET SHIMADA WHEN I WAS OUT DRINKING.

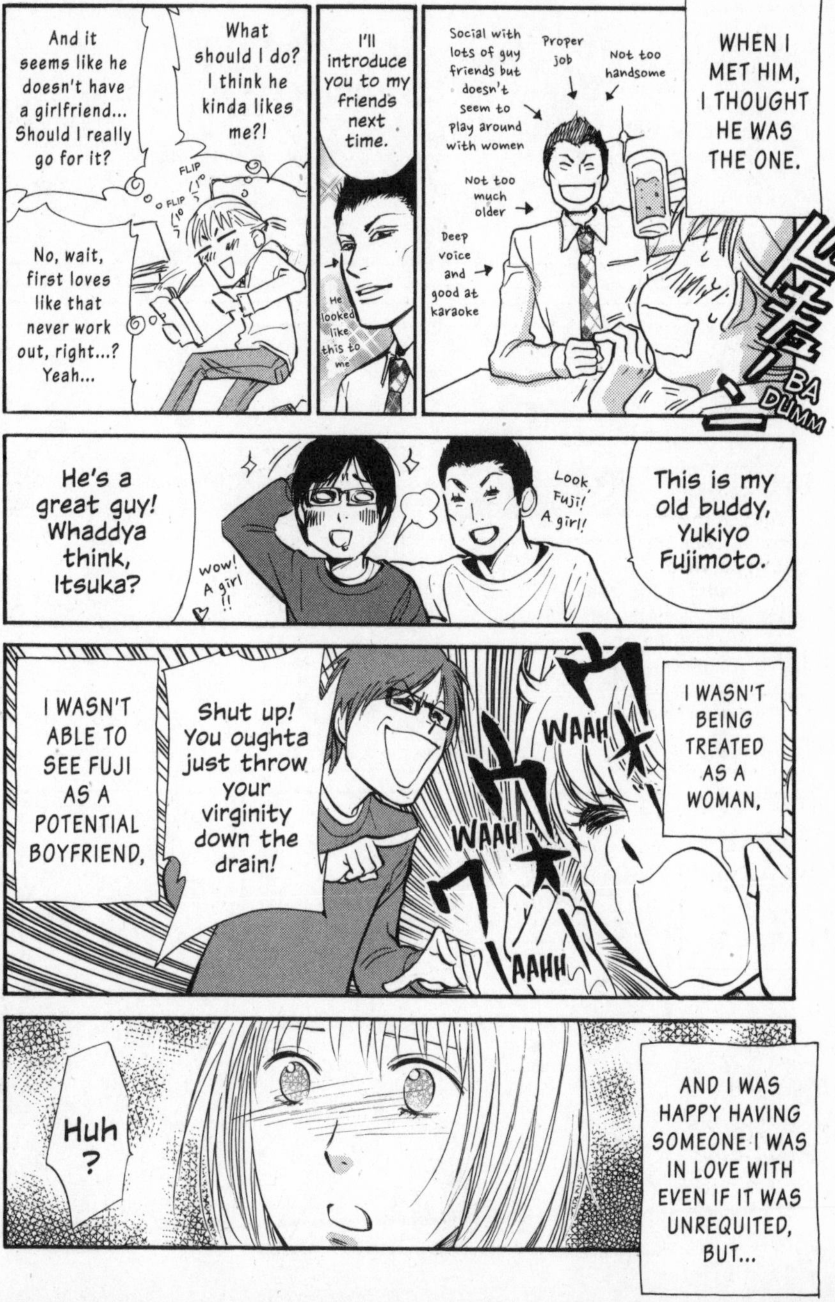
WHEN I MET HIM, I THOUGHT HE WAS THE ONE.
Social with lots of guy friends but doesn't seem to play around with women
Proper job
Not too handsome
Not too much older
Deep voice and good at karaoke
BA DUMM
I'll introduce you to my friends next time.
He looked like this to me
What should I do? I think he kinda likes me?!
And it seems like he doesn't have a girlfriend... Should I really go for it?
FLIP
FLIP
No, wait, first loves like that never work out, right...? Yeah...
This is my old buddy, Yukiyo Fujimoto.
Look, Fuji! A girl!
Wow! A girl!!
He's a great guy! Whaddya think, Itsuka?
I WASN'T BEING TREATED AS A WOMAN,
WAAH
WAAH
AAHH
Shut up! You oughta just throw your virginity down the drain!
I WASN'T ABLE TO SEE FUJI AS A POTENTIAL BOYFRIEND,
AND I WAS HAPPY HAVING SOMEONE I WAS IN LOVE WITH EVEN IF IT WAS UNREQUITED, BUT...
Huh?

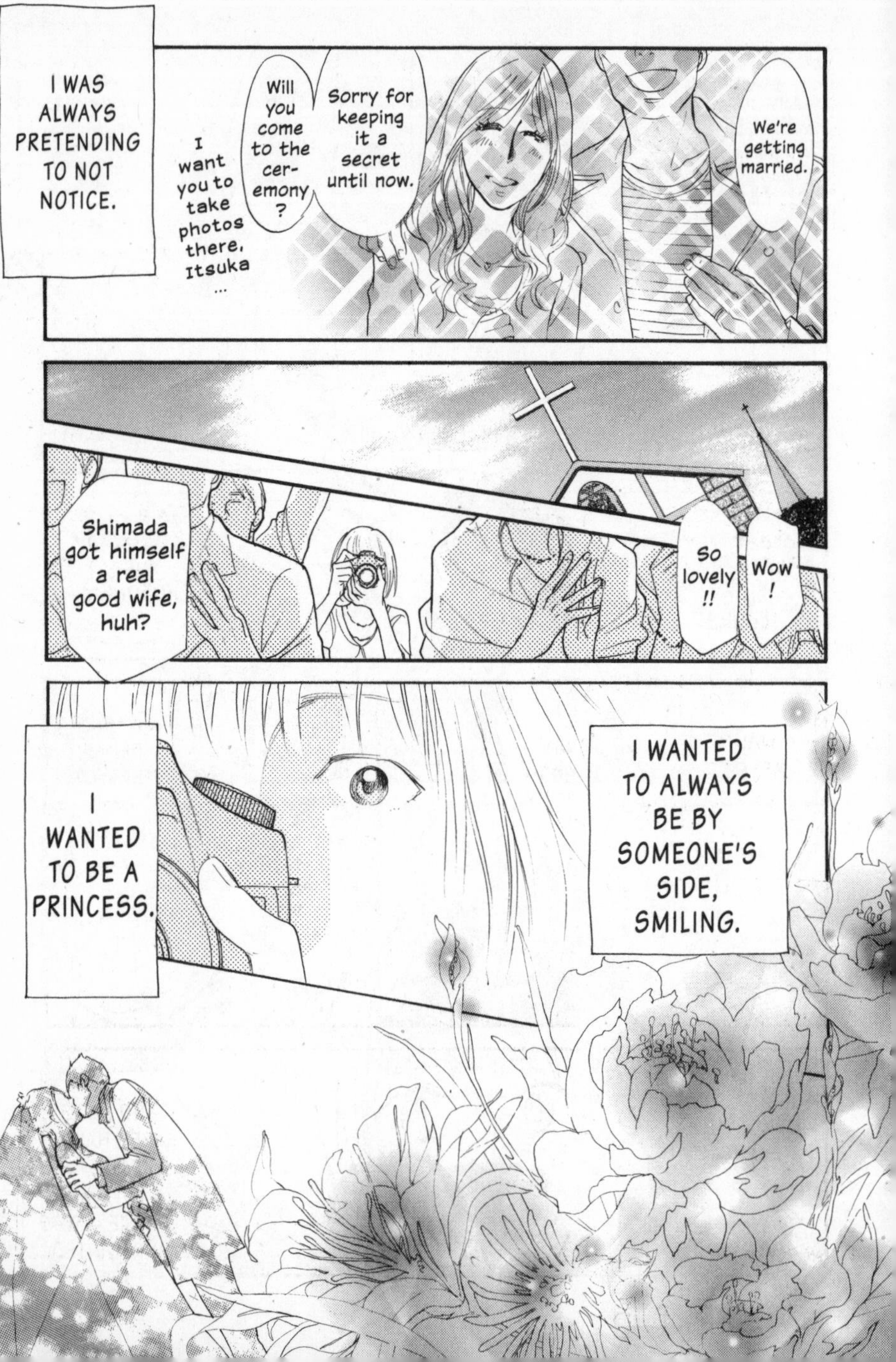
We're getting married.
Sorry for keeping it a secret until now.
Will you come to the cer-emony?
I want you to take photos there, Itsuka...
I WAS ALWAYS PRETENDING TO NOT NOTICE.
Wow!
So lovely!!
Shimada got himself a real good wife, huh?
I WANTED TO ALWAYS BE BY SOMEONE'S SIDE, SMILING.
I WANTED TO BE A PRINCESS.

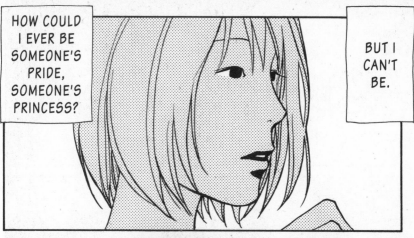

BUT I CAN'T BE.
HOW COULD I EVER BE SOMEONE'S PRIDE, SOMEONE'S PRINCESS?
I'm Cinderella without the bravery to go to the castle ...
I can't even wear glass slippers ...
GRASP
Hey! Your flashback has started getting super influenced by all kinds of romance comics! There's so much to poke fun at that I can't keep up...
OH, SHUT UP!!
Stop cutting me off and just listen !!
Hell no, I'm cutting this to pieces!! Don't you realize how self-absorbed you sound?!
JUMP
...
Well, yeah ...
Back then I was suuuuuper absorbed in how wounded I was... I guess ...
BLUSH
Then, when I ended up crying in a corner somewhere ...

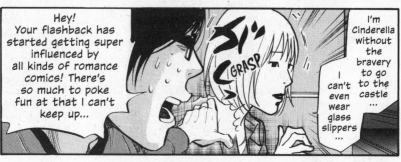

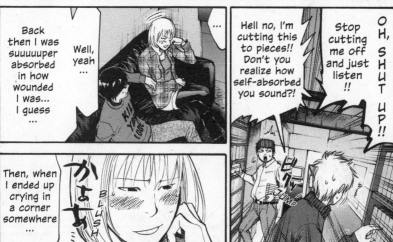

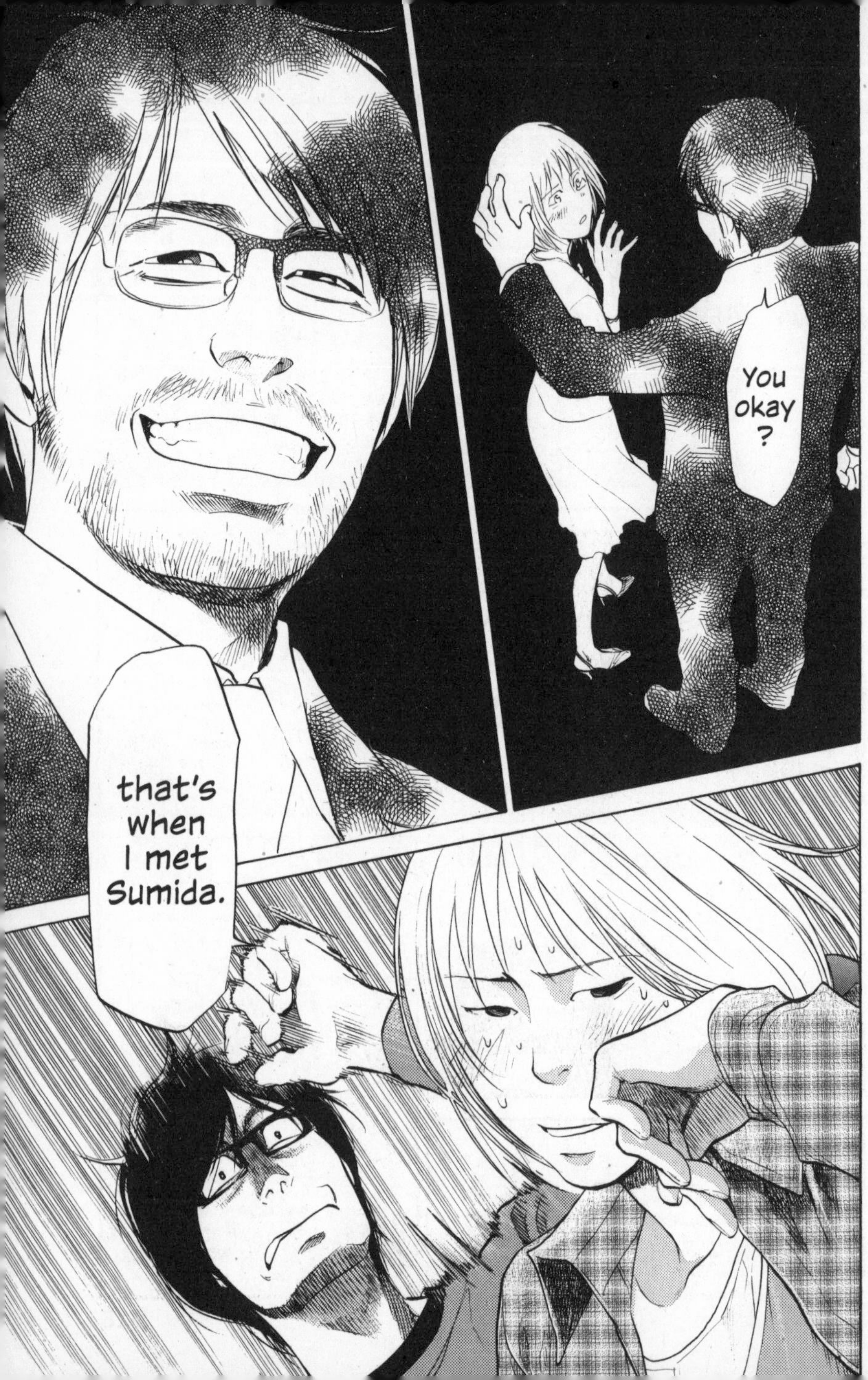
You okay?
that's when I met Sumida.

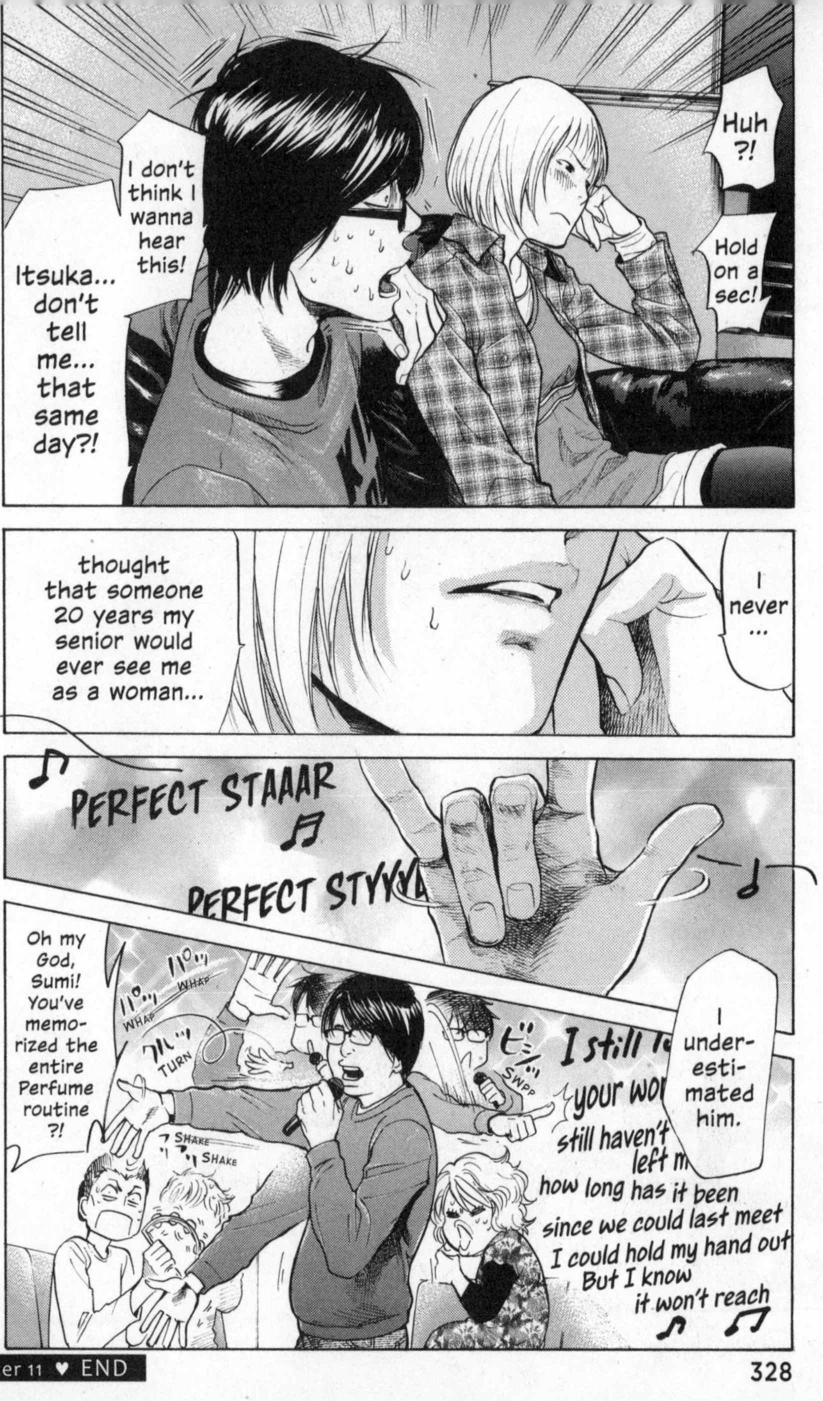
Huh?!
Hold on a sec!
I don't think I wanna hear this!
Itsuka... don't tell me... that same day?!
I never...
thought that someone 20 years my senior would ever see me as a woman...
PERFECT STAAAR
PERFECT STYYY
I underestimated him.
I still l
your wo
still haven't
left m
how long has it been
since we could last meet
I could hold my hand out
But I know
it won't reach
SWPP
パッ
WHAP
WHAP
TURN
Oh my God, Sumi! You've memorized the entire Perfume routine?!
SHAKE
SHAKE

Chapter 12 ♥ Love Cycle

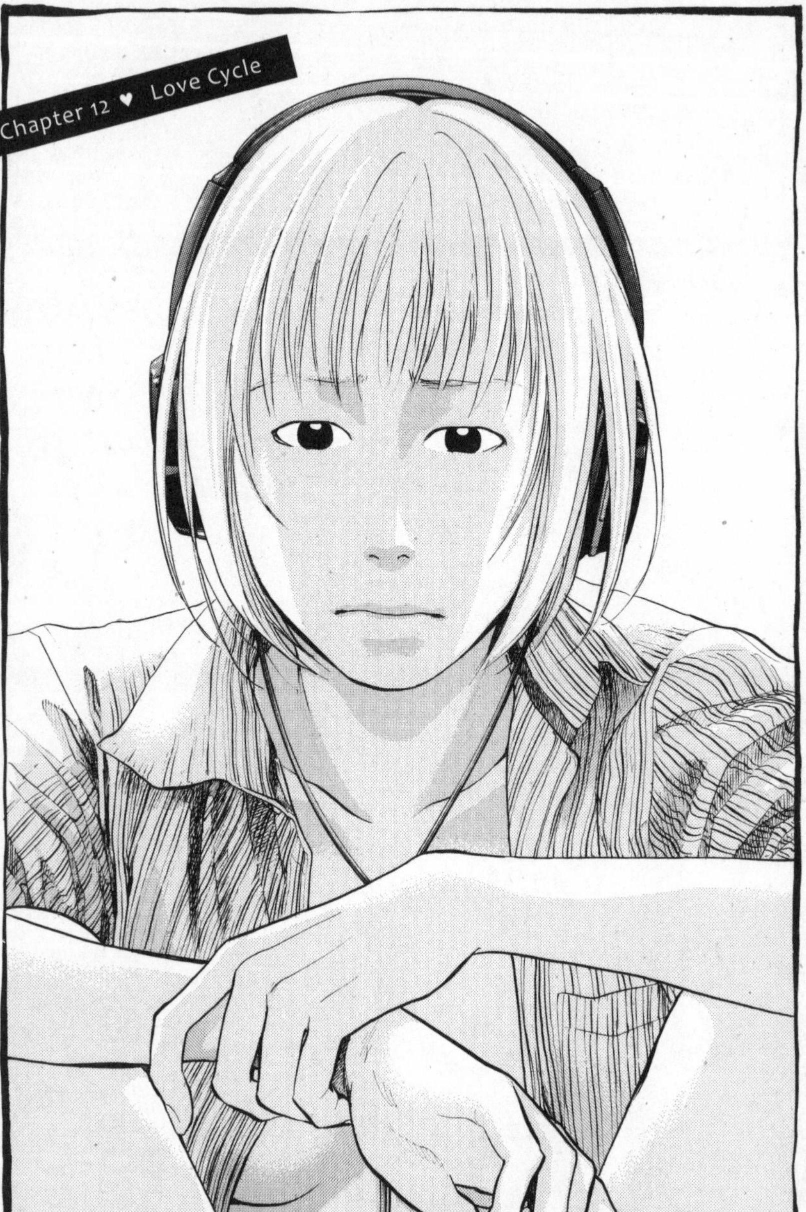

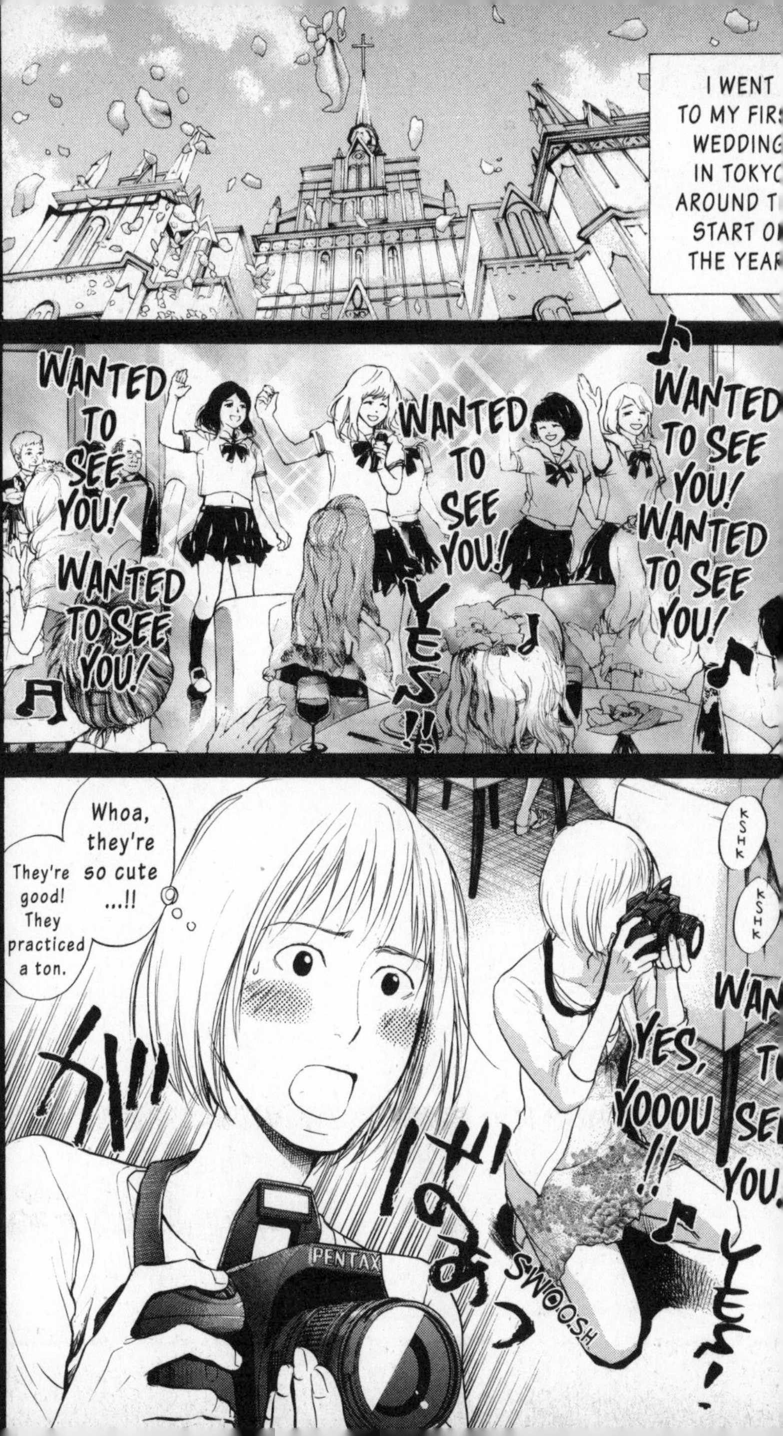
I WENT TO MY FIRS WEDDING IN TOKY AROUND T START O THE YEAR
WANTED TO SEE YOU! WANTED TO SEE YOU!
WANTED TO SEE YOU!
YES~!!
WANTED TO SEE YOU!
WANTED TO SEE YOU!
KSHK
KSHK
YOU.
YES, YOOOU!!
YES~!
SWOOSH
Whoa, they're so cute ...!!
They're good! They practiced a ton.

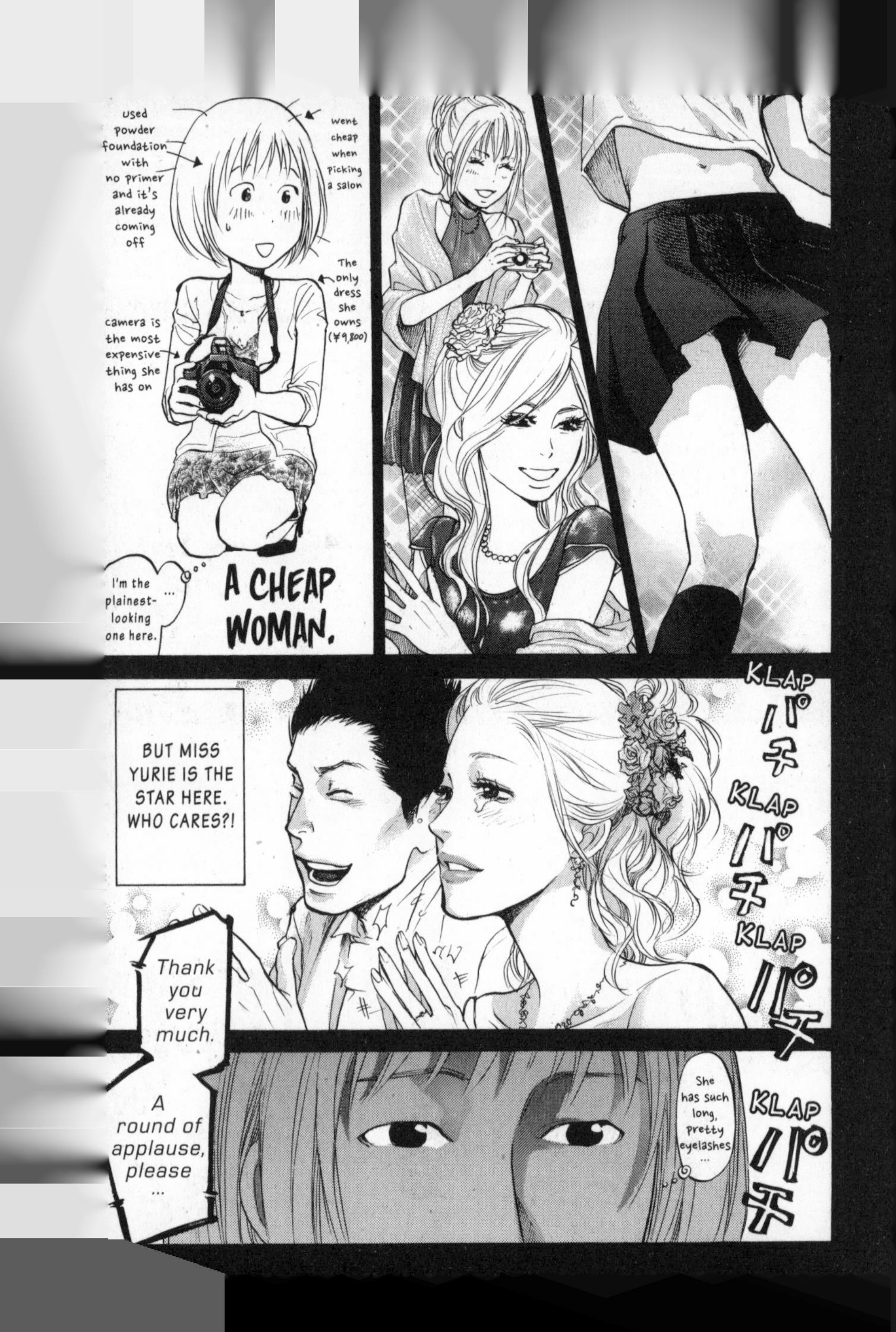

went cheap when picking a salon
used powder foundation with no primer and it's already coming off
The only dress she owns (¥9,800)
camera is the most expensive thing she has on
A CHEAP WOMAN.
I'm the plainest-looking one here...
KLAP
パチ
KLAP
パチ
KLAP
パチ
BUT MISS YURIE IS THE STAR HERE. WHO CARES?!
Thank you very much.
KLAP
パチ
She has such long, pretty eyelashes...
A round of applause, please ...

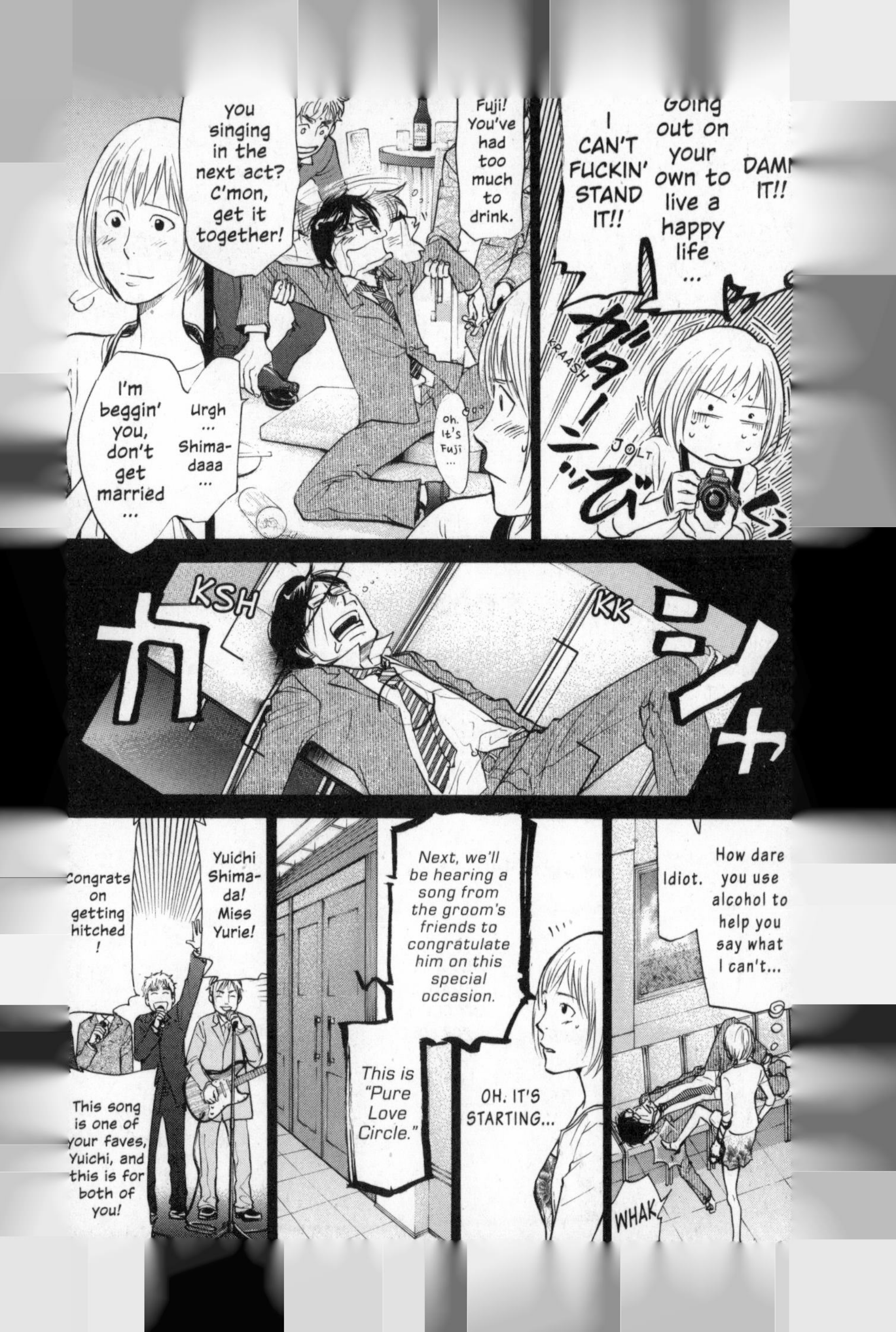
DAMN IT!!
Going out on your own to live a happy life ...
I CAN'T FUCKIN' STAND IT!!
KRAASH
JOLT
Fuji! You've had too much to drink.
you singing in the next act? C'mon, get it together!
Oh. It's Fuji ...
Urgh ... Shimadaaa ...
I'm beggin' you, don't get married ...
KK
KSH
How dare you use alcohol to help you say what I can't...
Idiot.
WHAK
Next, we'll be hearing a song from the groom's friends to congratulate him on this special occasion.
OH. IT'S STARTING...
This is "Pure Love Circle."
Yuichi Shimada! Miss Yurie!
Congrats on getting hitched!
This song is one of your faves, Yuichi, and this is for both of you!

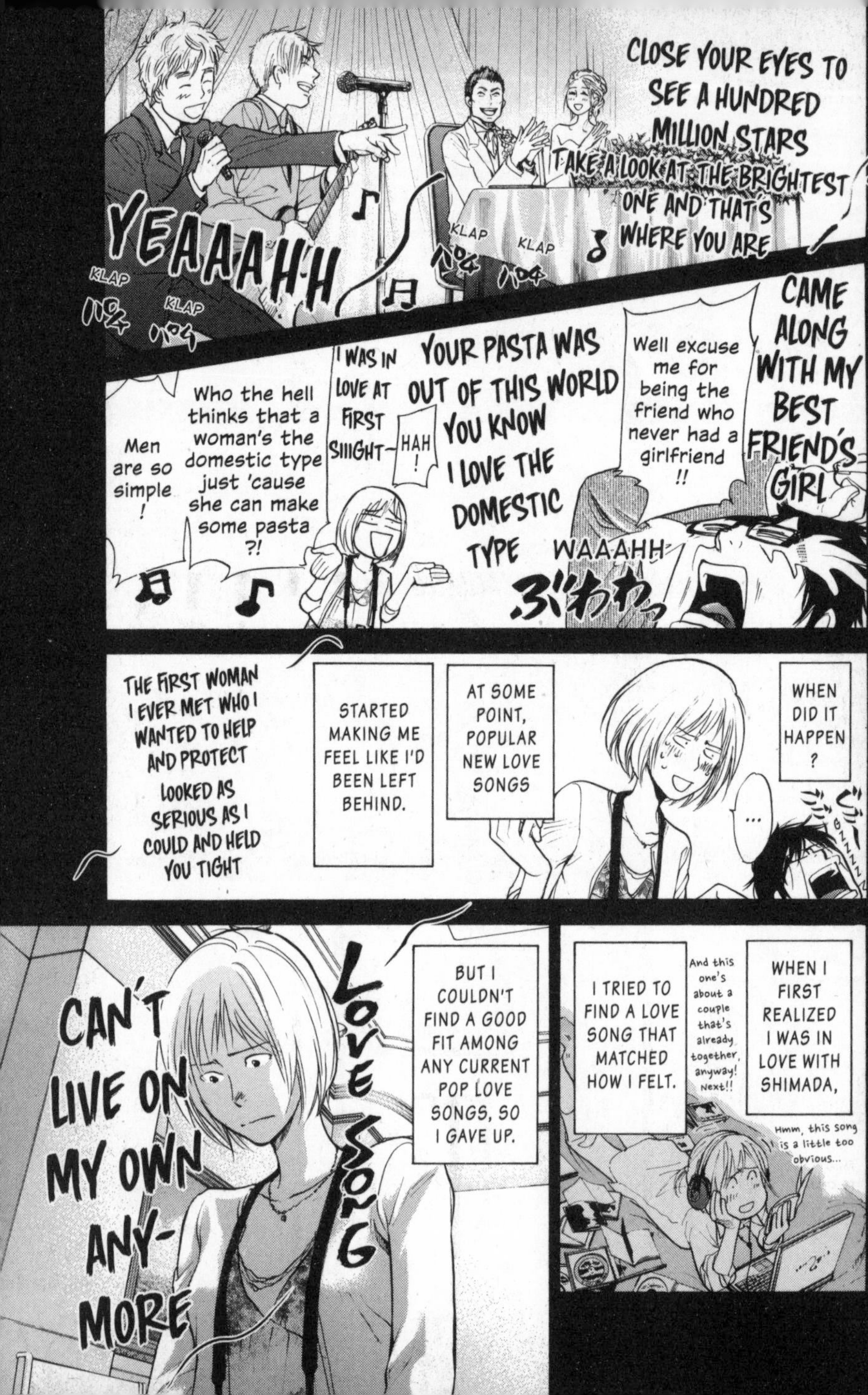
CLOSE YOUR EYES TO SEE A HUNDRED MILLION STARS
TAKE A LOOK AT THE BRIGHTEST ONE AND THAT'S WHERE YOU ARE
KLAP
KLAP
YEAAAAHH
KLAP
KLAP
CAME ALONG WITH MY BEST FRIEND'S GIRL
Well excuse me for being the friend who never had a girlfriend!!
WAAAHH
ぶわわっ
YOUR PASTA WAS OUT OF THIS WORLD YOU KNOW I LOVE THE DOMESTIC TYPE
HAH!
I WAS IN LOVE AT FIRST SIIIGHT-
Who the hell thinks that a woman's the domestic type just 'cause she can make some pasta?!
Men are so simple!
WHEN DID IT HAPPEN?
...
GNZZZZ
AT SOME POINT, POPULAR NEW LOVE SONGS
STARTED MAKING ME FEEL LIKE I'D BEEN LEFT BEHIND.
THE FIRST WOMAN I EVER MET WHO I WANTED TO HELP AND PROTECT LOOKED AS SERIOUS AS I COULD AND HELD YOU TIGHT
WHEN I FIRST REALIZED I WAS IN LOVE WITH SHIMADA,
And this one's about a couple that's already together, anyway! Next!!
Hmm, this song is a little too obvious...
I TRIED TO FIND A LOVE SONG THAT MATCHED HOW I FELT.
BUT I COULDN'T FIND A GOOD FIT AMONG ANY CURRENT POP LOVE SONGS, SO I GAVE UP.
LOVE SONG
CAN'T LIVE ON MY OWN ANY-MORE

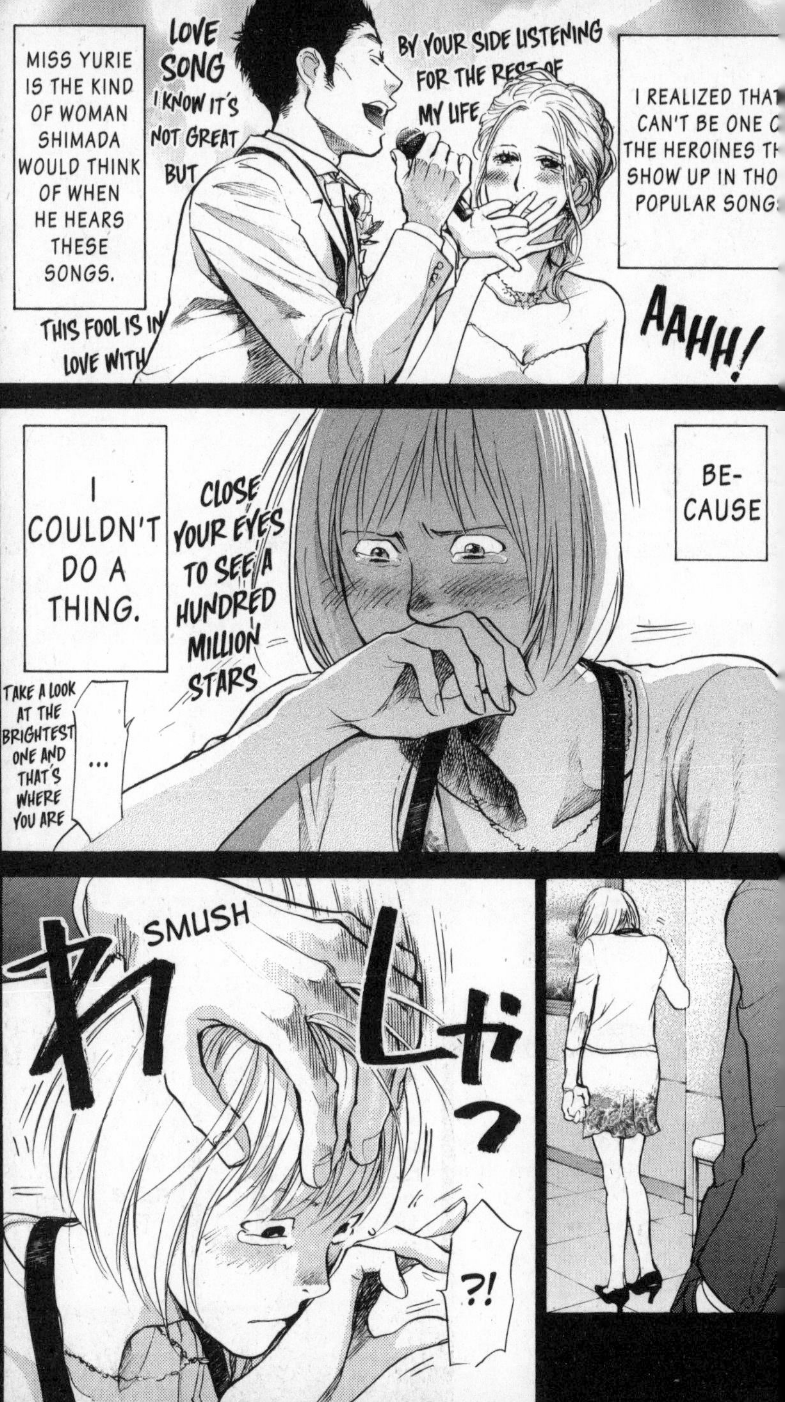

I REALIZED THAT CAN'T BE ONE C THE HEROINES TH SHOW UP IN THO POPULAR SONGS
BY YOUR SIDE LISTENING FOR THE REST OF MY LIFE
LOVE SONG I KNOW IT'S NOT GREAT BUT
AAHH!
MISS YURIE IS THE KIND OF WOMAN SHIMADA WOULD THINK OF WHEN HE HEARS THESE SONGS.
THIS FOOL IS IN LOVE WITH
BE-CAUSE
CLOSE YOUR EYES TO SEE A HUNDRED MILLION STARS
I COULDN'T DO A THING.
...
TAKE A LOOK AT THE BRIGHTEST ONE AND THAT'S WHERE YOU ARE
?!
わしゃっ
SMUSH

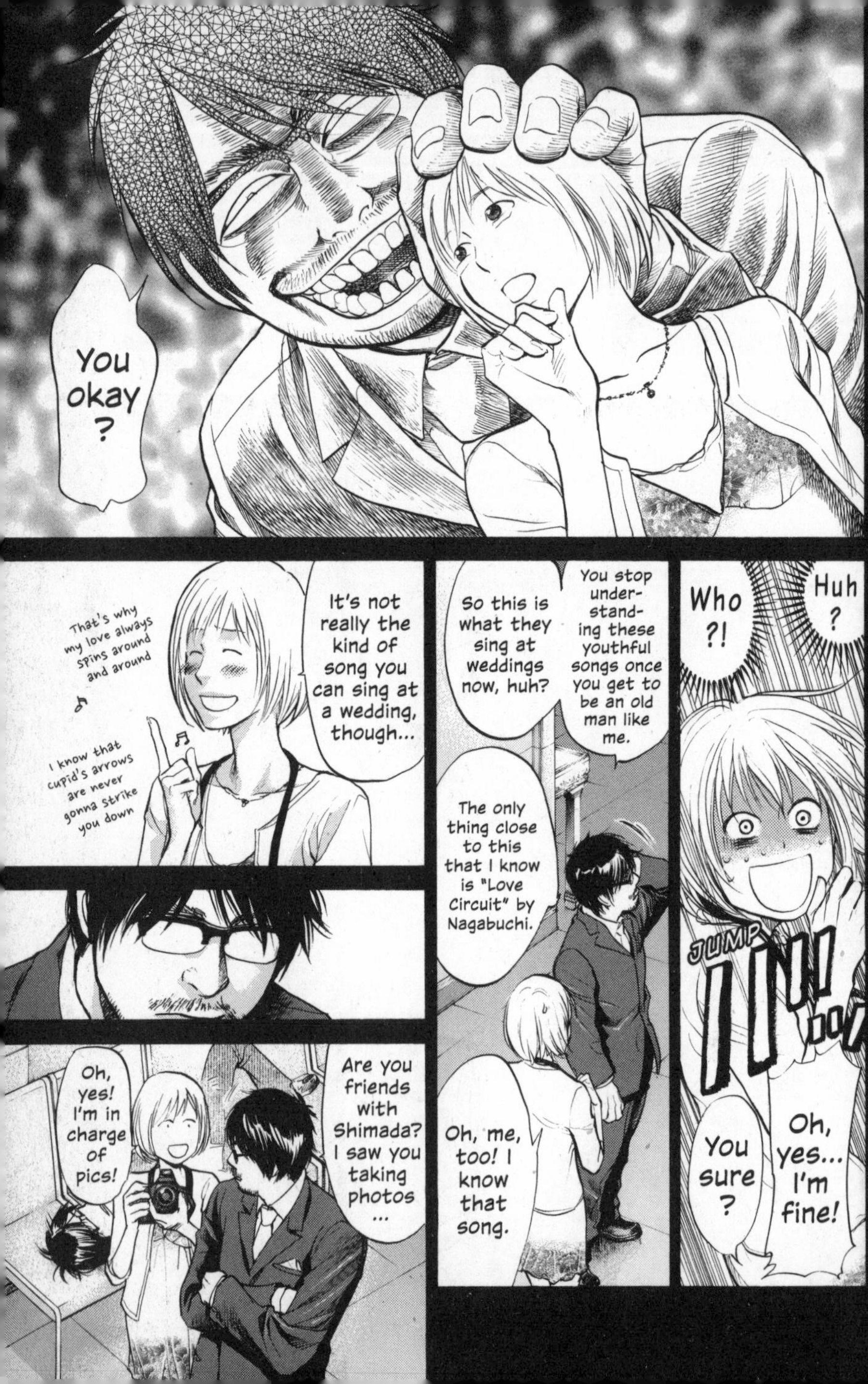
You okay?
Huh?
Who?!
JUMP
Oh, yes... I'm fine!
You sure?
You stop under-standing these youthful songs once you get to be an old man like me.
So this is what they sing at weddings now, huh?
The only thing close to this that I know is "Love Circuit" by Nagabuchi.
Oh, me, too! I know that song.
It's not really the kind of song you can sing at a wedding, though...
That's why my love always spins around and around
I know that cupid's arrows are never gonna strike you down
Are you friends with Shimada? I saw you taking photos...
Oh, yes! I'm in charge of pics!

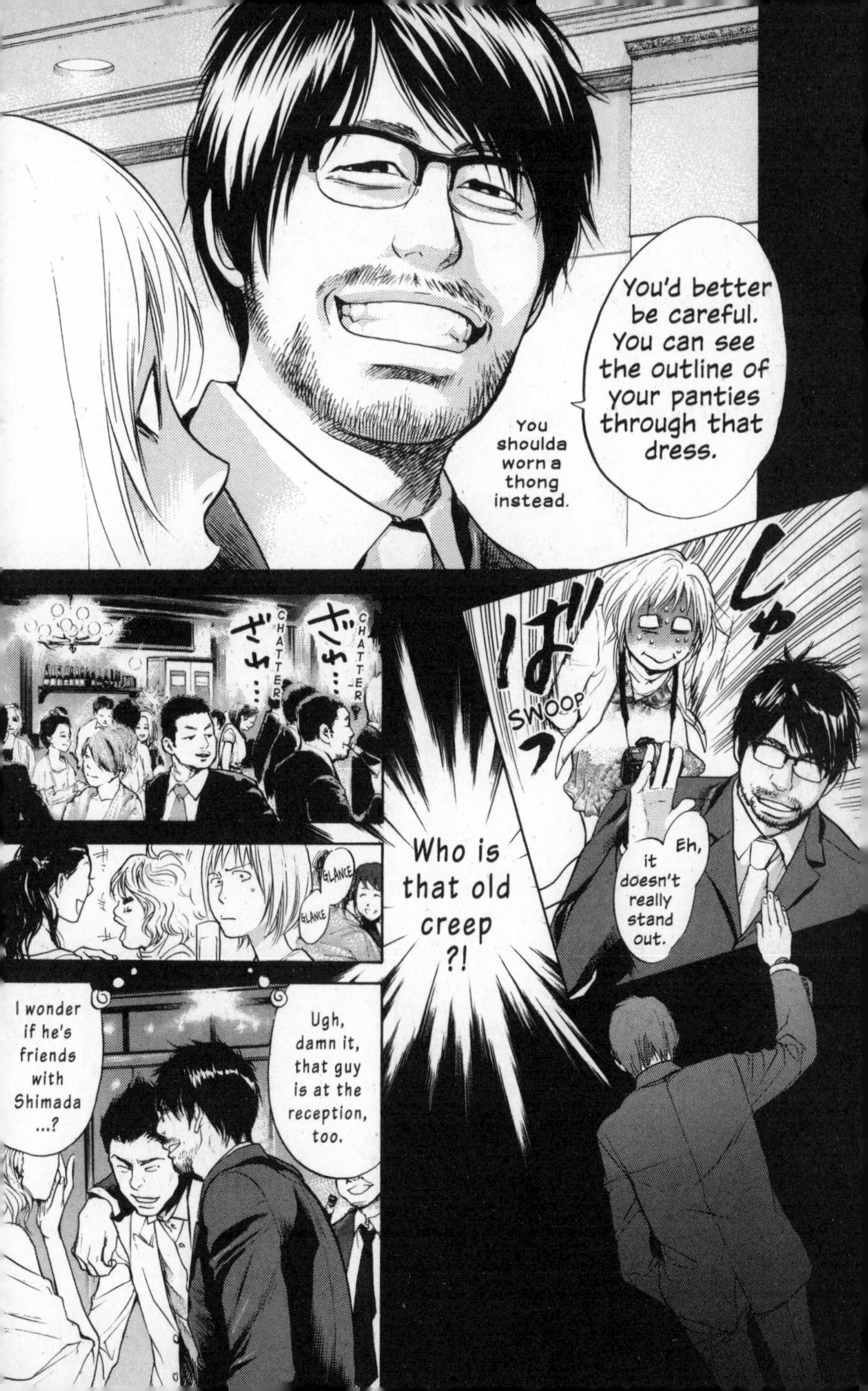
You'd better be careful. You can see the outline of your panties through that dress.
You shoulda worn a thong instead.
しゅ
ばっ
SWOOP
Eh, it doesn't really stand out.
Who is that old creep ?!
ざわ… CHATTER
ざわ… CHATTER
GLANCE
GLANCE
Ugh, damn it, that guy is at the reception, too.
I wonder if he's friends with Shimada ...?

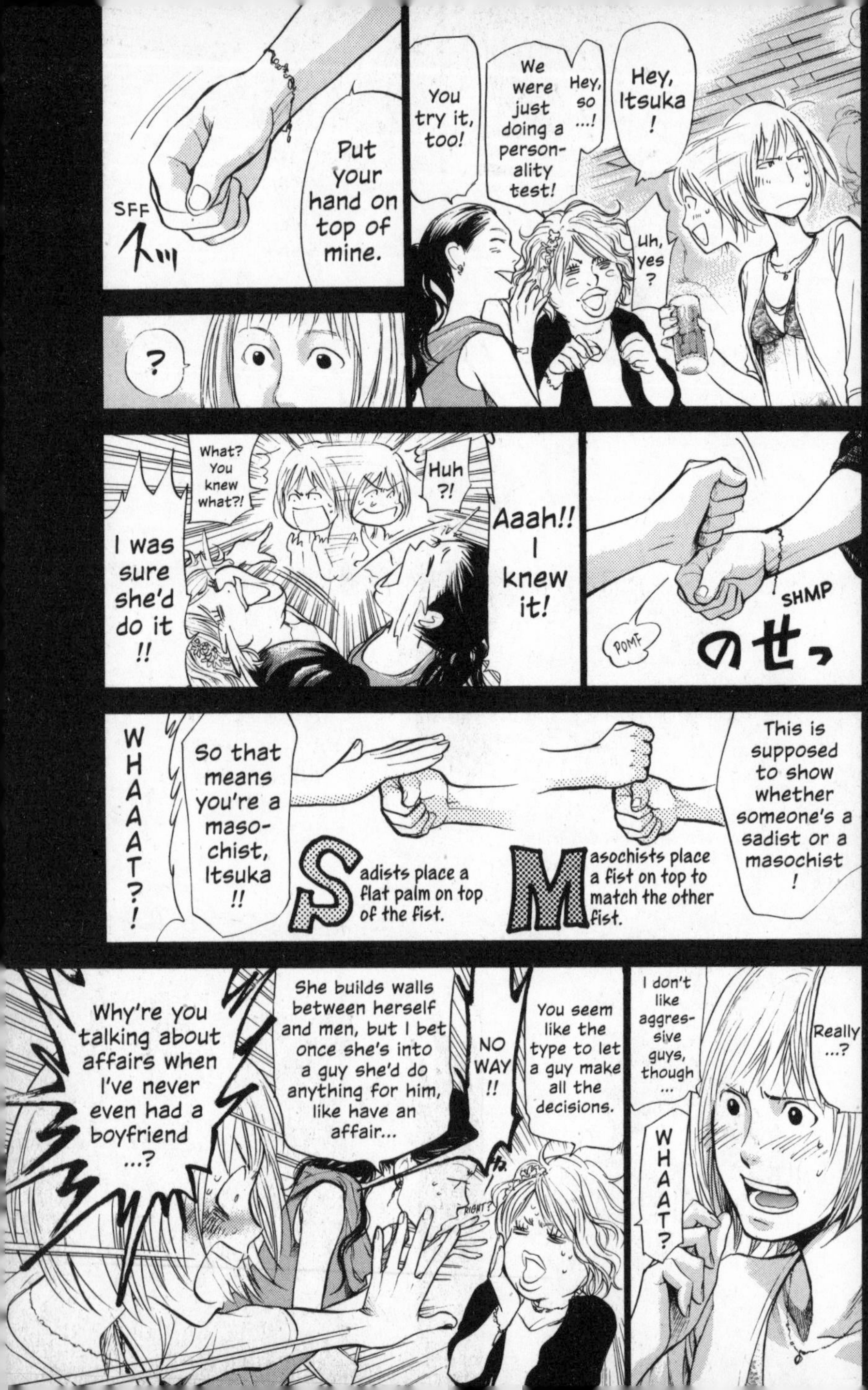
Hey, Itsuka!
Hey, so ...!
We were just doing a personality test!
You try it, too!
Uh, yes?
Put your hand on top of mine.
SFF
スッ
?
SHMP
のせっ
POMF
Aaah!! I knew it!
Huh?!
What? You knew what?!
I was sure she'd do it!!
This is supposed to show whether someone's a sadist or a masochist!
Masochists place a fist on top to match the other fist.
Sadists place a flat palm on top of the fist.
So that means you're a masochist, Itsuka!!
WHAAAAT?!
Really...?
WHAAT?
I don't like aggressive guys, though...
You seem like the type to let a guy make all the decisions.
NO WAY!!
She builds walls between herself and men, but I bet once she's into a guy she'd do anything for him, like have an affair...
RIGHT?
Why're you talking about affairs when I've never even had a boyfriend...?

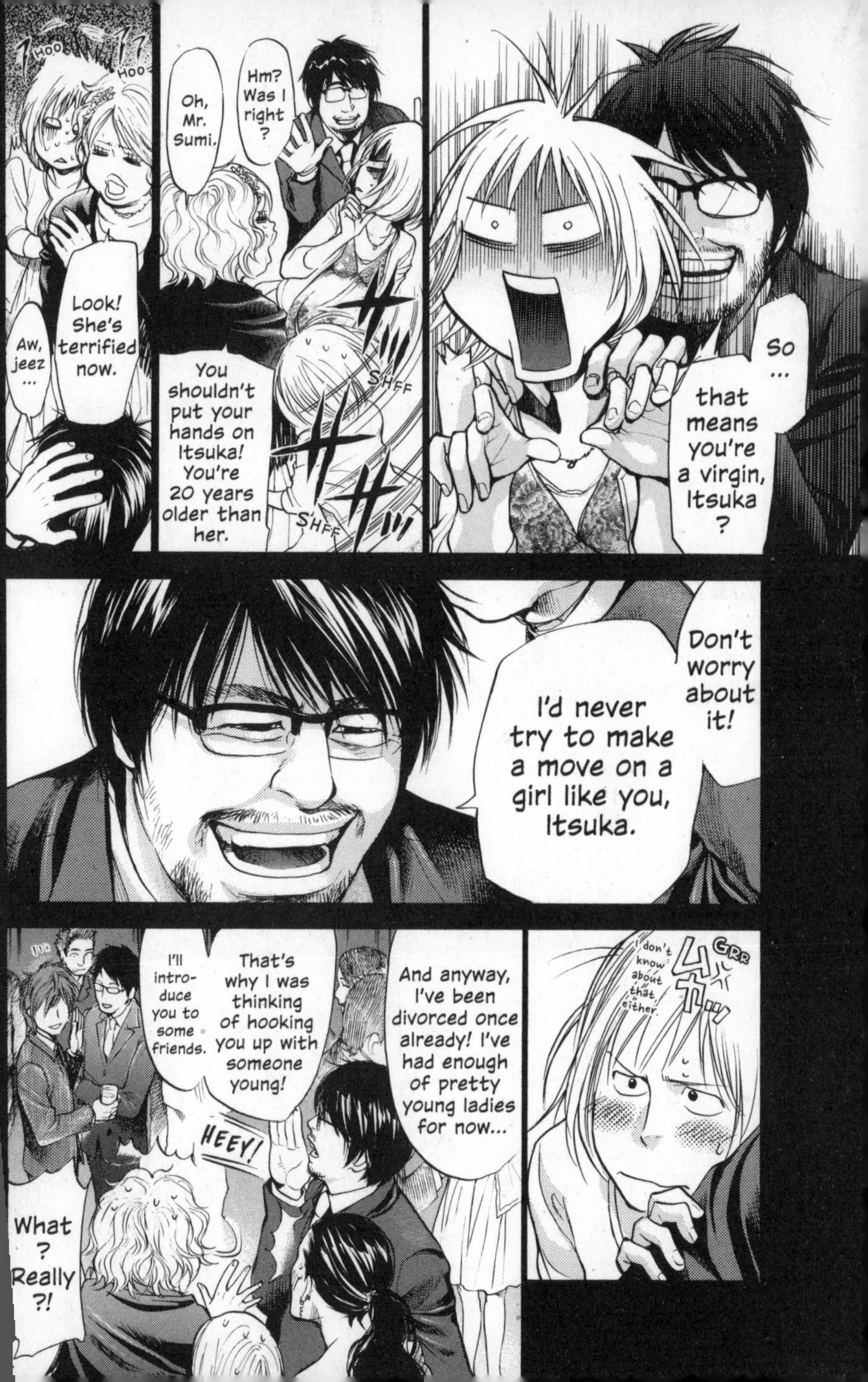
So ... that means you're a virgin, Itsuka?
Hm? Was I right?
Oh, Mr. Sumi.
You shouldn't put your hands on Itsuka! You're 20 years older than her.
SHFF
SHFF
HOO
HOO-
Look! She's terrified now.
Aw, jeez ...
Don't worry about it!
I'd never try to make a move on a girl like you, Itsuka.
GRR
I don't know about that either.
And anyway, I've been divorced once already! I've had enough of pretty young ladies for now...
That's why I was thinking of hooking you up with someone young!
I'll intro-duce you to some friends.
HEEY!
What? Really?!

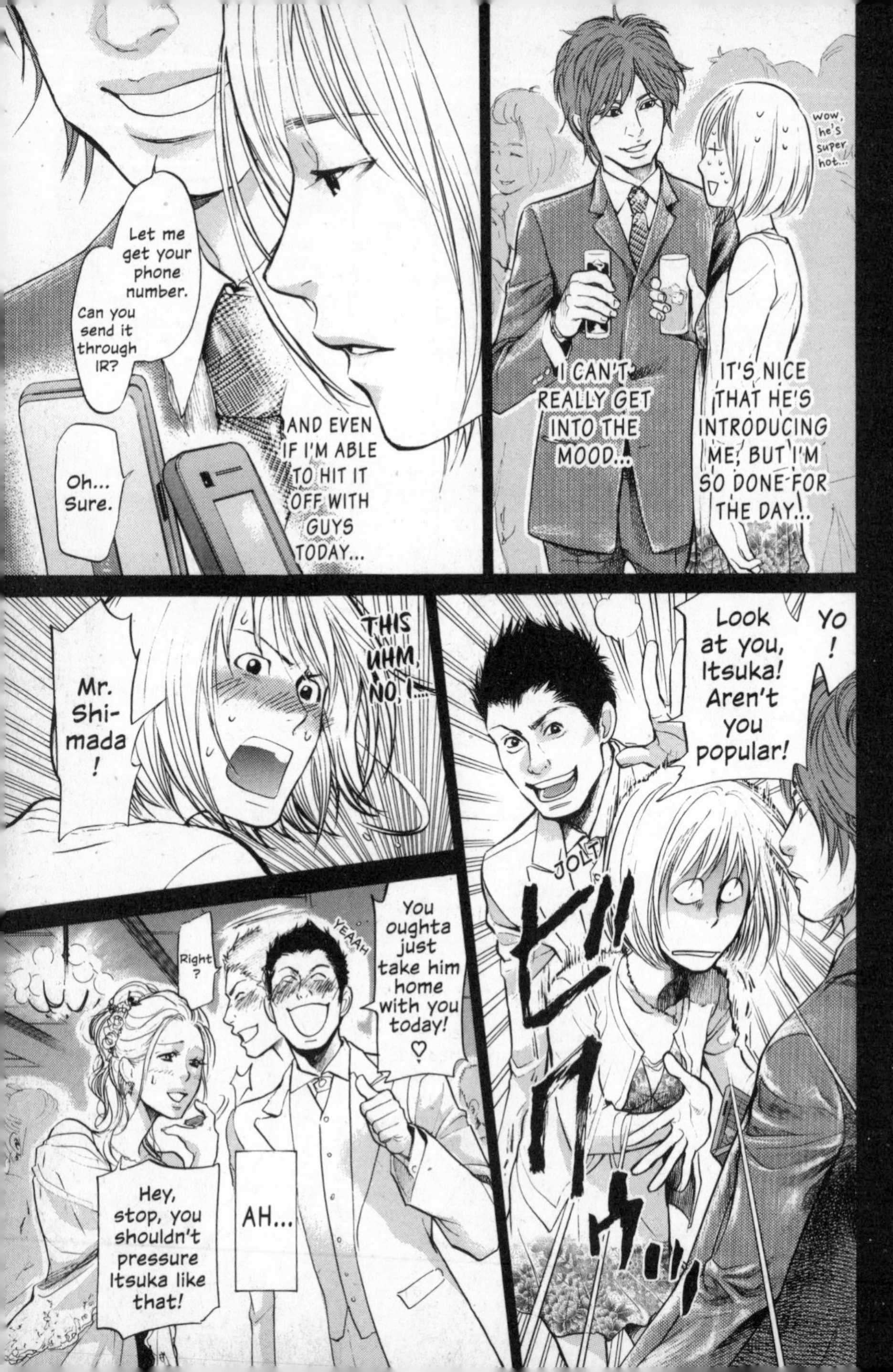
wow, he's super hot...
IT'S NICE THAT HE'S INTRODUCING ME, BUT I'M SO DONE FOR THE DAY...
I CAN'T REALLY GET INTO THE MOOD...
Let me get your phone number.
Can you send it through IR?
Oh... Sure.
AND EVEN IF I'M ABLE TO HIT IT OFF WITH GUYS TODAY...
YO!
Look at you, Itsuka! Aren't you popular!
JOLT
THIS UHM, NO, I...
Mr. Shimada!
You oughta just take him home with you today! ♡
YEAAH
Right?
AH...
Hey, stop, you shouldn't pressure Itsuka like that!

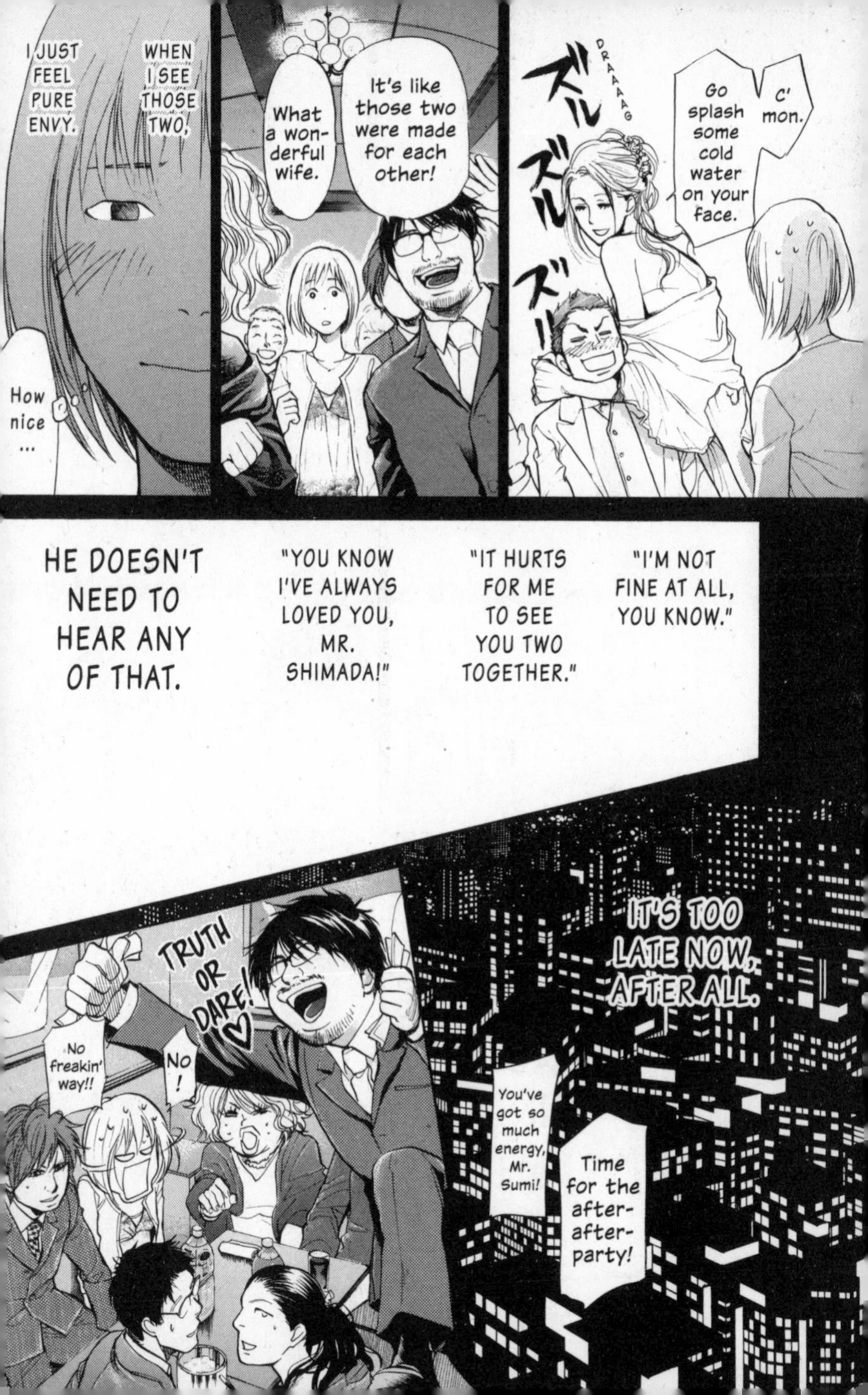
C' mon.
Go splash some cold water on your face.
ズル
ズル
ズー!
DRAAAAAG
It's like those two were made for each other!
What a won-derful wife.
WHEN I SEE THOSE TWO,
I JUST FEEL PURE ENVY.
How nice ...
"I'M NOT FINE AT ALL, YOU KNOW."
"IT HURTS FOR ME TO SEE YOU TWO TOGETHER."
"YOU KNOW I'VE ALWAYS LOVED YOU, MR. SHIMADA!"
HE DOESN'T NEED TO HEAR ANY OF THAT.
IT'S TOO LATE NOW, AFTER ALL.
Time for the after-after-party!
You've got so much energy, Mr. Sumi!
TRUTH OR DARE! ♡
No!
No freakin' way!!

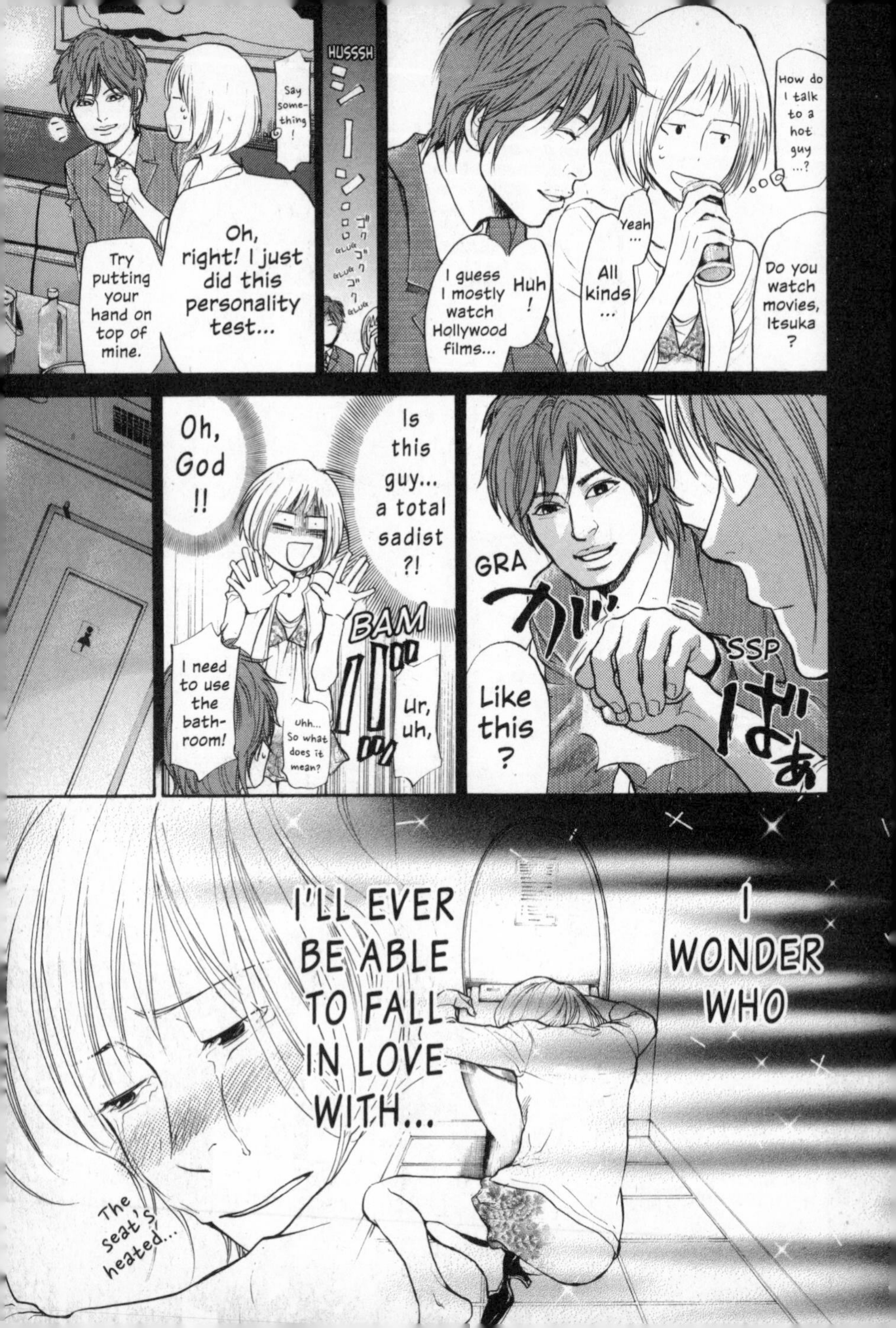
How do I talk to a hot guy ...?
Do you watch movies, Itsuka?
Yeah ... All kinds ...
Huh!
I guess I mostly watch Hollywood films...
HUSSSH
Say some-thing!
GLUG GLUG GLUG
Oh, right! I just did this personality test...
Try putting your hand on top of mine.
GRA
SSP
Like this?
Is this guy... a total sadist?!
Oh, God!!
BAM
Ur, uh,
Uhh... So what does it mean?
I need to use the bath-room!
I WONDER WHO
I'LL EVER BE ABLE TO FALL IN LOVE WITH...
The seat's heated...

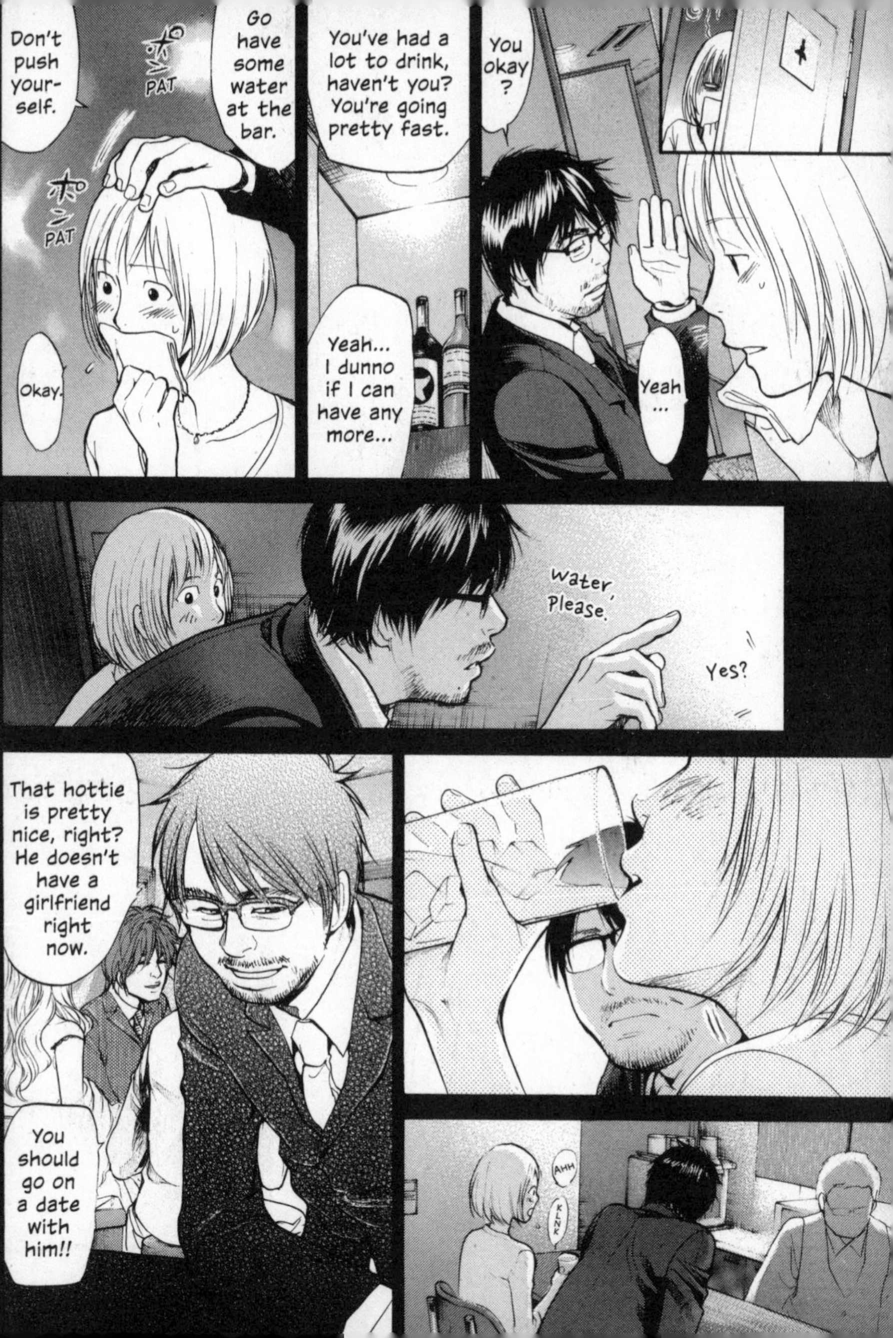
You okay?
Yeah...
You've had a lot to drink, haven't you? You're going pretty fast.
Yeah... I dunno if I can have any more...
Go have some water at the bar.
Don't push yourself.
PAT
PAT
Okay.
Water, Please.
Yes?
AHH
KLNK
That hottie is pretty nice, right? He doesn't have a girlfriend right now.
You should go on a date with him!!

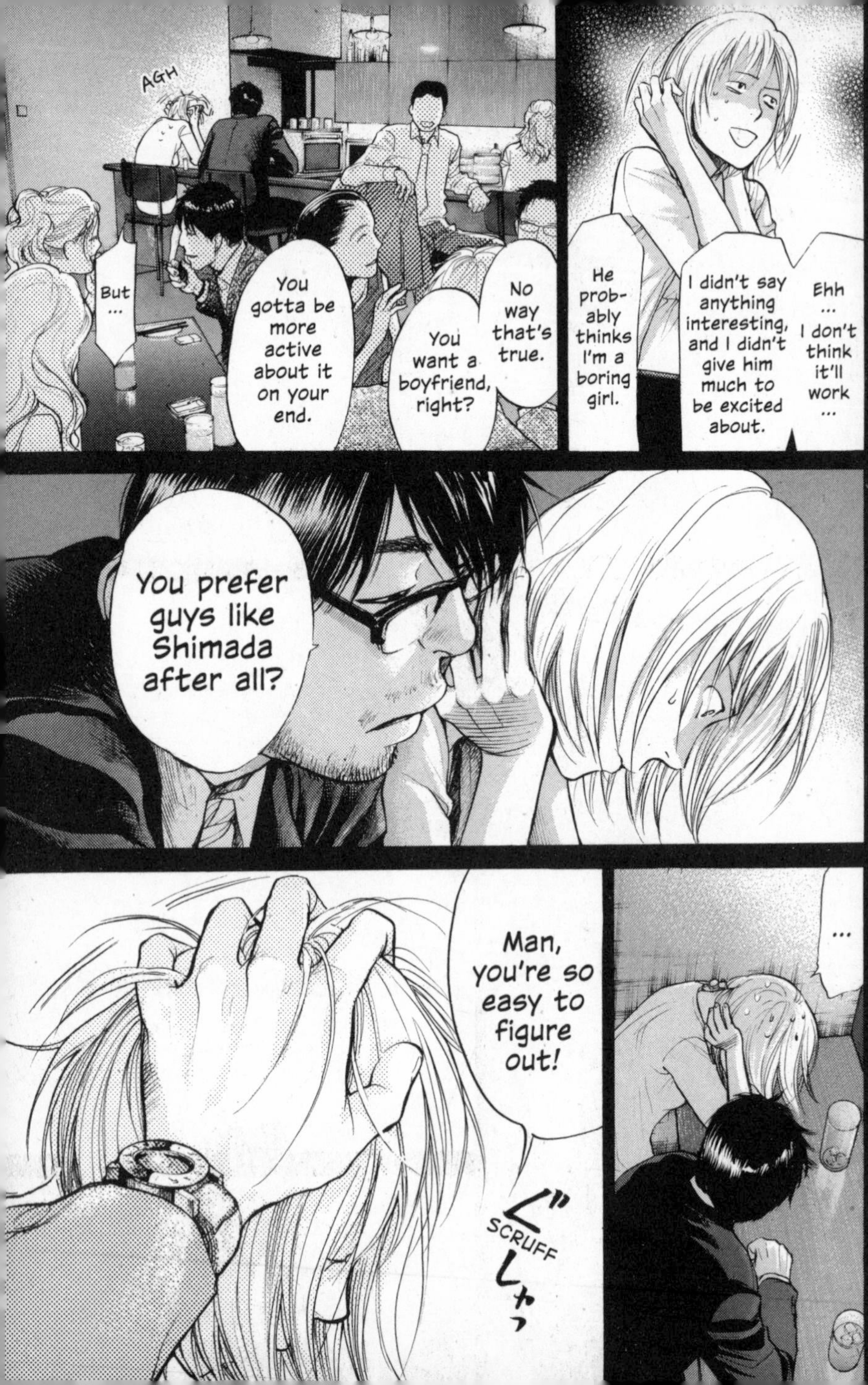
Ehh ... I don't think it'll work ...
I didn't say anything interesting, and I didn't give him much to be excited about.
He prob-ably thinks I'm a boring girl.
No way that's true.
You want a boyfriend, right?
You gotta be more active about it on your end.
AGH
But ...
You prefer guys like Shimada after all?
...
Man, you're so easy to figure out!
SCRUFF

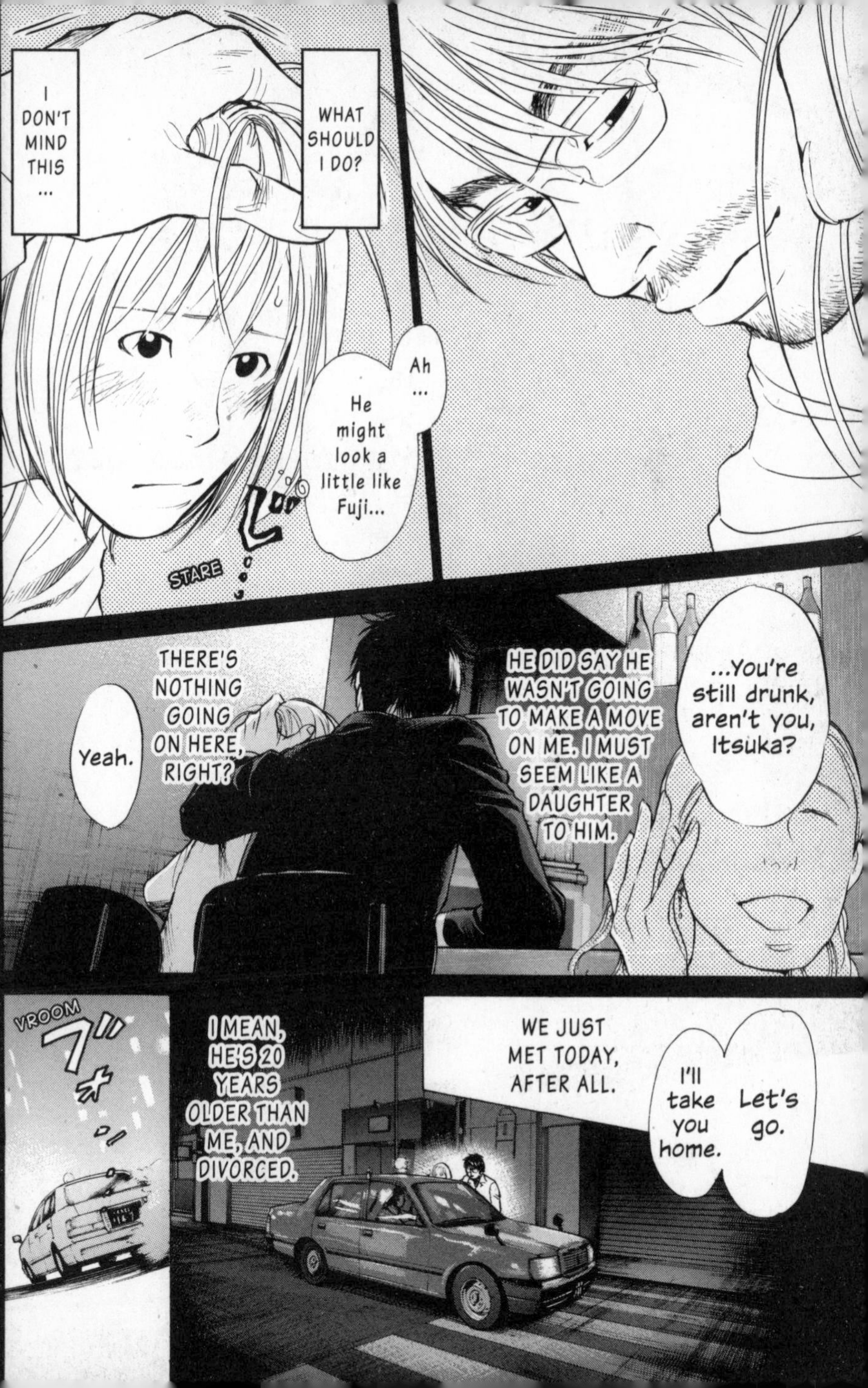
WHAT SHOULD I DO?
I DON'T MIND THIS ...
Ah ...
He might look a little like Fuji...
STARE
...You're still drunk, aren't you, Itsuka?
HE DID SAY HE WASN'T GOING TO MAKE A MOVE ON ME. I MUST SEEM LIKE A DAUGHTER TO HIM.
THERE'S NOTHING GOING ON HERE, RIGHT?
Yeah.
Let's go.
I'll take you home.
WE JUST MET TODAY, AFTER ALL.
I MEAN, HE'S 20 YEARS OLDER THAN ME, AND DIVORCED.
VROOM

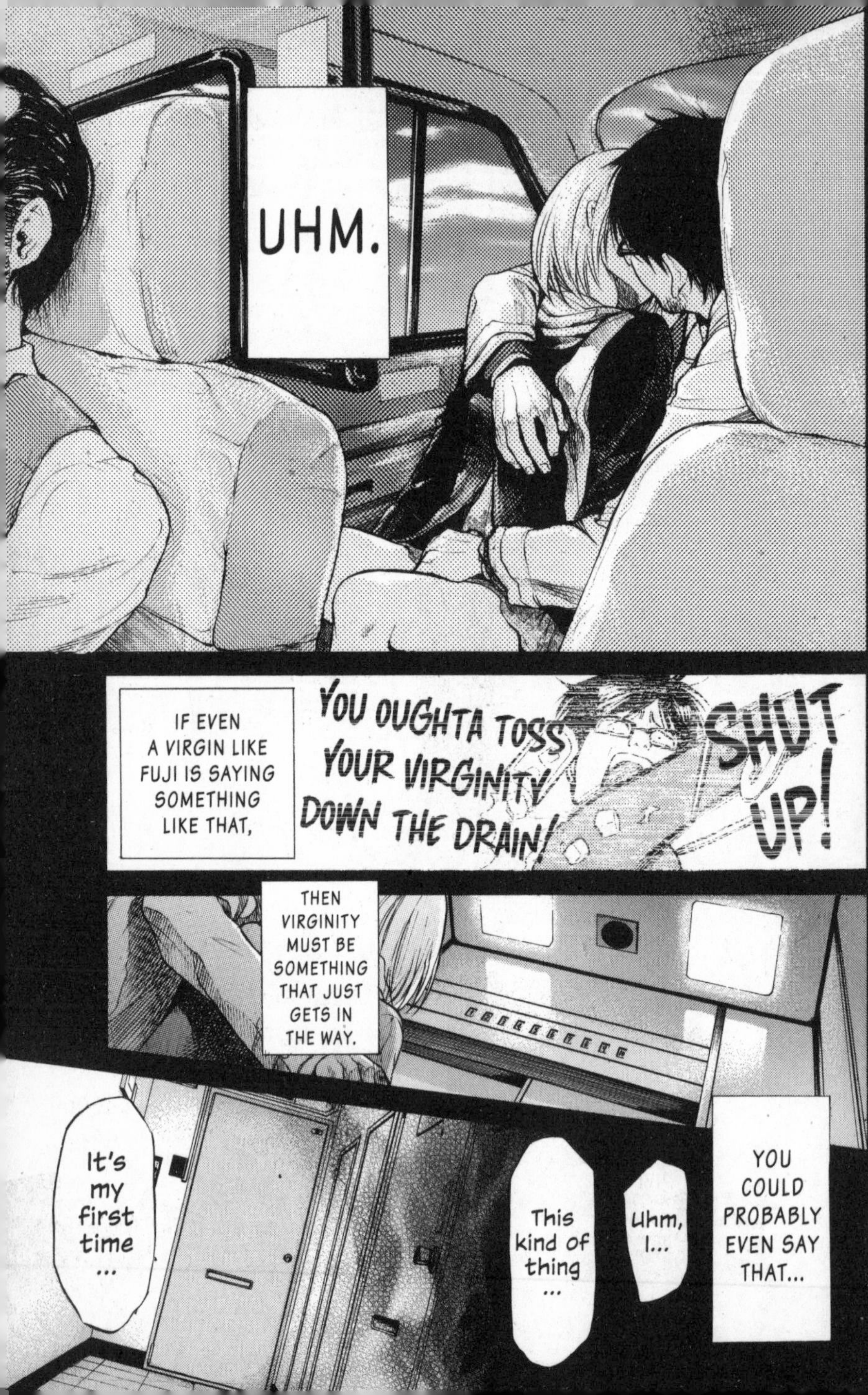
UHM.
SHUT UP!
YOU OUGHTA TOSS YOUR VIRGINITY DOWN THE DRAIN!
IF EVEN A VIRGIN LIKE FUJI IS SAYING SOMETHING LIKE THAT,
THEN VIRGINITY MUST BE SOMETHING THAT JUST GETS IN THE WAY.
YOU COULD PROBABLY EVEN SAY THAT...
Uhm, I...
This kind of thing ...
It's my first time ...

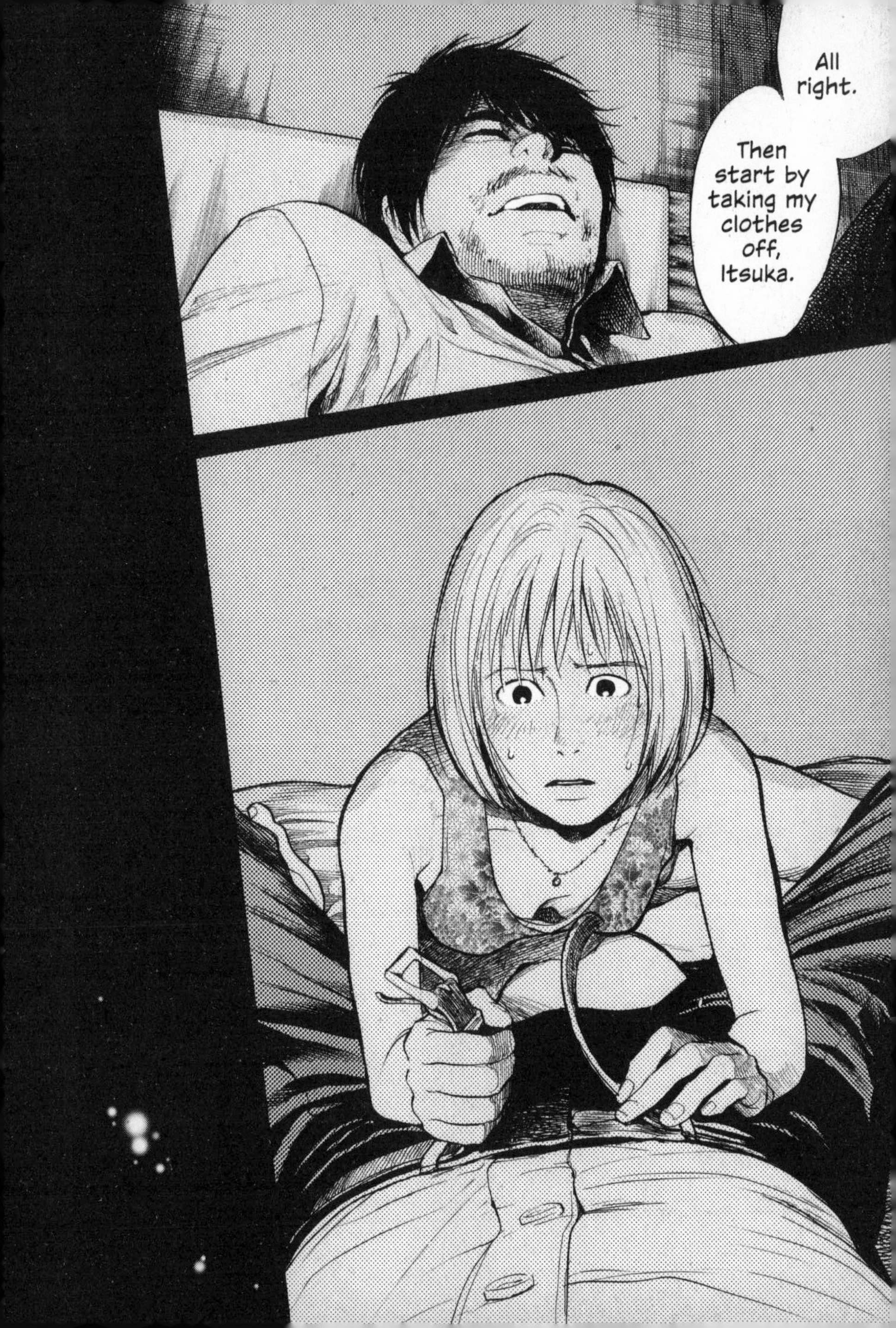
All right.
Then start by taking my clothes off, Itsuka.

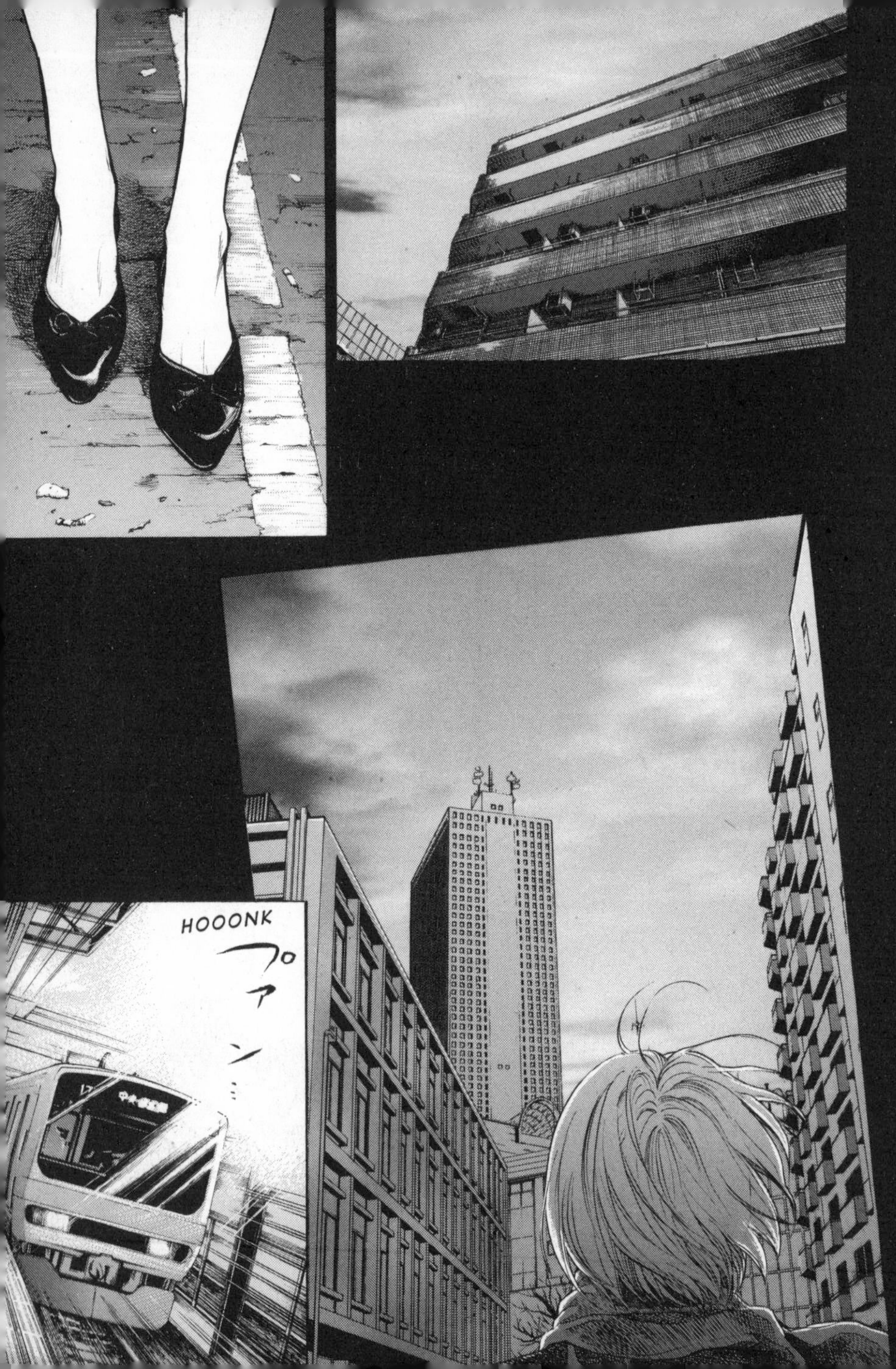
HOOONK
フアン

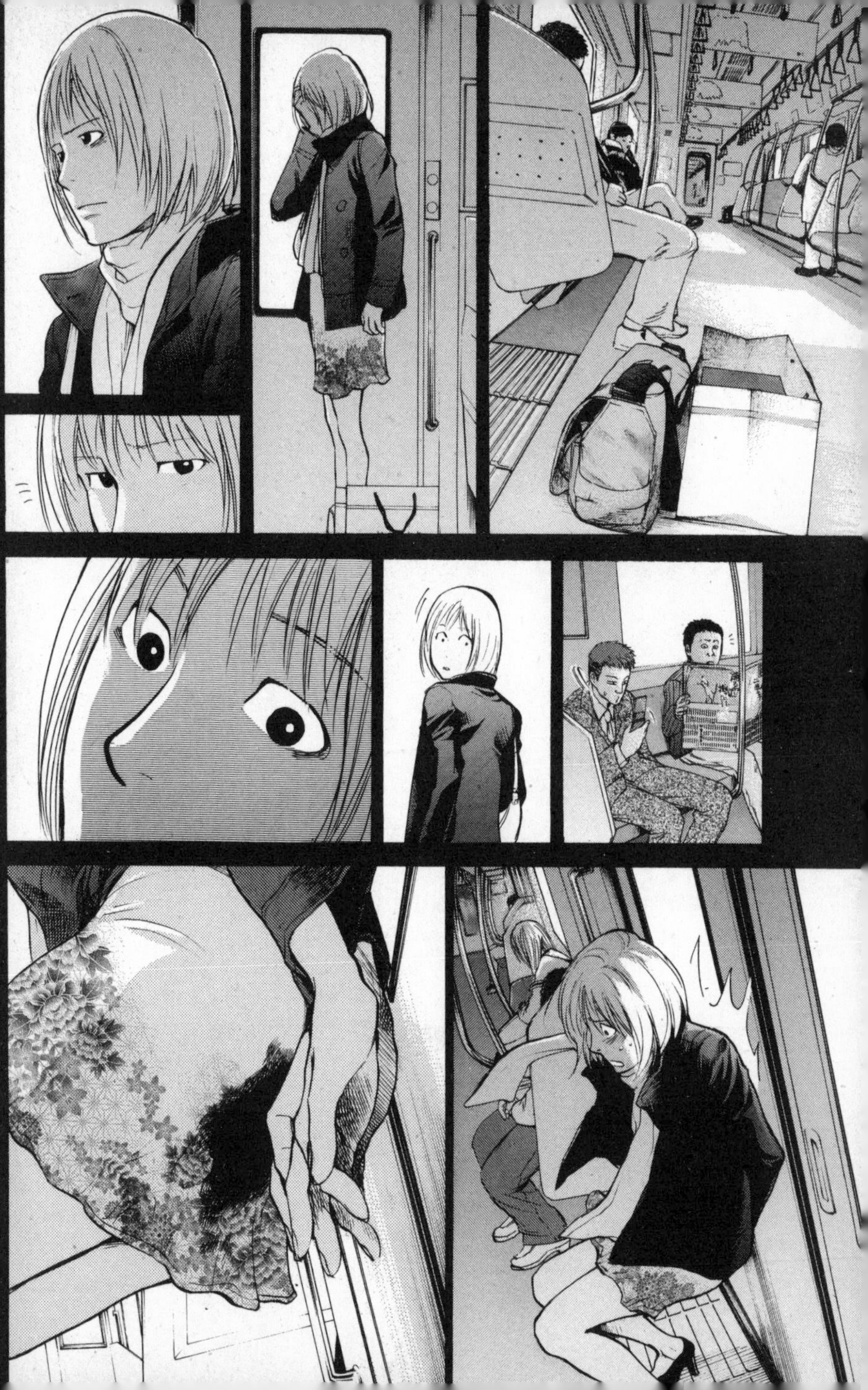

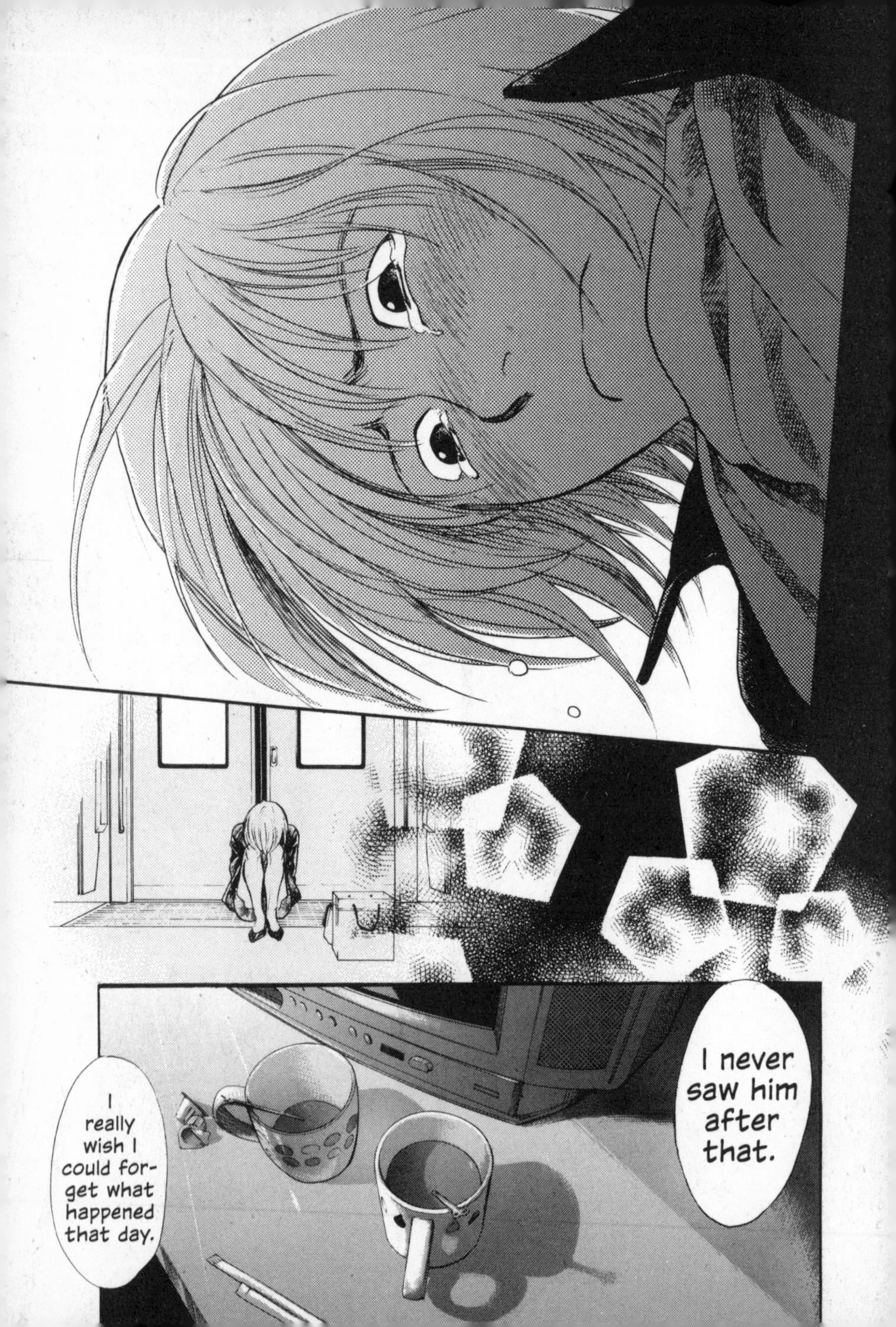
I never saw him after that.
I really wish I could forget what happened that day.

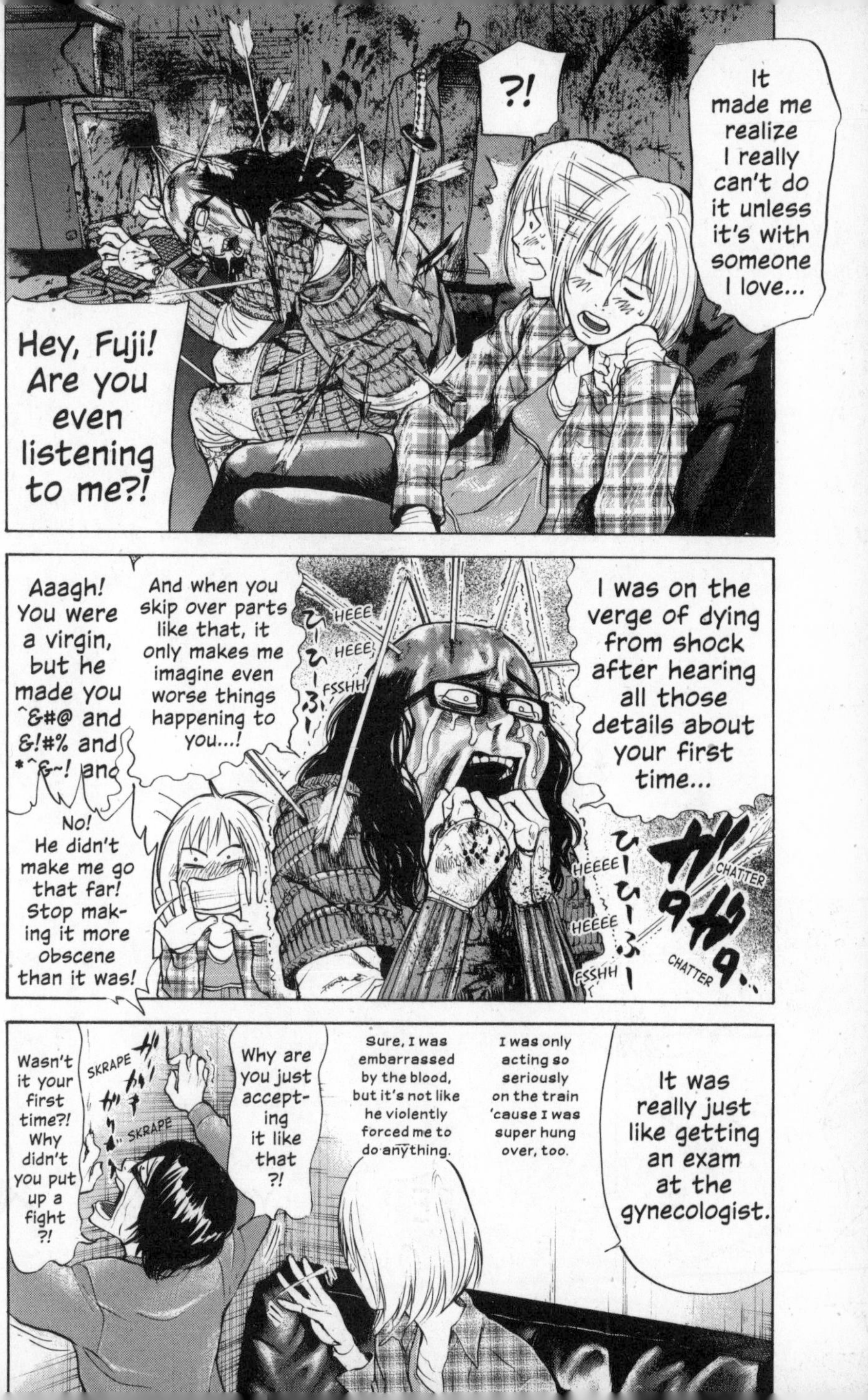
It made me realize I really can't do it unless it's with someone I love...
?!
Hey, Fuji! Are you even listening to me?!
I was on the verge of dying from shock after hearing all those details about your first time...
CHATTER
CHATTER
HEEEE
HEEEE
FSSHH
HEEE
HEEE
FSSHH
And when you skip over parts like that, it only makes me imagine even worse things happening to you...!
Aaagh! You were a virgin, but he made you ^&#@ and &!#% and *^&~! and
No! He didn't make me go that far! Stop making it more obscene than it was!
It was really just like getting an exam at the gynecologist.
I was only acting so seriously on the train 'cause I was super hung over, too.
Sure, I was embarrassed by the blood, but it's not like he violently forced me to do anything.
Why are you just accepting it like that?!
SKRAPE
SKRAPE
Wasn't it your first time?! Why didn't you put up a fight?!

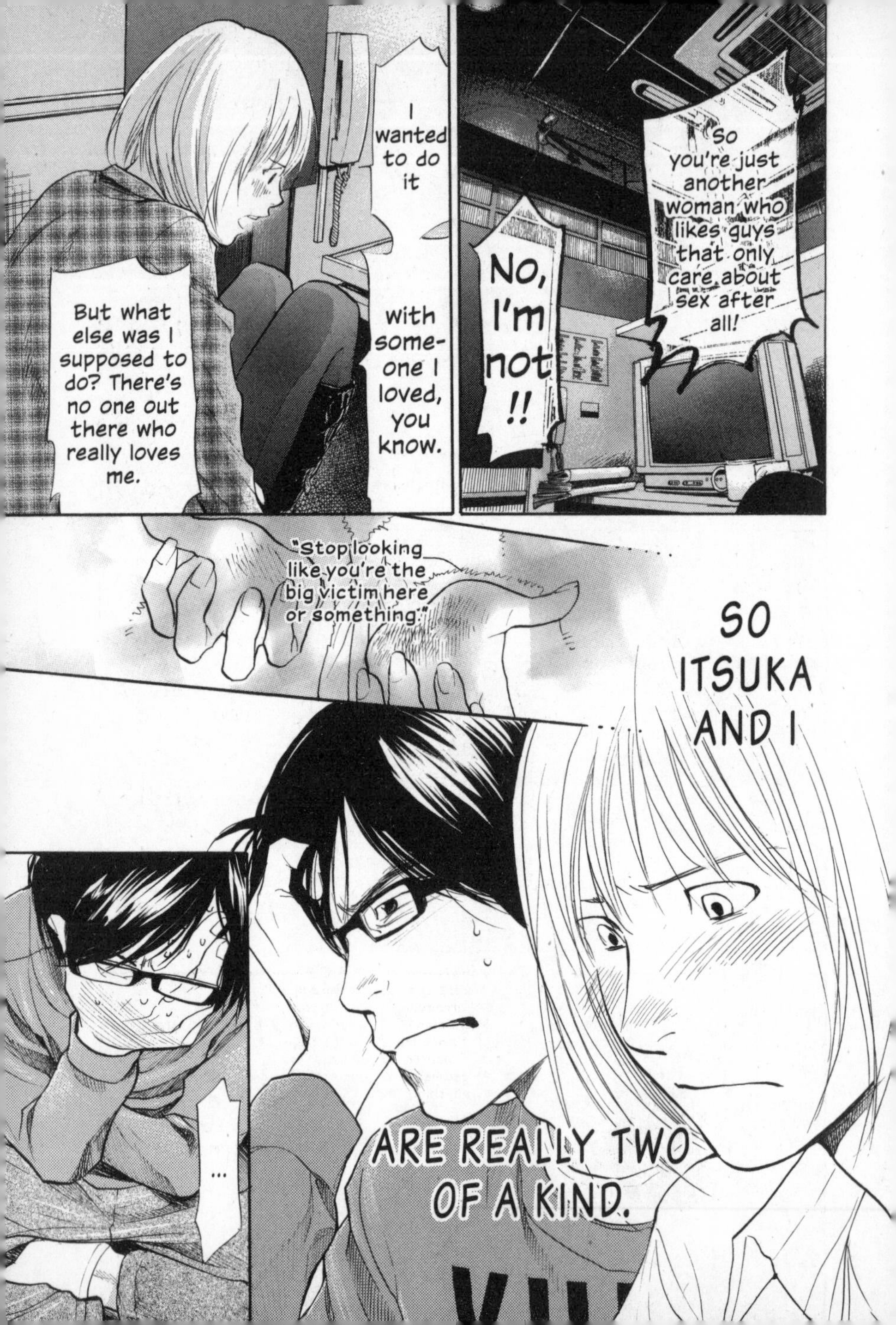
So you're just another woman who likes guys that only care about sex after all!
No, I'm not!!
I wanted to do it
with someone I loved, you know.
But what else was I supposed to do? There's no one out there who really loves me.
"Stop looking like you're the big victim here or something."
SO ITSUKA AND I
ARE REALLY TWO OF A KIND.
...

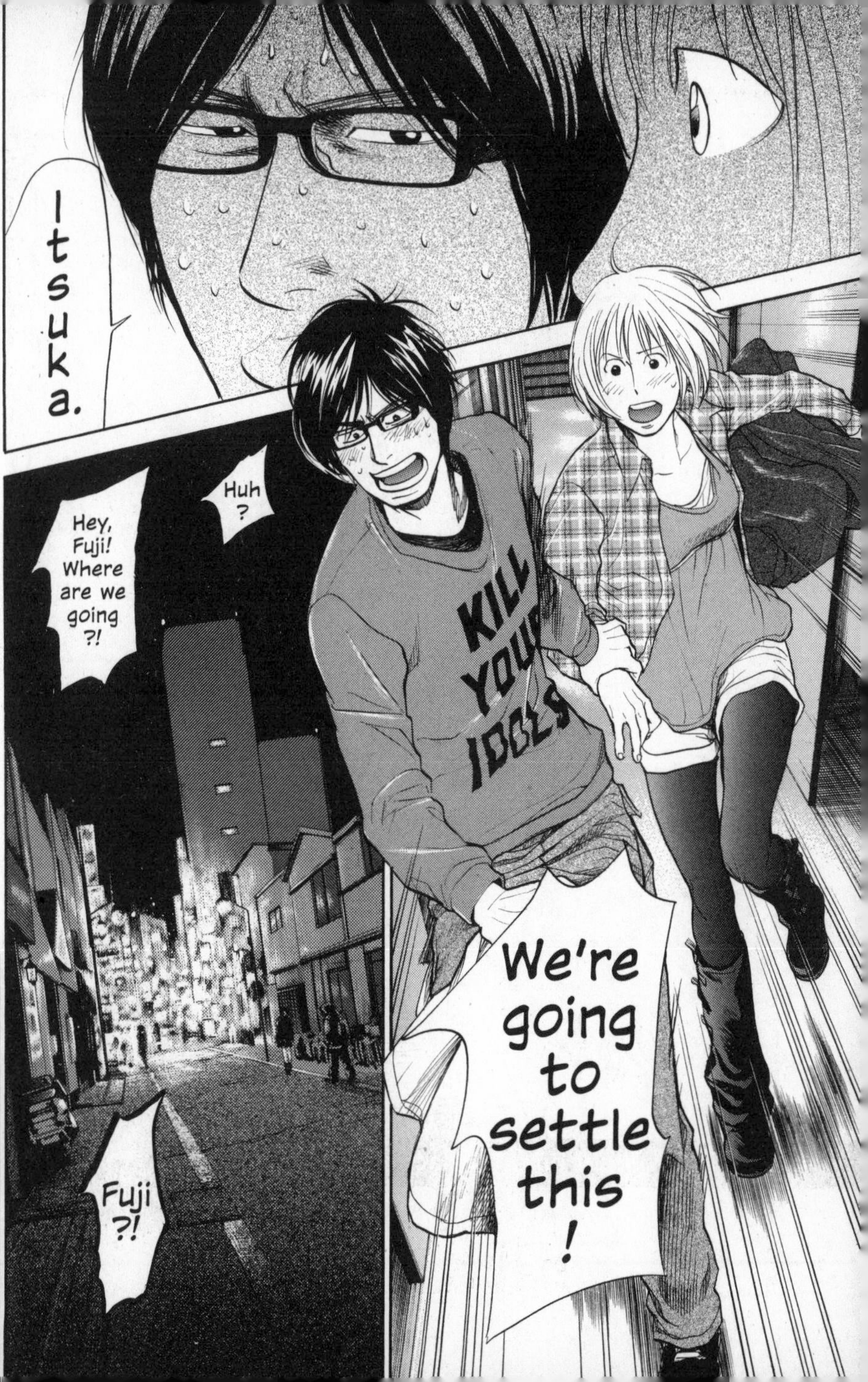
Itsuka.
Huh?
Hey, Fuji! Where are we going?!
We're going to settle this!
Fuji?!
KILL YOUR IDOLS

chapter 12 ♥ END

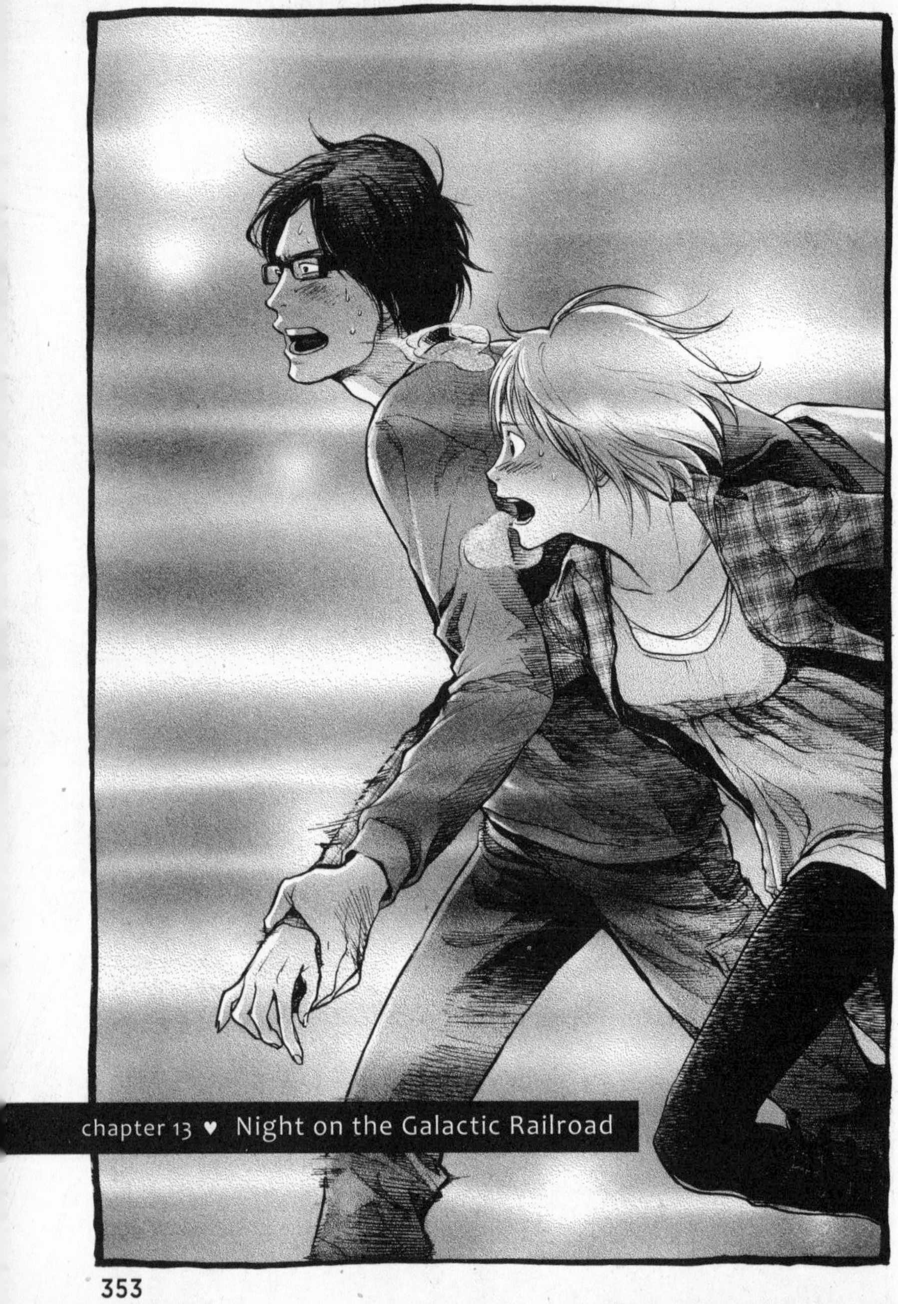

chapter 13 ♥ Night on the Galactic Railroad

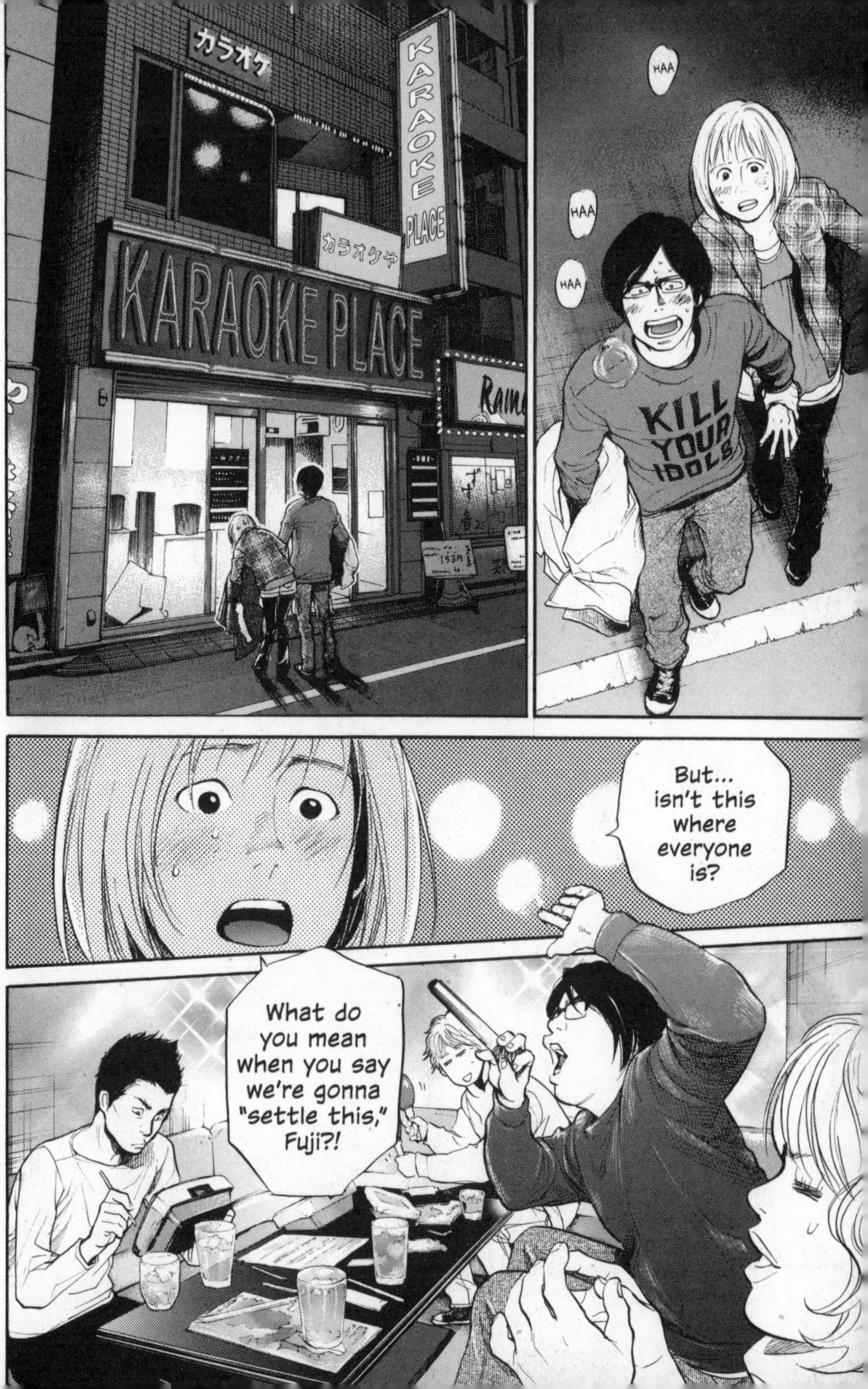
HAA
HAA
HAA
KILL YOUR IDOLS
カラオケ
KARAOKE PLACE
カラオケヤ
KARAOKE PLACE
But... isn't this where everyone is?
What do you mean when you say we're gonna "settle this," Fuji?!

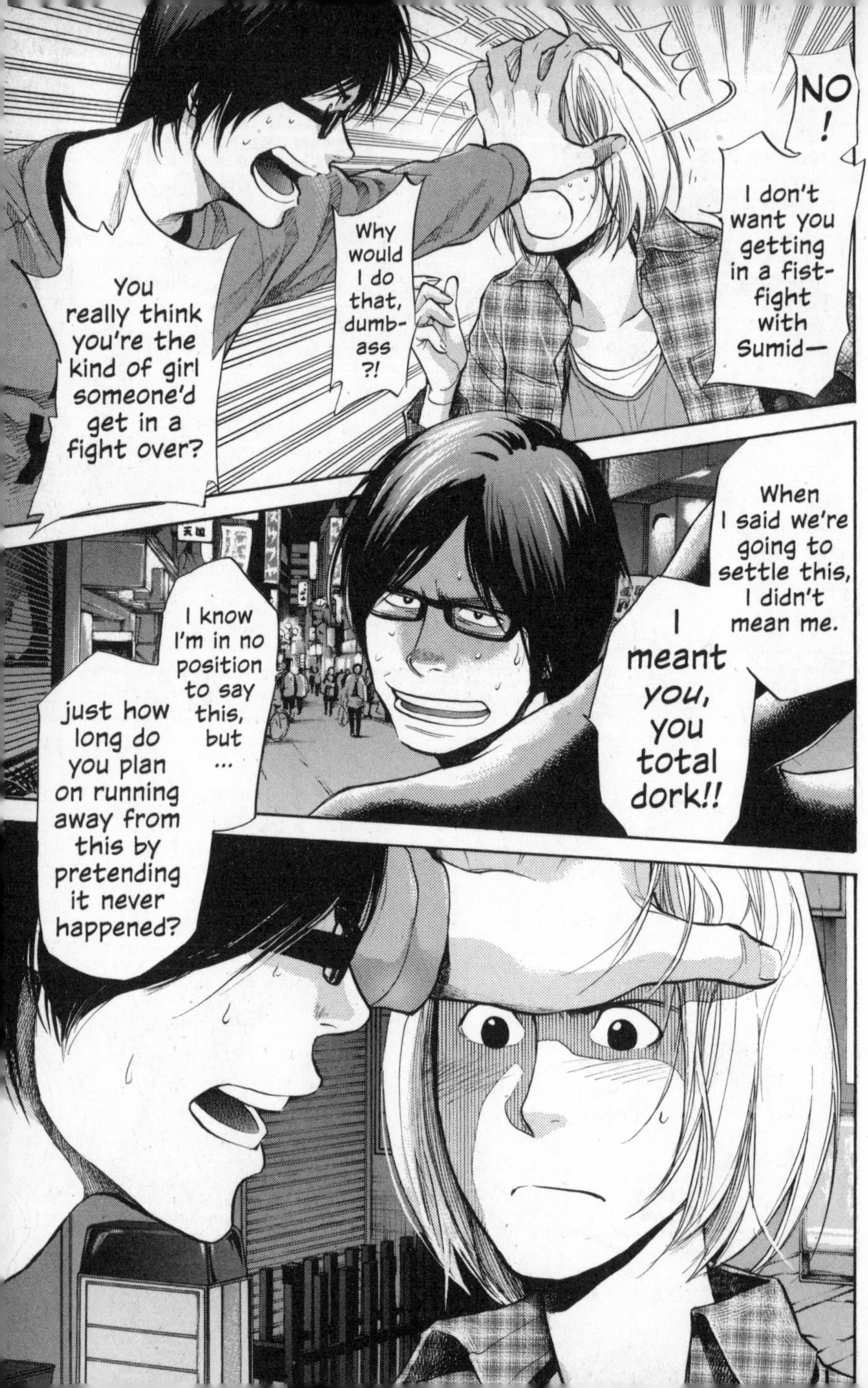
NO!
I don't want you getting in a fist-fight with Sumid—
Why would I do that, dumb-ass?!
You really think you're the kind of girl someone'd get in a fight over?
When I said we're going to settle this, I didn't mean me.
I meant you, you total dork!!
I know I'm in no position to say this, but...
just how long do you plan on running away from this by pretending it never happened?

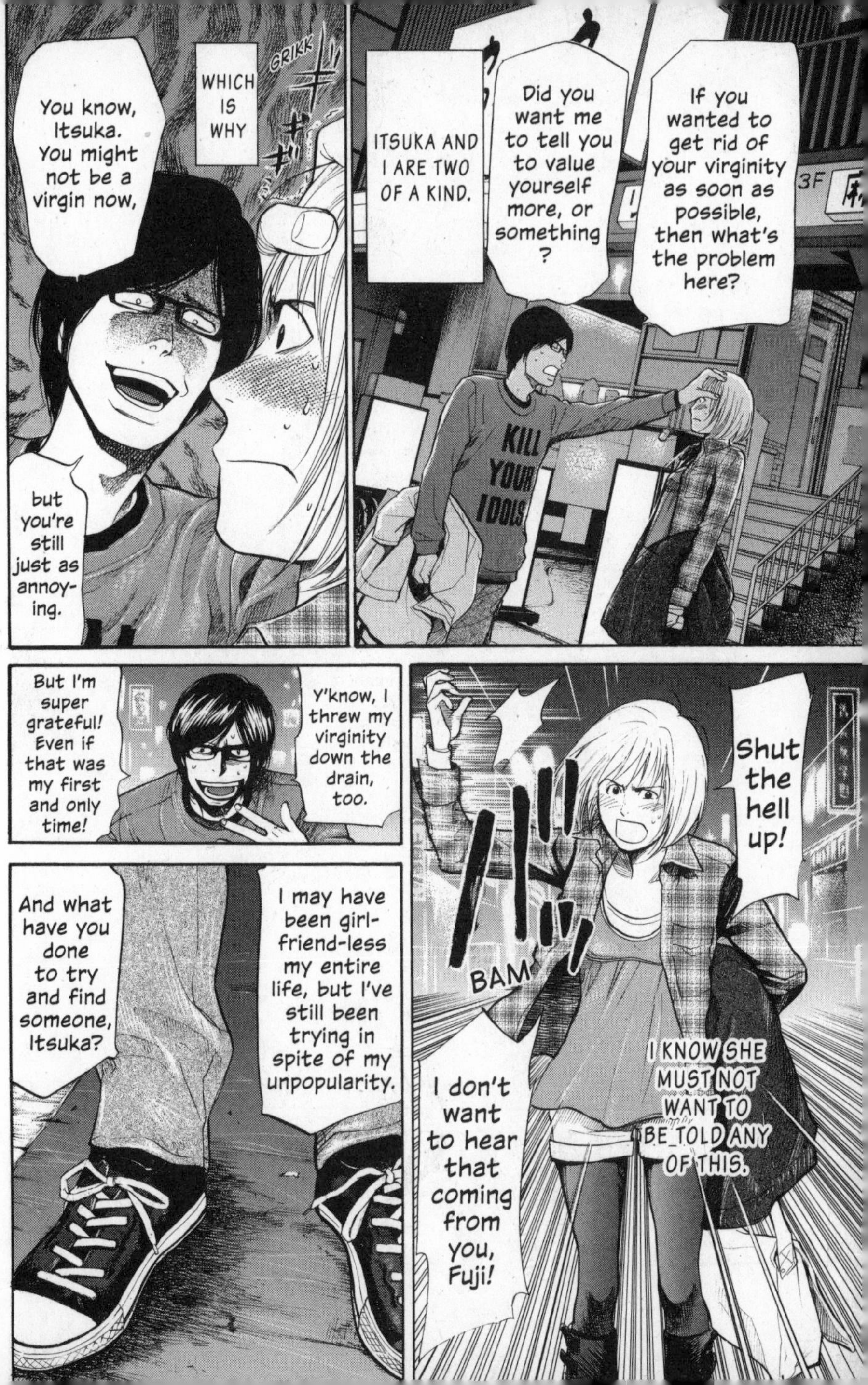

If you wanted to get rid of your virginity as soon as possible, then what's the problem here?
3F
Did you want me to tell you to value yourself more, or something?
ITSUKA AND I ARE TWO OF A KIND.
KILL YOUR IDOLS
GRIKK
WHICH IS WHY
You know, Itsuka. You might not be a virgin now,
but you're still just as annoying.
Shut the hell up!
BAM
I KNOW SHE MUST NOT WANT TO BE TOLD ANY OF THIS.
I don't want to hear that coming from you, Fuji!
Y'know, I threw my virginity down the drain, too.
But I'm super grateful! Even if that was my first and only time!
I may have been girlfriend-less my entire life, but I've still been trying in spite of my unpopularity.
And what have you done to try and find someone, Itsuka?

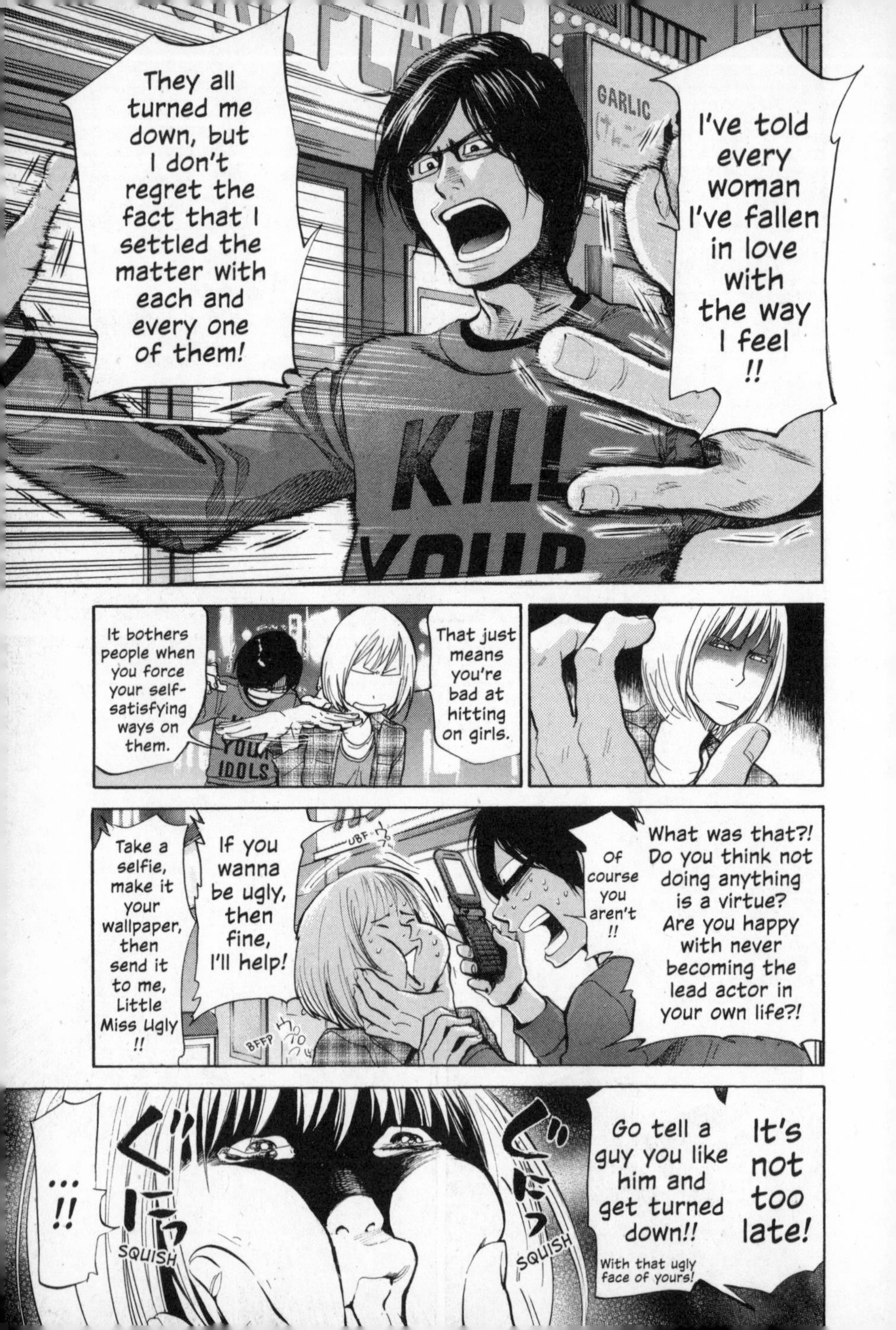
GARLIC
I've told every woman I've fallen in love with the way I feel !!
They all turned me down, but I don't regret the fact that I settled the matter with each and every one of them!
KILL YOUR
That just means you're bad at hitting on girls.
It bothers people when you force your self-satisfying ways on them.
YOUR IDOLS
What was that?! Do you think not doing anything is a virtue? Are you happy with never becoming the lead actor in your own life?!
Of course you aren't !!
UBF
If you wanna be ugly, then fine, I'll help!
Take a selfie, make it your wallpaper, then send it to me, Little Miss Ugly !!
BFFP
It's not too late!
Go tell a guy you like him and get turned down!!
With that ugly face of yours!
SQUISH
...!!
SQUISH

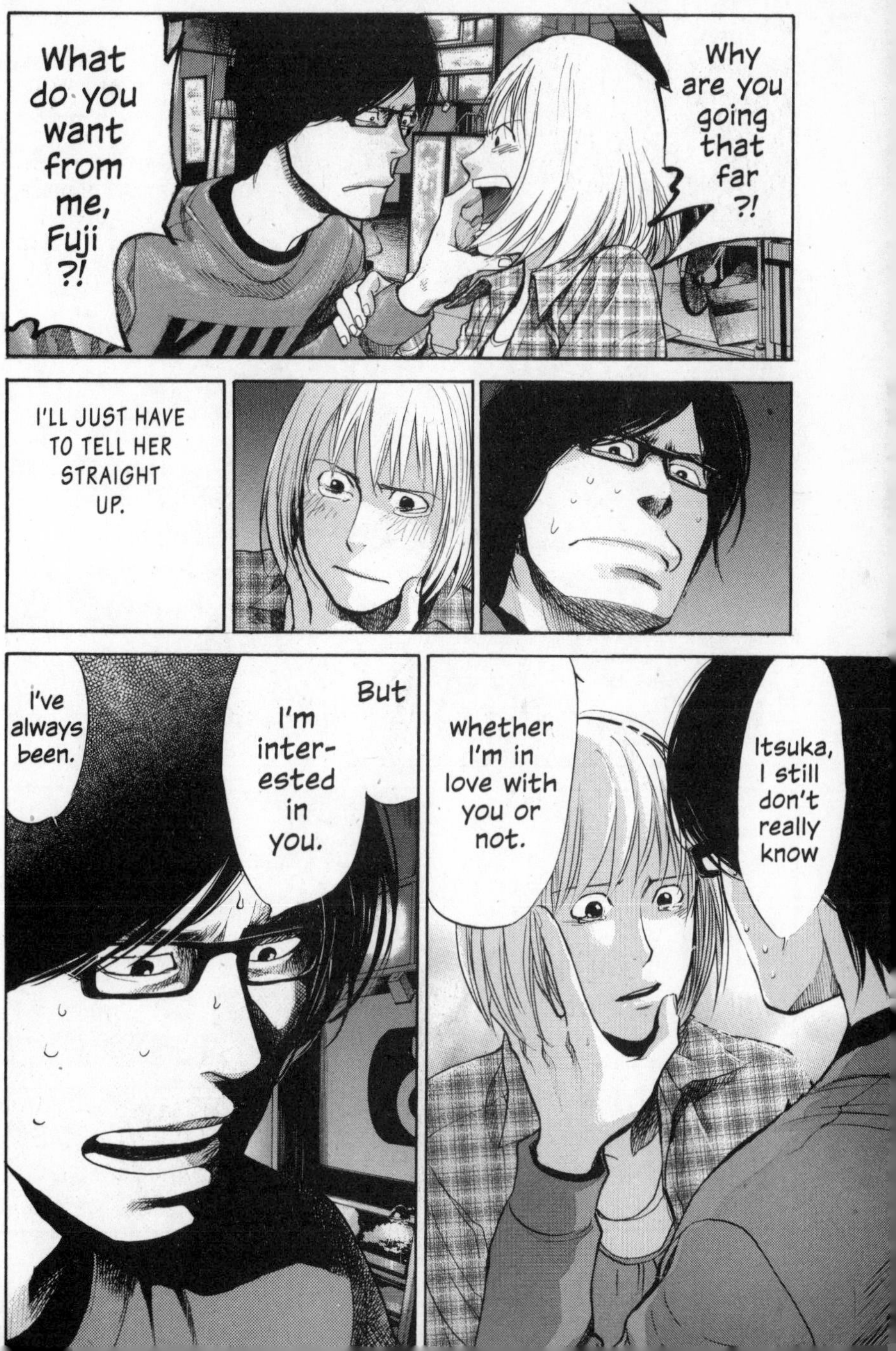
Why are you going that far ?!
What do you want from me, Fuji ?!
I'LL JUST HAVE TO TELL HER STRAIGHT UP.
Itsuka, I still don't really know
whether I'm in love with you or not.
But I'm inter-ested in you.
I've always been.

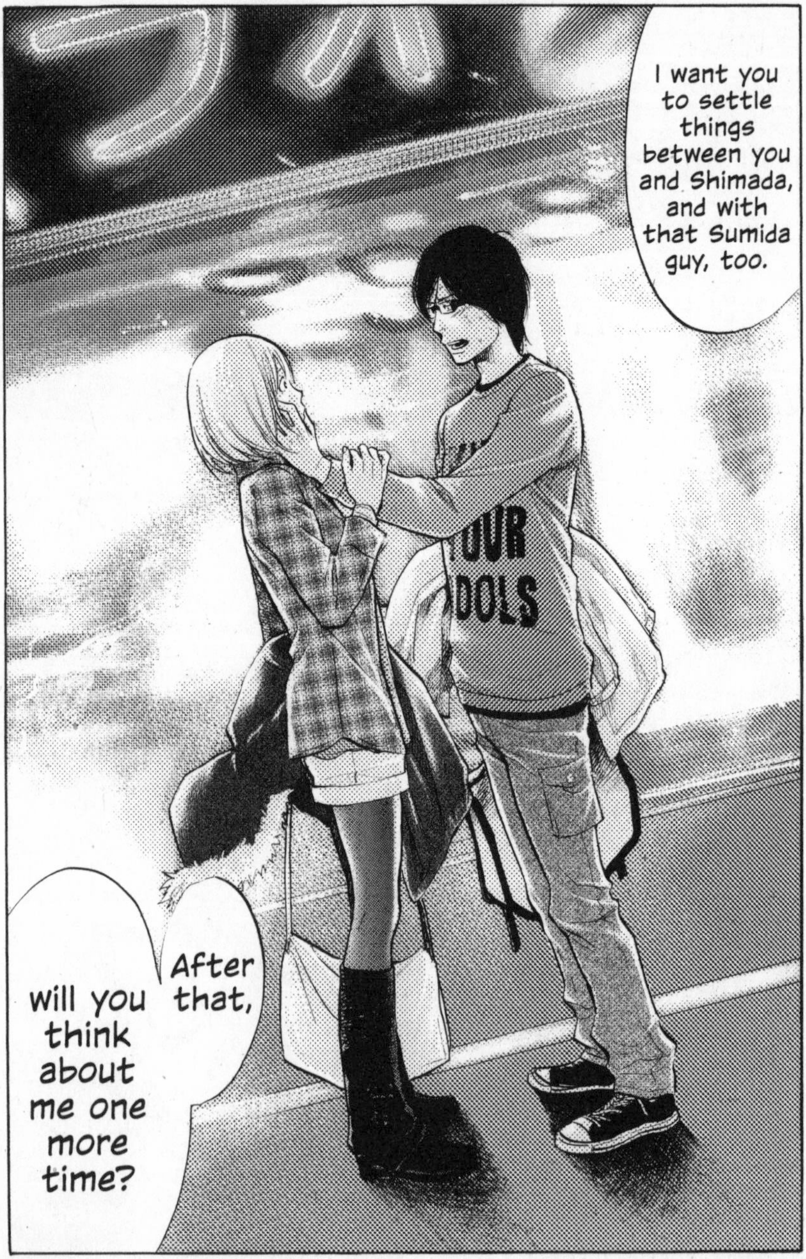
I want you to settle things between you and Shimada, and with that Sumida guy, too.
YOUR DOLS
After that,
will you think about me one more time?

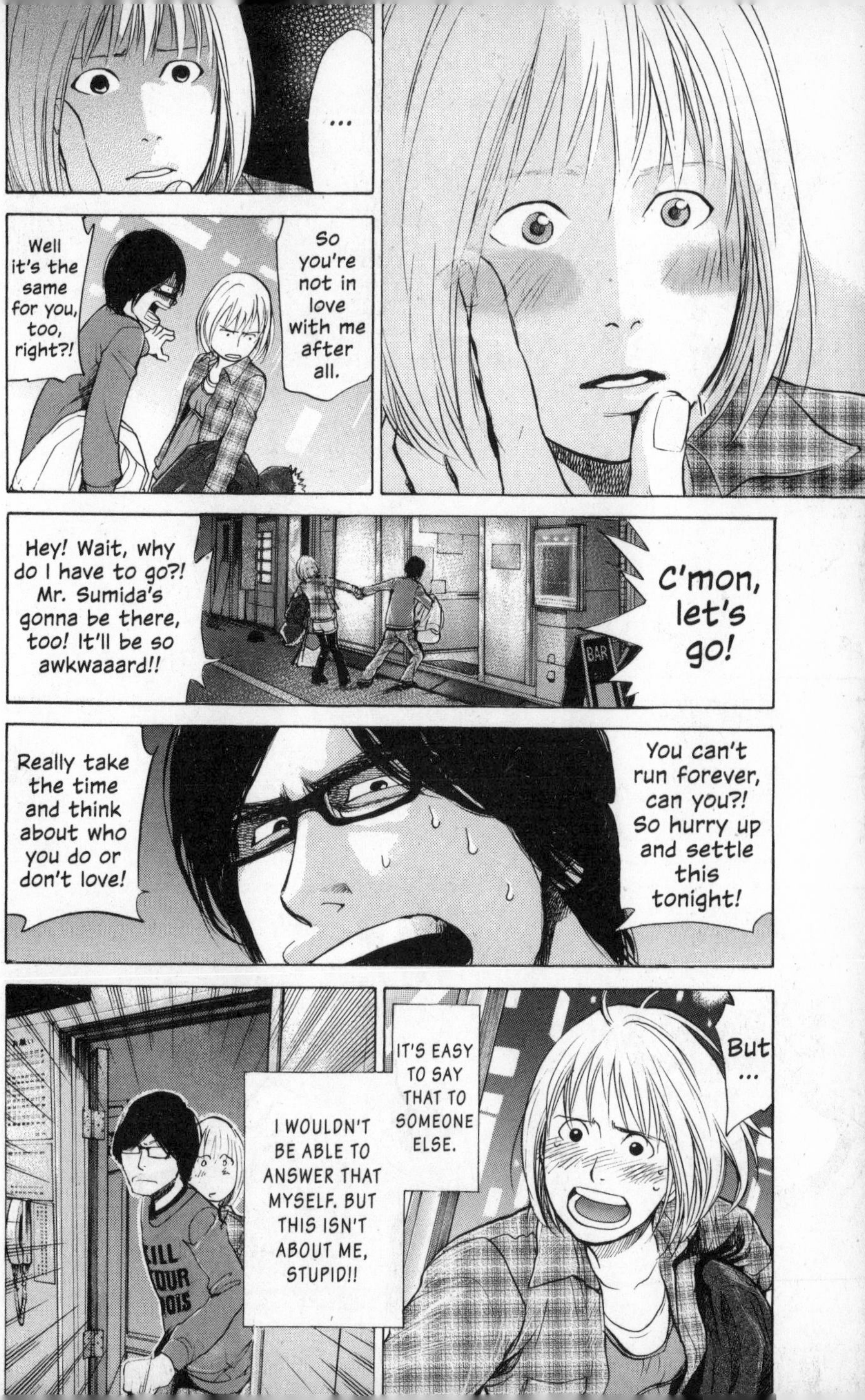
...
So you're not in love with me after all.
Well it's the same for you, too, right?!
C'mon, let's go!
Hey! Wait, why do I have to go?! Mr. Sumida's gonna be there, too! It'll be so awkwaaard!!
BAR
You can't run forever, can you?! So hurry up and settle this tonight!
Really take the time and think about who you do or don't love!
But ...
IT'S EASY TO SAY THAT TO SOMEONE ELSE.
I WOULDN'T BE ABLE TO ANSWER THAT MYSELF. BUT THIS ISN'T ABOUT ME, STUPID!!

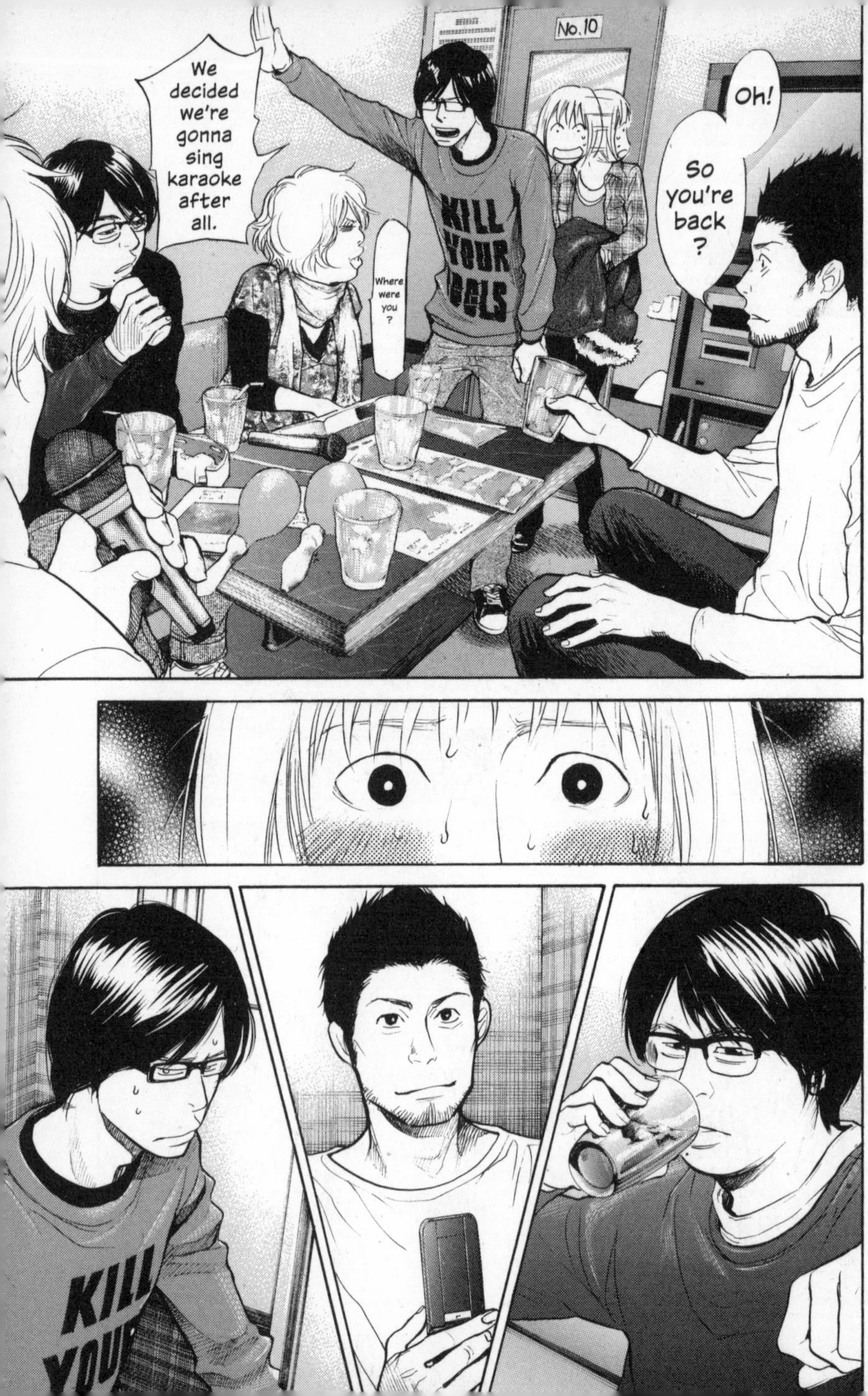
No.10
Oh!
So you're back?
Where were you?
We decided we're gonna sing karaoke after all.

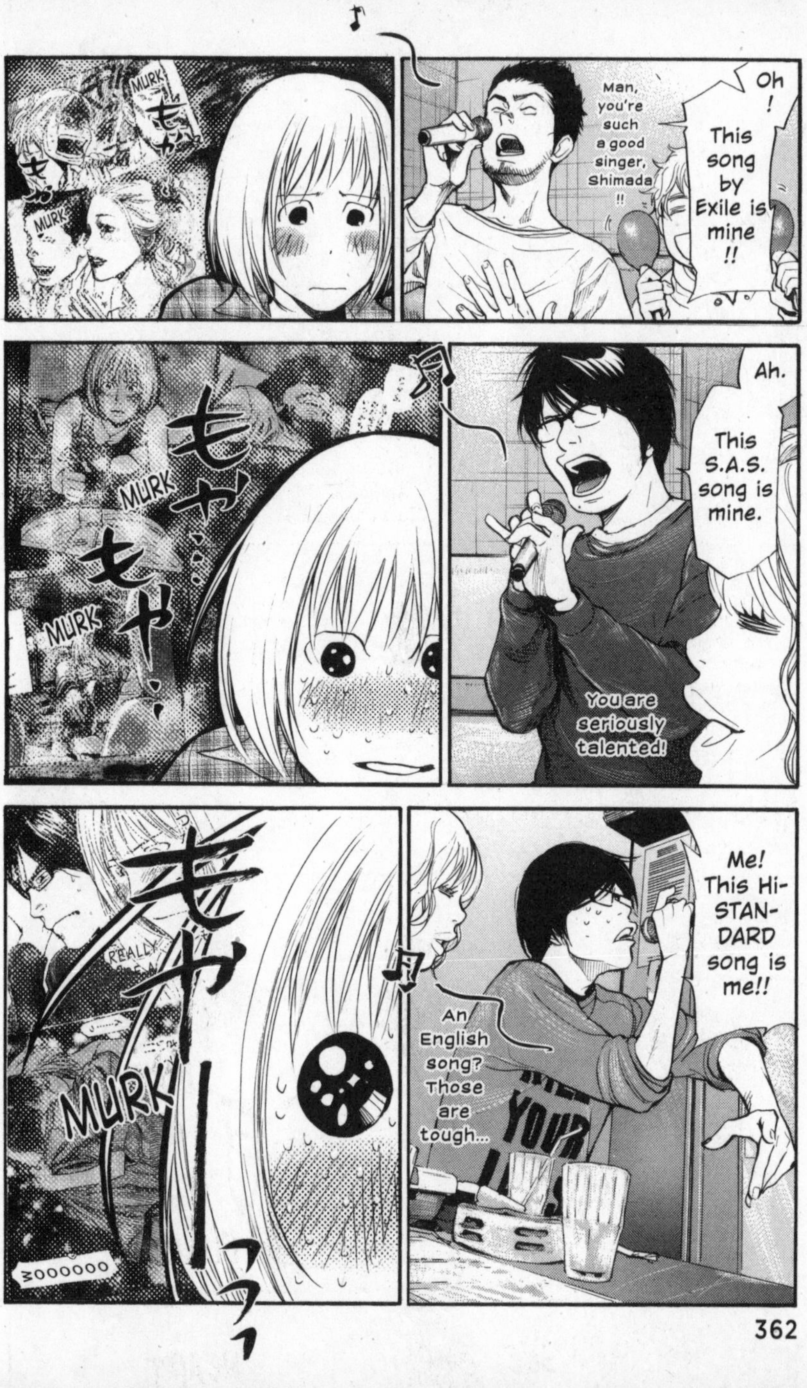
Oh! This song by Exile is mine!!
Man, you're such a good singer, Shimada!!
MURK
MURK
Ah. This S.A.S. song is mine.
You are seriously talented!
MURK
MURK
Me! This Hi-STANDARD song is me!!
An English song? Those are tough...
MURK

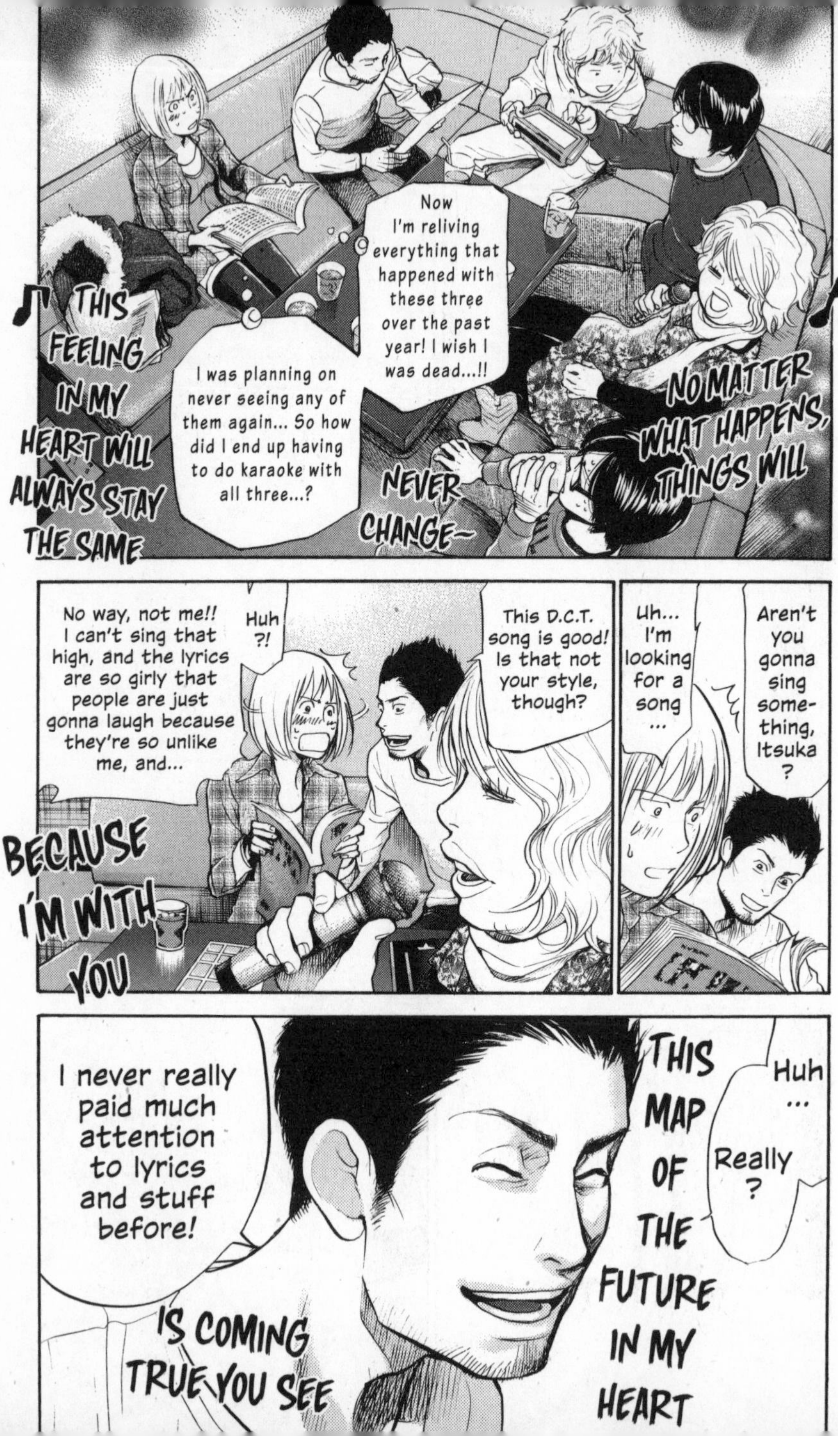
Now I'm reliving everything that happened with these three over the past year! I wish I was dead...!!
NO MATTER WHAT HAPPENS, THINGS WILL
NEVER CHANGE~
I was planning on never seeing any of them again... So how did I end up having to do karaoke with all three...?
THIS FEELING IN MY HEART WILL ALWAYS STAY THE SAME
Aren't you gonna sing something, Itsuka?
Uh... I'm looking for a song...
This D.C.T. song is good! Is that not your style, though?
Huh?!
No way, not me!! I can't sing that high, and the lyrics are so girly that people are just gonna laugh because they're so unlike me, and...
BECAUSE I'M WITH YOU
Huh... Really?
THIS MAP OF THE FUTURE IN MY HEART
I never really paid much attention to lyrics and stuff before!
IS COMING TRUE YOU SEE

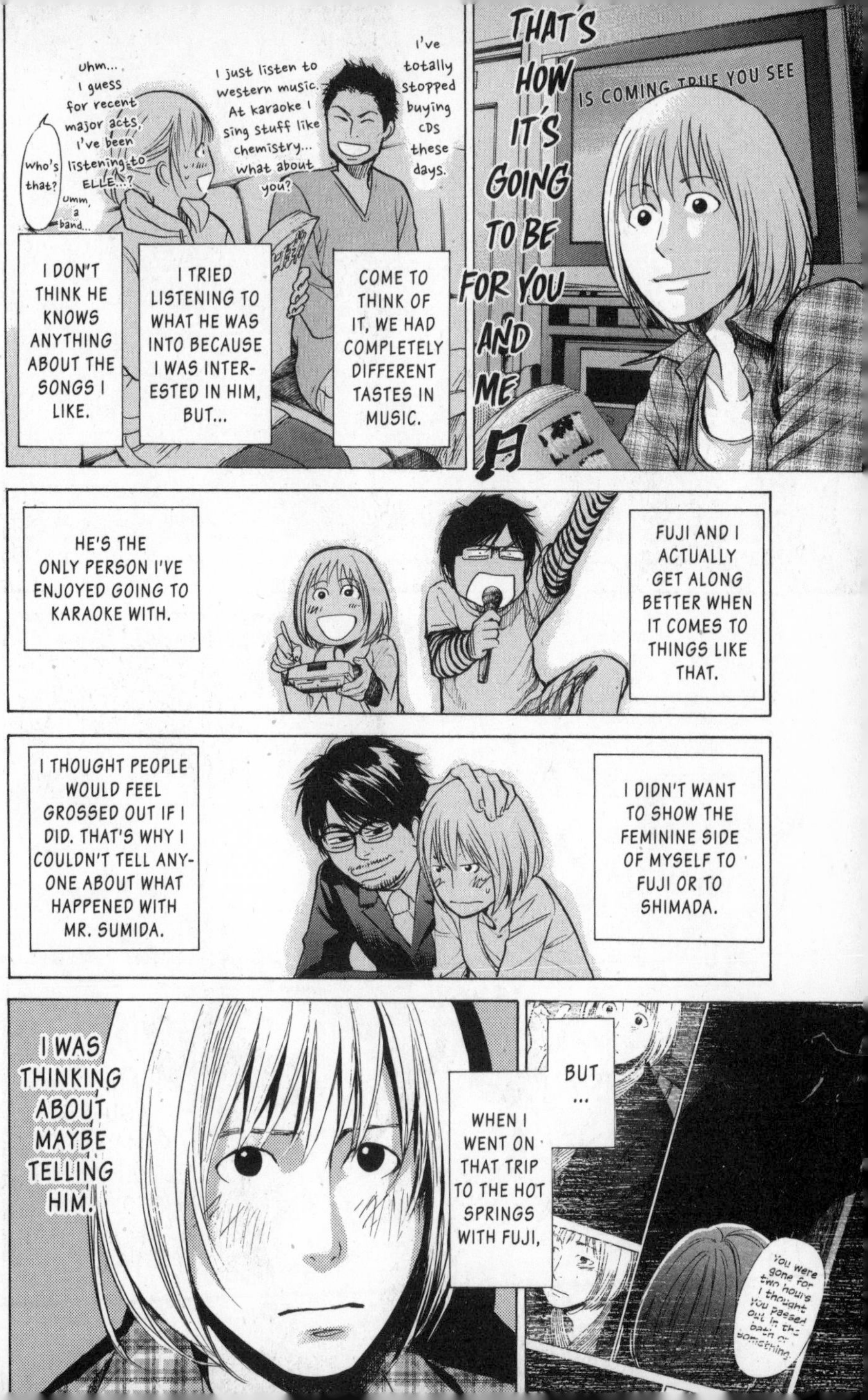
IS COMING TRUE YOU SEE
THAT'S HOW IT'S GOING TO BE FOR YOU AND ME ♪
I've totally stopped buying CDs these days.
I just listen to western music. At karaoke I sing stuff like chemistry... what about you?
uhm... I guess for recent major acts, I've been listening to ELLE...?
who's that?
umm, a band...
COME TO THINK OF IT, WE HAD COMPLETELY DIFFERENT TASTES IN MUSIC.
I TRIED LISTENING TO WHAT HE WAS INTO BECAUSE I WAS INTERESTED IN HIM, BUT...
I DON'T THINK HE KNOWS ANYTHING ABOUT THE SONGS I LIKE.
FUJI AND I ACTUALLY GET ALONG BETTER WHEN IT COMES TO THINGS LIKE THAT.
HE'S THE ONLY PERSON I'VE ENJOYED GOING TO KARAOKE WITH.
I DIDN'T WANT TO SHOW THE FEMININE SIDE OF MYSELF TO FUJI OR TO SHIMADA.
I THOUGHT PEOPLE WOULD FEEL GROSSED OUT IF I DID. THAT'S WHY I COULDN'T TELL ANYONE ABOUT WHAT HAPPENED WITH MR. SUMIDA.
BUT ...
WHEN I WENT ON THAT TRIP TO THE HOT SPRINGS WITH FUJI,
You were gone for two hours I thought you passed out in the bath or something.
I WAS THINKING ABOUT MAYBE TELLING HIM!

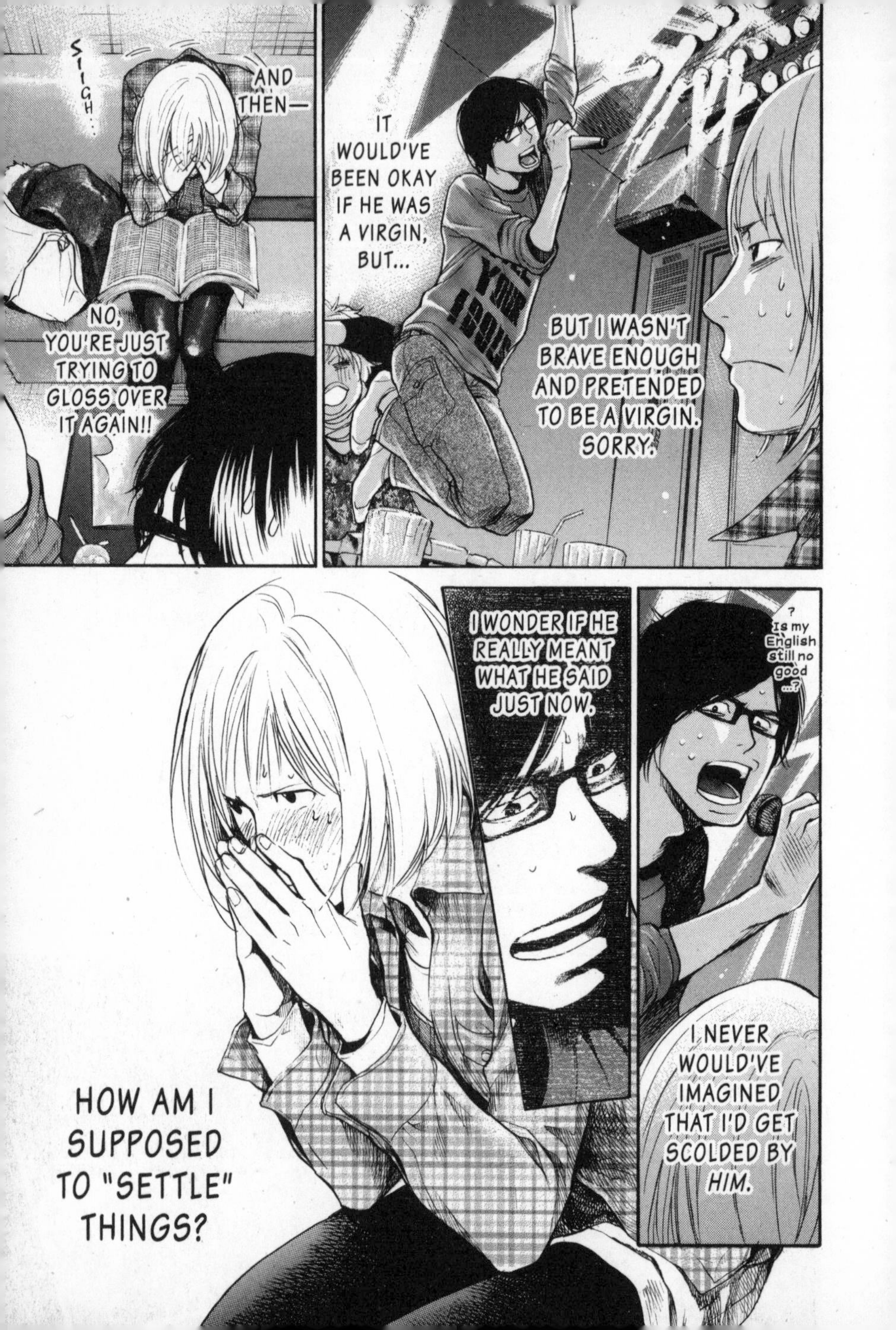
IT WOULD'VE BEEN OKAY IF HE WAS A VIRGIN, BUT...
BUT I WASN'T BRAVE ENOUGH AND PRETENDED TO BE A VIRGIN. SORRY.
AND THEN—
SIIGH...
NO, YOU'RE JUST TRYING TO GLOSS OVER IT AGAIN!!
? Is my English still no good...?
I NEVER WOULD'VE IMAGINED THAT I'D GET SCOLDED BY HIM.
I WONDER IF HE REALLY MEANT WHAT HE SAID JUST NOW.
HOW AM I SUPPOSED TO "SETTLE" THINGS?

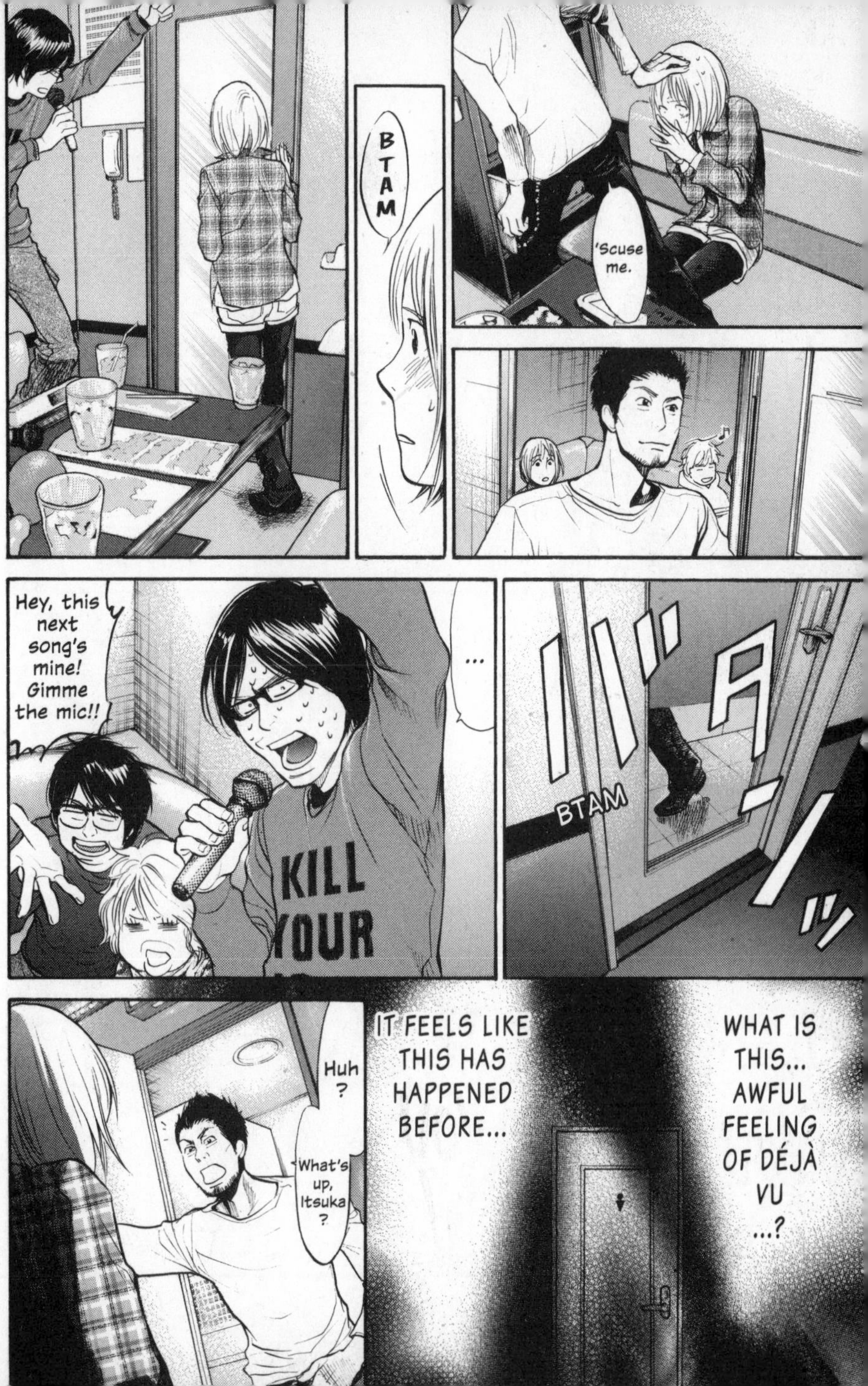
'Scuse me.
BTAM
BTAM
...
Hey, this next song's mine! Gimme the mic!!
KILL YOUR
WHAT IS THIS... AWFUL FEELING OF DÉJÀ VU ...?
IT FEELS LIKE THIS HAS HAPPENED BEFORE...
Huh?
What's up, Itsuka?

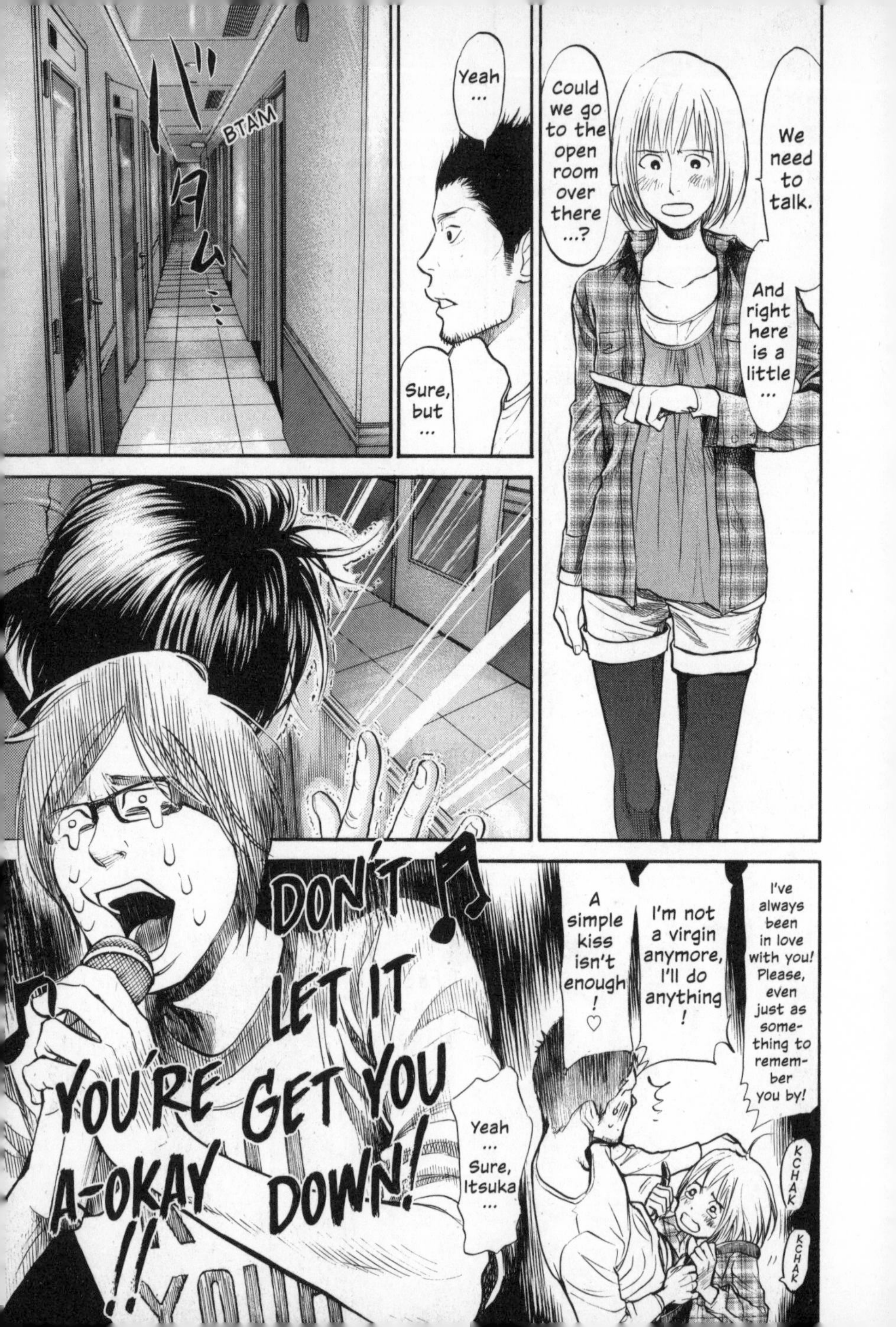
We need to talk.
And right here is a little ...
Could we go to the open room over there ...?
Yeah ...
Sure, but ...
BTAM
I've always been in love with you! Please, even just as something to remember you by!
I'm not a virgin anymore, I'll do anything!
A simple kiss isn't enough! ♡
KCHAK
KCHAK
Yeah ... Sure, Itsuka ...
DON'T LET IT GET YOU DOWN!
YOU'RE A-OKAY!!

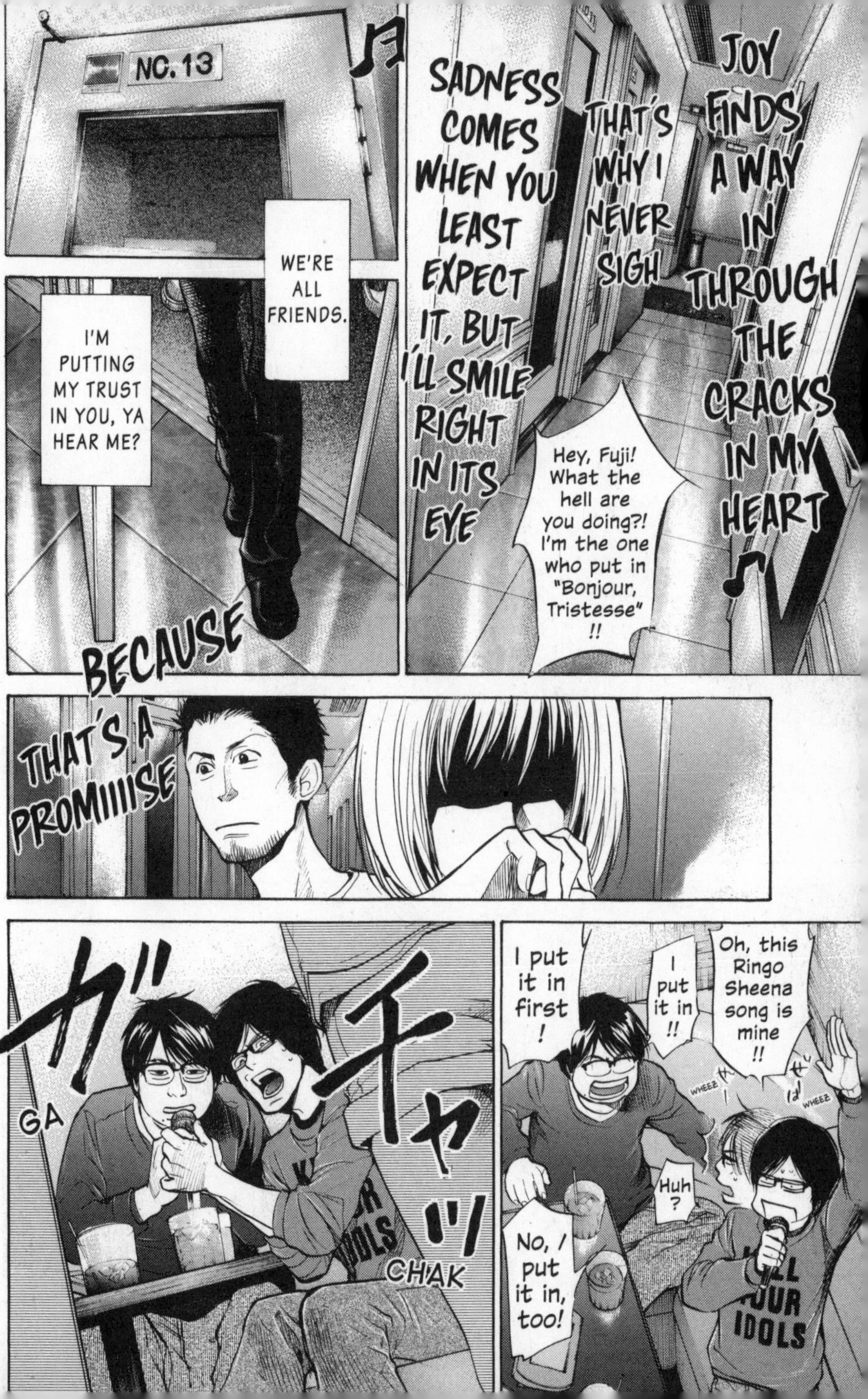

JOY FINDS A WAY IN THROUGH THE CRACKS IN MY HEART ♪
THAT'S WHY I NEVER SIGH
SADNESS COMES WHEN YOU LEAST EXPECT IT, BUT I'LL SMILE RIGHT IN ITS EYE
Hey, Fuji! What the hell are you doing?! I'm the one who put in "Bonjour, Tristesse" !!
NO.13
♪
WE'RE ALL FRIENDS.
I'M PUTTING MY TRUST IN YOU, YA HEAR ME?
BECAUSE
THAT'S A PROMIIIIISE
Oh, this Ringo Sheena song is mine !!
I put it in !!
I put it in first !
WHEEZ
WHEEZ
Huh ?
No, I put it in, too!
IDOLS
ガチャ
GA
CHAK
IDOLS

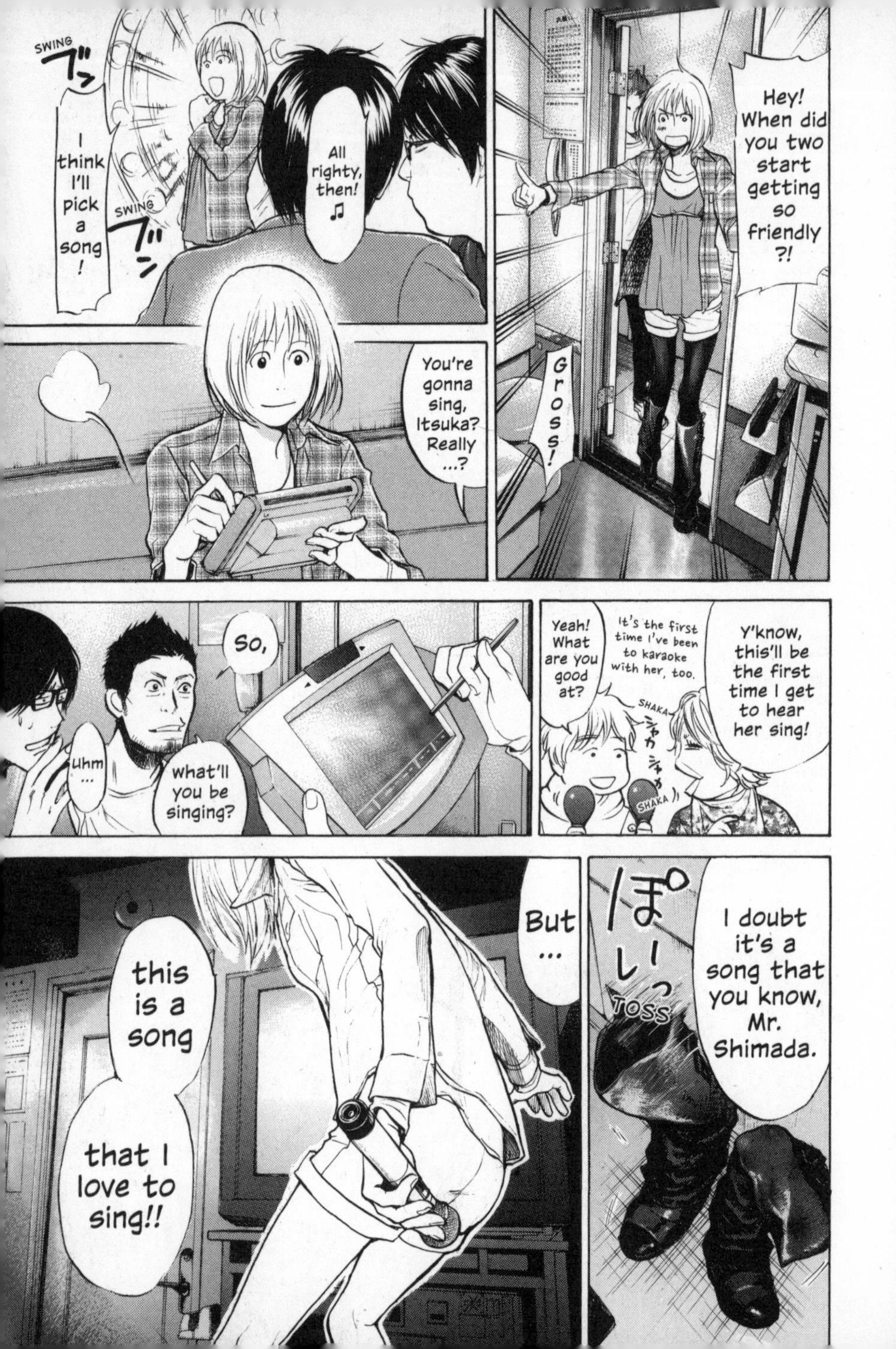
Hey! When did you two start getting so friendly?!
Gross!
All righty, then! ♫
SWING
SWING
I think I'll pick a song!
You're gonna sing, Itsuka? Really ...?
Y'know, this'll be the first time I get to hear her sing!
It's the first time I've been to karaoke with her, too.
Yeah! What are you good at?
SHAKA
SHAKA
So,
what'll you be singing?
Uhm ...
I doubt it's a song that you know, Mr. Shimada.
TOSS
But ...
this is a song
that I love to sing!!

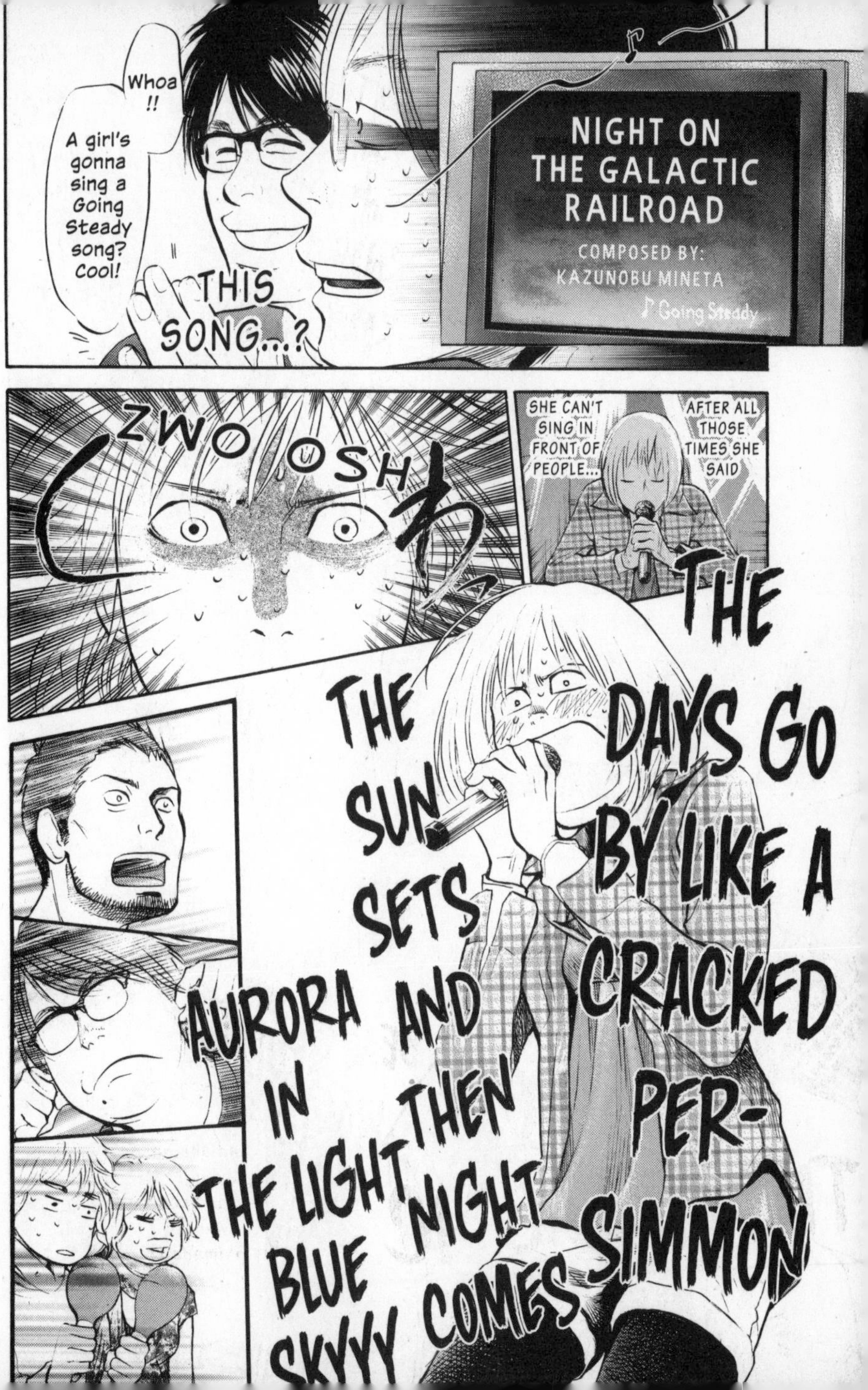
NIGHT ON THE GALACTIC RAILROAD
COMPOSED BY: KAZUNOBU MINETA
♪Going Steady...
THIS SONG...?
Whoa!!
A girl's gonna sing a Going Steady song? Cool!
AFTER ALL THOSE TIMES SHE SAID
SHE CAN'T SING IN FRONT OF PEOPLE...
ZWOOSH
THE DAYS GO BY LIKE A CRACKED PER-SIMMON
THE SUN SETS
AURORA AND
IN
THE LIGHT THEN
BLUE NIGHT
SKYYY COMES

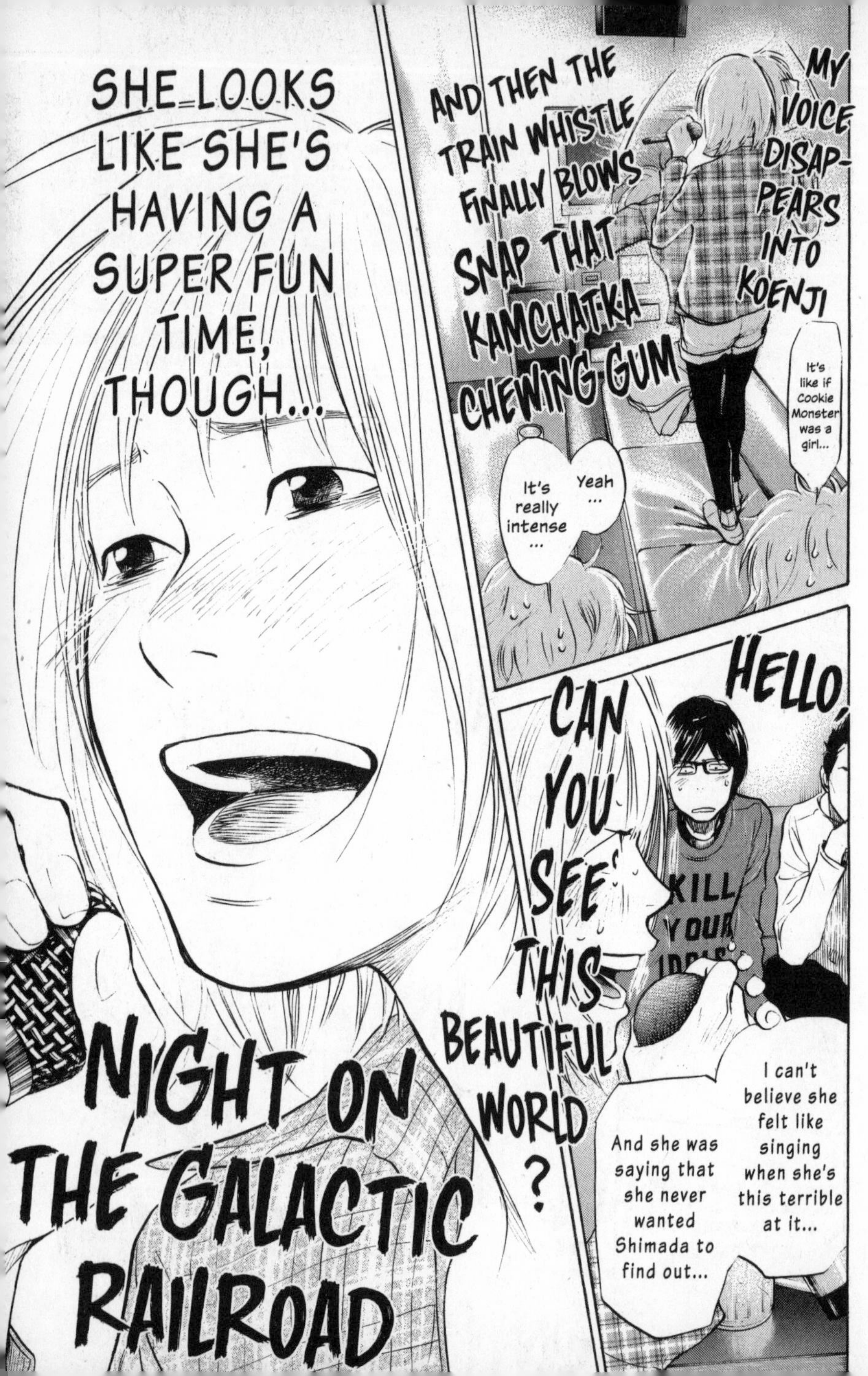
MY VOICE DISAPPEARS INTO KOENJI
It's like if Cookie Monster was a girl...
AND THEN THE TRAIN WHISTLE FINALLY BLOWS
SNAP THAT KAMCHATKA CHEWING GUM
Yeah...
It's really intense...
HELLO, CAN YOU SEE THIS BEAUTIFUL WORLD?
I can't believe she felt like singing when she's this terrible at it...
And she was saying that she never wanted Shimada to find out...
SHE LOOKS LIKE SHE'S HAVING A SUPER FUN TIME, THOUGH...
NIGHT ON THE GALACTIC RAILROAD

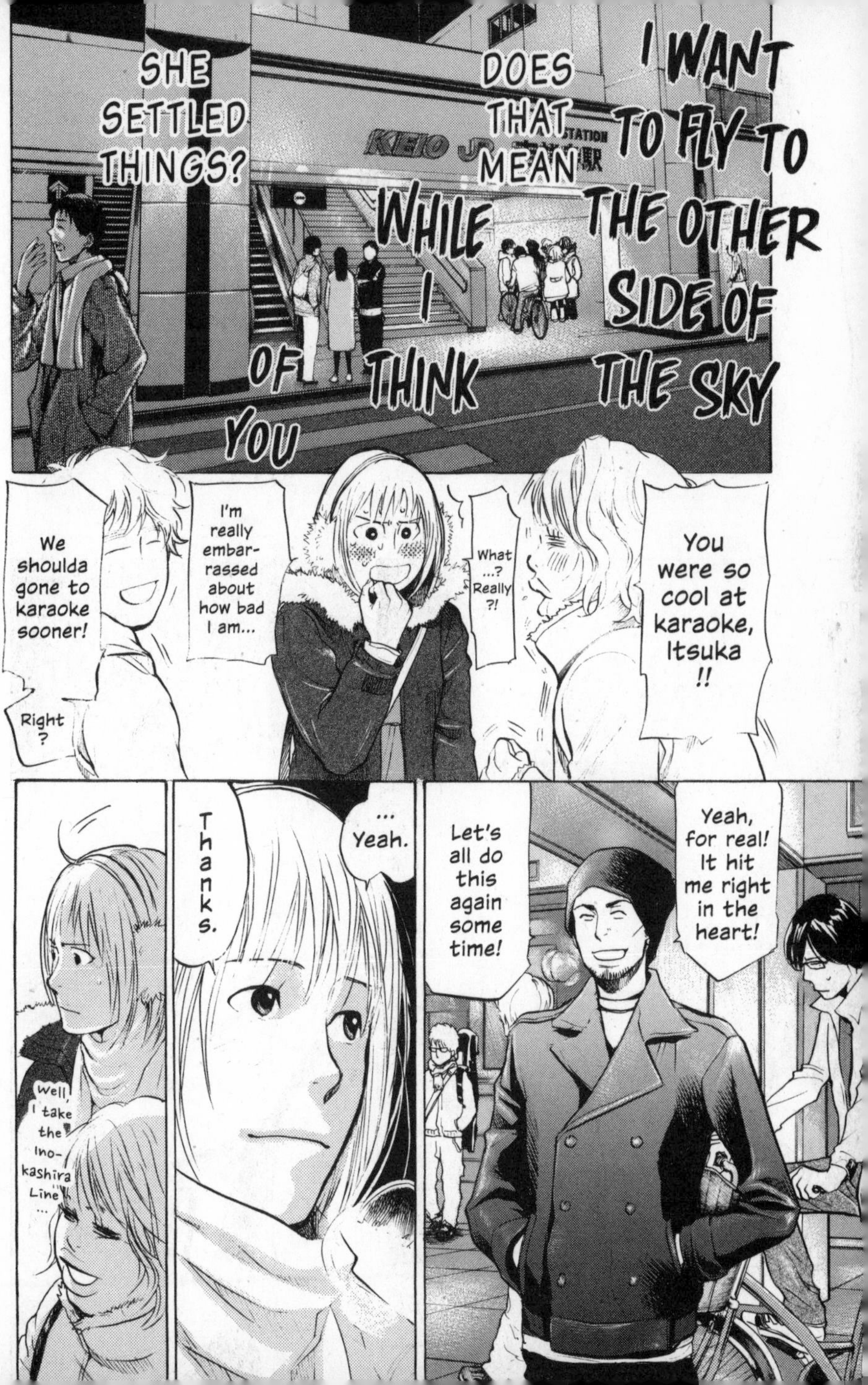
I WANT TO FLY TO THE OTHER SIDE OF THE SKY
WHILE I THINK OF YOU
DOES THAT MEAN
SHE SETTLED THINGS?
KEIO JR
STATION
You were so cool at karaoke, Itsuka!!
What...? Really?!
I'm really embarrassed about how bad I am...
We shoulda gone to karaoke sooner!
Right?
Yeah, for real! It hit me right in the heart!
Let's all do this again some time!
...Yeah.
Thanks.
Well, I take the Ino-kashira Line...

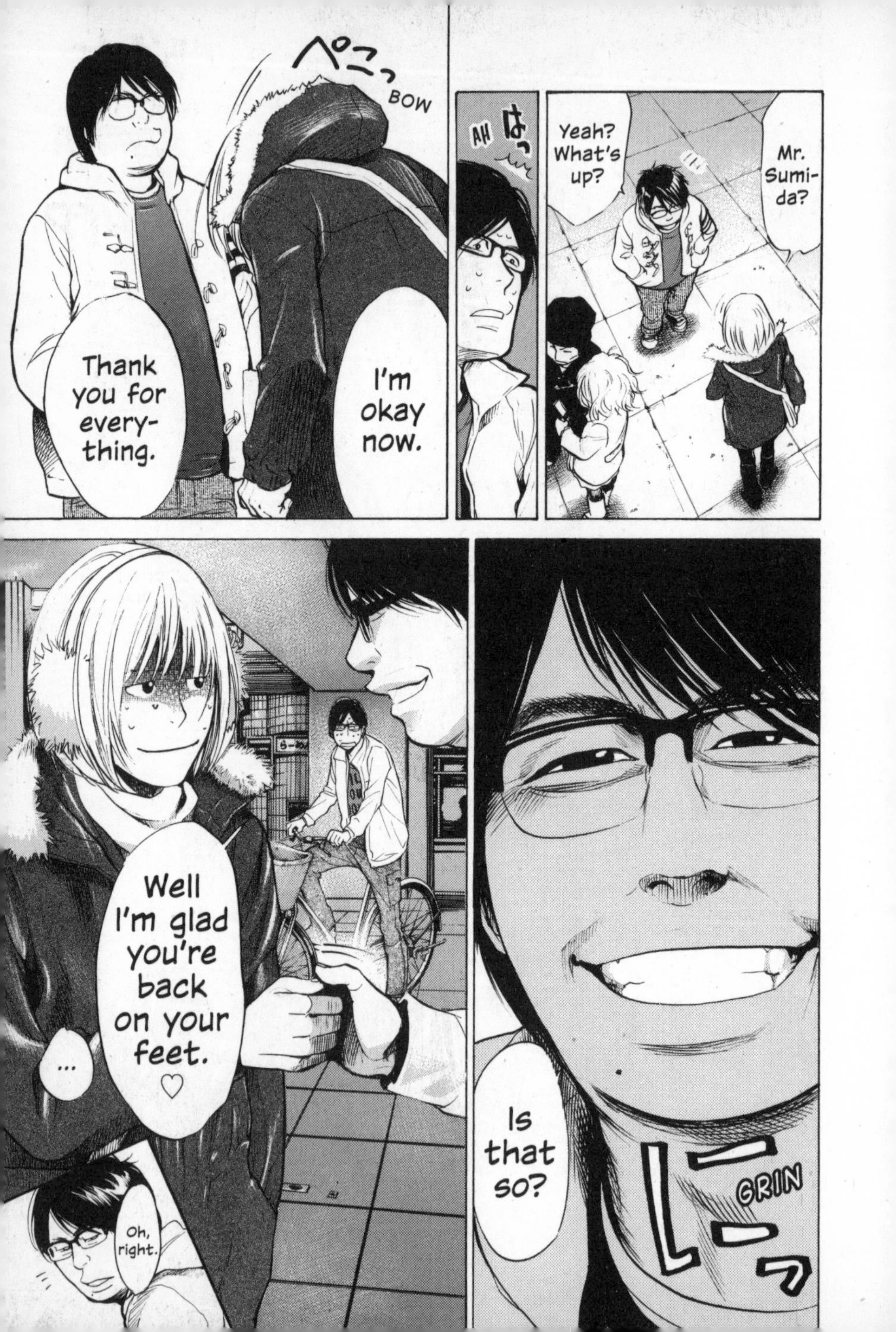

Mr. Sumi-da?
Yeah? What's up?
AH
はっ
ぺこっ
BOW
I'm okay now.
Thank you for every-thing.
Is that so?
GRIN
Well I'm glad you're back on your feet. ♡
...
Oh, right.

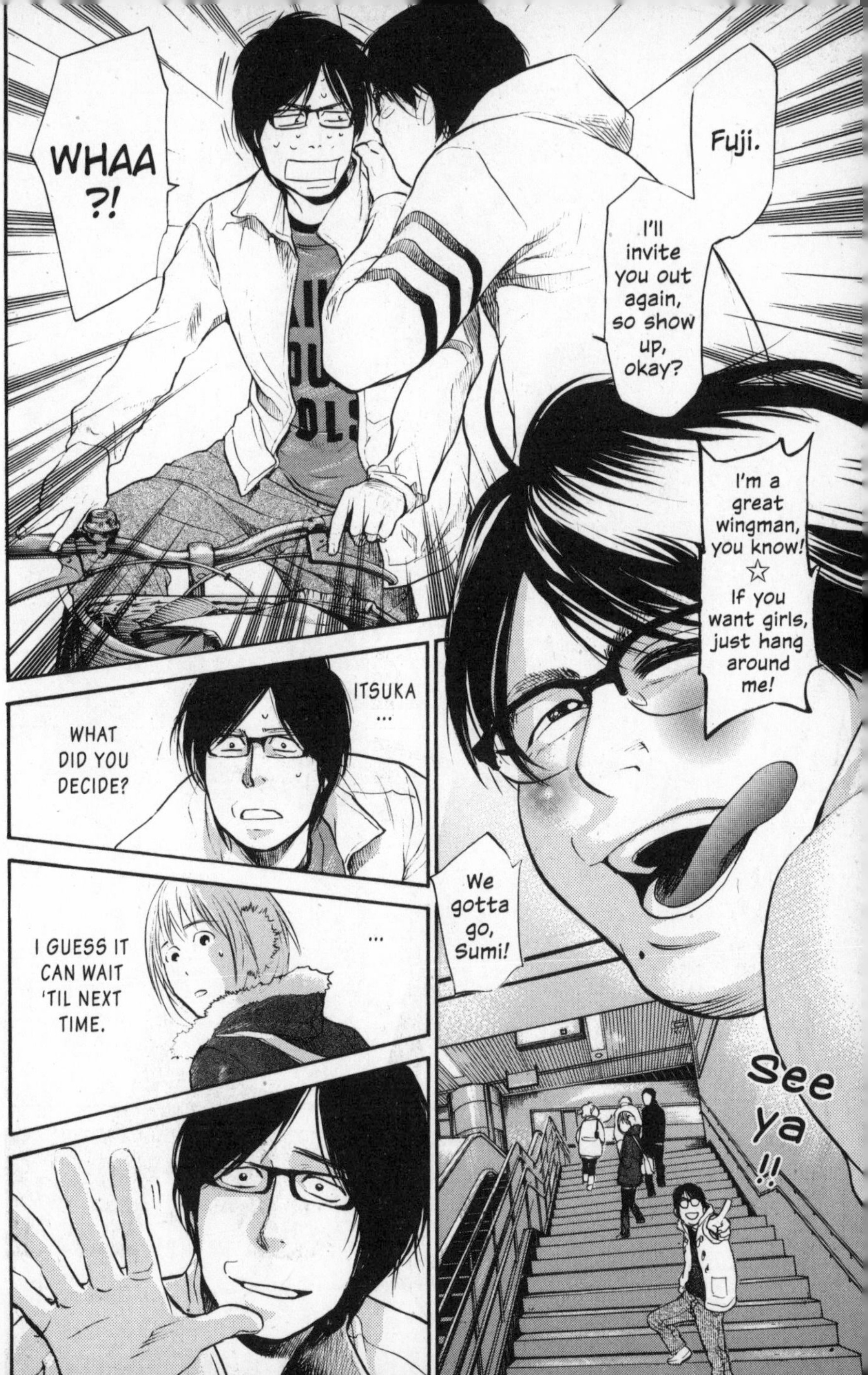
Fuji.
I'll invite you out again, so show up, okay?
WHAA ?!
I'm a great wingman, you know! ☆
If you want girls, just hang around me!
We gotta go, Sumi!
See ya !!
ITSUKA ...
WHAT DID YOU DECIDE?
...
I GUESS IT CAN WAIT 'TIL NEXT TIME.

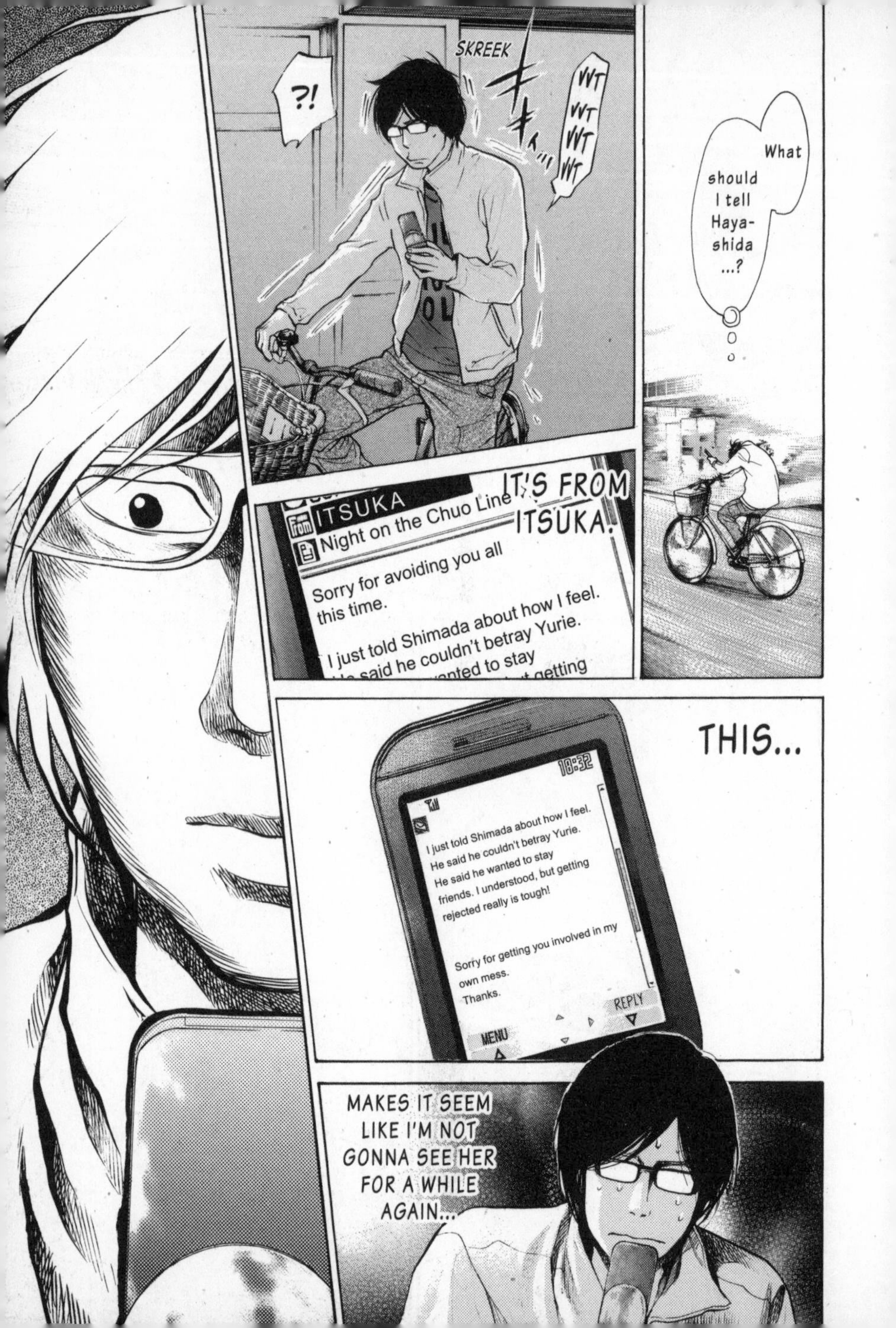

What should I tell Haya-shida ...?
?!
SKREEK
VVT VVT VVT VVT
IT'S FROM ITSUKA!
ITSUKA
Night on the Chuo Line
Sorry for avoiding you all this time.
I just told Shimada about how I feel.
He said he couldn't betray Yurie.
He said he wanted to stay
THIS...
18:32
I just told Shimada about how I feel.
He said he couldn't betray Yurie.
He said he wanted to stay
friends. I understood, but getting
rejected really is tough!
Sorry for getting you involved in my own mess.
Thanks.
REPLY
MENU
MAKES IT SEEM LIKE I'M NOT GONNA SEE HER FOR A WHILE AGAIN...

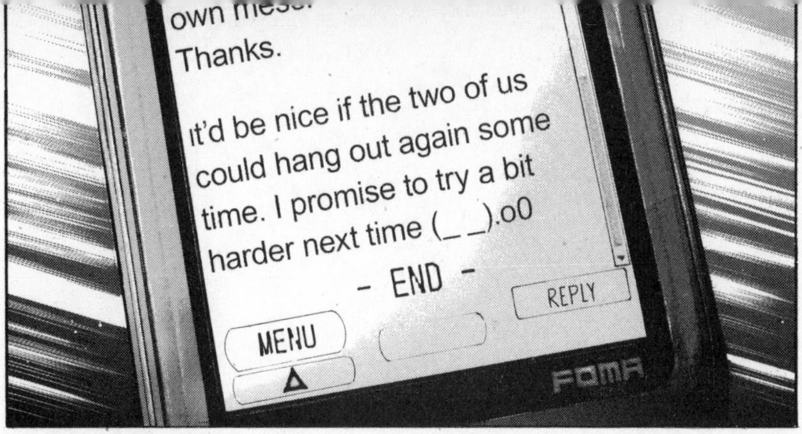
Thanks.
it'd be nice if the two of us
could hang out again some
time. I promise to try a bit
harder next time (_ _).o0
- END -
REPLY
MENU
FOMA

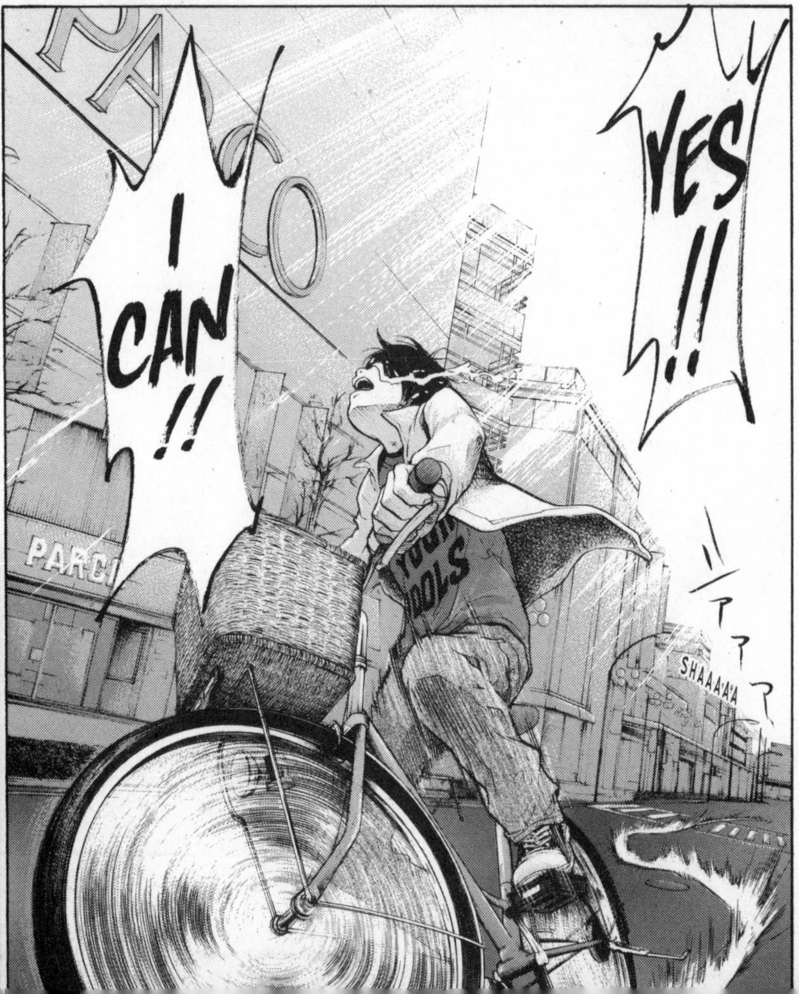
YES!!
I CAN!!
SHAAAAA
PARC

chapter 13 ♥ END

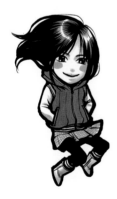

Moteki　Mitsurou　Kubo

M o t e k i

M i t s u r o u   K u b o

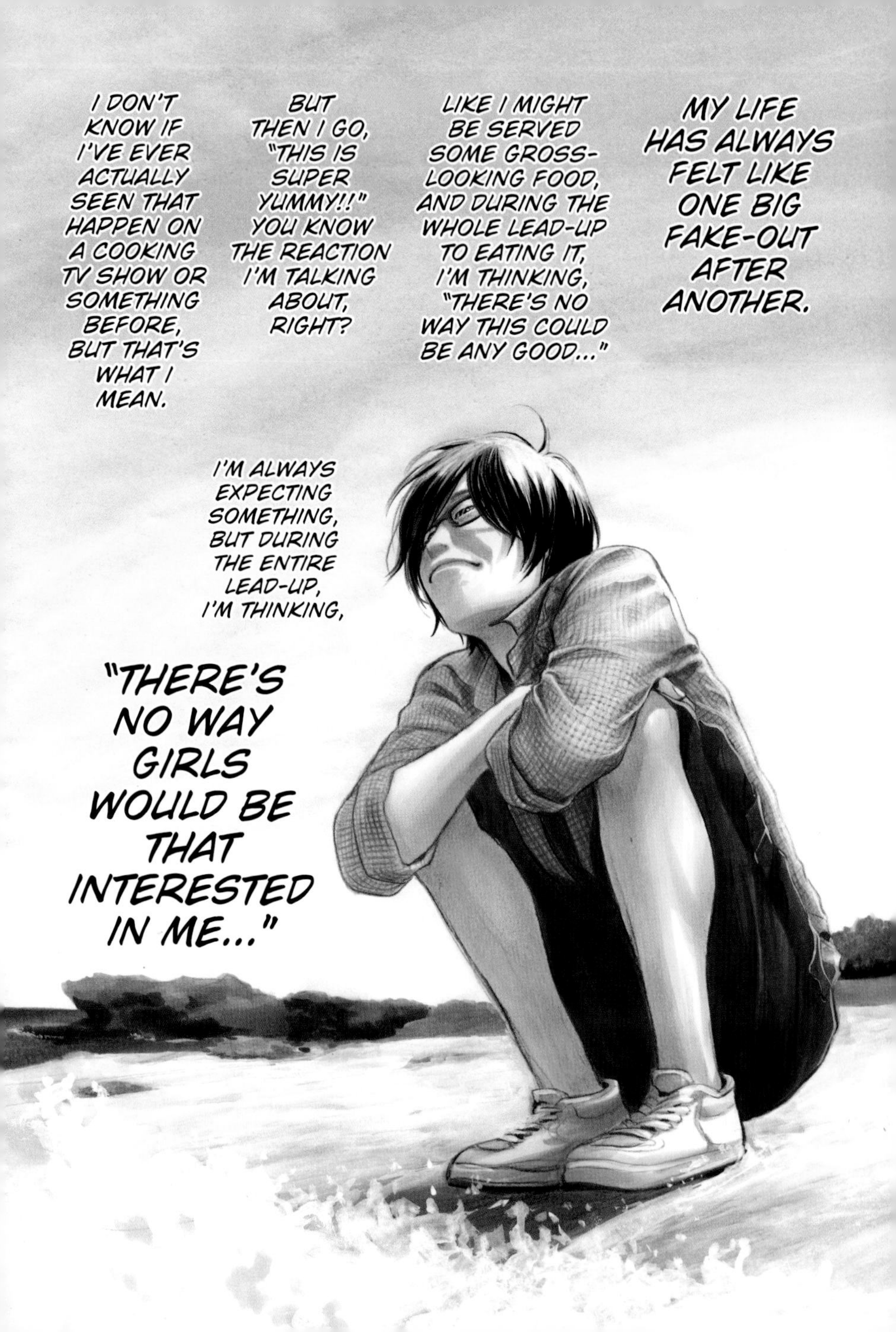
MY LIFE HAS ALWAYS FELT LIKE ONE BIG FAKE-OUT AFTER ANOTHER.
LIKE I MIGHT BE SERVED SOME GROSS-LOOKING FOOD, AND DURING THE WHOLE LEAD-UP TO EATING IT, I'M THINKING, "THERE'S NO WAY THIS COULD BE ANY GOOD..."
BUT THEN I GO, "THIS IS SUPER YUMMY!!" YOU KNOW THE REACTION I'M TALKING ABOUT, RIGHT?
I DON'T KNOW IF I'VE EVER ACTUALLY SEEN THAT HAPPEN ON A COOKING TV SHOW OR SOMETHING BEFORE, BUT THAT'S WHAT I MEAN.
I'M ALWAYS EXPECTING SOMETHING, BUT DURING THE ENTIRE LEAD-UP, I'M THINKING,
"THERE'S NO WAY GIRLS WOULD BE THAT INTERESTED IN ME..."

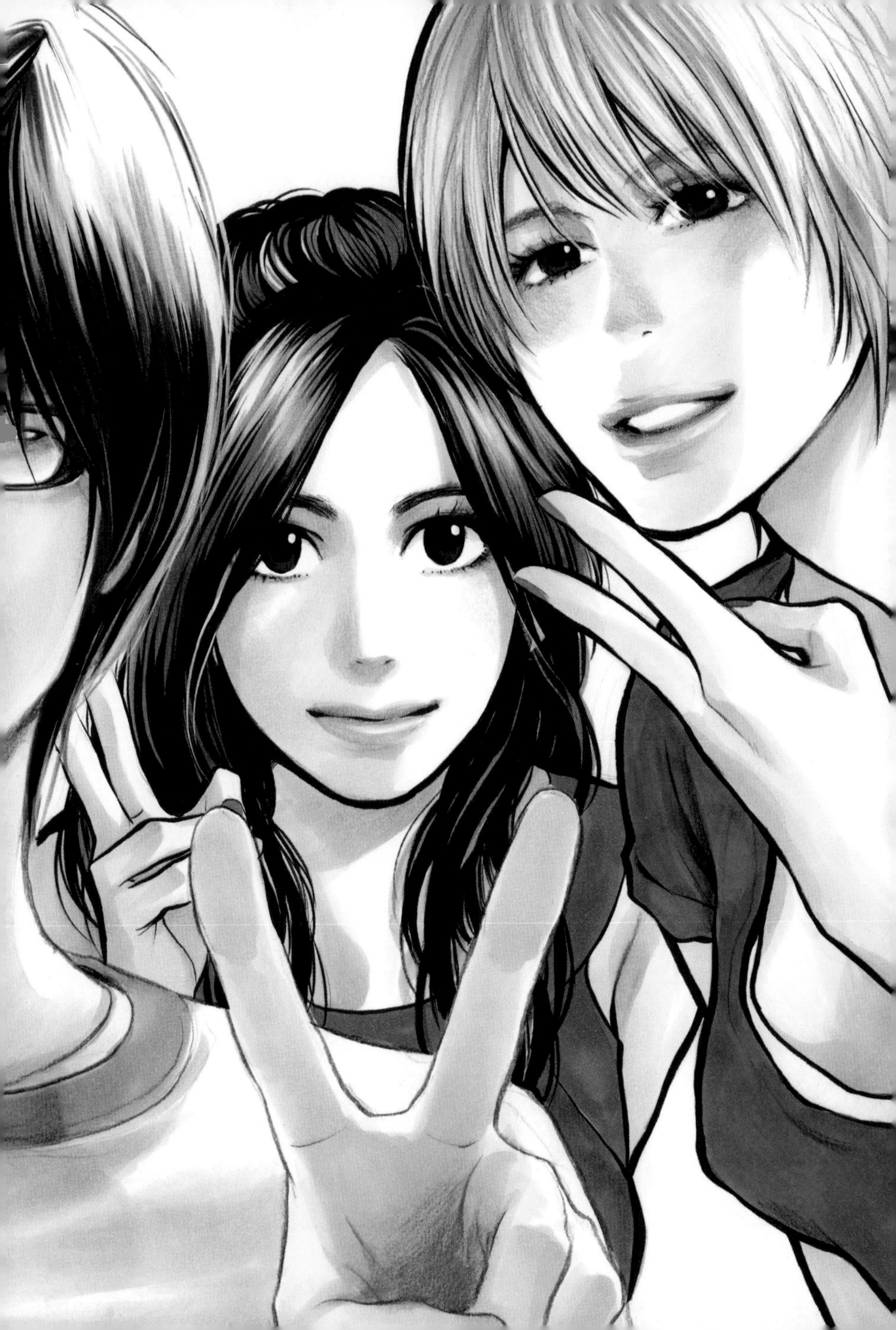

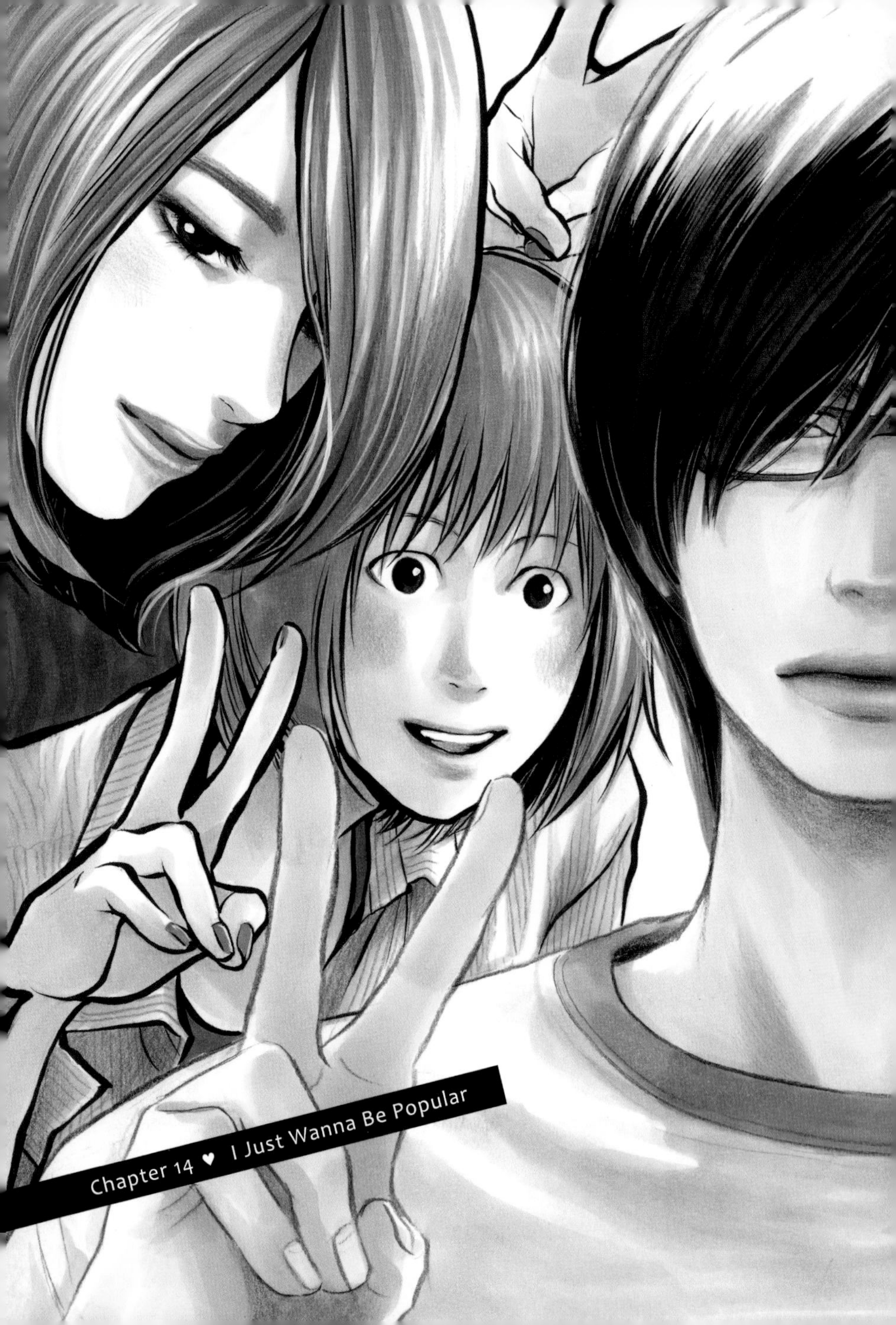
Chapter 14 ♥ I Just Wanna Be Popular

Moteki

Mitsurou Kubo

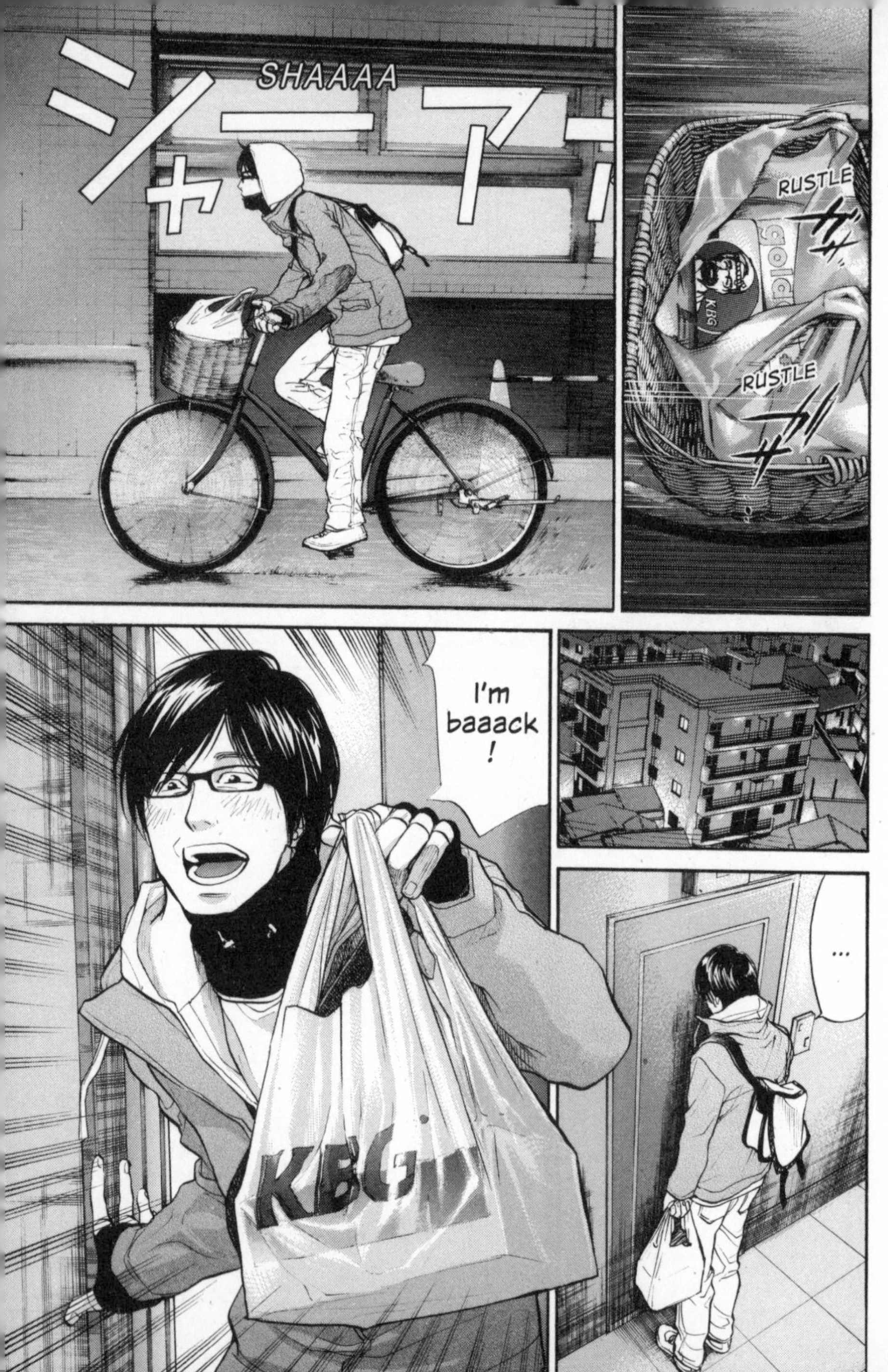
RUSTLE
RUSTLE
SHAAAA
...
I'm baaack!

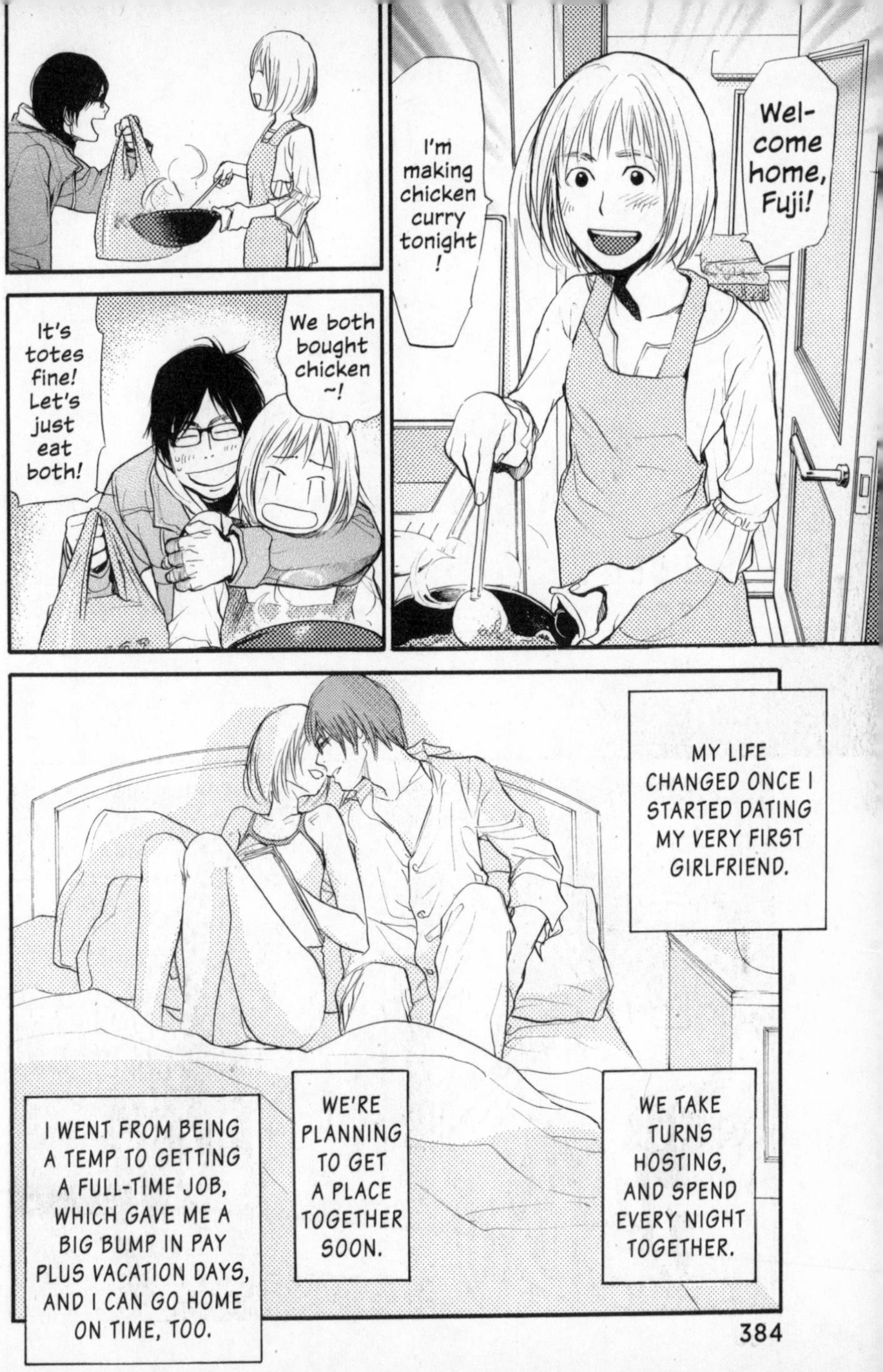
Wel-come home, Fuji!
I'm making chicken curry tonight!
We both bought chicken ~!
It's totes fine! Let's just eat both!
MY LIFE CHANGED ONCE I STARTED DATING MY VERY FIRST GIRLFRIEND.
WE TAKE TURNS HOSTING, AND SPEND EVERY NIGHT TOGETHER.
WE'RE PLANNING TO GET A PLACE TOGETHER SOON.
I WENT FROM BEING A TEMP TO GETTING A FULL-TIME JOB, WHICH GAVE ME A BIG BUMP IN PAY PLUS VACATION DAYS, AND I CAN GO HOME ON TIME, TOO.

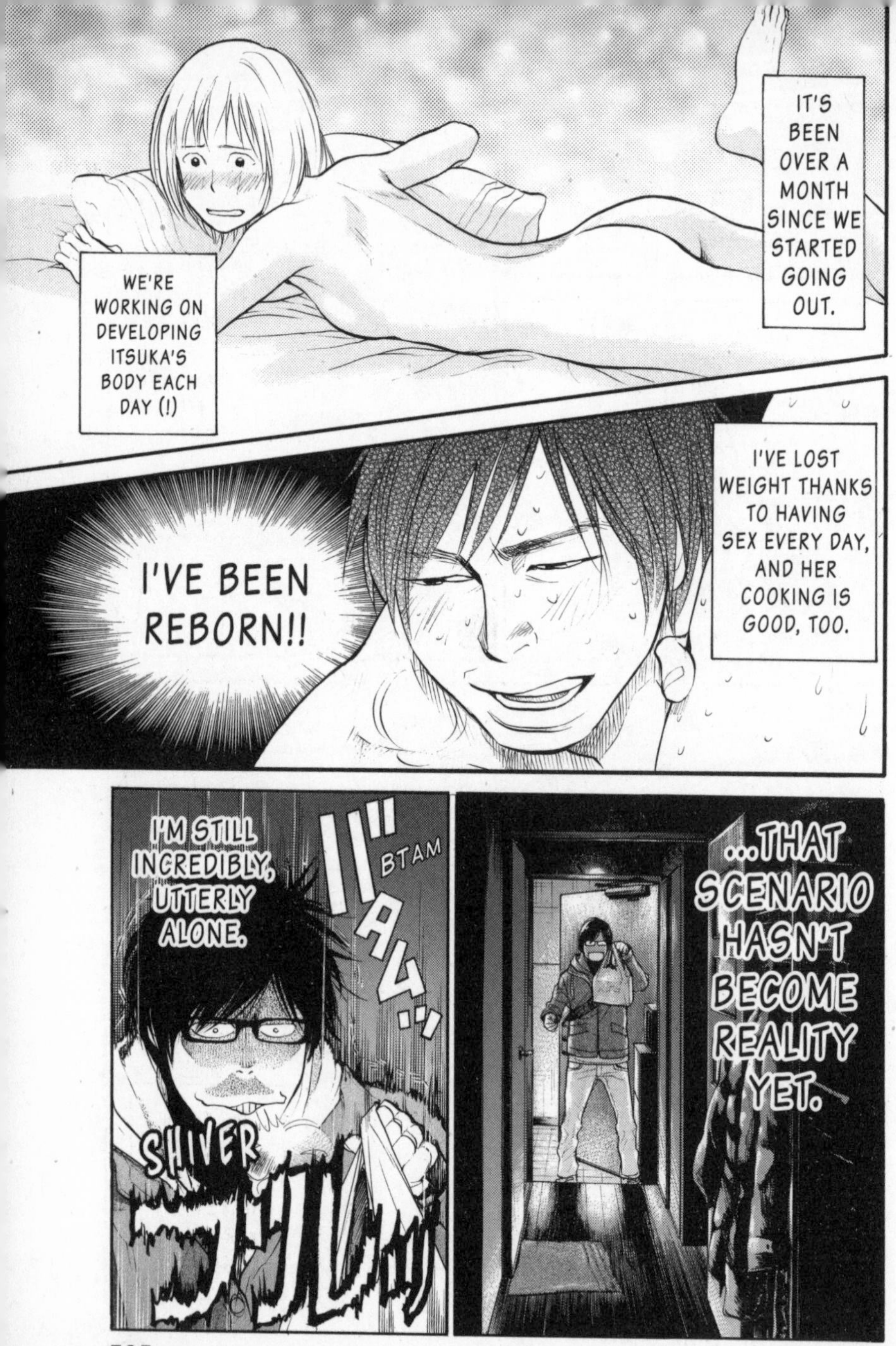
IT'S BEEN OVER A MONTH SINCE WE STARTED GOING OUT.
WE'RE WORKING ON DEVELOPING ITSUKA'S BODY EACH DAY (!)
I'VE LOST WEIGHT THANKS TO HAVING SEX EVERY DAY, AND HER COOKING IS GOOD, TOO.
I'VE BEEN REBORN!!
...THAT SCENARIO HASN'T BECOME REALITY YET.
I'M STILL INCREDIBLY, UTTERLY ALONE.
BTAM
SHIVER

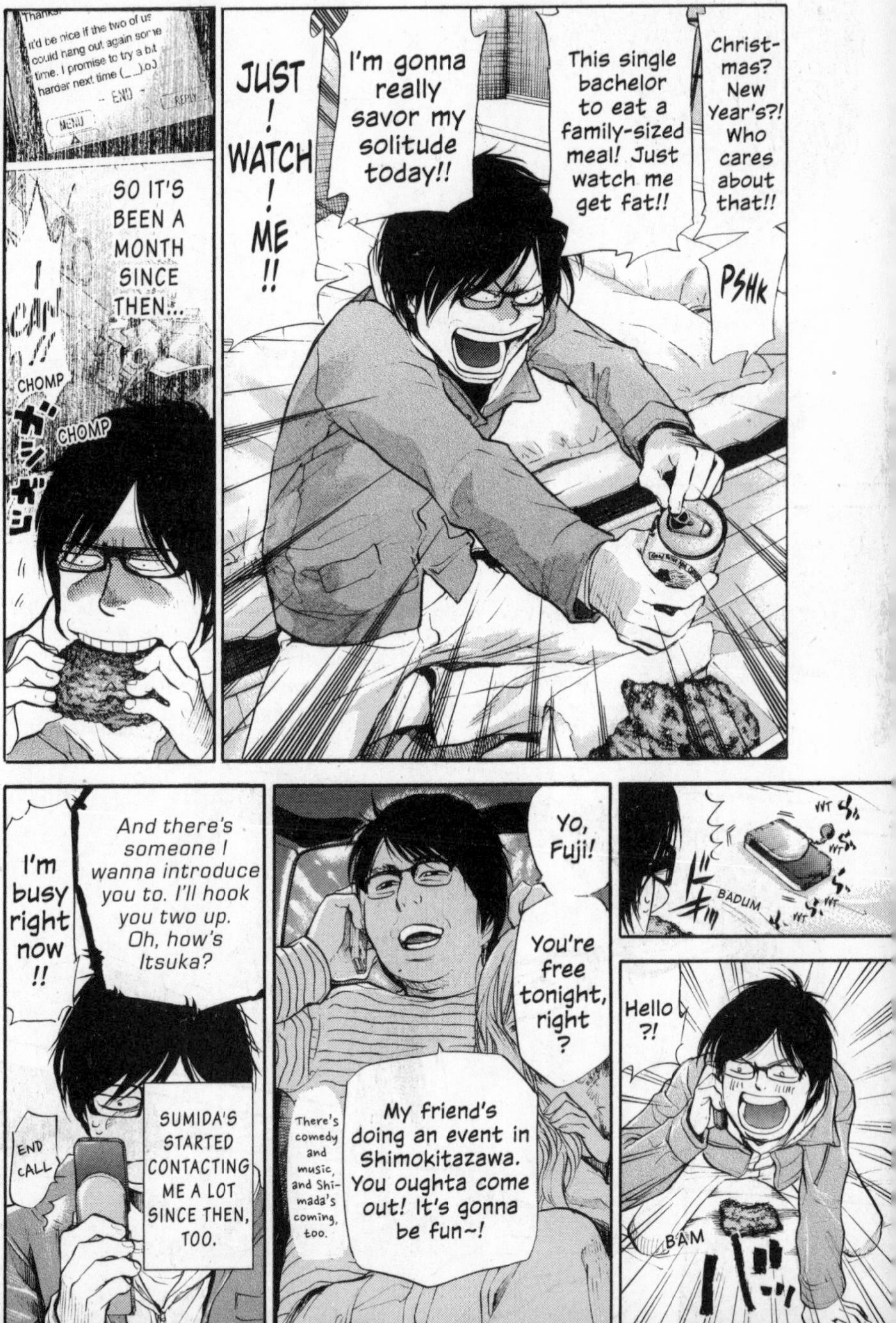
Christmas? New Year's?! Who cares about that!!
This single bachelor to eat a family-sized meal! Just watch me get fat!!
I'm gonna really savor my solitude today!!
JUST! WATCH! ME!!
PSHk
It'd be nice if the two of us could hang out again some time. I promise to try a bit harder next time (__).o)
END
MENU
REPLY
SO IT'S BEEN A MONTH SINCE THEN...
CHOMP
CHOMP
VVT
BADUM
Hello?!
BAM
Yo, Fuji!
You're free tonight, right?
My friend's doing an event in Shimokitazawa. You oughta come out! It's gonna be fun~!
There's comedy and music, and Shimada's coming, too.
And there's someone I wanna introduce you to. I'll hook you two up. Oh, how's Itsuka?
I'm busy right now!!
END CALL
SUMIDA'S STARTED CONTACTING ME A LOT SINCE THEN, TOO.

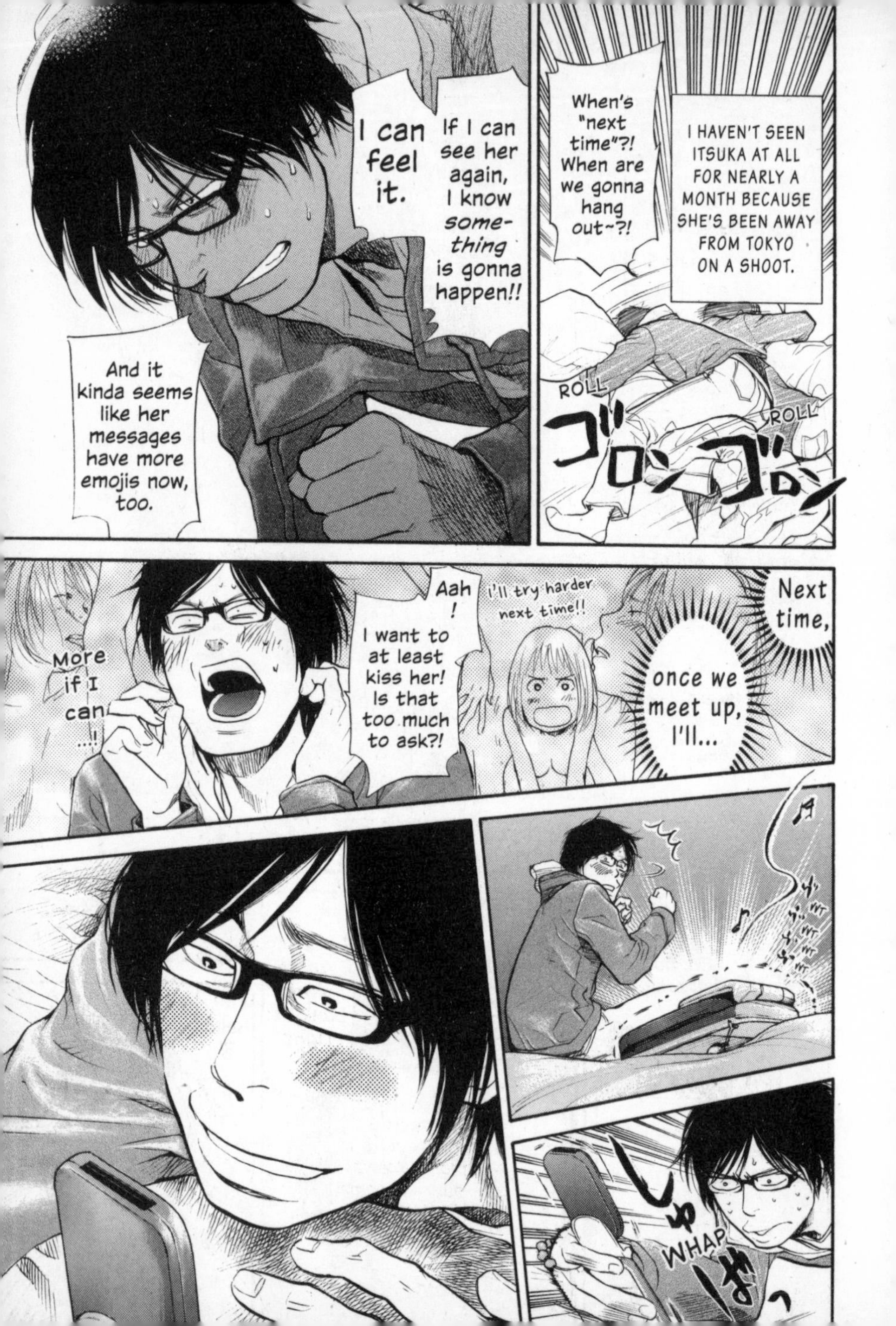

I HAVEN'T SEEN ITSUKA AT ALL FOR NEARLY A MONTH BECAUSE SHE'S BEEN AWAY FROM TOKYO ON A SHOOT.
When's "next time"?! When are we gonna hang out~?!
ROLL
ROLL
ゴロンゴロン
If I can see her again, I know *something* is gonna happen!!
I can feel it.
And it kinda seems like her messages have more emojis now, too.
Next time,
once we meet up, I'll...
I'll try harder next time!!
Aah! I want to at least kiss her! Is that too much to ask?!
More if I can ...!
WHAP

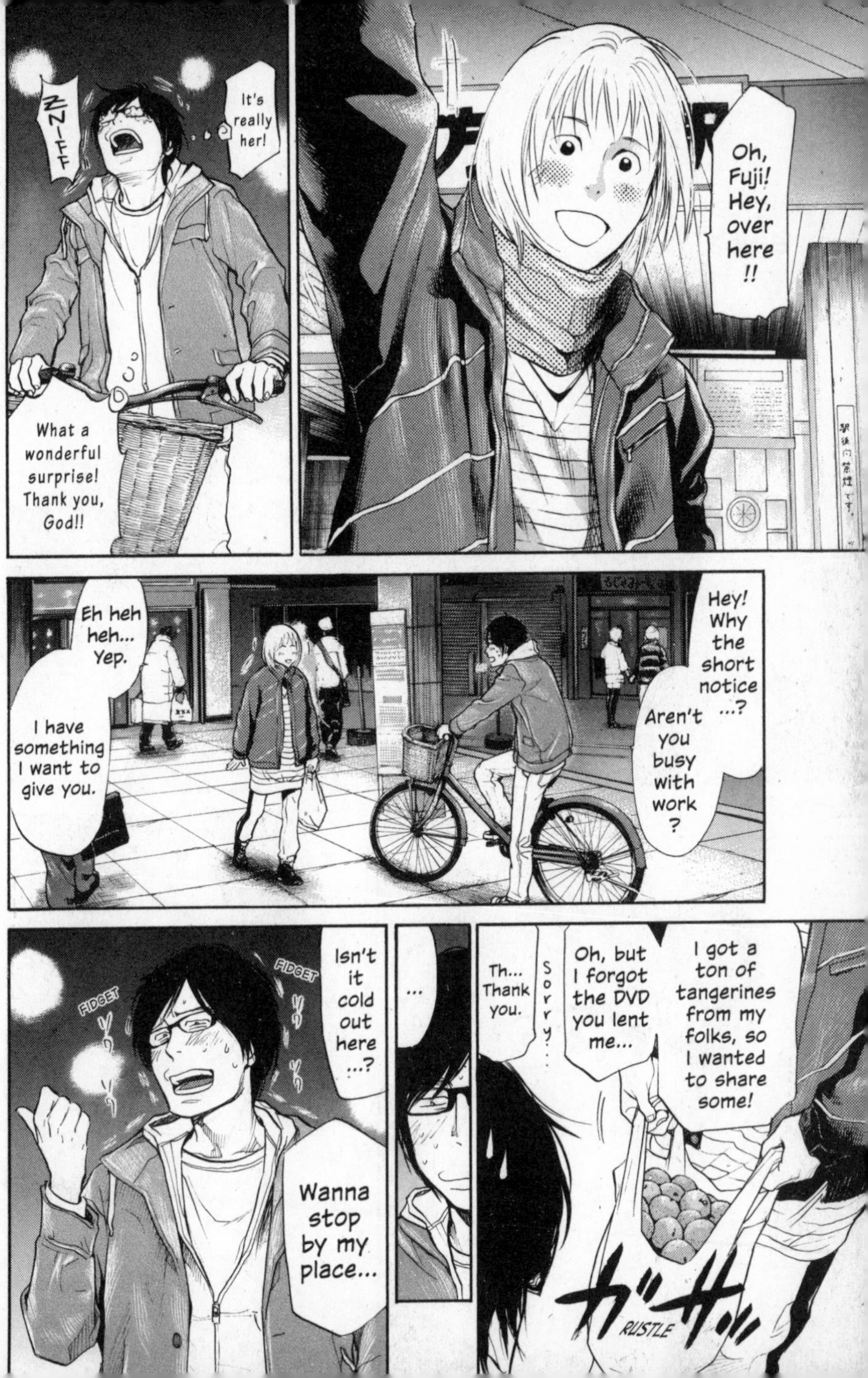
Oh, Fuji! Hey, over here !!
It's really her!
SNIFF
What a wonderful surprise! Thank you, God!!
Hey! Why the short notice ...?
Aren't you busy with work ?
Eh heh heh... Yep.
I have something I want to give you.
I got a ton of tangerines from my folks, so I wanted to share some!
Oh, but I forgot the DVD you lent me...
Sorry...
Th... Thank you.
RUSTLE
...
Isn't it cold out here ...?
FIDGET
FIDGET
Wanna stop by my place...

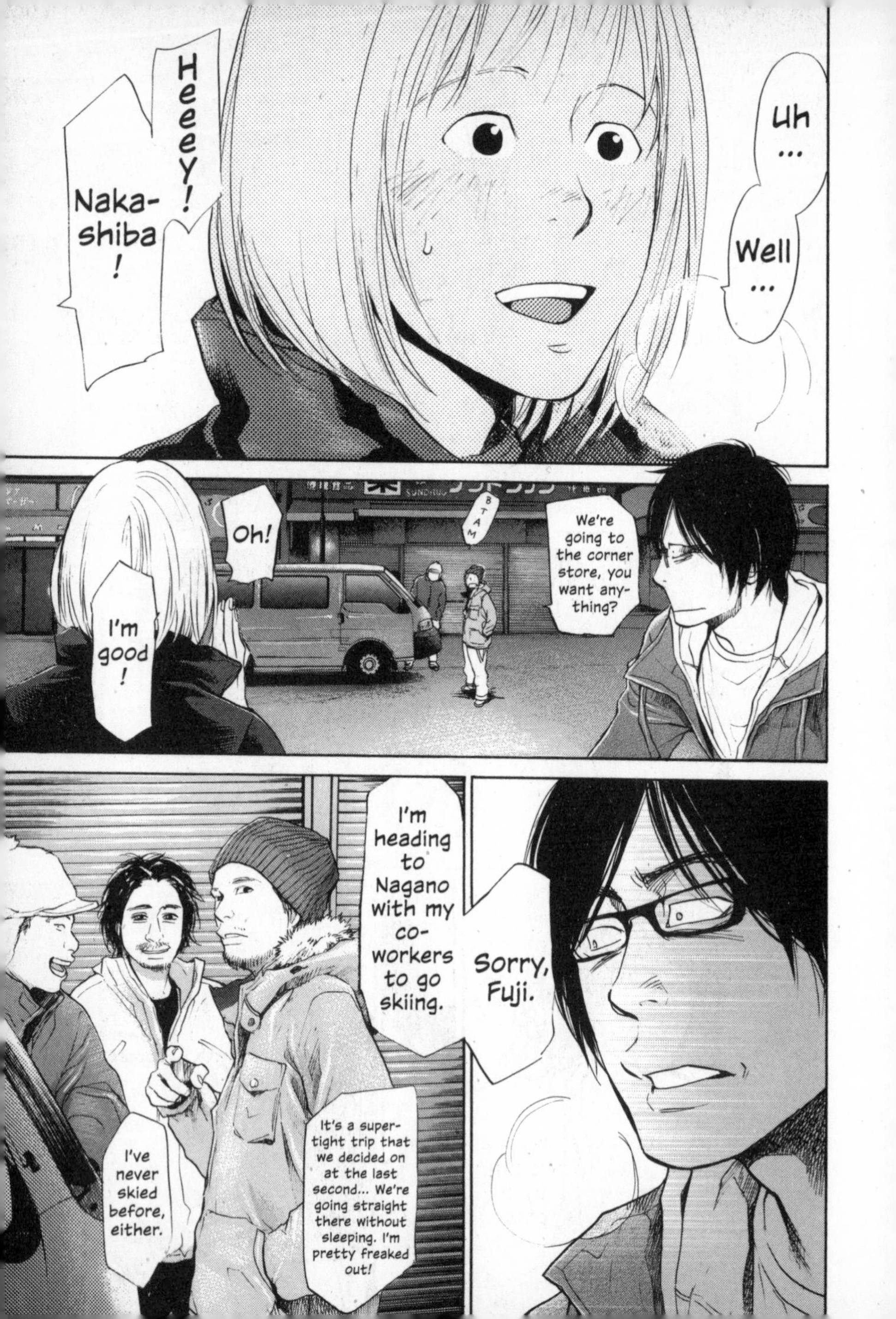
Uh ... Well ...
HeeeY! Naka-shiba!
We're going to the corner store, you want any-thing?
BTAM
Oh!
I'm good!
Sorry, Fuji.
I'm heading to Nagano with my co-workers to go skiing.
It's a super-tight trip that we decided on at the last second... We're going straight there without sleeping. I'm pretty freaked out!
I've never skied before, either.

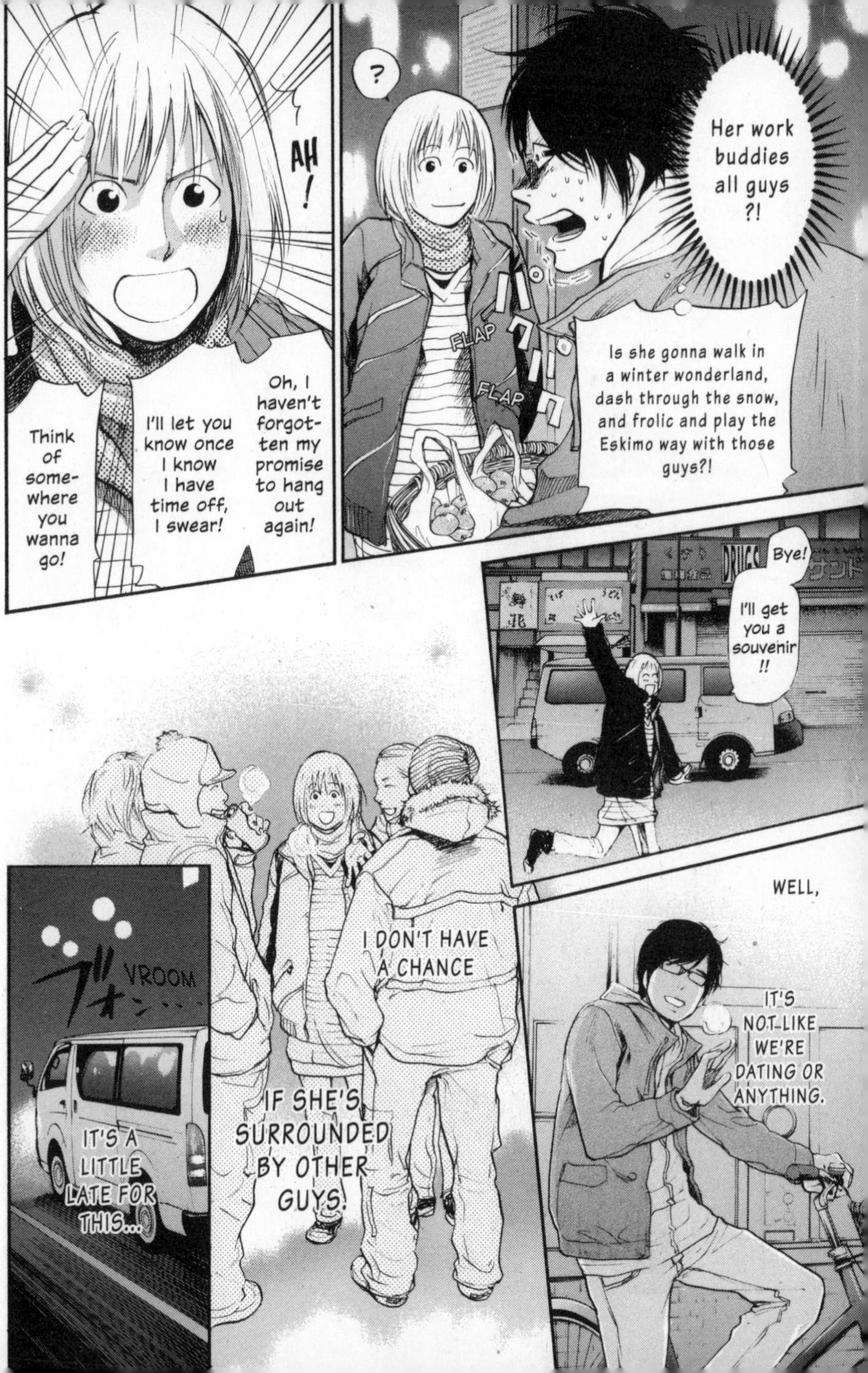
?
Her work buddies all guys ?!
FLAP
FLAP
Is she gonna walk in a winter wonderland, dash through the snow, and frolic and play the Eskimo way with those guys?!
AH!
Oh, I haven't forgotten my promise to hang out again!
I'll let you know once I know I have time off, I swear!
Think of somewhere you wanna go!
DRUGS
Bye!
I'll get you a souvenir !!
WELL,
IT'S NOT LIKE WE'RE DATING OR ANYTHING.
I DON'T HAVE A CHANCE
IF SHE'S SURROUNDED BY OTHER GUYS.
VROOM
IT'S A LITTLE LATE FOR THIS...

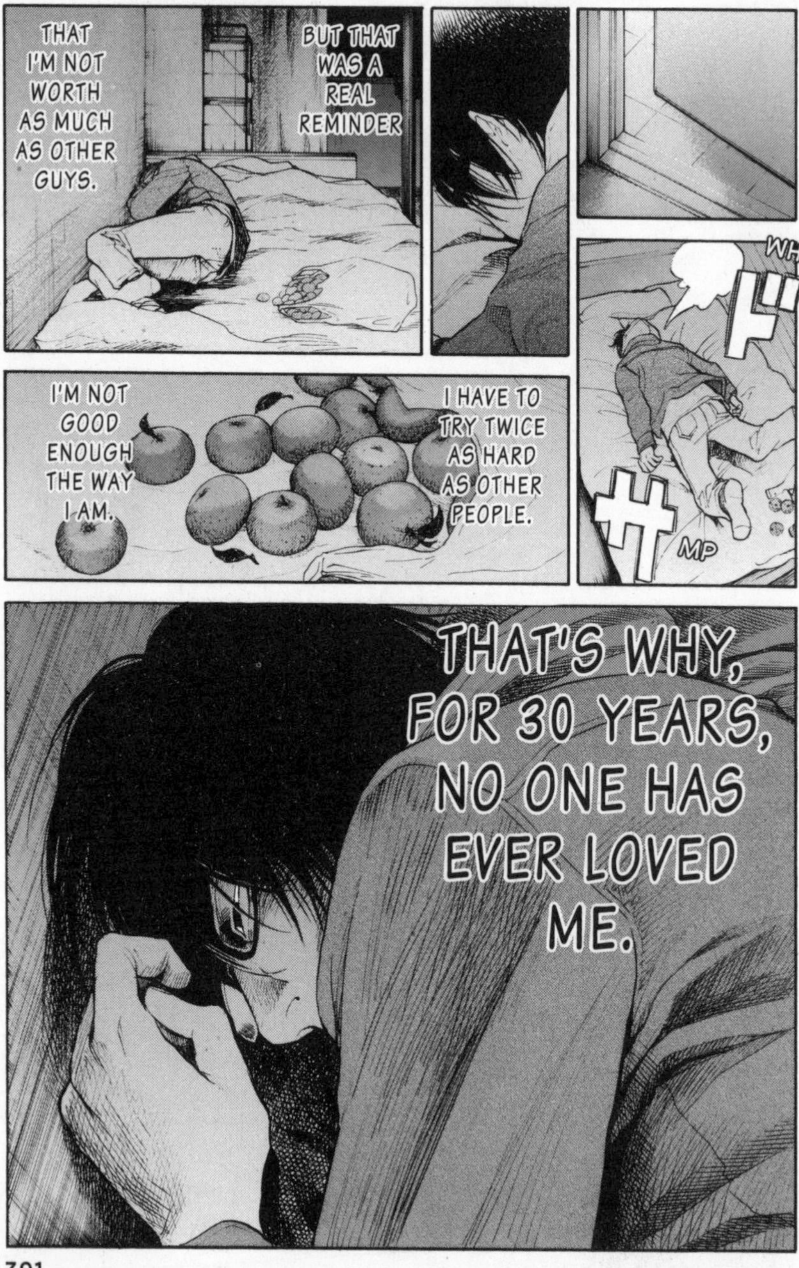
BUT THAT WAS A REAL REMINDER
THAT I'M NOT WORTH AS MUCH AS OTHER GUYS.
WHU
ド
サ
MP
I HAVE TO TRY TWICE AS HARD AS OTHER PEOPLE.
I'M NOT GOOD ENOUGH THE WAY I AM.
THAT'S WHY, FOR 30 YEARS, NO ONE HAS EVER LOVED ME.

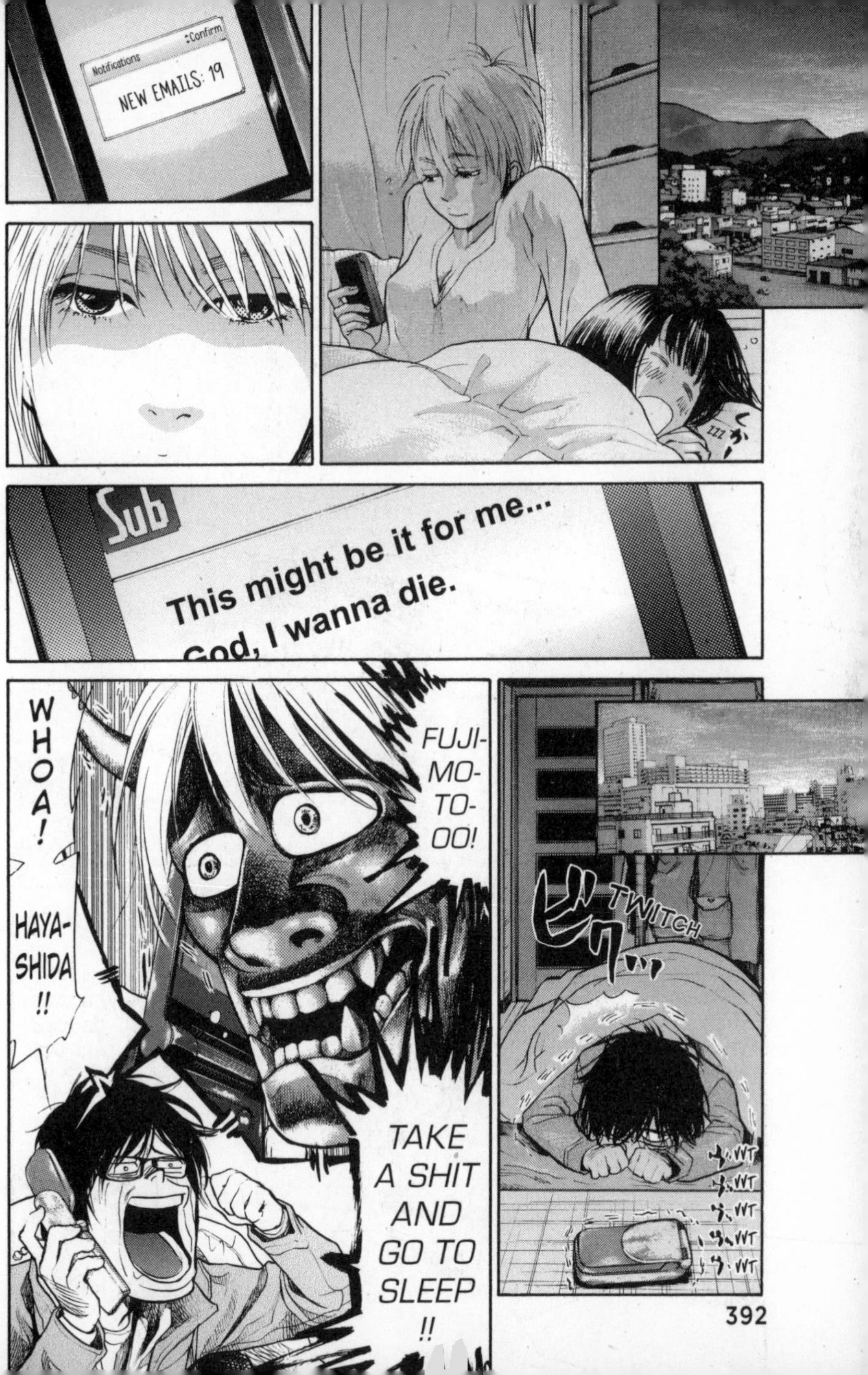
Notifications
Confirm
NEW EMAILS: 19
Sub
This might be it for me...
God, I wanna die.
TWITCH
VVT
VVT
VVT
VVT
VVT
FUJI-MO-TO-OO!
WHOA!
HAYA-SHIDA !!
TAKE A SHIT AND GO TO SLEEP !!

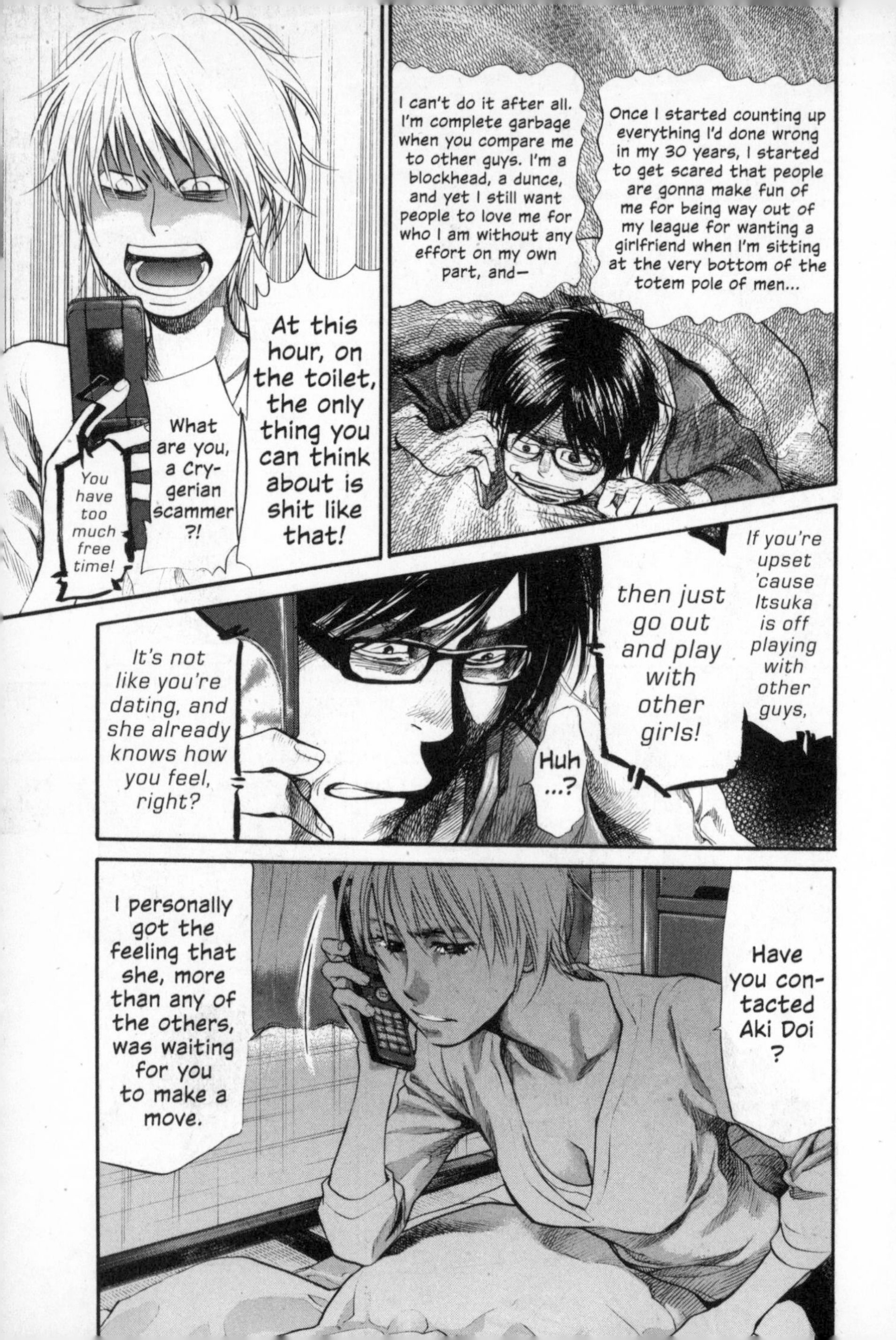
Once I started counting up everything I'd done wrong in my 30 years, I started to get scared that people are gonna make fun of me for being way out of my league for wanting a girlfriend when I'm sitting at the very bottom of the totem pole of men...
I can't do it after all. I'm complete garbage when you compare me to other guys. I'm a blockhead, a dunce, and yet I still want people to love me for who I am without any effort on my own part, and—
At this hour, on the toilet, the only thing you can think about is shit like that!
What are you, a Cry-gerian scammer?!
You have too much free time!
If you're upset 'cause Itsuka is off playing with other guys,
then just go out and play with other girls!
Huh ...?
It's not like you're dating, and she already knows how you feel, right?
Have you con-tacted Aki Doi ?
I personally got the feeling that she, more than any of the others, was waiting for you to make a move.

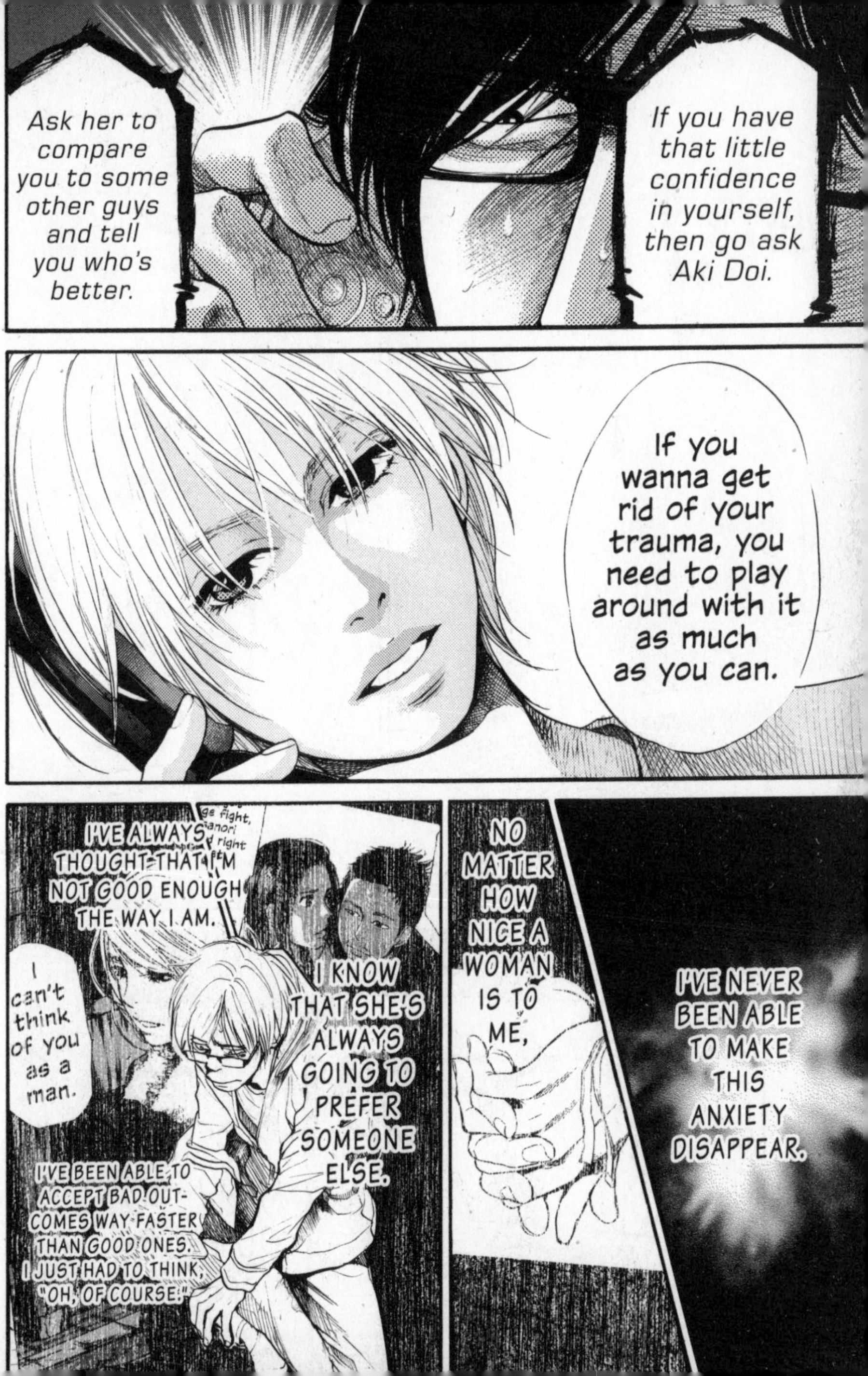
If you have that little confidence in yourself, then go ask Aki Doi.
Ask her to compare you to some other guys and tell you who's better.
If you wanna get rid of your trauma, you need to play around with it as much as you can.
NO MATTER HOW NICE A WOMAN IS TO ME,
I'VE NEVER BEEN ABLE TO MAKE THIS ANXIETY DISAPPEAR.
I'VE ALWAYS THOUGHT THAT I'M NOT GOOD ENOUGH THE WAY I AM.
I KNOW THAT SHE'S ALWAYS GOING TO PREFER SOMEONE ELSE.
I can't think of you as a man.
I'VE BEEN ABLE TO ACCEPT BAD OUT-COMES WAY FASTER THAN GOOD ONES. I JUST HAD TO THINK, "OH, OF COURSE."

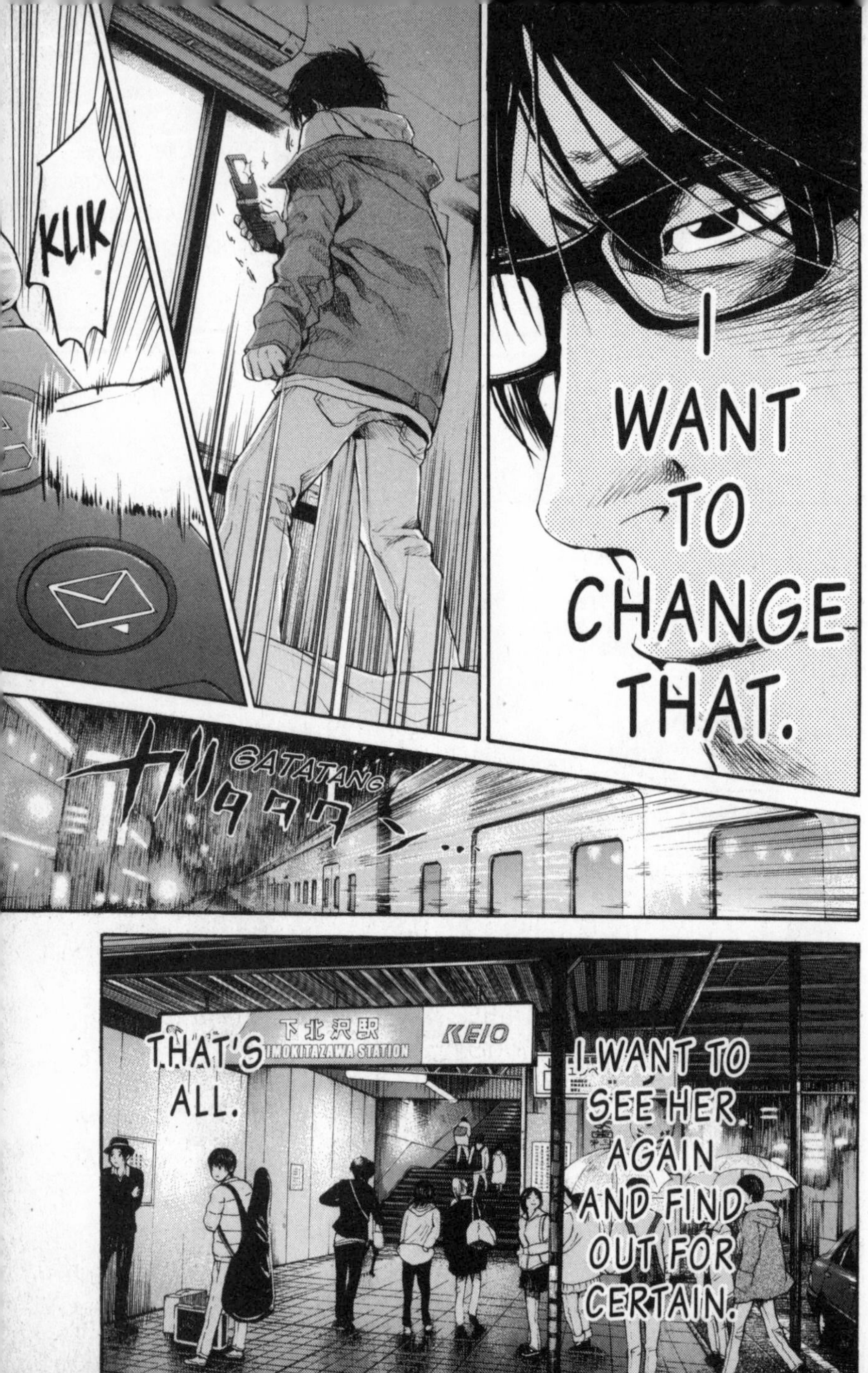
I WANT TO CHANGE THAT.
KLIK
GATATANG
I WANT TO SEE HER AGAIN AND FIND OUT FOR CERTAIN.
KEIO
下北沢駅
IMOKITAZAWA STATION
THAT'S ALL.

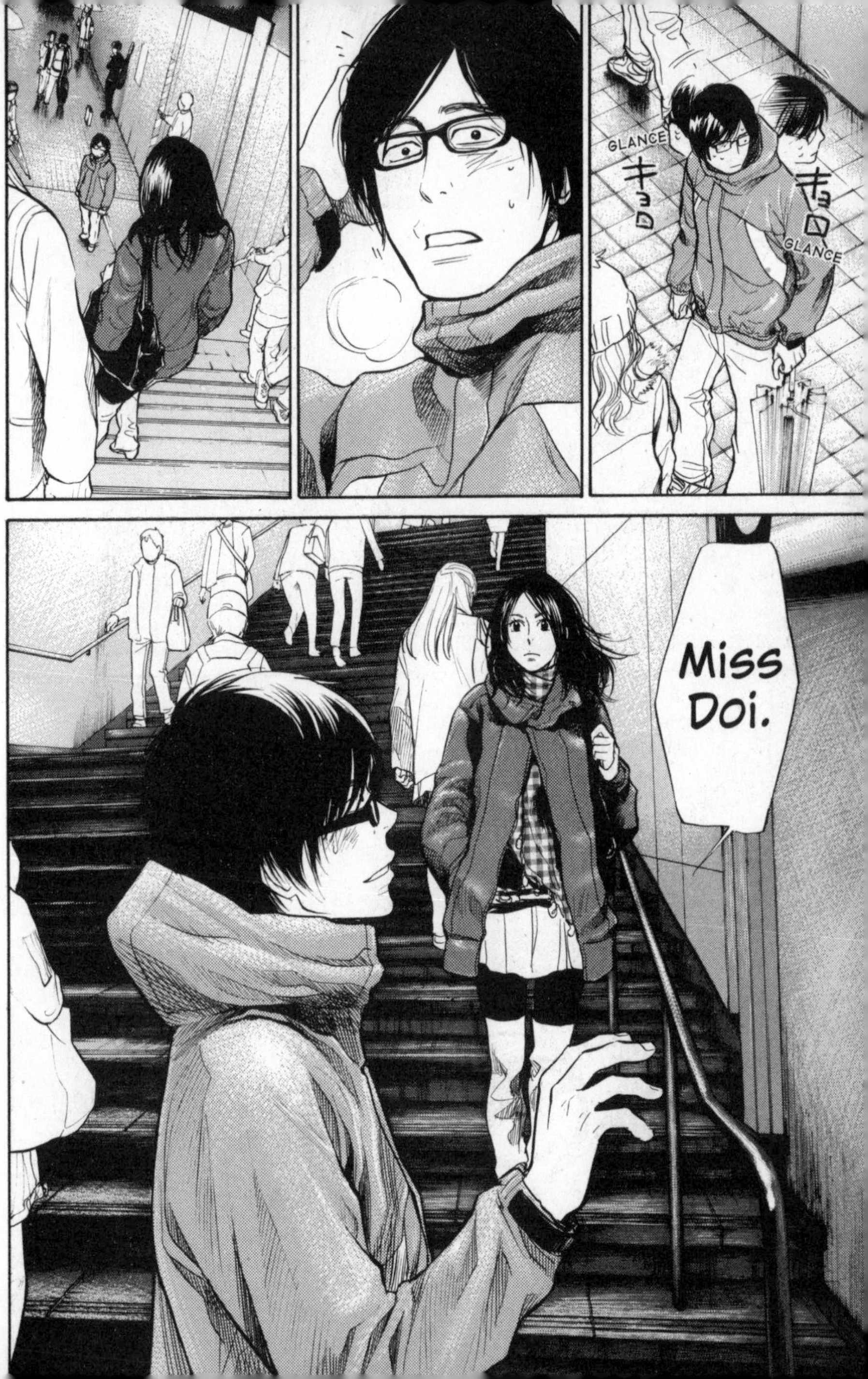
キョロ
GLANCE
GLANCE
キョロ
Miss Doi.

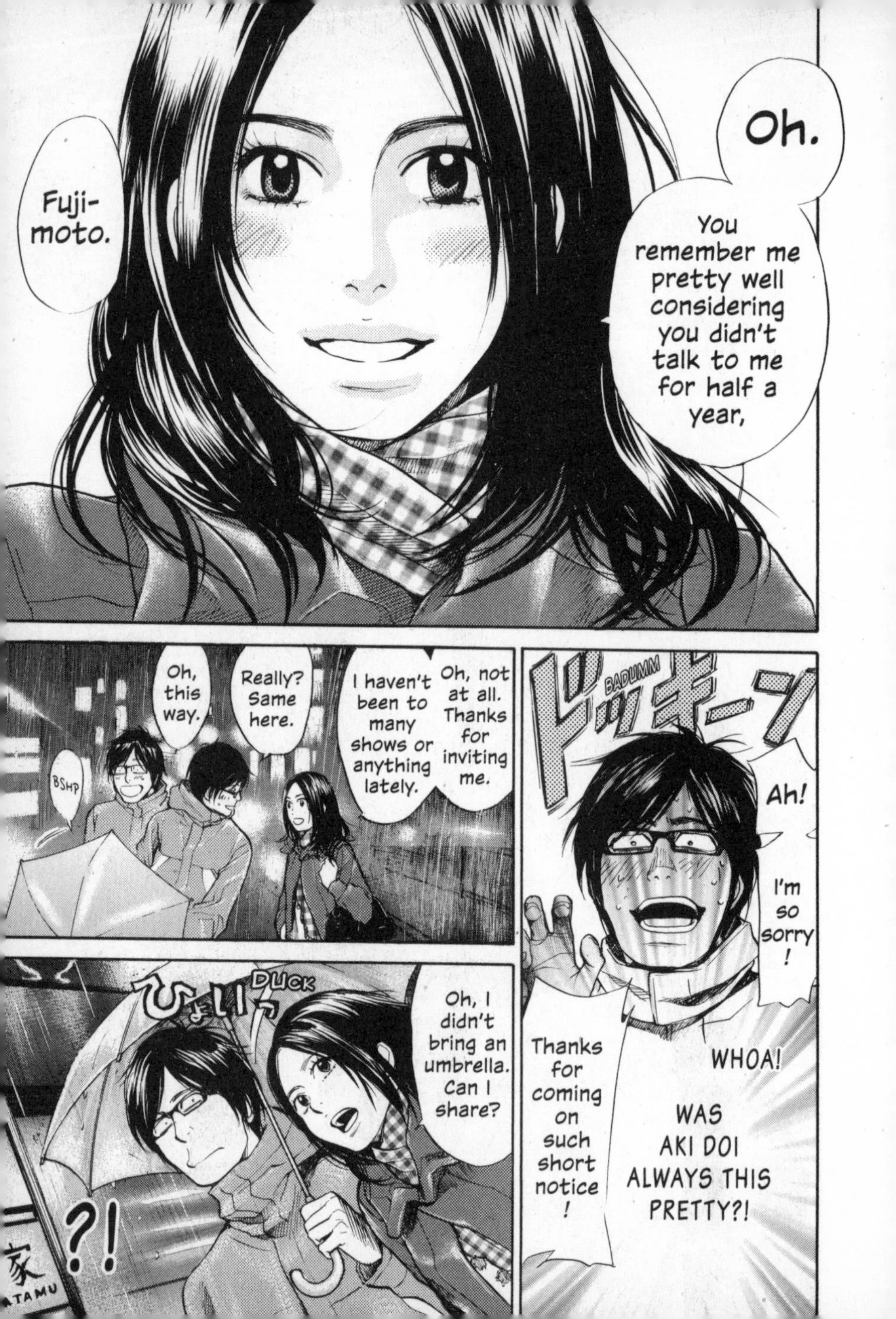

Oh.
You remember me pretty well considering you didn't talk to me for half a year,
Fuji-moto.
BADUMM
Ah!
I'm so sorry!
WHOA!
WAS AKI DOI ALWAYS THIS PRETTY?!
Thanks for coming on such short notice!
Oh, not at all. Thanks for inviting me.
I haven't been to many shows or anything lately.
Really? Same here.
Oh, this way.
BSHP
DUCK
Oh, I didn't bring an umbrella. Can I share?
?!

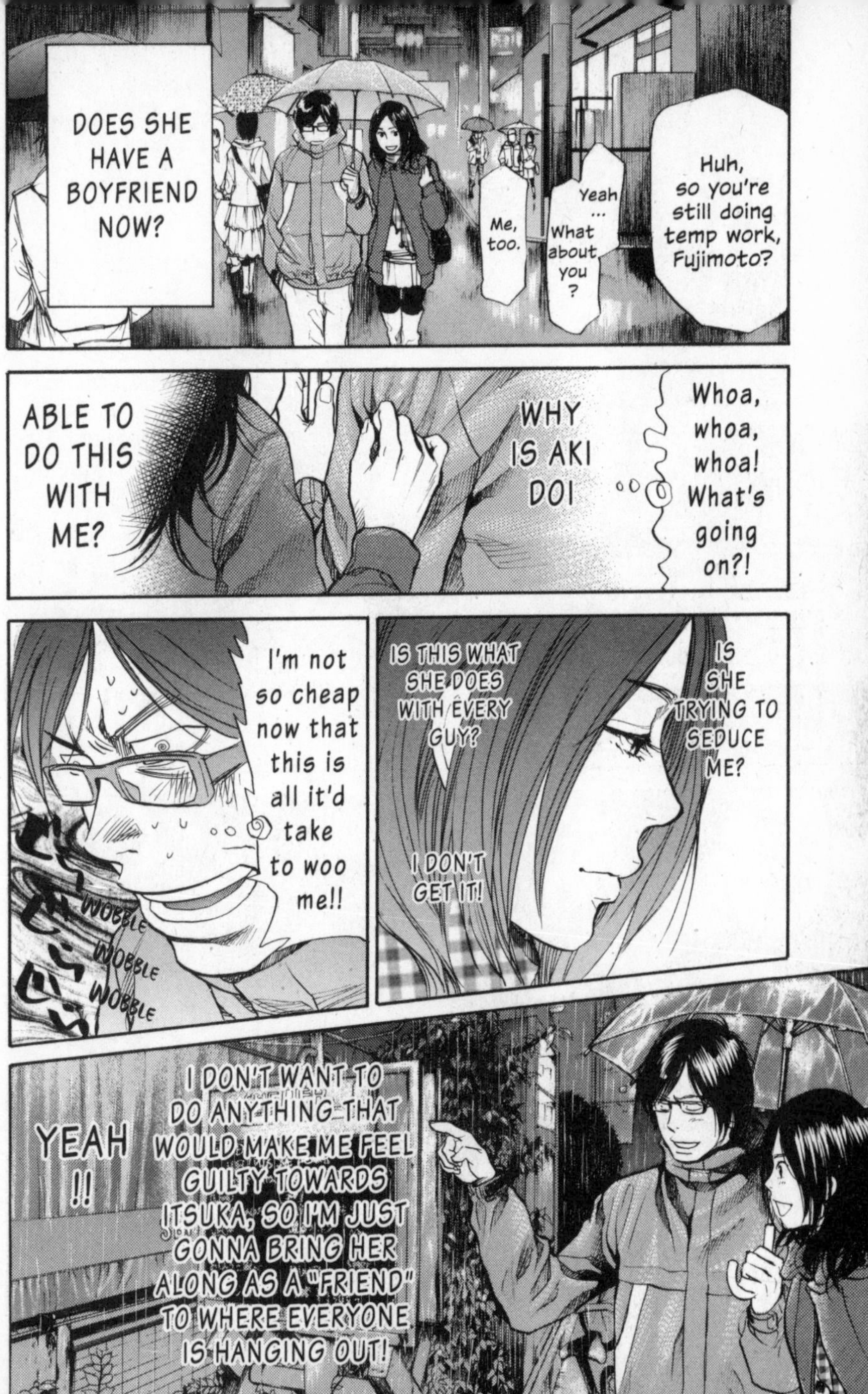
Huh, so you're still doing temp work, Fujimoto?
Yeah ... What about you?
Me, too.
DOES SHE HAVE A BOYFRIEND NOW?
Whoa, whoa, whoa! What's going on?!
WHY IS AKI DOI
ABLE TO DO THIS WITH ME?
IS SHE TRYING TO SEDUCE ME?
IS THIS WHAT SHE DOES WITH EVERY GUY?
I DON'T GET IT!
I'm not so cheap now that this is all it'd take to woo me!!
WOBBLE
WOBBLE
WOBBLE
I DON'T WANT TO DO ANYTHING THAT WOULD MAKE ME FEEL GUILTY TOWARDS ITSUKA, SO I'M JUST GONNA BRING HER ALONG AS A "FRIEND" TO WHERE EVERYONE IS HANGING OUT!
YEAH !!

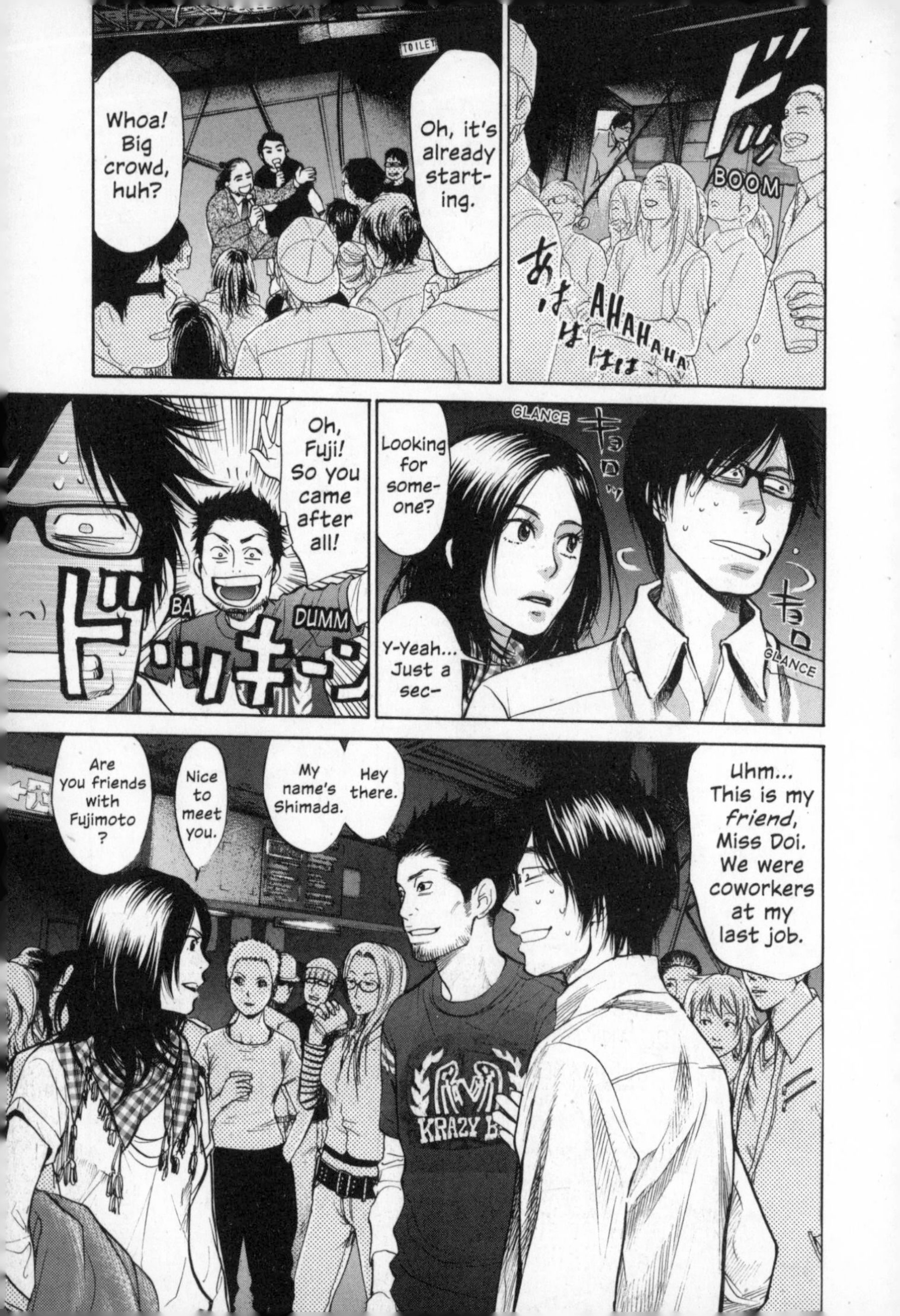
ドッ
BOOM
あははは
AHAHAHA
Oh, it's already start-ing.
TOILET
Whoa! Big crowd, huh?
GLANCE
キョロ
Looking for some-one?
Y-Yeah... Just a sec-
キョロ
GLANCE
Oh, Fuji! So you came after all!
ドッキーン
BA
DUMM
Uhm... This is my *friend*, Miss Doi. We were coworkers at my last job.
Hey there.
My name's Shimada.
Nice to meet you.
Are you friends with Fujimoto?
KRAZY B

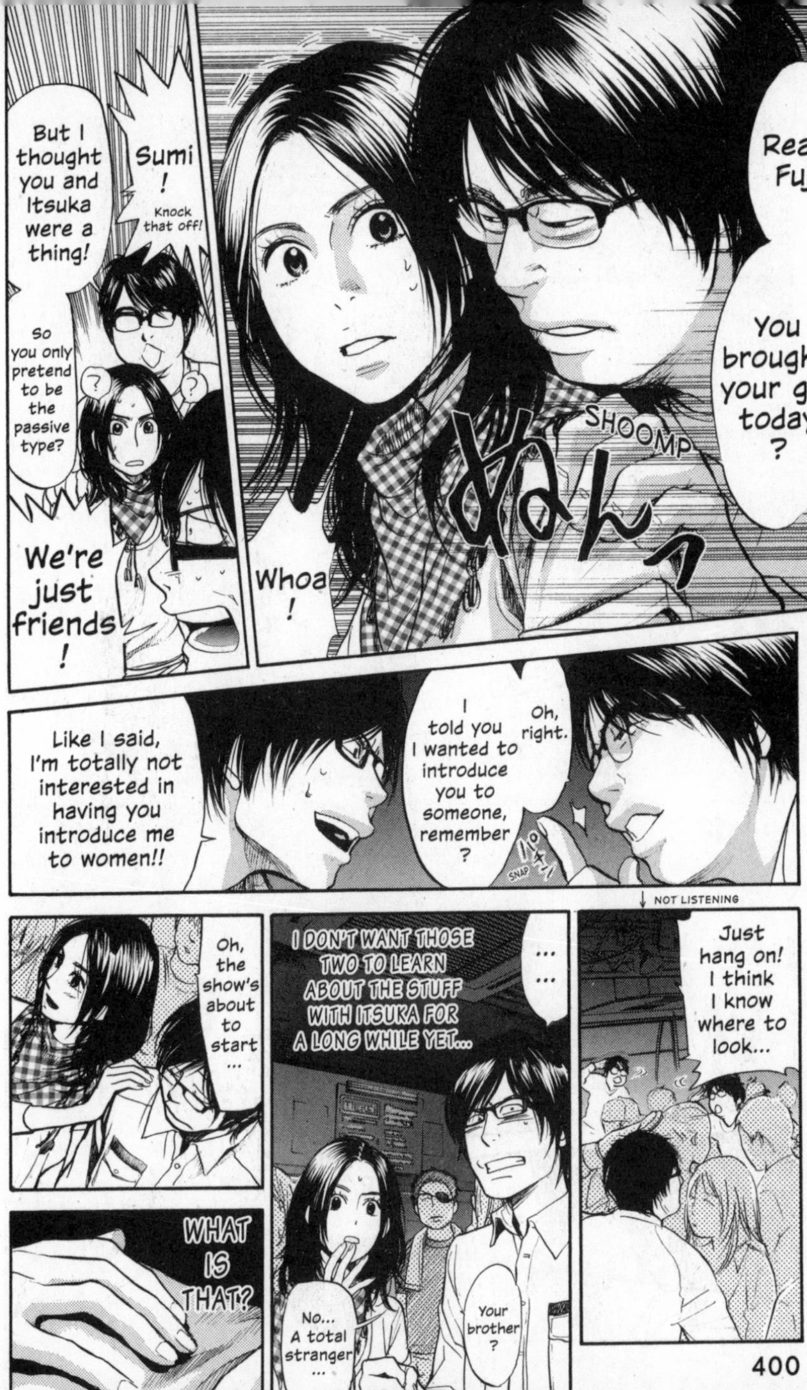
Really, Fuji?
You brought your girl today?
SHOOMP
Whoa!
Sumi!
Knock that off!
But I thought you and Itsuka were a thing!
So you only pretend to be the passive type?
We're just friends!
Oh, right.
I told you I wanted to introduce you to someone, remember?
SNAP
Like I said, I'm totally not interested in having you introduce me to women!!
NOT LISTENING
Just hang on! I think I know where to look...
... ...
I DON'T WANT THOSE TWO TO LEARN ABOUT THE STUFF WITH ITSUKA FOR A LONG WHILE YET...
Your brother?
No... A total stranger...
Oh, the show's about to start...
WHAT IS THAT?

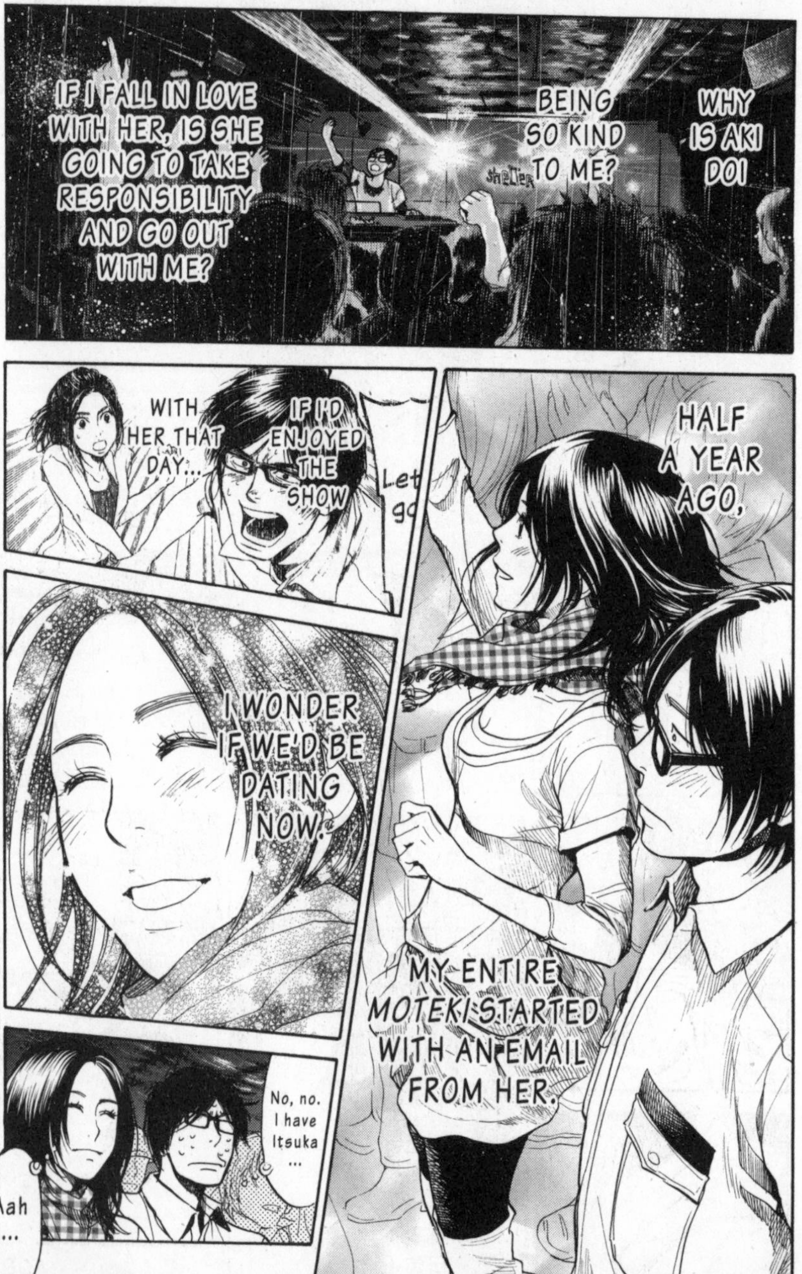
WHY IS AKI DOI
BEING SO KIND TO ME?
IF I FALL IN LOVE WITH HER, IS SHE GOING TO TAKE RESPONSIBILITY AND GO OUT WITH ME?
HALF A YEAR AGO,
MY ENTIRE MOTEKI STARTED WITH AN EMAIL FROM HER.
Let go
IF I'D ENJOYED THE SHOW
WITH HER THAT DAY...
I WONDER IF WE'D BE DATING NOW.
No, no. I have Itsuka ...
Aah ...

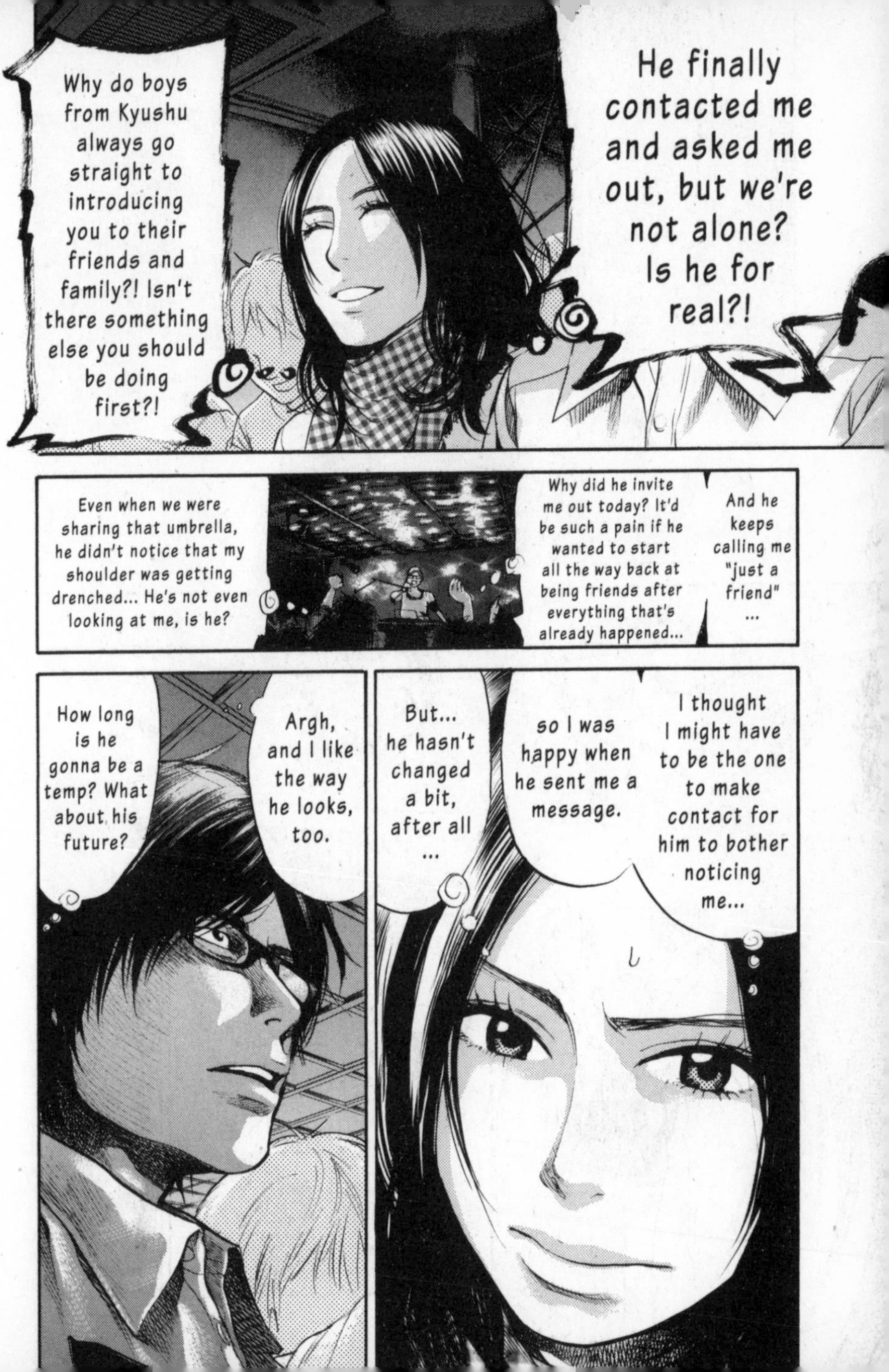
He finally contacted me and asked me out, but we're not alone? Is he for real?!
Why do boys from Kyushu always go straight to introducing you to their friends and family?! Isn't there something else you should be doing first?!
And he keeps calling me "just a friend"...
Why did he invite me out today? It'd be such a pain if he wanted to start all the way back at being friends after everything that's already happened...
Even when we were sharing that umbrella, he didn't notice that my shoulder was getting drenched... He's not even looking at me, is he?
I thought I might have to be the one to make contact for him to bother noticing me...
so I was happy when he sent me a message.
But... he hasn't changed a bit, after all...
Argh, and I like the way he looks, too.
How long is he gonna be a temp? What about his future?

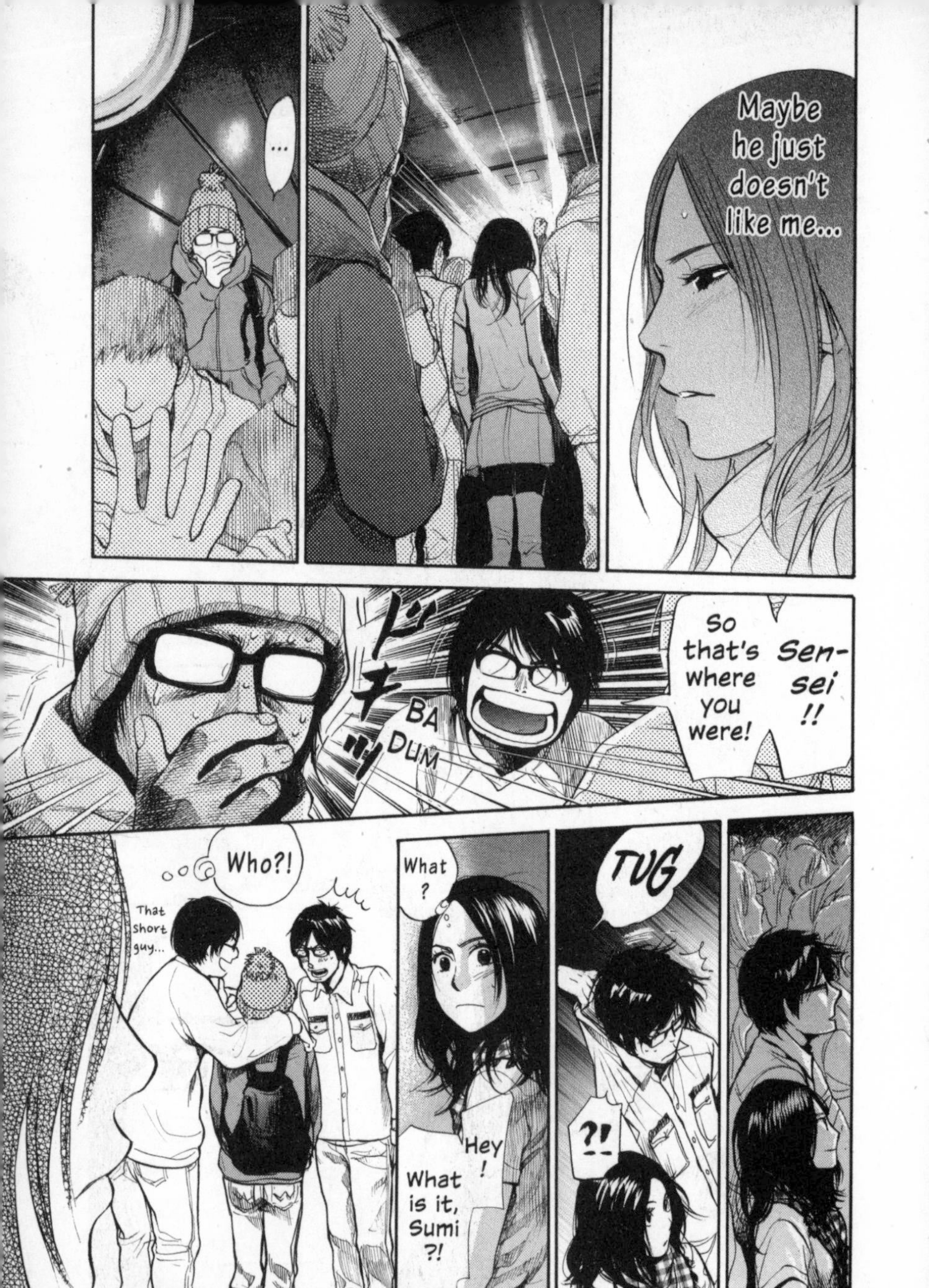
Maybe he just doesn't like me...
...
Sen-sei!!
So that's where you were!
BA DUM
TUG
?!
What?
Hey!
What is it, Sumi?!
Who?!
That short guy...

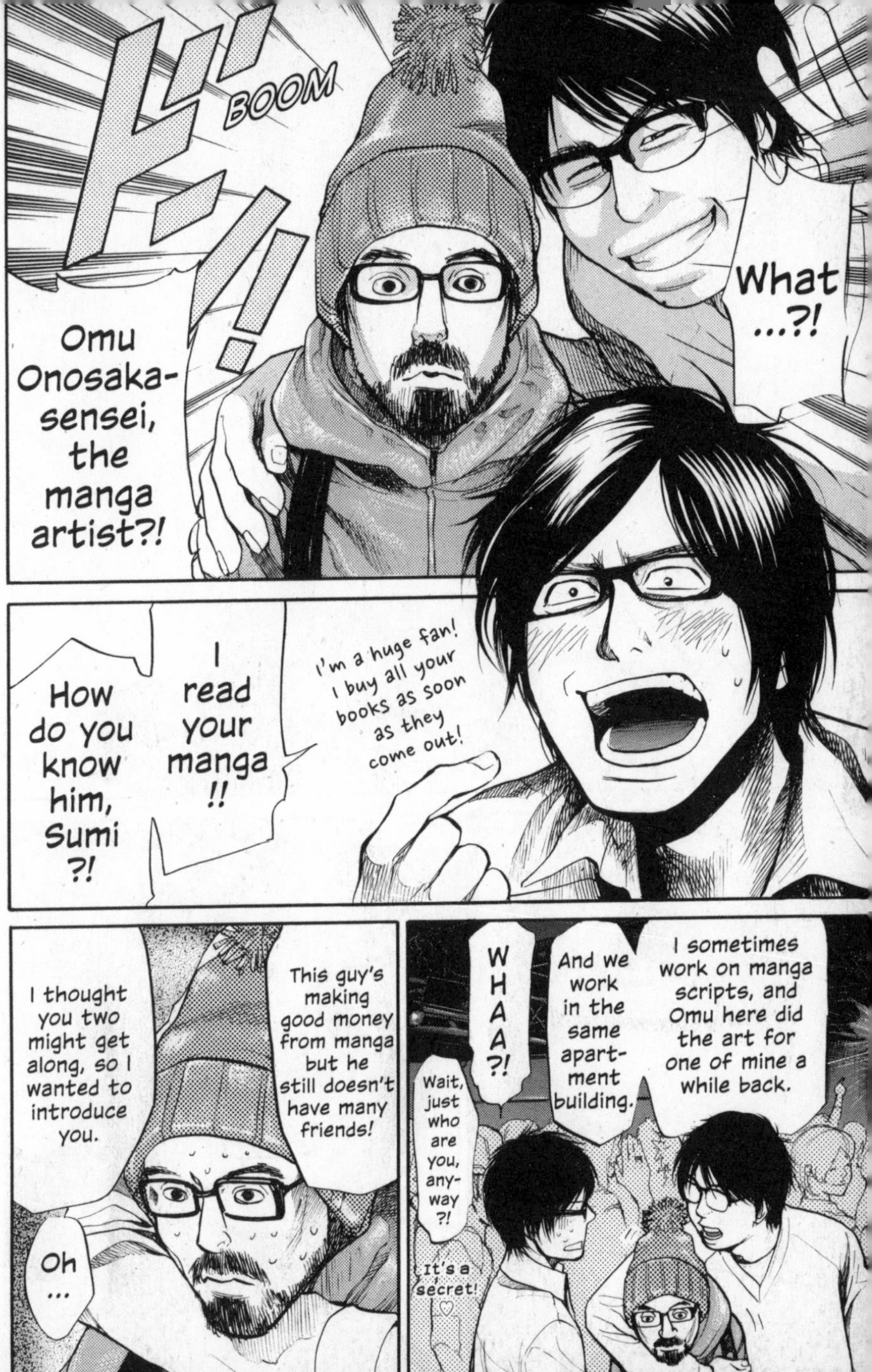
ドン!!
BOOM
What ...?!
Omu Onosaka-sensei, the manga artist?!
I'm a huge fan! I buy all your books as soon as they come out!
I read your manga!!
How do you know him, Sumi?!
I sometimes work on manga scripts, and Omu here did the art for one of mine a while back.
And we work in the same apartment building.
WHAAA?!
Wait, just who are you, anyway?!
It's a secret! ♡
This guy's making good money from manga but he still doesn't have many friends!
I thought you two might get along, so I wanted to introduce you.
Oh ...

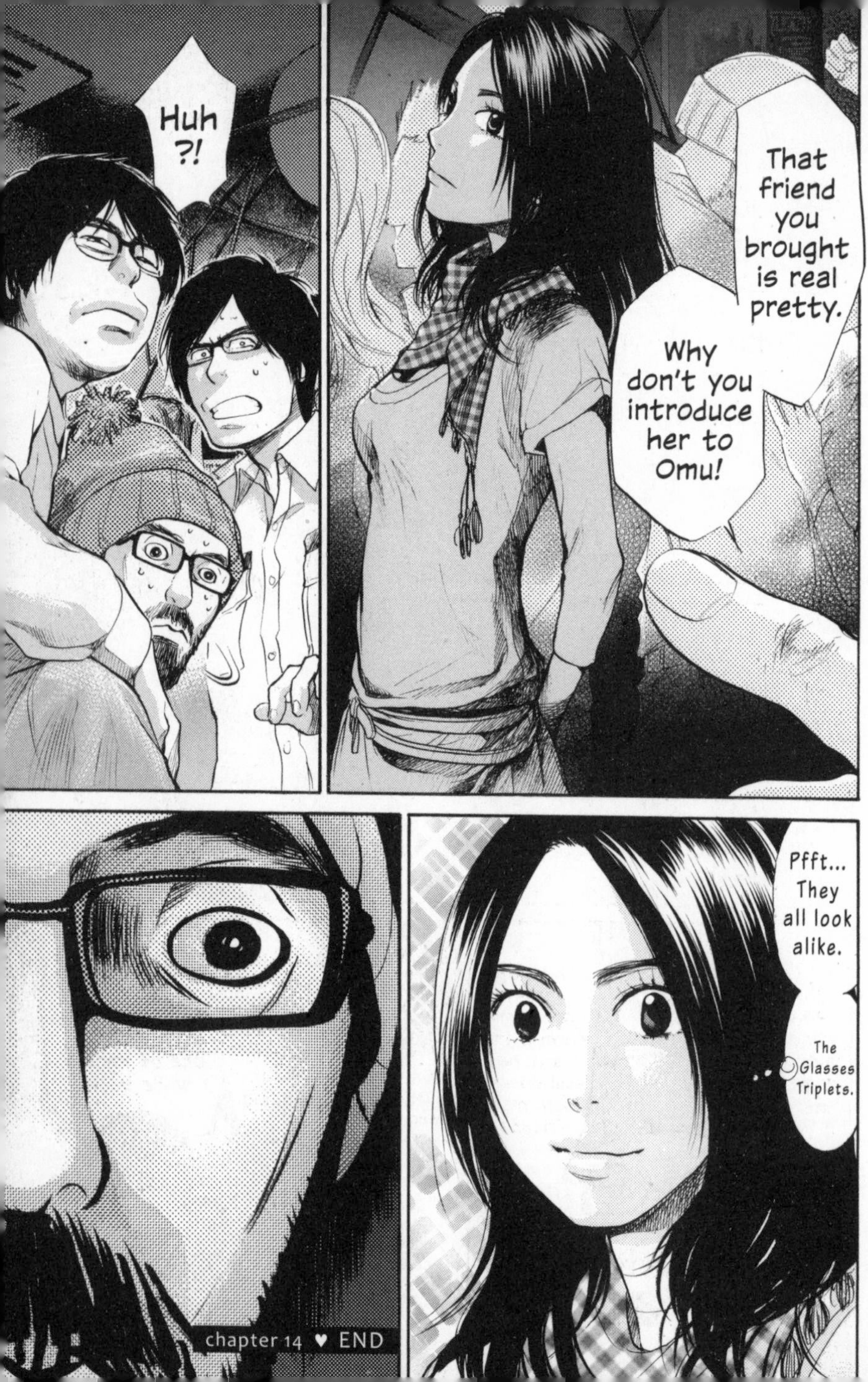
That friend you brought is real pretty.
Why don't you introduce her to Omu!
Huh ?!
Pfft... They all look alike.
The Glasses Triplets.
chapter 14 ♥ END

Moteki

Mitsurou Kubo

Chapter 15 ♥ Found a Girl I Love

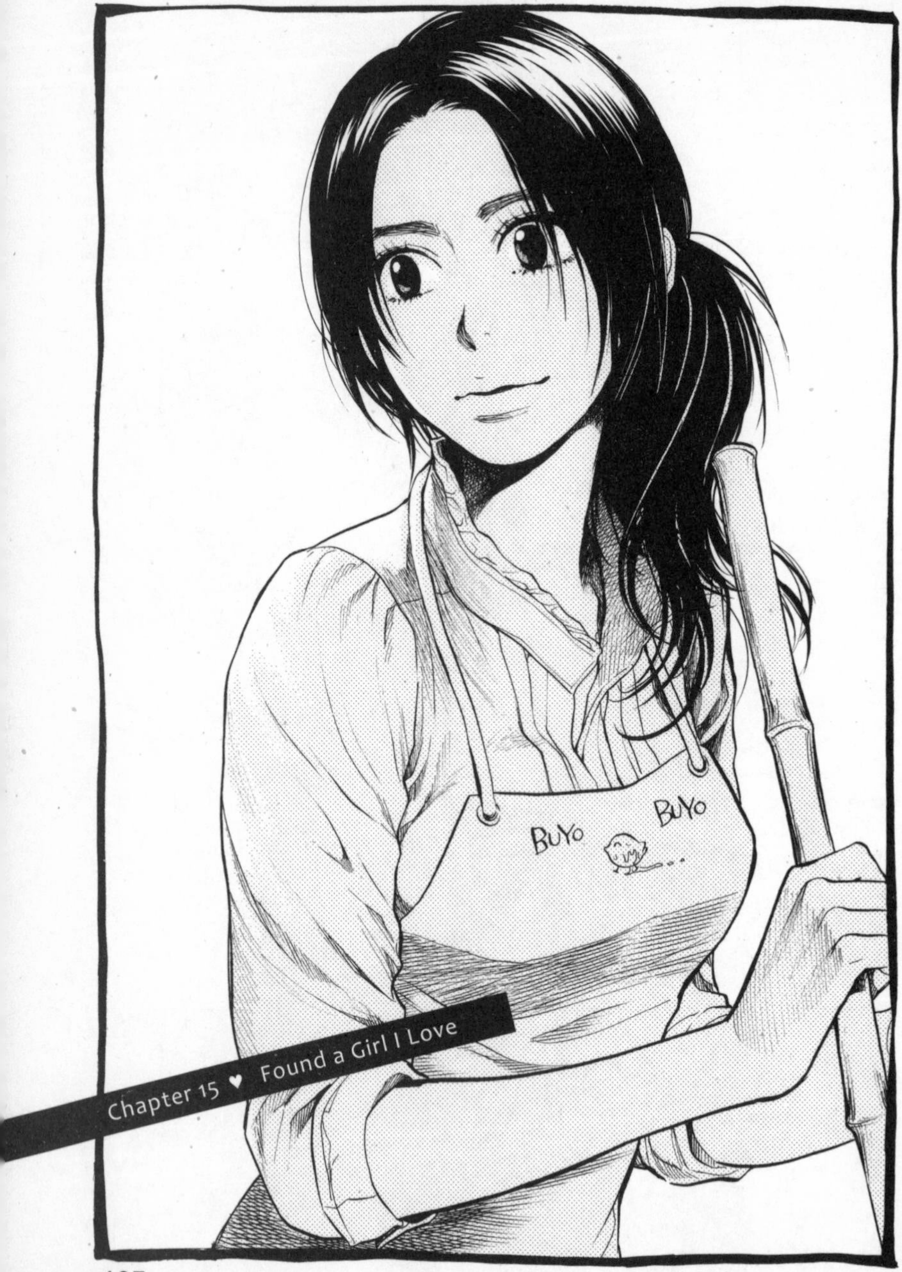
BUYO
BUYO

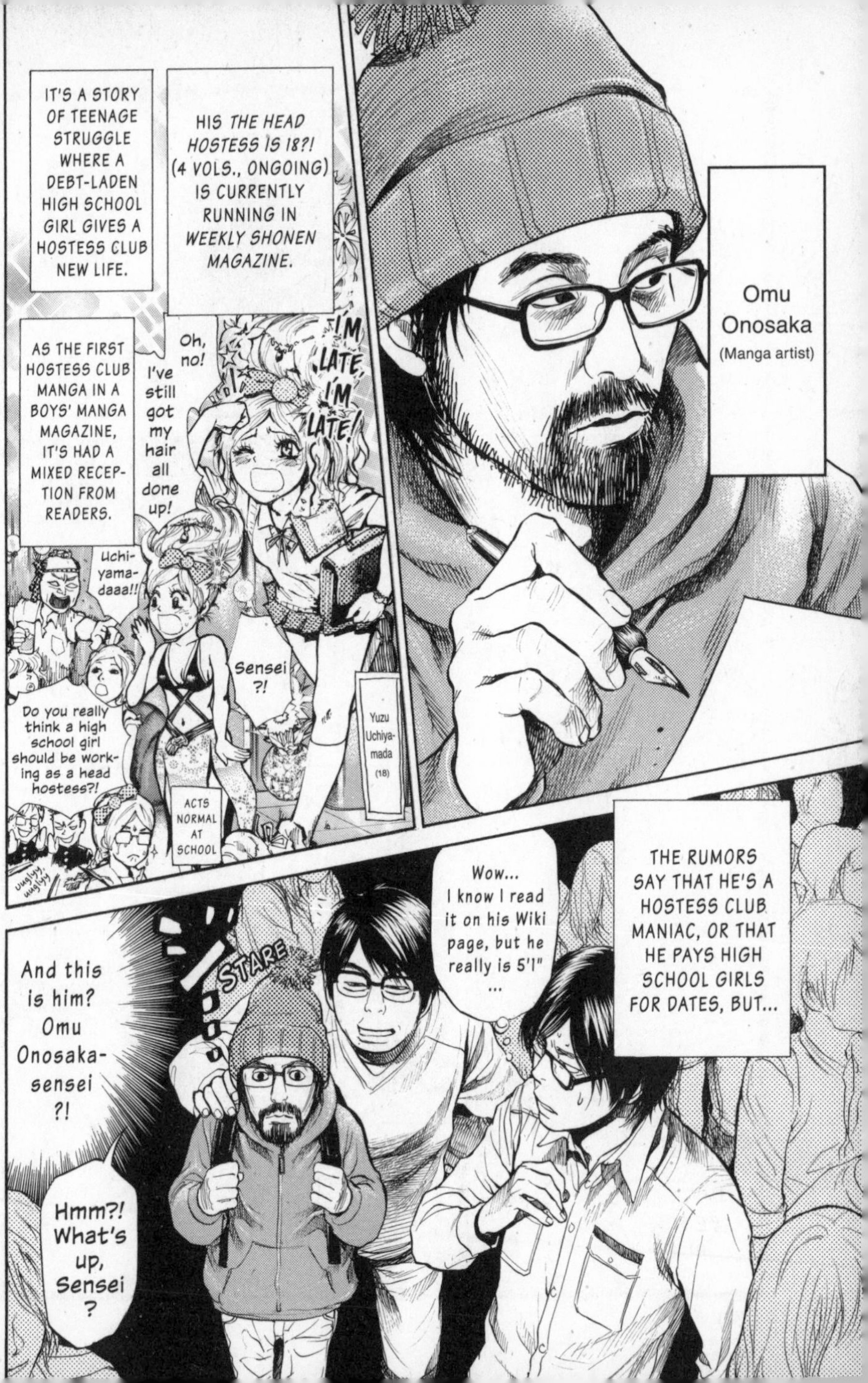
Omu Onosaka
(Manga artist)
HIS THE HEAD HOSTESS IS 18?! (4 VOLS., ONGOING) IS CURRENTLY RUNNING IN WEEKLY SHONEN MAGAZINE.
IT'S A STORY OF TEENAGE STRUGGLE WHERE A DEBT-LADEN HIGH SCHOOL GIRL GIVES A HOSTESS CLUB NEW LIFE.
I'M LATE, I'M LATE!
Oh, no! I've still got my hair all done up!
AS THE FIRST HOSTESS CLUB MANGA IN A BOYS' MANGA MAGAZINE, IT'S HAD A MIXED RECEPTION FROM READERS.
Yuzu Uchiyamada (18)
Sensei ?!
Uchiyamadaaa!!
ACTS NORMAL AT SCHOOL
Do you really think a high school girl should be working as a head hostess?!
THE RUMORS SAY THAT HE'S A HOSTESS CLUB MANIAC, OR THAT HE PAYS HIGH SCHOOL GIRLS FOR DATES, BUT...
Wow... I know I read it on his Wiki page, but he really is 5'1" ...
STARE
And this is him? Omu Onosaka-sensei ?!
Hmm?! What's up, Sensei ?

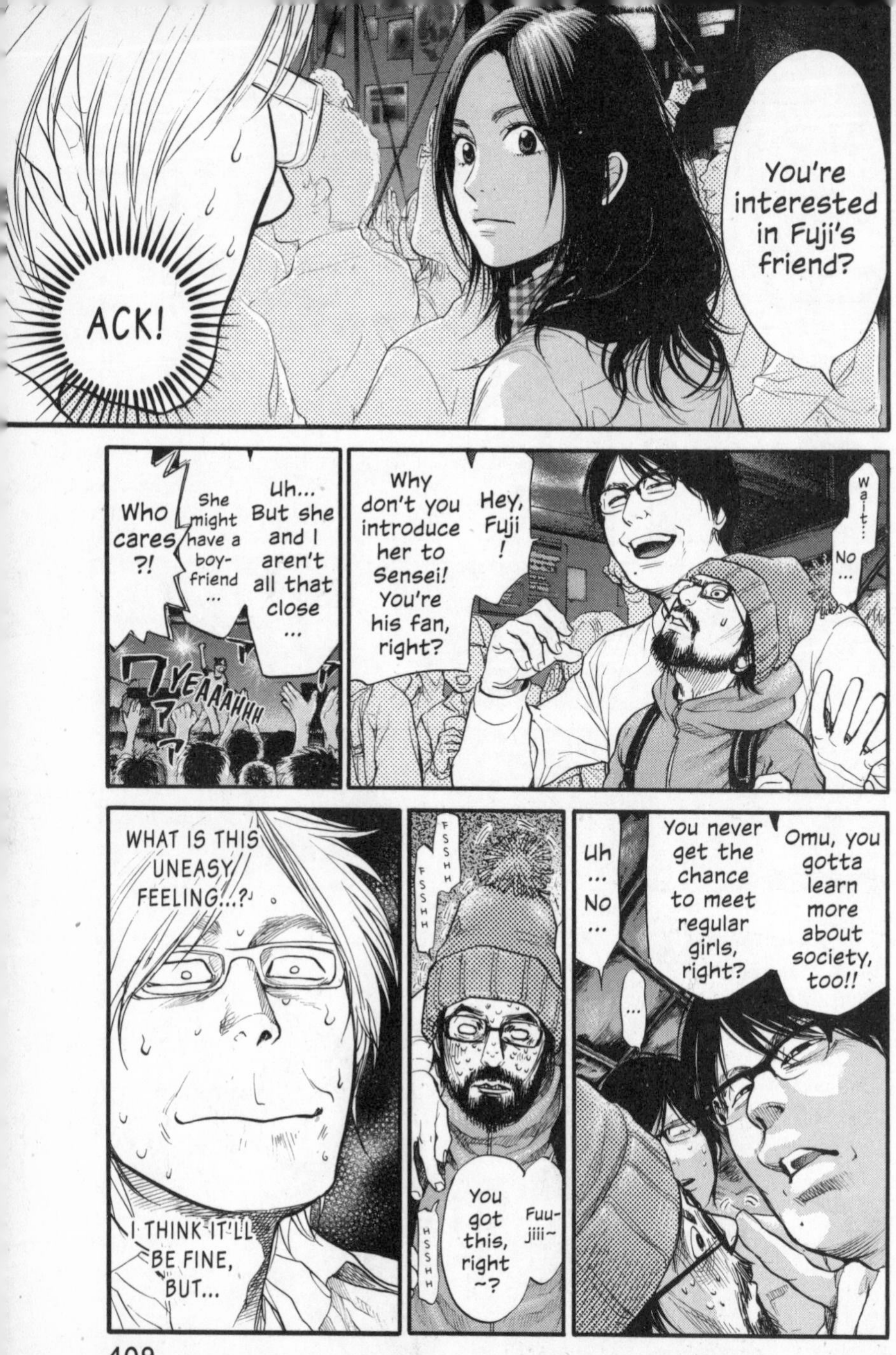
You're interested in Fuji's friend?
ACK!
Wait... No...
Hey, Fuji!
Why don't you introduce her to Sensei! You're his fan, right?
Uh... But she and I aren't all that close...
She might have a boy-friend...
Who cares?!
YEAAAHHH
Omu, you gotta learn more about society, too!!
You never get the chance to meet regular girls, right?
Uh... No...
...
FSSHH
FSSHH
Fuu-jiii~
You got this, right~?
HSSHH
WHAT IS THIS UNEASY FEELING...?
I THINK IT'LL BE FINE, BUT...

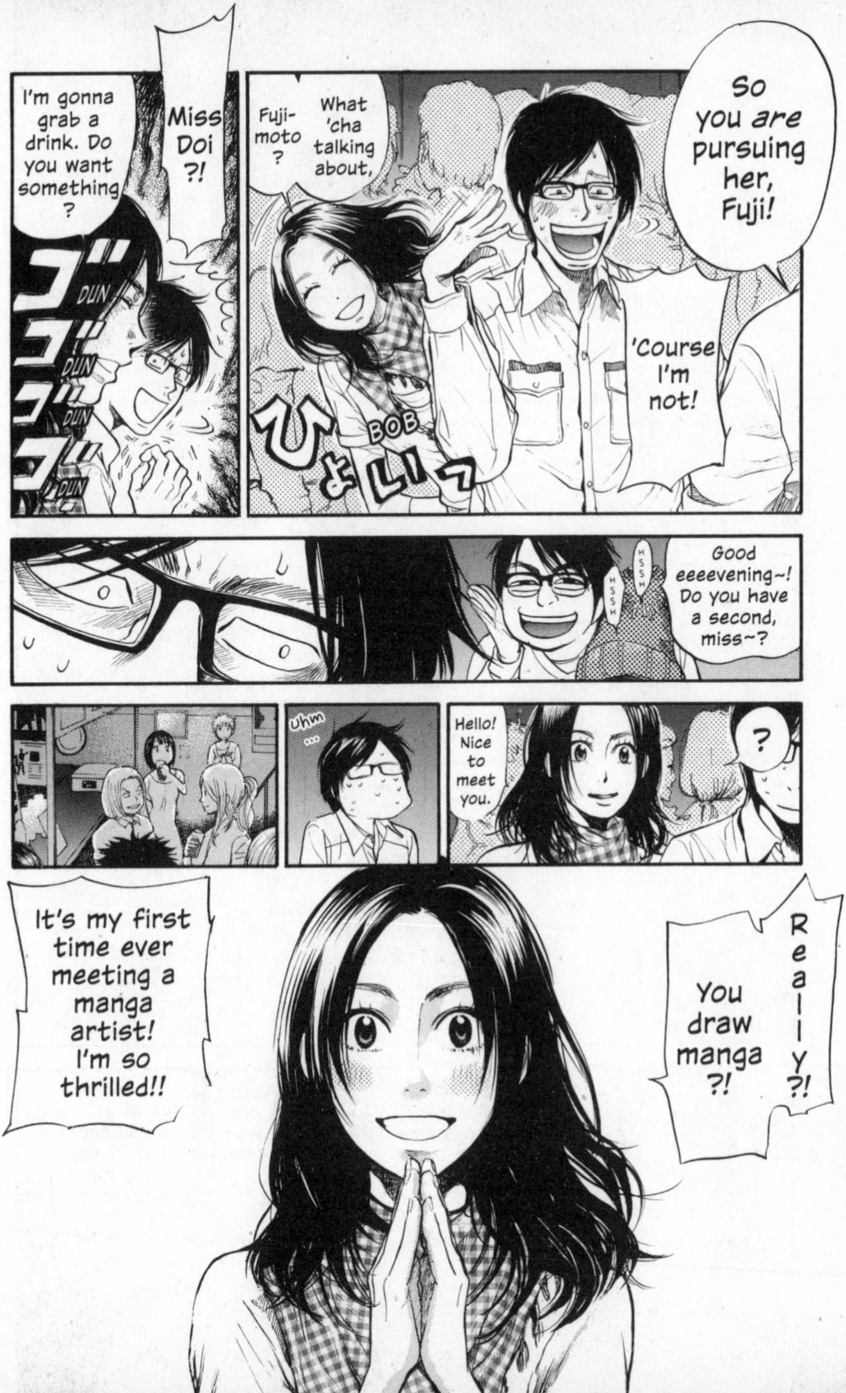
So you are pursuing her, Fuji!
'Course I'm not!
What 'cha talking about, Fuji-moto?
BOB
Miss Doi ?!
I'm gonna grab a drink. Do you want something ?
DUN
DUN
DUN
DUN
Good eeeevening~! Do you have a second, miss~?
HSSH
HSSH
?
Hello! Nice to meet you.
Uhm ...
Really ?!
You draw manga ?!
It's my first time ever meeting a manga artist! I'm so thrilled!!

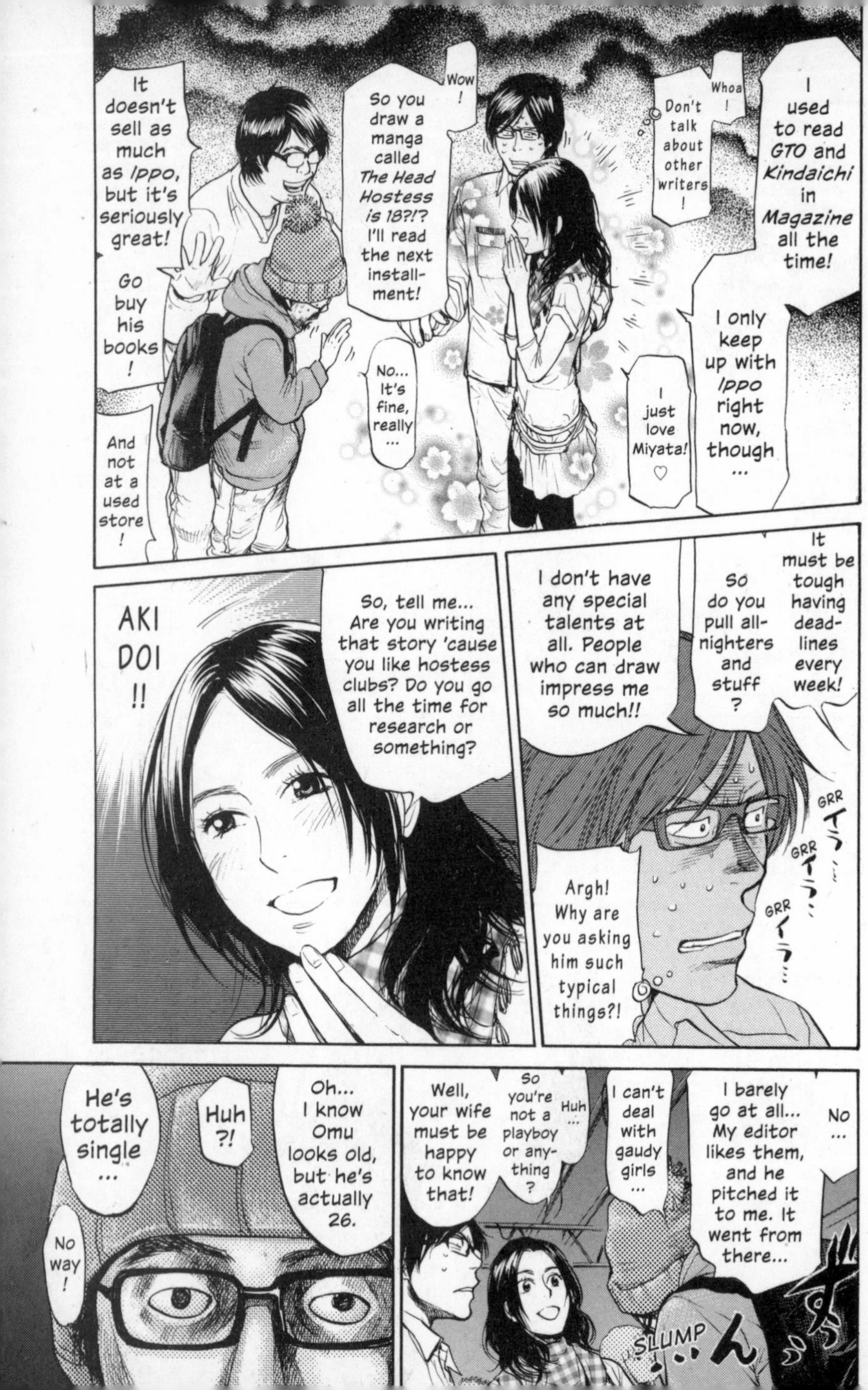
I used to read GTO and Kindaichi in Magazine all the time!
I only keep up with Ippo right now, though...
Whoa!
Don't talk about other writers!
I just love Miyata! ♡
Wow!
So you draw a manga called The Head Hostess is 18?!? I'll read the next installment!
No... It's fine, really...
It doesn't sell as much as Ippo, but it's seriously great!
Go buy his books!
And not at a used store!
It must be tough having deadlines every week!
So do you pull all-nighters and stuff?
I don't have any special talents at all. People who can draw impress me so much!!
GRR
GRR
GRR
Argh! Why are you asking him such typical things?!
So, tell me... Are you writing that story 'cause you like hostess clubs? Do you go all the time for research or something?
AKI DOI !!
No...
I barely go at all... My editor likes them, and he pitched it to me. It went from there...
I can't deal with gaudy girls...
Huh...
So you're not a playboy or anything?
Well, your wife must be happy to know that!
SLUMP
Oh... I know Omu looks old, but he's actually 26.
Huh?!
He's totally single...
No way!

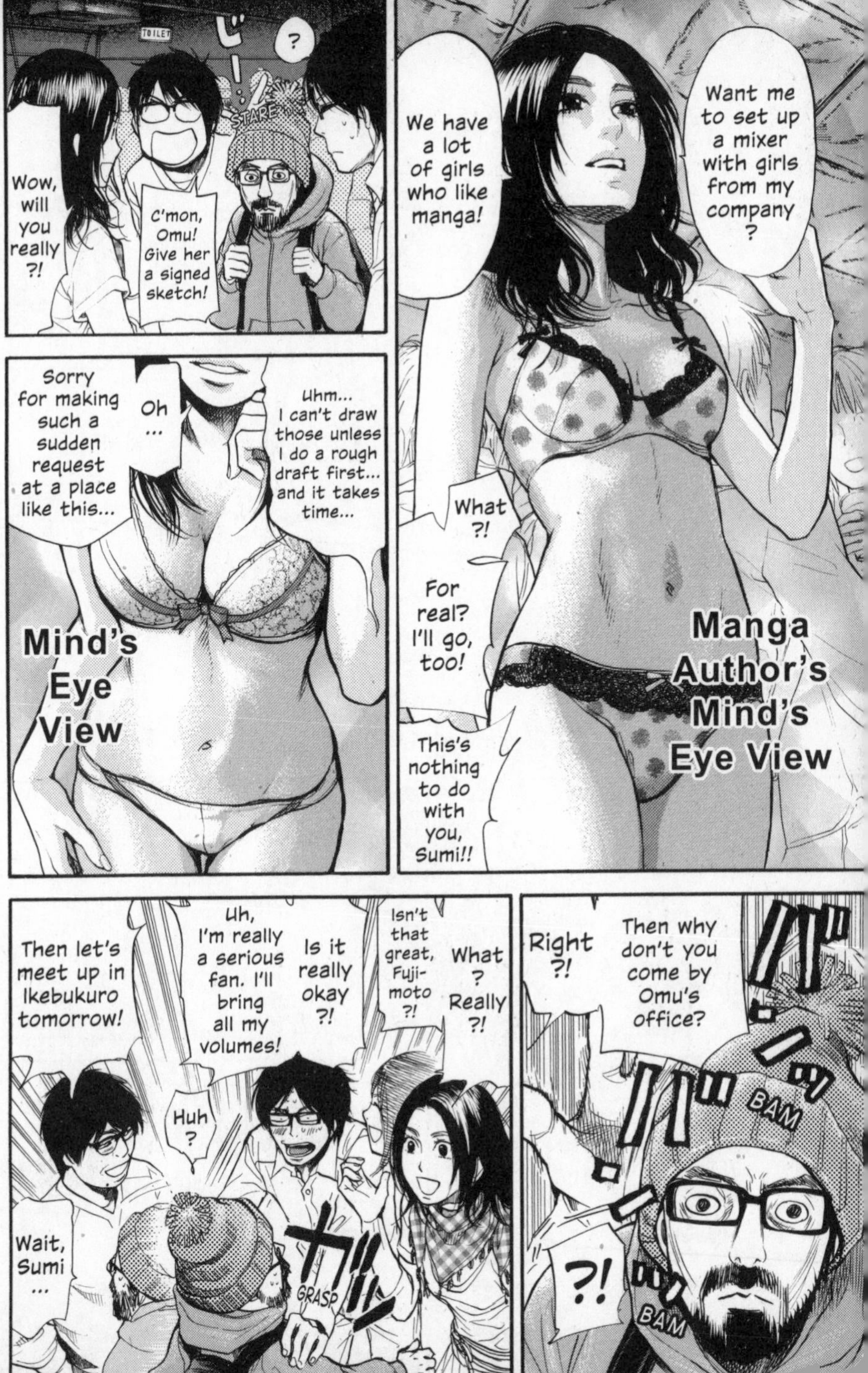
Want me to set up a mixer with girls from my company?
We have a lot of girls who like manga!
Manga Author's Mind's Eye View
What?!
For real? I'll go, too!
This's nothing to do with you, Sumi!!
TOILET
?
STARE
C'mon, Omu! Give her a signed sketch!
Wow, will you really?!
Uhm... I can't draw those unless I do a rough draft first... and it takes time...
Oh ...
Sorry for making such a sudden request at a place like this...
Mind's Eye View
BAM
Then why don't you come by Omu's office?
Right?!
?!
BAM
What? Really?!
Isn't that great, Fujimoto?!
Is it really okay?!
Uh, I'm really a serious fan. I'll bring all my volumes!
Then let's meet up in Ikebukuro tomorrow!
Huh?
GRASP
Wait, Sumi ...

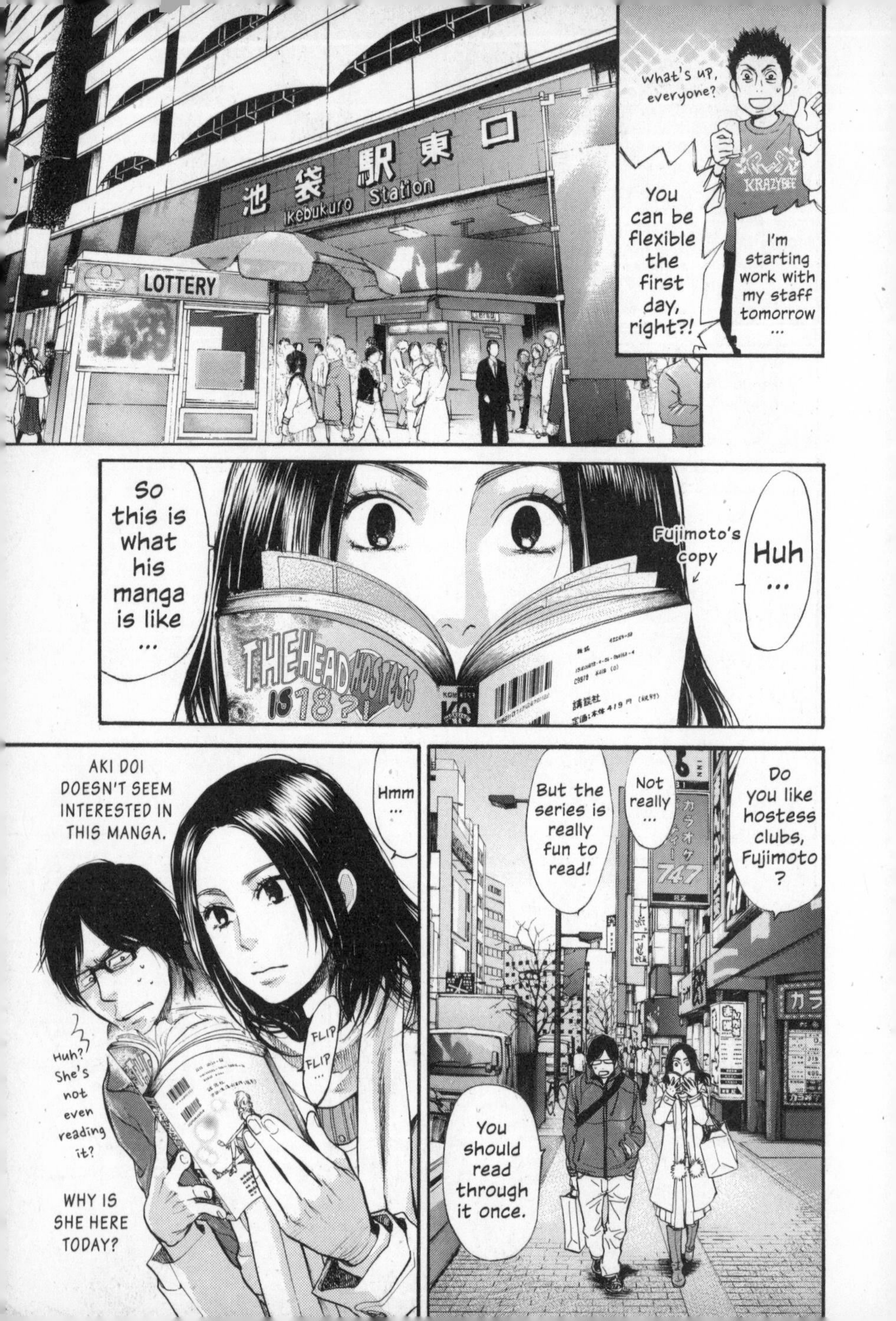
What's up, everyone?
I'm starting work with my staff tomorrow ...
You can be flexible the first day, right?!
KRAZYBEE
池袋駅東口
Ikebukuro Station
LOTTERY
Huh ...
Fujimoto's copy
So this is what his manga is like ...
THE HEAD HOSTESS IS 18?!
講談社
Do you like hostess clubs, Fujimoto?
Not really ...
But the series is really fun to read!
You should read through it once.
747
Hmm ...
AKI DOI DOESN'T SEEM INTERESTED IN THIS MANGA.
FLIP FLIP ...
Huh? She's not even reading it?
WHY IS SHE HERE TODAY?

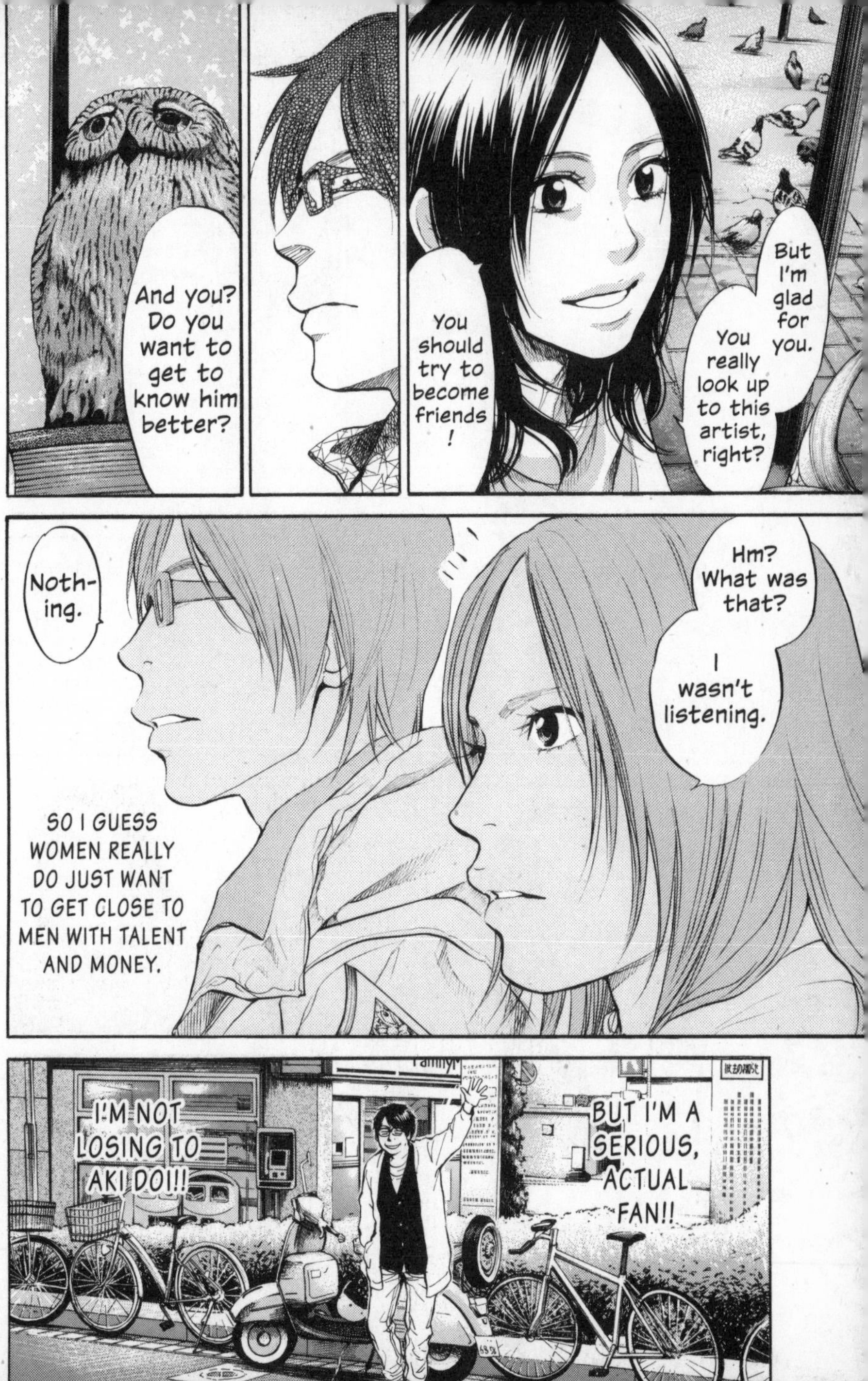
But I'm glad for you.
You really look up to this artist, right?
You should try to become friends!
And you? Do you want to get to know him better?
Hm? What was that?
I wasn't listening.
Noth-ing.
SO I GUESS WOMEN REALLY DO JUST WANT TO GET CLOSE TO MEN WITH TALENT AND MONEY.
BUT I'M A SERIOUS, ACTUAL FAN!!
I'M NOT LOSING TO AKI DOI!!

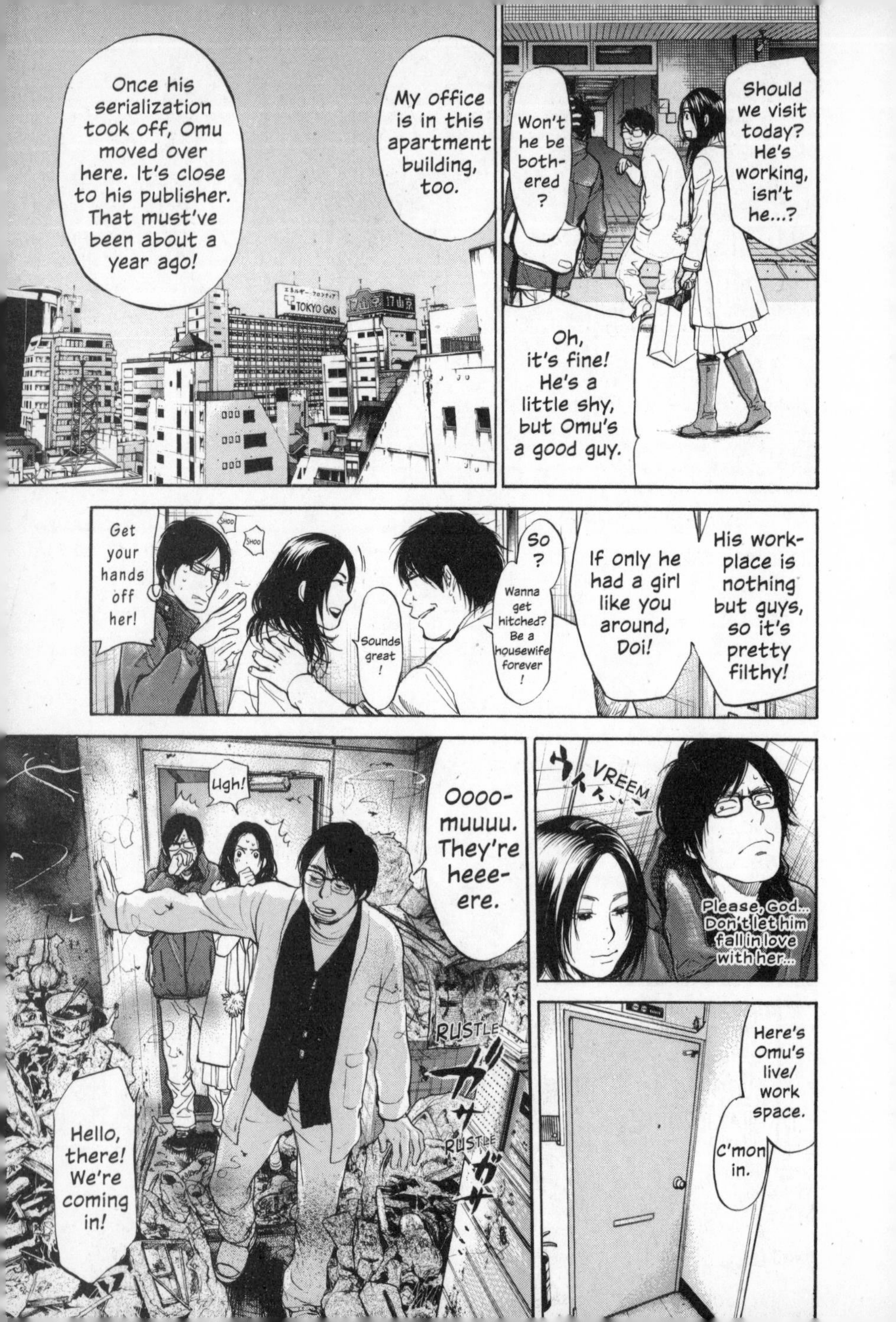
Should we visit today? He's working, isn't he...?
Won't he be both-ered?
Oh, it's fine! He's a little shy, but Omu's a good guy.
My office is in this apartment building, too.
Once his serialization took off, Omu moved over here. It's close to his publisher. That must've been about a year ago!
TOKYO GAS
His work-place is nothing but guys, so it's pretty filthy!
If only he had a girl like you around, Doi!
So?
Wanna get hitched? Be a housewife forever!
Sounds great!
SHOO
SHOO
Get your hands off her!
VREEM
Please, God... Don't let him fall in love with her...
Here's Omu's live/work space.
C'mon in.
Oooo-muuuu. They're heeee-ere.
Ugh!
RUSTLE
RUSTLE
Hello, there! We're coming in!

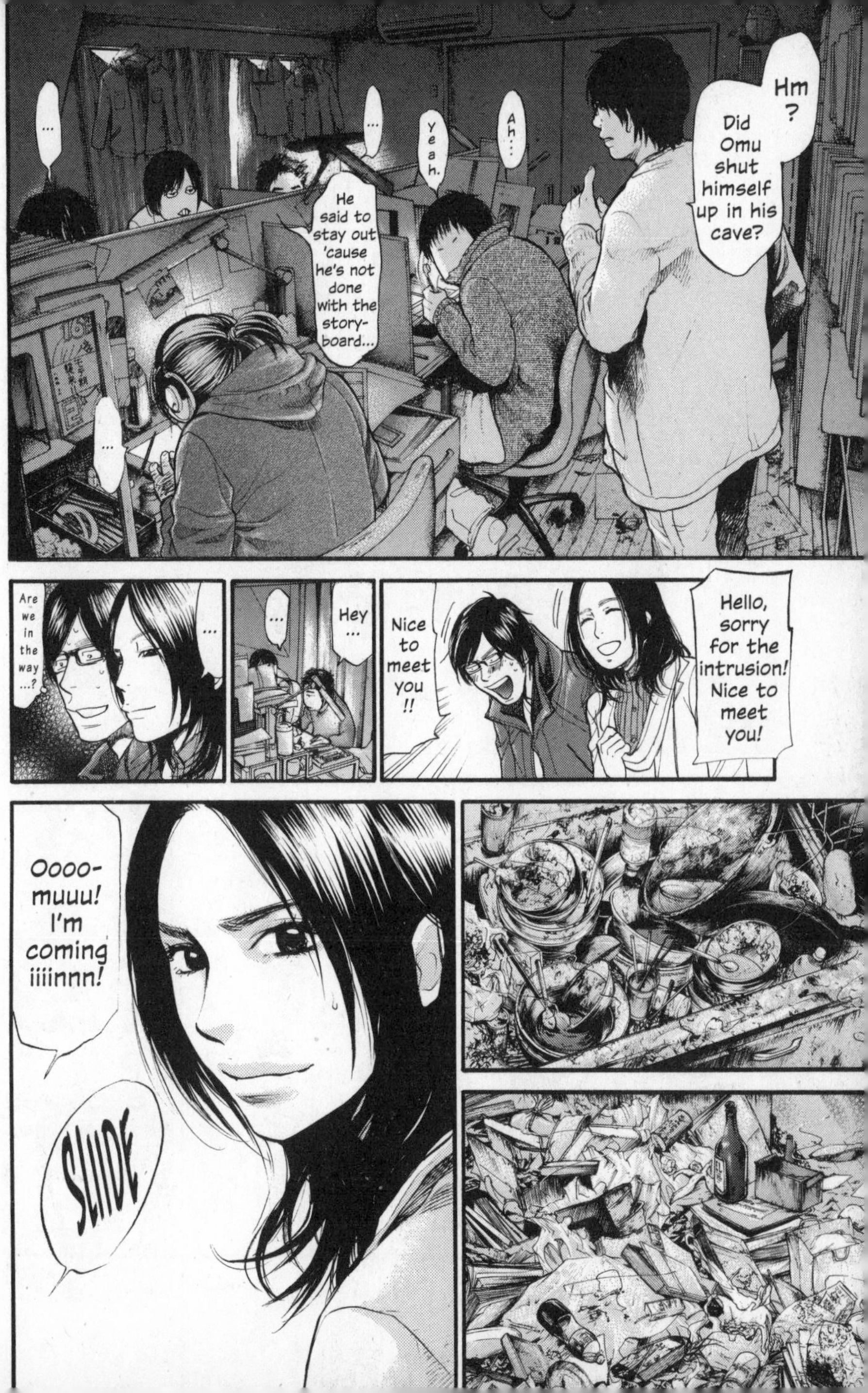
Hm?
Did Omu shut himself up in his cave?
Ah...
Yeah.
He said to stay out 'cause he's not done with the story-board...
...
...
...
Hello, sorry for the intrusion! Nice to meet you!
Nice to meet you !!
Hey ...
...
...
Are we in the way ...?
Oooo-muuu! I'm coming iiiinnn!
SLIDE

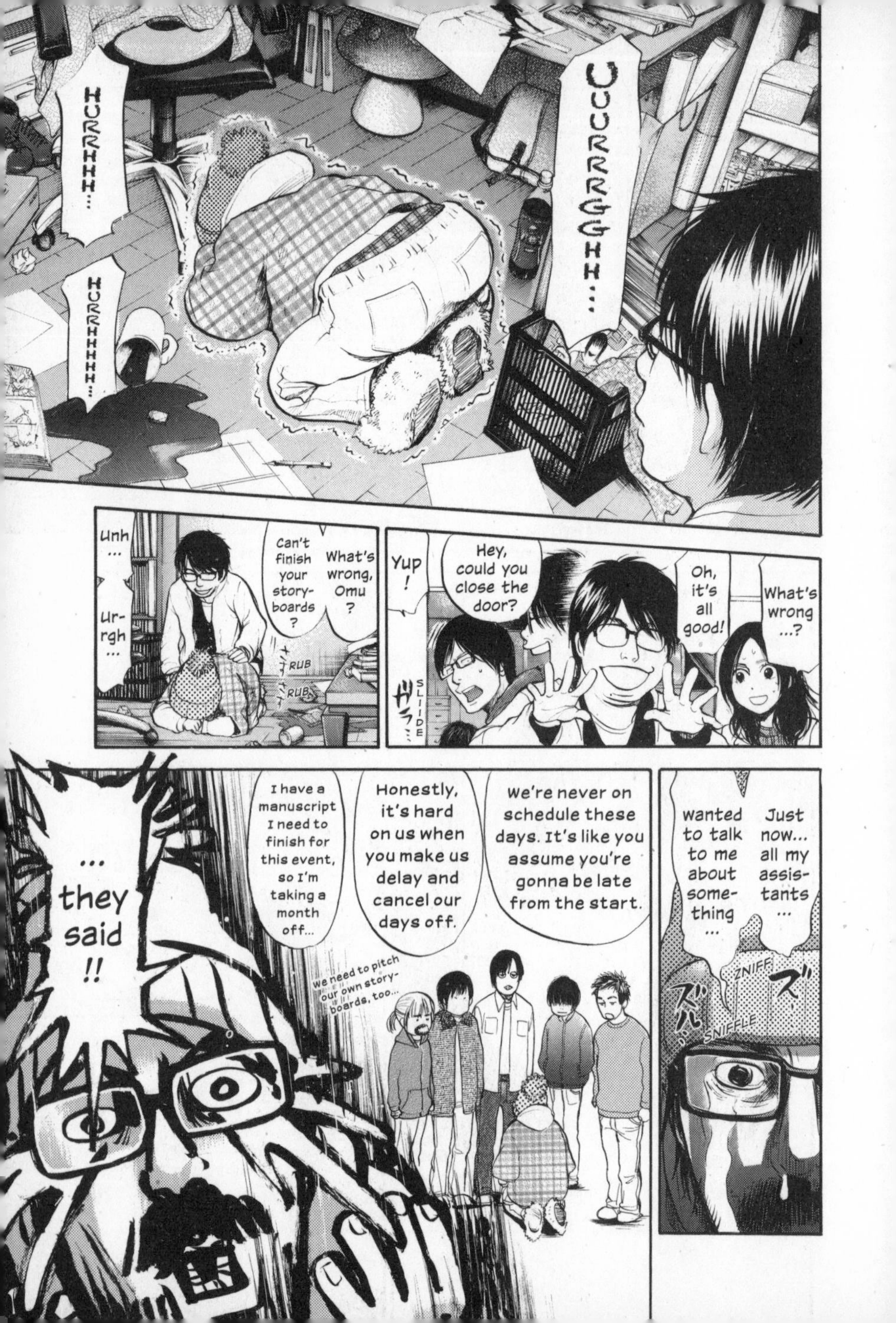
UUURRGGHH...
HURRHHH...
HURRHHHHH...
What's wrong ...?
Oh, it's all good!
Hey, could you close the door?
Yup!
SLIIDE
What's wrong, Omu?
Can't finish your storyboards?
Unh...
Ur-gh...
RUB
RUB
Just now... all my assistants...
wanted to talk to me about something...
ZNIFF
SNIFFLE
We're never on schedule these days. It's like you assume you're gonna be late from the start.
Honestly, it's hard on us when you make us delay and cancel our days off.
I have a manuscript I need to finish for this event, so I'm taking a month off...
We need to pitch our own storyboards, too...
... they said!!

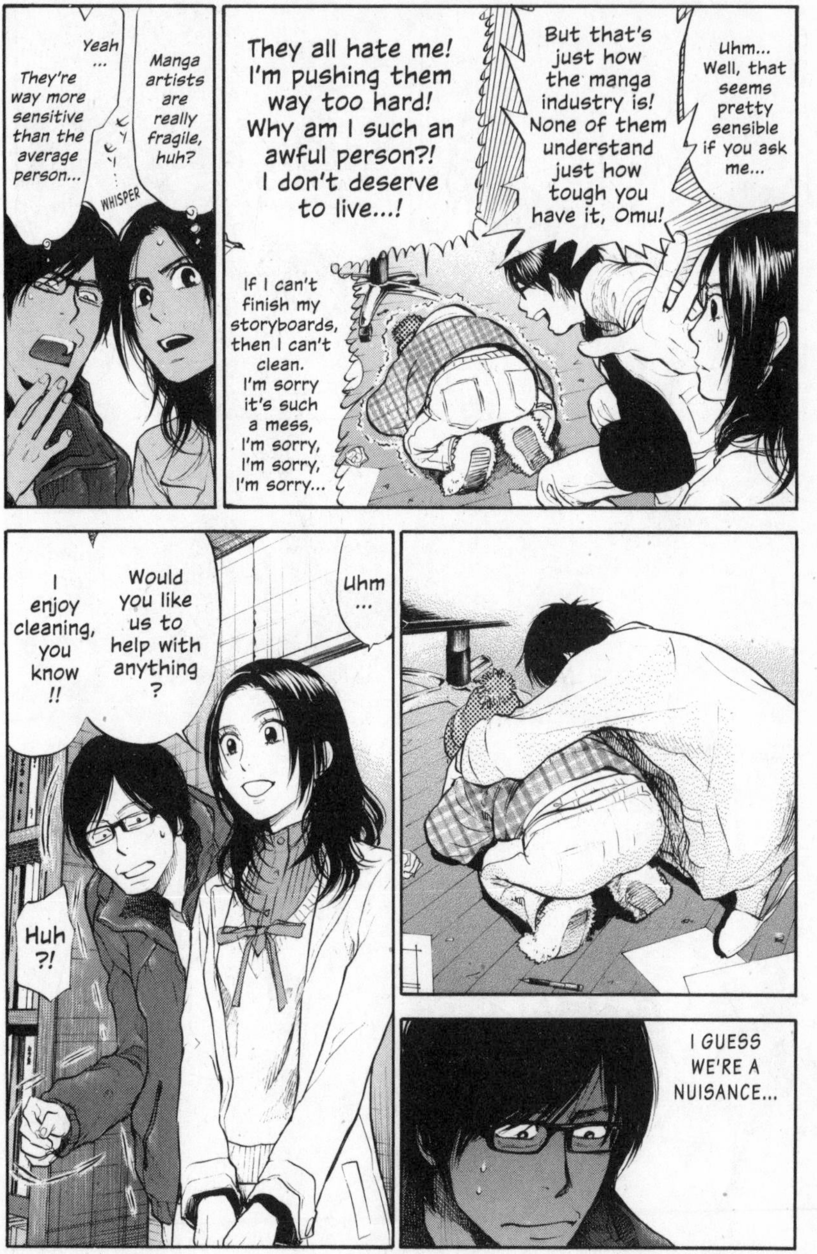
Uhm... Well, that seems pretty sensible if you ask me...
But that's just how the manga industry is! None of them understand just how tough you have it, Omu!
They all hate me! I'm pushing them way too hard! Why am I such an awful person?! I don't deserve to live...!
If I can't finish my storyboards, then I can't clean. I'm sorry it's such a mess, I'm sorry, I'm sorry, I'm sorry...
Manga artists are really fragile, huh?
Yeah ... They're way more sensitive than the average person...
WHISPER
I GUESS WE'RE A NUISANCE...
Uhm ...
Would you like us to help with anything ?
I enjoy cleaning, you know !!
Huh ?!

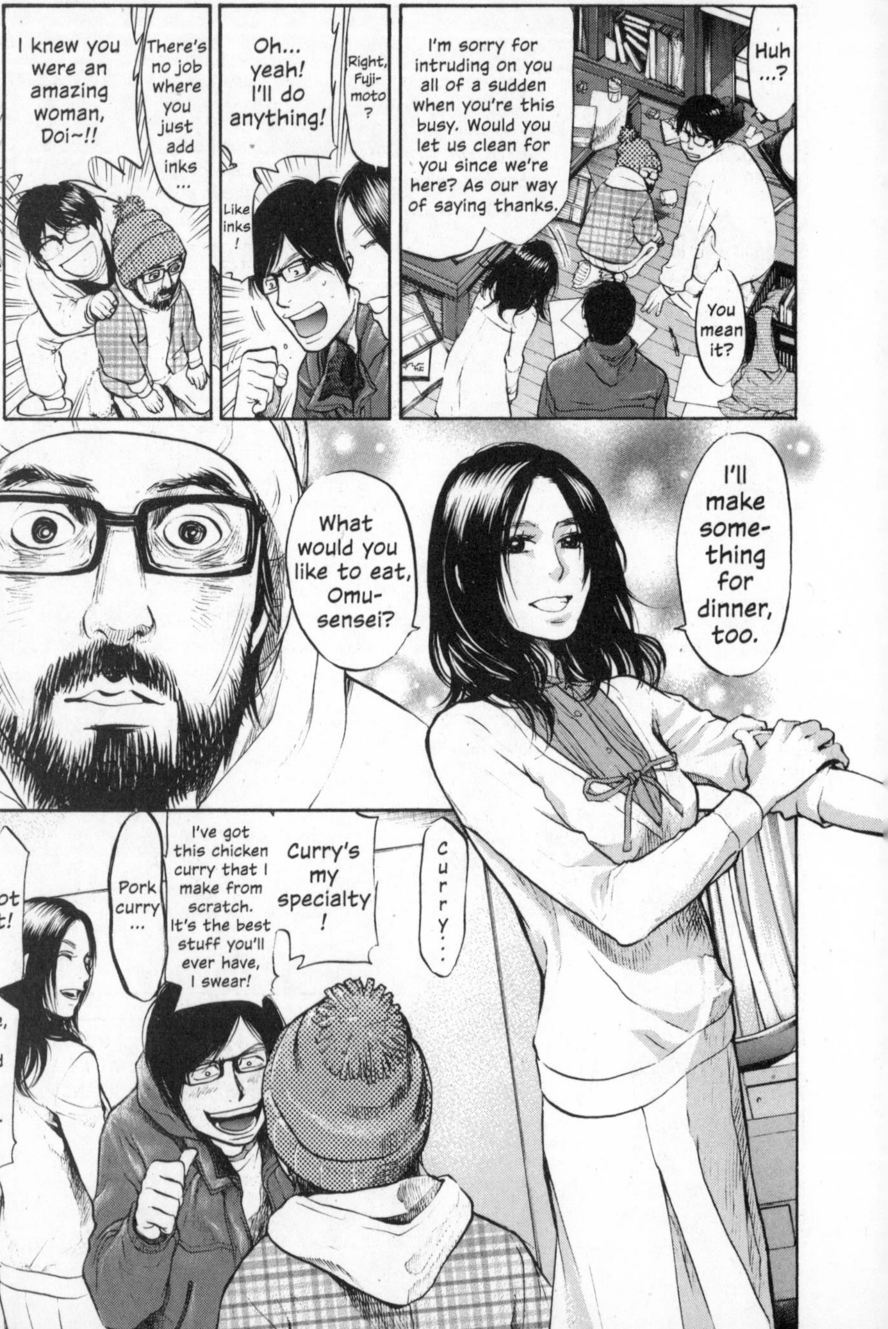
Huh ...?
I'm sorry for intruding on you all of a sudden when you're this busy. Would you let us clean for you since we're here? As our way of saying thanks.
You mean it?
Right, Fuji-moto?
Oh... yeah! I'll do anything!
Like inks!
There's no job where you just add inks ...
I knew you were an amazing woman, Doi~!!
I'll make some-thing for dinner, too.
What would you like to eat, Omu-sensei?
Curry...
Curry's my specialty!
I've got this chicken curry that I make from scratch. It's the best stuff you'll ever have, I swear!
Pork curry ...
Got it!
Please, go ahead and keep work-ing.

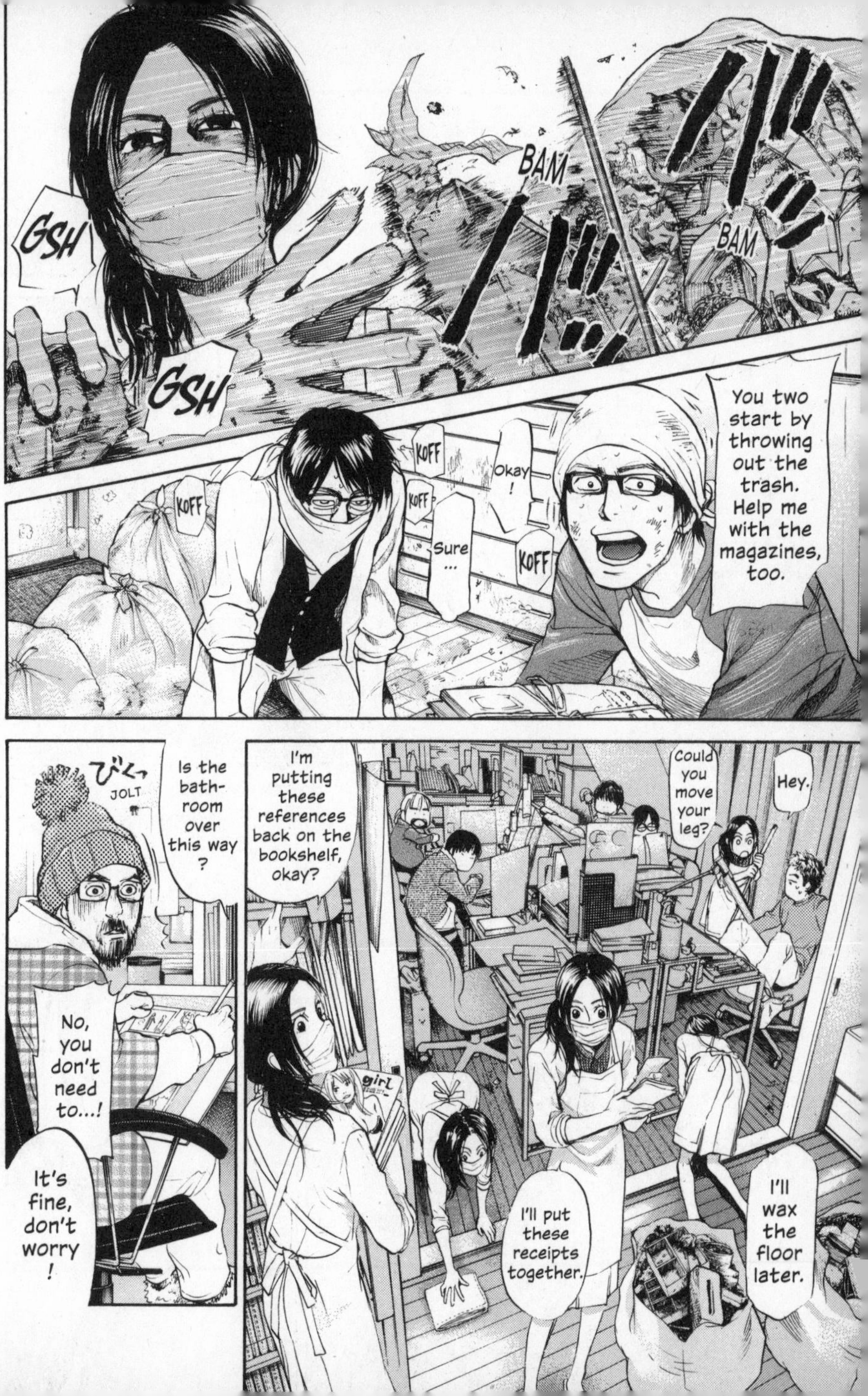
BAM
BAM
GSH
GSH
You two start by throwing out the trash. Help me with the magazines, too.
KOFF
Okay!
KOFF
KOFF
Sure...
KOFF
Hey.
Could you move your leg?
I'm putting these references back on the bookshelf, okay?
I'll wax the floor later.
I'll put these receipts together.
びくっ
JOLT
Is the bathroom over this way?
No, you don't need to...!
It's fine, don't worry!

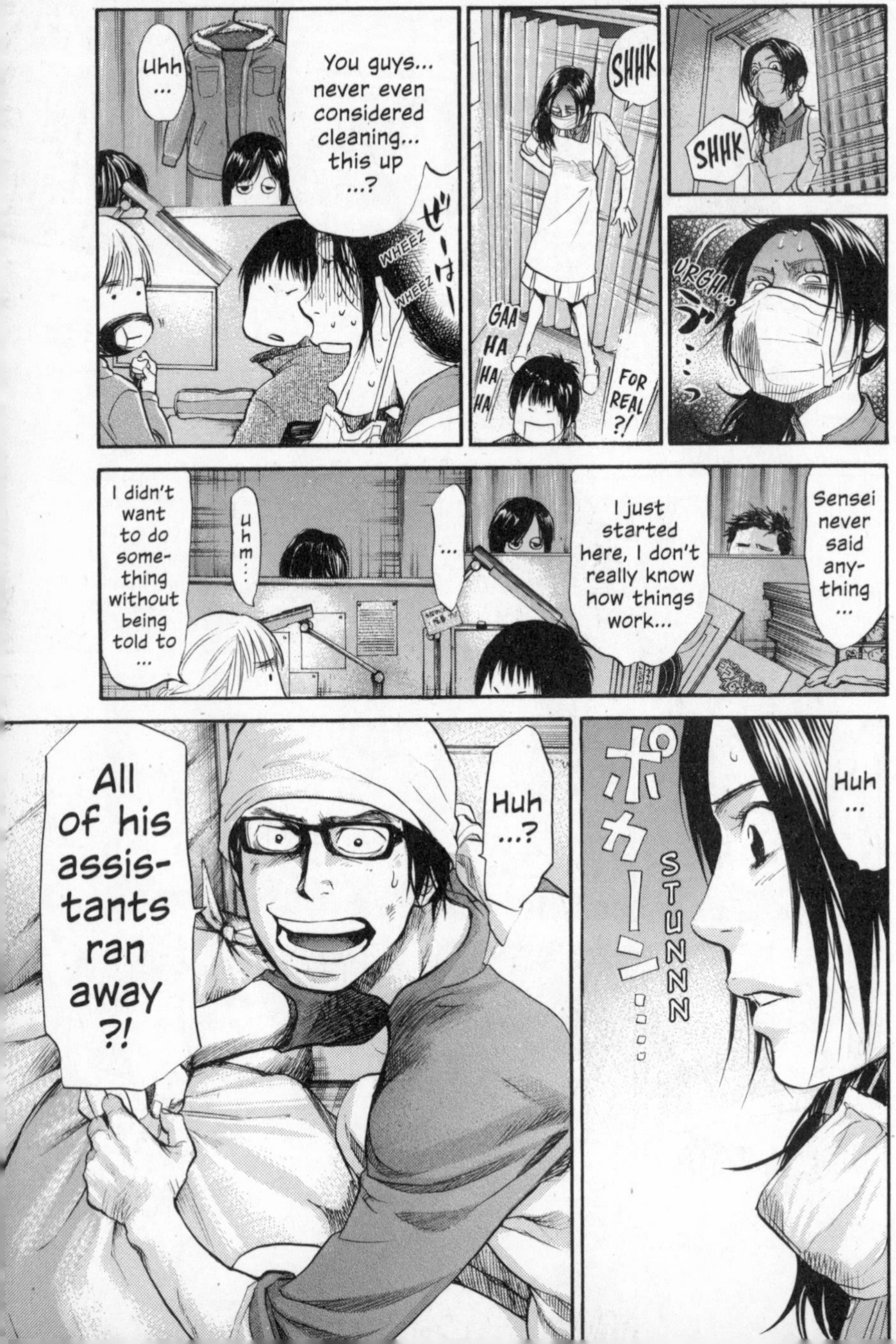
SHHK
URGH...
ヅ…
SHHK
GAA HA HA HA
FOR REAL ?!
Uhh ...
You guys... never even considered cleaning... this up ...?
ゼーはー
WHEEZ WHEEZ
Sensei never said any-thing ...
I just started here, I don't really know how things work...
...
Uhm...
I didn't want to do some-thing without being told to ...
Huh ...
ポカーン
STUNNN
Huh ...?
All of his assis-tants ran away ?!

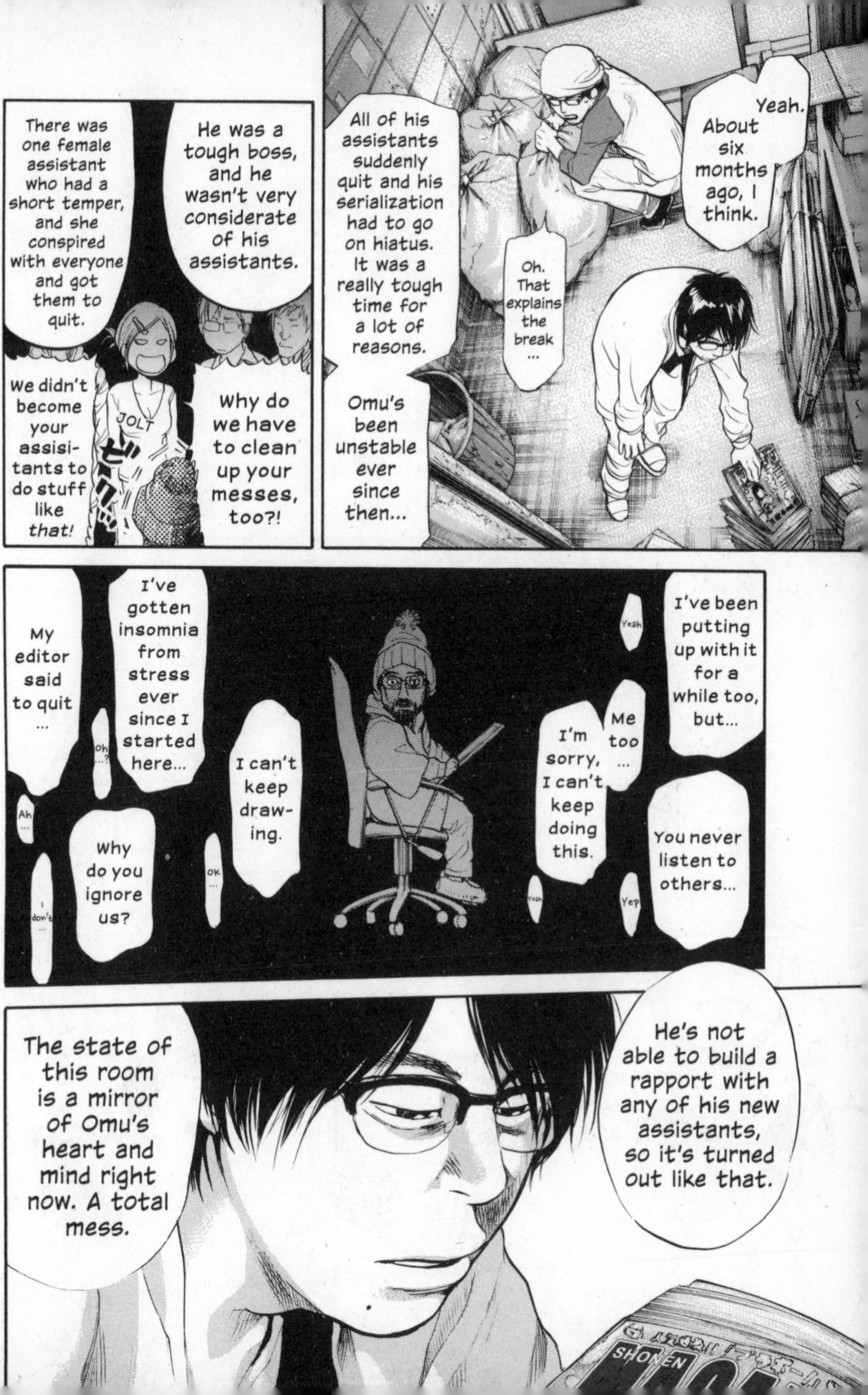
Yeah. About six months ago, I think.
Oh. That explains the break...
All of his assistants suddenly quit and his serialization had to go on hiatus. It was a really tough time for a lot of reasons.
Omu's been unstable ever since then...
He was a tough boss, and he wasn't very considerate of his assistants.
There was one female assistant who had a short temper, and she conspired with everyone and got them to quit.
Why do we have to clean up your messes, too?!
JOLT
We didn't become your assisi-tants to do stuff like *that!*
I've been putting up with it for a while too, but...
Yeah
Me too...
You never listen to others...
Yep
I'm sorry, I can't keep doing this.
Yeah
I can't keep draw-ing.
OK...
I've gotten insomnia from stress ever since I started here...
Oh...?
Why do you ignore us?
My editor said to quit...
Ah...
I don't...
He's not able to build a rapport with any of his new assistants, so it's turned out like that.
The state of this room is a mirror of Omu's heart and mind right now. A total mess.
SHONEN

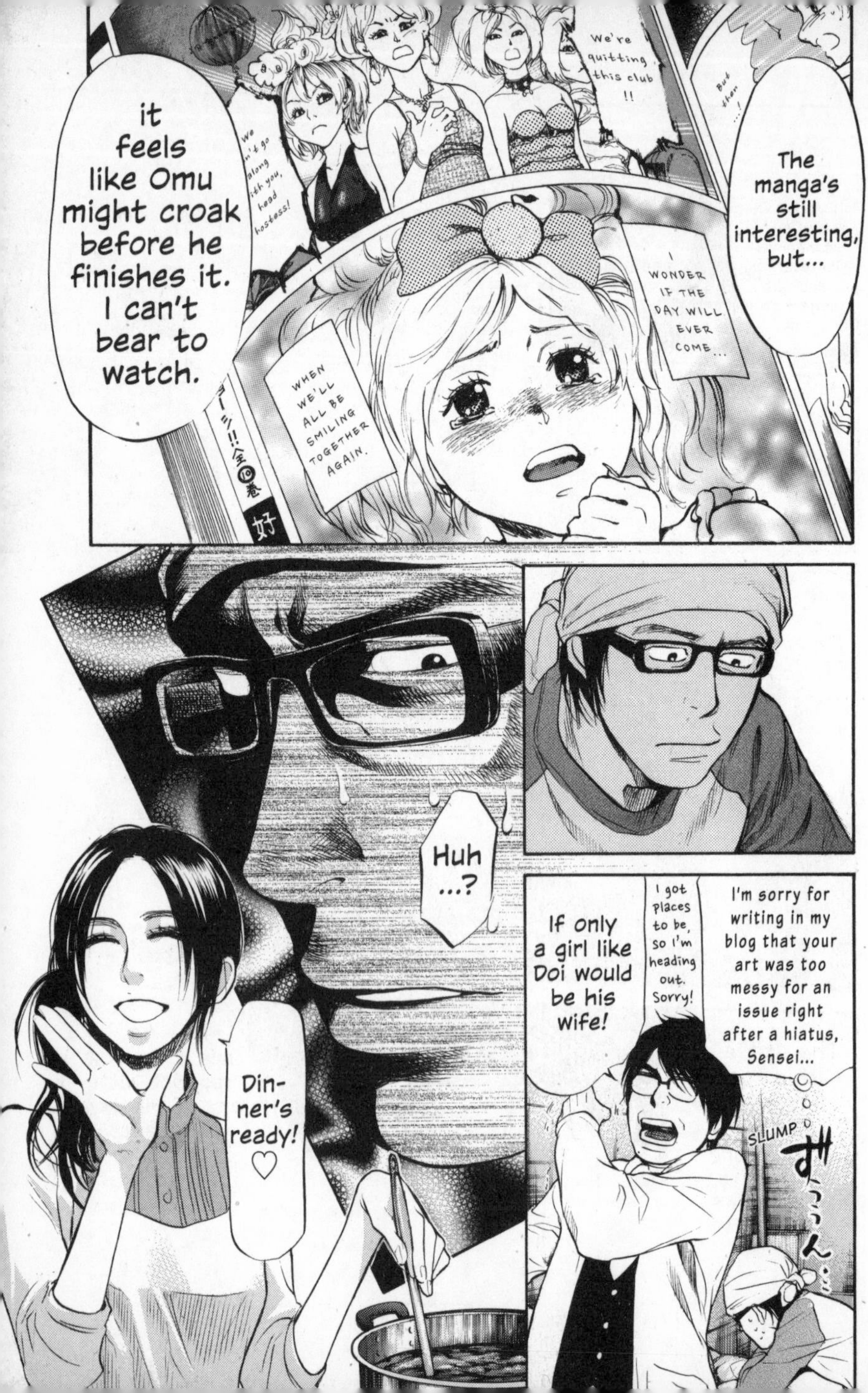
The manga's still interesting, but...
But then...!
We're quitting this club!!
We n't go along ith you, head hostess!
I WONDER IF THE DAY WILL EVER COME...
WHEN WE'LL ALL BE SMILING TOGETHER AGAIN.
it feels like Omu might croak before he finishes it. I can't bear to watch.
I'm sorry for writing in my blog that your art was too messy for an issue right after a hiatus, Sensei...
I got places to be, so I'm heading out. Sorry!
If only a girl like Doi would be his wife!
SLUMP
Huh...?
Din-ner's ready! ♡

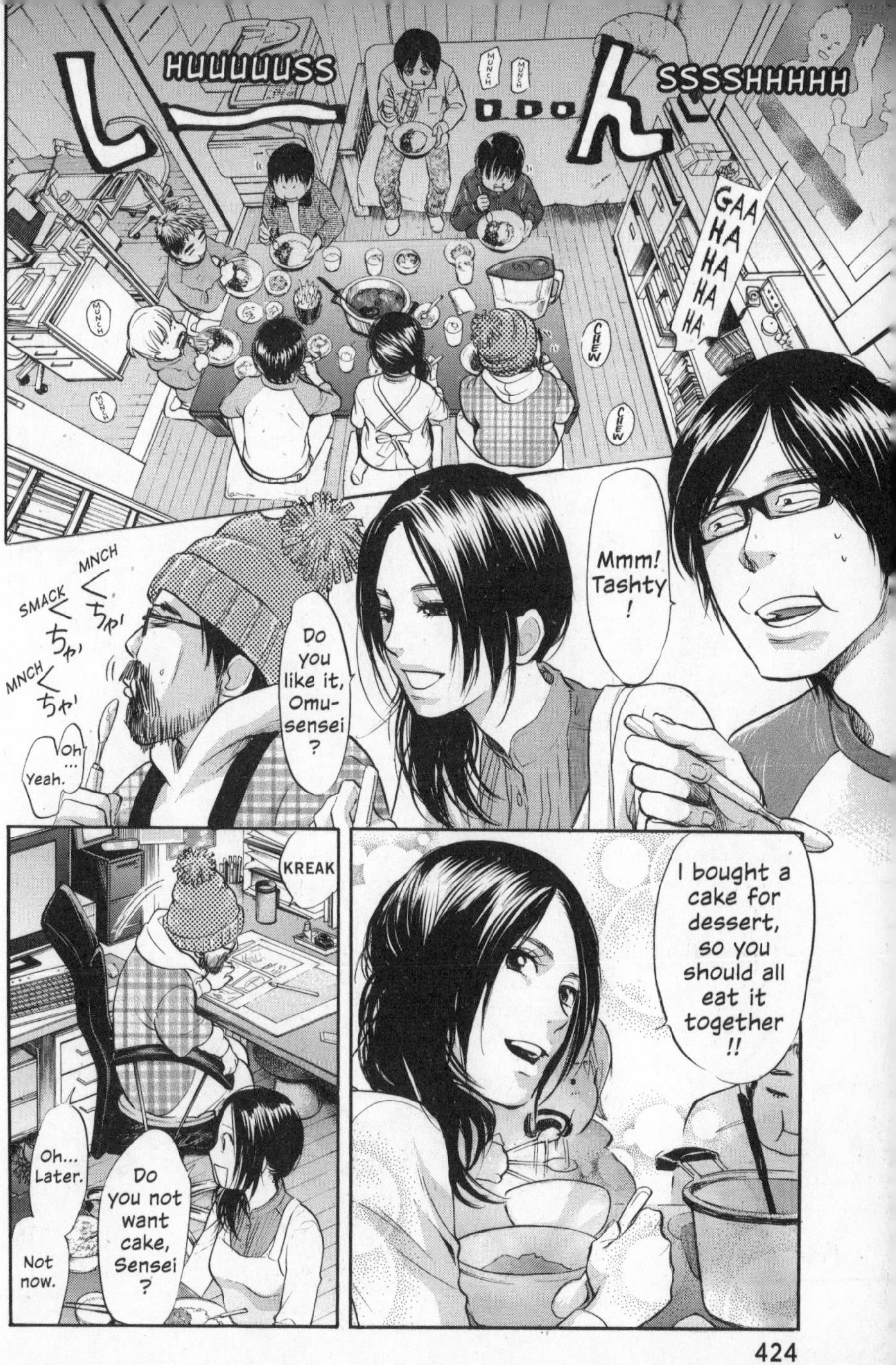
HUUUUUUSS
SSSSHHHHH
MUNCH MUNCH
GAA HA HA HA HA HA
MUNCH
MUNCH
CHEW
CHEW
Mmm! Tashty!
Do you like it, Omu-sensei?
MNCH
SMACK
MNCH
Oh... Yeah.
I bought a cake for dessert, so you should all eat it together !!
KREAK
Do you not want cake, Sensei?
Oh... Later.
Not now.

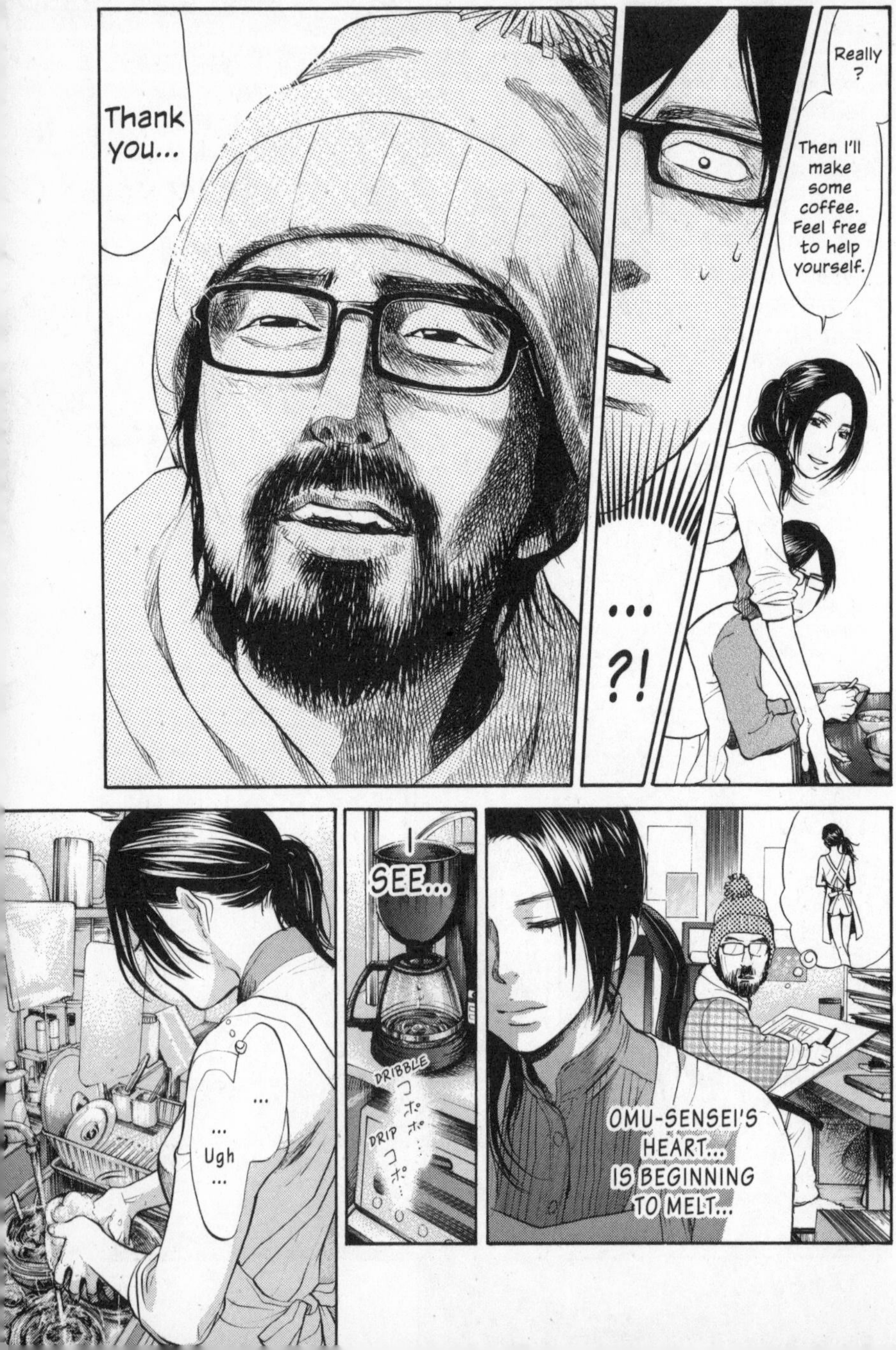
Really?
Then I'll make some coffee. Feel free to help yourself.
...
?!
Thank you...
OMU-SENSEI'S HEART... IS BEGINNING TO MELT...
I SEE...
DRIBBLE
コポポ…
DRIP
コポ…
...
... Ugh ...

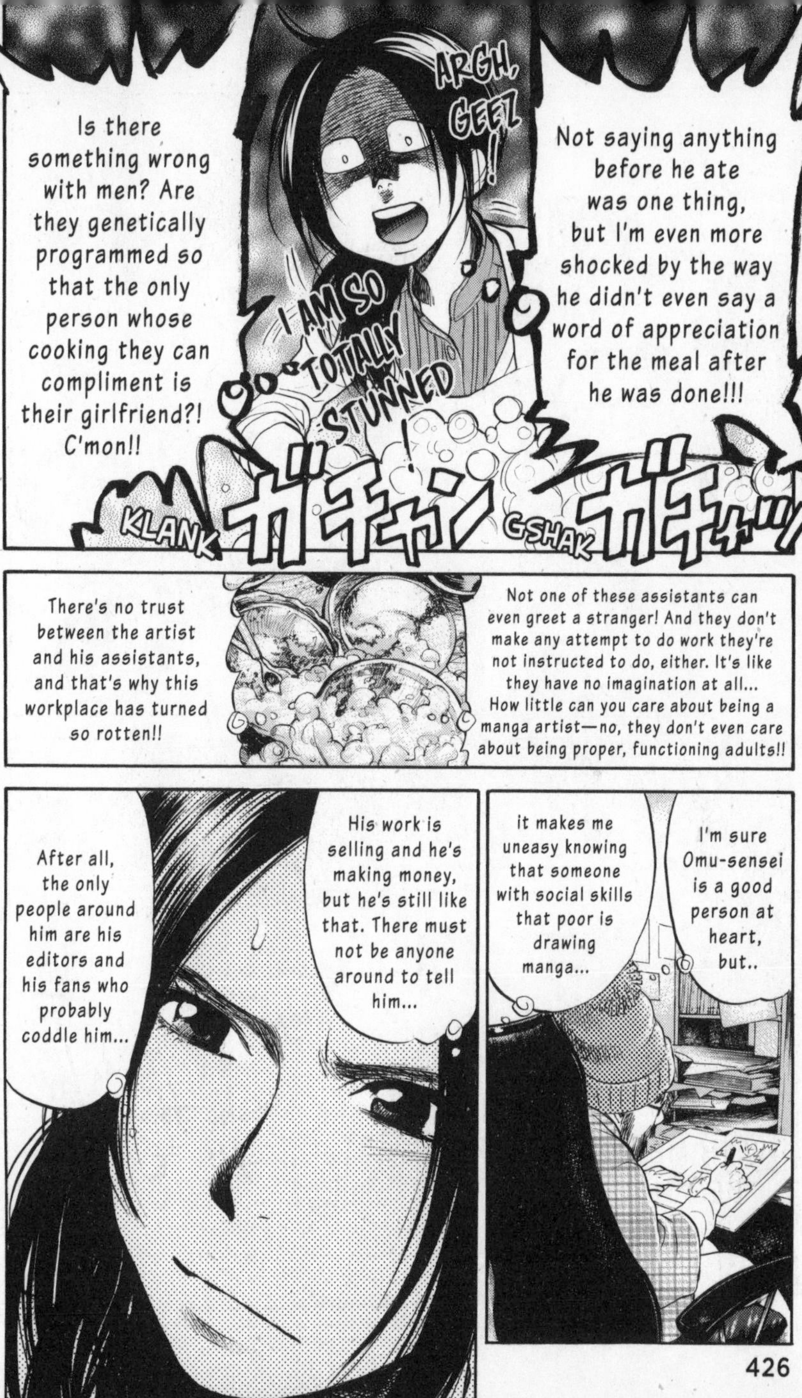
Not saying anything before he ate was one thing, but I'm even more shocked by the way he didn't even say a word of appreciation for the meal after he was done!!!
ARGH, GEEZ!
I AM SO TOTALLY STUNNED!
Is there something wrong with men? Are they genetically programmed so that the only person whose cooking they can compliment is their girlfriend?! C'mon!!
GSHAK
ガチャッ!
KLANK
ガチャン
Not one of these assistants can even greet a stranger! And they don't make any attempt to do work they're not instructed to do, either. It's like they have no imagination at all... How little can you care about being a manga artist—no, they don't even care about being proper, functioning adults!!
There's no trust between the artist and his assistants, and that's why this workplace has turned so rotten!!
I'm sure Omu-sensei is a good person at heart, but..
it makes me uneasy knowing that someone with social skills that poor is drawing manga...
His work is selling and he's making money, but he's still like that. There must not be anyone around to tell him...
After all, the only people around him are his editors and his fans who probably coddle him...

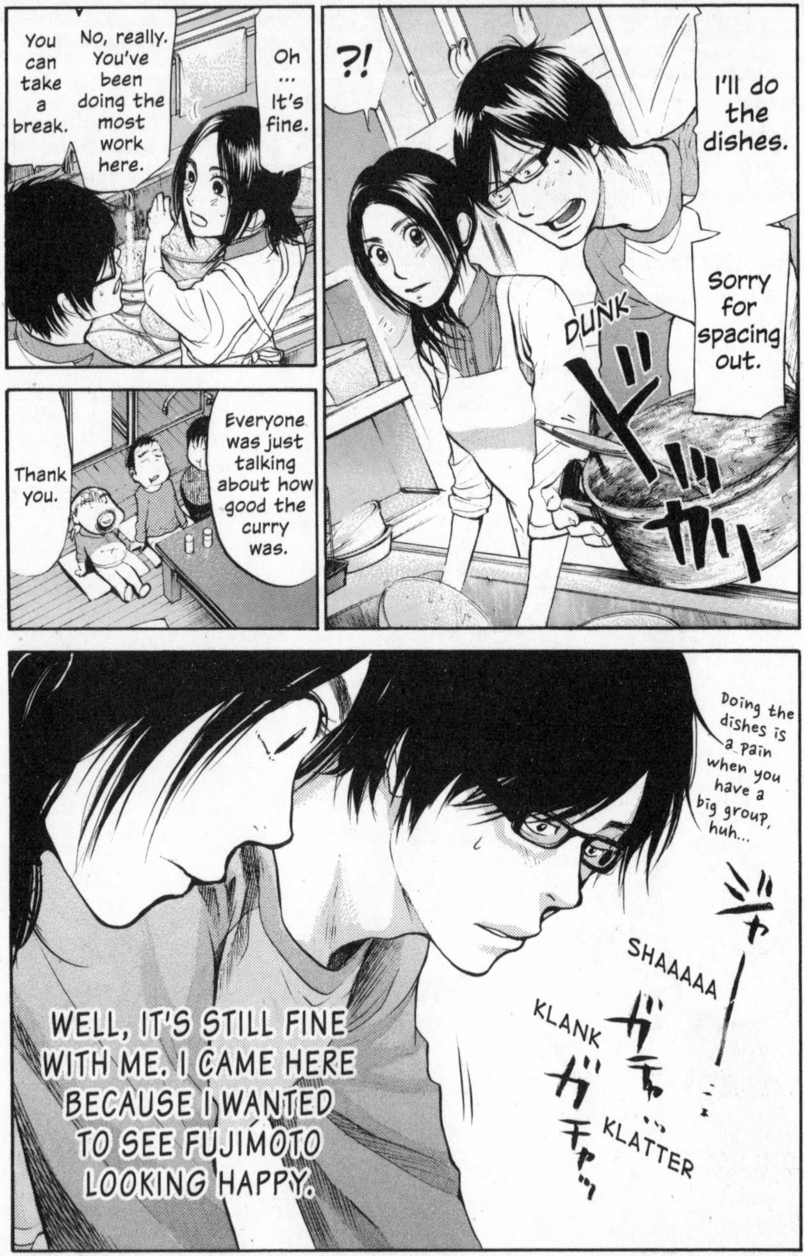
I'll do the dishes.
?!
Sorry for spacing out.
DUNK
Oh ... It's fine.
No, really. You've been doing the most work here.
You can take a break.
Everyone was just talking about how good the curry was.
Thank you.
Doing the dishes is a pain when you have a big group, huh...
SHAAAAA
KLANK
KLATTER
WELL, IT'S STILL FINE WITH ME. I CAME HERE BECAUSE I WANTED TO SEE FUJIMOTO LOOKING HAPPY.

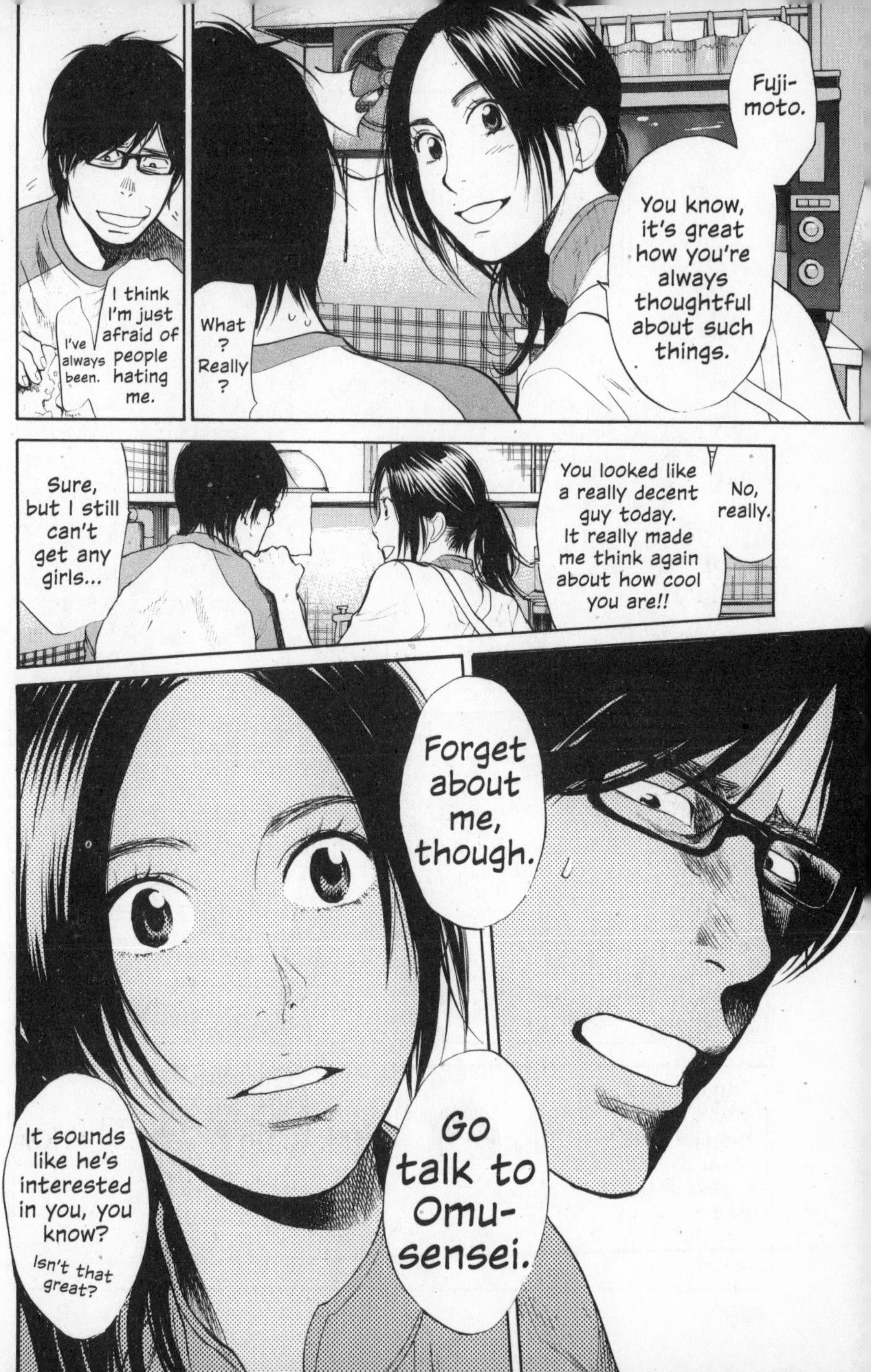

Fuji-moto.
You know, it's great how you're always thoughtful about such things.
What? Really?
I think I'm just afraid of people hating me.
I've always been.
No, really.
You looked like a really decent guy today. It really made me think again about how cool you are!!
Sure, but I still can't get any girls...
Forget about me, though.
Go talk to Omu-sensei.
It sounds like he's interested in you, you know?
Isn't that great?

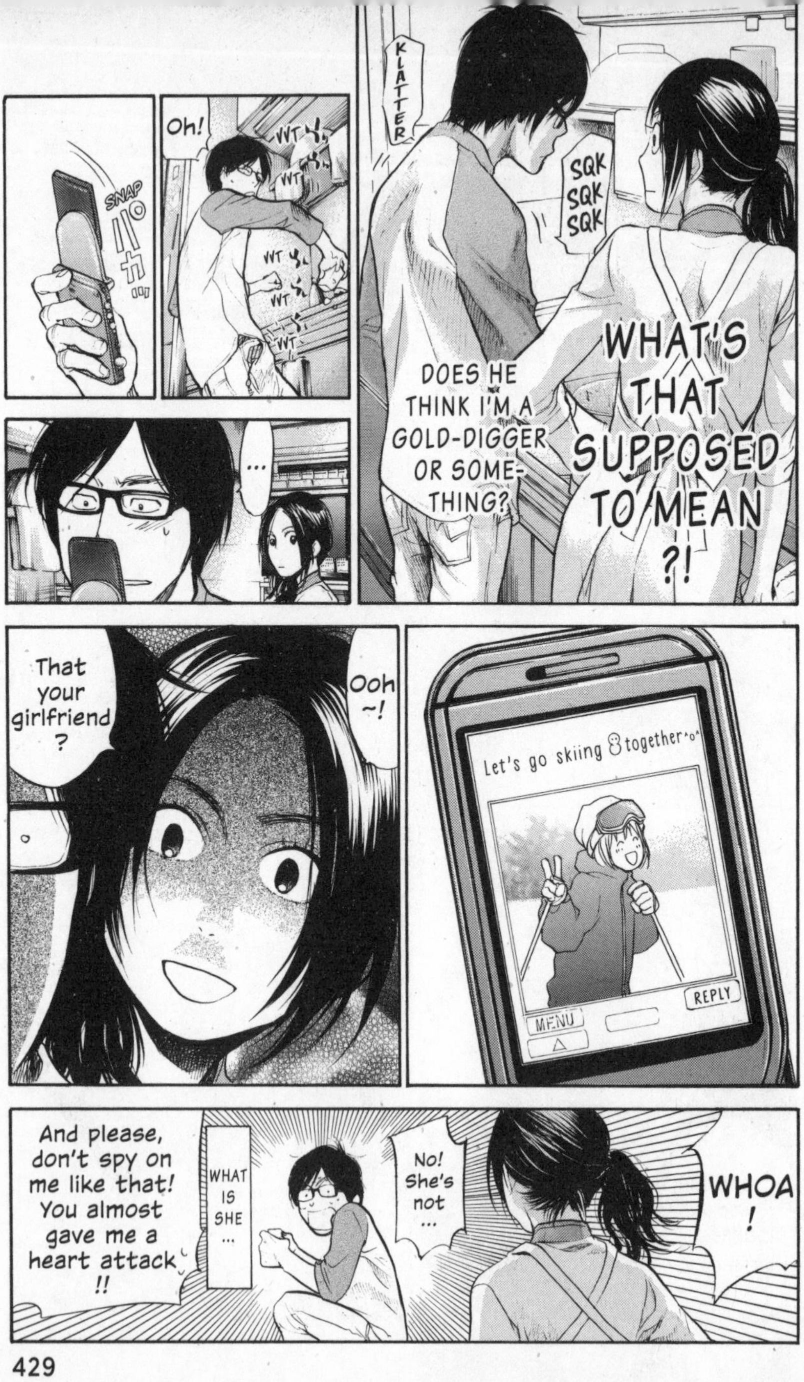
KLATTER
SQK SQK SQK
WHAT'S THAT SUPPOSED TO MEAN ?!
DOES HE THINK I'M A GOLD-DIGGER OR SOME-THING?
Oh!
VVT
SNAP
...
Let's go skiing together^o^
REPLY
MENU
Ooh ~!
That your girlfriend ?
WHOA !
No! She's not ...
WHAT IS SHE ...
And please, don't spy on me like that! You almost gave me a heart attack !!

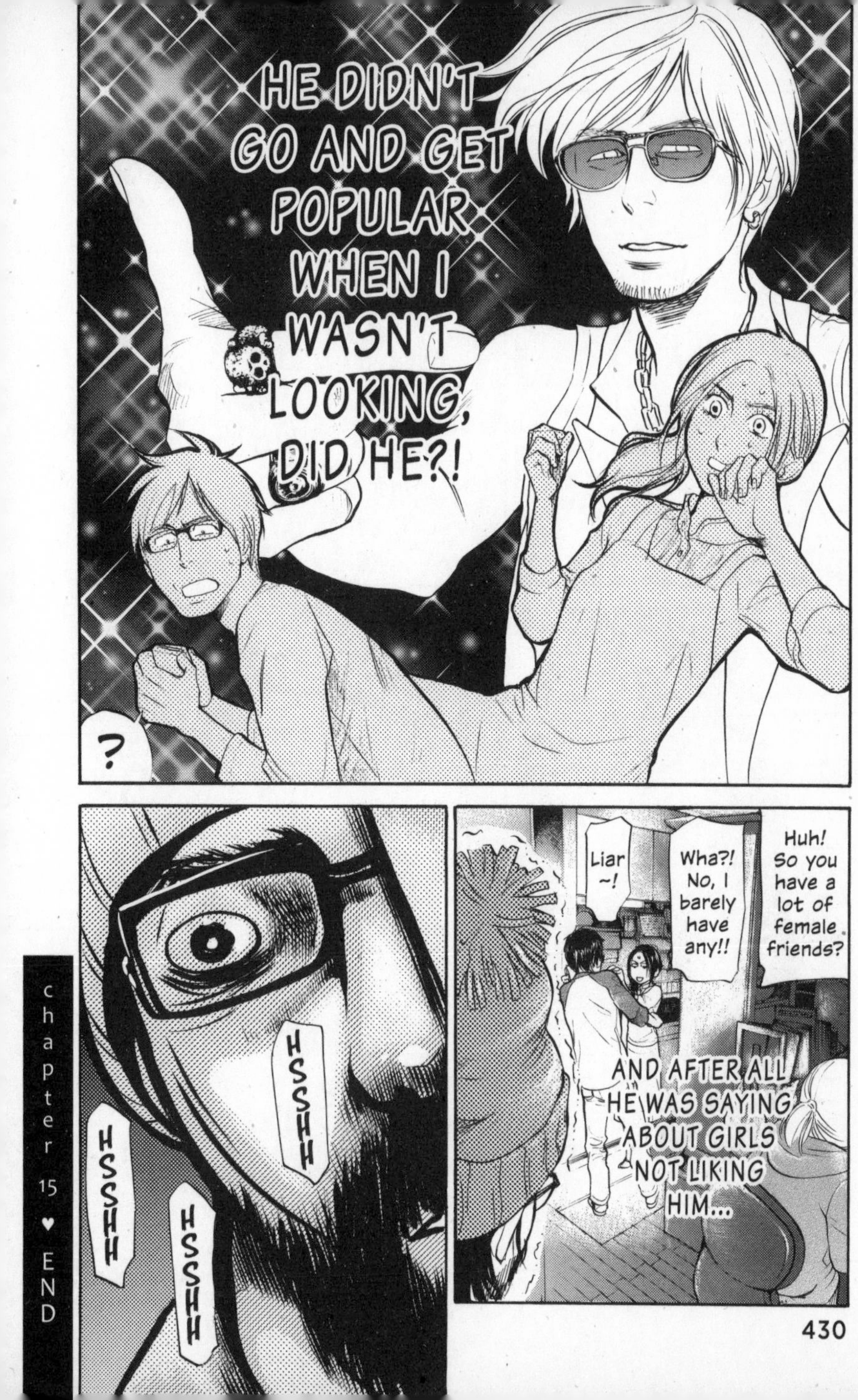
HE DIDN'T GO AND GET POPULAR WHEN I WASN'T LOOKING, DID HE?!
?
Huh! So you have a lot of female friends?
Wha?! No, I barely have any!!
Liar ~!
AND AFTER ALL HE WAS SAYING ABOUT GIRLS NOT LIKING HIM...
HSSHH
HSSHH
HSSHH

chapter 15 ♥ END

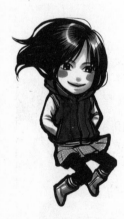

Moteki Mitsurou Kubo

Motekis You Wouldn't Want to Read ③

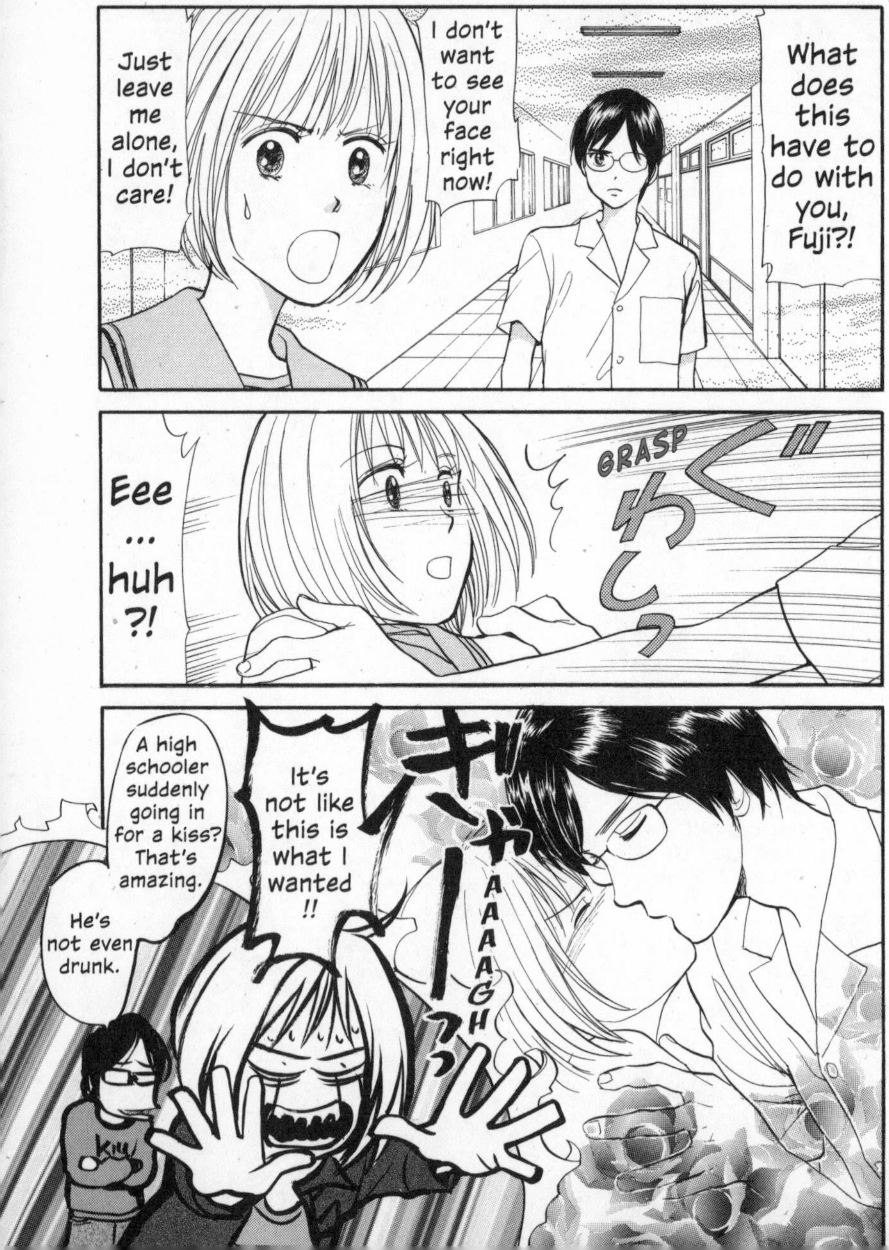
What does this have to do with you, Fuji?!
I don't want to see your face right now!
Just leave me alone, I don't care!
GRASP
ぐわしっ
Eee ... huh?!
AAAAAAGH
It's not like this is what I wanted!!
A high schooler suddenly going in for a kiss? That's amazing.
He's not even drunk.

Motekis You Wouldn't Want to Read ④

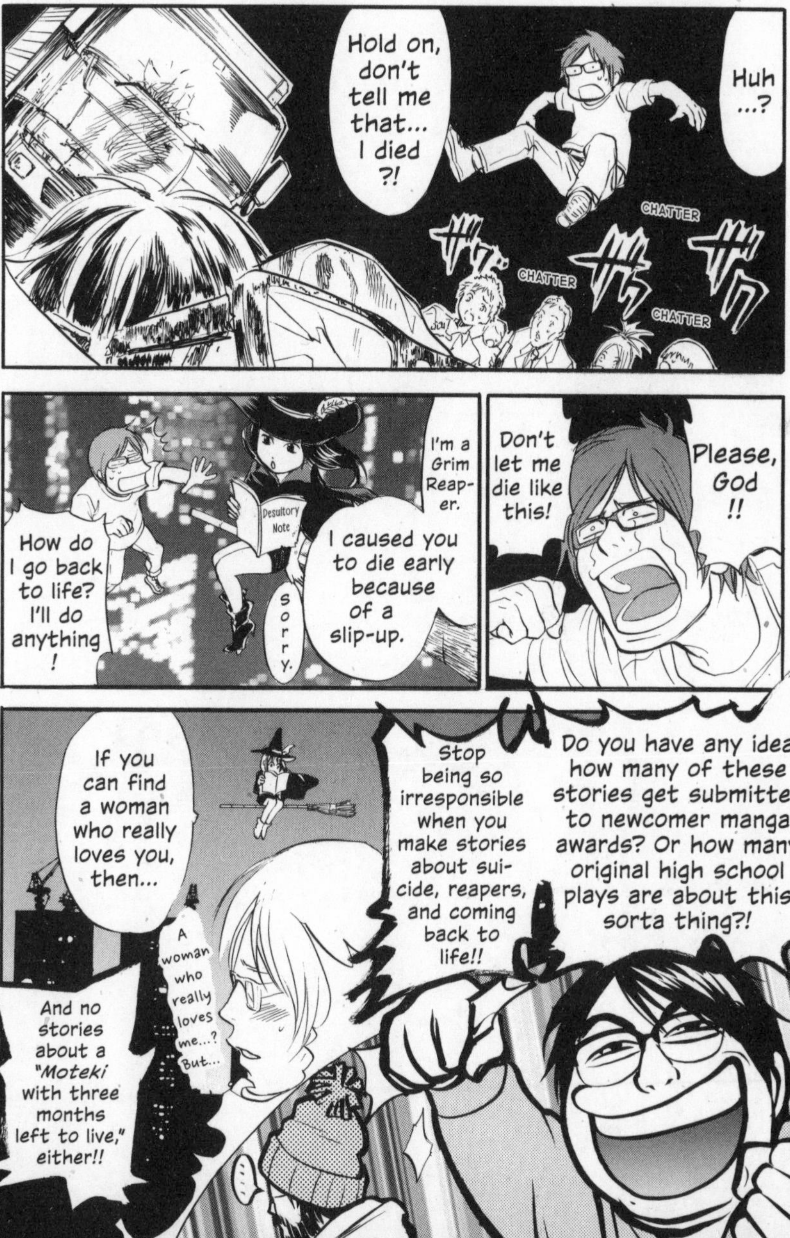
Huh ...?
Hold on, don't tell me that... I died ?!
CHATTER
CHATTER
CHATTER
Please, God !!
Don't let me die like this!
I'm a Grim Reaper.
Desultory Note
I caused you to die early because of a slip-up.
sorry.
How do I go back to life? I'll do anything !
Do you have any idea how many of these stories get submitted to newcomer manga awards? Or how many original high school plays are about this sorta thing?!
Stop being so irresponsible when you make stories about suicide, reapers, and coming back to life!!
If you can find a woman who really loves you, then...
A woman who really loves me...? But...
And no stories about a "Moteki with three months left to live," either!!
...

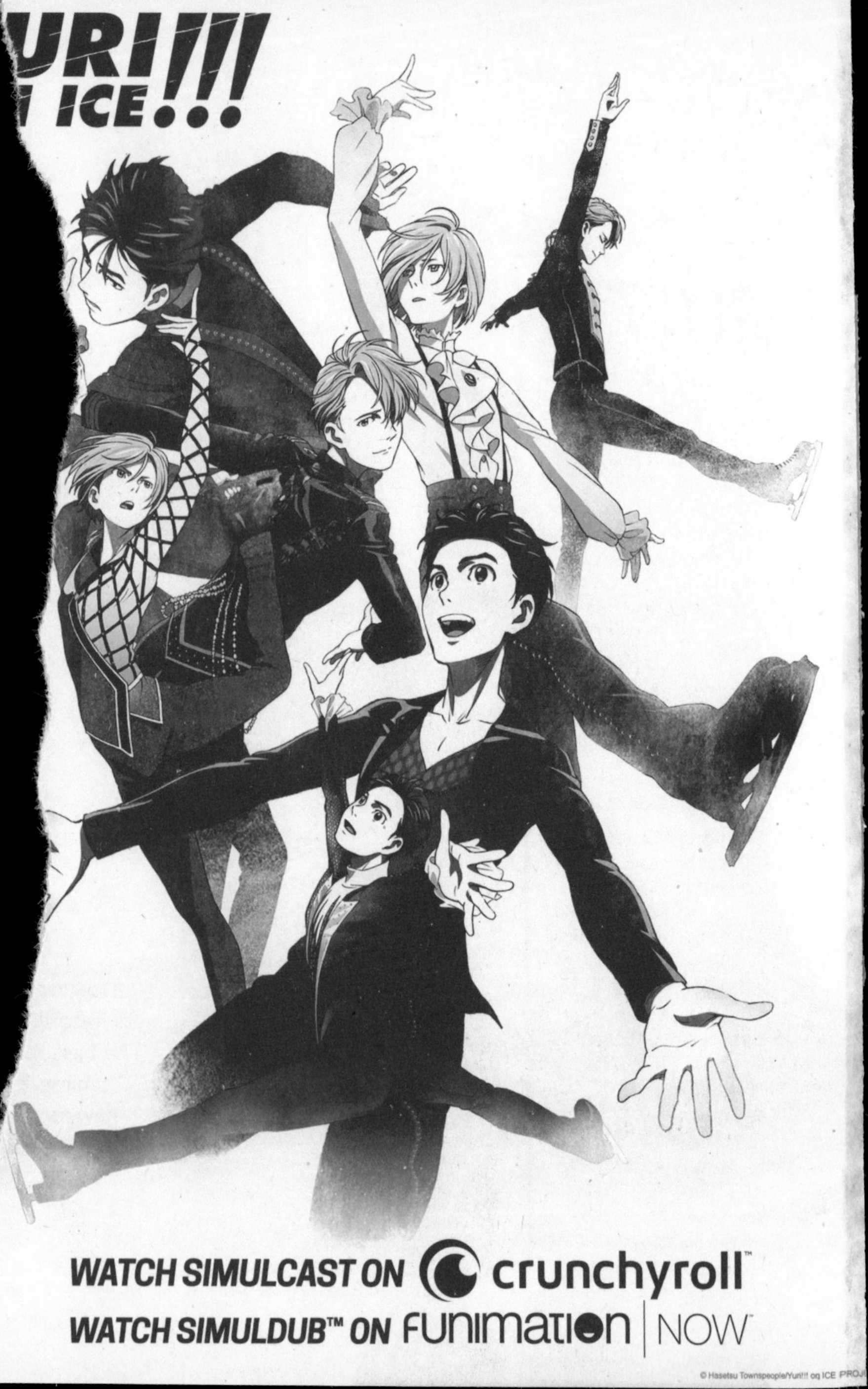
URI!!!
ICE!!!
WATCH SIMULCAST ON crunchyroll™
WATCH SIMULDUB™ ON Funimation | NOW™
© Hasetsu Townspeople/Yuri!!! on ICE PROJ

MOTEKI Love Strikes! 1

Translation: Ko Ransom
Production: Risa Cho
            Eve Grandt

Copyright © 2009 Mitsurou Kubo. All rights reserved.
First published in Japan in 2009 by Kodansha, Ltd., Tokyo
Publication for this English edition arranged through Kodansha, Ltd., Tokyo
English language version produced by Vertical, Inc.

Translation provided by Vertical, Inc., 2018
Published by Vertical Comics, an imprint of Vertical, Inc., New York

Originally published in Japanese as *Moteki 1 - 2* by Kodansha, Ltd., 2009
Moteki first serialized in *Evening*, Kodansha, Ltd., 2008 - 2010

Linda Linda
Words and Music by Hiroto Kohmoto
Copyright © 2009 GINGHAM MUSIC PUBLISHERS, INC.
All Rights Administrated by UNIVERSAL MUSIC PUBLISHING LLC
All Rights Reserved   Used by Permission
Reprinted by Permission of Hal Leonard LLC

This is a work of fiction.

ISBN: 978-1-945054-80-8

Manufactured in Canada

First Edition

Vertical, Inc.
451 Park Avenue South
7th Floor
New York, NY 10016
www.vertical-comics.com

Vertical books are distributed through Pengiun-Random House Publisher Services.

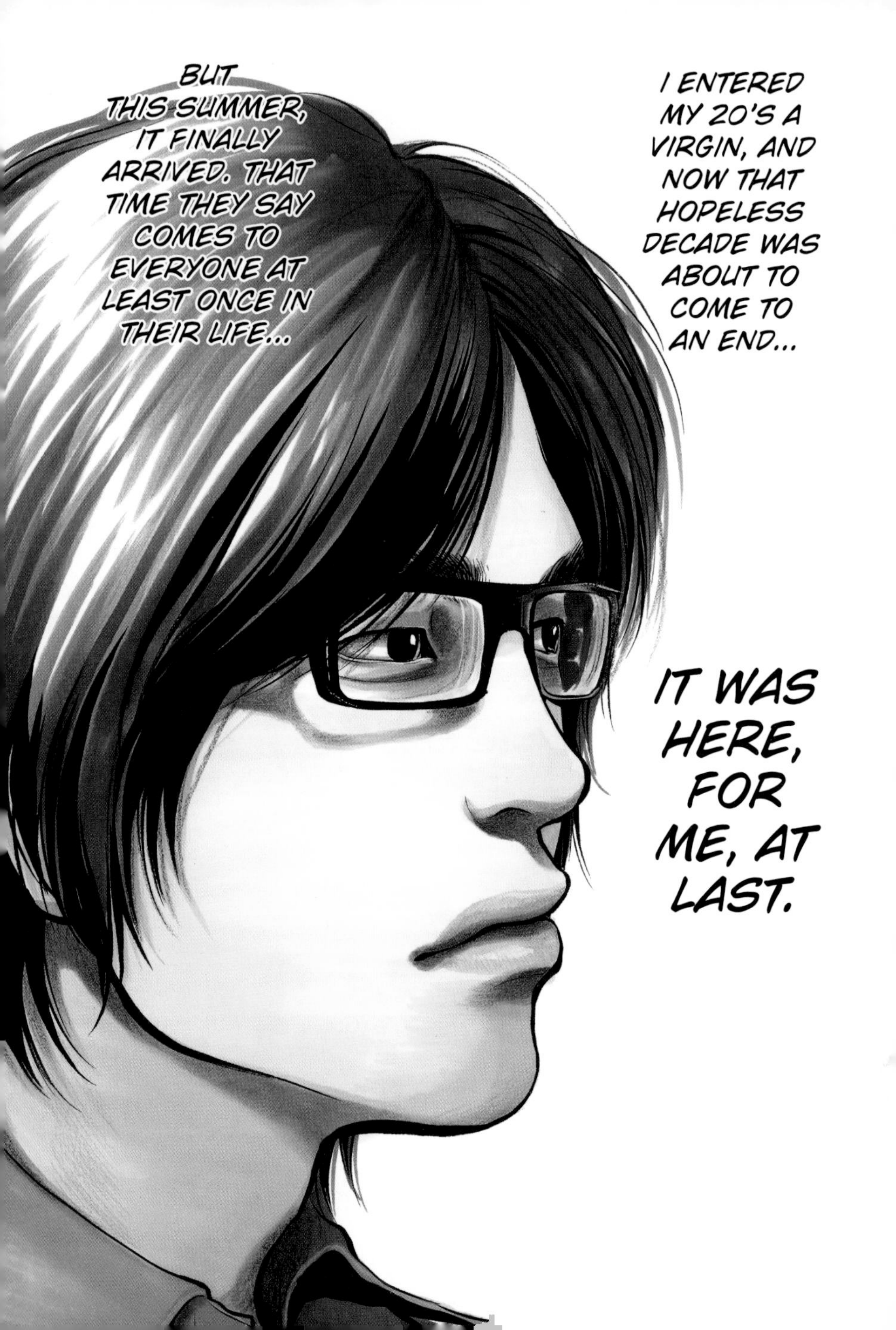
I ENTERED MY 20'S A VIRGIN, AND NOW THAT HOPELESS DECADE WAS ABOUT TO COME TO AN END...
BUT THIS SUMMER, IT FINALLY ARRIVED. THAT TIME THEY SAY COMES TO EVERYONE AT LEAST ONCE IN THEIR LIFE...
IT WAS HERE, FOR ME, AT LAST.

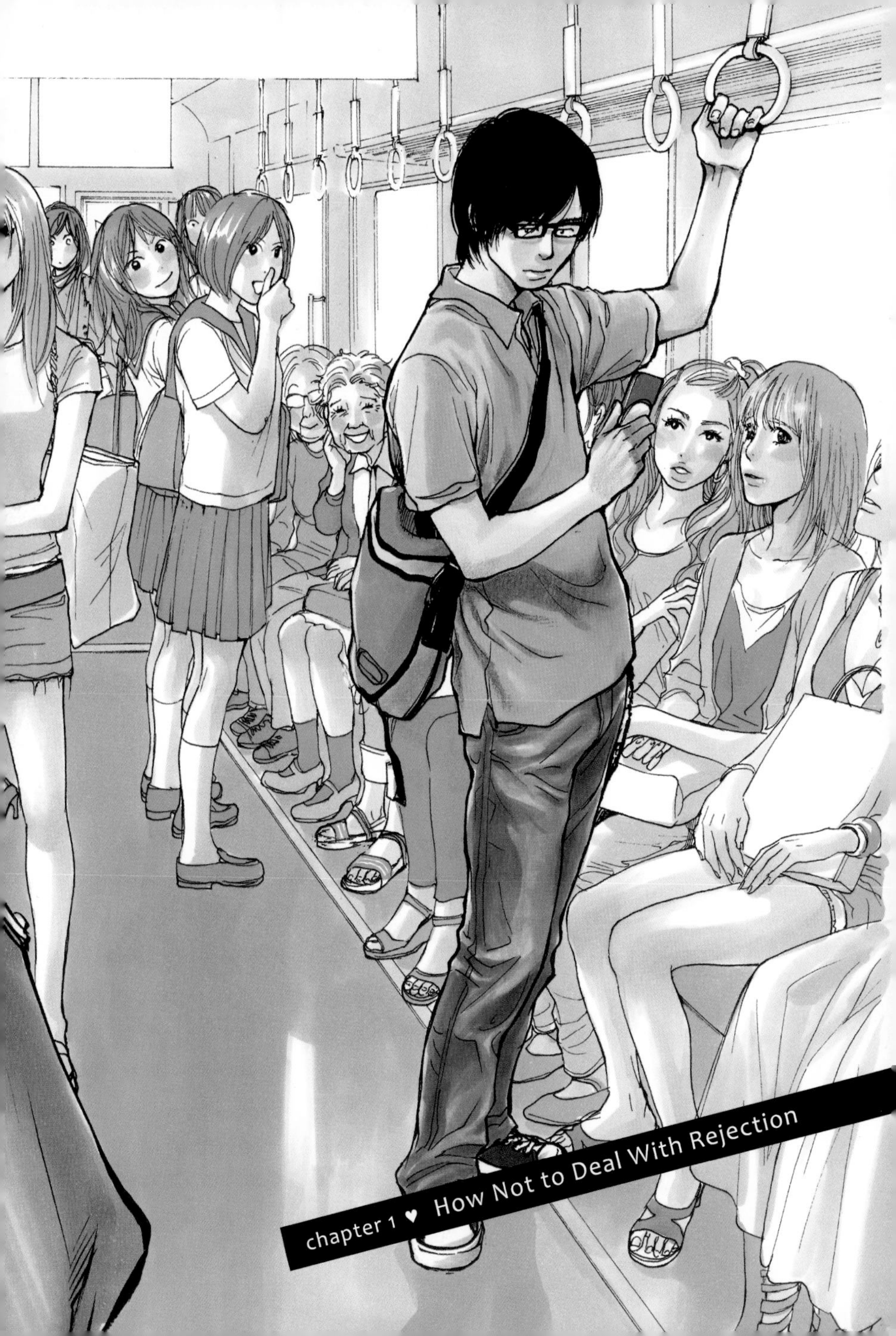
chapter 1 ♥ How Not to Deal With Rejection

contents

♥

Moteki
Mitsurou
Kubo

MOTEKI

Mitsurou Kubo

Love Strikes!

1

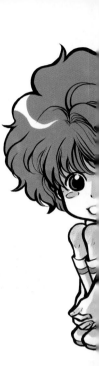

Moteki

Mitsurou Kubo

A NEW MANGA SERIES FROM YURI!!! ON ICE CO-CREATOR MITSUROU KUBO!!

Again!!

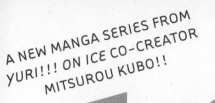

アゲイン!!

KC KODANSHA COMICS

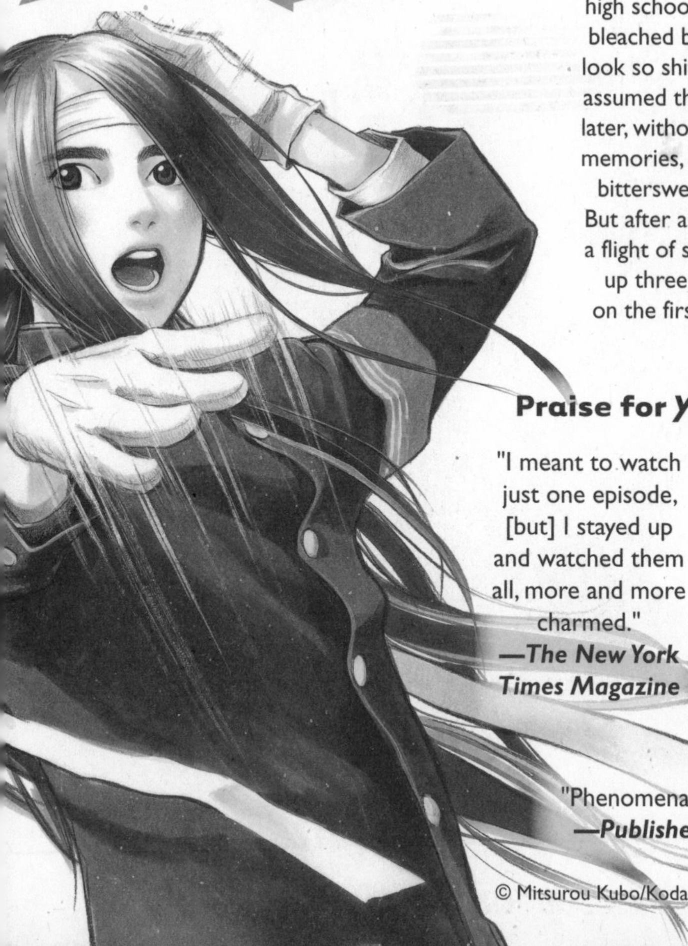

Kinichiro Imamura isn't a bad guy, really, but on the first day of high school his narrow eyes and bleached blonde hair made him look so shifty that his classmates assumed the worst. Three years later, without any friends or fond memories, he isn't exactly feeling bittersweet about graduation. But after an accidental fall down a flight of stairs, Kinichiro wakes up three years in the past... on the first day of high school!

Praise for *Yuri!!! on Ice*:

"I meant to watch just one episode, [but] I stayed up and watched them all, more and more charmed."
—The New York Times Magazine

"A smart show that frequently subverts your expectations in delightful ways... The best romance anime for newcomers."
—The Verge

"Phenomenally popular."
—Publishers Weekly